The Archer

Abigail Roux

Dreamspinner Press

Published by
Dreamspinner Press
4760 Preston Road
Suite 244-149
Frisco, TX 75034
http://www.dreamspinnerpress.com/

Cover Design by Mara McKennen

ISBN: 978-0-9815084-8-1

Printed in the United States of America
First Edition
April, 2008

eBook edition available in Adobe PDF, MobiPocket and MS Reader formats.

To my family, who have supported me
ever since I was writing A's
on the walls in purple crayon.

PART ONE: BIG BANG THEORY

I.

THIAGO idly mulled over his most recent assignment as he fiddled restlessly with his napkin. It had all the makings of a disaster waiting to happen, and Thiago could barely keep himself from cringing when he thought over the details.

The Organization ordered him to leave Argentina and meet with five other operatives in America. They were to form a team in order to track down a rogue covert called, simply, the Archer.

What kind of *pelotudo* name was that, anyway?

Thiago drew in a deep breath and chastised himself almost immediately for thinking that way. If the Organization thought this was a big enough threat to warrant a joint effort of this sort, then Thiago knew he should take it more seriously. He and the men he was supposed to meet were trained to be self-sufficient. They were trained to be loners; solitary warriors with no fallback and no safety net. If their handlers thought the only road to success was a rare joint effort between not two or three, but six highly trained agents, then this was a serious matter indeed.

His blue eyes moved slowly over the other patrons of the café, observing them carefully. He had no idea who he was meeting. He knew they were all male, but he had no other information save for the names of the town and the greasy spoon in which he was to wait. It was standard procedure, but Thiago was far out of his comfort zone here in the heartland of America. It was all he could do to hide his accent, much less blend in to the unfamiliar territory. He would much rather have been on the streets of Catamarca in the north of Argentina. Killing something, preferably. He would rather be doing anything but counter-intelligence. Thiago despised counter-intelligence. He preferred the action-oriented aspects of his job.

He shifted in his seat and glanced around the room for perhaps the hundredth time. Normally he would have been sitting in the corner like a good little spy, protecting his back and watching the room discreetly. But today Thiago sat in the middle of the little dining area with his back to the door, tearing his napkin into strips and sipping at a mug of coffee every so often. Today he didn't want to be spotted first by his fellow spooks, and behaving like a trained agent was the surest way of making that happen.

Thiago didn't like working with others, and he consoled himself with the fact that he'd already spotted two of his soon-to-be associates– they had each chosen to sit at tables in or near the corners– and Thiago could observe them freely.

One of them was a younger man with round spectacles and longish brown hair, streaked with blond highlights. Even sitting down, Thiago could tell he was short, probably a little over five and half feet. He looked harmless enough. There was nothing particularly outstanding about him, except perhaps for his crooked nose that had obviously been broken once upon a time and his rather outlandish way of dressing. He wore ripped jeans and a vintage punk rock T-shirt, complete with wristbands at his forearms and simple silver rings on almost every finger. His fingernails, Thiago noticed, were painted black. Thiago examined him with interest. He didn't look like the type to be in this business. Perhaps that was the point.

Thiago gave the man one last discreet look and then turned his attention to the man in the other corner. He was much larger, probably an inch or three over six feet, and well built. His muscles were clearly defined under the long-sleeved dress shirt he wore. He was handsome too, with short-cropped brown hair and perhaps a day's growth of facial hair. Even though he sat calmly reading a newspaper, one foot resting on his knee and bouncing to some internal tune, he looked entirely unapproachable. There was an air about him that screamed trained killer; dangerous and capable and ice cold.

Thiago thought briefly that if he looked like that, he'd sit with his back to the wall everywhere he went too.

He turned his attention to his own reflection and examined himself critically. He wondered what impressions these other men were forming about him. Pale blue eyes stared back at him appraisingly. For a 40 year-old spook he didn't look so bad. A myriad of scars covered his left arm all the way up to his neck, faded reminders of the time he'd lost a fight with a storefront window in his youth, but his body had remained remarkably unmarred otherwise. His hair had turned blond from all his time in the sun, and his skin was tanned and slightly weathered. The goatee he sported was blond as well, with hints of red and gold amidst the touches of gray. Most of his fellow South Americans thought him a *yanqui* because of his light coloring. Sometimes it helped with his missions south of the equator. Other times it found him hanging upside down in a warehouse on a dock in Cartagena.

"Anybody know another word for 'bellicose'?" someone asked suddenly, breaking the silence and actually making Thiago jerk slightly. "Ten letters," the kid at the far wall added, looking around the café with his pen held in the air expectantly. "Starts with a P? No? I think this thing is in Russian or something," he muttered as he turned his attention back to his crossword puzzle without receiving any aid.

Thiago stared at the man and found himself smiling slightly as he examined him.

He was a possibility. He was younger, possibly in his early twenties, and his hair and eyes were the same exotic brown that seemed to change from nearly auburn when the right light hit, to raven black in the shadows. The chameleon-like quality of it struck Thiago as something that must be useful to an agent. His most striking feature, though, was his high cheekbones, like his face had been chiseled from marble. They gave him an exotic quality that Thiago found hard to pinpoint. He wore faded jeans and a plain black T-shirt with scuffed cowboy boots and a drab green military surplus jacket that hung loosely from his wiry shoulders.

That made a probable third man, even though this one didn't appear to be observing anything but his crossword, but Thiago wasn't prepared to approach any of them just yet.

As he returned to his cup of coffee, Thiago watched in the mirror along the back wall as a man entered the café. He was old and stooped, and his long gray hair fell well past his shoulders, as did his ridiculous-looking, scraggly beard. As he hobbled up to the counter, Thiago couldn't help but groan inwardly.

It would appear they had a master of disguise in the group. That was all they needed. Thiago pondered the consequences ruefully as he chalked up a fourth man to his list. In his experience, the ones that disguised themselves did so out of vanity. They liked to show off their talent. Show off how clever they were. They were usually dumb as bricks, in the long run. This one was going to be a pain in the ass, Thiago decided. Oh well. You could choose your enemies but not your allies, he reminded himself.

One more ally to go.

He watched the old man order a cup of coffee and point to the wall behind the counter with a long, arthritic finger. Thiago had to give the guy credit; he was good. He looked every bit the fragile old man, and Thiago started trying to picture what the man beneath the disguise must look like. He was probably of average height even though he was stooped over, but he had to be slight of build to pull off that slightly decrepit look. That was as far as Thiago's guesses could go.

The blond man working behind the counter reached up to pull down a pack of cigarettes and Thiago sighed and looked away, observing the entirety of the café in the mirror once more.

The entryway to the café darkened yet again as Thiago pondered the scene, and Thiago's body tensed as he saw another man enter.

"Jesus," Thiago breathed before he could stop himself. He could see his own shocked expression in the mirror just as well as he could see the looks of concern and surprise coming from the two men he'd already positively identified as his future compatriots.

This guy was huge. He was at least six foot five with impressive musculature and a steady, graceful way of moving that belied his size. He reminded Thiago of a large cat, right down to his wavy black hair and full growth of beard. The fact that he was extremely good-looking, as well as a veritable behemoth, didn't help him blend in very well, either. Thiago caught himself gaping at the imposing figure and he looked down quickly, staring at the wiry muscles in his forearms and feeling inexplicably inadequate all of a sudden.

The giant strode easily up to the counter and spoke to the man behind the counter with a friendly grin that seemed out of place attached to such a large person. The blond nodded and went about fixing the order as the big man turned and leaned against the counter, blatantly scanning the room before turning his attention back to his fresh cup of coffee.

Thiago was pretty certain this guy was supposed to be their brawn. Not much finesse, but still effective just because of his size. Thiago pondered the big man for a moment longer before returning his attention to the back wall.

"Anyone know what the hell a 'nebbish' is?" the chameleon with the crossword asked, and Thiago found himself biting his lower lip so as not to smile.

Aside from dreading working with the master of disguise, Thiago felt very good about himself just then. He had all of the five other men pegged, and now all there was to do was decide how best to approach them. Although he was certain of his compatriots now, and apparently helping one of them with a crossword puzzle, it went against all of his training to simply approach another suspected agent and introduce himself.

'Hi, I'm Thiago; I'll be your trained killer for the day.' It didn't sit right.

Finally, Thiago decided on approaching the man with the crossword since he seemed to be trying to make contact, but even as he put his hands on the table to push himself to his feet, the old man stood with difficulty and began to make his way toward the side wall. Thiago eased back into his seat with a curl of his lip and watched. He already disliked this guy and they hadn't even begun to work together yet.

But the old man hobbled past the man in the glasses toward the trash receptacles. He deposited his napkins there, then made his way slowly to the counter to place his used mug on the scratched Formica surface. Thiago observed that everyone in the café now watched him, and he snorted aloud at the uselessness of the ridiculous costume. They'd all pegged the guy. What had been the point?

The big man stood to the side, still leaning on the counter and flicking a silver cigarette lighter open and closed repeatedly as he studied the old guy. The sound was almost deafening in the silence of the café.

"Can I get you anything else?" the blond behind the counter asked the old man politely, his voice suddenly audible and practically echoing in the tense silence. Thiago was slightly shocked to hear a British accent coming from him. It fit him somehow, he had the rough look and stubborn bearing of someone from the north of England, but they were in Bumfuck, U.S.A., and what Thiago thought might have been a Yorkshire accent was a little strange to hear.

The old man shook his head and pulled out a wad of dollar bills to pay for his coffee and cigarettes, then turned around and hobbled toward the exit on precarious legs. Thiago frowned, unsettled by the unexpected departure of a man he'd thought he had pegged. He turned to finally make eye contact with each of the other men. The two in the corners and the big guy at the counter looked just as baffled as Thiago, but the guy with the crossword seemed not to care and the blond behind the counter strode toward the door purposefully.

He reached to lock it with a resounding clink of metal and flipped the 'Open' sign over to read 'Closed.'

"There, now. Thought he'd never leave," he said cheerfully as he turned to look at them all with a large grin. Thiago couldn't help but be slightly flummoxed. The man behind the counter was their sixth man? And the old man was apparently nothing more than an old man after all. How had Thiago misjudged that?

"My name is Shawn Bennett," the blond said to them, "and I'll be your tour guide for the evening." He grinned, either oblivious to their shock or indifferent to it.

The young chameleon on the far side of the café flopped his crossword onto the table disinterestedly and ran his hand over his face.

"I swear, Beignet, if you didn't have your theatrics you'd turn *motier foux*," he said in a low, surprisingly deep voice that he hadn't used when he'd asked his questions. The accent was different as well, and Thiago couldn't place it. It sounded like slightly mangled French and deep American South that went about a hundred miles a minute. "Half-crazy," the man continued as if translating his own words for himself with a shake of his head.

"Oh, you're one to talk about half-crazy," the man called Bennett retorted with amusement.

The young man responded with a two-fingered salute and winked at Thiago conspiratorially. He had a fluid, graceful way of moving that seemed somehow compact, like he didn't use any more energy in moving than what was absolutely necessary. He reminded Thiago even more of a chameleon, moving in a manner similar to a small lizard.

"You two obviously know each other then," the big man said in a thick Australian accent.

"We've had a few encounters," the chameleon said as his dark eyes slid toward the blond. "I am Remy Bergeron. Class One. And that British *salaud* is Shawn Bennett, also Class One," he said with a nod toward the blond. Thiago finally placed the accent as being Cajun. He realized he'd only ever heard it in movies.

"Field operatives, eh?" the big Aussie said in response. "The real deal. Nice. Brandt Everett," he introduced himself, "Class Seven."

"Explosives?" Thiago asked in surprise when the man told them his classification. It was the first word he'd uttered to them.

"That's right. Love to blow shit up," Everett responded with a cheeky grin. "And you?"

"Thiago. Class One."

"You got a last name, Thiago?" the Cajun asked him with a drawl that was slightly unsettling.

"No," Thiago answered curtly.

A short silence followed, but Thiago refused to shift under the scrutiny of his new companions.

"Three Class Ones," the intimidating brunette in the corner finally observed neutrally. "They've loaded us down with you bastards, huh?" All eyes turned to him as he stood and walked over to sit back down at Thiago's table. He spoke with an accent similar to that of an Australian, but there were slight differences. New Zealand, if Thiago had to make a guess of it. The way he moved was just as frightening as the way he looked, smooth and alarmingly agile. "Must be one fuck of a snake we're after," he said as he sat down and offered his hand. "Carl Travers. Class Four."

"Ooh, munitions," Remy Bergeron cooed with apparent relish as he also stood up and joined them at the table in the middle of the floor. The others drifted over and crowded around, and Bennett nodded at the shorter man with the blond highlights encouragingly when he strolled up.

"Nikolaus Faust," the shorter man said softly, his accent laced heavily with German, "Class Ten." This brought a low whistle from Thiago and the others looked at Faust apprehensively. Class Tens, given only the most basic of training, were relatively harmless when in the field. Physically speaking. They were communications specialists, usually relegated to the O.R.G. hubs scattered across the globe. His presence here with them was slightly more frightening than he himself was.

Bergeron was the first to offer his hand to the man. "They brought you out of one of the Cellars for this?" he asked in disbelief, referring to the communications hubs that none of them had ever actually seen.

"That's right," Nikolaus responded curtly in the efficient manner all Germans seemed to possess. "You have been given your own comm officer. We are completely off the radar now. Not even Black Ops, yes?"

"Invisible Ops," Brandt Everett suggested, attempting humor as Thiago's mind reeled at the implications of having their own communications specialist on board. They reported to no one now and they had no one to call in for back up or support. They were completely and utterly on their own. Invisible Ops, indeed. As far as Thiago knew, this was unprecedented.

"How did you get behind the counter?" Carl Travers asked Bennett curiously as Thiago stared at the tabletop morosely. Bergeron snickered and the sound drew Thiago's attention to him once more.

"He got the owner tied up in the back office," the Cajun said with a laugh.

"Aye," Bennett said gleefully. "Crabby old bugger. I've half a mind to leave him there."

"He bite like a gator, than one. Shoulda shot him like I told you," Bergeron scolded.

"How do you two know each other?" Thiago asked. Their seemingly friendly relationship bothered Thiago to no end. He didn't like being out of a loop. And he didn't like Class One operatives who knew each other. They weren't supposed to have any contact with their peers.

"We've had a few dealings," Bennett answered cryptically. Bergeron responded with a 'pffft' noise.

"Dealings?" he echoed in a perfect imitation of Bennett's accent, barking a laugh at the end. "We're all on the same side now, Shawn. No harm letting 'em know our dirty little secrets, *non*?" Bergeron winked at Travers and Thiago found himself growing even more concerned. "We were given the same assignment a few years back, during that whole purging mess, you remember?" the younger man explained, waiting until everyone nodded before continuing.

The purging mess Bergeron referred to had indeed been chaotic, with agents assigned the same targets and some agents targeted by mistake. Eventually, O.R.G., affectionately called the Organization by its agents, discovered it was a computer virus, but not before nine O.R.G. agents lost their lives to friendly fire. Thiago was almost one of them. It was now referred to as the Purge, capitalization implied with the hushed way agents murmured the word.

"*Mais*, we started catching wind of each other as we tailed our mark, who it turned out was another covert, and finally we both decide that the other, he must be either a rival or a bodyguard."

"In a shocking example of how our training has brainwashed us," Bennett said, taking up the narrative with a smile. "We both hatched the same plan and ended up attempting to kill one another in frighteningly similar ways. Thankfully the virus was uncovered and put right before we could follow through, but barely."

"I had him in my sights when I got the message."

"Bollocks," Bennett responded grumpily. "You were dead to rights."

"Pffft."

"How many times have I told you– "

"Yeah yeah yeah," Bergeron said with a dismissive wave. "Anyways," he went on pointedly, "when I came in here to feel the place out last week who do I find but Shawn, sitting in the corner there, looking all *canaille* and out of place. We had us *une petite mêlée*. Anyway! We got the safe house all set up already, thanks to that. Nikolaus, you got everything you need?"

"In my car," Faust answered readily.

"Let's get going then, shall we?" Everett suggested as he stood and towered over the rest of them.

"*Laissez les bons temps rouler*," Bergeron drawled with a grin.

Thiago still wasn't very satisfied with the apparent history of two of his new companions as they gathered their few belongings and headed for their various modes of transportation, but he decided the information they had offered would have to do for now.

II.

THREE days after their initial meeting, Carl Travers thought he might like to kill each one of these blokes in their sleep while on watch and slink away into the horizon. He'd be done with this whole disaster waiting to happen and no one would ever be the wiser.

It was an idle thought, though, caused by the fact that they were all going a little stir crazy. The safe house Remy Bergeron mentioned upon their first meeting was simply a small cabin in the middle of nowhere. There were four bedrooms, each roughly the size of a matchbox, each with submarine-style bunks. They had drawn straws for their beds. Carl had wound up sharing a room with Bergeron, the crazy Cajun who talked too fast.

Being cooped up with five other very active trained agents was not helping Carl's sanity. He was pretty sure he wasn't the only one.

That big Australian bastard with the explosives wouldn't stop blowing up the tree stumps behind the cabin– or anything else he could get a hold of, for that matter. Carl was fairly certain it wasn't the captivity driving Brandt Everett insane, though. He seemed generally unstable regardless of the circumstances.

For the past two mornings, Carl awoke to the sounds of small explosions followed by maniacal laughter and whoops of delight. Carl would jump up, gun at the ready, and hit his head on the top bunk without fail. It was a bit disconcerting, to say the least. And painful.

Carl was also slightly befuddled by the general tone of the group. He'd expected an atmosphere of reticence and suspicion, something befitting some of the most highly trained black ops agents in the world. But this had to be the most open, trusting, ridiculously good-natured group of spooks in the history of covert operations. With the possible exception of Thiago, who was still slightly suspicious of everyone and generally grouchy, they seemed to be trying to accept that they were on the same side of this particular fight and become chummy.

Carl had never been chummy with anyone. He hadn't personally given a flying pigmy fuck about any of these blokes at first, either; he hadn't expected this assignment to last long enough to need to care. Now it was three days later, and he found himself not only wanting to kill each of them, but actually enjoying their company at the same time. It was an odd mixture of feelings and Carl wasn't accustomed to the latter, but he didn't really care about that. What he did care about was the fact that not a fucking thing had been done yet, and despite his notorious sniper's patience, he was ready to get started. You couldn't *finish* something until you got started.

He allowed himself to grumble this particular observation as he prowled back and forth in front of the fireplace, thinking he would simply implode if he didn't start to feel useful soon. The others sat in various stages of relaxation, ranging from Everett leaning forward on the edge of his seat looking ready to set fire to anything that moved, to Bergeron sprawled along the sofa with his eyes closed. Carl glared at the younger man as he made a pass by the stone fireplace and snorted like a bull preparing to charge.

"Calm down, lad," Bennett said in his soothingly gruff voice.

"Don't 'lad' me," Carl grumbled testily. "What are we waiting for?" he demanded

"Weapons. Communications. Mobility. Intelligence– "

"Remy."

Bennett's stern admonition cut off Bergeron's droning monologue. The younger man never even opened his eyes as he spoke, simply ticking off his words with long, slender fingers as he reclined.

Shawn Bennett's piercing green eyes pinned Carl with a hard stare, and Carl stopped his pacing short as Bennett began to speak calmly. "We don't know one another, Mr. Travers," he said in a low, soothing voice, the type usually reserved for small children and irate animals. "We have no idea how we'll operate as a team, or even *if* we'll operate as a team. We have very little information to go on at the moment regarding our target, and even if we knew exactly where he was or what he was doing, going after him in the state of disarray in which we find ourselves at the moment would be suicidal."

Bennett looked at them each carefully as he spoke, as if he were making sure that his words were sinking in, and Carl's ire began to noticeably ebb. His shoulders slumped and he sat down heavily on the hearth as Bennett continued speaking.

"The next two weeks should be considered a crash course for us all in how to work as a team. I know the other Classes are more accustomed to working in groups, Mr. Travers, but I for one have never done something even remotely similar to this mission."

"Is that why we were told to meet way the fuck out here?" Everett asked curiously.

"If by 'here' you mean in the middle of North Dakota where no one can hear you and your explosives," Bennett drawled with a smirk, "then yes, I would assume so. We're free to train out here without much chance of showing up on anyone's radar."

"How much more do you know about this situation than the rest of us do?" Thiago asked, leaning forward and unconsciously mimicking Everett's stance. Bennett looked at him blankly for several tense moments before responding.

"Well that's difficult to say, isn't it?" he finally answered with infuriating calm.

Thiago harrumphed unhappily and leaned back into his chair. Bennett looked back up at Carl and continued as if he had never been interrupted.

"Now this Archer bloke isn't going anywhere in two weeks, and in all honesty, we all know whatever damage he can do has long since been put under way. And all that's not to mention the fact that our mobile hub isn't even up yet."

"Uhhh...."

All eyes turned to settle on the German, Nikolaus Faust, who shifted uncomfortably under their collective gaze and cleared his throat. "The hub is up, actually," he said in clipped, precise tones. "Prepared for a test run whenever you are all ready."

Bergeron sat up suddenly and looked at the smaller man with interest. Carl watched him curiously and alarm bells began to sound in his head. Why, he wasn't quite sure yet. Something about the meerkat-like way the man moved. "What sort of test?" Bergeron asked with what Carl thought was undue enthusiasm.

Carl had always heard Class One agents were generally fucked in the head. Whether this condition was due to the stress of their job or to a trait with which most of them were born, Carl didn't know, but he hoped the rumors were exaggerated. He'd never had to deal with any of them for any extended period of time. Only one or two hour stints in the past, and then he'd been concentrating on his job, not his companions. If these three turned out to be half as mad as they were rumored to be, Carl could see himself having a hard time of it. Not to mention that Remy Bergeron seemed to be a bit of a livewire and Thiago the mysterious Argentinean was a sulky bastard. He had yet to find a fault with Shawn Bennett, unless you considered the ability to intimidate five men– all of whom were either bigger, younger, or both– a fault.

"Well, the easiest thing to do would be to take the radios out into the woods and, you know, test them," Faust said in response to Bergeron's query with apparent discomfort.

Carl snorted in amusement. Of course it was that simple. Just test them.

"That's it? Like they're fucking walkie talkies or some shit?" Everett asked incredulously.

"High tech doesn't always mean complicated," Faust replied defensively.

"Well, it's something," Carl said in exasperation. "Let's get to it."

"Now?" Faust asked in surprise.

"Why not? Have we got anything better to do?" Carl asked snappishly.

"Well," the German responded uncertainly, looking at Bennett first as if for permission to answer. "No, I suppose not."

"Good," Bergeron said as he unfolded himself gracefully from the couch and stood, stretching his arms to the ceiling. "This couch is chafing my ass end."

He winked at Carl as if to say he understood the need to get up and do something, anything, and Carl found himself reconsidering his opinion of the younger man. Being a livewire wasn't always a bad thing, especially if you could contain it well.

If the young Cajun felt half as antsy as Carl did, then he had an impressive amount of self-control. Perhaps that was why the kid was a field operative and Carl was a weapons specialist. In the field, they had to remain calm under any circumstances. Carl's duties allowed a little more temper to enter the picture. A flash of memory involving beating on a land-to-air missile launcher with an oversized monkey wrench accompanied Carl's thoughts, and he had to bite his lip to keep from grinning as the little group disbanded to gather equipment.

After almost an hour of what Carl thought was entirely too much discussion on the subject, they finally geared up for a little nature hike.

"We'll go in pairs," Bennett said as he tied a knife to his thigh. Carl listened to his orders respectfully, thinking it did the man credit that a group of headstrong warriors such as they were automatically accepted him as their leader. Even Thiago, who seemed a bit reluctant to head blindly into much of anything, hadn't questioned Shawn Bennett's authority.

Carl wanted to question that authority now, though, because Bennett had just told him to partner up with Everett and head off into the wild unknown. Carl gave the Australian a wary glance and a nod. The big man returned Carl's nod with a slightly snaggletoothed grin that made his eyes sparkle mischievously, and Carl wondered if it were too late to become a religious man.

In Carl's experience, some people were crazy, and you weren't aware of it until they opened their mouths to speak or tried to kill you. But some people were crazy and you could tell just by looking in their eyes. Brandt Everett's eyes fairly gleamed. Whether it was madness or something else, Carl wasn't yet certain. He almost hoped that it was madness, plain and simple. Madness he thought he could deal with.

"Nikolaus, you'll go with Remy," Bennett said. The two young men gave each other unreadable glances, and then Bergeron looked back at Bennett with a look that could only be described as *familiar*. Carl found himself wondering yet again about their relationship. He'd never heard of two Class One operatives being acquaintances, much less friends.

It was obvious just from the sour look on his face that Thiago wondered the same thing and didn't like the situation one bit. But Carl reckoned that it was none of his affair until his life was on the line. Even if these two blokes shagged each other senseless every chance they got, he didn't see how that really affected him.

Carl shrugged into his coat and took the earpiece Faust offered him. "We're on one," the smaller man said as he turned each receiver to the correct frequency and handed them out. "On we go then," he said, placing his own piece in his ear and heading for the door. Carl watched the smaller man with interest. He seemed nervous and a little shifty most of the time, but at other times he seemed cool and confident. It was a strange thing to observe.

Carl didn't know much about the different Classes of agent, but he knew each and every one of them had to pass rigorous tests, both physical and mental, every three months. Nikolaus Faust might be a glorified computer tech in many respects, but he was still a trained agent, Carl reminded himself.

Their plan was simple enough; just a little hike through the woods to make sure the comms worked. Regardless of simplicity, each of them went out armed. Carl and Everett were ordered to go west, Bergeron and Faust were ordered to go east, and Bennett and Thiago set out to the north.

"Go one kilometer," Bennett ordered as they stood in what Carl had come to think of as the courtyard, the area in front of the porch trampled to mere dirt. "Don't shut off unless you give us some forewarning." They all acknowledged the order and set off walking in their various directions.

"If you see dinner, don't be afraid to bring it back with you," Thiago added quietly, speaking through the comm unit.

"Dinner?" Carl heard Faust murmur questioningly.

"This should be interesting," Carl muttered to Everett as he tapped his earpiece and they headed west together.

"I think he means small, innocent, fuzzy creatures," Bergeron's voice supplied gleefully in Carl's ear. "Leave dem bunnies alone, *couyon*." the Cajun chastised, his accent deepening as he allowed himself to grow comfortable in the outdoors. It was apparently his natural habitat. "Go for them mean critters," Bergeron advised. "My maw maw used to walk into the bayou, whack a *caimon* with a wooden spoon, and make us skin him for dinner."

"*Caimon*?" Faust echoed questioningly, his voice tinged with dread as if he thought he didn't want to know the answer.

"Alligator," Bennett voice supplied with amusement. Carl idly wondered why Bennett would know that so readily.

"Gator's mighty tasty, *couyon*," Bergeron crooned.

"Stick with the bunny, lad, they don't bite as hard. You like bunny, young Nikolaus?" Bennett's gruff voice questioned teasingly.

Carl and Everett shared a look and kept walking, trying to drown out the other two conversations and concentrate on getting to know one another as they walked. They spoke idly about their own specialties for roughly half a kilometer, and Carl began to genuinely worry about Brandt Everett's sanity as the man joyously recounted many of the various things he'd blown up in the past.

At least he enjoyed his work.

As a Class Four operative, Carl Travers's job was to provide and operate the various armaments available, either for a group operation or working on his own. While all operatives were entirely capable of handling weapons of any sort, Carl was more than merely competent. He knew almost everything there was to know about almost every weapon ever created. He could just as easily work a medieval catapult as he could Darth Vader's Death Ray if the occasion called for it.

As a Class Seven operative, Brandt Everett served much the same purpose. But instead of wielding guns or knives or whatnot, Everett blew shit up. Carl knew the basics about explosives. He had limited experience with substances like C4 and nitroglycerine and dynamite, but Everett could probably blow up their cabin with a coffee mug and a pinch of salt if he felt so inclined.

Just the thought of what Everett might or might not be inclined to blow up made Carl shiver as they walked. They came to a stop as the path they followed forked, and they stood in the middle of the path listening to the chatter of the other four men. Bergeron and Faust were arguing over whether the tree they were walking past was an oak, and Thiago seemed to be trying to coax Bennett into telling him more about how he'd met the young Cajun. Carl blinked at the two paths and looked at Everett as the man began to hum slightly.

"*Two roads diverged in a yellow wood*," Everett murmured to himself. Carl cocked his head at him in concern, and Everett glanced over at him. Carl had to force himself not to retreat under the gleam in the large man's black eyes. He watched Everett's gaze slowly return to the fork in the road with growing concern. "And I," the Australian continued in a theatrical voice. "I took the one less traveled by… and I blew the other one all to Hell."

Carl heard the other two conversations grind to a halt, and the silence in his ears was tense and expectant as Everett looked at him again. He could just imagine the other four men standing frozen in the middle of the woods, listening intently for an explosion.

"Robert Frost," Everett offered before setting out once more and veering off toward the tree line. He stooped to pick up a pinecone as Carl took a cautious step forward.

"I'm not sure that's exactly how it goes," Carl offered carefully. Everett responded with a joyous laugh.

"It's how it goes in my world," he called over his shoulder. He tossed the pinecone in the air and caught it again. Carl followed him slowly, wondering just how far gone this bloke really was. Everett turned suddenly, and Carl tensed, expecting a blow. "Did you know that pinecones are explosive?"

"What?" Carl asked warily, not sure he'd heard correctly and almost hoping he hadn't.

"Yep," Everett went on, oblivious to the discomfort he was causing his companion. "You have to get them before they seed, of course," he said, holding up the sticky cone as an example. Carl could see that it had yet to open up and was covered in goo. "The pitch is flammable, you see. Add a little flame and bam!" Everett informed him with a delighted flurry of hand movements.

Carl knew he was gaping at the other man, but he simply couldn't help it. In his ear he heard Thiago asking Bennett if he was hearing correctly, as well as an amusing dialogue between Faust and Bergeron.

"Did he say pinecones?" Faust asked.

"I think so," Bergeron answered. "Seems like I heard about that before. Never had need of using it, though. Thank God. Fucking pyromaniac. Crazier'n a male crab, that one."

Carl wondered briefly how long the young man had been in the business and what the hell a male crab had to do with anything, but he didn't have long to ponder the questions before Everett withdrew a silver cigarette lighter from his pocket and flicked it open. Carl's eyes widened and he took a step forward, then retreated again indecisively.

"Uhh…."

Before Carl could get another sound out of his mouth Everett put flame to pinecone and tossed it into the path on the right of the fork where a smattering of other pinecones littered the way. Carl watched the flaming projectile in morbid fascination as it arced gracefully through the air. Surely it couldn't make that big of an explosion. Could it?

"Cover!" Everett shouted gleefully, and he tackled Carl to the ground. They landed with a pair of grunts and a cloud of dirt and pine needles. Carl was a little surprised to discover that Everett covered his body protectively with his own. His big hands shielded his own head as well as Carl's as he pressed his body down and his face into Carl's neck. Carl squeezed his eyes closed and tensed, waiting for the inevitable 'bam.'

III.

THE explosion was by no means earth shattering, but the sound of it both coming through the earpiece and echoing distantly through the forest caused adrenaline to rush through Shawn Bennett's body at warp speed all the same.

"*Mierda*! What the fuck did he blow up this time?" Thiago questioned in exasperation, not sounding all too concerned but obviously ruffled enough to slip back into his native accent.

"Hope it wasn't Carl," Shawn responded flatly as he unconsciously lifted his chin and sniffed at the air. It smelled like snow. He could hear Remy and Nikolaus Faust jibbering in his ear, and Thiago was saying something about Brandt Everett being mentally unstable. But Shawn was watching the birds fly over the trees and trying to figure out where the explosion had originated. He turned to look in the direction from which the birds flew and pressed the earpiece further into his ear. "Travers? Everett?"

There was an uneasy silence as they waited for an answer, and finally there was a cough and a muffled curse.

"Carl? Lads?"

More curses and sounds of a scuffle ensued. Shawn exhaled in relief and let his tense muscles relax.

"Hope Travers kicks his ass," Thiago muttered as he shielded his eyes against the setting sun. "*Boludo loco.*"

Shawn gave Thiago a worried glance, telling himself he probably didn't want to know what that meant, but from the tone he had to admit he was probably thinking close to the same thing. That big bastard was going to blow them all to Hell before this assignment was over.

The sounds of struggle died out and Shawn could imagine the two men lying on the ground, staring blankly at the sky and breathing heavily. He could hear them breathing, anyway, and it was enough to feed the visual.

"If these things will stand up to a blast and a tussle in the dirt then they're okay with me," Shawn said happily, tapping his ear to let Thiago know he was talking about the earpieces and not their two companions. Thiago nodded solemnly and watched the squawking flock of birds soar overhead. Shawn thought about reminding him to close his mouth, but then decided the serious Argentinean wouldn't think it was funny. "What do we think then, lads?" he finally asked of the rest of them. "Continue walking or trust that these gadgets work and go home before Brandt sets the whole of North Dakota on fire?"

Shawn expected a chorus of responses, but all he got was silence. He turned to look curiously at Thiago, who simply shrugged in answer.

"You're the boss, right?" the man asked, pulling at his ear in apparent agitation and almost dislodging his earpiece in the process.

"What?" Shawn asked, hoping he'd misunderstood the tone Thiago had used.

Thiago simply raised his eyebrows as if to say 'you heard me.'

"Shawn?"

Shawn pressed the piece closer to his ear in order to better hear Remy's voice. It seemed that the things weren't working so well after all. He could barely hear the younger man say his name, and now there was nothing.

"Copy," Shawn said after a long silence. He waited for Remy to say more, but when nothing came he looked at Thiago in concern. "Can you hear anything?"

"Nothing," Thiago said in a low voice.

"Problem?" asked Everett's voice nonchalantly.

"Damn, we were hoping Travers had put you out of our misery, Everett," Shawn said with a grin.

"Just cause I'm here doesn't mean he didn't try," came Everett's voice again.

"I did try. He threatened to stick a pinecone up my– "

"SHAWN!"

Shawn barely restrained himself from jumping out of his skin when Remy shouted at him through his earpiece.

"Christ, lad! I copy!"

"Oh. Sorry." There was a short silence during which Shawn swore Remy was groaning and he began to grow a bit more concerned. "Ouch. Dammit. I think Nikki and I have stumbled into a valley. We aren't receiving a fucking thing down here."

Nikki? Shawn smiled wryly to himself. He loved to watch his young associate win others over so quickly. It made him feel like less of a sap for being befriended so easily by the same man who'd repeatedly tried to kill him on their first meeting.

"I think… triangulate… then it'll… oh, for fuck's sake," came Nikolaus Faust's garbled voice, sounding much farther away than Remy's had moments ago.

"Have you two separated?" Shawn demanded almost angrily.

"No. I climbed a tree for high ground," Remy said testily. Thiago snorted before he could stop himself, and Shawn rolled his eyes.

"Watch out for the pinecones," Travers deadpanned.

"It's an evergreen. No pinecones," Remy responded with a little more heat than was strictly necessary, in Shawn's opinion. The attitude was explained though, when Faust's voice filtered through to them all.

"It's… fucking… pine… *blödes arschloch*!"

"It's an evergreen!" Remy shot back, seemingly unfazed by the use of a language Shawn knew he didn't understand.

"Evergreens have pinecones," Travers supplied, though he didn't sound very certain.

"No, they bloody well don't," Everett responded as Shawn watched Thiago close his eyes and shake his head tiredly. "That's why they're called bloody *pine*cones. Cause they come from bloody *pines*!"

"Isn't a pine a type of evergreen?" Shawn asked, unable to keep himself out of the discussion regardless of how much he hated to encourage it.

"Evergreen! *Maudit*!" came Remy's irritated voice in response to a comment that apparently only he had heard. Shawn loved to hear him get riled; it accentuated his unusual accent and made him sound like he'd just crawled out of the bayou.

Shawn watched Thiago carefully during the exchange of insults between Travers and Everett that followed the pinecone comments. The man didn't seem overjoyed about the prospect of working with them all for an extended period of time, but then who would after listening to this insanity? Shawn sure as fuck hadn't liked the idea at first. But when he'd seen that Remy would be with him to keep him sane, he'd warmed to the idea, actually looked forward to it, and now that he was getting to know the others, he felt even more comfortable. If anything, Shawn appreciated a good sense of invincibility, which was precisely what they all displayed. Thiago, on the other hand, seemed just as uptight and unyielding as he had the first day. Shawn wondered if it was a cultural thing or Thiago's personality.

Either way, he had to loosen Thiago up, and fast. If you couldn't smile while in the middle of the wilderness as you listened to two rather large, frightening men threaten one another with sticking various bits of shrubbery up one another's orifices, then you hadn't been in this business long enough. Shawn idly wondered how long Thiago had been at it. That had to be a question they were all asking themselves, in fact, and Shawn thought it would be a good idea to see to it that they all sat down, tonight preferably, and gathered a little background on each other.

They had to trust each other with their lives. That would start with learning something about each other.

Shawn was rather amused to hear Remy repeatedly insult the heredity of the unfortunate tree he'd chosen to climb as he attempted his descent. His young friend was a unique individual to be sure. Not many people were as secure with their position in life as Remy. Remy bordered on being oblivious to his own mortality.

Perhaps that had something to do with Thiago's discomfort. Perhaps the easygoing attitude of the rest of them made him more uptight rather than less so. Perhaps he read it as unprofessional or even incapable.

"Thiago," Shawn said quietly, getting Thiago's attention and nodding toward the way they'd come. "What do you think? Keep going or head back?"

Thiago stood stock still for a moment, returning Shawn's gaze unerringly. Shawn wondered once more what the Argentinean agent was thinking and why he always seemed to view the situation as a threat.

"Let's head back," Thiago decided finally. "Sounds like the others are getting their fill of the wilderness, and we're losing the light."

"Good man," Shawn said approvingly. "Me feet are killing me," he joked, offering a friendly smile as they turned around and headed back in the direction of the cabin.

Thiago simply nodded and marched along in silence. Shawn eyed him suspiciously. Surely they would have run strenuous screenings on this group. They were a highly specialized, highly covert team formed for a very specific purpose. They were to track down a dangerous operative who'd been recruiting and turning agents for almost six months now. It certainly wouldn't do to have a turncoat in their midst on such a mission. Could that be the cause of Thiago's reticence? Could he be working for the Archer, simply unable to hide his discomfort with the cover 24/7?

Shawn pressed his earpiece closer and listened in on the other two conversations as he and Thiago walked on in silence. Perhaps he'd watch Thiago closer than he'd at first planned.

Shawn shook his head in immediate disagreement with himself. He wouldn't have to watch Thiago. The man was already tense enough as it was, if Shawn went about observing him closely it would cause him even more discomfort and possibly turn him dangerous. Perhaps it was a job more suited to his talented young friend.

If anyone could smoke Thiago out, it would be Remy.

'Yes,' Shawn thought to himself contentedly. Remy would be quite useful in that respect. And knowing the young Cajun as Shawn did, Remy would thoroughly enjoy the psychological warfare.

One potential problem solved, Shawn turned his thoughts to the other most obvious problem they faced. Brandt Everett was certifiably crazy so far as Shawn was concerned, and to keep him under control they had to find something the man liked more than blowing shit up.

Shawn's senses zeroed in on the soft crunching of dry leaves beneath their feet and the vague chatter from the other two groups as he mulled over the problems. It was a pleasant feeling, he realized suddenly, one that was all too unfamiliar. He felt almost at ease here in the middle of nowhere.

Thiago cleared his throat restlessly, and Shawn glanced at him curiously. The Argentinean walked with his head down and his eyes darting from side to side. He positively looked about to spring.

"Remy? Carl?" Shawn queried suddenly, making a decision he hoped he wouldn't regret. "We're going silent," he continued before either man he'd spoken to could respond. Thiago stopped walking and looked at him warily. Shawn could see the beginnings of alarm spreading over the man's face as he turned his own earpiece off. He nodded for Thiago to do the same.

"What are you doing?" Thiago asked suspiciously.

"I want to speak with you privately. Turn your unit off."

Thiago stared at him, obviously weighing his options. Shawn could hear the small voices asking what the hell was going on coming through Thiago's earpiece, and he prayed that Thiago would trust him. After what seemed like an eternity of waiting, Thiago raised his hand slowly and clicked the earpiece off. Shawn released a relieved breath and gave his companion a wry smile.

"Well?" Thiago asked impatiently.

"You don't trust us," Shawn said bluntly. The only sign of surprise from Thiago was a quick succession of blinks. "I don't much blame you. I can't say that I trust you entirely, either. And God knows we aren't the most stable bunch of blokes I've ever had dealings with. But we have to start somewhere, Mr. Thiago. We're on the same side of this."

Shawn watched Thiago's reaction closely for any sign that he was getting through, but the man was a rock. His expression never changed, and he didn't even shift his weight. Finally Thiago's piercing blue eyes flicked to the horizon before settling back on Shawn with determination.

"How do you know Bergeron?" he asked challengingly.

It was Shawn's turn to blink in surprise, and he had to force himself not to lose eye contact with the other man. The slightest move could be misconstrued as guilt, and that would ruin any chance of building trust with the suspicious agent. Was that what was causing the problems, the manner of his relationship with Remy? Shawn had thought it was the bigger group issue.

"We've told you," he responded evenly. "We tried to kill one another. Several times, actually."

"What else?" Thiago demanded.

"There's nothing else."

"Bullshit," Thiago spat out angrily. "You talk about trust while you stand there lying to me. What– "

"I'm not lying to you," Shawn interrupted calmly.

"Omitting the truth is the same as lying when my life depends on it," Thiago stated in a low voice. Shawn had to concede that point, but Thiago went on before Shawn could respond. "What is there about any of you to trust? I don't know you. I've never worked with any of you. For all I fucking know you're all working together and–"

"I understand being cautious," Shawn interrupted in a soothing voice. "But I think you're being a bit–"

"Cautious? Ha! What the fuck do you know about caution? I haven't seen an ounce of caution from you! What the fuck kind of a shoddy covert are you anyway?

You blindly trust anyone you're thrust into close quarters with just because we're supposedly on the same side?"

"Just a minute," Shawn warned in a low voice. He didn't mind the other man being pissy, but he drew the line at being insulted needlessly.

"Well? Can you honestly tell me that you don't lie awake at night wondering if Everett is going to blow us all to Hell just to see if he can? Travers is a little too eager to get the show on the road, if you ask me, and Faust is a shifty little German bastard. Not to mention how fucking suspicious it is to find two Class One agents who not only know each other, but actually have some sort of… I don't even know what you call it, relationship? But I've never met another agent I would trust my life with so easily. There has to be something more to you two and I want to know what it is."

"You're right," Shawn said quietly before Thiago could go on with his rant. Thiago's mouth snapped shut and he stared at Shawn, waiting for him to elaborate. "You're right," Shawn repeated, more to himself than to Thiago. Shawn took a deep breath and wondered how much to tell the man. "I trust Remy for many reasons, some of which are professional, and some are personal." He looked at Thiago carefully and saw the man returning the look intensely. "What say we save this conversation so everyone can hear?" he asked.

"Okay," Thiago said with a nod after a few moments of consideration.

"Right, then."

"You can call me Thio," Thiago said abruptly, "not Mr. Thiago or whatever." Shawn looked at him curiously and simply nodded. He knew what a concession that must be for the other man.

"In all honesty, Thio, techs are almost always shifty, as are Germans. Travers has got every right to be antsy. And I'm terrified of Everett," Shawn mumbled as he lifted his hand to his ear to switch his earpiece back on. Thiago watched him suspiciously. "We'll have to deal with him. Soon," Shawn added. Thiago nodded and frowned slightly. "Lads," Shawn said as he switched his earpiece back on and began to walk again. "Double time it. I want everyone in before the sun sets."

"What's the problem?" Remy asked as soon as the last word had left Shawn's mouth. Shawn knew him well enough to be able to hear the concern underneath the casual query. He smiled suddenly, overjoyed at the mere thought of working so closely with the man once again after months of going solo.

"No problem here," he responded with a grin. "Not yet, anyway."

"Ah, the promises you make, my little crouton," Remy sighed into all their ears, causing outright laughter from several of them. Shawn looked over at Thiago again to see the man smiling slightly. Feeling eyes on him, Thiago turned to look questioningly at Shawn, the smile fading.

"You speak French, Thiago?" Shawn asked in amusement. Thiago shook his head in answer. "Don't worry. Neither does Remy," Shawn snickered. Thiago actually fully smiled at him then, and Shawn marveled at how much the wide grin changed the man's appearance. He looked almost relaxed.

"I heard that, *couyon*!" came Remy's voice one last time.

"That was the point, dear."

IV.

NIKOLAUS Faust hadn't been too keen on getting involved in this mission when he'd first been given his orders. But, he hadn't really had much of a say in the matter. When the higher ups said 'jump,' Nikolaus didn't even stop to ask how high.

As a Class Ten operative, Nikolaus didn't often put his actual life on the line. Only in missions like this that required a mobile communications unit did he actually leave the sterile gray room full of expensive equipment that field operatives affectionately referred to as 'the Cellar.' This was only Nikolaus's second mobile mission with the Organization, but true mobile operations were few and far between, and there weren't many Class Ten agents who had more field experience than Nikolaus. He also knew just as well as his handlers that he was the best at what he did.

Still. He didn't like the idea of Invisible Ops, as Brandt Everett called it. The mere thought made him nervous.

Nikolaus didn't mind putting his life in danger; that's what they'd all signed up for. What scared him to no end was that these other five men also appeared to be the best at what they did, and that meant the Archer was a serious threat. A very serious threat. What could the man possibly be up to that would warrant a crack team like this? Nikolaus was almost afraid to find out. He was even more afraid of their mission failing. God only knew what would happen if they weren't able to stop him.

Despite these worries, or perhaps because of them, Nikolaus found himself walking through the forests of North Dakota with five of the most peculiar, unstable men he'd ever encountered. And enjoying himself to no end. He could get used to the mobile life. As long as he didn't get himself killed.

"So, Nikki," Remy Bergeron said as they wove their way uphill through the dense undergrowth of the forest. "Do you mind my calling you that?"

"It's, uh, not a problem," Nikolaus replied as he stumbled over a log and reached out to steady himself. He was a little surprised to find Bergeron beside him and holding his elbow to keep him from falling. Nikolaus had never seen anyone move so quickly over such treacherous ground. He was impressed.

"It's just easier to say than Nikolaus," Bergeron went on almost apologetically, seemingly unaware that he'd ever moved. "That's a lovely name, though. You'd be surprised how many Joe's and Bob's you come across in this business."

"My friends call me Niko sometimes," Nikolaus offered as he looked upward at the fading light and then down at Bergeron's hand still on his arm.

"I even worked with a Joe Bob last year. In Hawaii. Niko, you say? I like that too. D'you mind my using that?"

"Uhh, that's... yeah, no," Nikolaus responded uncertainly as Bergeron released him and pulled ahead once more, seemingly oblivious to just how unusual his thought processes were. Bergeron seemed genuinely pleased at the concession, though, and Nikolaus wondered how effective a covert the Cajun actually was. He appeared to wear his emotions on his sleeve, and he wasn't half as solemn or reticent as the other field agents seemed to be. Nikolaus wondered how long the man had been doing this. He seemed so open and ingenuous, he couldn't have been in the business for long, Nikolaus decided.

"I've been called so many names during missions I've lost track of them all," Bergeron continued in the same rambling tone. "Lots of 'hey yous' and 'dammits' mostly. Shawn's always called me Remy, though, when he's not calling me an idiot or... anyway, you're welcome to do the same if you like. Call me Remy, that is."

Despite the cavalier way in which the invitation was extended, with Bergeron losing his train of thought periodically and not even paying attention to what he was saying, Nikolaus found himself touched by the offer. In his world of cold technology and shady colleagues, what Remy said felt like an offer of camaraderie and trust. Nikolaus was more than happy to accept. He also accepted the opportunity Remy's statement gave him to broach a subject he was extremely curious about.

"So what, um, what is the situation with the two of you?" he asked, hoping he sounded nonchalant and glancing at Remy out of the corner of his eye. He heard the other two conversations come to a halt and was comforted by the fact that he wasn't the only one curious about the association between the two men.

"Hmm? Oh. Shawn, you mean? He tried to kill me," Remy answered matter-of-factly. "Several times. In the most unimaginative ways, I might add."

"Yeah, you said," Nikolaus murmured after hearing an irritated snort that he assumed came from Shawn Bennett.

"I mean, using a gun to kill someone. How very unoriginal," Remy said with a little smirk and a wink at Nikolaus.

"Your problem is that you think you're bullet proof," Bennett's voice said caustically in response to Remy's jab. "It was no mere gun, lad. That rifle was a work of art. A classic. A beautiful– "

"Mm hmm," Remy said in a bored voice. "Hey, Brandt. You work much with plastique?"

Nikolaus heard what sounded suspiciously like an affirmative purr coming through his earpiece and he shivered involuntarily.

"I had his rifle rigged. One pull of the trigger and…."

"Bam," Brandt's voice finished in a frighteningly pleasure-laden tone.

"That's right. *Heureusement*, fortunately, it did not come to that."

"That's when you received the message, then?" Nikolaus asked, trying to get Remy to continue. Remy simply nodded and squinted into the distance. Nikolaus let the offer to continue hang in the air for a few moments, but Remy walked on, oblivious to all but his immediate surroundings as they picked their way through the thick undergrowth. After a while, the other two conversations quietly resumed, and Nikolaus thought they could try to whittle more information from the two cagey men later.

"Do you remember the way being this rough on the way down?" Remy finally asked in concern as he pulled up short and looked around. Nikolaus surveyed his surroundings in alarm as the steady droning in his ear ceased once more.

"You two have a problem?" asked Shawn Bennett's gruff voice.

"Not yet, my little onion," Remy responded in a voice close to irritation.

Nikolaus lifted an eyebrow to express his doubt in the other man's assessment of their situation, but he remained silent. Being in the middle of a dense forest with sketchy communications and unstable companions was bad enough, but not having a clear idea of where you were going in said forest, that was really high on Nikolaus's Oh Shit List. What was even higher, though, was pissing off one of those aforementioned unstable companions by questioning his judgment. So Nikolaus stayed silent.

"Yet?" Bennett asked without much concern.

"God, I hate being lost," Bergeron murmured.

"Lost? I thought you said we didn't have a problem," Nikolaus blurted worriedly.

"*Au contraire*," Remy said sagely. "Being lost is not always a problem. We have at least a week before we starve." He stopped and sniffed at the air. "Smells like snow, though. *That* may be a problem. I don't do cold well."

"Believe me, young Nikolaus," Bennett said with amusement. "When Remy gets well and truly lost, you will certainly know it. Watch your back though, he'd just as soon cook and eat *you* as he would some furry little woodland creature."

"Mind your own business, Beignet," Remy said in what appeared to be an automatic response to Shawn's teasing as he searched the trees for their location. "Don't go forewarning the prey."

"Did he just call you Beignet?" Thiago's voice inquired incredulously.

"It's a type of doughnut," Shawn muttered in answer. "It's a long story," he added. After a brief silence he blurted, "Remy really enjoys food, okay?"

Nikolaus tried not to snort in amusement as he watched Remy warily. He wondered about the man's competency once more and hoped his supposed super-spy skills would kick in or something and turn the homing beacon back on. He chastised himself for not having paid more attention to where they were going and mused about how long it would take Everett and his exploding pinecones to clear the area of all the trees in order to find them.

"Ah! Got it!" Remy exclaimed suddenly, pointing at the trunk of a tree some ten meters away. Nikolaus squinted in the half-light and could just barely see a pale, thin gash across the bark. He sighed in relief. "Just veered off course a bit is all," Remy continued as they walked toward the marker. Nikolaus hadn't even noticed Remy making the marks as they walked, and for the fourth time in ten minutes he found himself re-evaluating his opinion of Remy's abilities.

By the time Nikolaus and Remy made it back to the cabin the sun was beyond setting, and Nikolaus cringed at the thought that Bennett might be angry with them for being late. He really needn't have worried. It seemed that Shawn Bennett wasn't so much the bastard that Nikolaus pictured him to be, and he genuinely liked the man whenever he was around him. It was just when they were separate that the unwarranted image of the ill-tempered, nasty veteran spook haunted Nikolaus's imagination. Nikolaus knew that it was a stereotype; a preconceived notion of what their leader would be like. But he was having difficulty shaking it.

He thought it rather ironic that as he had these thoughts Thiago came out onto the porch to light a cigarette. Now there was the cranky covert Nikolaus had imagined.

"You're late," Thiago said in a flat voice. Nikolaus opened his mouth to apologize, but Remy smiled cheekily and shocked Nikolaus by wrapping his arm around him and pulling him closer as if they'd been friends all of their lives.

"I was teaching Niko the proper technique for getting lost in the woods," Remy claimed seriously. "He took to the lesson real well."

Nikolaus saw Thiago shake his head in the low light coming from within the cabin. He wondered whether the man was smiling. He followed Remy past Thiago and into the cabin to find the other three men sitting around the fire and talking quietly.

"Ah," Carl Travers said as he lifted his head and glanced at them with a grin. "The trailblazers are back."

"We didn't have smoke signals to work with like you did," Remy responded with a smirk. Carl's lips twitched in amusement and he resumed his job of stoking the fire. "Throw a pinecone on that if you're having trouble. I hear they're flammable," Remy offered as he headed for the kitchen.

"Only the pitch," Everett said knowingly as he leant back on the sofa and stretched his arms behind his head. Thiago returned from the porch and pulled the door shut behind him as Nikolaus perched on the arm of the sofa.

"It'll snow tonight," the Argentinean announced. The others nodded in agreement and Travers poked at the fire absently.

"All right, lads," Bennett finally said as Remy returned with two cups of steaming coffee. To Nikolaus's surprise, Remy handed one cup to him and sipped from the other carefully. Nikolaus thanked him quietly and sniffed at the coffee. The Cajun made his coffee the consistency of tar. He sipped at it carefully and shifted to get comfortable as Bennett tried to settle them all down.

"We may as well do this now, lest it become an even bigger problem," the blond said, looking as if he were gearing up for battle.

"What problem is this?" Everett asked distractedly. Nikolaus was slightly worried to see that the man stared at the fire with something akin to lust and had trouble concentrating on what they were saying. Nikolaus wasn't the only one to notice, apparently, because Thiago and Remy moved almost simultaneously to sit with Travers on the hearth of the fireplace, effectively blocking Everett's view.

As soon as the flames disappeared behind their bodies it was as if a spell broke, and Everett snapped to attention. Nikolaus glanced warily over at his equipment set up in the corner. He knew in his heart Everett was going to try to blow his shit up. He just knew it.

Nikolaus returned his attention to the group as Bennett gave Everett one last worried sidelong glance and then began to speak.

"I know you all have a problem with the nature of our relationship," Bennett started bluntly, indicating Remy Bergeron with a tilt of his head. "I can understand why you do. If I were on the other side of it, I would have a problem too. So if you have questions, ask them now," Bennett went on in an even voice.

"Was the story you told us before true?" Travers asked immediately.

"Yes," Bennett responded readily. Nikolaus decided right then that he was going to have to take what they said as the truth. He had no hope of deciphering whether a trained agent was lying.

"That's all I need then," Travers shrugged negligently. Nikolaus was fairly shocked at the Kiwi's easy acceptance, but then he realized he didn't really give a damn, either. Yes, he was curious. But not to the extent that he absolutely had to know.

"Same here," Everett added quietly.

"Yeah," Nikolaus agreed as he looked back at Bennett. "Unless it's something that may come back and bite one of us on the ass," he added, "then I see no reason to get into it. Unless you just feel like sharing," he offered cheekily, risking

Bennett's ire to lighten the mood. To his relief, Bennett smiled a little and nodded.

All eyes turned to Thiago, and the man looked back at them unflinchingly.

"I'd like to know," he said steadily. "But like Nikolaus said," he continued with a small sigh, "if it's not life-threatening I don't suppose it's necessary. And as much as I hate to admit it, if it doesn't pertain to this mission then, then it's none of our business."

They were all silent for a moment, and Nikolaus watched Remy and Bennett share an indecipherable look. The connection they shared was unmistakable, and Nikolaus found himself slightly envious of it.

"It's been roughly five years since we met," Bergeron told them suddenly, startling even Bennett. "Since then we've worked together off and on. Whenever two or more agents are needed, and we're available, they send us in. We're the closest thing to a permanent team in the Organization, I suppose, and I believe that's the reason they've put us on this." Nikolaus saw a small smile play over the Cajun's lips as he paused for what was apparently dramatic effect. Bennett shook his head but Remy spoke anyway. "And yes, during our very limited down time we tend to have quite a lot of sex."

This last statement shocked the hell out of Nikolaus. Thiago too, it seemed, was left dumbfounded. His mouth hung open as he stared at Remy, much as Nikolaus reckoned his own was doing. Neither Travers nor Everett seemed to be shocked or to care overly much. Nikolaus briefly wondered if Remy was poking fun at them for being so nosy. But then he decided that the Cajun probably told the truth. It explained their easy manner with one another anyway.

It wasn't so much the fact that they were two men that surprised Nikolaus. In fact, he didn't know many agents who weren't at least bisexual. It had something to do with the recruiting standards of coverts; you had to be willing and able to seduce any mark, no matter their gender. It wasn't the sexual aspect at all. It was the fact that these two agents would completely trust not only their operations, but also their lives to one another repeatedly. It boggled Nikolaus's mind. Not to mention the fact that they were apparently rather accustomed to working as a team. That was unheard of in the Organization. O.R.G. field agents were solo operators. Period.

"Well," Bennett finally said with a huff. "That's not exactly how I would have put it, but you've always been succinct, if nothing else, lad."

"Thank you."

"That wasn't exactly a compliment."

Remy made a face that clearly said 'who gives a shit' and stood up gracefully. "Who else has a problem I can solve?" he asked happily as he stretched his hands over his head. "Anyone?" Everyone shook his head. Remy nodded in acknowledgement and winked cheekily at Nikolaus.

Nikolaus couldn't help but smile in return. But then Remy was all seriousness again, and he turned around and knelt in front of Thiago, placing his hands on the other man's knees. Nikolaus wondered briefly if he did it to make Thiago uncomfortable and gain the upper hand. Surely he wouldn't be that calculating, even if he were an operative. Would he?

"What about you, *papere*?" Bergeron asked. The word was obviously one Remy was accustomed to using when speaking to someone with respect. Nikolaus was pretty certain he used it on purpose.

"Don't call me that," Thiago said in a flat voice, apparently getting the same impression. "And I have no problem," he said almost as an afterthought. "You two fucking is much more innocent than anything I was imagining."

"*Excellent*!" Remy exclaimed, and he stood and strolled into the kitchen once more, leaving behind a slightly befuddled group of spooks.

Surely it wouldn't be that painless. Thiago had been too bothered by it to accept that explanation so readily.

Nikolaus watched in interest as Bennett and Thiago shared a nod of acknowledgement. Perhaps it *was* that easy. Perhaps it wasn't, but Nikolaus wouldn't have to deal with any future fallout. Either way, Nikolaus hoped their little session would end the tension he'd sensed between the two senior members of the group and they would be able to get on with it.

"Remy!" Bennett called suddenly, almost causing Nikolaus to fall off his precarious perch on the arm of the sofa. "Get back in here. We have some research to do."

"Research?" Travers repeated hopefully, leaning forward and practically bouncing in place. Nikolaus knew the man was spoiling for something to do, and he smiled at him sympathetically. Bennett nodded as Remy returned to the room with a quizzical look on his face and a bag of chocolate covered-pretzels in his hand.

"Carl," Bennett said as he shifted to look at Travers. "Tell us about yourself."

"What?" Travers responded stupidly.

"Tell us about yourself," Bennett repeated patiently. "You're a Class Four, yes? I doubt any of us know much about the other designators except the basics, so tell us about yourself. How long have you been in the business? How old are you? Where are you from? What are your duties?"

"Uhh…." Travers looked around at the others in confusion. Nikolaus thought that it was a safe bet to say that Carl Travers had never been asked a personal question during a mission before, and he could relate to the man's reticence.

"Okay, I'll start then," Bennett continued amiably. "We'll make this simple. I was born in 1969 in Sheffield, South Yorkshire. Recruited into the Organization in October '87."

"You've been in the Business for almost twenty years?" Nikolaus asked before he could stop himself. That was one hell of a record. People in this line of work didn't usually live that long, much less stay in it for that long.

"That's right."

"Jesus," Thiago said softly. "That makes you one of the most senior field operatives in the Organization, doesn't it?"

"Other than Mac? I suppose it does."

"Mac?" Nikolaus questioned.

"Sir John McTiernan," Bennett supplied.

"The Grey Ghost?" Everett asked keenly. "You know him?"

"He was my recruiter," Bennett answered softly.

"Wow," Nikolaus said almost to himself. He had never met Sir John McTiernan, the man they referred to as Mac or the Grey Ghost or sometimes merely Sir. But he had heard the stories about him. He'd earned the appellation the Grey Ghost in his early days. Nikolaus had never heard why, and now it was used to put the fear of God into the new recruits. Like folklore used to frighten small children into going to bed. For Shawn Bennett to actually know him was incredible.

"I'm based in North America for the most part," Bennett continued with a wry smile. "America and a little of Canada. They tend to think I'm Irish," he added with a private, disgruntled sneer.

There was a short silence in which each man was surely thinking about the Grey Ghost and being even more intimidated by Shawn Bennett, but Nikolaus finally took a deep breath and offered his own information.

"Born in Berlin, Germany. 1980," he said with a nod at Remy Bergeron. They were the babies, so to speak, and Nikolaus felt a certain kinship with the other young man. Remy smiled and nodded back in acknowledgement. "Recruited in 2003. Based in Germany. Should I go into my duties?"

"Nah," Travers answered with a wave of his hand. "You do all the shit the rest of us don't understand. That's all we need to know." The others murmured in agreement, and Nikolaus smiled. At least they seemed to respect his abilities. Most operatives didn't appreciate the intricacies of communications and the gadgets he worked with.

"I was born in Auckland, New Zealand. 1975," Travers offered as he looked around. "Recruited in '97. My home turf is Russia mostly. I get sent into Europe and the Pacific regularly. I'm the man you call when you can't kill someone easily."

"You're the Specialist, yeah?" Remy said in a low voice. "The assassin?"

"That's right," Travers responded with a hint of pride. Remy gave him a nod and Nikolaus looked at Carl Travers carefully. He looked more frightening now than he had five minutes ago. Knowing that a man could kill you without batting an eye or breaking a sweat was a bit unnerving.

"I was born in Buenos Aires in 1967," Thiago offered after a moment of silence. "Recruited in 1992. I suppose that makes me the old man of the group," he added with a smile. Nikolaus thought perhaps he could like the man after all, now that he seemed to be growing more comfortable with them. He really did have quite an endearing manner about him when he relaxed.

"Nothing wrong with being old," Bennett practically growled. Nikolaus caught a glare shot toward Remy and saw the younger man snap his mouth shut and look at Bennett innocently.

"Most of my territory is in South America. Spain, sometimes. Argentina mostly, though," Thiago added. Nikolaus allowed himself to admire the almost complete lack of Thiago's accent. He supposed a Class One field operative had to lose their accent at times. Even Remy Bergeron's less noticeable Cajun accent, Nikolaus had noticed, would disappear here and there.

"I was born in Sydney, 1970," Brandt Everett offered after another moment of silence. "Recruited in '94. Territory is Asia mostly, out of Australia. You all know what Class Seven does?"

"You blow shit up," Travers supplied in a long-suffering voice that drew snickers from the rest of the group.

"All kinds of shit," Everett growled with relish, the gleam returning to his eyes in full force.

There was an uncomfortable silence in which it seemed even the fire was afraid to crackle. Then Remy cleared his throat, and Nikolaus was of the opinion that the as-of-yet unflappable young man was perhaps uncomfortable for the first time.

"Is Brandt your real name?" he asked the Australian, and Everett looked up at him and nodded with a smile. "It means firebrand, *non*?" Everett nodded again and Remy smirked. "Was it the chicken or the egg, then?" he asked, producing a bark of a laugh from the big man but no answer.

"*Mais, jamais d'la vie*," Remy muttered in amusement. "I was born in Bayou Lafourche, Louisiana. 1981," he went on curtly, suddenly all business once more. Nikolaus was a little surprised to learn his age. Remy was less than a year younger than he was. His accent changed suddenly, and his voice softened until he sounded like the perfectly stoned surfer dude. "Working in North America, mostly the lower 48. Recruited…," he hesitated, and his voice was once again the drawling, easy Cajun accent when he spoke. "Recruited in the summer of '97."

"You were sixteen?" Travers exclaimed after a moment's calculation.

"*Oui*."

"Remy has special talents," Bennett informed them with a small grin.

"Meaning?" Thiago asked curiously.

"I'm sure you'll find out soon enough," Bennett said with an enigmatic grin.

V.

SHAWN'S words echoed through Brandt Everett's head like a pebble tumbling down a never-ending chasm.

Special talents, eh? That could be fun.

With Remy's spot on the hearth vacated, Brandt's gaze was drawn back to the flames, and the rest of the conversation that consisted mostly of Nikolaus asking about Class One duties faded into background noise as the hissing and spitting of the flames called to him like a siren's sweet song.

Brandt enjoyed demolition. He enjoyed having the power to control the fate of anything within the blast radius. He enjoyed putting *his* special talents to work and creating chaos and destruction.

He knew what the others thought of him. They thought him mad.

Well, perhaps they were right.

Brandt *was* mad. Well and truly mad. Gleefully, joyously, certifiably, insanely mad.

But he wasn't stupid. Only rarely did he well and truly lose himself to the madness. Being thought mad had the advantage of making people wary of you, while at the same time causing them to underestimate you. Brandt's madness was controllable, and it had always served him well in the past.

He shook his head and blinked away the image of the flames as he realized that he was zoning out once more.

He returned his attention to Nikolaus and focused his still slightly glazed eyes on the other man. Nikolaus's eyes met Brandt's, and his words ground to a halt.

"What were you saying?" Brandt asked him, and the man snapped his gaping jaw closed and cleared his throat.

"I was asking about the other Classes," he answered as Remy moved discreetly to sit once more on the hearth in front of the fire. "I don't really know much about them."

"Ah. Well, Sevens blow shit up," Brandt offered with a wink.

"As previously established," Carl muttered.

"Do you sleep with a stick of dynamite?" Remy asked in amusement.

"Dynamite would tend to confuse me in bed," Brandt answered seriously. The others shared puzzled looks, but Remy lifted an eyebrow in interest and inclined his chin challengingly.

Yes. The young man was definitely driving on the wrong side of the road.

"Class Ten is a glorified computer tech. Communications, gadgets and what have you," Nikolaus provided self-deprecatingly, though Brandt could hear the pride beneath the words.

Could poke fun at himself while still having pride in what he did. Brandt liked Nikolaus.

"Has anyone ever met a nine?" Nikolaus asked curiously after several moments.

"There's no such thing," replied Shawn.

"Huh?"

"Nine is a decoy for field ops. If you're not certain about your contact you class yourself as a Nine. If they don't question it, then…." Shawn trailed off and looked at Remy and Thiago cautiously.

"Then what?" Nikolaus asked.

"You kill them and abort the mission as blown," Remy answered bluntly. Nikolaus's eyes widened, but Remy winked at him and twirled the ring on his finger absently.

Straightforward and almost nonchalant about death and destruction. Brandt liked Remy. A lot.

Shawn and Thiago continued to explain the different classes to Nikolaus, and Brandt listened with interest. He'd never paid much attention to the other designators. They didn't get to blow shit up and therefore were of little consequence in Brandt's world.

"Eight is strategy," Shawn went on.

"Non-mobile operatives who like to tell the rest of us how to do our jobs," Thiago clarified.

Blunt with a little bitty chip on his shoulder. Brandt hadn't made up his mind about Thiago yet. He had potential, though.

"Seven is… obviously…." Shawn trailed off again and looked at Brandt, who still gazed at Thiago thoughtfully.

"We blow shit up," Brandt provided without removing his gaze from Thiago's handsome face. Thiago gave him a small, amused twitch of his lips.

"Right," Shawn said uneasily as he watched Brandt. Finally he shook his head and continued the lecture. "The Six designator provides field intelligence when the agent in the field can't obtain it himself."

"That's usually where the women in skimpy red dresses come in," Carl added with a smirk, "sent to seduce the bigwigs when they won't go for a bloke."

Brandt couldn't quite get a read on this one. He liked Carl regardless, and even the fact he was a Kiwi and quite possibly straight didn't dampen the growing fondness.

Carl raised an inquiring eyebrow as Brandt's gaze transferred to him.

"Have a lot of experience with Sixes, do you, Trigger?" Brandt asked the man.

"Not as such, no," Carl responded with a grin. Brandt smiled back at him and winked. Maybe not straight. Even better.

"Five," Shawn said loudly, trying to inject some semblance of order back into the discussion. "Provides transportation. Planes, trains, and the like."

All eyes turned to Remy as he began to snicker. Brandt saw Shawn glare at the younger man, but Remy was oblivious and continued to try ineffectively not to laugh.

"And the like," he said in a deep voice, a fair mimicry of Shawn's delivery. "Do you remember," he stuttered, trying to catch his breath as his eyes began to tear up, "that motorbike? When you were caught that one time… and I had to come rescue you… called in transport for two… the… the motorbike with… with the sidecar?" Brandt smiled at the vague image Remy's nearly incoherent laughter painted. "Shawn… with the…." Remy put his fingers into circles and placed them around his eyes to illustrate. "Goggles," he snickered and finally lost it, falling against Thiago in a fit of raucous laughter.

"Bloody sidecar," Shawn grumbled.

"I saved *ton tcheue* with that sidecar," Remy laughed.

"Aye. Destroyed me dignity though," Shawn muttered.

Stoic, kind of grumpy, and obviously able to give as good as he got. Brandt thought maybe he liked Shawn most of all.

"Fours," Shawn said with a gesture toward Carl. Carl simply nodded, and Shawn continued, "Four is the weapons specialty. They're also used as specialized assassins, as I think we've established."

"I could kill you with a pinecone," Carl told Nikolaus seriously. Brandt was quite pleased to see the man's eyes twinkle with amusement, and for the first time in years he felt like he could fit in with a group of people. They were *all* slightly mad– Brandt reasoned that you had to be in this business– but unlike other coverts with whom he'd worked, these blokes had a good time of it.

"The three is cleanup," Thiago continued the lecture with a hint of amusement as he glanced sideways at Carl. "Basically, if someone fucks up, *cogidas,* they're sent in to fix the mess."

Nikolaus nodded and looked around at the group. When no one continued with the lecture he asked, "What about the Two designator?"

Brandt sat back and watched the other men carefully. This was one of the moments he'd been waiting for. This was a very telling moment.

Remy cleared his throat and Thiago examined the ground between his feet carefully. Carl appeared to be clueless as to the cause of their discomfort, and Shawn, well, his was the most interesting reaction of all. He simply didn't have one. Not a tic or flash of movement or worried sound. Nothing. Brandt was impressed.

"Has anyone ever dealt with a Two?" Nikolaus asked again innocently.

"No," Shawn finally responded with confidence.

"How do you know?"

"The Two designator is the one given to agents who have turned. Or are known to be moles," Thiago answered. Carl shot a slightly confused glance at Brandt, and Brandt shrugged in return. Carl apparently didn't know about the Two designator either, but then, usually only Class One coverts did.

"So then, why would no one have dealt with one?" Nikolaus asked persistently. "There are obviously moles around."

"They don't live long after they're given the designation," Shawn answered quietly. The soft tone of his voice gave the conversation a grim tone Brandt found unsettling.

Nikolaus nodded in understanding, and the conversation died away. Remy rolled his head from side to side and his neck emitted several popping sounds that made the hair on the back of Brandt's neck stand up.

"So the Archer… he's a Two then?" Nikolaus asked after a long silence.

"That's right," Shawn answered as Remy began to mutter and grumble in that odd French that wasn't quite really French.

"It is a death sentence," the Cajun hissed, sounding as if he didn't agree with the Organization's methods where Two designators were concerned. Brandt could see that. If you were labeled a traitor there was no trial to prove your innocence. It was indeed a death sentence.

"And we are meant to kill him?" Nikolaus asked in an oddly innocent voice

Brandt watched Shawn closely for his reaction to the query. Shawn pressed his lips together and slapped his hands against his thighs before standing up.

"We'll deal with that first thing in the morning," he declared. Everyone mumbled their agreement and began to stand and stretch. "Brandt? You've got first watch," Shawn informed him as the others began to drift toward the bedrooms, muttering wishes for a good night and other, less civil things. “No playing in the fire,” Shawn ordered with a smile.

“Right. No worries,” Brandt said as he glanced once more at the flames. Shawn stood there looking at him for a long moment, and Brandt could tell that he wanted to say more. These field agents were all the same. So very predictable in the way they handled an apparent roadblock like Brandt. The older man looked back at the bedrooms and the retreating forms of their comrades briefly before turning and opening his mouth to speak. “Hey, Beignet?” Brandt said quietly before he could do so. “I’ll be here when you need me,” he said simply.

Shawn snorted in amusement, not at all bothered by the use of the nickname Remy had used earlier. “0400,” he informed Brandt softly. “Just the two of us. I have a proposition.”

Brandt nodded and watched Shawn walk away. The fire spoke to him with a hiss that sounded like laughter in Brandt’s head, and he smiled happily at his flickering companion.

Several quiet and uneventful hours later Brandt looked at his watch and stretched. He stood up slowly and cracked his back and neck, and then squinted to look down the dark hallway.

He’d been instructed to let the fire die down– to make them look like a group of hunters with no concern for keeping watch– and he’d let it though it had pained him not to play in it. Now it simply smoldered as he made his way on the creaking floorboards to the first room on the left.

He scratched lightly at the heavy wooden door, and it opened almost immediately. Shawn stood there in a worn pair of gray sweatpants and nothing else. His hair told of the few hours of sleep he had managed.

Before Shawn could open his mouth in greeting, Brandt pinned him neatly against the wall beside the doorway and nudged the door gently closed with his foot. Shawn hadn’t made a sound, even though his striking green eyes registered alarm, and Brandt grinned at him. This bloke was a real pro.

“You have an offer to make me?” Brandt asked in a barely audible voice.

“I do,” Shawn said softly.

“You seem fairly certain that I’ll accept it,” Brandt observed in amusement.

“Call it hope,” Shawn answered easily, not attempting to free himself from Brandt’s grasp.

“And just what exactly are you hoping to get?” Brandt asked as he held Shawn pinned against the wall.

“Some peace of mind,” Shawn whispered in answer.

“And what piece is mine?” Brandt inquired with a slowly spreading grin.

"You tell me what it'll take," Shawn murmured as his eyes took in Brandt's features in the low light.

"Oh?" said Brandt absentmindedly, becoming distracted by the way Shawn's accent deepened when he was in a slightly heightened state of awareness.

Shawn nodded then said, "I was actually going to offer you Remy."

Brandt's eyes flashed in interest, but he pressed his body closer to Shawn's to let him know that what he had here might just be better. "Why does Remy call you Beignet?" Brandt asked instead of responding to the statement.

Shawn snorted in consternation and amusement. "I think it started because it sounded like my name and he knew it annoyed me," he answered with a shrug of one shoulder. Brandt's grip tightened. "He would tell you it's because I remind him of a doughnut. Whatever the hell that means," Shawn grumbled as he rested his head against the wall.

"Well, you don't look like a doughnut," Brandt murmured with a tilt of his head as he examined Shawn critically. "You don't feel like one either," he added as his fingers dug into the hard muscles of Shawn's arms. "I think you'll do, just the same," he decided as he tilted his head and slowly ran his tongue along the line of Shawn's jaw. "I could see the resemblance," he purred low in his throat, "if we had some powdered sugar."

"Well, then," Shawn whispered distractedly, at a loss for the first time that Brandt had seen. Brandt smiled and tightened his grip on Shawn's biceps. "How did you know what I planned to offer?" Shawn asked curiously as he shifted and slowly tried to twist away from Brandt's grasp.

"I always get bribes from you field people if I'll leave the fire alone," Brandt answered as he raised his head again. "Sexual bribe, though, that's a new one. Do I look that desperate?" he asked curiously.

"It's not for your benefit that I'm bribing," Shawn said as his eyes came back into focus. "If we can keep you centered long enough to keep you from blowing us all to Hell then I'll be happy."

"Ah, so you're a distraction. A replacement for my other interests."

"I am," Shawn answered in a low voice. "Every day you go without blowing something up– something that doesn't deserve it anyway– you'll get a treat," Shawn propositioned, and Brandt found himself loosening his grip and staring as if mesmerized by the prospect.

Brandt had never encountered someone so commanding as this man, and it fascinated him. Even standing there pinned against the wall by a larger man and offering his body as a bribe for good behavior, Shawn's manner demanded both respect and obedience.

Brandt was simply fascinated.

"Treat," he repeated quietly.

"That's right," Shawn nodded. Brandt licked his lips. "Now you've not been behaving yourself, but I'm going to show you what you'll get if you do, understand?"

"Yes," Brandt breathed. Before he could try to capture Shawn's mouth in the brutal kiss he wanted so badly to take, he found himself hitting the floor with a muffled thud.

Shawn hovered over him and held him down quite easily, and Brandt wondered if he could have even gotten free if he really tried.

He didn't want to get free, though.

"What do you want?" Shawn asked in barely a whisper.

"You," Brandt responded readily. "Right now."

"You want to take me?" Shawn asked with what could have been wariness.

Brandt's cock twitched at the thought, but that wasn't what he wanted tonight. He enjoyed being in charge and having power. Power to destroy. Power to create. Power to make another man scream in pleasure or pain.

But right now he wanted to be overpowered, and this was just the man to do it.

"No," he said.

Before Brandt really registered what was happening, Shawn had him on his feet once more and simultaneously pushed him toward the bed and patted him down skillfully.

"I've never had to strip search someone for explosives before fucking them," Shawn whispered in irritation. "You're not packing any C4 or some shit, are you?"

"Not tonight," Brandt responded distractedly as Shawn deftly pushed his briefs to the ground and shoved him at the bed.

"Stay quiet, understood? Get on your knees," Shawn ordered gruffly, and Brandt hurried to obey.

He buried his face in Shawn's pillow to keep from crying out as Shawn prepared him roughly. How the man knew he liked it hard and fast Brandt didn't know, but he was grateful all the same.

Brandt liked the burn.

He enjoyed experiencing the pain along with the pleasure. It was like braving the heat of the flames in order to witness the beauty of the destruction. Although Brandt expected a lot of pain, he was sadly disappointed. Shawn was very good at what he did in all aspects of his life, and the brief flash of pain Brandt craved was soon replaced with immense pleasure.

Brandt found he didn't mind the loss of the burn so much.

VI.

THE Archer was restless tonight. He itched to make a move. To strike before they had the chance to do so.

That was the last thing he should do, though. To start being impulsive now would be the death of him. He'd known they put a team together to sniff him out, but he hadn't expected it to be so skilled or varied a group. And he hadn't expected them to mobilize so quickly. He'd barely had time to reposition himself before they were meant to rendezvous.

They had the best agents in the Business after him, and he had to admit he was a little scared. He was walking a tight rope without a net, so to speak, and he was completely off the map now. No real allies in sight.

He did have one advantage. More than one, really. He knew who they were, while they grasped at straws as to his identity. He knew where they were, while they were having their 'getting to know you' sessions. And he knew how they would go about finding him, because the same people who had trained him had trained all of them.

He had time to plan.

He would leave them just enough of a trail to make them overconfident. To make them feel as if they were on the right track and that he wasn't quite as crafty as they thought. He would lull them into a sense of false security and success and then he would strike hard and fast. He would leave such a mess that the Organization would never know what hit them

His biggest advantage? These men were accustomed to working alone. All he had to do was stir them up a bit and make them suspect one another. Pit them against each other.

With any luck, they would take care of each other before he even had to lift a finger.

VII.

THE early morning proved to be unusual in that Remy Bergeron wasn't awakened by an explosion. He wasn't particularly alarmed by this. He also wasn't unduly concerned when he padded into the main room at first light to find nothing but embers in the fireplace and Brandt nowhere in sight.

Despite Shawn's hopes for stealth, Remy had heard almost every move the two men had made in the early hours of the morning from the top bunk of the room he shared with Carl. As soon as the noises coming from Shawn's room started, Remy had climbed down and checked that Carl really was asleep. Making certain of that, he had then shuffled sleepily to the door and cracked it open, sitting with his back against the wall to hear better.

It wasn't that Remy was a voyeur– not in many senses of the word anyway– it simply helped his peace of mind to know that if Shawn called out for help he could be there before too much blood spilled. The last thing he wanted was for Brandt to try to kill the man before they even got under way.

Despite his nonchalance over the whole matter so far, there was only one person in the world Remy trusted, and that was Shawn Bennett. He couldn't have anything happening to him and he would intervene if he heard the slightest hint of trouble.

Thankfully, nothing of the sort was necessary. He remained awake long after the noises from Shawn's room died, despite his exhaustion. Their remote location notwithstanding, Remy figured it wouldn't do to let their guard down completely.

Did it bother him that Shawn was even now curled in a single bed with another man? It probably would have if theirs was a normal relationship. But theirs was not a normal relationship, and it didn't bother Remy. Much. They'd each had their share of partners while on the job, and they'd both enjoyed many of the trysts.

He knew getting Brandt under control and keeping him there was a necessity, and he agreed with Shawn that the best thing to do would be to simply distract the man with something better than his explosives. Remy knew from his experience with other pyromaniacs that if it didn't blow up or flame, it had better be fuckable. And Remy wasn't particularly interested in being blown up. He had to smile at the way Shawn handled it, though. Behave yourself and get a treat. Remy snorted in amusement.

He knelt in front of the fire and poked at the ashes absently as he mulled over the coming mission. For the first time in his career, Remy found himself regretting the intel he'd gathered. Usually the intelligence was just a bunch of facts you had to put in proper places, like pieces of a puzzle. But the information Remy put together in preparation for this mission seemed to tell its own story before Remy could even try to decipher the pieces. Whether it was real or imagined on Remy's part, it caused the mission itself to have a strange feeling to it, like the end to something.

He even knew what that something was.

Remy loved what he did. He loved the adventure and the danger and the subterfuge. He loved the mind games and loved the challenges he faced with every mission. He couldn't imagine living any other way. He knew that would probably change in due time. He could see it in the older operatives. Shawn and Thiago, while both still very capable, both looked and acted weary at times.

A sudden wave of melancholy swept over Remy as he thought about the day that Shawn would retire. It was coming.

What would he do with himself then?

The soft creak of a floorboard alerted Remy to another's presence, but he remained motionless, poking idly at the ashes of the fire. It took a great deal of effort not to be completely on guard out here. Old habits died hard. But Remy was doing his best to remain casual and easy in the presence of the others.

From the light, tentative tread of the steps, Remy suspected it was Thiago standing behind him, and Thiago was the last person he wanted to seem jumpy around.

"I see Everett refrained from playing in the fire," Thiago's soft voice observed directly over Remy's shoulder. If Thiago expected to get a startle response of some sort, he would be disappointed this morning. Remy knew he should play up the appearance of ineptitude he'd been cultivating, but he just didn't have the energy at that particular moment. He had to stop depressing himself with thoughts of the future and try to stay in the present.

"I gave him a break around 0400," Remy said simply, a half-truth at best. He turned his head and looked up at Thiago. He looked tired, and Remy wondered if he too heard the deal struck in the early hours of the morning and decided to stand his own guard as Remy did.

"Wouldn't do to have the fire going all night," Thiago said approvingly as he met Remy's eyes. "Must keep up appearances, *sí*? Just in case," he added bitterly.

Remy noted the resentful tone and raised a questioning eyebrow. Thiago was even wearier than Remy thought, apparently.

"They did it to you too, *non*?" Remy asked with a note of sadness in his voice that he couldn't quite stamp out. Thiago looked at him sharply and knelt beside him.

"Did what?"

"Told you this could be your last assignment if you took it," Remy clarified as he returned his gaze to the dark fireplace. Thiago remained silent. "They offered Shawn the same thing," Remy continued quietly. "*Retraite*. Retirement. 'Find the Archer,' they told us. 'We'll set you up in a nice villa in Italy,' they said, 'or a little spread in the Caribbean. Just don't come back to haunt us, lads. Stay gone.'"

Remy found himself disgusted by his own bitter tone as he mimicked his handler, but he refused to restrain himself. Perhaps a mutual embittered attitude would help him win Thiago's confidence.

"Coverts, they are a thing of the past, Thiago," he said as he jabbed at the remains of the fire. "Agents like Niko, they will be taking over before long. That, or we'll blow everyone all to Hell on our way down."

Thiago was silent. Remy suspected he'd shocked the older man with his little outburst.

"Did they offer you the same deal?" Thiago finally inquired curiously. Remy nodded and stood up to retrieve the box of matches from the stone mantle. "Did you take it?" Thiago asked as Remy knelt back down. Remy looked down at the box of matches in his hands, then looked up and met Thiago's eyes steadily. For the first time he noticed the odd color of Thiago's eyes; somewhere between gray and blue. They were really quite striking.

"*Non*," he answered distantly, still slightly distracted by Thiago's piercing gaze. "They offered, but I couldn't… couldn't give this up yet."

Thiago nodded and his brow wrinkled in a sympathetic gesture.

"Did you take it?" Remy asked carefully, watching Thiago closely in order to gauge how willing the man was to share with him. There was a tense moment in which Remy felt sure he'd trampled over every ounce of trust Thiago might have formed. Thiago's countenance clouded over, and he broke their eye contact to stare at the ashes of the fire. Then he took a deep breath and nodded slowly. Remy had the fleeting impression that perhaps he was ashamed to admit it.

"I took it."

Despite the answer being what he'd been expecting to hear, Remy was a little shocked. How could anyone give up this life? And for what? Retirement in the country where nothing ever happened?

"You've been in the game for quite a while," Remy responded in a low, soothing voice, trying to ease Thiago's mind and gain a little more confidence from him.

"Not as long as Shawn," Thiago argued as he let his head hang. Remy felt pity for the inner turmoil the man must have been experiencing and made a decision that could very well do him in if Shawn ever found out.

"Shawn took it, too," he told Thiago regretfully. Thiago's head snapped up and Remy looked away before the man could see the sadness in his face. "We need more firewood," Remy observed in a dazed voice, not quite believing he'd just told Thiago a fact even he himself was not supposed to know. He'd tipped his hand too early, but he just couldn't stop himself.

He stood up and walked over to the row of hooks where their coats hung and plucked his from its spot.

"I'll go with you," Thiago offered, coming over to take hold of his own jacket and his hiking boots.

"*Mais oui*, I'll wake one of the others," Remy muttered as Thiago pulled one of the heavy boots on.

The man nodded and Remy made his way to Shawn's door. He listened carefully but could hear nothing. He was pretty sure Shawn and Brandt moved to Brandt's room after their bargaining session, but Remy was still at a loss as to why.

He pushed the door open and peeked inside anyway. Both bunks were empty.

He turned around and stared at Brandt's door. The problem with waking Shawn was in entering Brandt's room. God only knew how many booby traps there might be. He steeled himself and stepped up to the door, pushing it open slightly and peering inside. The first thing he saw was the blurry barrel of a gun, pointing directly at his nose. He crossed his eyes and the tip of the .38 came into focus.

"Christ, lad," Shawn whispered in exasperation. Remy cocked an eyebrow at the gun and smirked at Shawn.

"I see that you are up," he said cheekily. Shawn gave him a withering glare but it didn't really faze Remy much. "Coast will be clear in a minute," he whispered.

He pulled the heavy door closed before Shawn could respond with anything other than an affirmative nod and went to the door of the room he shared with Carl. He tapped lightly and opened it when he heard a soft greeting from the other side.

"Thiago and I are going for firewood," he said softly as Carl rubbed his tired eyes and blinked at Remy sleepily. "How did you sleep?" he asked, even though he knew Carl had been restless and fitful.

"Not used to a soft bed," Carl mumbled as he sat up carefully, glancing up at the bottom of the top bunk warily and rubbing the back of his neck. "Do you need help?"

"*Mais non*. Just letting someone know we'd be gone. The fortress," Remy sighed theatrically, "it is unguarded."

"Where's Everett?"

"*Fais do do*. Sleeping. I relieved him earlier. I think Shawn's awake but he is dangerous when he's half-conscious so...," Remy said wryly. Another half-truth. Shawn was dangerous all the time.

"Okay," Carl said sleepily. He swung his legs out of the bed to land lightly on the wooden floor. "Cold!" he hissed and drew his feet back into the warm cocoon of his covers. Remy snickered and pulled the door closed.

He turned to find Shawn standing directly behind him, silent as a ghost. Remy gave a theatrical little start and immediately wrapped his arms around the other man's neck as if he were about to faint from the shock. He inhaled deeply and relished the comforting feel and scent of the other man for a brief moment.

"You should know not to sneak up on a spook like that, Beignet," Remy whispered in a hoarse voice.

"Mm hmm," Shawn responded as he hugged Remy tightly and then released him slowly. "Turn your radar on, Dixie," he admonished softly, "you're too distracted. How was your night?"

"Highly frustrating," Remy whispered as he remembered spending the early morning listening to Shawn and Brandt's muffled moans. "You owe me, *non?*"

Shawn snorted in amusement and gave Remy's finger a friendly nip before mouthing a belated good morning and then disappearing into his own bedroom.

Remy sighed heavily as he watched the door close. He heard a light scuffle and looked down the hall to find Thiago standing there, his head lowered slightly and his shadowed eyes on Remy.

"Sorry," Remy offered softly as he realized Thiago had probably seen them capering around in the hallway.

"No worries," Thiago responded in a voice that barely carried to Remy. "Ready?"

Remy nodded and started forward with his head down. He was a little angry with himself for not being aware of Thiago's location. He was certain the man hadn't heard their conversation, and even if he had, it wouldn't have really mattered, but it pissed him off nonetheless. Four days without a threat, and he was already losing his edge? Fucking ridiculous.

"It's a bit more than just sex, isn't it?" Thiago asserted almost as soon as they reached the edge of the woods. Remy looked at him intently through the cloud of his frozen breath to try to decipher what the man thought of the situation. There was no threat or judgment in Thiago's eyes, and Remy was convinced Thiago was simply curious. Perhaps still a bit suspicious, but he had every right to be.

"Yes," Remy answered simply.

Thiago gave a tilt of his head that made him look a little like a confused puppy and asked, "You love him?"

Now there was a tricky question. Remy's morals were certainly sketchy in most respects, but he didn't like to lie unless it was strictly necessary. And that didn't have much to do with his morals either, come to think of it. He simply enjoyed the challenge of getting out of sticky situations using nothing but the truth. He had been known to stretch the truth when needed, to say what needed to be said and leave the rest for the listener to erroneously fill in. Or he prevaricated until the original question was forgotten. The truth, he had found, was a diamond of many facets.

But this was different. Shawn was Remy's best friend– his only friend– and Remy would die for him if the occasion called for it. He could answer Thiago's query truthfully and say yes, he did love Shawn, and let Thiago assume what he liked.

But for some reason, standing there in the falling snow and looking into those odd blue eyes, Remy wanted to explain. He wanted to use as many words as possible to tell Thiago exactly how he felt about Shawn and what their relationship entailed.

He wanted to tell Thiago that Shawn had saved his life too many times to count.

He wanted to tell Thiago that Shawn had followed him blindly into almost certain death on at least three occasions for no other reasons than loyalty and love, only to miraculously escape and go back to do it again.

He wanted to tell Thiago that in everything they did, he and Shawn were partners, and that if Shawn decided he wanted to blow them all away and attempt to take over the world with a pellet gun, Remy would have been there at his side with a homemade slingshot.

He wanted to make Thiago understand how complex and important and devoted the relationship between himself and Shawn was. That it went far beyond the occasional tumble in bed and that it was far more complicated than love.

He didn't know why he wanted Thiago to know all these things. He just knew he felt an overwhelming urge to confess how important Shawn was to him. He suspected it had nothing to do with Thiago, but rather the fact that he knew this was Shawn's last mission. The sense of finality around the man was palpable.

Whatever the reason, Remy wanted to clarify their relationship out loud once and for all, if only for himself if nothing else. But Remy Bergeron was nothing if not a creature of habit, no matter how much he wanted something.

"Yes," he finally answered somberly.

VIII.

THE six restless coverts sat around the blazing fire as Nikolaus clicked away at his keyboard and Carl attempted to light what was apparently a faulty burner on the stove in order to cook dinner. Brandt was forbidden to even try. The man was okay until something sparked, and then the look in his eyes made Thiago genuinely want to piss himself.

Thiago knew now he had underestimated every single one of these men. He'd tried to convince himself that the threat was somehow less than it appeared, and in so doing convinced himself that the agents assigned to the job came from the bottom of the barrel. But they were all the very best at what they did, and out of the three field operatives present, Thiago was fairly certain that he himself was the weakest link. It didn't help his confidence much that Shawn and Remy were apparently able to read one another's minds and anticipate what the other was going to do before he did it.

Despite the way Remy described them as working 'off and on' together over the years, Thiago thought maybe it was more on than off. But in love? Thiago didn't buy it. People of their ilk didn't fall in love.

But why would Remy lie about something that was essentially inconsequential to their working relationship? Thiago asked himself that all day, risking curious glances at the young Cajun every now and then and frowning as he thought through every permutation of his various theories.

In the end, it all came down to one truth: Remy Bergeron couldn't be trusted.

The only thing that felt natural about the man was his genuine loyalty to Shawn, and in Thiago's mind that meant that Shawn Bennett couldn't be trusted either.

Thiago could tell there was already something the two men were keeping from the rest of them, and he suspected it had something to do with Brandt. Thiago thought perhaps they'd drugged the man or something. He'd been calm all day, much too calm for Thiago's peace of mind, and it had been over twenty-four hours since something had caught fire or blown up.

Whatever they did to him or threatened him with, it worked. Make no mistake, Thiago was grateful for their efforts, he just didn't like being left out of the loop.

He realized he was probably looking fairly morose as he sat and stared into the fire, and he shifted uncomfortably, hoping he wasn't being observed. He seemed to be the only one still suspicious of the others. They were all quite comfortable with one another. Thiago was desperately trying to trust them, but he simply couldn't. He'd lived too long without trustworthy allies to change his habits so quickly. He wondered how Shawn managed to find it in himself to trust Remy to the extent he did. He wondered what transpired between 'we tried to kill each other' and what they were now.

As he pondered, he unconsciously took a count of the men in the room, as he did every ten minutes or so, and was a little shocked to find Remy gone.

The little *pajero* was unnaturally quiet. Humans weren't supposed to move like that, even if they were trained to be silent. Thiago looked around the room discreetly, turning around to check on Carl in time to see the man kick the stove in frustration. Thiago snorted in amusement and sympathy and returned his gaze to the rest of the room as Remy came strolling back down the hall wrapped up in a fuzzy white blanket. It looked to be faux sheepskin or something similar, and Thiago shivered as he looked at it. He hadn't even realized that he was cold.

"You better take that off," Brandt warned casually.

"*Mais oui*?" Remy asked in obvious amusement as he plopped himself down gracelessly between Brandt and Thiago on the couch.

"If you know what's good for you. The Kiwi in there might mistake you for a sheep and try to do unnatural things to you."

Remy snickered, and Thiago rolled his eyes, trying to hide his amusement.

"Fuck you, Wally!" they heard from the kitchen, followed by another clang from the abused stove.

"Any time, Trigger!"

Thiago didn't know when or where the little feud between the two men had started. He assumed it was due simply to their nationalities and their various frightening similarities, but he didn't really care all that much. It remained harmless enough, and at least it was amusing.

"I don't see how Carl doing unnatural things to me would be at all bad," Remy mused. "I'd even 'baaa' for him," he added, making a fair imitation of a sheep's bleating as he spoke. Thiago was once again struck by how skilled Remy appeared to be at mimicking sounds and voices and he added that to his list of observations. The talent probably came in handy.

"What was that?" Carl called from the kitchen. He sounded amused.

"You heard me!" Remy shouted back, adding another 'baaa' for good measure and wrapping the blanket tighter around his body.

"Careful," Brandt said in a deep, growling voice. "That's turning me on a little."

Remy laughed, but Thiago noticed him leaning away from the big man as he looked at him. "Baa means no, Wally," he intoned with a wag of his finger in Brandt's face.

Before anyone could say anything else regarding sex or sheep– or, God forbid, both– Nikolaus let out a little shout and looked at them all triumphantly.

"I've made it into the main files and disabled the detection system," he announced with a hint of pride in his voice. Thiago felt Remy's body stiffen against his, but just as quickly as it happened he was loose again and turning around to peer back at Nikolaus excitedly. Thiago watched Remy suspiciously.

"The Organization's main files?" Remy asked eagerly.

"Yep," Nikolaus said proudly as he continued to click away. Thiago was impressed by the feat, but distracted by Remy's reaction. Why did he tense? Was it just a tic or did it mean something more significant? Did Remy have something to hide in those files?

As he watched Remy, a little more intently than he liked to admit, Carl thumped into the room, wiping his hands on a dishtowel and huffed loudly.

"Fucking stove," was all he said.

"No supper then?" Remy asked as he flopped around and tilted his head back to look at Carl.

Carl looked down at him in disgust and shook his head.

"Mind if I take a stab at it?" Remy asked.

"Be my guest."

Remy got up, tossed his sheep blanket haphazardly over Brandt's face, and strutted into the kitchen.

Thiago watched him go and wondered how in the world the younger man survived to this point. He seriously hoped the whole puppy-like attitude was an act the younger man just wasn't accustomed to dropping, but he seemed genuinely excitable, and that was dangerous as hell.

"And I have it," Nikolaus announced smugly, and they all snapped to attention. "I've found it already!"

Thiago and Shawn scrambled to their feet, and Remy hurried back into the room as they all crowded around Nikolaus's chair to peer at the computer screen.

"What do you mean you've got it?" Carl asked excitedly. "What's 'it'?"

"New Zealand grammar," Brandt murmured wryly, earning a discreet jab in the ribs. Brandt snickered and wrapped Carl up in his arms in retaliation. Thiago watched distractedly as they struggled and couldn't help but grin.

"I mean I've found the drop spot. The file we use to communicate."

"Why did we have to hack in?" Thiago asked, thinking he already knew the answer but wanting to make certain.

"Well, the Organization has completely cut us off in order to weed out any moles, but we can still communicate. They'll leave whatever information they have for us in predetermined spots within the main files, and we do the same whenever we need to report in. It just depends on my getting into the system and finding the right file. Which I've just done," Nikolaus explained with a cheeky little smile. "Now, we've been following the Archer's communications," Nikolaus began explaining.

"You know how he communicates?" Remy asked. Thiago tried to interpret the tone, but all he could tell was that Remy was impressed.

"We have for weeks now. But we can't decipher the code."

"Oh."

"Now, we know that the Archer communicates with his operatives through an online chat room."

"What?" Shawn said disbelievingly.

"Yeah. It's very simple, and almost impossible to trace if you do it right. Which he does."

"What kind of chat room?" Remy asked curiously.

"Wait, wait, lemme guess," Brandt said in amusement, releasing Carl and holding up his hand dramatically. "An archery chat room."

Nikolaus snorted and nodded. "Makes you think maybe he wants us to catch him, doesn't it?"

"How did he get the name, anyway?" Thiago asked curiously. The name bothered the shit out of him for some reason.

"Through the chat room, as far as I know. That's where we first caught wind of him. But he's refused to change methods. The code he uses is apparently random, so I suppose he sees no need."

"That or he's got other methods and we just don't know about them," Carl corrected drearily. Thiago nodded his agreement.

"Well, yes," was all Nikolaus said as he pulled up a file for them all to see. "This is his last communication. We know they're orders, but we don't know what for."

Thiago leaned in and read the message as Remy continued to ask questions about how they knew which messages were his and other things Thiago knew he should care about. But the message itself was distracting him. It was a mixture of jibberish and seemingly random numbers.

"The hell?" Shawn murmured right next to Thiago's ear.

"Exactly," Nikolaus said in a frustrated voice. "It appears to be a stream cipher but–"

"Wait, a what?" Brandt asked with a confused frown.

"A stream cipher," Nikolaus answered as he pointed at the series of numbers and letters. "You might know it as a state cipher?" he ventured. They all looked at him blankly, and he sighed. "Well, it's a symmetric cipher where plaintext is combined with keystream and converted one at a time, and the following plaintext varies depending on–"

"Do it in English, you bloody Kraut," Brandt demanded with a smirk.

Nikolaus huffed and looked at the computer screen, pursing his lips thoughtfully. "Basically," he finally sighed, "it's a complicated form of encoding where the key varies every time. Which makes it difficult to crack without serious mathematical functions if you don't know the key."

"So each code requires a different key to read it?" Shawn ventured.

"That's right," Nikolaus nodded.

"And we don't have any keys," Remy observed in a flat voice.

"Correct," Nikolaus confirmed.

"So we have to look at them from another angle," Remy murmured almost to himself. "The back door."

"Right," Shawn agreed. "Do we have an event to compare it with?" he asked as he too leaned forward and read the message.

"What do you mean by back door?" Carl asked, sounding slightly lost.

"Well, if we have the event that this message produced, we can come at it in reverse," Remy explained.

"Use the answer to form the question," Shawn provided.

Nikolaus typed in a command and brought up a list of dates, locations, and names.

"These are all the hits on our agents in the past year," he said.

"Jesus," Thiago breathed as he looked at the list. It was longer than he'd imagined, and Thiago was beginning to understand the fuss over the Archer. "Surely he's not responsible for all these?" he asked weakly.

"Not all of them, I'm sure. But we're not taking any chances by underestimating him."

They all nodded in approval of the reasoning, and Thiago scanned the list again.

"When was that message posted? Can you take out all the events that occurred before that?" Remy asked. Thiago marveled at the change in his demeanor. He was all business now. Brandt and Carl were looking on in interest, but it was obvious they were accustomed to simply being told where to point the gun or how long to set the timer. They just waited for their orders.

Nikolaus did as Remy requested, and only one line was left on the screen. The only hit to occur after the last order from the Archer.

"So there we have it. We just need to figure out how the two of them match up, right?" Brandt asked hopefully.

"If this is indeed the hit the Archer was ordering in his last transmission," Shawn said grimly. "It could be from a previous communication, and the latest orders just haven't been carried out yet."

"Ah."

"How many days between the message and the last hit?" Thiago asked, squinting slightly at the screen.

"Looks like five," Nikolaus answered after a moment.

"That's not much time to elapse between order and hit," Shawn murmured.

"Does anyone else think maybe we're overreaching here?" Carl asked. "I mean, they have their best techs on this code, am I right? I don't think any of us is going to have some sort of Indiana Jones epiphany and suddenly figure it out."

Remy snorted and stood up to look at Carl over Thiago's back. Thiago was jostled a bit as the younger man grabbed Carl around the shoulders and pulled him closer, saying, "We'll just find you a nice whip, *non*?"

"We'll start somewhere else then," Shawn said with a sigh as he watched Carl struggle to extricate himself from Remy's grasp.

"Where?" Nikolaus asked, his fingers poised over the keyboard.

"Is that all they've left us in the drop?"

"Yeah."

"Damn. Okay. Do we have a list of agents we know to've turned?"

"Yeah." Nikolaus repeated as he typed in the commands to bring up the requested list. This list, too, was longer than Thiago would have supposed. The Archer had been a busy boy according to the Organization.

"Now, can you bring up lists of the agents these have worked with in the past year and cross-reference them?"

"Ooh, nice," Remy said appreciatively, and Thiago couldn't help but to agree.

Nikolaus busily typed away, and when he finished he said, "It may take a while."

"I'll be kicking the stove then," Remy said almost immediately, and he turned to head for the kitchen.

"I think I'll help him," Brandt said in an eager voice, but Shawn grabbed him by the front of his shirt to stop him.

"No fireworks," he said in a stern voice.

Brandt put his hand over Shawn's hand at his heart and looked at Shawn innocently. "You wound me," he said pitifully. Shawn simply rolled his eyes and released the bigger man. "I made a promise," Brandt sniffed haughtily as Shawn shoved him almost playfully toward the kitchen.

Thiago watched him creep up behind Remy and grab him, and he wondered if the younger man was playing the same game with Brandt as he had with Thiago that morning. Thiago knew Remy wasn't as inept as he made out to be, but it was damn difficult to tell which reactions were genuine and which were affected. Remy rewarded Brandt with a little squawk, as if he hadn't heard him coming, and the two of them snickered and playfully shoved one another back and forth as they jostled for space in front of the stove.

Despite his suspicions, Thiago couldn't help but smile at their antics.

"Okay," Shawn said quietly, and he gestured for them to gather around him. Carl and Thiago exchanged wary glances and leaned forward to listen as Nikolaus tore his eyes away from the computer screen.

"I've struck a deal with Brandt," Shawn told them, getting right to the point. "I was going to keep it quiet, but there's really no point. He doesn't seem the type to care one way or the other."

"Is that why nothing's blown up today?" Carl asked distractedly. He was watching Brandt and Remy out of the corner of his eye, and Thiago thought perhaps he secretly hoped they wouldn't be able to get the stove working, either. It was probably a matter of pride.

"Yes."

"What sort of deal?" Thiago asked.

"Bribery," Shawn answered with a slight flush.

"What are you bribing him with?" Thiago asked pointedly.

"To put it bluntly?" Shawn questioned wryly. Thiago nodded. "Myself. And Remy. And whoever else is willing," he said, giving them each a second's stare from clear green eyes before glancing back at Brandt warily. Shawn's eyes were truly unique, Thiago decided. The only problem was that you couldn't read them.

"You mean sex?" Nikolaus asked, sounding thoroughly scandalized.

"Yes. It was the only thing I knew he would give up his explosives for. And really…," Shawn smiled at them and shrugged. "Brandt's quite a bit of all right, isn't he?" he said with a wink. Carl laughed, and Thiago smiled a little. He couldn't argue with that, and Thiago had used his body to ensure the success of missions in the past. He had no problem with this arrangement.

"Count me in then," he offered readily enough.

"If it keeps my ass from being blown up," Carl added with a nod, "I'm in."

Nikolaus looked at them with wide eyes when they all turned their attention to him. "I'm not really qualified for that sort of thing," he protested in a hoarse whisper.

"I think the four of us should be able to keep him happy," Shawn responded with a grin, giving Nikolaus a comforting pat on the back. Nikolaus looked back at his computer screens, relieved.

"What do *I* have to do to be bribed with sex?" Carl asked with a huff.

"I don't think you'll need to bribe anyone in this group," Thiago muttered wryly.

IX.

SHAWN finished filling them in on the details just as there was a shout from the kitchen and a gusty whoosh of air and heat.

"Well," Shawn sighed in a flat voice, "he's blown the stove," he muttered as they all turned toward the kitchen.

There wasn't much smoke. The flames had simply leapt up and then receded back into the burner, but Remy hopped around the kitchen trying to rid his hand of a flaming oven mitt as Brandt danced around him comically, trying to grab hold of him.

Brandt finally caught him and threw him to the ground in a move Carl was pretty sure came straight from wrestling on television, and he beat out the flames with his hands as they all looked on impassively.

Carl looked around at the other three men and smiled at the fact that not one of them had moved to help. Either they were all slightly sadistic, or they trusted Brandt to handle the situation. Carl was pleased to realize that the coherency they needed to work as a team was already forming. Perhaps they'd get out of this place sooner than the allotted two weeks after all.

They gathered around in the smoky kitchen to look down at Remy and Brandt, who were both on the floor breathing heavily, their clothing slightly blackened and singed in places. Thiago went to the window over the sink and fought with it, trying to open it. Nikolaus turned and headed back into the living room after rolling his eyes.

"Tsk, tsk," Shawn offered in disappointment as he looked down at Brandt. Carl was briefly reminded of being scolded as a boy when he was naughty.

"Wasn't me, mate," Brandt responded in amusement.

"Sorry," Remy said as he shook the now crusty mitt from his hand and sat up slowly. "Didn't know it would do that exactly." Carl put out a hand to help one of them up, and Brandt grasped it firmly and pulled himself to his feet.

"Thanks, Trigger," he said softly.

"Uh huh. You all right?" Carl asked automatically.

"Mmm," Brandt practically purred. "Was a nice flare up," he answered as he looked at the stove wistfully. Carl gave him a wary glance and turned to Shawn, who was helping Remy carefully to his feet.

"Your back okay?" the man asked quietly.

"Yes," Remy answered curtly. "Like a fucking trip to the chiropractor."

Before they could question why Remy's back wouldn't be okay, Nikolaus's voice called out uncertainly from the other room.

"Gentlemen? The list. It's up."

They moved quickly into the other room, curious about the reason for Nikolaus's strained tone of voice.

"What have we got then?" Shawn asked as he leaned over Nikolaus's shoulder. Nikolaus sat back and gestured to the screen.

"We've got eleven agents at the top of the list, each of whom has worked with every single agent that is known to have turned in the past year," Nikolaus told them for the benefit of those who couldn't see the screen clearly. "We're each on it."

"What?" Remy asked in shock as he squeezed in between Carl and Thiago to see the screen. "That can't be a coincidence," he mumbled as if he were talking to himself.

"See those markers there?" Nikolaus asked as he pointed to a row on the screen with three red symbols in it. "Those indicate a deceased agent. The green ones indicate an agent on an active mission. You'll notice none of us have a green indicator."

"They don't want anyone knowing we're out here," Shawn murmured with a nod.

"So that just leaves the two suspects?" Carl suggested hopefully.

"No. That leaves the eleven," Thiago said grimly.

"Surely you don't still suspect one of us?" Nikolaus asked him in exasperation. Thiago's jaw clenched and he had the good grace to look slightly ashamed. Remy stared at him intently, and Carl watched in fascination as the younger man squared his shoulders in front of Thiago and stood almost nose-to-nose with him.

"If one of us was a double agent," he said in a smooth, icy voice, "don't you reckon you'd be dead by now?"

"Dixie," Shawn chastised in a soft voice. Again, Carl marveled at the change in the young Cajun and the control Shawn exerted over him when he seemed about to snap. Remy immediately relaxed and any hint of the dangerous man Carl had just caught a glimpse of was gone.

Remy looked Thiago over calmly one last time before returning to his former position, leaning over Nikolaus's other shoulder and looking intently at the screen.

"We can't assume that the dead agents are out of the picture," he said softly. "If it were me I would have faked my death in order to throw people off."

Carl had to agree with that logic. He didn't like to think of the possibility that one of these five men was the man they'd been sent to kill, and he decided he would follow Remy's logic on that matter as well. If the Archer were among them, surely he would have tried to rid himself of their presence by now.

"Do any of you know of these other five?" Nikolaus asked as he eliminated their own names from the list, leaving the names and designators of the other five agents on the screen.

"McTiernan," Shawn breathed in disbelief. The red marker beside the name glared back at them, and Carl's heart hurt for the man. If Sir John McTiernan really was dead, then Shawn had just learned of the loss of his mentor. Carl saw Remy give Shawn a worried glance before looking closely at the list once more.

"I have a contact who worked with Kincaid in Central America on a job," Thiago offered as he pointed at one of the names. "Gray Kincaid. He's a Class One as well. Based around the Gulf Coast, I think. Florida and the Caribbean. Very good at what he does. One of the best in the Organization, from what my man told me."

"Never heard of him," Remy muttered almost sulkily, as if he were insulted that someone else might be one of the best.

"Evan Washburn works out of Tokyo mostly," Brandt offered after a moment. "Worked, that is," he added, taking note of the red marker beside that name as well. "He was a class 10 sub something or other. Did audio stuff."

"Sub Five," Nikolaus provided with a nod.

"Yeah, that," Brandt agreed in a tone that clearly said he didn't care. "Always bitching about the decibel level of the explosions."

"Fletcher Barclay is a cleaner," Shawn told them in a slightly gruff voice as the others studied Brandt warily for any signs of impending madness. None came, though, and Shawn went on. "Class Three. He works in Scotland and Ireland mostly."

"He moonlights as a hitter too," Carl supplied absently. Shawn looked at him curiously and Carl smiled back abashedly. "We made a mess of it in Glasgow last winter," he said by way of explanation for his association with the cleaner. "A right massacre. Needed the services of a sweeper."

"Why would a cleaner moonlight as a hit man?" Nikolaus asked as he tapped a pen nervously against the arm of his chair.

"I never asked," Carl responded vaguely. "I couldn't hardly understand what the bloke was saying most of the time."

"Lydia Ashton," Remy provided absently as he pointed at the screen. Nikolaus swatted his hand away before his finger could touch it, and Remy looked at him with a wounded expression.

"No touching," Nikolaus said sternly as he gestured toward the charred remnants of the oven mitt on Remy's hand. Remy looked down at his blackened fingers and wiped them on his jeans absently as he refocused his attention on the screen.

"Lydia's a piece of work. A real *bonne fille*. She's one of those," Remy looked back and smirked at Carl, "sexy women in the skimpy red dresses Carl is so fond of," he finished. "Class Six, that is. I can't believe someone could have gotten to her," he added almost sadly as he gestured at the red designator by her name.

"Where was she based?" Thiago asked.

"North America. Atlantic seaboard, for the most part, around D.C. Used her on a political assignment once."

"You actually met a mark you couldn't seduce?" Shawn asked in mocking amusement.

"Long story," Remy mumbled.

"Hasn't it been confirmed that the Archer is a man?" Nikolaus asked curiously.

"Nothing's been confirmed until *we* confirm it," Thiago said authoritatively. They had to give him that at least, and Carl was more than willing to make the concession. He wasn't fond of the idea of going on information provided by a questionable source, and there was no doubting the Organization's files were questionable. The Archer had already proven himself a clever opponent; Carl had little doubt that the man could hack into their files just as easily as Nikolaus did.

"This is getting us nowhere," Brandt said irritably. "Who's to say the Archer actually worked with all the agents he's turned? Maybe he's networking."

"Networking?" Carl snorted in amusement, but he took Brandt's point all the same. It was entirely possible the Archer had turned only one or two agents, then let it spread like a disease throughout the Organization. Brandt nodded, and Carl sighed in frustration.

"So basically, we've got nothing to go on that's concrete?" Carl asserted, not really expecting an answer.

"Well," Nikolaus said defensively, but he couldn't come up with a response.

Carl let his shoulders sag. "Who's got watch tonight?" he asked, giving up the hunt, for the moment, to exhaustion.

"I do," Remy said absently as he pointed for Nikolaus to return to the screen with the Archer's last message on it.

"Oh no, you don't," Shawn corrected commandingly. Remy straightened and looked at the man defiantly. Carl wondered if perhaps he should back away so as not to be caught in a spat. But Shawn's pose wasn't threatening, and he smiled at the younger man rather than puffing up combatively. "You didn't sleep last night," he reminded Remy. "I'll take watch."

"You didn't sleep, either," Brandt observed with amusement.

"I'll take watch," Thiago muttered irritably. Carl watched him stalk over to the couch and take hold of Remy's blanket. "I'm a little wired anyway," he huffed as he wrapped the blanket around his shoulders. Carl watched him curiously as he went about stoking the fire and then made himself comfortable on the couch.

"Who's got Spark Duty?" Carl asked in amusement as he tore his eyes away from Thiago to look at Brandt curiously.

"Go get your sheepskin, Trigger," Brandt ordered with a cheeky grin.

"We're just leaving this?" Remy asked in disbelief as he gestured at the screen that once again displayed the message from the Archer.

"There's nothing for it tonight," Shawn answered with a shrug.

Nikolaus slid out of his chair and trudged over to the couch to flop down beside Thiago and stare into the fire. Obviously computers were more exhausting than Carl thought they were.

Brandt shrugged and grabbed Carl's arm, yanking him toward the hallway and pulling him close to whisper in his ear.

"I need a word with you, Trigger," he said softly.

Carl wondered how serious Brandt was about being treated with sex every night for being good, as Shawn had put it, and thought how ridiculous it was for the man to expect it. But then again, Brandt was certifiable in Carl's opinion, and he certainly didn't want him upset. It wasn't like it was all that great a sacrifice, right?

"What, uh…."

"Shh. A word," Brandt hissed, and he practically threw Carl into his bedroom and slammed the door behind them. Carl didn't mind being roughed up a bit; it was actually quite fun if done right, and Brandt was certainly an acceptable partner. But something wasn't right, and it made the hair on the back of Carl's neck stand up.

He stood stock still in the middle of the room, watching Brandt warily and tensing almost unnoticeably.

"Down, boy," Brandt whispered in amusement. "I'm tired. Besides, the stove wasn't entirely the Ragin' Cajun's fault," he added with a grin. Carl cocked his head in confusion as Brandt sat down on the bed and rested his head in his hands. He thought about prompting Brandt to speak with a question, but then thought better of it. He sat beside the man and waited impatiently. "I don't know about you, Trigger," Brandt said softly after what seemed like an eternity. "But I don't trust him."

Carl's brain whirred to life once more and his senses went into overdrive. To whom was Brandt referring? Had he picked up on something Carl missed? Was he trying to smoke Carl out and see if he had his own suspicions about one of the others? Carl wasn't accustomed to mind games. He simply killed who and when he was told. Carl believed Brandt was the same way. He decided to trust his instincts and have faith that Brandt wasn't into the games, either.

"Who?" he finally asked.

Brandt looked up, his eyes registering surprise that Carl hadn't been able to read his mind, but then he gave him a wry grin and looked away. He was silent for some time, staring into the distance, and Carl was afraid he'd lost him. Finally, Brandt turned to look at him once more, and his black eyes flashed dangerously as he spoke.

"I don't trust him," he claimed. "He's too damn quick. And he's too eager to please everyone. He's just too goddamned easy."

"Who are you talking about?" Carl asked impatiently.

"Honestly, Trigger, you're the only one I trust out here," Brandt murmured. Carl gaped at him. "We're from the same mold, you and me. Those blokes, they're too used to playing the game," Brandt went on, unconsciously echoing Carl's thoughts from just moments before. "I've got a bad feeling about him. He gives off a… I don't know. Vibe. Too damned perfect," he repeated disconsolately. "Every reaction is too fucking perfect. Like he knows what we're thinking before we do it, and he plays right into our expectations."

Carl was still trying to grasp the fact that Brandt apparently trusted him and no one else, but he was slowly beginning to realize which of their companions Brandt was talking about.

"Do you trust me, Trigger?" Brandt asked suddenly. Carl snapped back to the present and looked at the man intently. The gleam was nowhere to be seen. Carl decided to go with his gut once more.

"Yes."

"Good," Brandt said, genuinely pleased. "Do this for me? Take Spark Duty every night."

Carl opened his mouth to question the request, but Brandt stopped him. "If Remy is the Archer, or even one of his men, then we're in danger. I'll watch your back, you watch mine."

Carl was silent for a moment, considering his options. Finally, he nodded slowly, and a slow smile began to spread over his face. "Right then," he said decisively. "So they'll just think you really enjoyed my company, yeah?"

"What makes you think I wouldn't?" Brandt asked with a truly frightening grin.

"Well, I hear Australians are very stupid," Carl answered with a sad shake of his head, "you may not be able to comprehend just how good I am."

Brandt grinned, and Carl found himself intrigued by the predatory way the man moved.

"Are you a screamer, Trigger?" Brandt asked in a low voice that had Carl's entire body tingling with anticipation.

"Not normally," he managed to respond with difficulty.

"You will be tonight."

X.

SHAWN cocked his head at Remy as they stood facing one another, left alone by the others. Neither man had so much as twitched since the others scattered. Shawn knew the best thing was to wait Remy out. The younger man had a bug up his ass about something, and it was obvious to Shawn that he wanted to discuss it. But this was the game they always played, a game in which each man challenged the patience and sanity of the other, and so Shawn waited.

Finally, Remy rolled his eyes and his shoulders sagged as he looked back toward the computer. *'Like clockwork,'* Shawn thought with what could only be described as a shit-eating grin. Remy usually didn't have the patience to wait him out, especially when he had something important on his mind.

"Quit grinning like a *bioque*," Remy mumbled as he tried to hide his own smirk. Shawn reached out and pulled Remy to him, forcing them closer together, and affectionately ran his nose along the stubble of Remy's cheek.

"Something I can do for you, lad?" Shawn purred.

Remy shivered theatrically as Shawn's breath gusted over his ear. Shawn glanced over at the sofa where Thiago and Nikolaus sat talking quietly, wondering how much privacy he and Remy could hope to find. Remy's hand slid under his chin and gently pulled his attention back.

"What about this message?" Remy asked almost petulantly as he held Shawn's chin firmly with one hand. Shawn's gaze slid to the computer screen briefly before returning to rest on Remy's perturbed countenance. He loved psychological warfare, but he almost always met his match in Remy. Now he'd gotten himself all worked up, and Remy was going into code-breaking mode.

Fucking great.

"Massive computing machines running on the power of a small village have failed to break it, but if it'll make you feel better, go right ahead and study it," Shawn suggested with a smirk.

Remy huffed, but he turned to copy the message onto a notepad anyway. Shawn walked over to sit on the hearth of the fireplace, watching Remy in exasperation. Thiago and Nikolaus stopped mid-conversation and looked at him with blank expressions.

"We never had dinner," Thiago observed, as if having missed dinner really didn't bother him all too much, but he needed something to talk about.

"No, we didn't," Shawn responded, a little surprised he hadn't noticed the lack of food. Remy had that effect on him at times. He forgot what he was doing and why he was doing it and knew nothing but the force of nature that was Remy's presence. The distraction had grown to the point that he was now more concerned with Remy's well-being than his own. It was one of the many reasons he'd decided to take this assignment, regardless of the almost inevitable likelihood that most of them wouldn't live through it, and why he'd decided to do what he was doing.

Although he hated himself for his decision, he knew it was the only thing he could do to save himself or Remy in the end. The lad wasn't the type to live until retirement. He was too unaware of his own mortality and too willing to do the jobs others refused to do for the very reasons those less reckless individuals refused to do them. Shawn had to get him out before his sense of adventure killed them both.

He was brought out of his reverie as Remy thumped down beside him.

"Is that the Archer's message?" Nikolaus asked as he sat forward and stared at Remy intently. Remy nodded, and Shawn watched Nikolaus curiously.

He hadn't really paid much attention to the man, and he knew he should be observing all of his companions a little closer than he had. He couldn't simply take it for granted that they were all true to the Organization, and he also knew if he were hiding something from them like he was, no matter how trivial or critical it may be, then they could all be doing the same.

Nikolaus seemed harmless enough, though, and very genuine at that. Of course, that could mean very little, considering Shawn's experience with Remy and others like him. But still, Shawn didn't get the psycho killer vibe from Nikolaus.

Thiago, on the other hand, was a different matter. Out of all five men, Thiago worried Shawn the most. The man was suspicious to start with, which wouldn't help Shawn's cause all that much, but he was also very shrewd. If one of them were going to figure out what Shawn was on about, it would be Thiago. And there were times when Shawn watched him that the man's eyes glazed over and he reminded Shawn disturbingly of Brandt. Being crazy as fuck was one thing. Being able to hide it under a normal exterior? That was deadly.

Thiago watched Nikolaus in much the same way as Shawn watched him and, for a brief moment, Shawn entertained the idea of pulling him aside and asking the man what he thought about the young tech. Not only would he get the chance to feel Thiago out, but he also might even be able to begin to build a bit of trust with him. But then Thiago turned to look at him, and Shawn thought he'd never seen a more guarded expression in all his years. No. Tonight was not the night to get Thiago to open up. Something weighed heavily on the Argentinean's mind, and Shawn would just as soon not get into that area just yet.

"I'm convinced that the letters have something to do with it. Like a designator or a… uh… shit, I can't think of the word."

"A key?"

"Yeah!"

"Remy?"

"Huh?" Remy responded innocently in response to Nikolaus's soft words. Shawn got the feeling that perhaps Remy had a bit more on his mind than just the message and he shifted uncomfortably. Remy wasn't stupid, and when he was acting that way it meant that trouble was coming. Something weighed heavily on Remy's mind too, and Shawn *had* to get into that area. Soon.

"There's not much point in worrying over that until we have the other half to the code. I've got the computer running on it."

"But–"

"Come on, Dixie," Shawn huffed before Remy could go into a whole diatribe over how important breaking the code was. "I've got something you can help me with," he added with a wink at Thiago.

A shout emitted from Brandt's room as if on cue and Thiago grinned crookedly.

"If he can make Carl scream like that, I'm quite worried about my turn," Thiago told them softly, and Shawn wondered whether he was joking. He thought not. Carl certainly didn't seem the type to scream.

"Uhhh…."

Shawn looked at Remy inquiringly as he stood and stretched his sore back, but the younger man remained sitting and looked up at him blankly.

"What's the problem?" Shawn asked curiously.

"It's just…," Remy trailed off and his eyes slid from Thiago and Nikolaus on the sofa to the message in his hand, and then back to Shawn. "Oh, fine," he finally conceded.

Thiago actually snorted in amusement. "*Che*," he said sarcastically, "*mierda*, Shawn, you must be a real treat in the bed to warrant such enthusiasm."

Shawn shot him his most lascivious grin and winked. "You could only be so lucky," he claimed enigmatically before grabbing Remy and hauling him to his feet. He then picked him up and threw him over his shoulder like a sack of potatoes, gave the two surprised men on the couch a cheeky bow, and strolled out of the room.

Remy didn't protest the high-handed treatment. The younger man didn't even fight him or utter so much as a squeak as Shawn carried him down the hall and into the bedroom Remy shared with Carl, and Shawn really began to worry that something was truly wrong. Normally, Remy at least put up a token struggle.

As soon as the door slammed behind him, Shawn set Remy down none too gently and shoved him. Remy wheeled backward but managed to catch himself before he tumbled to the floor. He looked back at the bag of ammunition and hunting knives and various and sundry other deadly instruments that he had almost fallen onto and then looked back at Shawn accusingly.

"What's all this then?" Shawn demanded before Remy could say anything.

"What?" Remy asked defensively, backing away a step and nudging the bag with his heel. He suddenly reminded Shawn of a caged animal, and Shawn narrowed his eyes in suspicion.

"What have you done?" he demanded.

"What?" Remy repeated, a little surprised now.

"You've done something you know I wouldn't like," Shawn asserted. A nasty thought began to creep into his mind, but he did his best to suppress it. "And what the fuck was that act you were pulling out there?"

"What act?" Remy asked, his tone once again defensive.

"Cut the crap! The act!" Shawn clarified forcefully, struggling to keep his voice down. He brought his hands up and let his wrists go limp and began flailing and speaking in a high-pitched, mocking Cajun accent. "'*May wee,* I don't know what I'm talkin' about. What's going on? Why do we need this? Oh, what's the word I'm thinking of? Key, is that it?'" he said in mimicry of Remy. "It's bullshit, and you're well aware that I know it," he finished disgustedly.

"*Mon tcheue*!"

"Shut up," Shawn ordered as he began to prowl around the small room. He saw Remy's wide brown eyes following him, and he finally turned to face the younger man once more. "Why are you playing games?" Shawn demanded suspiciously.

Remy opened his mouth to speak, but snapped it closed again. Shawn's eyes narrowed further, and the nasty thought that had been merely creeping before slammed into him in full force.

"What are you hiding?" he asked hesitantly, hoping Remy either wouldn't answer or would tell him 'nothing.' Anything but a hesitation.

"I...." Remy's shoulders sagged, and he looked guiltier than Shawn had ever seen. Remy didn't usually show what he was feeling unless it suited his purpose, but Shawn had enough experience with him to be able to decipher the real from the fake. His heart sank as he realized the guilt he was seeing was real.

"What've you done?" Shawn whispered.

Remy's eyes hardened and he straightened his sagging shoulders.

"Why don't you tell me?" he demanded, his voice nothing more than a harsh whisper. "What have *you* done, Shawn? Hmm? Why don't you tell me that!"

"Keep your voice down," Shawn hissed.

"Why?" Remy challenged. "Hiding something?"

Shawn closed the distance between them and gripped Remy by the shoulders. Remy started to protest, but Shawn held him firmly and threw him at the bed. Remy stumbled and fell against the side of the mattress, sliding down and landing on one knee to look up at Shawn in confusion. Shawn's heart ached as he saw the betrayed look in Remy's eyes, but he grabbed Remy's shirtfront and pulled him roughly back up to his feet, pinning him against the bunks and putting his face just inches from the younger man's. "Are you accusing me of something, lad?" he snarled in the most threatening voice he could muster.

Shawn had to admit he was impressed with Remy's reaction. He had seen men fall to their knees and beg in the face of his most threatening personas, but Remy simply blinked and swallowed with slight difficulty.

"You certainly are defensive for a man who's done nothing wrong," Remy observed softly. It was Shawn's turn to blink, and he released Remy's shirt slowly as if he just realized what he was doing. Remy had certainly won that round.

They remained that way for several tense moments, and finally Shawn stepped away and knitted his brow inquiringly.

"How much do you know?" he asked sadly.

XI.

NIKOLAUS didn't know whether to be amused or annoyed by the behavior of his comrades. If he were being honest with himself, he would have admitted it was a little bit of both. If these first few days were any indication, then they would never quit fucking one another long enough to get out of this fucking cabin.

He and Thiago sat silently for some time, watching the dark hallway where Shawn and Remy had disappeared and straining to hear snatches of their conversation. All they could hear, however, were the sounds coming from Brandt's room. Finally, Nikolaus turned to look at Thiago, and he found the man sitting and smiling oddly.

"They really are endearing, once you get past thinking they may want to kill you," Thiago said to him in amusement. Nikolaus smiled and nodded. But he couldn't honestly say he agreed. At first he'd taken comfort from Shawn and Remy's unusual bond, but now Nikolaus thought he sensed something that perhaps the others were missing. The tension was obvious, but it could be chalked up to many things. Sex, for instance. Or lack thereof. It could also be chalked up to knowing the others were suspicious of them.

Nikolaus shook his head irritably. He didn't want to get into the psychology of the others. Just the thought of trying to diagnose Brandt made Nikolaus's head hurt. But what Nikolaus was sensing between Remy and Shawn was not only the very obvious and understandable tension, but also a very subtle hint of suspicion. And if Shawn and Remy were suspicious of one another, then what hope did Nikolaus or any of the others have of trusting either of them?

What had caused the sudden shift, anyway? They were certainly comfortable enough with one another yesterday, and even this morning nothing seemed out of the ordinary. But as the day progressed Remy seemed to grow more and more tense. Nikolaus wondered if perhaps the Archer's message had anything to do with it.

And if it did, then why? Nikolaus's brain revved to life as he tried to think through the problem.

He glanced at Thiago as the shadows from the firelight danced across the man's handsome face. Could he trust the cagey Argentinean? He desperately wanted someone with whom to confer, to whom he could relay his suspicions. In all honesty, he wanted someone to allay his fears, tell him there was nothing to worry about and their only enemy was the Archer.

He wanted someone to talk to.

Several hours ago, Nikolaus would have gone without a second thought to Remy to voice his concerns, but now with his new suspicions in mind, Thiago seemed the most likely candidate.

Especially considering Thiago was the only one here.

Nikolaus tried to forget that he was slightly intimidated by the older man, and he cleared his throat. Thiago looked at him inquiringly.

"May I…," he cleared his throat again as Thiago waited patiently, and he started over. "May I speak with you candidly?"

Thiago raised one eyebrow in amusement, but he seemed to sense Nikolaus was a bit jumpy, and he apparently took pity on him.

"Of course you can," he said gently. "What would you like to speak of?"

Nikolaus looked down the hall once more, then back at Thiago. He wondered how far he should go, how much he should confide in Thiago, but then he decided this was an all-or-nothing situation.

Thiago followed his gaze and apparently anticipated what Nikolaus had on his mind. He smiled crookedly and returned his eyes to the fire. "I don't like what's going on in there any more than you do," Thiago said with a nod toward the bedroom. "Yes, I've noticed something wrong between them. No, I don't know what it is. And God knows what they could be plotting or… but I'm trying to come to terms with the idea of working with other people, and I'm trying to come to terms with whatever it is Remy and Shawn have together. Remy says it's love, but…."

"You don't think so?" Nikolaus prompted as Thiago trailed off, not caring that they were getting off the subject. It felt good to have Thiago speaking openly about anything. Thiago looked conflicted for a brief moment before his stony exterior returned.

"Do you trust me, Nikolaus?" he asked suddenly.

Nikolaus stared at him. What to say? If he said yes, would Thiago believe him? Should he appear to think it over before answering? Should he offer his reasons behind what was essentially his blind trust? Nikolaus had never been one for face-to-face tactics. He was more of a behind-the-scenes operator, and he wasn't sure how to handle himself with the experienced field agent.

"Yes," he finally answered with as much conviction in his voice as he could muster. Thiago gave him a faint smile.

"I'd like to say that it makes me happy to hear you say that," the Argentinean sighed sadly. "But if you trust me so easily, what's to say you won't trust others as well? What if one of them is a mole?"

"I do trust them," Nikolaus insisted, wondering how Thiago turned him around so easily. One minute he was thinking of how suspicious two of the others were, and now he was defending his own trust in them.

"If you trust them, then why are you sitting here asking me questions about Shawn and Remy?" Thiago asked slyly.

"I don't know. I think you've talked me into a circle," Nikolaus admitted candidly.

Thiago chuckled, and they sat in silence for some time. Eventually the sounds from Brandt's room faded. Nikolaus sat waiting for something to happen.

He looked at Thiago again and cleared his throat. Thiago smiled and looked at him sideways.

"Yes?"

"What if the message is the reason they're being– "

"Weird?" Thiago supplied. Nikolaus nodded, and Thiago shook his head. "I think it's just a full moon or something."

"I'm serious. I've been thinking it over. Since they know each other so well, isn't it possible that if one of them were the Archer, then the other might be able to break the code? Maybe that's why Shawn didn't want Remy working with the message."

Thiago frowned and opened his mouth to reply, but let it shut again and returned his gaze to the fire. "That's entirely possible," he murmured.

"They're loyal to one another, that much is obvious, but the Archer has been killing off agents. Agents just like you and Shawn and Remy. If I found out that my best friend was really the enemy…." Nikolaus let the assertion hang in the air for Thiago to decipher. Thiago turned to look at him intently.

"When was the last message sent?"

A cry from the other bedroom almost made Nikolaus jump out of his skin. It wasn't a cry of pleasure like the ones Carl made, but a plea for mercy.

"No!" the voice called out softly.

"Jesus," Nikolaus breathed in horror. He got to his feet and lunged forward, but was halted by an iron grip around his elbow. He looked back at Thiago to question him, but the man was staring intently into the darkness of the hallway, his body taut as a bowstring.

"Leave them to it," Thiago whispered. "If they're fighting then they have good reason."

"And if one of them kills the other?" Nikolaus questioned incredulously. Thiago looked at him, and his oddly colored eyes flashed in the firelight.

"Then we hope the one who lives is on our side."

XII.

BRANDT rested his head on the pillow beside Carl's, breathing heavily and smirking as the tingling in his body receded once more.

After a few more moments Brandt raised his head to look down at Carl appraisingly. The man still had his eyes closed, but his breathing had returned to normal and his body had gone limp. Most of it, anyway. Brandt always appreciated a lover who could keep up with him, and Carl could certainly do that. Brandt leant down and nipped lightly at the other man's nose.

"Your methods worry me," Carl mumbled as he cracked one eye open.

"I didn't hear you complaining before."

"That's because I was too busy screaming. I should have figured you for a biter, you crazy fuck," Carl observed with a slight smile. Brandt creased his brow in confusion. He could tell before they'd begun that the man wasn't accustomed to being on the receiving end of such attentions, and Brandt had been reasonably gentle. Carl wasn't bleeding, was he? Or on fire? What was he complaining about? What was wrong with biting? And for that matter, what was wrong with his methods?

"What's wrong with my methods?" he asked in a hurt voice

Carl cracked open his other eye slowly and tried to focus his gaze on Brandt's face. Brandt lifted himself further so Carl could see him better without going cross-eyed and Carl hummed warningly.

"You've got quite a lot of stamina, Sparkplug," Carl observed in amusement. Brandt rolled and crawled back on top of Carl and looked down at him in confusion.

"That was just the warm up," he informed Carl unashamedly.

"Warm up?" Carl repeated incredulously as he shifted his hips, planting his feet flat on the mattress as if preparing to be slammed into again.

Brandt grinned at him and felt Carl shiver in response. He reached down to the area of the bed near his knees and grabbed the covers they'd pushed aside during their earlier struggles. He pulled them up over their bodies to help stop the shivering, and Carl moaned wantonly as the motion produced some pleasing side effects.

"Ready for more, are you?" Brandt asked in amusement. "It reminds you of that sheep blanket, yeah?" he asked, gesturing to the white quilt he held in his hand before wrapping it tightly around their bodies. It felt good to press against Carl in the warmth of the blankets. "I could go get it from Thiago," he offered in a growling voice, and Carl snorted in irritation. He lifted his hips, and Brandt felt his body go momentarily weak.

There was something very gratifying about making a man like Carl call out, especially when it was a scream of pleasure. A plea for more.

Brandt really liked fucking Carl.

"If you make any bomb jokes I may have to kick you out of the bed," Carl warned him sleepily. It was a single bed, and it probably wouldn't take much effort to do just that. Brandt rolled to his side and took Carl into his arms, nuzzling his neck affectionately.

"If I go, you're coming with me, Trigger," he whispered just before they heard a soft cry coming from the other room.

"No!"

Brandt looked blankly up at Carl, who shot to a sitting position and stared at the door of the bedroom like a cat stalking a mouse.

"Was that Remy?" Carl whispered after several seconds of tense listening.

"I think so," Brandt answered nonchalantly. "I wouldn't worry. Shawn is... vigorous." Carl looked at him sharply before rolling his eyes and lowering himself slowly back onto the mattress. "If something's wrong Thiago will look into it," Brandt said assuredly. "And if Shawn's gone crazy and attacked that damn Cajun, I rather like the odds of that fight."

"In our favor, though?"

"Of course."

They stayed motionless, listening for more cries or any sounds of movement, but they could hear very little through the thick wooden doors of the old cabin.

"No shots or screams," Carl observed in a murmur.

"Or explosions," Brandt added in a disappointed voice as he nuzzled into Carl's neck once more.

Brandt managed to suppress a yelp when he found himself being shoved to the ground. He sat up and peered over the edge of the bed at Carl, who was now propped on one arm and looking at him bemusedly.

"Can't say I didn't warn you, Wally."

Brandt grinned and climbed back into the bed.

"My ass," he mumbled plaintively.

"No, mate. *My* ass. Rug burn is no contest."

Brandt grinned again and this time he snuggled into Carl's arms, resting his head against Carl's shoulder.

"Your turn next time, Trigger," he said in amusement. Carl hummed in response.

"What are we going to do about him?" Carl asked abruptly, reverting back to the discussion they'd been having before Brandt tackled him. Brandt hated to admit it, he was terrified of the man, Archer or not, but there was really nothing they could do. It could be that he was just simply dangerous, no matter whose side he was on. Brandt could feel it.

He could feel the Cajun's madness, and it scared him.

"Wait him out, I suppose," he said uncertainly. "Just because he acts as if he has something to hide doesn't mean he's the Archer, or even that he's working for the Archer. He really hasn't done anything to warrant suspicions. He's just been too– "

"Perfect."

"Yes," Brandt agreed. He held his breath, wondering if he should say what he thought. But then he decided that either he trusted Carl or he didn't, and he hoped the other man would understand his meaning. "It's just a feeling I get when I look at him," he explained tentatively. "Like a… a grenade that didn't go off after the pin was pulled."

Brandt felt Carl nod his head, and he was relieved to have found someone he could relate to in his own way. He supposed his life would be much easier if he simply put a little effort into wrangling in his own madness. Because he could do so. And did, when necessary. He could be perfectly normal when he had to be.

But where was the fun in that?

Carl understood weapons. He even understood fire. More importantly though, he understood Brandt and apparently understood the way Brandt's mind worked.

But most important of all, Carl shared Brandt's suspicions. He understood Remy Bergeron was a little unhinged; a ticking bomb with a broken timer. Brandt was happy to have found an ally in this improbable group, and with that thought in mind, he drifted off into a light sleep.

XIII.

REMY questioned his methods for the first time in years as Shawn watched him sadly. What was so different about this situation that he needed to resort to such drastic measures? Against Shawn, no less? He was playing a very dangerous game with the only man he trusted, and if he lost the game, he would not only lose his only friend, but probably his life as well.

Shawn stood looking at him, waiting for an answer. How much to tell him? Should he tell Shawn all he knew about his activities over the past months? Should he tell him everything or keep certain things to himself? Remy decided the truth was the only way to go now. They'd been hiding too much from one another for too long.

"I know that this is your last mission," he admitted. Shawn looked slightly taken aback for a brief moment, but then he recovered and lowered his gaze. "How could you not tell me?" Remy asked, hating the pleading quality of his voice, but for once letting his own emotions take control. "How could you just pack up and leave without a word to me? Abandon me? We were partners, Shawn!"

"How did you find out?" Shawn asked in a hoarse voice, his green eyes glinting a little as he looked up at Remy.

"That won't work on me. I know you too well," Remy said, referring to the oldest method of diversion in the world. Classic change of subject. Remy was almost insulted. He continued. "Answer my question. Please," he begged, hoping it was merely shame that kept Shawn from telling him his plans to retire after this mission.

"I…." Shawn couldn't seem to get the words out and Remy's heart sank a little further. He'd hoped Shawn would confide in him without having to prompt him, but it looked like that wasn't going to happen. Did he have something more to hide? A bigger betrayal? Something more serious than simply abandoning him?

"Shawn?" Remy ventured tentatively. Shawn took a step back and looked away from him, and Remy swallowed hard before continuing. "I never asked you this. I never thought I had to," he said in the same hurt tone of voice. "Are you the Archer, Shawn?"

Shawn's head snapped back around and he looked at Remy as if the younger man had just stabbed him in the heart.

"I would follow you," Remy continued in a low voice. "You know that. I would follow you to Hell and back. Just tell me the truth." He looked into Shawn's clear green eyes and waited for the axe to fall.

Shawn didn't answer, though. He stood staring at Remy in shock for what seemed an eternity. Just when Remy was about to ask again Shawn lunged at him and took him into his arms, pressing their mouths together and holding Remy so tightly the younger man thought perhaps he was trying to crush the breath from him.

"You're a bloody fool, lad," Shawn ground out as soon as their lips had parted. Remy's eyes widened at the tone of voice. He sounded angry, almost desperate. Remy didn't think he'd ever heard Shawn sound quite like that, but he didn't have much time to think it over before Shawn once again kissed him and pawed desperately at his clothing.

"Shawn," Remy finally managed to gasp as Shawn started to fumble with his belt buckle and nip at his earlobe. Remy's knees started to go weak, and he cursed Shawn for knowing how to press his buttons so well.

He was quite handily rid of his jeans as Shawn thrust his tongue roughly into his mouth and maneuvered him back to the bed. Remy moaned into the kiss and held Shawn tighter, briefly entertaining the thought that they could avoid the discussion they'd been having and simply curl up in bed together for the rest of their lives.

They were both breathing heavily, and Shawn finally pinned Remy's legs to the mattress behind him and pulled his T-shirt over his head. Remy twisted to help when the shirt seemed to catch on his nose, but Shawn held him tight and pressed their bodies together. Remy's arms caught in the material of the shirt, and his vision was cut off.

Remy belatedly realized his mistake. He'd let his emotions cloud his judgment and now he was at Shawn's mercy. The man would no doubt be getting answers now.

Shawn shoved him backwards, and he felt himself falling, landing on the mattress with a grunt. His arms were still trapped by the T-shirt and Shawn's iron grasp no matter how much he struggled to free himself, and his eyes and nose were covered as well as Shawn took both his wrists in one hand and held them against the bed.

Remy hated not being able to see almost as much as he hated not being able to move.

He began to struggle to free himself, pondering the advantages and disadvantages of kneeing Shawn in the groin, but then Shawn's callused hand brushed gently over his chin and soft lips grazed his own. Remy shivered uncontrollably and groaned despite his best efforts to the contrary.

Perhaps he had been wrong?

"How did you find out?" Shawn asked, his voice a threatening whisper in the darkness.

Nope. Not wrong then.

"Fuck," Remy breathed in agitation.

He felt Shawn's hand on his face, gentle and almost loving in the way it caressed his cheek. The thumb rubbed over the fabric covering his cheek as the other four fingers dug beneath his jaw line, and then Shawn shifted and the fingers drifted down his cheek and rested on his lips.

"How did you find out that I had taken the deal they offered me?" Shawn questioned again. Remy answered by biting Shawn's finger. A pained hiss came from the other man and then an amused chuckle. "You want it that way then, do you?" Shawn murmured, almost to himself. Remy shivered again and smiled around the finger he was still sinking his teeth into lightly. He felt Shawn shift again and Shawn's lips were moving at the shell of his ear. "I don't want to hurt you, lad," Shawn murmured. "Just tell me what I need to know and we'll be done with it."

The finger was pulled from his mouth as the weight of Shawn's body lifted from his chest, and Remy tilted his head back and forth, desperately trying to see. Shawn's hand still held his wrists down, but the other lightly caressed his ribs, tickling him and sending an anticipatory shiver through his body. He snorted lightly and then clenched his jaw stubbornly. It was going to take more than that to get answers from him. He heard Shawn sigh sadly.

"Am I going to have to torture you again?" he asked softly.

"Fuck," Remy breathed again, remembering the last time Shawn had 'tortured' him. It always culminated in being uncomfortably sticky in hard-to-reach places.

"Tell me, lad," Shawn coaxed. Remy winced and squirmed and shook his head back and forth in answer to Shawn's plea. He wasn't about to break that easily.

Shawn's knee was summarily shoved into his ribs, and Remy bit down hard on his lip, only to have Shawn's tongue lap at it gently and coax his teeth to loosen their grip. Remy groaned again as Shawn's mouth met his.

His mind spared a moment's thought to appreciate how difficult the position must have been for Shawn to get into, but then Shawn moved away again, and Remy felt the man's breath gust across his own damp lips as he spoke. "How did you find out?" he queried again.

Remy's jaw clenched again.

"Dixie," Shawn murmured against his lips coaxingly, "quit being stubborn."

"St. John told me," Remy murmured as soon as Shawn's voice took on the serious note. The games were over.

"Why would Thierry tell you that?"

"I don't know," Remy murmured as he shifted his hips and tugged at his wrists. "Let me go, Shawn."

"Not yet."

"I'm getting twitchy!" Remy protested plaintively.

"Not until you tell me the truth."

"I told you the truth!" Remy huffed as he tried to move the T-shirt enough to be able to see.

"I don't believe you," Shawn told him matter-of-factly.

"*Maudit!*"

"Tell me and maybe I'll fuck you, hmm?" Shawn practically cooed.

"Everyone got it," Remy admitted finally as the blood rushed through his body at warp speed with the offer. "Thierry was trying to convince me to take the same deal. He thought if I knew you'd accepted it then I would, too." Shawn was silent, and Remy thought he was either processing the information or trying to figure out something painful to punish him with. "Shawn, please," he murmured, deflating with the memory of that scene in Thierry St. John's office when his handler had told him about Shawn's retirement.

"Did you take it?" Shawn asked in an oddly strained voice.

"Shawn," Remy pleaded, wanting desperately to be done with this conversation.

"Did you take the deal they offered?" Shawn asked again, more forcefully this time.

"No!" Remy called out in frustration, not caring whether the others heard now, but simply wanting to be done with this.

Instantly, Shawn was gone, leaving him alone on the bed and tangled up in his own T-shirt. He began to struggle inelegantly to free himself so he could locate Shawn and possibly kick him a few times.

"Hey," he finally said in irritation. "Can I get some help here?"

Shawn chuckled from somewhere in the little room, and Remy finally freed himself in time to see Shawn sliding his jeans to the ground. He stayed on his back, his weight resting on his elbows as he watched Shawn crawl back onto the bed.

"That was a dirty trick there, Beignet," he admonished as Shawn straddled him and grinned at him playfully. "You could have just asked."

"You always did respond well to torture, though. Besides, dirty tricks are my specialty," Shawn said as he crawled up the bed and kissed Remy almost tenderly.

Their kiss broke, and Shawn looked down at Remy's stomach as he ran his finger gently along Remy's ribcage.

Remy knew what he was thinking. They'd certainly discussed it often enough. Shawn was feeling the scars of three different bullet wounds, numerous knives, and a burn made by a chain during one particularly interesting car chase, and he was remembering the missions they'd been on together. Even worse, he was pondering the missions they'd been on without each other, always wondering if the other would come back. He was trying to think of a way to convince Remy of his own mortality. Remy knew he was doing this because he almost always did it when they were together. Then the finger moved from Remy's ribs to his navel and Shawn pushed up to his hands and knees once more.

"How's your back?" Shawn asked absently as he let his eyes roam over the various blemishes on Remy's otherwise perfectly tanned torso.

"You're not trying to get out of fucking me, are you?" Remy accused with a small smirk. Shawn rolled his eyes and flopped back onto the bed, curling beside Remy in feigned exhaustion.

"Interrogations take so much out of me," he complained.

"Pansy," Remy accused in amusement.

He inhaled the scent of Shawn's hair fondly as he dug his blunt fingertips into Shawn's back. Shawn responded by raising his head and kissing Remy's jaw and neck.

"No more secrets," he murmured into Remy's ear. Remy held him tighter and nodded.

They lay there for some time, each man entertaining his own thoughts and trying to work up the energy to grope each other. Shawn finally rose up onto his elbows and looked down at Remy. His green eyes seemed liquid in the half-light. If Remy hadn't known him better, he would have thought the man was going to cry. "This is a fool's errand, lad. A suicide mission."

"I know."

"And yet you took it without any promise of compensation?"

"Shawn, I–"

"Why didn't you take the deal?"

Remy remembered in vivid detail the conversation he'd had with Thierry St. John regarding retirement and shook his head sadly, not sure of how to explain his decision. Especially to Shawn.

"Why?" Shawn pressed as he ran his fingers through Remy's hair. Remy closed his eyes and tried to think of a plausible explanation. He couldn't possibly use the real one. Not with Shawn. "Remy, you could come with me," Shawn said hopefully. "We can leave all this behind," he continued, his hand coming to gently rest on one of Remy's many battle wounds.

Remy blinked at him in surprise. "Come with you?"

"Yeah," Shawn said excitedly, as if he hoped that he was finally getting through to the younger man. "We can go back home to England. Or you could take me into the bayou and we could disappear if… if it would be enough to get you out."

"Shawn," Remy murmured uncertainly. He'd never dreamt that Shawn would think along those lines. If he'd known Shawn would be willing to put up with him indefinitely, he would have taken retirement in a heartbeat. The knowledge that he couldn't possibly do it now made his stomach clench uncomfortably and he squeezed his eyes closed. "I… I signed another contract. I'm theirs for five more years… at least."

Remy felt as if his heart were being compressed in a vice as he watched Shawn blanch in the half-light of the moon. The contracts agents signed weren't really contracts in the legal sense of the word. They basically outlined the rules of engagement, and promised that if the agent fell out of contact for any length of time, went AWOL, or went rogue, he would be hunted down by the Organization and 'discharged.'

That word was the most feared word in Remy's or any other agent's vocabulary. He couldn't even think it without shuddering uncontrollably. Shawn held him closer and buried his head in the waves of Remy's dark hair, inhaling deeply and exhaling a slow, measured breath.

"You won't make it five more years," he mumbled sadly.

Remy knew he was right.

XIV.

NIKOLAUS got up and retired to his room shortly after they'd heard Remy's shout, and Thiago figured he'd been gone for roughly thirty minutes before he came staggering back out.

"I cannot sleep," he mumbled disconsolately, his German accent heavier with his exhaustion as he plopped back down beside Thiago on the couch.

Thiago smiled and nodded understandingly. He didn't know that he would be able to sleep either, considering the various things running through his mind. Aside from his brief walks around the perimeter of the cabin to keep him awake, Thiago's mind had been free to wander.

Nikolaus sat up with Thiago, ostensibly to keep him company, and they conversed sporadically as they waited to see if any of the others would emerge again. The young tech was curious and seemed eager to learn a new skill set. Thiago approved.

"Do you suppose you could show me some moves?" Nikolaus asked hopefully.

"I'm sure out of the five of us we can teach you some things," Thiago responded with a laugh. "Carl would probably be the one to ask about fighting, though, considering he's the expert in all things lethal."

"Are you really going to fuck Brandt?" Nikolaus asked abruptly. His eyes were as wide as saucers and Thiago found himself trying to decide what color they were. That was something that people didn't normally notice unless it was a particularly outstanding feature. Like the green of Shawn's eyes.

"If he wants me to," Thiago answered distractedly. "And like Carl said, if it'll keep *mi asno* from being blown up, I'll do anything. Besides, Shawn was right, was he not? Brandt is quite– "

"Crazy."

"'Attractive' was what I was going for."

"He made Carl scream."

"I heard."

"Carl. The very large assassin who could kill me with a button and a teapot."

"Yes."

"Made him scream like a little girl."

"*Sí, eso*–"

"Repeatedly."

"Nikolaus!"

"Sorry. It's just… he is very– "

"Large?" Thiago supplied with a smile.

"I was going for 'insane.'"

"That too. But mental stability has never impeded ability in bed, so far as my experience goes, so I'm not going to worry about it."

"You've bedded many mentally unstable people, have you?"

"I was married once," Thiago deadpanned.

"Really?"

"That was sort of a joke, Nikolaus. You know agents don't have families."

"Oh. Right. Well, maybe Brandt's taken a liking to Carl, and you won't have to worry about it," Nikolaus ventured hopefully.

"One can only hope."

"Didn't anyone ever tell you not to stare into a fire when you're on watch?" Remy asked softly from the darkness of the hallway. Thiago barely restrained himself from jumping.

"*Mierda*," he hissed, a little more harshly than he'd intended. "No sneaking!" he admonished as he sat forward and looked around the room as if there could be more people hiding in the flickering shadows.

"Sorry. Old habits die hard, I s'pose," Remy responded in a tired voice as he walked noiselessly over to sit on the hearth in front of the dying fire. "So used to skulking in the shadows I hardly ever notice when I'm doing it anymore," he added as he sat gingerly, leaning forward to take the pressure off his lower back. Thiago watched him in the firelight, and even as the shadows and flame danced across his features, Thiago could see that Remy was drawn and weary. His accent was heavier as well, and Thiago took a moment to be amused.

"Are you okay?" Nikolaus asked him quietly, leaning forward to peer at him.

Remy looked at him and smiled weakly. "I'm tired," he answered. His voice was hoarse.

Thiago looked inquiringly at Remy and pursed his lips. "Shouldn't you get some rest? You were up most of the night last night."

"Can't. Beds are too fucking soft," he responded grumpily.

"Did he hurt you?" Thiago asked seriously.

"Shawn? No," Remy answered in surprise. "Shawn would not hurt me. Not on purpose anyways," he added with a smirk.

"*Ein geiler Schuft*," Nikolaus mumbled in apparent amusement.

"Don't know what that means, *Peeshwank*, but I'm sure it hurt my feelings if I did," Remy whispered playfully.

"Complains the trained killer about his hurt feelings," Nikolaus scoffed. Thiago gave him a hard look, but he realized both Nikolaus and Remy were smirking at each other.

"I got feelings," Remy challenged in a hurt voice. "They right here," he explained as he pointed to his shoulder and patted himself gently. "That's where I like to shoot people," he added as if it were an afterthought. "Hurt them on their feelings first give them a chance to say sorry."

"A chance to say they're sorry?" Nikolaus laughed softly.

"Even trained killers have their moral quirks," Remy responded in a haughty tone. Thiago's lips twitched in amusement.

Nikolaus nodded. "So what was the…," he mumbled, gesturing toward the bedroom and giving Remy a confused look.

"The scream for mercy?" Remy provided with a wry grin. "Shawn was torturing me for information."

Nikolaus's eyes widened comically. "Torturing you?"

"Not wholeheartedly. A mere tiff," Remy told them dramatically. "It's okay now."

Thiago boggled at him. "Tiff?" he echoed hollowly.

Remy looked up at him and Thiago saw him sigh and close his eyes as he looked away again.

"Look," he said quietly, serious once more, "I don't expect you to understand how we work. Just know that Shawn, he my *podna*. My partner, my friend, *comprenez*? I trust him with my life. I trust him with *your* lives," he said with an emphatic point at them in the firelight.

Thiago met Remy's dark eyes and held his gaze by sheer force of will for several moments, but he could read nothing in them in the darkness and so he turned to look at Nikolaus for guidance.

"As long as you two don't go crazy on us, whatever you do in your bed is fine with me," Nikolaus said offhandedly as he stifled a yawn.

"Why don't you get some sleep, Niko," Remy suggested softly.

Nikolaus looked thoughtful for a moment before nodding. "Yes, I think I may. You two should think about sleep too, yes? Especially you," he said with a teasing finger wagged at Remy.

"We have to have a guard," Thiago muttered.

"Do we? Really?" Nikolaus asked innocently as he stood up. "Do we really need someone to keep watch out here in the middle of nowhere? Not a soul at the Organization knows we're here, much less anyone outside of it. Just the six of us know the location, and we've already discussed that issue, no?"

Remy and Thiago shared a look, and Remy gave a little shrug.

"He's probably right," Remy said to Thiago in a low voice, as if maybe Nikolaus couldn't hear him. "The only threat right now is from Brandt and that broken stove," he grinned.

Nikolaus headed for the hallway, muttering in German.

Thiago sat examining Remy for a moment as the fire hissed and popped in the silence.

"If you want to get some sleep," Remy said to him in a low voice, unmoving as he spoke, "I will take your watch." Outlined by the fire and masked in shadow, Remy seemed to transform into something more menacing as the words emitted from the darkness.

The effect gave Thiago chills. "Is there a reason you want to take the watch night after night?" he asked evenly. "It would worry a more suspicious man, no?"

"*Non*, is just insomnia," Remy answered. He sniffed and shook his head. The movement broke the eerie effect given to him by the fire and Thiago licked his lips and frowned. Remy stood slowly, stretching his back and twisting from side to side before heading toward the hall. Thiago lunged to his feet and grabbed his arm. He stepped in front of him and glared at the younger man menacingly.

"I know you enjoy playing games," he snarled in a barely audible tone, "but playing games with me is a dangerous way to die. Understand?"

Thiago was slightly surprised he didn't get more of a reaction from Remy. He knew he was frightening when he needed to be, and he knew his tone of voice brooked no argument. But Remy didn't seem at all fazed. The younger man was actually grinning.

"I'm not playing games with you, *che*. I been honest with you at every turn. Even when I was trying to deceive you I was being honest." Remy cocked his head and narrowed his eyes. "Can you say the same thing?"

"Of course," Thiago said defensively as his mind tried to evaluate the truth of his own statement. He was pretty certain he hadn't misled any of the others in any way, aside from… well, the obvious.

He knew Remy wasn't as inept as he made out to be. And he knew Brandt wasn't as crazy as he made out to be. They all had their protective coatings, and though Thiago hadn't yet deciphered what the other three men were using as their shields, Thiago readily admitted that his was his suspicion. Some of his questions had been warranted, like wanting to know about Shawn and Remy, but the truth was that Thiago *did* trust these men. He trusted them with his life at this point. He had to. Their knowledge and acceptance of his suspicion simply gave him some much needed leeway to work with.

Remy made an odd hissing sound, like one used to shoo away a cat, and he looked pointedly at Thiago's hand still on his elbow.

"Shall I take you to bed with me, then? Or are you going to let go of my arm now?"

Thiago looked down at his hand but didn't remove it. When he looked back up Remy was smiling at him, one eyebrow raised questioningly. "When you said you did not take the Organization's offer," Thiago murmured, his fingers digging into Remy's wiry muscles as he met his dark eyes, "what did you take instead?" he inquired curiously.

"Why?" Remy asked in confusion. Thiago could see a wariness creeping into the Cajun's eyes that he had yet to see.

"Humor my curiosity," Thiago murmured.

Remy gave his head a jerk to the side as his eyes searched Thiago's countenance. "I took five more years of service," he answered finally.

"*¿Cuál era ése?*" Thiago questioned in a stunned voice as he let his hand drop from Remy's arm.

"I signed on for five more years," Remy repeated slowly.

"*Gilún,*" Thiago breathed in something akin to horror. "You fool."

The kid was either crazier than Brandt or suicidal. All of Thiago's contracts had been six-month contracts in case of the very real possibility of burning out. A commitment that long was simply *loco*.

Something clicked as he looked into Remy's eyes, and Thiago finally understood.

Remy didn't expect to live through this mission. He hadn't expected to live through it before he had even accepted it.

Thiago studied Remy's face intently in the flickering firelight.

"Why are you here, Remy?" he asked softly.

"Where Shawn goes, I follow," Remy whispered in answer, not even hesitating to answer.

"Bullshit," Thiago responded, though it came out uncertain and questioning.

"Truth," Remy corrected. "This is not a mission we will all live through if we do not work together. I will not see him die. And so, I will say nothing but the truth. And I ask for it in return."

"Truth."

"Trust, Thiago. We must trust."

"Trust," Thiago repeated doubtfully.

"Are *you* the Archer, Thiago?" Remy asked suddenly, with a glint of mischief in his eyes.

Thiago creased his brow in confusion and found himself smiling at the straightforward query. "No," he answered in slight bewilderment. "No, I am not."

"Good," Remy said happily. "I asked Shawn the same thing. Now you can ask me, if you like."

Thiago didn't quite know what to say. "Are you?" he asked.

"Am I what, Thiago?" Remy asked, sounding like a teacher speaking to a child. "Leave no room for prevarication, now, I am very good at it."

Thiago snorted in amusement. "Are you the Archer, Remy?" he asked with a grin.

"No," Remy responded with something akin to glee. "See how easy that was? Any more questions?"

"Does Shawn have any idea that you're completely insane?" Thiago asked in amusement.

"Probably. He is wicked quick like that," Remy answered with a grin.

Thiago huffed and shook his head in exasperation. Remy looked at him sympathetically and reached out to grasp his forearm. He squeezed it and then let his hand slid up Thiago's arm until their hands were joined. Thiago stared down at their joined fingers, wondering just how long it had been since someone had touched him in order to comfort or console, and not just to fuck. He honestly couldn't remember.

"You will see," Remy told him quietly. "Life is a whole lot easier when you're not all alone, Thiago. All you have to do is trust us. And we'll earn it. I promise you, we'll earn it."

Thiago looked up to see Remy's sincere brown eyes watching him closely. He nodded and Remy let his hand go and moved away.

"Get some sleep, Thi," Remy said as he moved the ashes of the fire around just enough to douse the flames. "Can I call you that? You mind?" he asked as he stood back up and turned to look at Thiago in the darkness.

"No, not at all," Thiago said, his voice gruff with an emotion he couldn't quite place. Was it… happiness? Relief? Camaraderie?

Thiago watched Remy shuffle away toward the dark hallway and prepared to follow him to bed when he thought of one last question.

"Hey, Remy?" he whispered.

Remy turned around to look at him. Thiago could barely see him in the darkness; he was merely a darker shadow against the charcoal background of the hallway.

"We'll talk more in the morning, my little bay leaf," Remy drawled with a dismissive wave of his hand. Thiago could hear the smile in his voice.

A bright flash of light blinded him as he watched the Cajun. He threw up his arms to protect his eyes and felt a great whoosh of hot air. He went to his knees and covered his head as the muffled blast of an explosion rocked the cabin.

XV

CARL'S eyes snapped open as Brandt shook him roughly and shouted something Carl's sleep-addled brain couldn't quite understand. He didn't have time to question the rough treatment, though, as Brandt rolled him to the side, pulling the twin mattress with them and landing them on the floor with the mattress covering them just as the blast sounded.

"Tell me you did not just blow up the cabin!" Carl shouted as the heat and noise washed over them. Brandt's body covered his protectively, and Carl pressed his face into Brandt's neck and squeezed his eyes closed even as he wondered how much good a mattress was going to do in shielding them against whatever explosive had caused the destruction.

An unnatural silence followed the explosion. It was as if someone had pressed the mute button, and Carl had the briefly terrifying thought that he was dead. But then his ears seemed to pop and he could clearly hear Brandt's steady breathing, only slightly faster than normal in the excitement.

"No, I did not just blow up the cabin," Brandt responded in a disturbingly calm voice as the silence lengthened. "But the cabin is definitely on fire," he added as a round of smaller explosions sounded, followed by another unearthly silence.

"Are you indirectly responsible?" Carl asked as Brandt pushed up onto his hands and knees and looked down at him through the darkness. Carl was struck by the difference in this time and the last time he had been under Brandt.

The last time had been much more fun.

"Not this time, Trigger," Brandt said just before he gave Carl a quick, hard kiss and pressed his body to Carl's once again as another, smaller explosion sounded.

The panic began to rise in Carl's chest. He started struggling to get up as Brandt fought with lifting the mattress off their bodies.

"How'd you know?" Carl demanded as the sounds of falling debris and burst water pipes began to intrude upon the second odd silence. He was surprised at how calm his voice was. He'd been in explosions before, but never awakened by one. It was a surprisingly different experience altogether, and he could feel his entire body shaking with adrenaline and nerves.

"Had to use the toilet," Brandt said as they lifted the mattress up together and hefted it back onto the bed. It slumped half off the bunk and bounced slightly, but Carl had a pretty good idea that they wouldn't be caring about the condition of the beds after tonight. Brandt walked slowly to the door, which was miraculously still intact and closed.

"Let's get the fuck out of here, Wally," Carl said in agitation as he came up behind Brandt's still naked form and reached for the door. Brandt's hand flew out and gripped his wrist.

"Get some clothes first," Brandt responded calmly. "We'll have to go out the window. See the smoke?" he asked, pointing to the small billow of smoke issuing from under the door.

"Oh, yeah," Carl said as he pulled back and looked wildly around the room, trying to get his brain to catch up with Brandt's. He lunged toward the bed and fumbled around on the floor for his and Brandt's clothing, and then he tossed Brandt his jeans and pulled his own up over his naked hips before grabbing his shirt and putting it on inside out in his agitation. "When the oxygen hits it, right? It'll catch fire?"

"Not in this case," Brandt said, shaking his head as he calmly put on his jeans and cast around for his T-shirt.

Carl still shook with adrenaline and near-panic, and he took a moment to inhale several soothing breaths and admire Brandt's calm attitude. Of course Brandt would be calm as the cabin burnt down around him. He was fucking insane.

"That's only when the area is enclosed, you see. And I doubt the hallway is enclosed any longer judging from the size of that blast." Carl gave him a questioning look as he gathered up all the equipment in the room that he could get his hands on and threw it on the floundering mattress. "Smoke's bad for you," Brandt explained with a wink. Another round of smaller explosions sounded and Brandt took Carl by the arm and propelled him toward the small window. "Move it, Trigger! Can we fit through that?"

"Only one way to find out!" Carl shouted in response. He braced his hands on the footboard of the bed and the dresser and lifted himself into the air, swinging his legs and kicking out the fixed glass windowpanes in one fluid movement. "You first!" he called as the sounds of the destruction grew louder and the door to their room began to smolder.

Brandt shook his head, and Carl knew they didn't have time to argue, so he hefted his body into the windowsill and swung himself out of the room. The drop was a bit longer than he'd thought, but nothing any more life-threatening than the blazing fire he'd just left behind.

"The bags!" he called as Brandt stuck his head out and looked down. Brandt's shadowed form disappeared, only to be replaced with a large black bag Carl knew contained just about every explosive device known to man. He debated briefly over whether to catch it and risk it exploding in his hands or to let it fall and risk it exploding at his feet.

He caught the bag with an expectant wince and laid it at his side with a relieved breath as another bag appeared in the window. It was a smaller one of brown leather, and Carl didn't know what was in it, but he caught it nevertheless and set it with the first.

Two more bags of Brandt's equipment came through, and Carl piled them far enough away from the cabin that they wouldn't catch fire. He mourned the loss of his own equipment, still in the room he had shared with Remy, but knew he should be thankful for just being alive. The roof above his own room was even now blazing merrily and he experienced a brief, terrifying moment of panic as he hoped that Remy and Shawn had been in Shawn's room.

Brandt made it through the window easily enough and landed with a grunt. Carl helped him to his feet and they stood watching the flames on the roof lick at the dark night sky for several tense moments before Carl pulled himself together and shook Brandt out of his little trance.

"We need to get to the others," Carl said hastily.

XVI.

SHAWN stood with his eyes averted from the flames in order to ensure that his night vision wasn't compromised, his gun drawn and at the ready and his senses on high alert for any sign of movement from within the cabin or from without.

When Brandt and Carl came slinking around the corner of the cabin they were dead to rights as Shawn swung around and lined the two shadowy figures into his sights.

He managed to stop his trigger finger just in time as he realized who they were. His heart pounded in his throat and the blood rushed through his ears as he realized what he'd almost done. He pointed the muzzle into the air, resting the piece against his shoulder as they both skidded to a halt and looked at him in momentary indecision. Shawn knew he must have looked quite interesting to say the least, standing there motionless with a gun aimed at them in the middle of a mysterious blazing fire.

"Are you two all right?" he called over the noise of the fire. They both hesitated briefly, looking at one another uncertainly before trotting up to him.

"Just a nice bruise on my ass," Carl answered as they all three turned to look up at the flames in momentary fascination. Shawn blinked and shook his head, looking away once more and scolding himself as he blinked the white lights from his vision.

"Brandt?" he queried worriedly.

"Hmm? Fine," Brandt murmured dazedly as he watched the fire eat through the wooden walls of the cabin like a knife cutting through melted butter.

Despite the affirmative responses, Shawn looked them over carefully all the same. They both seemed relatively unharmed, despite their various stages of undress. "Have you seen the others?" he asked, his heart jumping into his throat once more when they both shook their heads.

What had happened to Remy? He was supposed to have been in bed with Shawn. Safe in bed with him. If anything had happened to the younger man, Shawn would never forgive himself.

"Where's the Ragin' Cajun?" Brandt asked as he looked at Shawn with black eyes.

"I don't know," Shawn answered hoarsely. "When I woke up he was gone."

"And Nikolaus?" Carl questioned. "Was he still up with Thiago?"

Shawn shrugged as he searched the area desperately for any sign of Remy.

"We should go around to the front. Thiago may have gotten out okay," Carl suggested.

"If Thiago was on watch…," Brandt said, stopping in mid-thought and shaking his head. Shawn knew what he was thinking, though. If Thiago had been on watch, then he'd probably been killed before the bomb went off by whoever set it.

That or the bomb had been set by someone already in the cabin. Shawn hoped that the latter option hadn't occurred to Brandt or Carl just yet. That would make things even more difficult.

"This way. Hurry now," Shawn ordered as he set off at a wary trot around the other corner of the cabin, keeping an eye on the dark line of trees to his right. The other two followed close behind him.

XVII.

NIKOLAUS felt very lucky at that particular moment. He stood by the tree line and watched in dismay as the cabin went up in flames. He could understand why Brandt found fire so fascinating, but then thoughts of his companions filtered through his stunned mind and a wave of profound shock and sadness hit him.

Perhaps they'd all survived? It wasn't looking particularly promising from

Nikolaus's angle. Another small explosion rocked the frame of the cabin, and Nikolaus shielded his face from the heat.

Not promising at all. He should go in and look for them. The blast seemed to have originated from the back of the cabin, and it was possible that Thiago and Remy had lived. If they were still by the fireplace when the explosion happened then they would have been okay. Maybe. They'd still been in the main room when he'd snuck out the front door for a smoke; what was to say they hadn't remained out there? They could still be alive. But he hadn't seen anyone come through the doors, and if they were still alive, they would need help.

Nikolaus shook the cobwebs from his mind and his limbs and started forward, having no real idea of what he should do, but wanting to do *something*. He almost jumped clear out of his skin when Shawn rounded the corner of the cabin, his gun up in front of him commando style, with Carl and Brandt right on his heels. Relief washed over Nikolaus at seeing at least three of his companions safe.

If he couldn't endure the thought of losing them after just five days together what must Shawn be feeling, knowing Remy was still in there?

"Hey!" he shouted, throwing up his hands instinctively as Shawn swung around and aimed at him.

"Are you okay?" Carl called as he and Brandt swooped down on Nikolaus and began feeling him over and checking him for injuries.

"I'm okay!" he shouted, shaking his head and swatting at Carl and the pawing hands. He grabbed Shawn by the elbow and shook him, disregarding the gun in the man's hand as he tried to pull his attention away from the flaming front door. "They haven't come out!" he yelled over the surprisingly noisy fire. "I've been out here the whole time! They haven't come out!"

XVIII.

"CAN we get through the door?" Shawn asked anxiously as they stood watching the fire consume more and more of the structure. His voice was the closest to panic Brandt had ever thought to hear from the man.

Brandt had apparently underestimated how much Shawn really cared for Remy. Of course, Brandt was also noticing that Carl and Nikolaus were a little on the frazzled side as well.

'Silly boys, letting a little heat get to them,' Brandt thought in amusement, but he had to admit there was a nagging pain in his stomach whenever he thought that the other two men might still be inside.

Yes, he was worried about Remy and Thiago, because oddly enough he found that he did care for them, just as he did Shawn and Nikolaus and Carl, regardless of his various suspicions. He didn't want to see any of them hurt. It was an odd sensation for Brandt, who'd gone through most of his life not giving a flying fuck about anything or anyone. It was terrifying. He finally had someone to care for, five someones, in fact, even if one of them was probably trying to kill him, and the thought of losing one of them was terrifying. He didn't know how Shawn was functioning.

"Brandt!" Shawn shouted, snapping his fingers in front of Brandt's face. "Can we get through?"

Brandt nodded and grabbed Carl by his shoulders, taking the thin T-shirt the man wore in his hands and tearing it in half. Carl was too stunned to protest as his only shirt left in the world was ripped from his body. Brandt tore the shirt to shreds, knelt, and rubbed the shreds in the snow until they were soaked through as they all stood and gaped at him.

He handed them each a piece of soaked cloth and tied his own around the bottom half of his face, covering his nose and mouth and nodding to them to do the same. He then dropped to the ground and rolled in the snow, soaking his body as best he could, and the others followed his example as realization of what he was doing dawned.

"This won't help much," he told them calmly. "So if you find yourself on fire, get the hell out of there," he advised as he stood back up and looked to the flaming cabin with something akin to glee. Nikolaus's eyes widened slightly, and Brandt thought that Carl went slightly pale. But Shawn's jaw clenched in determination, and he began to give orders like the true leader they all knew he was.

"Brandt, gather as much equipment as you can. You know the signs," Shawn said through his soaked piece of Carl's T-shirt.

Brandt nodded his understanding. Shawn was giving him the hardest job because he knew how to see the danger. That, or Shawn was hoping he'd be killed in the fire.

"Carl, Nikolaus. Find Thiago," Shawn ordered as the fire blazed merrily behind him. They all nodded, and Brandt noticed the despair in Shawn's eyes as he failed to mention his own mission. It was almost physically painful to see. Brandt actually felt badly for thinking that Shawn was trying to kill him.

He knew the others were panicking, as much as a trained agent could panic anyway. But Brandt's mind was working on a slightly different plane as the fire whipped about in the darkness and the smell of burning wood permeated the air. He led them into it without blinking, his mind almost elsewhere as he kicked the heavy door in and slipped between the flames.

The most likely suspect out of the six of them to have started this particular little blaze stood in Brandt's unlaced boots. Brandt knew that. And he knew the others would come to the same conclusion as soon as they calmed and started thinking rationally again. So as he moved almost mechanically, carrying out the orders Shawn had shouted at him, he tried to work out the problem in order to defend himself when the accusations started to fly. And they would. Carl had questioned him and he had been naked in bed with Brandt. To Carl's credit though, it must have been a little... disconcerting to be awakened in such a manner. Maybe he hadn't been thinking clearly.

Assuming the bomb– and it was definitely a bomb– hadn't been on a long-term timer or a remote control, then Brandt could easily narrow the possibilities.

He knew he hadn't set off the bomb. Even *he* wasn't so far gone as to not remember setting a charge of this magnitude. Check that. Of any magnitude.

He knew Carl hadn't set off the bomb. Carl had been in bed with him the whole time, and Brandt was a very light sleeper. If Carl had moved Brandt would have known.

Those were the only things he could be sure of. Those were the absolute certainties. Now, the questions. Why had Shawn been standing calmly outside the cabin, with every one of his bags sitting around his feet and his gun out? And why had Nikolaus been out front? He said he'd been out there the whole time. Why? How?

Brandt almost tripped over a lump on the ground, and when he bent over to investigate, he immediately recognized Remy's unmoving body.

"Hey!" he called into the smoky chaos of the outer room. "I found Remy!"

Shawn was by his side in a heartbeat, and Brandt watched him gather the younger man carefully into his arms in a fireman's carry, nod in thanks, and disappear into the smoke as he carried Remy outside to safety.

If Shawn had set off the bomb in the assumption that Remy would be out of harm's way with him when it went off, then now that he was assured of Remy's relative safety, he would most certainly be gone by the time Brandt was done gathering what little equipment he could find.

Brandt knelt on the floor as the fires raged around him, struggling with indecision. Should he follow Shawn out and lose what little supplies they would be able to salvage, or should he trust the older man to still be there and get on with his job?

Brandt cursed colorfully and lunged to his feet, heading into what was left of the hallway toward the worst of the flames.

XIX

REMY struggled against the arms that held him. There was something wrong. There was danger, and he had to get to Shawn. But the arms held him firmly, and though he struggled to the point that his abused lungs sent him into a fit of pitiful coughing, he eventually ran out of the energy to fight them.

"It's okay, Remy. You're fine," the voice belonging to the shockingly strong arms told him soothingly.

Were the arms that strong, or was there something wrong with him? Remy was having difficulty seeing clearly, and his lungs and throat burned as if Brandt had lit a pinecone and stuffed it down his throat.

Out of the corner of his eye, Remy could see Thiago on the ground coughing and struggling to get up from his hands and knees. Carl knelt with him, patting him on the back and trying to convince him to eat what looked like a handful of snow.

"Shawn," Remy gasped desperately as his glazed eyes took in the flames and the destruction of the cabin. Fuck! Explosion! Bedrooms! "Shawn!" he tried again, his voice a mere croak as his fingers dug into the hard muscles of the arm draped across his chest, trying to pry it loose so he could get up.

"He's in there," Nikolaus said as he tightened his grip around Remy's body. He pointed to the flaming doorway as the sound of a falling ceiling timber echoed throughout the forest. "He went back in to help Brandt gather equipment."

"No… let me up," Remy begged, finally managing to sit up slightly before crying out as pain tore through his body.

"You're hurt bad, Remy. Stay down. They'll be okay… know what they're… be… Remy? Remy!"

Remy's world began to fade into black, and though he could hear Nikolaus's desperate voice calling to him, he couldn't return to it no matter how hard he tried.

XX.

THIAGO looked up from his kneeling position and stared at the flames as they flared more and more out of control. Carl held him up and rubbed his back in an automatic gesture as he shivered in the snow. Thiago distantly wondered how you could be so cold and yet so hot at the same time. He looked over just in time to see Remy going limp in Nikolaus's arms.

"*Carajo*," he gasped. Carl turned him loose and they both scrambled through the snow to the other two men.

"He won't wake up," Nikolaus said in a surprisingly calm voice as he cradled Remy's lolling head in his hands. "He started struggling, calling for Shawn. Then he just…."

Thiago scooped up a handful of snow and began to gently smear it over Remy's forehead and cheeks as Carl put two fingers to the younger man's neck, searching for a pulse.

"It's strong," Carl murmured.

Thiago seemed to be doing nothing more than mixing the soot and melting snow over Remy's smooth forehead. He nodded and wiped his abused eyes as if it would clear away his muddled thoughts before looking Remy's body over for injuries.

"His leg, Thiago," Nikolaus said softly, nodding his head at Remy's bloody thigh. "It's the only injury I can see. Are you hurt?"

"No," Thiago said distractedly as Carl grabbed him and yanked at his belt. Thiago raised his hands the let Carl yank it out of his belt loops.

"What happened?" Carl asked as he tied the belt tightly around Remy's thigh just above the shrapnel wound.

"I was in front of the fireplace," Thiago explained needlessly to the two men who had found him. "Remy was standing just in front of the hallway. I thought for sure it had killed him. I was looking right at him and then…."

"When the fires calm I'll go back in," Brandt announced breathlessly as he and Shawn staggered up and dumped several bags of equipment on the ground.

He fell to his knees and huffed, and Thiago was a little shocked at how normal he appeared, covered in soot and singed around the edges. His bare chest shone with sweat, and Thiago realized that he was gawking at the impressive sight. Shawn wasn't in much better shape, but Brandt carried off the crispy look much more naturally.

"We'll try to see where it originated," Brandt was saying. "From the amount of damage it looks as if it was one of the back bedrooms… or maybe the washroom. Won't be able to tell for sure 'til I can look at it, though."

"Did you set this fire?" Thiago demanded angrily.

"If I had started this fire, there would just be a crater," Brandt answered heatedly, "and none of us would be sitting here breathing in all this lovely smoke because I would have made damn sure to blow us all to Hell!" he shouted. It was the first time Thiago had seen the big man perturbed, and he instantly regretted his hasty accusation. "So no, I didn't start this fire, but fuck you very much, all the same."

Shawn put a hand on Brandt's shoulder and Thiago saw the fingers dig into the muscle. As if by magic Brandt was once again calm, and Thiago blinked at him uncertainly.

"I'm sorry," he offered sincerely. He tried to think of something more to say, but Brandt apparently didn't need more because he nodded and looked at Remy in concern.

"Is he… bad?" Brandt asked hesitantly. Shawn swallowed with difficulty, and Thiago's heart went out to him. He himself wanted to kill the person who had done this. He couldn't even begin to fathom what sort of murderous rage must have been going through Shawn's head. He shivered as he thought about the look in Shawn's green eyes and shook himself out of the rather frightening images that graced his imagination.

"I think he passed out. Shock, maybe," Nikolaus supplied as Shawn gestured for him to move. Nikolaus complied and Shawn settled himself beneath Remy's head and shoulders and held him close, keeping him warm in the snow.

"Does anyone know what happened?" Shawn asked in a low voice as he gently ran his hand over Remy's forehead. Thiago didn't like his tone at all. He'd dealt with some of the most ruthless and dangerous individuals in the world without batting an eye, but Shawn's tone scared him. Thiago made a mental note never to cross the man as he shook his head in answer.

"Nikolaus?" Shawn said in the same terrifyingly low voice.

"Hmm?" Nikolaus responded as he tore his gaze away from Remy's face.

"Why were you out here?"

"What?"

"Why were you out here?" Shawn repeated deliberately as he finally looked up and pinned Nikolaus with a dangerous glare.

"You were outside?" Thiago asked in surprise. That was news to him. How had Nikolaus gotten outside?

Nikolaus looked like the proverbial deer in the headlights as he looked from Shawn to Thiago and back.

"I needed a smoke," he squeaked.

"How did you get past Thiago?" Brandt asked as he eyed Thiago suspiciously. Thiago creased his brow and shot a nervous look at Shawn. Nikolaus had to have slipped out when he and Remy were having their little discussion about trust. How very ironic.

"He...," Nikolaus started uncertainly. He looked guilty as hell, and Thiago suddenly realized why. Nikolaus knew he was in serious trouble if he couldn't get them to believe his story, but he was actually risking his life to cover for Thiago. Thiago couldn't have that.

"I was having a discussion with Remy," Thiago said softly. "We weren't paying attention. He could have easily walked by us without us noticing."

Behind them the last timbers of the cabin began to crackle merrily.

XXI.

"DID he?" Carl demanded.

"Well, I didn't crawl out a fucking window," Nikolaus insisted with a scowl.

Carl merely nodded at Nikolaus and looked back down at Remy in concern. He wasn't really concerned with Nikolaus. He didn't like the little German for this mess. And Remy was a bigger worry at the moment. If he had been standing in front of the hallway when the explosion happened, then he had probably taken the brunt of the force directly. The thick log walls of the bedrooms had protected the rest of them, and Thiago's sheer distance had kept him safe, but if Remy had been in the open....

"We should check him for internal injuries," Brandt said softly, as if he had been reading Carl's mind and thinking along the same lines.

Shawn gently placed Remy's head in the snow as they laid him flat, and Thiago began to probe gently at his torso.

"How did you get out so quickly, Shawn?" Carl asked regretfully. It almost caused him physical pain to question the man. Shawn looked up at him in surprise.

"What do you mean?"

"Brandt and I moved pretty fast, but you were out with all your gear and just... standing there like it was a walk through the park. With your weapon out, no less. Who were you planning to shoot, Shawn? You weren't expecting the blast, were you?" he asked doubtfully. He hated to play the interrogator at this point, but he had a feeling that he was the only one who would.

Shawn stood and faced Carl, his face calm once more. "I got out quickly because I'm very fucking good at what I do. Just like the rest of you," he growled dangerously. "I had all the gear out because I happened to have been in Remy's room at the time, and not only is he the most organized person I know, but he also procrastinates, so his bags were all sitting under the window, still packed. I got your shit out, too, by the way. You're fucking welcome. I had me gun out because someone had just tried to blow us up!" he shouted, finally losing his temper. "And I don't take kindly to people who try to blow me up!"

Carl put up his hands in a placating gesture. Shawn's explanations were entirely plausible, and besides, Carl found that he trusted Shawn implicitly. He was the last person Carl would suspect of being out to hurt any of them.

"I had to ask, Shawn," he murmured apologetically.

Shawn seemed to tense slightly, but then he deflated visibly and nodded. "You're right," he said calmly. "You're right," he repeated softly, turning back to place a hand on Nikolaus's shoulder as if he had just realized he had insulted the younger man in the same way Carl had done him.

Nikolaus nodded in acknowledgement of the silent apology, and the three of them stood and watched Thiago and Brandt's hands move gently over Remy's body as the cabin behind them smoldered in the freshly falling snow.

XXII.

SHAWN was the closest to a full-fledged breakdown as he had ever been, which was to say, he was a little nervous. In the five years Shawn had known him, Remy had been shot, stabbed, hit by a particularly lovely blue Jaguar, dragged behind a motorbike, thrown off a roof, and attacked by a nasty turkeyduck thing that had ended up being supper that night. Among other things. Shawn had rarely been so worried about him as he was now.

Shawn thought perhaps it wasn't so much the possibility that Remy could have internal injuries and that he was bleeding pretty profusely and that there wasn't a doctor for miles, but that Shawn felt guilty. Guilty as fuck, actually. If he hadn't tried to hide anything from Remy in the first place, Remy would never have felt the need to seek Thiago out and lecture him on trust. He would have been happy to stay in that tiny single bed, curled up with Shawn, and he would have been safe there. He would have been able to calmly roll out of bed, gather his things, stroll out into the forest, and remain just as unscathed as Shawn.

It didn't occur to Shawn that Remy might have had other reasons to be out of bed.

"There's really no way to tell," Thiago said as he looked up at them finally. "I don't feel any broken ribs, which is good, I suppose. But I'm no doctor. We won't be able to tell if there's bleeding anywhere until it's too late. Unless he wakes up soon to tell us where he hurts, we'll have to get him to a hospital."

Brandt stood and dusted the snow off his knees, but he said nothing as he looked down at Remy thoughtfully. Shawn avoided eye contact with the others, knowing that his guilt was written clearly on his face. He sat down, weaving his arms under and around Remy and pulling him close once more to keep him warm. Brandt and Carl exchanged a look that Shawn was too tired to try to decipher, and Nikolaus and Thiago scooted closer and began fussing over the man like mother hens.

"Should we move him if he could be bleeding?" Carl asked in concern.

"If we don't move him out of the snow he'll die anyway," Thiago responded grimly.

"If he's bleeding internally," Shawn said softly, "he's already dead."

Shawn rocked slowly back and forth as he held Remy to him– a habit that he had picked up from Remy in their early days of working together– and tried to wrap his mind around what had just happened.

XXIII.

NIKOLAUS couldn't begin to describe how relieved he was at seeing all five men out of the cabin and relatively safe.

The blast had shaken him, but he kept trying to force down the grin that wanted to appear every time he heard his mother's voice in his head telling him that cigarettes would kill him one day.

It certainly hadn't been today.

"Does anyone have any information we can go on from here," Carl asked after they had moved Remy to Shawn's Land Rover. He seemed to sense that Shawn would be useless until Remy awoke, so Carl momentarily took charge. "Anything at all?"

"I managed to grab Remy's paper," Thiago said as he patted down his pockets.

"Paper?" Carl repeated questioningly.

"Yeah, he… he wrote the Archer's transmission down," Thiago mumbled as he pulled the sheet of paper out of his back pocket. Nikolaus looked at it curiously. The pad was gone, as if Thiago had ripped it away in his haste to leave the burning structure, and it was just a single charred sheet now. But it was certainly still legible.

"It'll do," Nikolaus murmured as he watched Thiago fold it carefully and place it in the front pocket of Remy's flannel shirt. "Not like the computers were giving us much anyway."

"What else? With the fire? No one heard anything? Saw anything? Thiago? You were on watch."

"To be honest with you, I wasn't all that alert," Thiago said to Carl, somewhat testily. "Between the God-awful sounds you two were making and talking with Remy…," he shook his head and rubbed his hand over his eyes irritably. "Besides, Nikolaus was with me most of the time. We didn't hear anything."

Brandt turned to look at Nikolaus, and he tried desperately not to back away from him in alarm.

"What about you, Gizmo?" Brandt asked in a reasonably normal voice. "What's 'for the most part' mean?"

"I, uh… well… I tried to get some sleep after… after, uh…."

"He was gone for roughly thirty minutes after Remy called out," Thiago supplied, being careful not to meet Shawn's eyes. "I assume you both heard it?"

Brandt and Carl both nodded, and Nikolaus was relieved to be out of the rather dangerous spotlight once more.

"About that," Carl said as he looked down at Shawn. Nikolaus saw the same look cross the assassin's face as he had seen before, one of pity and regret. Nikolaus could tell that Carl didn't want to ask Shawn what he was about to ask. He didn't want to cause Shawn any pain as Remy lay unconscious in his arms, and Nikolaus liked the man all the more for it.

"I would never hurt him," Shawn mumbled as he continued to rock back and forth slightly and began to speak softly into Remy's ear. The rocking was almost imperceptible, it was so slight, but it worried Nikolaus all the same. Was it just a nervous habit or was it a nervous breakdown?

They all stared at Shawn for what seemed like forever, each of them undoubtedly wondering about his sanity. They had all they could handle with Brandt being half off his rocker, if they lost Remy and Shawn went mad because of it, they were as good as dead.

The Organization did not tolerate failure in any form, and Nikolaus thought of the repercussions for a setback such as their safe house being compromised less than a week into the mission. He looked up and into Thiago's intense gaze, and he knew that the older man was thinking the same thing from the look in his odd blue eyes. Just the thought of what would be done to them if they failed so miserably made Nikolaus's blood run cold.

XXIV.

BRANDT catalogued what he'd learned during the night as he picked through the charred remains of the cabin in the early morning light. The fire had burned fast and hard, just like Brandt liked it, and he'd thoroughly enjoyed watching it burn down to nothing as the sun rose over the tree tops.

He kicked aside the burnt corpse of a door and bent over to examine the ashes beneath it. He'd not yet found the device that was responsible, but he hadn't expected to just yet. He was still in the outer room, after all. The door appeared to be the washroom door. It was thicker than the others, and Brandt thought that its being at the end of the hall, at least a full ten meters away from its original location, was even more evidence that the bomb had been behind the toilet.

He continued slowly picking his way through, and finally he found what he was after. To the untrained eye, it would probably have looked like any other debris after such an explosion, but to Brandt it looked like pay dirt.

"Clever bastard," he murmured as he knelt to pick up what remained of the corrugated steel pipe. It was the thinnest pipe you could get, and therefore gave off the biggest blast. It had been placed amongst the plumbing as far as Brandt could tell, and it would have passed unnoticed in a brief inspection of the room. Attached to it were the shattered remains of an old-fashioned pocket watch.

He cradled his find in his arms and picked his way back out to the vehicles where the others milled about, waiting for him. They'd transferred Remy to the back of one of the Land Rovers, and now Shawn sat in the storage compartment with the younger man's head in his lap. The others paced back and forth in front of the tailgate like uneasy guard dogs. The whole scene struck Brandt as wildly funny.

"I've found the timing device," he announced as he walked up to them. They all turned to look at him expectantly. "Old time pocket watch. No remote on it from what I can see. The way the timer works," he told them as he held up the remains of the pocket watch, "you attach one wire to the hour hand, another wire to the minute hand, and boom when they connect. It can't be set for more than twelve hours," he explained. "Want my Big Bang Theory? Whoever blew this bastard was here with us," he concluded grimly, not wanting to admit that one of them could have done it. Probably *had* done it.

He hated harboring the suspicions he had voiced to Carl, but they were there all the same. Now, though… Remy wouldn't have set this bomb and then knowingly stood in its path like he had. Would he? Brandt could think of three plausible explanations.

One; his suspicion that Remy was working for the Archer had been wrong. God, how he hoped he'd been wrong.

Two; Remy had mistimed the device. The fact that his bedroom, where Shawn had just happened to be when the bomb went off, was even now relatively unscathed despite the fact that the roof had burned away, was very suspicious. Brandt could conceive of Remy luring Shawn to his room in order to keep him safe, going out to do whatever he'd been doing to Thiago to deflect suspicion, but then getting caught in the blast because he'd made a mistake. He'd been up, and even Thiago had admitted that Remy had surprised him and Nikolaus. There was no telling how long he'd been up and moving about before he made his presence known.

Or three; Remy hadn't made a mistake. This was the most frightening scenario of all, and if Brandt was right then it meant Remy was even more unbalanced than he was, if that were possible. If Remy had set that bomb and then stood in its path with a bull's eye painted on his fucking ass, trusting in the fates that he wouldn't be killed just to deflect suspicion from himself, then he was crazy as hell. And smart. And dangerous. And downright fucking scary.

A bomb with a broken timer. Though Brandt respected the thinking behind it, and admired the balls required for it, he didn't like it.

Brandt had never been scared of an opponent before, and he didn't like the feeling. He looked at Remy closely, as if he could see into the other man's soul. But no miraculous insights came. He shook his head and moved away from his suspicions for a moment, trying to get a better angle.

He tried to think of times during the past twelve hours in which any of them had been alone. But because the bomb had been in the fucking toilet, it made them all suspects merely by location and opportunity.

Unless, of course, the bomb had been set by an outsider, which was quite frankly hard to fathom. No one knew they were here. And anyone who could get past six trained agents and sneak into the bathroom, of all places was… well, nonexistent, really.

Brandt realized he was drifting once more, and he looked down at the remains of the bomb in his hand. So out of his five suspects, because he knew that he himself hadn't done it, Brandt had two real suspects. Carl was the only one with express knowledge of making explosive devices aside from himself, but he was out of the question. Brandt trusted him implicitly, and his reaction to being awakened by the explosion had been genuine. Nikolaus had managed to quietly slip out of the cabin only moments before the blast under the guise of having a smoke, miraculously saved from any danger. And then there was Remy.

Brandt sighed. And then, of course, there was the possibility that Shawn had gotten up as soon as Remy had left him, and that would also explain why the room which he'd occupied had been spared, as well as why the fuck he'd been standing in the woods with a gun in his hand. Of course, if he'd been trying to kill them all, he'd have taken the gun and shot them as they came around the corner. They never would have known what hit them.

Brandt shivered and shook his head. No. He trusted Shawn. He trusted him with the same certainty that he now trusted Carl. They were both out of the question.

Thiago had the same opportunity as the rest of them and, as a Class One agent, possessed the knowledge to make a pipe bomb, but for some reason Brandt believed him when he said he'd done nothing all night but walk the perimeter. In fact….

"Thiago, is it possible that someone could have entered the cabin when you were on rounds?"

Thiago blinked at him. "I saw no signs. But yes. Like I said, I thought we were safe. I was going through the motions, really, and I can't be everywhere at once, now can I?"

"Well, fuck," Brandt whispered. All that rational thinking had to be thrown out the window. This was why he liked irrational thinking so much better. It took less effort and the conclusions you came to were harder to refute.

XXV.

REMY was struggling with consciousness. He didn't want to be conscious. He didn't want to be cold and in pain. He quite liked the comfort of the dark and he would have preferred to stay unconscious, thank you very much.

But it was not to be. His face was wet and very cold, and there was a steady, pleasant rumbling in his ear that slowly brought him back to the land of the waking. There was also a fiery pain in his thigh, and it was this pain that finally brought him around.

"I think he's coming to," Remy heard a voice say.

"This looks bad, Shawn. We have to–"

"He's seen worse," Shawn's wonderfully familiar voice rumbled into his ear.

Remy opened his eyes with difficulty and looked up to see all five of his companions staring down at him. It would have been comical if he hadn't hurt so badly.

"Cold," he managed to croak. Shawn pulled him closer, and Remy realized that Shawn was holding his head and shoulders in his lap like you would someone who you thought was about to die. Well, fuck that. Remy started to struggle to remove himself from Shawn's grip, but Shawn held him firmly around his chest and whispered soothing words into his ear.

"It's all right, lad. You're just fine," he said, seeming to sense why Remy was panicking. "I'm just trying to keep you warm, lad. Stop struggling."

Remy did as he was ordered.

Thiago sat with difficulty in the cramped space beside him and Carl knelt at his knee. He untied a leather belt from around Remy's thigh and checked the wound. Remy uttered a pitiful cry of pain as the blood rushed back to the wound. The belt was hastily tied tightly around his leg once more, and Carl looked at him apologetically. Remy tried to smile at him, but he thought that it possibly came out as more of a grimace.

"What happened?" he asked in a horribly hoarse voice.

"Big bang," Brandt answered as he paced restlessly back and forth, in and out of Remy's limited vision.

"Is everyone okay?" Remy asked, not thinking that it was a fairly stupid question as all five of them stared at him.

"Only casualties were the electronics and most of our clothes," Nikolaus said mournfully as he settled in beside Thiago. How many grown men could you fit in the back of a Land Rover? Remy didn't really care. "Brandt and Shawn managed to rescue most of it."

"Shawn," Remy groaned, remembering the blinding fear he'd felt when he'd thought Shawn was in danger.

"I'm here, lad."

"Bastard."

"I know, lad," Shawn said with a laugh that sounded oddly like a sob. "I know."

"Well… what now?" Nikolaus asked after several minutes of silence.

"We have to get him some sort of medical attention," Thiago said. "This bleeding has to be stopped. And disinfected. We can't go to a hospital. Maybe a vet or…."

Remy snorted despite the pain he was in. "A vet… where's my sheep blanket?" he slurred with an amused look at Carl and Brandt. He saw them both smile affectionately, and Shawn's arms tightened around him once more.

"You'll have to get well soon then, if you plan on romping around in that blanket," Carl said softly as Brandt walked around to the driver's side of the Rover and got in.

"What do we do with the other vehicles?"

Remy opened his eyes again and looked at Nikolaus. "We should separate," he said in a hoarse voice. He cleared his throat, trying to recover his voice, but when he continued to speak it was no better. "Can you ride my bike?"

"*Ja.*"

"Keys are in the bag. Be careful with her," Remy murmured as Nikolaus squeezed his foot and then slid out of the back of the Rover. Remy looked up at Thiago, who was hovering over him, and then at Shawn, who was holding him so tightly that Remy almost couldn't breathe.

"Carl, you and Thiago take the truck. We may end up needing it," Shawn ordered in a soft voice. "We're going for speed, not stealth, so don't worry about being seen."

They both nodded, and Thiago let his fingers brush Remy's as he slid out.

"You all right back there?" Brandt asked as he turned around to peer over the seats. Carl closed the back door and Shawn answered affirmatively as he ran his hand over Remy's forehead and threaded his fingers through his hair.

"Thought I'd lost you," he said softly as Brandt cranked the Rover up.

"Same here, Beignet," Remy muttered as the fingers in his hair threatened to put him back to sleep.

"Where to, Beignet?" Brandt asked with a little smirk.

Shawn gave him instructions to find the nearest no-tell motel he could as he rocked Remy slowly back and forth, and Remy couldn't have really cared what they did next, so long as Shawn never let go of him.

Part Two: Three Roads

I.

THIAGO sat by Remy's bed and stared blankly at the cheap burgundy comforter as he thought over their situation. It had been roughly two weeks since their safe house was compromised, and they'd traveled what Thiago estimated to be about 700 miles since that morning. They'd finally gone to ground in the city of Sioux Falls, roughly fifty miles from their original rendezvous point.

They weren't certain who was after them or how they had been tracked in the first place, but after the shock of the fire had worn off, they'd realized that they needed to move, often and fast.

It had been difficult, but they'd managed to get Remy to a backwoods veterinarian, who'd looked him over and pronounced that he would 'probably live.' He'd patched him up, given them illegal painkillers and antibiotics for the fever that was even now tearing through the young man's body, and taken their money with a promise to keep the incident to himself. It had taken everything in Thiago and Carl's considerable combined power to convince Brandt that they didn't need to kill the man.

Then they'd continued on, bouncing from one little town to another, trying to lose themselves in a city of fairly decent size. Six men of their sort traveling together didn't really blend in well, and they'd been forced to continue moving even though they risked Remy's health and life by doing so.

Now they were holed up in their fifth motel of the week, and Thiago was on deathwatch. He hated to think of the duty of sitting up with Remy as deathwatch, but that was what it was, regardless of how well Remy was doing now. The watch wasn't necessarily to sit up with Remy in case he died or anything, but to sit up with him and smother him if he started making too much noise. His body was battling back to health at a remarkable speed, but the fever was what worried Thiago. It made Remy a little on the delirious side, and the last thing they needed was to have him call out in the middle of the night and compromise their position. Again.

But tonight it looked like the fever was breaking. Remy had been restless and sweating and just downright pitiful for the first hour or so of Thiago's watch, but now he was calm and quiet, and Thiago absently stroked his hand in what he hoped was a comforting fashion.

Their group seemed to be floundering. They didn't have a plan or even so much as a goal other than the very long-term one of not getting dead. Thiago worried that, like his own and everyone else's, Shawn's planning ability was hindered by his concern for Remy's well-being. It spoke volumes about the group's coherency that no one seemed willing to do the most obvious thing and move on, leaving Remy to fend for himself. Thiago felt sick just thinking about it.

After the shock wore off, they'd suffered through another short bout of accusations and an interesting little tussle between Brandt and Shawn, from which Shawn surprisingly came out the victor, hovering over Brandt and threatening him with a pinecone he managed to grab as they rolled on the forest floor. Brandt had questioned whether Remy could have been responsible for the bomb, and Shawn had taken exception.

They'd all eventually decided that Remy couldn't have done it, and what was more, he'd had no reason to do it. After this last seed of mistrust was uprooted, they'd slowly but surely grown to trust one another. And yes, care for one another.

Yes, they were a team. And yes, they'd become good friends in a short time. And yes, they'd formed a close bond and all that shit, but they still had no plan and no purpose. If they didn't set up shop again soon they'd really be in the shit.

Remy shifted and groaned, bringing Thiago out of his depressing thoughts.

"*Hola, aguante*," Thiago whispered gently as he leaned in and brushed the curls away from Remy's damp forehead. Remy looked back at him blankly for so long that Thiago began to worry that the fever had caused some sort of amnesia, but then Remy blinked and a smile ghosted across his lips.

"*Aguante*?" he repeated in a weak voice. "What the hell does that mean? Oh, God, does it mean I'm dying?"

Thiago smiled and laughed in relief. "It's better than 'Dixie', isn't it?"

Remy closed his eyes and smiled. "There is history behind that one, *mon vieux*. What's your excuse for calling me a lizard, huh?"

Thiago cocked an eyebrow and grinned. It sounded as if the old Remy was beginning to shine through once more, and Thiago couldn't remember many times that he'd felt more relieved. The sooner Remy could move the sooner they'd be on their way.

"It simply means a rebellious or spirited person," he explained with a dismissive wave of his hand. "I could think of no word that fit you better," Thiago said softly as he scooted his chair forward and rested his elbows on the bed. He enclosed Remy's hand with both of his own and rubbed the man's cold fingers as he looked down at them absently. Remy watched him warily, but then the caution seemed to seep from his features and he smiled again.

"Has he told you any stories yet?" Remy asked in a hoarse voice. He cleared his throat as Thiago looked back up at him.

"Who? Shawn?" Thiago asked in surprise.

"*Oui*," Remy answered, his voice still hoarse and pitifully weak.

"No. He has been… quiet," Thiago said hesitantly. He didn't want Remy knowing how worried everyone was about him. It wasn't just Shawn. There'd been a definite funereal air about the group as they'd waited for Remy to either improve or die, but that was the last thing Thiago wanted Remy knowing. From the little he knew of the younger man's personality, Thiago thought Remy would probably just rush his recovery and end up getting even sicker than he was now if he knew that they were all concerned and that Shawn was almost out of his mind with worry.

Remy simply nodded and closed his eyes as if it took effort to keep them open. Thiago was about to offer to go and fetch water. Or food. Or painkillers. Or Shawn. Whatever would make him feel better, but then Remy started talking.

"Usually when he think I'm dying, he start babbling nonsense and telling embarrassing stories," Remy mumbled. Thiago had noticed that his way of speaking changed with how lucid or exhausted he was. The intriguing accent was nearly always present, unless Remy actively tried another, but there seemed to be a difference in the way he put emphasis on different parts of words. He also seemed unable to pronounce the hard sounds when they came at the end of his words. Ask became *ax*, next became *nex*, desk became *des*, some of his *the* sounds became *de* sounds. It was slightly endearing to hear his natural dialect. "*Rahdoht, non*? Talking that got no end to it," Remy explained with a fond smile.

"I cannot imagine Shawn… babbling," Thiago murmured with a smirk.

"*Mais oui*, he do. I figure he'd tell you how we met, since you wanted so bad to know. He'd tell you different, but I caught his scent before he caught mine," Remy started without preamble.

Thiago perked up and leaned forward attentively. Remy had been babbling a lot, but he seemed coherent now.

"I started following him instead of the target, and one day when he was out on surveillance I broke into the building where he had set up camp. I did just like I told Niko that day out in the woods, you remember? I put little charges in the firing pins of each of his long-range rifles. It was perfect, *mon ami*, beautiful. As soon as he pull the trigger, whether it was me or *my* target he be shooting at, the gun would self-destruct and take him with it."

Thiago wondered whether he should try to get Remy to clarify that he was talking about how he and Shawn first met, but Thiago feared bumping the younger man's train of thought off track, and so he remained quiet and simply listened.

"But the more I saw of him; the way he work, the way he carry himself, the way he…." Remy trailed off and opened his eyes to stare at the ceiling with a faraway look. "The way he stopped and helped little old ladies cross the street, even when he was supposed to be tailing a mark. I could not have someone like that just blow up, *non*? I became enthralled by him, I think. By this time, I had almost forgot the target. And let me tell you, that *salaud* was hard to tail," he added as he looked over at Thiago. "Neither one of us ever even got so much as a look at his face. He was an agent, too. Like us. Another one of the fuck ups from that Purge mess… bad *gris-gris*. Lucky bastard, too, to have two agents on him and live through it.…"

Remy seemed to drift off a bit, but Thiago waited patiently. He thought of how lucky he himself had been during that mess. He'd been one of the agents assigned as a target, and he hadn't known just how lucky he was until later when he'd found out about it. He'd never known why the agent on him hadn't taken him down. Thiago had found out later that the agent had been called the Hunter, and for some reason the name made Thiago shiver even now.

"Anyway, by then he had caught sight of me as well," Remy continued, his voice getting a bit stronger the more he talked. "And I knew I had to make the first move, so I set a decoy in a vacant building near his."

"A decoy?" Thiago asked with interest, his professional curiosity getting the better of him.

"Mm hmm. The buildings, they were real close together, see, so I let him track me going into the one next to his a couple of times. I don't think he really thought me a threat," Remy said thoughtfully, his mind very obviously wandering as he slurred slightly throughout his story. Thiago thought about getting him to stop, but his curiosity won out over his concern and he let Remy continue. "I mean, look at me," Remy instructed with amusement. "Five years ago I look like a baby, *non*?"

"I believe it," Thiago nodded with a small smile, taking in the Cajun's features. There were only faint laugh lines around his mouth and eyes. There were no blemishes on his smooth face aside from a barely discernible scar that ran over his left eyebrow. He did not look like a man who'd lived such an eventful life.

"That was one of my advantages," Remy murmured. "But he set up regardless of how young I looked, wanting to get me out of the way in order to take care of his mark and get on with it. That's what he tell me later. That I was a 'damn nuisance', always showing up and distracting him from *his* mark." Remy laughed weakly and closed his eyes once more. "I went through the fire escape to the roof while he was trained on the front door, jumped the gap between the buildings and kicked open his door as he stood there looking for me through his scope." Remy started snickering again and opened his eyes to look up at Thiago. "You should've seen his face. Like a deer in the headlights."

"Can't imagine he was pleased," Thiago murmured.

"So I taunt him some, *non*?" Remy admitted with an errant little flip of his hand. "It piss him off like you would not believe. I was feeling pretty good about myself at that point, so I forget to tell him not to throw down his gun."

"*Ay, Dios mio*," Thiago muttered with a hint of a laugh.

"As soon as I saw his hand move to toss that fucking rifle my way I yelled at him not to drop it. It would have blown us both back to the bayou." Remy smiled and shook his head, remembering what he obviously considered a good memory now that time had washed it clean of the fear and uncertainty. "*Canaille*. He must have known because he got this… self-satisfied… smug little… shit-eating grin on his face, and then the shitwit tossed the fucking thing at me."

Thiago put his hand on Remy's forehead to check how warm he was, and Remy nuzzled up into the contact as if the action were automatic. He definitely looked better, but he was still warm. "What happened?" Thiago prompted after Remy remained quiet.

"I catch it," Remy sleepily as he let his eyes drift shut once more. "Dropped my own gun and catch that one. Shawn, he dive behind a couch, and when he come back up he have a handgun."

"What'd you do?" Thiago asked after Remy was silent for several more moments.

Remy sniffed and finally opened his eyes again to turn and look at Thiago. "I turned tail and run away."

II.

CARL hadn't slept too soundly of late. He seriously doubted any of them had, actually. Agents rarely slept soundly, with the possible exception of Brandt, who couldn't be moved when they shared a bed even when Carl kicked and shoved him. But this sleeplessness was a little different. It wasn't just wariness, it was worry. Concern over a comrade. They didn't deal with that often. Carl, in fact, had never dealt with it.

None of them were sleeping soundly, but Carl thought that perhaps his reasons were a little different. He had a lot on his mind that the others were either not thinking about or weren't openly discussing.

Yes, he was worried about Remy just as much as they were.

Yes, he was frustrated with their lack of options, just like the others were.

And yes, he wanted revenge, not only for almost being killed, but also for the sheer fact that someone had gotten the upper hand on them.

But unlike the others, Carl wasn't as certain of whom exactly he wanted to kill for it all. Carl rolled to his other side for perhaps the fiftieth time in the last hour and earned himself a swift kick to the leg.

"Ow! Son of a bitch!" he hissed quietly, rubbing his calf and turning to glare at Shawn through the darkness.

"Quit moving. Tosser," Shawn mumbled grumpily as he turned his back to Carl once more. When Carl sat up and rested back on his elbows to look at his cranky bed mate a menacing growl emitted from somewhere in the vicinity of Shawn's head, which was now buried under a pillow.

They were essentially doing a round robin with the sleeping arrangements. Every two hours someone new would go into the connecting room to look in on Remy, and whoever got up would concede their spot in bed. Carl began the night with Nikolaus, and Shawn took the first shift. But then it was Nikolaus's turn, and Shawn replaced him next to Carl. Apparently Nikolaus was too scared of him to say anything about his restlessness, but Shawn didn't seem to have that problem.

"Bastard," Carl grumbled as he flopped heavily onto his back. He flopped again and made as much fuss as he could manage, causing the mattress to bounce up and down as he scooted up behind Shawn and threw his arm and leg over him. Then he started to breathe heavily against the back of Shawn's neck until the other man started to snicker sleepily.

"What the bloody hell are you doing?" Shawn grumbled, trying to hide his amusement as he turned halfway over and let his fuzzy cheek rest against Carl's nose.

"I'm seeing how far I can push you until you blow up," Carl whispered back against his skin matter-of-factly.

"Blowing up is a bad term," Shawn muttered as he turned his head even more, his lips just barely brushing over Carl's as he spoke. "Brandt would blow up. I would probably snap." Carl smiled against Shawn's lips. "You got something on your mind, I promise I'll listen in the morning," Shawn said softly as he pulled back slightly and gave Carl's shin one more kick for good measure. "Now go to sleep!" he hissed.

Before Carl could retaliate, the door to the adjoining room opened and the room was briefly flooded with light as Thiago stepped in. It was Brandt's turn to sit up with Remy, but the man snored lightly as Nikolaus fought to keep from being pushed off the bed. Carl rolled his eyes. Brandt was an active sleeper, as they had all discovered during the bed rotation.

"Fuck, I'll take this one. I can't sleep anyway," Carl said with a smile as he retreated from the warmth of Shawn's body just in time to narrowly miss being kicked again. He didn't even bother to pull his jeans on over his briefs as he shuffled past Thiago. "How is he?" he asked the Argentinean quietly.

"He was awake earlier," Thiago said quietly as he glanced at the spot in the bed Carl had just vacated. Or perhaps he was glancing at Shawn, Carl wasn't certain in the low light. "He talked for a bit."

Carl nodded and gripped Thiago's shoulder. Then he pulled him close and whispered, "Beignet's a grumpy bastard tonight. Careful that you don't move at all."

"You and Brandt deserve to be bed mates," Shawn grumbled from beneath the bedcovers he'd thrown over his head in a huff. Carl gave Thiago one last pat on the back and disappeared into the adjoining room.

The lamp beside the bed was on, and one of the others had pulled a chair to sit beside the bed at Remy's head. Carl stood motionless for several seconds, holding his breath as he looked at Remy's still form.

When Remy didn't move at all, Carl walked on cat's feet over to the chair and eased himself into it. He rubbed his eyes and stared at the horrid painting above the bed as his thoughts wandered.

They'd managed to replenish their wardrobes as they moved, and they had enough loose cash to keep on renting cheap motel rooms for the next few weeks at least, but they were still in trouble.

Carl had been going over the various scenarios they'd contemplated together, and he just didn't think any of them fit.

Yes, the Archer could have known that they'd formed if he had a contact in the Organization. A mole. Yes, any agent worth a flying fuck would want to strike first, and Carl thought the Archer fit under that category. And yes, the bomb could easily have been placed by an outsider. But how had he known where they were?

This was the question that kept Carl awake at night. How had anyone known where they were?

"You look bored stiff," Remy's hoarse voice observed from the bed. Carl shook himself out of his thoughts and looked down at him in surprise.

"I thought you were asleep," he admonished quietly.

"I was. I think I was, anyway," Remy murmured blearily. "What were you thinking about so profoundly?" he asked in a tired, teasing voice.

Carl frowned and hesitated. Should he confide in Remy? From the night Brandt had taken Carl into his confidence, Carl had had a difficult time trusting the Cajun. But over the last week, watching him struggle through the pain and the fever and offering only jokes and weak smiles when he was lucid, Carl had developed a slow but sure change of heart. They'd thought his cover a little too perfect to be genuine at first; the endearing, occasionally bumbling young man with an innocent smile was possibly the best performance Carl had ever seen. His reactions to everything they said or did to him had been perfect, and Carl could understand why he and Brandt had become suspicious.

But now Carl could see that Remy's act had been dropped, and surprisingly most of it had been genuine after all. He *was* endearing. He *was* upbeat. He *was* a little on the clumsy side, though the few incidents Carl had witnessed during their hurried travels could have been due to the injury. And in Carl's opinion, he *was* trustworthy.

"I was just thinking… I was thinking about the Archer, actually. And the fire."

Remy nodded slightly and began to shift uncomfortably. "Will you help me up?" he asked almost ashamed after several moments of struggling. Carl could sympathize. It must have been difficult for a man like one of them to ask for help. But he shook his head.

"No," he said bluntly. "Keep your broken ass in bed."

"I'm not getting out of bed. Just… just help me sit up. Please? My ass is killing me and so is my back. Usually when I'm on my back I'm having a lot more fun than this, *non*?" Carl suppressed a snicker and took pity on him. He stood up, rearranging the pillows to offer more support before wrapping his arms around Remy gently and helping him prop himself against the pillows at the head of the bed. Remy buried his face against Carl's neck as the pain from his injured thigh and his broken ribs washed over him, but he didn't make a sound of complaint. Carl sat on the bed beside him after he made sure Remy was steady and looked at him worriedly.

"That was more effort than I was expecting," Remy muttered wryly, a small grin on his lips despite the fact he'd gone completely white.

Carl was once again struck by Remy's attitude, and he found himself liking the younger man even more for his perpetual buoyancy. He put his hand gently on the other man's forehead and made sure that Remy's temperature felt normal.

"Do you want water? Food? Anything?" he offered, feeling helpless in the face of Remy's stoicism.

Remy just shook his head and waved his hand through the air. "Go on with what you were saying," he said as he sat up straighter and leant forward with a grimace.

"Are you sure?"

"*Absolument*."

"Well… I don't really know where to begin. I have this idea, but… it just sort of flits across my mind and I can't grab it long enough to be able to express it properly," Carl explained with difficulty. He saw Remy frown slightly and knew he wasn't being clear. "I mean, I know what I want to say, and where I want it to end, but I don't know how to get it there in explaining it to you."

"Uh huh," Remy responded flatly, biting his lips as his frown deepened. "*Mais quelle est l'extrémité*? What's the end then?" he asked finally.

"What do you mean?"

"You said you didn't know where to begin? So, start at the end. *Merde*, I probably won't remember this in the morning anyway, *non*?" he added with a little laugh.

Carl smiled and nodded. "Okay," he murmured, rubbing his hand thoughtfully over his mouth and cheek. Finally, he exhaled and cocked his head to the side. "I don't think the Archer was the one who set that bomb," he stated as he looked sideways at Remy to gauge his reaction. To his surprise, Remy was nodding eagerly and looking at him with wide brown eyes.

"I thought that's what you were getting at. Neither do I," he told Carl excitedly. His voice was still weak, but his face had a healthy flush to it that Carl had yet to see until tonight.

"You don't?" Carl asked in surprised.

"*Mais non*. Too many pieces, they do not fit. Tell me what you think."

"Well…." Carl looked at Remy uncertainly.

"Come on, the only thing my mind has to do these days is wonder who I have to kill to get revenge for what will no doubt be a nice painful limp. Humor me, Trigger," Remy pleaded with a wry smile. "Please?"

"Okay, okay. Just don't use those puppy dog eyes on me again."

Remy nodded and smiled in pleasure, and Carl licked his lips absentmindedly, wondering where to start.

III.

THIAGO stood in the darkness for some time after Carl had closed the door, and Shawn assumed he was allowing his eyes to adjust before he tripped his way to bed. With this crowd, it was dangerous to go stumbling through a dark room. You never knew what sort of sharp, explosive, or disturbingly gooey objects might be on the floor. Shawn had taken some of the Silly Putty out of Remy's bag– it didn't do to think about why Remy kept it– and gave it to Brandt to keep him from playing with the C4. They'd been finding it everywhere ever since.

"There's nothing in front of you," Shawn offered groggily as he rolled onto his back and rubbed his tired eyes until little white lights began to shoot across his vision. Thiago grunted in response and took a tentative step. Shawn laughed softly at his reticence and let out a surprised little woof when Thiago leapt onto the bed instead of walking the three steps required to get into it like a normal person.

He began to bounce around a little on his hands and knees and Shawn was jostled on the mattress, completely against his will. "Carl sent you to torture me, didn't he?" Shawn groaned in a long-suffering tone.

"Yes," Thiago said as he flopped onto his stomach and stared at Shawn like a little kid waiting for a story. Even in the darkness Shawn could feel the odd blue-gray eyes on him, and he wondered what in the hell had gotten into Thiago. He was usually so… normal.

"What do you want?" Shawn asked warily after several moments of silent staring.

"*Un favor*."

"Uh huh," Shawn said in the same wary tone.

"Remy is doing better," Thiago offered. Shawn closed his eyes and breathed out an inaudible sigh of relief. He'd known the lad would pull through. There had never been a doubt in his mind. Not at all.

"You said he was talking?" Shawn asked nonchalantly after a few seconds, digging for information without seeming to be overly hysterical about his partner's health.

"Yes, hence the favor I would like from you."

"Uh oh. What has he been babbling about now?" Shawn groaned uncomfortably, trying to divert Thiago from this mysterious favor.

"You."

Shawn blinked and turned his head to look at Thiago's shadowy form in the darkness.

"What was he saying about me?" he asked carefully, almost afraid to hear the answer.

"He was telling me about how you two met. The whole 'we tried to kill each other and that's it' nonsense won't work anymore. I want the whole story. The rest of it, anyway."

Shawn gave an inaudible sigh of relief over the fact that their initial meeting was all Remy had talked about. He looked from Thiago to the other bed where Nikolaus had given up trying to fight Brandt for the covers and was staring at them, listening intently. Shawn could see the reflection of his glasses in the little bit of moonlight seeping through the heavy drapes, but not much else.

"Come on over here, Niko," he said finally. "Leave him to that bed for tonight, yeah?"

Nikolaus got up almost instantly and looked at Shawn gratefully before wrestling his pillow from Brandt's arms and flopping into the bed with Shawn and Thiago.

"Aww, now I'm cold," Brandt murmured in amusement.

"Have you been awake this whole time?" Nikolaus whispered harshly. "*Arschloch*!"

Shawn couldn't help but laugh as Brandt snickered shamelessly.

"Come on, then," he called softly to Brandt. Brandt got up and ripped the covers from his own bed, then came over to pow-wow with the others. Shawn and Thiago huddled under their own bedspread as Brandt and Nikolaus sat opposite them, sharing the covers Brandt had pilfered from the other bed.

"Story time?" Brandt asked wryly, his eyes shining gleefully in the darkness as he held a pillow to his chest and leant forward expectantly. He reminded Shawn of a five-year old on Christmas Eve. Thiago nudged Shawn with his foot beneath the covers, and they both burrowed their cold toes beneath Brandt's body, wiggling them until Brandt began to laugh again, finally culminating in a few helpless snorts and a minor fit as he fell onto Nikolaus and batted at their wiggling toes.

Shawn smiled, thinking that a man of Brandt's mentality and stature shouldn't be allowed to giggle, but the smile faded as he thought back on his first meeting with Remy. They *had* nearly killed one another.

"Where did Remy leave off?" he asked Thiago as soon as they'd all settled back down and the snickering died away. Thiago told him, and Shawn smiled fondly and nodded. He picked up in the telling where Remy left off. As he spoke his mind flew over the sea of his memory to that day five years ago, and he relived it in the telling as if it had been just yesterday.

Remy wasn't stupid now, and he hadn't been then, either. He knew when he was beaten and when he should retreat, and he wasn't too proud to do it. In perhaps the fastest series of movements Shawn had ever been witness to, the rifle had been tossed back at him and the other man had disappeared into the hallway before it had hit the ground.

Shawn flinched and ducked, but the rifle landed harmlessly on the cushions in front of him. He blinked at it, then vaulted over the back of the sofa and took off after the other man, determined to rid himself of this nuisance before he was caught with his proverbial pants down again.

The stairwell door clanged closed as he skidded into the hallway, and Shawn was just seconds behind the kid when they reached the roof.

Shawn clearly remembered thinking about how much of an action movie cliché it was to be running in hot pursuit over the rooftops of a city, but he did it nonetheless. The kid was fast, and as Shawn struggled over the many hindrances and gravel-filled patches of roof, the other man seemed not to be bothered by them and he was swiftly pulling ahead.

Shawn got off several shots, but as the kid zigzagged across the rooftops, his hands covering his head protectively as bits of concrete and gravel exploded around him, not one came close to actually hitting him. Shawn knew that his only chance was to catch the other man as he made the jump from one building to the other. Shoot him right out of the air. He was like a fucking mountain goat.

Shawn skidded to a halt at the edge of the building that he stood on and steadied his hand, aiming for the gap that the kid would have to leap across. But as he came to the knee-high wall at the edge of the building the kid ducked out of sight behind an electrical conduit of some sort and did not re-emerge.

"The fuck?" Shawn murmured to himself. His gun stayed at the ready, but his gut began to tell him to run. This was unfamiliar territory and he was up against an obviously experienced opponent. He should be retreating. Now.

Just as he lowered his weapon and began to back away, the kid popped up only meters in front of him, a small gun aimed at him and a smile on his face.

"Son of a bitch!" Shawn shouted in frustration, his gun whipping back up to train on the other man. The corners of the kid's mouth twitched, and finally a snort that he just couldn't contain escaped as they stood pointing their guns at one another.

"My sentiments exactly. What's your name?" the kid asked him in the same pleasing baritone. He had regained the deep southern drawl, but Shawn still thought that it didn't fit him.

"Fuck you," Shawn replied in a polite voice, making sure he employed the heavy Boston accent he had been using with his cover, as much as the five words he had uttered could have an accent, anyway.

"Alright then. Where are you from, Mr. You?" the kid replied in an amused voice. "Your accent is... off."

Shawn snorted in irritation. "Why do you want to know? Do you keep a tally of your kills or something?" Shawn had asked in his real Yorkshire accent.

"Ooh, now that one's better," the kid had said appraisingly in a new, posh English accent. "Yorkshire? Your own, perhaps?"

"Could be."

"I've been watching you."

"I know."

"I watched you to the point that I'm not sure I can kill you."

"Is that so?" Click. *Shawn blinked at the sound of a gun cocking. The kid hadn't moved. Had that been his own gun cocking? Had he meant to do that? The kid stiffened almost imperceptibly, but he went on with the surreal conversation as if nothing untoward had occurred.*

"Yes. I watched you walk a little old lady across the street and lose track of your mark for your trouble. Now, after that... you can't be all that bad, can you?"

Shawn's eyes narrowed suspiciously. That had been days ago. He was beginning to shake, he was so angry with himself. He had been watched for two whole days before he had caught wind of it?

Just as his body tensed their two mobile phones began to vibrate simultaneously. The jarring vibration caused the kid to jump slightly in the tense atmosphere. But Shawn was already so on edge that the vibration in his pocket caused his trigger finger to convulse. The gun didn't make a sound other than the soft thump allowed by the silencer, but that hadn't lessened its effect.

A disembodied shout sounded from somewhere close and pulled Shawn violently back to the present. He stopped short in his telling of the memories he'd been reliving. The four of them scrambled from the bed with difficulty, their limbs and bedcovers getting them tangled up together, and they rushed towards the door to the other room.

IV.

NIKOLAUS was the first into the room adjoining theirs, and he stopped short when he saw Carl sitting on the bed with Remy, both looking perfectly innocent and quite frankly stunned at the sudden ungainly arrival of their colleagues.

The others ran into Nikolaus one at a time in a comedic little domino performance, with Shawn and Brandt just barely keeping their feet and Nikolaus ending up on the floor beneath Thiago.

"What the hell?" Carl asked in confusion.

"Did you call out?" Brandt demanded as Nikolaus pushed his face off the floor and looked up at the bed. All he could see was Carl's head, as if it were floating above the bed and looking extremely confused while doing so. Thiago pushed up onto his hands and knees and looked down at Nikolaus, but Nikolaus couldn't turn enough to see the expression on his face. As Thiago grunted in agitation at not being able to untangle their legs, Nikolaus began to laugh silently. Thiago grabbed him around the waist to help him up, but when he felt Nikolaus laughing, he too began to shake silently, trying valiantly to hold the laughter in.

"No. Must have been from a different room," Carl shrugged as he watched Nikolaus and Thiago flounder on the floor. "We didn't hear anything. What in the hell are you two doing?"

The question finally broke through their defenses, and Nikolaus and Thiago both burst into little spurts of snorts and laughter as they tried to help one another off the floor.

"These damn walls are too thin," Shawn grumbled as he disentangled himself from Brandt and stepped around them and into the room. "Will you two get it together please?" he shouted at them.

"Sorry," Thiago wheezed as they finally found their feet. Nikolaus quelled his laughter into two or three short little snorts and bit his lip in order to keep quiet as Shawn stared them down. Thiago cleared his throat and schooled his features into a frown. "Sorry," he repeated in a deeper, serious voice that sent Nikolaus into another fit of giggles.

Shawn rolled his eyes and shook his head. He gave them one last look before walking to the bed and crawling in to sit beside Remy at the head of it.

"Are you okay?" he asked quietly. The emotion in his voice immediately silenced Nikolaus and Thiago's laughter, and as Nikolaus watched Shawn worriedly place his hand on Remy's forehead, he wondered what he'd found funny in the first place.

"I'm fine. Feeling much better, actually," Remy said, and his voice did sound much stronger than it had when he'd spoken to Nikolaus several hours earlier. His fever must have finally broken. "Carl and I were just having quite an interesting discussion," he added, clearing his throat again and looking at Nikolaus and Thiago curiously.

"As were we," Brandt said before striding to the bed and sitting down beside Carl. Nikolaus noticed that he was careful to avoid Remy's hurt leg as he sat.

"Oh, yeah? Talking about the Great Shooting of Remy, were you?" Remy asked with a smirk.

Nikolaus blinked in surprise, and Thiago asked, "How did you know?"

Remy sniggered, which by all accounts was a good thing. This was the most activity they'd seen from him since the explosion. If Remy was getting better, then they could move on and take care of business. Whatever that business happened to be, now.

"You're so easy to predict, Thi," Remy snickered. There was a moment where Thiago tried to look affronted, but he couldn't hold it for long.

"Well?" Shawn prompted.

Remy turned to look back at him, and as his face turned into the light of the lamp, Nikolaus could see the dark circles under Remy's eyes and how drawn he still looked. He was either looking worse than he felt or he had caught wind of how worried Shawn was and was putting on a pretty damn good show of being better.

Remy and Carl shared a look that Nikolaus didn't even want to try to decipher, and then Carl shrugged. Remy raised his eyebrows questioningly, then looked around the room at the lot of them.

"Well, where should we start?" Remy asked Carl as he looked at him once more.

"You think it over while Shawn finishes his story, yeah?" Nikolaus suggested as he and Thiago moved closer and sat on the other bed. "'Cause he stopped with his gun going off and I, for one, would really like to know how you two went from shooting at one another to being…," Nikolaus trailed off and gestured vaguely at the bed, "… you."

Shawn smiled and looked down at his hands almost as if he were embarrassed, and Remy allowed himself a private little smirk that told Nikolaus they'd never get the full story.

"He didn't shoot *at* me," Remy announced in a sarcastic voice. "He *shot* me. Shot me! And not only did he shoot me, but he stopped to check the message on his phone before he came over to check on me!"

"I was working!" Shawn said in exasperation. "How many times are we going to have this discussion? When you get a message from your handler in the middle of a fucking mission, you know it's a life and death situation."

"Being shot is sort of a life and death situation, too, Beignet."

"Yes, but when it's my life instead of yours I tend to care more," Shawn responded haughtily.

"Pfffft."

Nikolaus and Thiago both snickered quietly. It seemed that things were swiftly returning to normal.

"Anyway, I had only shot him in the side, just there," Shawn said as he pointed to an old scar on Remy's ribcage. "It was so nearly a miss that it grazed off his rib and kept on going."

"It was close," Remy said in a voice close to a sulk.

"What was it you always said? Close only counts in horseshoes and hand grenades?" Shawn admonished sarcastically. Nikolaus saw every eye in the room flicker to Brandt's still form and back.

"Close counts in handguns as well, in my book," Remy argued.

"Your book is written in purple crayon. No one cares. Now where was I?"

"You were reliving the joys of shooting me."

"Ah, yes," Shawn said with mock relish as he tilted his head back and closed his eyes in apparent pleasure.

"It wouldn't be so bad if that had been the only time," Remy protested to the rest of them. Shawn's eyes snapped open and his head whipped around to glare at Remy.

"I told you, that were an accident!" he declared in agitation as he pointed his finger in Remy's face and waved it around.

"You said the first one was an accident, too!" Remy yelled as he pointed his finger back at Shawn. "I've never had an accident with a gun, *couyon*! And you're a better shot than I am! Please tell me how, in twenty plus years of service, have you only had two accidents and I happened to be the target of both of them? Hmm? You shot me in the ass!"

"I wasn't aiming for your ass," Shawn argued meekly as the rest of them laughed raucously. Remy's eyes widened and his mouth dropped open.

"You were actually *aiming* for something?!" he cried.

"I think you need to rest," Shawn said hastily as he started to tuck the covers in around Remy's body.

"Fuck that, you were aiming? You actually *missed* something badly enough to shoot me in the ass?"

"Well– "

"My ass isn't that big, Shawn! How could you hit it and not be aiming for it?"

Thiago started to snicker helplessly at Nikolaus's side. Watching Shawn and Remy bicker was like sitting down to a sitcom, and they were all thoroughly enjoying watching the typically imperturbable older man squirm under Remy's wagging finger.

"I told you it was an accident!" Shawn finally shouted defensively. "It was three years ago, for chrissake! It's water under the bridge!"

"Ha! Well it's *blood* under my fucking bridge, *grand bioque*!" Remy harrumphed and crossed his arms. He was definitely feeling better, Nikolaus decided. He'd heard several of Remy's Cajun curses, but he'd understood none of them. He knew enough to know that the 'grand' in front of one made it bigger, though.

"What happened after Shawn checked his message?" Thiago asked in a voice still shaking with laughter.

"The message had been that massive all-stop that was sent out, you all remember?" Remy inquired, still sulking slightly.

They all nodded. Nikolaus had been one of the engineers of that message. It had been his first month with the Organization, and even then, he'd known that sending out a mass message of that sort was a major security risk. It had saved countless innocent lives though, and miraculously no real harm had ever come from doing it. Not that anyone had detected, anyway.

"When I fell after being *accidentally* shot," Remy continued testily, "my cell went flying across the gravel of the roof top, as did my gun. When Shawn finally came prancing over to check on me–"

"I resent the implication that I prance anywhere."

"You prance in my mind, Mary," Remy snapped. Shawn snorted irritably, and Remy continued. "When he got to me he just stood over me, looking at me like I was some poor creature in a zoo."

"I was actually marveling over how young he looked," Shawn informed them defensively.

"Whatever, *couyon.* I know you were perving on me," Remy declared haughtily.

"You were bleeding quite profusely," Shawn pointed out.

"And you like that, don't you," Remy purred as he let his head rest on Shawn's shoulder contentedly. "Turns him on," Remy said to them in a conspiratorial stage whisper.

Their relationship was unlike any Nikolaus had ever witnessed. One minute they were bickering like an old married couple and the next they were flirting and seemingly on the verge of screwing in front of everyone. Nikolaus inhaled deeply as he thought about them, smelling the scent of Thiago's cigars.

"You're fucking mad," Shawn mumbled contentedly as he petted Remy's cheek with the hand Remy wasn't leaning on. "I was trying to decide what to do with him."

"Took you forfuckingever."

"It wasn't really that long."

"It's a long time when you're lying there bleeding all over yourself, wondering if this *bioque* is going to blow your balls off any second."

"True," Shawn conceded carelessly. "Anyway, I finally decided that we had to be on the same side, so I took his hand in mine and introduced myself."

"As I lay there bleeding and in pain," Remy supplied.

"But how did you end up being…" Carl motioned randomly with his hands much like Nikolaus had done, and finally he let them fall to his lap. "You," he finished.

"Shawn brought me in," Remy answered. "The order had been for every agent to cease and desist all activity; leave your shit where it is and come home," he explained needlessly.

They'd all lived through it. It was the only time in the history of the Organization that every agent had been called home at the same time. Agents were rarely recalled to the main Facility located in a very remote locale in the wilds of New Zealand, and when they were, you could bet it was serious. All of them at once? That was catastrophic.

"But instead of dropping all his shit and going immediately," Remy continued, "Shawn helped me."

"I couldn't in good conscience leave him to fend for himself when we didn't know what the threat was, now could I?" Shawn argued as if any of them thought he had done the wrong thing. "Especially after shooting him like I had," he muttered.

"It took us a full week to get in. What a fucking disaster that was. We were the last agents in and we had actually been written off as killed in action. By that time, we had had plenty of time to… bond, I suppose. It's a cliché, but it was like we had known each other all our lives."

"This 'bonding' was of course after he quit bitching about being shot."

"*Va-t'à la merde*," Remy muttered. "When we were debriefed," he continued, "they took an interest in how we had worked together. That's when they asked about the possibility of partnering us."

"That's it?" Nikolaus asked after a thoughtful silence.

"Well, we could go into every detail, but there is no point, *non*?" Remy said, and though it was said in the friendliest of tones, Nikolaus could tell that it was more of an order than a suggestion. Story time was over.

V.

BRANDT nudged Carl with his elbow to get his attention.

"What were you two talking about?" he asked curiously when it became apparent Remy and Shawn were done sharing. He thought he had a pretty good idea, but he was going to play dumb just now.

"Oh. Well," Carl looked back at Remy and shrugged. "We were sort of having a conspiracy theory chat."

"What sort of theory?" Thiago asked from where he and Nikolaus sat on the other bed.

"We were talking about the explosion," Remy said quietly. His voice seemed to have gotten weaker, and if Brandt had suspected he was putting on a show for Shawn's benefit before, then he was sure of it now. Brandt could tell he was hurt, tired, and still painfully weak. Oh, he was probably healthy enough by a normal person's standards, with the possible exception of that hole in his thigh, but to keep up with five well-trained agents he would have to be a lot better, and soon.

"What about the explosion?" Shawn asked in the same quiet voice, and Brandt got the sudden impression that Shawn was angry. They'd been joking just seconds ago, but now Shawn's entire presence changed. Why would he be angry?

"Remy and I don't think the Archer was responsible," Carl announced, and though Brandt wasn't truly surprised, hearing the words out loud was a bit of a shock. The other three were obviously surprised though, and Brandt slipped his arm around Carl's waist protectively as Shawn stared at him blankly.

"You don't?" Nikolaus asked innocently. "Who do you think did it then?"

Remy licked his lips nervously and looked at Carl. Brandt's grip tightened around Carl's waist reassuringly and he nuzzled the back of the other man's neck.

"Here's our thinking," Carl said as Brandt inhaled his clean scent deeply. "The first thing we did in order to find the Archer was look at his message."

"Which we've been working on, by the way," Remy interjected.

"Yeah. Let them see it, Dixie," Carl suggested. Brandt raised an eyebrow at the nickname, and he saw Shawn do the same thing. Was it possible Shawn was the jealous type? Brandt could just smell trouble coming from those two.

Remy picked the charred little piece of paper up and put a blue Bic pen into his mouth as he handed the message over to Shawn. He explained the marks they'd made as the paper was passed around carefully.

"Niko said the key changes with every transmission. So, we figure the key has to be in the message itself. I wrote that down when I thought of it in case... anything happened to me," he said, trailing off in a low voice and giving Shawn a sideways glance before continuing. Thiago handed Brandt the paper and he looked it over as Remy spoke.

"I have a tendency to scribble," he muttered apologetically as Brandt examined the flurry of doodles covering the singed piece of paper.

"Still," Shawn sighed as he shook his head and examined the dark ceiling, "that gets us nowhere."

Remy lowered his head, looking fairly crestfallen at Shawn's lack of response. Brandt felt badly for him. It was a pretty nice observation on his part, if it was true, but Shawn hadn't really acknowledged it.

"Well, that's about where we got to when we were interrupted by the clown parade," Carl muttered. Brandt thought maybe Carl was getting a little annoyed with Shawn, too. He had spent all week mooning over the kid and now he couldn't even give him a pat on the head for a job well done? What the hell? "After hitting a dead end with that, we went to the list of agents who had turned, and then the agents who had worked with all of them."

"We know this, mate. We were all there, remember?" Shawn said testily.

"Bear with me," Carl said a soothing voice. "Now, if that list of names was our top suspect list, then who's to say that it wasn't theirs as well."

"'Theirs?'" Thiago repeated questioningly.

"The Organization's," Carl offered with a nod. "What if they took that list, saw our six names at the top of it, and said that we were expendable if it would rid them of the Archer? What if– "

"What if we were set up," Remy supplied hollowly.

"You think they got us together in one place to make us easier to kill?" Brandt asked, unable to keep the shock out of his voice. He hadn't gone this far with his theories, but he had to admit that it made sense.

Remy was nodding, and Carl turned his head to the side to glance at Brandt. "It makes a hell of a lot of sense," Brandt agreed quietly.

"But how would they have tracked us?" Thiago asked skeptically. Shawn was scowling heavily, and Remy was shooting him worried glances.

"Niko, is it possible that your equipment could have been traced?" Remy asked despite his concerned looks at Shawn.

"Very," Nikolaus said with a nod. "By the Organization? Most certainly. The equipment I used was theirs, not my own. I didn't even check it for bugs or tracers because it came directly from a secure area."

"Did they give you a choice of which equipment you could use?" Thiago asked with a frown, "or did they issue it to you?"

"They issued it, come to think of it," Nikolaus answered in a troubled voice.

"They could have had tracking implants– sort of a…'if you steal me you're screwed' kind of thing– already in them," Thiago suggested.

Shawn's scowl deepened and he looked at Remy, but he said nothing. Brandt watched them curiously, wondering what was going on between them that had Shawn so tense. As he pondered, he leaned forward and let his arm tighten around Carl's waist. Carl shivered in his arms, and Brandt kissed the back of his neck impulsively before standing up abruptly and shuffling over to the other bed in the room.

"It's late," he pronounced as he shooed Nikolaus and Thiago away and threw back the covers on the bed. He turned to face them all. "I've been up all night irritating Gizmo and I'm tired. Trigger, come keep me warm. Dixie looks like hell. Mary, you should sleep there tonight in case he needs you," he declared.

"Did you just call me Mary?" Shawn asked incredulously.

Brandt looked at Thiago and winked. "You two go do something interesting," he said to Thiago and Nikolaus dismissively.

At first, it seemed that they would all simply stare at him. But then Carl smiled slowly and got up, gave Remy's head an affectionate rub, and walked over to crawl into the bed beside Brandt.

Remy grinned and winked at Brandt, though he still looked pale and drawn. Brandt worried about him regardless of the brave front he was putting up.

Shawn stared expressionlessly at him. If Brandt could ever get Shawn to show any sort of bewilderment, then he would consider his life complete.

"Fine then," Thiago huffed, feigning annoyance as he nodded at the door. Nikolaus gave a little sniff and turned to go, flipping Brandt the bird as they disappeared through the door.

"Well," Brandt said uncertainly, at a loss for words now that his orders had actually been followed. His orders were never followed.

"Well," Remy repeated in a tired but amused voice. "Maybe Thiago will be a little less cranky if he gets laid, hmm?"

"Hell, Mary over there is the cranky one," Carl offered as he snuggled into the cold sheets and pulled Brandt into bed by the waistband of his sweatpants. "Grumpy, too."

"Is he grumpy or is he cranky? Make up your mind," Brandt demanded as he allowed Carl to manhandle him and pull him beneath the covers.

"Are you cranky?" Remy asked Shawn innocently as Brandt settled into Carl's arms.

"Very."

Brandt snickered and Carl pulled him closer. "Shawn wouldn't hurt from getting laid either," Brandt murmured teasingly.

"Fucking firebug," Shawn mumbled, and he leant over and switched off the lamp at the side of the bed, throwing the room into darkness.

VI.

REMY waited until the steady breathing of the other two men indicated that they were asleep, and then he turned onto his side with difficulty and ran gentle fingers over Shawn's bare chest.

"What's on your mind, Dixie?" Shawn asked softly. He sounded sleepy, but not as if he had been asleep.

"I'm sorry," Remy whispered sincerely, his voice barely audible in the darkness.

He felt Shawn move slightly and imagined the other man had turned his head to peer through the darkness at him. It was pitch black, and Remy assumed the night had clouded over since the moon no longer sent rays of light through the heavy drapes.

"Sorry?" Shawn repeated incredulously, his quiet voice bordering on anger. But when he spoke again his tone was calm and cool. Professional. It was like a slap in the face. "No need to be sorry for anything, Remy. We're all doing a job here, after all."

Remy closed his eyes and let the pain of Shawn's words wash over him. That had been an intentional hit, and usually Remy would have had a barb just as painful to toss back. Tonight, though, he just didn't have the heart or the energy for a fight.

"I tried to talk to you, Shawn. You kept drugging me. I–"

"Remy," Shawn whispered harshly. The angry sound was like the report of a pistol to Remy's ears, and he glanced over at the other bed even though he knew he wouldn't be able to see Brandt or Carl in the darkness. "I don't want to fight with you. You're sick and you're injured and it wouldn't be a fair fight. I would end up winning and feeling guilty as fuck and then I'd be fucked off about that as well. Just drop it."

Remy gritted his teeth angrily and flopped back onto his back, wincing at the white-hot pain that shot through his wounds but not daring to call out for fear of injuring his pride.

Shawn must have been paying closer attention than he thought, however, because he was hovering over Remy just seconds later, one hand gripping his and the other resting on his forehead.

"Are you okay?" Shawn murmured, the breath gusting across Remy's face even as the heat of the pain flushed his cheeks.

"Yes," Remy answered weakly. He felt Shawn's tense muscles relax as the other man rested the upper half of his body on Remy's chest. The pressure felt good after days and days of fearing the pain in his ribs, and Remy gripped Shawn's hand and slid his free arm around Shawn's waist to keep him from moving. "Don't be angry with me, Shawn. I couldn't deal with it just now," he pleaded in a low voice.

Shawn lowered his head and let his nose and mouth come to rest against Remy's cheek.

"Just tell me," he started in a defeated voice. He kissed Remy's cheek gently and went on. "Tell me you didn't go to Carl first because you thought I had something to do with it."

Remy's body went cold and his mouth went completely dry at hearing Shawn's whispered words.

"Jesus, Shawn," he breathed as he tightened his hold around Shawn's waist. "I thought you would know better than that," he whispered.

Shawn lifted up and looked down at him, and Remy could just barely make out his glittering green eyes in the darkness.

"We were the only ones who knew where the safe house was prior to the rendezvous, Remy," Shawn said seriously. "Just you and me."

"I know that," Remy said as he regained some of his composure. "And I also know that neither of us would have called in the coordinates."

"None of the others know that," Shawn argued. "Why would you fuel suspicions by going behind everyone's back to discuss it?"

"I didn't," Remy protested quietly. "Carl looked like he had something on his mind and I…."

"What?" Shawn asked in surprise.

"What?" Remy echoed, not sure what he had said to prompt the reaction.

"Carl came to you with the idea?"

"Well… actually we had both been thinking it, we just happened to start talking about it and–"

Remy's explanation was cut off by the noise of shuffling bed sheets from the other bed, and he and Shawn froze. They weren't really talking about anything that couldn't be overheard, if it had been that sensitive they would simply have waited, but it was habit all the same. Shawn's hand moved to Remy's hair and his fingers automatically twirled around Remy's unruly curls.

"You need a haircut," Shawn mumbled absently. "And a shave," he added after a short, gentle kiss.

"I thought you liked me scruffy," Remy responded in a weak voice. Usually he would have made a retort calling attention to Shawn's own state of dishevelment, but Shawn was angry with him, and the mere thought made him feel a bit sick.

"I do," Shawn said tenderly as he ran his fingers through the curls. "Hey," he said as their fingers twined together and Remy closed his eyes against the angry look he kept seeing flash across Shawn's face in his mind. "Hey, I'm sorry," Shawn said softly. "I know you're not well. I overreacted."

"Well, Carl did say you were cranky," Remy offered weakly. Shawn snorted and lowered his head to nuzzle against Remy cheek once more.

"So you really think we could have been set up?" he asked against Remy's warm skin. "You think they would put six of their top agents together and rid themselves of them before ever even investigating it?"

"We don't know that they didn't investigate," Remy said matter-of-factly as he tried not to be turned on by Shawn's actions. He was in no state for such an endeavor, and he didn't suppose that was what Shawn was after. "I mean… we're some shady characters, the six of us." Shawn laughed silently, but Remy wasn't smiling. "The more I think about it, Shawn," he said seriously, "the more I think we're right. I think we were set up. I think they sent some amateur to blow us all to Kingdom Come, and I think they think we're all dead. I don't think anyone will be coming for us."

A shout sounded from somewhere in the seedy motel and halted their discussion. They both held their breath. In the silence, the sounds of pleasure were easily distinguishable, though, and they both relaxed noticeably.

"They'll want proof that we're dead," Shawn continued regretfully. It took Remy a moment to get back on track after visions of Thiago and Nikolaus doing all sorts of dirty things in the other room danced through his head. Maybe he wasn't recovered from that fever just yet after all. "It's too big a risk to take to assume that they'll just write us off," Shawn added helpfully.

"So is running back to New Zealand and jumping up and down outside the Facility, letting them know we're still alive," Remy whispered back. "I say we all break and run for it, Shawn. Let the Archer keep killing their fucking people and they'll know they made a mistake. We'll be on an island in the Caribbean sucking down drinks with little umbrellas in them and trying to keep Brandt from blowing up the tiki hut."

"It's not… it's not *their* people who're being killed here, Remy," Shawn said in a stunned voice. "It's *our* people. Got that? Our people. And I won't sit idly by while that bastard goes around taking down agents as if they were clay ducks at a carnival."

"Shawn–"

"No!" Shawn whispered harshly. "If you want to break and run then that's your affair. But I've never known you to cower in the corner when there was a perfectly good opportunity to get yourself killed lurking around the next turn."

"Two weeks ago you were pleading with me to quit and run away with you off to Paradise! Now I'm suggesting the same thing and I'm a coward? Was all that bullshit then?" Remy demanded angrily. Shawn opened his mouth to speak, but he snapped it back shut again and removed his body from atop Remy's. Remy watched his dark form move away in disbelief. "Huh uh," he objected heatedly and rolled again, wincing with the pain in his leg and ribs. He took hold of Shawn's arm, squeezing a pressure point in what he knew was a painful grip even though he was as weak as he was, and pulled at him. Shawn gasped and then growled angrily. "Give me one good reason to stay in this," Remy whispered demandingly, still mindful of waking the others even through his anger.

Shawn rolled back onto his back and looked up at Remy silently. Remy could just barely make out his features in the darkness, but he couldn't tell what sort of expression Shawn wore.

"Stay in it for me," Shawn requested quietly after several moments. "I need you with me. I need to know that you're safe."

Remy blinked in surprise. He hadn't been expecting that argument. King and country and honor and pride and camaraderie and all that shit, he had expected. But not this.

"Shawn," Remy responded pleadingly, frantically searching his brain for a response but coming up empty.

"I can't spend the rest of me life wondering if someone is coming after us," Shawn whispered thickly, his hand coming up to cup Remy's cheek and his accent thickening. His thumb rubbed across Remy's cheekbone in a familiar, tender motion that made Remy's eyes flutter closed. "I would never be able to rest. If you're right and we were set up, then they'll keep coming until our bodies are delivered. But if you're wrong and we run, they'll come after us anyway. You know this. Our only chance is to finish the job and prove that we're loyal. Please stay with me on this, Remy. I need you. I need you more than I can say."

Remy forced his eyes back open and stared at the other man for what seemed an eternity.

"You know we'll still have to find the Archer," Remy said finally, unable to express the emotions roiling through his mind and unwilling to let Shawn know that he doubted his sincerity.

"You still want to catch him then?" Shawn asked in surprise.

"*Mais oui*, we'll catch him, no doubt. And then we'll join him."

VII.

THIAGO wasn't certain what had gotten into him tonight. Jumping on the bed and playing footsy with Shawn and Brandt? Tumbling clumsily to the floor and laughing hysterically about it? He hadn't laughed uncontrollably in years.

Perhaps it was relief over Remy's apparent recovery. Perhaps it was exhaustion or stress, which didn't seem likely considering how easy he'd had it thus far compared to the life Thiago usually led. Perhaps he had just finally cracked and he was going Brandt's route.

Thiago didn't think Brandt's route seemed all that bad, actually.

He and Nikolaus lay in the same bed they had vacated earlier, too tired and lazy to retrieve the blanket Brandt had pilfered from the other bed. Neither man could seem to sleep though.

They were passing each other in the darkness on the path to the toilet when they heard murmurs from the other room. Thiago looked at Nikolaus through the inky darkness, and as if they could read each other's minds, they both started for the adjoining door at the same time.

They pressed their ears to the door– their noses just inches from each other– just in time to hear the tail end of what sounded like a whispered argument.

"Join him?" hissed Shawn's voice through the thin separation.

"Do you've a better idea?"

"Yes."

"I'm all ears, *cher*," Remy challenged sarcastically, the strange word pronounced like 'sha'. Thiago knew it was a mongrelized form of the French word that meant 'dear.' It was both touching and disturbing to hear Remy use it when arguing.

"Well, we could *not* turn traitor. That might be fun," Shawn shot back in a sarcastic hiss.

"Fuck that. They tried to kill us, Shawn, in case you'd forgotten."

"I'm not likely to forget that, Remy, and we don't know that for sure. Don't try to change the subject on me."

There was a long silence, and Thiago imagined that the two of them were staring each other down like he had seen them do the night of the explosion.

"Remy wants to turn traitor? Is that what I'm hearing?" Nikolaus whispered after more silence.

Thiago frowned. That couldn't be right. If Remy was planning on turning he wouldn't be openly discussing it like he was. No doubt Brandt was still awake. The fucker never slept.

"I don't think so," Thiago whispered back finally.

"I'll stay with you, Shawn," Remy finally said in a voice so low Thiago had to strain to hear it. "But if I get killed I am *so* going to come back to haunt you."

VIII.

THE Archer lay awake long after the excitement had died down. Every so often, he would cast a wary glance at his bedmate, but he was fairly certain that he was the only one still awake.

This most recent discussion was an interesting turn of events. Join forces with him? Well… he wasn't sure what he thought of that now. He would worry over their loyalty if they were to join his ranks, of course, but he did that about most of his agents anyway.

On one hand, if they thought they'd been betrayed by their beloved Organization then they'd probably be all fired up for revenge, and if he were honest with himself, that was a very enticing scenario.

On the other hand, these other five men scared him like no other force he'd ever encountered. They'd become cohesive. They cared for one another and they worked extremely well together when they weren't trying to kill each other.

The fact that they'd all become comfortable enough to indulge in their various and sundry little romantic encounters spoke volumes about how much they trusted one another. Life and death situations did interesting things to people, and these men's lives were a constant life and death situation. During battle you had to trust your colleagues with your life. After that trusting them with your body was nothing.

No, the copious amounts of sex were nothing new, in the Archer's experience. They could fuck each other from here to the end of time for all he cared–so long as he got to watch and participate every now and then. What bothered him was the fact that they were still together at all. After the explosion, he'd felt sure that they would scatter, but they had clung to one another with an odd sort of loyalty; that, quite frankly, scared him shitless.

If he could have such a group working on his side, fueled not only by anger and fear and revenge, but also by their loyalty to one another, then his would be an unstoppable force.

The question was; what would they do once they found out who he was? They thought he was one of them. They trusted him. Would they turn on him when he revealed himself as the Archer? Or would their loyalty to him by that time negate the sting of the betrayal?

It was quite the conundrum the Archer found himself dealing with.

Was there a way, perhaps, he could mask himself? He had loyal men, men who he trusted who would pose as him if the other five demanded a face to face with him before he was ready to reveal himself. Yes. The Archer liked that plan.

He smiled in the darkness as the man beside him moaned and shifted restlessly in his sleep. The Archer put his hand out into the darkness and laced his fingers through the man's hair in a soothing gesture without really noticing what he was doing.

The Archer's smile widened as he pulled the man closer. He liked that plan very much.

He would cease the wedging tactics he'd been employing. He would no longer attempt to subtly breed fear and suspicion amongst the five other men. He would instead encourage their loyalty, their cohesion. And he would encourage them to find him.

Find him and join him.

IX.

CARL sat at the head of the bed, leaning against the headboard and watching with a strange, detached fascination as Brandt and Shawn proceeded to verbally tear each other new assholes.

Halfway through the argument, Thiago came to sit beside him, and they merely nodded at one another in acknowledgment and sat in identical poses; their arms crossed and their heads cocked to the side as they watched. Nikolaus was in the other room with Remy, playing music loudly on the cheap clock radio and trying to distract him from the noise Shawn and Brandt were making.

"If you were awake then you should have said something!" Shawn shouted angrily as he paced back and forth. Occasionally he would stop and glare at Brandt, and Brandt would cross his arms and glare right back.

"And when was I supposed to announce my presence, hmm? Before or after you reamed him for having the *audacity* to actually contemplate our little predicament when none of us were bothering with it?" Brandt questioned sarcastically.

Carl cleared his throat pointedly, but they either didn't hear him or took no notice of it.

"We had *him* to worry about, in case you'd forgotten. And he's not thinking clearly! And I'm not angry that you listened, just that you didn't fucking back me up!" Shawn hissed as he stopped for one of his glares. "He wants to… to run off and… and join the fucking Archer for Christ sake!"

"And if we *were* put together just so we'd be easier to exterminate?" Brandt argued. "I'm with Dixie on this one, mate, I don't want to go waltzing up to the Facility and announcing my still-breathing status until I am one hundred-percent certain that they won't gun me down."

"And what if this was a mole hunt, huh? What if they're waiting for us to turn up and clear ourselves? What if by going to ground we're unknowingly professing our guilt?"

"I'd much rather be professed guilty than dead," Thiago murmured to Carl.

Carl shook his head absently and continued to watch the two men circle one another like prizefighters as they argued. He really didn't feel like stepping between them again. The last time he tried, he'd been conked on the head with a stick and then had his shirt sleeve set on fire. He reckoned that he and Thiago would probably just sit this one out and watch if it came to blows. It would make for fine afternoon entertainment to watch them pound on one another again.

"Are you not even considering the possibility that we were set up?" Brandt asked disbelievingly. "Not even–"

"Twenty years!" Shawn shouted suddenly, loud enough that Carl and Thiago both jumped and Brandt snapped his mouth closed. Shawn ran his hand through his hair and looked disgusted with himself as they all sat in the uncomfortable silence. "Twenty fucking years, and they would just… I refuse to believe it."

So that was Shawn's problem. Part of it, anyway. He had lived over half his life in the employ of the Organization. Carl couldn't even begin to imagine how betrayed he must feel. It was apparent then that Shawn knew Remy had probably been right. He was arguing against himself, not Brandt.

When Remy's quiet voice broke the silence that followed Shawn's mumbling Carl almost jumped out of his skin. Even injured, the kid could move like a ghost.

"We really only have one option, you know," Remy said to them as he leant against the doorframe that separated the two rooms. He had a blanket draped over his shoulders and was looking better than he had since before the explosion. Shawn stopped his agitated pacing and turned around slowly to stare at him, and Thiago and Brandt seemed to be just as shocked as Carl had. Nikolaus stood slightly behind Remy, looking a bit guilty for his failure to restrain the injured man.

"What are you doing up?" Shawn asked quietly, the anger and vehemence suddenly replaced by concern.

"I'm fine. The wound has closed, and I can walk fine. The fever's gone. If I stay in that bed much longer, I'll never get out of it. You know what we have to do, Shawn," Remy murmured, switching gears so smoothly that his amenable tone never even changed as he went from one subject to the other.

Shawn looked around at them all hesitantly and then rubbed his eyes in a tired manner as he sat down heavily onto the end of the bed. Brandt was still standing, looking as if he were about to pounce on Remy, but Carl suspected he was waiting for the younger man to fall over so he could catch him.

"We have to find the Archer," Thiago provided softly. Carl looked over at him and saw that he had his head down as if he were ashamed of suggesting it. He looked up at Remy through his eyelashes, and Remy nodded grimly at him in return.

"We have to find the Archer," Remy repeated.

Shawn opened his mouth but Remy took an unsteady step into the room and placed his hand on Shawn's shoulder. Carl watched in fascination as Shawn immediately closed his mouth and slumped his shoulders as the hand made contact, and he found himself wondering just which one of them was the leader of the pair. Most of the time it seemed that Remy yielded to Shawn's decisions without much of a problem, but when something major like this came up it appeared that Remy called the game. It was an amazing dynamic.

"I know your objections. But regardless, Shawn," Remy was saying soothingly, "we only have two options here. Either we were betrayed or we've been wrongly accused. Now, if we were set up, then we have to join the Archer, for reasons of self-preservation, if nothing else. And if not, in that case we'll still have to deliver the real Archer in order to clear ourselves."

"Either way, we'll have to track the bastard down," Brandt added quietly.

"Do you have a plan?" Carl asked curiously. He had gotten to know Remy pretty well, and he knew that the younger man was not only sharp as a tack, but that he was quick to formulate once he got going.

"Well, in order to track him down we'll need equipment," Remy said as he wrapped the blanket around his shoulders tighter. "Weapons, communications, money. Now I don't know about all of you, but I keep a hide. Several, actually. There're only a few weapons and such, but combined there's roughly eight hundred thousand American dollars in them, and I'm betting we'll need every penny of it."

Carl watched the reactions of the others carefully. Nikolaus looked stunned. As a tech, Carl assumed he didn't have use for such a thing, or the resources to accumulate that much money. Thiago and Shawn were both nodding, and Brandt was unreadable. Carl had a hide in which he kept a variety of weapons. A large variety. They would need those too. Weapons specialists didn't make that kind of money, though. Not many agents did.

"So you're suggesting we hit each of our hides and clear them out?" Carl asked as he wondered how Remy had accumulated that amount. Shawn, yes. He had been in the business for a long time. But Remy?

"Yes," Remy responded. "But not together."

"Now, wait a minute," Shawn objected hurriedly.

"I know," Remy soothed. "I know, but let me finish. How many are there?" he asked the others.

"I have just the one," Carl answered.

"I don't have one," Thiago told them. "It's easier to use what I buy on the street," he explained as Remy and Shawn looked at him in surprise. "Most of my hits look like they're drug related that way. But I've got money that can be accessed from just about anywhere."

"As do I," Brandt said as he finally sat down on the end of the bed. "I acquire my equipment as I go. No need for a store of it anywhere."

"And Shawn and I have six between the two of us," Remy concluded finally. "Nikolaus," he said as he turned slightly to look at the other man. "Can you get into the main files again if you have the right equipment?"

"Of course," Nikolaus responded readily. "Getting in is no problem. It's being detected that's the hitch. Unless I have secure equipment or we're really fucking mobile it could get us all killed."

"So if we went into say, one of those internet cafés, you could access the main files of the Organization?" Thiago asked incredulously.

"Yes. I'm an insider, I know all the routes and codes and all that. The problem, like I said, is not getting killed while you're doing it. Two, maybe three seconds after I get in without my scramblers they'll have our location."

"Seconds?" Shawn asked incredulously.

"So," Remy said, as if it should be obvious, "we'll keep you moving. While you do your thing, the rest of us will gather our resources and then we'll regroup."

"You mean separate?" Nikolaus repeated uncertainly.

Shawn was rubbing his face again, and Carl finally identified the gesture as one of agitation.

"Yes," Remy answered confidently. "We've got enough cash to get us all to our various destinations, so–"

"We can't split up," Shawn interrupted in a low, patient voice. "We'd be as good as dead on our own with both sides looking for us. That's not to mention if we've been black-flagged!"

"Black-flagged?" Nikolaus echoed.

"Wanted, dead or alive. They'll put a bounty on us if they think we're a major threat," Brandt supplied happily. Nikolaus looked devastated, but Brandt went on cheerfully. "Not only will O.R.G. agents be looking for us, but we'll have mercenaries after us as well. I've never had a price on my head, wonder how much I'd be worth?"

"A pinecone or two, I'd wager," Shawn murmured.

"It's all the more reason to scatter, Shawn," Remy went on persistently.

"No."

"But–"

"I don't like it, Remy!"

"Hear me out," Remy requested patiently. Carl had the feeling that they played this game quite often. And he was pretty sure he knew who would win this round. "We'll split into three pairs. Shawn, you and Brandt will clear out your three hides, Thiago and Carl will get Carl's as well as two of mine, and Nikolaus and I will get the last one and then lead them on a chase with the computers," he explained with apparent relish. "We can meet again in three months, when everything has died down."

"Three months?" Nikolaus repeated again in horror. Remy nodded.

They were all silent for some time, and finally Carl watched Shawn's impassive face break into a slow, sad smile. "Well done, lad," he sighed quietly. "Even if I don't like the idea, it's a good one. If we're doing this we need to be under way," he added as he looked around at all of them for their opinion of the plan.

Thiago scratched his head and looked at Carl inquiringly. Carl shrugged in return and they both turned to look back at Shawn, offering a simultaneous, "Sounds good."

Brandt was nodding his head in acquiescence, but Nikolaus looked doubtful.

"By 'chase' you mean…."

"You and I will hop all over the map," Remy said, turning to face Nikolaus and taking him by the shoulders, obviously enjoying relating the scenario dramatically, "and access the files at random intervals to get them chasing their tails."

"Remy," Shawn warned worriedly.

Remy turned to look at him, and Carl could see the light back in the young man's eyes. Here was another one who enjoyed his job. It was almost more frightening than Brandt.

"That's without a doubt the most dangerous part of this," Shawn pointed out. "Maybe–"

"Niko and I are the same age," Remy argued. "We'll attract much less attention than you would if you were escorting him," Remy said, anticipating what would obviously be an attempt by Shawn to get Remy into a more passive role.

Carl couldn't blame him. It *was* the most dangerous role in that plan; whoever was with Nikolaus would need to be extra alert in order to evade pursuit for three months while constantly accessing the system and guarding the inexperienced tech. It would be like running around and around a giant, poking him with a stick all the while. With Remy injured, it was risky, but Remy also made a good point.

"The less attention they attract the better, Shawn," Carl observed out loud.

"We'll be okay," Remy said with a reassuring smile.

"Very well," Shawn acquiesced finally as he looked at Remy. "Let's hammer out some details then."

An hour later, they were all either sitting on the floor or hanging off the edge of the bed as Brandt and Shawn argued over the details of Remy's plan. Nikolaus and Remy lay on the bed with their faces propped in their hands, looking down at the rest of them. Brandt sat against the end of the bed, and Remy absently twirled the big man's hair as he peered down at them. A map of the United States was spread out on the floor, and they all sat scowling at it and the many blue marks Shawn had made with Remy's pen.

"They should get as far away as possible," Thiago argued.

"That would put them in New Zealand, genius," Brandt retorted. "Right in the Organization's back yard. Look, they know our last known location was Whereverthefuck, North Dakota. I think if they pop up on the grid somewhere close it might give the impression that we took a bigger hit than we did."

"Like we're crawling, so to speak?" Shawn said as he stared at the map.

"Exactly," Brandt nodded. "And if they do spot them, they'll only be seeing the two of them. Being underestimated in this case would be a good thing, I think."

"It's hard to reckon," Remy mumbled as he furrowed his brow and looked up at Shawn. Carl was of the opinion that the further they went the better, but Brandt did have a point. It would serve them better if their resources and their abilities were underestimated. "Shawn, let me see the pen," Remy demanded suddenly, reaching out to take it as Shawn held it up and wagged it teasingly. Remy made an odd hissing noise, like he was pushing air between his teeth. It was a surprisingly jarring sound, like someone would make to scare a wild animal.

Shawn handed the pen over and watched Remy fondly as he hefted himself up onto his elbows and closed his eyes. Carl watched him curiously, wondering what the hell he was up to. Remy wrapped one arm around Brandt's neck to steady himself and held the pen out. Then he jabbed down at the map, opening his eyes finally to look down at the little hole it had made.

"Salt Lake City," Shawn announced as he peered down at the hole.

"Utah?" Nikolaus asked. They all turned to look at him.

"Got you a problem with Utah?" Remy asked him curiously.

"No. Sorry," Nikolaus said as he shot Remy an apologetic glance. "I'm just never present for the planning part."

Remy had the good grace to look ashamed. "Well… usually we don't do it with our eyes closed," he mumbled as he rested his chin on the top of Brandt's head. Carl managed to suppress the smile that threatened, and he looked back at the others in time to see Thiago hide a grin behind his hand.

Shawn and Brandt still scowled at one another, though Brandt looked much happier as a headrest than he had before, and Nikolaus and Remy intermittently exchanged playful scowls and snickering.

Carl had a feeling that it was going to be a long three months for all of them.

He wondered how they would all make it through. He and Thiago seemed to get along well enough, but Brandt and Shawn were eternally having a tiff, and when Remy and Nikolaus were together their combined mentality seemed to equal that of a twelve-year-old.

Also, if anything were to happen to one of them, the others wouldn't know until they reunited.

Carl didn't even want to think about that.

"Should we have a way to communicate?" he asked hesitantly. "In case… something happens to one of us?"

"We could… how about pre-paid mobile phones?" Nikolaus suggested tentatively. Remy, Shawn and Thiago were all nodding.

"That's good, Niko," Remy said proudly. "The pre-paid thingies can be traced if they try hard enough, but we'll just use them in emergencies. And we can discard with every new city if the need arises."

"I saw a sign down at that petrol station," Shawn offered. "They sell them there."

"What else?" Carl asked as he twisted back and forth slowly, stretching his back.

"When do we leave?" Nikolaus asked, looking at all of them in turn.

Silence and a regretful glance from Shawn to Remy met his query. Finally, Shawn got slowly to his feet and looked down at them all.

"Get your things together, lads, we leave at first light."

X.

SHAWN checked everything in the bags for the third time as the others sat on the beds conversing softly. The other two bags were in the other bedroom, and Shawn told himself that he needed to get those too before he forgot them. They only contained clothing and toiletries, but he still needed to have everything together.

In truth, he was trying to distract himself.

He knew this was their best plan of action, but he wished there had been some way to keep Remy with him. Thiago or Carl would have been acceptable. Nikolaus seemed to be terrified of him, but even he would have suited Shawn better than the firebug. He was probably going to end up getting Shawn killed.

"Shawn? Would you please come over here and relax?" Remy requested softly. "Your shit's not going to get up and run away."

Shawn sighed and turned around to look at them all.

"Are you always this nervous before a mission?" Thiago asked teasingly.

"No," Shawn responded tersely as he rubbed his eyes and began to pace the length of the room. Usually before a mission he was getting laid. It was like a tradition. A good luck charm, even. Oh, God, was it good luck? Was it necessary? Would something go wrong if he didn't get laid before a mission? Fucking hell.

They watched him pace, looking like a crowd at a tennis match in slow motion until Remy squeezed his eyes closed and shook his head. He added a flailing of his hands to accentuate his point and started struggling to get out of the bed. Shawn watched him curiously as he crawled over Carl's body and rolled off the bed to land on his feet right in front of Shawn. Like a fucking cat even when he was lame.

"I know what your problem is," Remy said as if it had just occurred to him.

"Oh?" Shawn responded, his interest peaked by the seductive undercurrent in the younger man's voice.

"Yeah. You haven't shot anyone in the ass lately!" Remy shouted as he punched lightly at Shawn's chest. The others snickered as Shawn rubbed at his chest in surprise.

"That's not fair," he said in a hurt voice. "I can't hit you back."

"That was sorta the point," Remy said as he thumped Shawn playfully on the nose. Thiago tossed Shawn a pillow as Remy turned away, and he promptly used it to whack Remy over the head. "Hey!" Remy shouted as he turned and grabbed at the pillow. They grappled over it as Remy got in a few jabs to Shawn's ribs with his finger. The little bastard knew he was ticklish and he knew Shawn wouldn't risk hurting him by jabbing back.

Shawn wasn't sure how it happened, but as his hands got tangled in the pillowcase and Remy's body moved closer to his in their struggles, one minute Remy was right there in front of him, the next the back of his fist was connecting with Remy's face and Remy was falling to the ground.

Remy landed on his side and sprawled out onto his stomach in a classic slapstick pratfall as the rest of them watched, frozen in shock to their various spots.

Shawn had hit Remy before. And vice versa. But he'd never done it by accident. He stood over him with his hands out as if he were about to pick up a fragile object, but Remy shook as he buried his face in the cheap carpet.

"You hit me!" he cried in disbelief, the laughter slowly but surely creeping into his voice.

"I didn't mean to hit you! It were an accident! Your face were in the wrong place!" Shawn yelled back almost pleadingly, his accent getting thicker as he got agitated.

Remy wallowed and floundered on the floor as he truly began to laugh. "I hit your fist with my face!" he cried in a dramatic half-sob before breaking down and giggling and rolling onto his back.

"Are you okay?" Shawn asked in exasperation, finding that the more Remy laughed the less he cared.

"My elbow," Remy said with a huff as he pointed to quite an impressive rug burn on said appendage.

"Well, that's your own fault," Shawn responded haughtily as he tossed the pillow back to Thiago, who was barely containing his own laughter. "I just hit you, it were your own fault you hit the ground."

With this, the others really began to snicker, and Remy practically doubled over laughing. "*Pardonnez mon* poor balance," he wheezed as Shawn helped him to his feet. "You hit me," he repeated. "I think you should feel worse about hitting me than you do."

"Uh huh. Excuse us, lads," Shawn said to the others as he took Remy's face in his hands and kissed him right there in front of everyone. Shawn had been determined to keep any sort of physical relations out of sight and therefore out of mind in order to maintain some semblance of order within the group. But this was possibly the last night he would ever be with Remy, and he intended to make good on it. If Remy felt well enough to wallow all over the floor, then he could help Shawn with his good luck charm.

The messy, open-mouthed kiss earned several low whistles and one impressive wolf call from their companions. If Remy was favoring his hurt leg, Shawn neither noticed nor cared at that moment.

He also didn't care what the others were doing as he dragged Remy's willing body through the door and slammed it closed behind them.

"I thought–"

"Not now," Shawn growled as he pressed their mouths together once more. Remy responded with a sort of detached amusement, and they moved their way clumsily across the room, stumbling every few feet and finally falling onto the bed, barely missing rolling off the edge.

Remy struggled beneath him, and Shawn spared a brief moment to let him speak as he proceeded to practically rip the clothing from both their bodies.

"I thought you wanted to keep it low-key?" Remy asked in amusement.

"To hell with low-key," Shawn murmured.

"You're not worried about hurting me?" Remy asked innocently, the beginning of a smirk making his lips twitch.

"Am I hurting you?" Shawn asked pointedly, growing tired of the game Remy was trying to play to cheer him.

"No," Remy said thoughtfully. "Shawn… I… I don't know what to say to
"

"Shh… now's not the time for that. We can deal with that tomorrow," Shawn murmured as he kissed up and down Remy's neck.

"So is this is your good luck fuck, or is it a goodbye fuck?" Remy asked conversationally.

"You really know how to kill a mood, don't you," Shawn grumbled as he ceased his kissing and looked down at Remy once more.

"I know how to kill a lot of things," Remy responded cheekily. "You always get so keyed up right before a mission," he observed with amusement. "If we're doing the good luck fuck *and* the goodbye fuck, you may want to get started," he ordered haughtily.

Shawn couldn't think of a thing to say to Remy, so he simply kissed him once more to shut him up.

The next morning was a different story. There was so much Shawn needed to say. So much he wanted to hear. But they just didn't have the time.

They decided to leave in staggered pairs to avoid a suspicious-looking mass exodus from the Roach Motel. Remy and Nikolaus were leaving first.

They stood in the parking lot next to Remy's Harley. Nikolaus and Remy gave each man a hug as they prepared to leave.

"Are you sure you can handle that thing with your injuries?" Shawn asked doubtfully as Remy wrapped his arms around him and held him tight.

"I'm fine, Beignet, no worries," Remy with a smile as he released him and ran his knuckles lovingly down the side of Shawn's face. "We're stopping at the first place we see to pick up another bike for Niko, and after that the strain won't be so bad."

Shawn nodded and looked off to his right, staring into the distance instead of looking at Remy. He knew it was another habit of his that surfaced when he was unsure of what to do, but he couldn't help that just now. The deep brown of Remy's eyes was too painful to look at.

"Hey," Remy said, trying to sound cheerful but not exactly pulling it off. "We'll see you on the first of March. I promise."

Thiago cleared his throat. Shawn saw him nod his head to the others before walking away, and he told himself to remember to thank the man for his discretion. He and Remy were left alone to say their goodbyes. As alone as you can be standing in a parking lot with four other men just meters away trying to look as if they aren't listening, at any rate.

"Come back to us," Shawn said sternly as he took Remy's face in his hands. He had expected a clever retort of some sort, but Remy merely looked at him fondly.

"I'll follow you, Shawn," Remy murmured finally. "You remember that, if you decide to go getting yourself dead or some such nonsense. I'll follow you anywhere."

Shawn closed his eyes against the moisture that threatened. He certainly wasn't about to start crying, but he was about as close as he'd been since he was seven or so.

"Get out of here. Before I change me mind," Shawn said roughly as he pushed Remy toward the Harley. Nikolaus stood waiting, and Remy mounted the bike as he took the helmet and handed it to the other man.

"You're more likely to fall off than I am," Shawn heard him say to Nikolaus. "Rougarou, he don't like strangers. *Allons!*"

Shawn smiled despite the melancholy of the moment, and Remy looked at him intently as he revved the Harley up. Shawn watched in fascination as Remy mouthed the words 'be careful' before giving them one last grin and a wink, and then the two youngest members of their group were swept away in a cloud of exhaust and sloshed snow.

Thiago walked up to stand beside Shawn, and Shawn was surprised to find Brandt's hand resting on his shoulder comfortingly as they watched the Harley speed off into the distance.

"He calls his bike 'Rougarou?'" Thiago finally asked incredulously. "What the hell's that mean?"

"It's a… Cajun folk thing," Shawn sighed as he watched the bike grow smaller. "Like a werewolf that went around eating bad Catholics or something."

"What?" Thiago and Carl both asked in bemused confusion.

Shawn couldn't help but laugh.

XI.

NIKOLAUS and Remy did exactly as they promised the others. They stopped in the first major city they came to and purchased Nikolaus a used Honda. Remy paid in cash and then they drove on to Salt Lake City, Utah.

Nikolaus spent most of the drive repeatedly refusing to allow Remy to give his beautiful new bike some off the wall Cajun nickname. He came to the conclusion that Remy was for some reason obsessed with giving inanimate objects names and personalities, but he decided early on not to delve deeper into that bit of potentially frightening psychoanalysis.

In Salt Lake City, they promptly found a café that offered the use of free wireless internet, and Nikolaus easily accessed the main files of the Organization as Remy stood watch outside the little building. He downloaded the lists of both the agents that were suspected of having turned and the agents who had worked with them all. The lists had not changed, but now beside each of their six names on the latter list there was a foreboding little red mark.

"They think we're dead," Nikolaus concluded after he had exited the café. He handed the lists to Remy and walked down the sidewalk a bit to get away from the door.

"Possibly," Remy responded as he looked the papers over and offered Nikolaus some of his fries. "They certainly won't after today. But they might just be trying to lower our guard. Lesson Number One, Niko," he said, shaking a fry in Nikolaus's face, "never take anything at face value, and never take information for granted."

Nikolaus nodded and followed Remy as he headed back to the bikes.

"I left a trail," Nikolaus reminded Remy pointedly. "They'll be here soon," he added when Remy didn't seem to be bothered by it.

"*Oui*. It's fucking cold, *Peeshwank*," Remy observed absently as he leant against his bike. "We should get some more heavy clothing. And we'll snag you a laptop while we're at it, *non*? Some gear and shit. Maybe some of those little Motorola two-ways. How do you feel about a shopping trip?"

"Did you hear me, Remy?" Nikolaus asked incredulously. "They'll be here any minute."

"Ya. I want to time them, find out what we're up against." Remy responded as he tossed the remainder of his food into a nearby trash receptacle and brushed his hands together. "Utah isn't exactly a hotbed of intrigue or anything, but we'll see. C'mon."

Nikolaus nodded absently and glanced back at the café before they headed off in search of the necessary supplies, including bedrolls and heavy winter jackets. When they came back, their arms laden with their purchases, they watched in interest as the café was thoroughly searched by men with dogs in blue ATF windbreakers.

"ATF?" Nikolaus questioned worriedly as Remy checked his watch with a frown.

"Department of Alcohol, Tobacco and Firearms," Remy supplied absently.

"I know what the fuck it stands for," Nikolaus snapped. "But what the hell is the ATF doing here?"

"Took them a full three hours," Remy murmured, shaking his head. "Hmm? Oh, they're not ATF. You can get those things just about anywhere. I've got one myself. I did, anyway. Lost it. Let's get going before those fucking dogs catch our scent."

They quickly evacuated Salt Lake City, taking out their map and using the scientifically proven method of jabbing it with a pen to decide their next destination.

"Where in the fuck is Truth or Consequences, New Mexico?" Remy pondered aloud as they gassed up the now heavily loaded bikes just outside of town.

"It's in Canada," Nikolaus deadpanned. Remy burst out laughing and gave him a pat on thc back and a little squeeze.

"You're coming around, Niko! Pretty soon you'll be speaking in whole sentences again!"

Nikolaus smiled and nodded. He had to admit he was more comfortable now that he was with just Remy. It made it so much easier to breathe when you weren't constantly worried about being blown up or shouted at.

"That's an appropriate name, no doubt," Nikolaus mused.

"Yeah," Remy agreed in a distracted voice as he looked out at the stretch of highway they were about to start down. The sudden change from laughter to solemnity was astonishing. Remy should have been an actor or something. That or he was a freaking sociopath. "Unfortunately the truth has its consequences too," he mumbled to himself.

Nikolaus wasn't sure what Remy was talking about, but he decided he would rather forget it than worry about it.

At least New Mexico offered warmer climes, and he soon realized that the smaller the city, the bigger their window of time. When he mentioned this, Remy explained that the lesser towns didn't have agents posted there, and therefore they were forced to come in from more populated areas whenever the two of them pinged the system.

"So why don't we stick to smaller towns?"

"No. We stick to the Holey Map," Remy responded with a shake of his head, indicating the map filled with holes, which was laid out on the table of their booth in the grimy little diner. The pen was even now sticking up out of New Haven, Connecticut.

"Why?" Nikolaus questioned curiously.

"There's safety in being random," Remy answered seriously. "If they realize we're staying with the smaller cities and towns they'll start finding a pattern and stationing agents in the smaller towns, too. Our best bet is to not know where we're going until we're almost there. You want the rest of your ice cream?"

"Take it," Nikolaus answered with a grin. He wondered if he would ever start thinking like Remy did. Probably not. It seemed to require a certain madness Nikolaus just didn't possess.

XII.

BRANDT wasn't exactly sure what he had done to get Shawn's knickers all in a twist this time. It seemed that every little bitty flare up sent Shawn's sanity careening over the edge of a cliff and he always ended up trying to do Brandt harm.

Brandt certainly didn't see what the big deal was. Things caught fire; it wasn't always Brandt's fault. Brandt expressed this opinion breathlessly as Shawn held him pinned against the wall with his gun pressed against the hollow of Brandt's cheek.

"Yes, *things* catch fire," Shawn ground out as he switched the safety off and cocked the gun threateningly, letting it dig even further into Brandt's cheek. "But *hotel rooms* do not just catch fire! *Automobiles* do not just catch fire! And my favorite pair of sweatpants do *not* just catch fire!"

"I said I was sorry about those," Brandt responded assertively. Shawn let out a low, plaintive growl that ended up sounding more like a miserable howl as he pushed Brandt against the wall once more in disgust and turned away.

"We have to move again," he groaned as he began throwing things into his bag.

XIII.

AFTER Connecticut, Remy and Nikolaus made their way to Canada, purchasing a map of the country as they got further north and poking it full of holes as well as they travelled over the country. Remy amused himself with teaching Nikolaus as they went, and Nikolaus vowed never to ride a motorbike through Canada in January ever again so many times that Remy lost count.

Remy became particularly melancholy in Toronto, telling Nikolaus that being there brought back memories of Shawn, and he wondered how the others were faring, and did Nikolaus want the last of his pie?

It was also in Toronto that their pursuers finally caught up to them. It was then that Remy's true genius began to shine through. His methods of evasion were unique and inventive, and the calm, almost nonchalant manner in which he faced almost certain death was quite admirable. Nikolaus began trying to emulate Remy's example; he'd soon gotten quite good at the whole business.

From Canada they followed the Mississippi River to the Gulf of Mexico, stopping and sidetracking wherever the Holey Map told them to, and then followed the coastline until they crossed over the border in Texas. Mexico proved to be more trouble than it was worth, and Remy found himself wondering why Shawn liked to work down there so much. They crossed the border again, local style– wading through the Rio Grande– then it was back up into the States once more and on to Marietta, Georgia, just outside of Atlanta.

They refrained from accessing the files there, hoping for a respite from the chase, and instead holed up and analyzed the information they'd collected. So far, they had very little. Remy sat and stared at his crispy little piece of paper for hours during their various pit stops, but had rarely written anything on it. When he finally passed it to Nikolaus over Chinese takeout one night Nikolaus expressed his frustration with their lack of progress by teaching Remy several interesting German curses.

"You still think the key is embedded in it somehow?" Nikolaus finally asked him in frustration.

"I have no idea. I've stared at that fucking thing for so long I can't even make any sense of what I've writ, much less the code," Remy responded with a careless shrug. "I've been wracking my brain searching for something that could provide key codes but would be mobile enough for his operatives to take with them. Books, movies, even music. Well-known manuscripts… what about archery? Are there any, like… archery manuals?" he asked as he reached across the table and snagged a fortune cookie.

"I'm sure there are," Nikolaus responded absently as he stared at the message.

"Fuck it. They'd still need some way of finding them!" Remy huffed as got up to go throw away the take-out boxes.

Several hours later and they both rested their heads on the table morosely and stared at the piece of paper.

"Maybe he's high when he writes these," Remy suggested. "Maybe you have to be… I dunno… under the influence to be able to read them."

Nikolaus raised his head and stared at his companion.

"You really think he'd order his operatives to go on a binger right before receiving their orders?" he asked incredulously, a smile playing at his lips.

"Maybe not. But it's a good excuse to get plastered, *non*?"

That led to their first trip to the liquor store down the street from their hotel. After two bottles of vodka shared between the two of them, they decided that it probably wasn't going to help them crack the message.

"We have two options," Nikolaus murmured seriously as Remy bit his lip to keep from snickering at him. "We can either keep frustrating ourselves with this for a few more hours until we're too tired to fuck each other, and then get dressed again and go for more vodka. Or we can forget the message, go get the liquor now, and then fuck all night. Your choice."

Remy didn't display his shock at Nikolaus's pronouncement. In the time they'd spent together, Nikolaus had not expressed an ounce of interest in sex. Not with Remy, anyway. They'd been moving nonstop, staying permanently exhausted and in fear of being caught. Remy supposed that this, their first real night of feeling safe, was a logical time for Nikolaus to finally bring it up. It would be a good way of releasing all the pent-up stress. And the knowledge that Shawn was probably fucking Brandt every time he managed not to blow something up went a long way to assuaging any guilt.

"Why do I have to make all the tough decisions?" he sighed dramatically.

"Closing your eyes and jabbing at a map is not a tough decision!" Nikolaus shouted as he began to laugh.

Remy laughed as well and stood up, stretching his wiry muscles languidly. "Vodka first," he decided with a mischievous grin. He leaned over the table and placed both palms flat on the tabletop. "Then you can fuck me 'til the sun comes up," he murmured with a glint in his black eyes. Nikolaus merely grinned at him.

With that, they made their precarious way back to the liquor store and were miraculously sold another two bottles of liquor. It was in getting back to the hotel that they ran into problems.

When they made it to their room– and had checked the room number three times– they couldn't get in.

Nikolaus leaned against the wall and snickered as Remy pressed his forehead against the door and repeatedly ran their card key thingy through. The red light blinked morosely at them with each attempt.

"Do you've it downside up?" Nikolaus asked. Remy snickered and hissed drunkenly as he flipped the thing every which way it would go, but to no avail.

A clang in the stairwell near their room drew Remy's attention, and he stopped his movements and cocked his head to listen intently. Someone was climbing the stairs.

Remy turned to look at Nikolaus, who'd tensed as well. He licked his lips and looked around the hallway, cursing himself for allowing them both to get so drunk. They'd left their weaponry inside the room. All he had on him was a small pocketknife.

"Come on," he hissed, taking Nikolaus's hand and tugging him down the hall. He shoved Nikolaus into the alcove that housed the drink and snack machines and then went to the decorative hall table. He grabbed the flowers and yanked them out of their vase, then dumped the water on the floor as he glanced back at the stairwell door. No one had appeared yet.

He moved faster, taking the empty vase and wrapping it in his shirt hastily before pressing it hard against the mirror that hung over the table. The mirror cracked and splintered, and Remy dug out a piece of the broken mirror and then moved back into the alcove, the flowers still in his hand.

Nikolaus stood behind him, breathing unevenly as Remy used the mirror to peer around the corner.

The stairwell door opened and a man stepped out into the hallway slowly, peering left and right as he held his wrist up to his mouth.

Remy held up his hand to Nikolaus as another man followed the first out of the stairwell. Down the hallway, the elevator dinged to announce its arrival.

"Hallway clear," the first man murmured into his wrist. "They must have gotten into the room. Moving in," he informed whoever was listening as he began to move toward Remy and Nikolaus's room. "Copy," he whispered in response to some unheard order.

The man pulled out a key card and slid it through the lock. It turned green on the first try, and Remy cursed to himself. He should have seen the trap. He had used it himself in the past. Killing someone in their own hotel room was like child's play in a moderately priced hotel. In the movies, you saw men using advanced gadgets as they tried to gain entry, wiring them to the locks and letting the digital readout find the code and unlock the door. But that was mostly theatrics.

All you had to do to gain entrance to someone's room in a place like this was go to the front desk and tell them you locked yourself out. They would ask you for your room number, you give it to them, *et voilà*, your keys would open their doors and their keys no longer work.

The elevator doors opened, and Remy pushed Nikolaus further into the alcove. They couldn't hide. They would have to fight their way out. And Remy knew the fucking hotel would be surrounded. He looked around desperately, and his eyes landed on the courtesy phone beside the ice machine.

He reached for it hastily and watched with his mirror as one more agent made his way warily down the hall. The front desk answered his call, and he spoke in a hurried whisper, his accent heavily southern. "Yeah, uh, I'm up here in 407 and there's these two guys out by the ice machine?" he drawled in an annoyed voice. "I think they're fuckin' or somethin'. That's right, two guys," he said in apparent disbelief, "right out in the hallway! I got kids up here!" he whispered angrily.

The flustered woman stuttered a response, and Remy hung up the phone as the last agent got closer. The first man had entered their room and was even now searching through it and realizing they weren't in it, the second stood guard at the stairwell as the third blocked the way to the elevators.

Remy took in a deep breath and let it out slowly, then stepped into the middle of the hallway, right in front of the third man. The agent raised his gun in alarm, and Remy held out the flowers to him with a cock of his head.

"Allergies can be a bitch," he said to the agent as he wagged the flowers in his face, then jammed the heel of his hand through the flowers and into the man's nose. The crunch practically echoed in the silent hallway and the ruined flowers fluttered to the ground and stuck to the blood pouring from his face as he stumbled back. Remy grabbed him by his wrist, spinning him around as if they were performing some morbid tango, and he wrapped his arm around his neck and held him as the guard at the stairwell opened fire.

The silenced shots caught the agent in the chest, and he and Remy both stumbled back slightly with the impact. The shots did little damage, though, thumping against the Kevlar vest the man wore. He groaned and struggled weakly, and Remy's hand tightened on the man's chin as he jerked his arm to the side.

He crumpled to the ground, his neck broken, and left Remy without a human shield. Remy cursed and tossed the piece of jagged mirror in his hand, underhanded as if it were a horseshoe. It caught the other agent in the neck. He reached up and touched the piece of glass with wide, startled eyes. The spurting blood oozed through his fingers, and he stared at Remy in shock as he stumbled through the door and disappeared back into the stairwell.

The last man, the one who had been searching their room, raised his gun from the cover of the doorway. Remy sidestepped and snatched the vase from the hall table. He turned and tossed it, throwing it like a baseball pitcher, and hit the man's gun hand to send the weapon flying.

Remy was already moving, and before the man could draw his backup Remy was on him. One swift kick to the Adam's apple was all it took and the man went down in a heap.

"Niko," Remy hissed as he pounced on the body and began dragging it into the room. Nikolas crept out into the hall, and Remy hurriedly instructed him to get into the room and gather everything they had. Nikolaus hurried to obey.

They dragged the bodies into their room, hastily wiped down the blood in the stairwell, and then ran down the stairs to the fourth floor.

Remy yanked Nikolaus into the fourth floor alcove, and they hurriedly stashed their documents behind the ice machine. Then Remy pressed Nikolaus against the wall, unzipping his fly as they both panted for breath after their mad dash down the stairs. He dropped to his knees and enveloped Nikolaus's cock with his mouth, and he held Nikolaus's hip firmly with the other. Nikolaus groaned and let his head fall back against the wall as he tangled his fingers in Remy's curly hair automatically.

"Is the intention to get caught?" Nikolaus asked in a strangled voice.

Remy merely hummed in response and the vibrations rippled though Nikolaus's body. Surprisingly, he'd understood the message. They had just spent the last month living in almost constant fear of being killed; getting caught giving a guy a blowjob in the hallway of a Holiday Inn was not going to faze Remy much. Plus, they would be assured a police escort out of the hotel.

They spent the night in the Fulton County lockup for their trouble, with several large, inebriated men who were curious as to how two such 'pretty boys' had ended up in jail on public lewdness charges.

When the guards finally came to break up the brawl that ensued, three of their cellmates were in various stages of injury, and Remy was close to choking the life out of the fourth man as the fifth cowered in the corner. After that, they were given their own little solitary cells in which to sober up, and after posting their own bail in the morning, they promptly retrieved their things and disappeared once more.

A joyously proclaimed "So much for keeping under the radar," was the only comment Remy ever offered on the experience.

XIV.

THIAGO wondered how the others were faring as he stared at the dark ceiling. He was amazed at how quickly he'd become attached to the other five men. Thiago rarely became attached to anyone; what had made him suddenly turn full circle and actually start caring now? Thiago didn't know, but it had happened regardless.

He liked the feeling.

At the same time, though, he hated it. He hated worrying and wondering. He hated not knowing how the two younger men were faring in their deadly game of cat and mouse, and he missed the camaraderie that Shawn's presence had offered. Hell, he even missed Brandt and his damned explosives.

Carl was a good man, though, and Thiago was glad for his company. Thiago didn't know where Remy and Nikolaus had ended up, but he was fairly certain he and Carl had traveled the farthest distance of the three groups, if not the longest time. Clearing the money out of the two hides Remy had directed them to, one in Washington, D.C. and another in Baton Rouge, Louisiana, had been easy enough. Thiago had wondered about Remy's sanity when they had finally found the address in Louisiana.

"Bergeron's Storage?" Carl read incredulously as they pulled up to the little store-it-yourself establishment. "He's got to be kidding, right?"

Thiago simply shook his head and muttered, "Guess it's a common name."

There had been close to $200,000 stashed there amongst the cushions of an old sofa and the drawers of an old armoire, and any doubt as to Remy's mental stability in Thiago's mind was wiped away. He was definitely crazy.

The real travel came because Carl was based in Russia, and they'd been forced to fly all the way to St. Petersburg to retrieve his stash of weaponry. The tricky part was getting the damn things out of the country. Carl had all the papers required to transport them, saying that he was a dealer heading for a show in Los Angeles, but there had been a lot of unusual weaponry that raised a lot of eyebrows. It was also a bitch to move– physically– with just the two of them.

Now they were in Los Angeles at one of the more high-end hotels, cooling their heels and awaiting a call from Remy or Shawn. It had taken Carl an entire day, but he'd found a storage unit under the name 'Travers Storage' and they stashed the weapons there, snickering to themselves all the while.

Thiago just hoped Remy lived to hear about it.

XV.

CARL stared out the window at the haze that hovered over Los Angeles. He pressed his lips together tightly and glanced back at Thiago, who was spread eagled on the bed and drifting in and out of sleep.

It was not in Carl's makeup to worry. It went against his training to brood over a problem he could do nothing to fix. But the ice he'd been accused of being carved from in the past was beginning to melt, and he found himself unable to completely relax as concern for his companions constantly assaulted him.

He ran a hand through his hair and let his foot bounce restlessly.

He hadn't thought he was ready to get out of this business. Now, though, he wasn't so sure if he still had the nerve to watch the people he cared for lose their lives around him. And lives would be lost, that much he did know.

XVI.

SHAWN sat staring morosely at the television in the cheap hotel room in Toronto. He despised being in Toronto with Brandt– a city that had been the backdrop to several important events for himself and Remy– when it should have been Remy. He despised not knowing where Remy was or what he was doing or even if he was still alive.

But most of all, Shawn hated that he'd begun to enjoy Brandt's company. His presence– larger than life and boisterous and outlandish and insane– was like a soothing balm over the wound Remy's departure had left.

They could have been brothers, Shawn found himself thinking. They were so very much alike.

It was as far as he would allow his thoughts to wander down that road.

XVII.

AFTER landing themselves in jail, Nikolaus and Remy knew they had to get out of the States for a while. They left the bikes in the long-term lot of Hartsfield International Airport in Atlanta, and Remy took an inordinate amount of time saying goodbye to Rougarou, a word Nikolaus still didn't know the meaning of.

The more time Nikolaus spent with him, the more endearing Remy became.

From Atlanta, they flew to Glasgow in search of Fletcher Barclay, the first of the agents on their suspect list, in order to question him. They never found any trace of him.

Next they flew to Prague, where they searched for and found Evan Washburn, who was supposed to be dead, according to their lists.

"Please don't kill me, man," Evan begged as Remy held him pinned against the wall of his flat. "I'm just an audio tech, I don't know a thing."

Nikolaus stood behind Remy, watching in fascination. Evan Washburn was an American. He was a smaller man, a little shorter than Nikolaus, with impossibly blue eyes and dark hair. Remy held him off the ground, and his feet dangled just barely above the carpet. Just enough to tantalize, apparently, because he kept pointing his toes and kicking his legs, trying to find solid ground.

"If you answer our questions, we won't kill you," Remy told him matter-of-factly. "Deal?"

"You're a fucking hired killer, man! How do I know you'll keep your end of the deal?"

"I always keep my word, and I promise you that if you don't answer my questions, I will kill you. Slowly."

Evan's eyes widened impossibly further. When Evan's tongue apparently didn't allow him to respond Nikolaus saw a slow, evil smile spread across Remy's handsome face. "Nikolaus," he murmured pleasantly. "Go in there and find me a spoon, will you?"

"A spoon?" Nikolaus repeated, not certain he'd heard correctly.

"*Mais oui*," Remy hissed with relish, his piercing gaze never leaving Evan's. "I'd like to take his eyes with me when we go."

"I'll talk!" Evan screamed almost immediately.

"Who is the Archer?" Remy asked without dropping the other man.

"I don't know." When Remy tilted his head as if to give Nikolaus another request, Evan shouted a panicked: "Seriously, man! I never met him! It all went through back channels and shit."

"Did you receive messages from him?"

"No, man. One of his agents contacted me. Said if I helped him with a bugging job he'd get me out."

"Out?"

"Out of the business, dude. I just wanted out."

Nikolaus saw the muscles in Remy's jaw jump as he clenched his teeth, and then he released the American so suddenly that the smaller man fell to the floor with a thud.

"So he helped you fake your death," Remy concluded softly.

"Right," Evan gasped as he rubbed his throat where Remy had been holding him.

"How?" Remy demanded.

"An explosion. They pulled out my fucking teeth, man, and then planted them in the van I was supposed to be in. Thing burned forever."

"What did you bug?"

"I didn't do the actual bugging. I just taught the guy and gave him the equipment."

"Do you know what it was?" Remy asked patiently. Evan licked his lips nervously.

"It was… it was the operations room of the Facility in Paris."

This was met with stunned silence. No fucking wonder the Archer was always one step ahead.

"Christ, *Peeshwank*, we're running in circles," Remy murmured to Nikolaus.

"You're not gonna… you're not gonna tell the Organization I'm still alive, are you?" Evan asked miserably as he struggled to his feet.

Remy was shaking his head as he walked away, and Nikolaus watched him go in confusion. He turned to look at the other man and smiled. "No worries," he offered with a small smile, "you're safe."

The look of relief on the younger man's face did wonders for Nikolaus's conscience.

"Are you really going after the Organization?" Evan asked tentatively. Nikolaus made sure his features were schooled into a passively blank mask, but Remy came storming back into the room and started growling in what Nikolaus had begun calling Frenglish.

"Where did you hear that?" he asked dangerously.

"Well, it's all over the underground. That six operatives got screwed over and now the two that lived are gunning for the bad guys. That's you two, right?" Nikolaus and Remy shared a look. "If you ever need help, you can obviously find me," Evan offered wryly. Nikolaus let his lips twitch into a smile. Now that was brave. Remy nodded and mumbled and moved back out of the room silently.

Nikolaus hustled after him, throwing a, "Sorry about the… y'know, torturing thing," over his shoulder as he went.

"*Two* that lived?" Nikolaus murmured worriedly as they left the building and walked quickly to their stolen car.

"Obviously the others are doing a better job than we are of remaining under," Remy answered under his breath. "That, or whenever they're spotted they're simply taken for 'the two' that lived."

There was really nothing they could do about it, and so they carried on.

They had several close calls in France and England before finally returning to the States. But as they strolled casually through the airport in Atlanta upon their re-entry into the U.S., Remy turned to Nikolaus and said possibly the most frightening thing Nikolaus had ever heard.

"It's good we're back in the States," he said with a large grin. "I feel like I know what I'm doing now."

"You feel like you know what you're doing now?" Nikolaus repeated hollowly. "*Now*?"

"I mean, I spent me some time in Paris and all, but this is my region, you know?"

"*Now*?" Nikolaus repeated angrily as memories of their last frantic dash through the crowded avenues of Calais and the subsequent dive into the freezing waters of the Channel flashed through his mind.

"*Mais oui*. Hey, look! Pretzels!"

They'd made the fatal error of thinking they had covered their trail to Atlanta.

They hadn't even made it through the security gates before Remy spotted the two men milling about near the end of the long queue of people. He immediately drew Nikolaus into the men's restroom and dragged him into a stall.

"You know," Nikolaus murmured cheekily as Remy frantically scrabbled at his own belt buckle. "Last time we were in Georgia we had a little problem like this. I don't think we should make the same mistake twice."

"Shh," Remy hissed as he pulled a small plastic bag out of a patch sewn into the waistband of his briefs.

"What are you doing?" Nikolaus whispered.

"This is a health supplement called inosital. You remember all that money we dropped at that supplement shop?"

Nikolaus nodded. Remy had gone in and spent well over fifty euro for a little bottle of white powder. It looked suspiciously like cocaine.

"It's supposed to improve communication between the cells or some shit like that," Remy continued in a hurried whisper as he took out a little roll of one-hundred dollar bills and wrapped them around the bag with a rubber band. "It's also used to cut cocaine 'cause it looks like it, see? If we can plant this on them and have security detain them we should be able to get far enough away before they've caught our scent again."

"Jesus, Remy."

"It's all I've got," Remy told him regretfully as he opened the stall door cautiously.

Nikolaus jumped when Remy was grabbed and yanked out of the stall, and he found himself unable to react as he too was pulled roughly out into the open.

They were both forced to their knees, and the two men held guns to their heads as a tall, distinguished-looking older gentlemen strolled into the room.

"Fuck," Remy breathed shakily.

Nikolaus didn't know the man, but he knew that if Remy was frightened, then he was frightened.

"Hello, dear boy," the man said in an educated British accent.

"Hello, Sir John," Remy responded shakily. The name hit Nikolaus like a load of falling bricks. He was sure that he paled noticeably. It was the Gray Ghost. Nikolaus began to tremble where he knelt, paralyzed with awe and fear.

Sir John McTiernan tsk'd at them.

"You have been very naughty, my boy," he said to Remy as he took Remy's chin in his hand and lifted his head. Remy probably could have killed him just then, Nikolaus was sure of it, but he thought probably the gun digging into the Cajun's cheek was a major incentive for him not to move. "What have you done with Shawn? It's been ages since I've seen him."

"He's dead, John," Remy said as his voice wavered quite convincingly. "They're all dead."

A shadow flashed across McTiernan's face, but he recovered quickly. "That is a shame," he murmured sincerely.

"Shame?" Remy repeated angrily. "They killed him, John! They would have–"

"He was a traitor, dear boy. As are you, I'm afraid."

Before Remy could form a retort the sound of dress shoes clicking against the tile floor sounded. Remy and Nikolaus took advantage of the momentary distraction to rush their captors. Remy grabbed John and rolled backwards, taking out the legs of the man holding the gun to his head as Nikolaus flung his own body at the other man and toppled him. In the chaos, the two of them scrambled to their feet and past the unsuspecting citizen who'd just saved their lives.

It hadn't been pretty by any stretch of the imagination, but it had worked. They fled toward the security checks, but Remy took hold of Nikolaus as they skidded to a stop at the end of the line and yanked him toward a door that read 'Airport Personnel Only.'

"This leads to the roof," Nikolaus hissed as he and Remy fled up the sterile gray staircase.

"Right. We have to hide. We can't outrun them and get through security too."

Nikolaus was now seriously considering trashing his plans and his loyalties and killing Remy. He didn't think it would be so hard. Just a little nudge and Remy would fall off the side of the building they were even now clinging to. Just a kick of his leg and Remy was a goner. Too bad Nikolaus was so fucking attached to the cheeky bastard.

"I was so looking forward to seeing my Rougarou," Remy murmured mournfully.

They both tried to control their inappropriate snickering, and Nikolaus pressed his forehead against the rough wall to which he was clinging in order to control them. They were standing on what was essentially a decorative ledge, roughly eight feet below the top of the building. The heels of their feet jutted out into thin air, and their hands were pressed to the wall in a vain attempt to suction themselves to it. Nikolaus had the horrifying thought that if a plane were to come by they would simply be blown off the side of the building. The thought made him snicker even more.

As the sound of gravel crunching beneath a heavy boot echoed above them, they both instantly quieted. Remy had his cheek pressed to the wall, and Nikolaus did the same, unconsciously trying to make himself flatter. His eyes locked with Remy's, and Remy discreetly moved his hand until it was resting atop Nikolaus's. They twined their fingers together and waited breathlessly, wondering if they were finally caught.

They'd had plenty of close calls, and during one tense moment in Calais a man actually got close enough to brush his fingers against Nikolaus's jacket. But this situation was by far their most desperate. They were cornered, hiding, and hoping they wouldn't be found.

They listened intently to the crunching of the boots. Nikolaus's entire body began to shake with adrenaline. Remy's fingers tightened around his as little bits of dust and gravel were kicked over the side of the roof, and for one tense moment Nikolaus thought that all was lost. But then the crunching faded into the distance, and Remy's body relaxed next to his.

Neither man dared to move for five more minutes, but when nothing more came of the encounter Remy pointed upwards and reached tentatively for the edge of the roof. They pulled themselves up slowly and peeked over the top before hefting their bodies over and kneeling there at the edge, slowing their breathing and calming their racing hearts.

"That was a nice little move you showed back there," Remy finally said quietly, a smile on his face as they both stood.

"Yeah well, I may be a computer nerd, but I'm still a trained agent, *ja*? I can take care of myself," Nikolaus said proudly with just a hint of sarcasm.

Remy raised an eyebrow and smirked. "Keep talking like that and you may have to fuck me into the mattress tonight."

Nikolaus grinned and snickered. "I will never understand how nearly dying can turn you on so much," Nikolaus observed fondly as they made their way carefully to the door through which they had fled earlier.

"It's a psychological thing," Remy said with a dismissive swipe of his hand. "Look, here's the plan. If we run into these blokes again, we'll be a little on the screwed side."

"Yeah," Nikolaus said uneasily, afraid that he knew what was coming next.

"I still have–"

"No."

"What?"

"I will not let you use me as bait. Again."

"But you're so good at it," Remy protested.

"Don't care. It scares me."

"Well, okay then. I'll be the bait, and you can plant this on the big scary guy with the gun, *non*?" Remy suggested as he held up the roll of money and the plastic bag.

"Err… fucking hell. What do I have to do?"

"Make sure they see you. I want them running after you, got it?" Remy instructed as they made their way slowly down the stairs. "Then make sure you find a security officer. You have to tell them that you saw these men with weapons. Now, they'll probably have them stashed somewhere by now, but they won't know they have the bag so they'll surrender to the search thinking they're clean. This much cocaine would be enough to get them put away for a lot longer than a drunken blowjob, I can tell you that."

"Right. Run. Security. Tattle. What else?"

"That's it. Oh, and don't get killed, okay? That would really ruin my plans for the night."

"Right."

Thankfully they never had to implement their risky plan. McTiernan and the other two goons were nowhere in sight when they re-emerged, and they easily slipped out of the airport and back to their bikes. Remy stroked the seat of his Rougarou affectionately, and Nikolaus couldn't help but grin.

"Where to?" he asked as he they revved up the bikes and let them idle, letting them warm up after nearly two weeks of non-use.

"We'll go north a bit, I suppose," Remy said thoughtfully. "Stop at the first motel we see that allows screaming and blowjobs in the hallways, and then we'll consult the Holey Map after that."

Nikolaus nodded and donned his helmet.

XVIII.

"WHERE do we plan to go, oh fearless leader?" Brandt asked as he casually walked over to his bag and began packing as if nothing untoward had just occurred.

This had become the norm for them. Brandt would destroy something, usually something little and inconsequential, and Shawn would go apeshit and try to kill him. Then after a few minutes of threats and growls, which would inevitably have Brandt's libido going into overdrive, they would separate amicably and pick up the conversation they'd been having as if none of it ever happened. More often than not it would end in a nice brutal shagging.

Brandt really liked Shawn Bennett. A lot.

"We should go south a bit. It's fucking cold up here," Shawn said as he stuffed his things haphazardly into his leather bag. Brandt counted his grenades carefully as he thought about their previous travels. They'd gone to Los Angeles directly after splitting with the others in search of Shawn's first hide, and then they'd dipped down to Mexico City for the second. Lastly, they'd travelled back up to Vancouver to clear out the third.

They were now trying to remain stationary with the loot until it was time for their reunion with the others, but Brandt kept 'accidentally' setting things on fire and so they were forced to keep moving.

He needed the flame, he couldn't help it. It would start with a flick of a lighter or the ticking of an alarm clock, and Brandt's mind would haze over, only to return with Shawn frantically putting out the flames and screaming at him.

Those times were few and far between; Brandt could count only three of them in the last seventy-nine days.

The other twelve incidents Brandt had instigated intentionally to keep Shawn on his toes. When they were down for too long with nothing to occupy them, Shawn would begin to brood, and when the brooding started Brandt would light something aflame. The pants had been a real accident, actually, but the effect had been the same. Brandt was pretty sure Shawn caught on after the second time, but the fact that he'd never said anything told Brandt he probably enjoyed the little game, the distraction. Until his favorite pair of pants caught on fire, anyway.

Brandt loved Shawn. He was crazy as hell under that normal exterior and Brandt loved him for it. Now he understood where Remy's fierce loyalty to the man came from.

"When do we find out where we're doing the rendezvous?" Brandt asked as he looked around the room for an errant grenade.

"Remy is supposed to call us at eleven thirty-two exactly on the 29th and let us know where to meet them. What are you looking for?" Shawn asked suspiciously, sounding as if he was almost afraid to ask.

"Eh? Oh, nothing. It's probably rolling around in the Rover somewhere," Brandt answered in an off-handed manner as he continued to stuff his things into his bag.

"By 'rolling around' do you mean ticking, by any chance?" Shawn asked as he stopped what he was doing and turned to face Brandt.

"It should be fine," Brandt assured him with a swipe of his hand. "Although I suppose if the pin gets caught on something it could be a problem, but I wouldn't worry about it." A low growl emitted from Shawn's direction, and Brandt shivered happily. "You are one sexy beast when you're teetering on the edge, you know that?" he observed casually as he turned around to face the other man.

"You're close to driving me permanently insane."

"I hate to tell you, mate, but that'd be a short trip."

"Kinda like your trip to Hell, yeah?" Shawn responded with a smirk as he turned back around and zipped up his bag.

"Exactly. It's warm down there. Hey, we've got some time before we have to leave, you–"

Before Brandt could complete his sentence, Shawn kicked his legs out from under him and he landed on the floor of the hotel room hard enough to make the pictures on the walls rattle. Shawn knelt and straddled him, effectively pinning him with his ankles crossed over Brandt's knees and his hands wrapped firmly around Brandt's wrists. Not that Brandt was about to start struggling. Shawn was an excellent top, the best Brandt had ever encountered in fact, and he had no problem with being overpowered.

"You think you're getting shagged after setting me pants on fire?" Shawn asked incredulously as he leant over and peered at Brandt's face bemusedly.

"Well. It's not like you were *in* them at the time," Brandt argued. Shawn snarled and his grip tightened around Brandt's wrists. "Besides, burns give clothing character," Brandt added with a cheeky smile.

"Stop talking before I change me mind," Shawn growled before biting down on Brandt's lower lip to emphasize his point. Brandt groaned appreciatively and squirmed as if he were trying to get away. He'd learned that they both enjoyed this little game of sexual cat and mouse immensely, and he gladly played along. "We don't have time for this," Shawn grumbled against Brandt's lips even as he reached between their bodies and untied the knotted string at the top of Brandt's track pants. The other hand gripped Brandt's wrist so hard Brandt knew there would be bruises there soon. Probably before they were done fucking.

"Quickly then?" Brandt asked eagerly as he used his newly freed hand to tug at Shawn's shirt. Shawn simply nodded and continued to struggle with the knot, and Brandt ran his hand beneath the thin material of the T-shirt and over the hard muscles of Shawn's stomach and chest. "Both hands," Brandt grunted in suggestion, and when Shawn released his other wrist in order to untie the knot Brandt ran his hand over Shawn's thigh and tugged at the back of his knee demandingly.

"That's how you want it then?" Shawn purred. Brandt nodded his head and licked his lips in anticipation. Over the last two and a half months, they had gotten pretty good at working together and communicating. Brandt found that Shawn was easy to work with and easy to predict since he always chose the most unusual and unlikely route, which was generally Brandt's way of operating too. And their understanding wasn't just physical.

Brandt had found that he truly enjoyed Shawn's presence, which wasn't that surprising. What had surprised him was that Shawn truly enjoyed Brandt's presence as well. It didn't matter to Brandt that the other man had threatened to kill him numerous times; he could tell that Shawn liked him. He also enjoyed the fact that Shawn seemed to be able to read his mind as well as his actions. Shawn understood Brandt's cues as if they were written on his forehead, and Brandt loved him for it. When Brandt was wanting hard and fast Shawn gave it to him gladly.

Brandt really liked being fucked by Shawn. He was actually able to make Brandt cry out for more, and Brandt couldn't begin to describe how much he liked *that*. The best thing, though? Shawn had seemingly forgotten their deal that Brandt only got sex when he behaved himself, and so usually even when he set something on fire or had an 'accident' like they'd had at that gas station in Albuquerque, Brandt still got fucked more often than not.

He got to blow shit up *and* get laid. Life was good.

XIX.

REMY had been in several situations where he'd awakened in a strange place. He'd been in even more situations where he'd awakened with his wrists and ankles tied and a gag in his mouth. And he'd lost count of how many times he he'd awakened naked.

But Remy was pretty sure this was the first time all three had happened at the same time.

It took him several moments to remember that they were in a little town in central North Carolina and that Nikolaus had just spent half the night fucking him into oblivion. Remy smiled at the memory, but it soon faded. This was the first time he'd fucked someone besides Shawn for the simple pleasure of fucking, and he was shocked to find that he felt guilty. Guilt. That was also a first.

Remy closed his eyes and batted that thought away.

They'd left Atlanta and stopped at the first truck stop they'd come across and gone over the bikes with a fine-toothed comb, looking for tracking devices. They had found three on each bike, which Remy knew was pretty standard, and he had taken the six little pieces and attached each to a different truck trailer. He made sure that they were all going in different directions, and that one of them was definitely headed for Los Angeles.

"Aren't *we* going to Los Angeles?" Nikolaus had asked.

"Yes. Sometimes the secret's in what's *not* there, Niko," Remy had replied, knowing full well that it probably hadn't made much sense to the other man. He had to keep Nikolaus thinking, though, just in case something happened to him before they could meet up with the others and Nikolaus was forced to go it alone.

As soon as their tracers realized that all six devices were heading in different directions they would probably examine each target, determine that it wasn't Remy and Nikolaus, and then move on. No agent in his right mind would send a tracer to his intended destination. And that was why Remy had done it. Hopefully, Nikolaus would catch on.

Where was Nikolaus anyway? Remy was definitely alone in the room. He examined the bonds at his wrists as he lay on his stomach, and decided that if he got to the point that his shoulders hurt before Nikolaus returned he would wriggle out of them.

Remy had never met a rope, chain, handcuff, newfangled plastic zippy thing, or silk scarf from which he couldn't escape. That was one of his many special talents. The Cajun Houdini, as it were.

"Speaking of special talents," he murmured out loud against the bandana in his mouth as he lifted his head with difficulty and looked over at Nikolaus's laptop. Did he have time before Nikolaus got back? After a split second of deliberation Remy decided that he did, and proceeded to neatly remove himself from Nikolaus's knots and leap across the room to sit down at the laptop, never even removing the gag.

When Nikolaus came back with two cups of coffee and a box of Krispy Kreme donuts Remy was once again lying face down on the bed with the knots retightened as they had been. He was mentally cursing himself for getting the left one too tight. His fucking fingers were going numb and there were sure to be bruises on his wrist.

"Well, it's about damn time," he mumbled into the bedspread through the gag.

Nikolaus wandered over and set his goodies down carefully onto the table before he reached down and undid the bandana.

"I'm hot, thirsty, and– ooh, are those donuts?" Remy asked as he craned his neck to see the table beside him.

Nikolaus grinned and nodded as he tapped the box. He then wandered over to throw the gag onto the chair in the corner and remove his coat.

"A little help?" Remy requested as he tapped his fingers against the mattress impatiently. Those donuts smelled too good to pass up.

XX.

"ONE more heavy sigh and I might start to get the wrong idea," Carl mumbled from Thiago's side. Thiago hadn't realized he had been sighing at all, and he glanced at Carl apologetically.

"Sorry. I just… I'm a bit worried."

Carl rolled over and rose up onto his elbow, looking down at Thiago. Thiago couldn't see his face, but he assumed the other man was frowning.

"You didn't expect to hear from them, did you?" Carl asked curiously.

"I suppose not. It's just… *mierda, no se*."

"Tell you who I'm worried about," Carl said as he readjusted his position carefully and rolled onto his stomach, propping himself up on both elbows now. "I'm thinking Shawn has probably killed our mad bomber in his sleep. That or they've both been blown up."

Thiago grinned and snickered at the thought of the trials and tribulations their two comrades were probably enduring.

"What else do you have on your mind?" Carl asked shrewdly.

"Am I that transparent?" Thiago asked sadly. "One more reason to get the fuck out of this business then," he said at Carl's responding nod.

"Out?" Carl questioned in surprise.

"Yeah. They offered you retirement too, right?" Thiago questioned. Carl nodded and made a sound of acknowledgement, and Thiago continued talking as his gaze focused on the tense muscle of Carl's bicep. "Well, I took it. So did Shawn, from what Remy said."

"So did Brandt," Carl offered as he looked at Thiago intently. Thiago's eyes shot to Carl's in surprise, but Carl was smiling softly. "As did Nikolaus… as did I. It's nothing to be ashamed of, Thi. When you have a chance to get out, no strings attached, then you fucking take it."

"Remy didn't take it," Thiago argued as his fingers reached to brush over the line of muscle he had fixated upon.

"Remy's still young. And a bit unusual."

"As is Brandt," Thiago argued with a smile.

"Brandt may be easily distracted, but he's not stupid. Nor is he mad. Not entirely. But Remy?" Carl mused. "I have my doubts as to how appropriate it would be to reinsert him into society."

"Yeah," Thiago murmured with a touch of melancholy. As his thoughts turned more and more morose, his hand traveled freely over the parts of Carl that he could easily reach; rubbing gently over the defined muscles of his chest before trailing down through the light fuzz to dip below the waistband of Carl's briefs and then travel slowly back up. "What's your take on the Archer?" Thiago finally asked quietly.

"That's a difficult question to answer while your hand is doing that," Carl purred contentedly before raising his head to stare at Thiago intently. Thiago grinned mischievously and cocked his eyebrow, waiting for a response. "I don't know, to be honest," Carl finally said as he shifted happily and placed his body over Thiago's in a gesture that was no longer unusual. "Part of me wonders what his agenda is," Carl said as he brushed Thiago's hair away from his eyes. "Why is he doing it? What profit can come from taking out other agents? Another part wonders if he's really the man behind the action, or if he's just the spearhead of a bigger organization. We don't even really know if the Archer is one man. He could be a group. Or it. It could be a group."

Thiago blinked up at Carl as his eyes unfocused slightly. Carl was right. There were so many questions they just didn't have the answers to.

"And the more I think on it the more I'm sure it wasn't the Archer who came after us," Carl continued. "I understand striking first, but if you strike you better damn well make sure you hit, y'know? I can't imagine that a man as shrewd as the Archer supposedly is would miss so badly. That bomb was in a place that was certain *not* to kill any of us unless we were in the toilet. What do you think about the whole thing?" Carl asked him as they stared at one another in the half-light.

Thiago blinked again. What should he say to this? The truth was Thiago had no idea what he should think. He had no idea who'd set the bomb. He had no idea whether the Organization had turned on them. He had no idea what the six of them should do regarding the Archer. He was more clueless now than he'd been since his very first day on the job, and the feeling was frustrating as hell. He was confused as fuck and he knew that Carl could tell as they gazed blankly at one another.

"I… I'm not sure," he admitted finally.

"If we find the Archer, what do you plan to do?" Carl asked hesitantly. Alarm bells began to sound softly in Thiago's mind. "Would you kill him and hope that the Organization keeps their deal, or would you want to join him like Remy does?"

The alarm bells were sounding so loudly now that Thiago could almost feel his nose vibrating. His nose itched, actually. He leaned upward and rubbed the end of it on the stubble of Carl's cheek, and felt the other man smile and laugh slightly.

"Is that another 'I don't know?'" Carl asked in amusement as he nuzzled against Thiago's face.

"*Sí.* I mean…" Thiago let his head fall back against the pillow. "Right now? We have nothing to go on. *En bolas*. But so far as I can see, if we can make the Archer believe that we're on his side, he poses less danger than the Organization. If they think we've turned, they'll do anything in their power to be rid of us."

Carl was nodding solemnly.

"You make good sense there, Zed," he said with an easy smile. Thiago snorted. Where the nickname had come from, he didn't know. It was something akin to Carl calling Brandt Wally. Thiago assumed it was a cultural thing.

"Why don't you quit talking and give my poor, old, troubled mind something else to ponder?" Thiago challenged as he shifted under Carl's body. "Is that a gun in your briefs?" he asked incredulously. Carl grinned broadly.

"Yeah. Sorry 'bout that," he said as Thiago reached into his briefs and retrieved the little handgun. "Habit."

"You know, I've never actually been able to use that line," Thiago mused to himself as he examined the gun. Carl took it gently from Thiago's hand and laid it on the table beside the bed.

"You would do better to play with the other one," Carl suggested cheekily.

"I can't believe you sleep with a gun in your briefs," Thiago responded, staring at the piece as if it might get up and start dancing a tango. "Have you always done that?"

"Usually."

"I mean, every night we've been together? You've had a gun in your fucking underwear?" Thiago asked, his voice getting slightly higher when he thought about the amount of damage *that* misfire could cause.

"Not until we got to L.A.," Carl answered defensively. "Something about this place gives me the colly wobbles."

"The what?"

"Makes me nervous."

"It's probably the gun being held to your dick!"

"I keep it at my hip," Carl responded with a little laugh of amusement. It seemed to Thiago that Carl couldn't quite understand why he was upset. Carl was crazy as fuck, too!

"Jesus!"

"Are you going to keep bitching?"

"Are you carrying any other weaponry I should know about?" Thiago asked, half in amusement. Carl laughed and kissed him affectionately. Thiago closed his eyes and murmured in pleasure as Carl placed soft kisses at the side of his mouth and along his jaw line, and all the way down his neck. "Is it loaded?" Thiago asked curiously as he enjoyed the soft nibbling and kisses that were now at his collar bone.

"Depends on which one you're talking about," Carl murmured happily before grinding his erection against Thiago's hipbone.

It had amazed Thiago their first time together, how gentle Carl was. After sitting through hearing Brandt make Carl scream like he had, Thiago had been almost reluctant to get into it. But Thiago had very little resistance when it came to such matters, and he'd been pleasantly surprised.

Thiago did not often wander far from the duties of being a top, and when he had in the past it had been with fairly brutal men who he'd ended up having to kill, so to find a man as deadly as Carl and feel nothing but pleasure when he was with him was indeed a treat.

Thiago wasn't a particularly proud man either. He had the unusual and amazing ability to admit when he was wrong, ask for help, and beg another man to fuck him if he thought it would make it happen sooner. He trusted Carl, with both his safety and his pleasure, and he also knew that the needy sounds he tended to make turned the younger man on. He had no problem with begging Carl to fuck him.

Carl reached up and pinned his wrists to the bed, his grip so hard that Thiago knew there would be bruises there in the morning. Thiago, though, didn't really care.

XXI.

THE Archer was completely and utterly confused. He'd become severely attached to the man with whom he'd spent the last three months, and just the thought of the other four in danger now made his skin crawl.

He had a new problem. He not only had to get the other five to join him, but he had to get them out of the game and as far away from danger as he could. All of them.

Even if he couldn't turn them in the end, he knew now that he wouldn't be able to kill them. If it ended up costing him his own life, then so be it. The battle would go on with or without him. Without him, though, his side didn't have a chance at victory.

Was victory worth the lost lives?

He reached through the darkness and gripped the other man's hand tightly. He looked down at their joined hands and could see the bruises from their earlier escapades on the pale wrist even in the moonlight coming through the sheer drapes. He closed his eyes and sighed heavily.

Would he still feel the burn for that all-important triumph if the man beside him ended up dying because of it?

The Archer really didn't think so.

XXII.

CARL shot out of bed and immediately reached for the gun at his hip, but the gun wasn't there and he stood staring wide-eyed at Thiago as the other man knelt at the opposite side of the bed in a defensive position.

"What wassat?" Carl demanded, his mind slowly clearing of the fog of sleep and finally registering the high-pitched droning sound that woke them.

"*¿Teléfono?*" Thiago suggested hoarsely as he hurried to his bag and began rummaging through it in search of the prepaid mobile phone Shawn had bought them. "*¿Hola?*" he answered in a shocked voice as soon as he found the thing. Carl had discovered very early on that Thiago only spoke English after a certain hour in the morning. It made mornings interesting since the closest thing Carl knew to Spanish was Croatian.

Carl walked up to stand beside him and watched him intently, waiting for any sign that something had gone wrong. There was a very specific time that Remy was supposed to contact them, and that wasn't for another four days. Hearing from any of the others before then meant something was wrong. Something couldn't be wrong.

'Please don't let something be wrong,' Carl pleaded mentally.

Thiago turned to look at Carl with a little frown on his face, and Carl raised his eyebrows inquiringly. After a few more seconds, Carl made an impatient noise in the back of his throat and Thiago nodded in understanding

"It's Remy," Thiago informed him finally as he listened to the voice on the line. "Hold on, I think there's a speaker phone option on this thing… Remy… Remy! *¡Parada*! *Jesus*," Thiago muttered as he studied the buttons. Finally, he found what he was looking for and Remy's irritated voice echoed hollowly through the speaker.

"I think the son of a bitch hung up on me," he was saying.

Carl grinned happily at hearing the younger man's voice, and at the fact that he was obviously talking to someone. That meant that Remy and Nikolaus were both intact, at least.

"Thiago?"

"Yeah, we're both here now, start over."

"Oh. *Bonjour*, Trigger!" Remy yelled happily into the phone.

"Hey there, Dixie. You two alright then?" Carl asked with an indulgent smile.

"Oh, we're just swell," came Nikolaus's sarcastic voice from somewhere in the background.

"Don't mind him, he just gets sort of queasy. Listen, we have some–"

"Queasy?" Carl echoed questioningly.

"*Oui*. He's not much for the blood. Listen, I realized this morning that these things have cameras in them and–"

"Remy?" Thiago interrupted haltingly, obviously wanting to know more about the blood and not really caring about Remy's morning realizations.

"I mean the phones. They have cameras in them," Remy explained distractedly, as if he hadn't understood Thiago's intentions. Carl shook his head and smirked at Remy's ability to do that so well. The younger man understood perfectly well, but only when it suited his purposes. "Niko's uncovered another message from the Archer, sent out some time about four months ago or thereabouts, and today's events made it pretty apparent that we needed to get it to you fast so–"

"Today's 'events?'" Thiago questioned again.

"He got shot!" came Nikolaus's distant shout. Remy hissed into the phone as if he were in pain.

"Would you watch what you're doing? No getting excited while playing with the needle, *s'il vous plaît*," Remy requested irritably. "Anyway, I wanted to let you know that we're sending pictures of these two messages, in case we hit another roadblock. Hey, can we send other stuff too?" he asked Nikolaus curiously.

Carl was beginning to feel like a parrot as he asked hoarsely, "Roadblock?"

"Look, we're a little short on time, so nix the questions and let me explain," Remy said, his tone suddenly completely different. He no longer sounded like the cheerful and slightly oblivious young man they had just been speaking with. His accent was almost completely gone, and he sounded like a hardened general giving orders to his troops. It was a disconcerting change, and Carl found himself battling with the sudden urge to salute the phone. "They've zeroed in on us somehow and they have us land locked. We're trying to slip through the net but so far we've not found a way. Now, we're going to send you photos of everything we've been able to extract from the Organization's files and then we're destroying this phone and we'll be on our way. If all goes well, we'll meet you in Sydney on the first of March at four pm. Repeating. Sydney, 1-3, 1600."

"Got it," Thiago and Carl chirped obediently

"*Bon.*"

There was a shuffling sound, and Carl assumed they were looking for something as they spoke quietly to one another.

"All right, *mes petits amoureux*," Remy said finally, his voice once again cheerful and untroubled. "Niko's going to get those pictures to you. How have you two been managing? Are you looking out for one another?"

"Smooth sailing," Thiago answered with a frown at Carl. "Remy? Are you really okay? How badly are you wounded?"

"Hmm? Oh, it's nothing serious. Some cowboy new recruit dickhead with terrible aim. It grazed my arm, nothing serious at all. Have you heard from Shawn and Brandt?"

"Not a word."

"No mushroom clouds in the desert or any such disasters?"

Carl smiled and laughed. "We did hear about a petrol station going up in flames down in... New Mexico was it? Arizona maybe? That was about a month ago."

Remy laughed joyously and Carl and Thiago both grinned at the sound. "That'll be them, I suppose. We spoke to them very briefly, sent them the same stuff for redundancies. Barely got time to ask how they were."

"Good idea," Thiago agreed softly.

"They said to tell you hello. You two look after each other," Remy responded sternly. "We'll see you in six day's time Down Under," he said with a perfect Australian accent. "Here's Nikolaus."

"Take care, Dixie," Carl murmured in parting, and he and Thiago just looked at one another and shook their heads. It was like being hit by a wave whenever you dealt with Remy, and Carl felt exhausted from it.

"Nikolaus?" Thiago asked after several seconds of silence.

"Yeah. Yeah, sorry, I was waiting until Remy closed the door to the toilet. Look gentlemen, we're in the shit out here, and Remy knows it. Instead of the phones I want you to get to a computer, can you do that?"

"Uhh... does it have to be secure?" Thiago asked tentatively.

"No. Just go out and buy a cheap laptop and find a hotel with a wireless internet system. That'll be enough. It's got to be a hotel, though, those at least have some security to them."

"Okay. Why did you have to wait 'til Remy left the room?" Carl asked suspiciously. When it came to the computers they were all light years behind Nikolaus, and it wasn't easy to delve blindly into something you didn't trust completely.

"Because he thinks he's shielding me from the fact that we're probably going to die. I'd like to keep his spirits up by playing into the illusion a little," Nikolaus said hastily. He sighed and suddenly Carl's throat tightened as he listened to Nikolaus's voice. "Remy's worn himself thin protecting me, so I'd like to repay him a bit. Now, here's what you're to do."

Carl grabbed the little pad of paper Thiago always seemed to have and began copying down Nikolaus's instructions, along with a web address that appeared to lead to a chat group of some sort.

"What is this?" Thiago asked as he watched over Carl's shoulder to make certain he got it right.

"If the Archer is communicating this way, we might as well do it too," Nikolaus explained. "The file you'll download will include scans of everything we've collected so far. One thing Remy didn't tell you though, and this is very important, is–"

"Niko!" Remy's distant voice called as a door banged shut. "We gotta move. *Now*!"

"What's going on, Niko?" Thiago asked as they both leant over the phone and listened intently.

"They've found us again," Remy's calm voice informed them as he apparently snatched the phone from Nikolaus's hand. "*Adios*, lads!"

The line went dead, and Carl and Thiago were left staring at the phone in numb horror. Finally Thiago walked back to the bed and sat down heavily.

"They'll be okay," he mumbled. Carl looked at him doubtfully and then back at the phone as if it would magically bring Remy and Nikolaus back to them if he glared at it hard enough.

To go all this time without a word, and then to finally hear from them only to have their brief time together cut short by a life-threatening situation was heartbreaking. To think that it could have been the last time they would hear the other men's voices made Carl's throat tighten miserably once more.

"They'll be okay. Remy knows what he's about. They've made it this far," Thiago murmured repeatedly, as if he were trying to convince himself. "Let's get to a computer store," Thiago finally suggested as he went about dressing himself.

An hour later, they were all set up and the file had finished downloading.

"They didn't leave many stones unturned, did they?" Thiago muttered as he clicked through the pages of scans.

Carl could see lists and lists of names, scans of notes and messages, and lists marking the suspected hits. He wondered when Nikolaus had done all this if he'd been trying to keep it from Remy, but there were too many questions raised to linger on that now.

"What's that one?" he asked, pointing to an unusually colored scan at the side of the screen as he leant over Thiago's shoulder. Thiago brought it up and they peered at it curiously.

"Is that Remy's note?" Thiago asked in amusement. "From the cabin?"

"Is that blood?" Carl asked, zeroing in on the more important aspects.

"Hmm. Wait there's another," Thiago mumbled in a troubled voice. He clicked on it and looked it over. "Looks like the back of the first one."

Carl nodded. There were so many notes and doodles jotted down that there was no making sense of any of it.

"Their notes are almost as hard to figure out as the original message!" Thiago grumbled.

"They said there was another one? A new message?" Carl asked as he bent over and settled his chin on Thiago's shoulder.

"Yeah," Thiago said as he found the right file and brought it up as well.

It was nothing but another note just like the original, full of jumbled letters and numbers.

"That's not much help," Carl mumbled, causing Thiago to shiver involuntarily. "Sorry."

"Niko must not have had time to leave any notes to explain or anything for us," Thiago mumbled. "This doesn't really get us anywhere without someone to explain it all, does it?" Thiago asked irritably as he slumped back in the chair and rubbed his face in a tired manner.

Carl wasn't as ready to write all this off just yet, but in the end they still hadn't answered the biggest question, the one they had to answer before they could go any further. Were they after the Archer or was the Archer after them?

'Who else is after us?' Carl wondered idly as he stared at the screen.

XXIII.

REMY had called them earlier, and the brief conversation Shawn had with the younger man had been nearly enough to satisfy him as to their relative safety. They were apparently having a time of it, but Shawn wasn't too worried about them after receiving repeated assurances from Remy. The other man knew his way around a net, and besides, if Shawn continued to worry over them he would probably end up killing Brandt just to relieve the tension.

"Next time you tell me a direction, I will gladly go that way if you'll just shut your trap!" Shawn shouted in exasperation as the newly purchased computer whirred away happily on the end of the bed.

Brandt stopped in mid-pace and turned to look at Shawn with an amused smile.

"Not right now," Shawn said before Brandt could even suggest the one activity that was always at the forefront of his mind– aside from destruction and mayhem. Brandt huffed and threw himself onto the bed beside Shawn to peer at the computer screen. "Have some sort of brilliant epiphany when we get these files and I'll fuck you from here to Sunday," Shawn promised as Brandt's body bounced them both on the springy mattress.

"Are we sure this is safe?" Brandt murmured as Shawn followed the directions Nikolaus had hastily relayed as Remy had been in the bathroom tearing his shirt into strips for a bandage.

When Remy told them he'd been shot Shawn's stomach had flipped uncomfortably, but he seemed in good spirits so Shawn let it pass. What Brandt was talking about was the computer itself. Nikolaus's reasons for secrecy had been enough for Shawn, though. Besides, as soon as they had all they needed the laptop would be staying behind at the hotel in a little puff of destroyed metal anyway, so they had little to worry about as far as being tracked went. Shawn nodded and let his free hand rest on Brandt's head as he typed with the other.

As the download started, Shawn looked down at Brandt affectionately. His finger twined around one long curl, and he idly wondered if any of the others had disregarded such trivial things as haircuts and razors like they had. He rather liked Brandt a little scruffy.

The big Australian had surprised him in more ways than one in the last three or so months. The man was shrewd and cunning, and he was deadly fast. Not to mention that the madness wasn't a cover so much as a reality. But he was also affectionate and caring, and extremely protective. Yes, they had their encounters where Brandt merely wanted to be fucked into next week, but there were also times when Brandt would simply hold Shawn at night and offer his silent reassurance, or brush his fingers along the side of Shawn's face and instigate a sweet, undemanding kiss.

"He'll be okay," Brandt assured him quietly as he let his head rest on Shawn's thigh like a dog with his master. Shawn petted him slowly before sliding his hand down Brandt's back and then back up under his fleece pullover to caress his skin lightly. Brandt sighed contentedly.

"Actually, it wasn't Remy that I was thinking of," Shawn murmured as his eyes flicked toward the screen to check the progress of the download. Brandt rose up and Shawn let the motion force his hand back down to rest on Brandt's hip.

"Oh?" Brandt asked curiously. "What's on your mind then, Beignet?"

Shawn stared at him for long seconds, drinking in the deep brown eyes that looked so similar to another pair he knew, and yet at the same time were so completely different. The nickname coming from Brandt's lips had that same quality; familiar and yet different. Tender when it should have been mocking and sensual when it should have been friendly. It was intoxicating, and even though Shawn could feel the guilt wash over him as he thought about Remy, Shawn couldn't help what he was thinking.

"You," Shawn finally answered softly.

Brandt cocked his head curiously, and Shawn leant forward to brush his lips gently over the other man's. Brandt remained stock still, but Shawn could feel his breath coming in short, quick gasps, and he pressed forward, letting the kiss progress slowly. Brandt's breath caught in his throat and his hand tightened over Shawn's hand that was gripping his hip.

This was not an undemanding kiss. Something about this one was different, and Shawn knew that Brandt could feel that too. He was the most perceptive individual Shawn had ever come across. That included Remy and his uncanny abilities, and Shawn was constantly amazed by what Brandt noticed. It would take little effort for Brandt to recognize the need behind this particular kiss.

The computer whirred away as Brandt got to his knees and cupped Shawn's face gently. They sat there almost motionless and simply kissed, tongues and lips moving gently together as their hands gripped at one another possessively. When the computer beeped at them to signify that the download was finished, they parted reluctantly and sat with their noses pressed together, breathing unevenly. Shawn's stomach was doing somersaults and he wasn't exactly sure why. It wasn't like this was their first kiss. Far from it.

It was almost like the feeling he got right before a mission. One of impending danger.

XXIV.

"TECHNICAL difficulties?" Nikolaus practically screamed as they skidded to a halt and Remy looked around the abandoned construction site wildly before calming himself and glancing at Nikolaus.

"Well," Remy huffed, slightly out of breath from the running they'd been doing for the past fifteen minutes. "What would you like me to say?" He turned to look at Nikolaus pointedly once more and then scanned behind them as Nikolaus caught his breath. "You would rather I run around waving my hands in the air and screaming 'we're all gonna die?' I'd much rather think of it as a… nuisance than a–"

The silenced pop of the shot kicked up the dirt at their feet and they immediately divided before veering off to the left together, like a flock of birds evading a predator.

"Niko! This way!" Remy called as he dove behind one of the large drainage pipes that littered the deserted construction site. Nikolaus scuttled across the gravel and slid to a stop beside Remy, resting his back against the concrete tube and reloading his gun.

"Is it McTiernan?" Nikolaus asked breathlessly.

"I can't tell. I don't think so. He likes to play with his prey a little more. He has more… finesse, you might say."

Another shot clanked against the concrete and Remy and Nikolaus covered their heads protectively with their hands as they ducked and huddled together.

"Come out, lads!" the authoritative voice rang out and echoed off the framework of the unfinished houses around them.

"It's McTiernan," Remy said, his voice cracking slightly.

"Finesse, huh?" Nikolaus panted.

"We don't want to hurt you!" McTiernan's voice asserted through the dark night. "We know what's happened. We simply need you to come Home. We'll straighten this out in no time!"

"They said McTiernan was dead. Why isn't he dead?" Nikolaus yelled in a near panic as the concrete splattered around them from another well-placed shot. It didn't seem that the shots were aimed at them. Simply near them.

"Two things," Remy said calmly as he dug in his little bag of supplies. "One; he was tagged intentionally as a backup, in case we weren't killed. If I had known he was still out there, I would have been a fuck of a lot more cautious. If that's true, then he's lying and they're trying to kill us." Another shot punctuated his point and he continued to dig. "Two; he's turned and is now working for God knows who. We don't know how many people are after us now, Niko. And if *that's* true, then he's lying and he's trying to kill us," Remy concluded as he looked into Nikolaus's eyes briefly before continuing his quest for whatever the fuck it was.

Nikolaus was terrified to see a spark of fear in Remy's eyes.

"We won't make it, will we?" Nikolaus asked resignedly as another shot hit just above their heads.

"No," Remy responded curtly. "*We* won't." He looked up into Nikolaus's eyes once more and smiled sadly as his hand pulled out of the bag. Nikolaus's eyes widened as he saw the grenade. "We won't make it, but you will," Remy said assuredly.

"Remy, what–"

"Listen. See that irrigation ditch there?" Nikolaus followed Remy's eyes discreetly in case they could be seen. Remy pointed to a building in the distance, in the opposite direction of the ditch for the same purpose. "There's a pipe that you should be able to get through. You have to move fast, Niko. I won't be able to hold them off for long."

"But–"

"When I say go, Niko, if your ass isn't tearing it across that pavement I'll kill you myself, I swear to God," Remy growled as his gun came to rest against Nikolaus's nose. Nikolaus's eyes crossed as he looked down the barrel, but then he looked back up at Remy and saw the fear there once more.

"Remy, I can't just–"

The gun cocked, and Remy's jaw tightened. Nikolaus nodded and licked his lips nervously. Another shot hit, much closer this time. It seemed that negotiations were over.

"Now, when you get free, you go under and you stay under, you hear me? You stay so far under you be eating worms for breakfast. You know what to do. Get to Sydney, then get the others and get them the hell away."

"But what if–"

"No ifs. Don't wait for me past 1600. If I ain't there by then I ain't coming. You got to get them away. Do *not* let Shawn wait for me."

Nikolaus nodded and swallowed hard. His blood raced through his body at warp speed, and he felt the pounding of adrenaline as he got to his knees and knelt low. Remy hunkered down behind the concrete, his gun now on the ground beside him and the grenade clutched in his hand. Remy's free hand came up to grip the font of Nikolaus's shirt, and he pulled him down for one last, violent kiss.

"Make sure I can't find you, Niko," Remy hissed as their lips parted. Nikolaus didn't understand. He was about to question the order when Remy looked at him angrily. "Take them somewhere else," he said through gritted teeth. "Make sure I can't ever find you!" he growled emphatically. He pushed him away and yelled, "Run!"

Nikolaus saw Remy lunge to his feet behind the concrete tube as he took off, and moments later Remy shouted a mocking challenge and the blast of the grenade whooshed past Nikolaus's body as he slid safely into the ditch. The pipe was there, but he couldn't bear to crawl into it. Not yet.

He turned to look for the familiar slim figure, and was just in time to see four men overpower Remy and take him down to the ground. Nikolaus managed to remain down and out of sight as a tall figure in a gray overcoat and hat walked up to Remy's struggling body and looked down at him impassively. He stood there, seemingly talking, for several moments, and Nikolaus heard Remy shout several creative obscenities in his colorful native language.

The move was so smooth that Nikolaus barely registered the gun being drawn from beneath McTiernan's overcoat, and when it popped quietly in the silence and Remy's body jumped from the impact, Nikolaus ripped his gaze away from the scene and scurried into the pipe. Tears stung his eyes as the image replayed as if on a loop in his mind.

Now Nikolaus understood Remy's words. Go where Remy couldn't find him. Go where Remy wouldn't be able to give them away once he awoke from the tranquillizer and they began to torture him.

Remy was as good as dead, but the other four could still be saved. And so, Nikolaus pushed on into the night.

XXV.

BRANDT wasn't certain what was going on in his head. He knew he wasn't in love, not in the traditional sense, but he didn't know what the feeling was that he was struggling with. Was it a sense of safety? Was it trust? Was it loyalty? Brandt had rarely experienced these feelings, and perhaps the combination of them all was wreaking havoc on his mind.

All Brandt knew was that since the afternoon Shawn had kissed him in so loving a manner he hadn't felt one single urge to light something on fire. Not one. It was frightening, and Brandt felt just a tad lost because of it.

"Shall we continue on tonight, do you think?" Shawn asked as they walked through the airport terminal in Los Angeles. They had flown in from Cincinnati, Ohio, and now they had the choice of purchasing a plane ticket to Sydney and going on that night or bedding down for the night in Los Angeles and continuing on the next day.

"We risk being late if we stop," Brandt pointed out as they stopped walking at the same time and turned to look at one another blankly. The fatigue was taking over now, and their brains were taking longer and longer to process information.

"Sydney then?" Shawn asked finally.

"I suppose, yeah," Brandt responded as he hitched his bag higher onto his shoulder. He felt naked without his gear. They had stashed every bit of their equipment before leaving Cincinnati, and they now each traveled with only a fake Air Marshall's badge and a handgun each.

Brandt missed his grenades.

They stared at one another for another brief moment as the exhaustion of travel caught up with them, and then simultaneously turned around the way they had come and headed for one of the Qantas desks to purchase tickets.

They had just enough time to get something to eat and have a couple lagers, and then they were on their way once more.

It was a long flight. Very long. Brandt's legs were killing him by the time they landed in Sydney. As was his ass, which was still a bit sore. Not that he was complaining about that, mind.

"You okay?" Shawn murmured in his ear as the plane taxied across the runway. Brandt nodded and turned his head slightly to the side to give Shawn's fuzzy chin a nip before settling his head back on Shawn's shoulder in order to close his eyes and rest. Shawn bounced his shoulder slightly to get Brandt's attention. "Hey, what's wrong?"

"Hmm? Nothing," Brandt responded flatly, knowing that it didn't sound convincing but hoping that Shawn was just as tired as he was and wouldn't notice

"You look a little ill. When we get on the ground, I promise you can light something," Shawn murmured with a smile. "As long as I'm not wearing it, that is," he added hastily.

Brandt rewarded his efforts with a little half-smile, but even the prospect of destruction didn't completely lift Brandt's spirits.

What was wrong with him?

He wasn't the type to sulk.

He usually killed the type that sulked.

Shawn wasn't exactly bright-eyed and bushy-tailed, either. Maybe a good night's sleep would do them both a load of good. Then again, if Brandt were completely honest with himself, he did have a vague idea of what his problem was. He'd seen the way Shawn's eyes lit up when Remy phoned them. He'd seen Shawn worry over the other man almost constantly for three months, and even though the kiss they'd shared had definitely signified something of import, Brandt knew it couldn't contest with what Shawn and Remy had.

"Brandt?" Shawn ventured in concern.

"I dunno really," Brandt answered miserably as he sat up straight and looked intently at his hands. "I think… I think maybe…." He looked around the cabin of the plane desperately, as if he could find some method of escape. "Never mind," he amended finally, hoping Shawn would just disregard what he'd started to say.

"What?" Shawn pressed as he leaned forward and turned in his seat, trying to make eye contact. He looked worried and he sounded… suspicious? Yes. Suspicious. Brandt decided perhaps this wasn't the time to be reticent with sharing his feelings, considering how wary they'd all been of one another at first. He looked up at Shawn apologetically.

"I'll miss you, I think," he admitted with a shrug.

"Miss me?" Shawn repeated with a little smile. "Where am I going then? You're not planning on killing me, are you?" Shawn asked with mock panic, his hand gripping Brandt's elbow playfully.

"You're going back to him," Brandt said quietly, lowering his voice in the hopes Shawn wouldn't really hear him. He knew he sounded pathetic. Clingy and over-dependent and just pathetic.

He wasn't the clingy, dependant, pathetic type.

He usually killed the clingy, dependant, pathetic types.

Shawn was apparently dumbstruck. He simply sat and stared at Brandt for what seemed like hours, his fingers still gripping Brandt's arm and his lips slightly parted as if he were about to speak. They sat there locked on each other as the fasten seatbelt light turned off and the other passengers began to mill about and retrieve their bags. They sat there frozen, mesmerized by one another as people filed past them.

Finally, after the stragglers had scooted past, Shawn leant toward him and kissed him gently.

Again, the sparks flew through Brandt's body as Shawn's lips touched his own. His entire body flushed with that strange cold heat that it seemed only Shawn could produce. He parted his lips, willing Shawn to deepen the ill-advised kiss, and Shawn did. He shifted over in his seat and Brandt did the same until their upper bodies touched, and Shawn could better access every surface of Brandt's lips, tongue and teeth.

It was a slow, passionate kiss, and Brandt savored the taste of the other man as they traded off control of the kiss.

When they separated, Brandt found that he was having trouble breathing, and the only thing he could clearly think was that he wanted more. So very much more.

But what was Shawn doing? Brandt didn't like being played any more than the next man, and while he was all for the occasional off-duty fuck, that wasn't what this felt like.

"What… is… I…." Brandt couldn't finish any of the questions he wanted to ask, but Shawn apparently knew what he was trying to express.

"I don't know," Shawn murmured as his eyes flickered toward the queue of people exiting the plane. "I don't know what we're doing," he admitted softly as his startling green eyes turned back to look into Brandt's.

"And Remy," Brandt whispered breathlessly, not certain whether it was a question, an accusation, or simply a statement, and not certain what the point of saying it was.

"I know. I… I just don't know what…," Shawn said, his voice lowering with every word until he tapered off with a frustrated sigh. Brandt wasn't sure why, but Shawn's obvious confusion made him feel better about his own. Brandt couldn't help himself. He pulled Shawn's face towards him once more and kissed him passionately, heedless of the few passengers still awaiting their turns to disembark.

"We'll figure it out together then," Brandt murmured against Shawn's lips. "We'd best go now, though."

Shawn nodded and they gathered their few belongings and made their way down the aisle to the exit, their fingers brushing inconspicuously as they moved one after the other.

Brandt was intrigued by Shawn and Remy's relationship, but he'd never imagined he would somehow be inserted into it. How was this going to work? Brandt wasn't a particularly possessive person; he didn't mind sharing the few things in life that he cared about.

He wondered idly if Remy would share just as easily.

Brandt knew one thing for certain, though; he certainly couldn't see how he would manage going back to being solo after this experience.

A soft call from behind them startled Brandt out of his musings, and he whirled around in alarm. Shawn turned slowly, his face a study of impassivity.

"Trigger!" Brandt exclaimed happily.

Without even thinking, Brandt walked the few steps down the aisle and drew Carl and Thiago into his arms, actually lifting Thiago off his feet in the process. Thiago and Carl laughed happily and returned his embrace as best they could in the narrow aisle.

"Lads."

They all turned, grinning, to look at Shawn, who stood at the entrance grinning back at them. He nodded his head and they all followed him obediently, chittering excitedly about their unexpected reunion like school children on an outing.

Brandt hadn't realized just how much he had missed the other two men, and he kept an arm around both of them just to make sure they didn't disappear on him as they walked through the airport terminal. They had roughly twelve hours before they were to rendezvous with the other two, and they all seemed to be in agreement that the best thing to do would be to get a hotel room and some much needed rest.

"I can't believe we were on the same flight all that time," Carl said he inserted his card key into the door of one of the two rooms they had paid for. "Were you the ones making all that racket in the loo?"

"Not us," Shawn laughed. "Imagine trying to move about with the two of us in there," he said, indicating Brandt and himself with a flick of his wrist as he unlocked the other room.

"True that," Carl said in amusement. He turned to Brandt with a spark in his dark hazel eyes and winked. Brandt grinned happily, his previous mental ramblings all but forgotten as he reveled in the company of the only men in the world he really considered his friends.

Yes, life was good.

The next day, they arrived at the airport roughly an hour before they were supposed to meet the others, and Brandt immediately began scanning the busy terminal. His height gave him a bit of an advantage in that area, and he listened half-heartedly to the light conversation of the others as he concentrated on trying to spot the two familiar forms. He zeroed back in when Thiago's voice pinged one of Brandt's internal alarms.

"Speaking of, what's the time?" Thiago asked in concern. It was then and only then that Brandt's elation over being reunited began to ebb and the prickling of foreboding began to attack the back of his neck.

"They are a bit tardy, aren't they?" Shawn mumbled as he looked at his watch. "They have thirty minutes, though. Remy's nothing if not punctual. He said 1600, he meant 1600."

As soon as Shawn said it, Brandt caught sight of Nikolaus walking slowly through the terminal, looking just a bit lost.

"There they are," Brandt said happily. He strolled through the little pub and out into the main terminal, the others trailing behind him, and as Nikolaus turned to look at him in surprise he simply picked the smaller man up and squeezed him as hard as he could. "Gizmo!" he beamed in greeting.

As the others came up to join them, they each took their turn in picking up the unfortunate little German and hugging him. All the while Nikolaus was trying desperately to speak.

"Where's Remy?" Shawn asked with a grin once he had set Nikolaus down. "You didn't walk past food, did you? That snags him every time. If he catches sight of a Tim Tam he's done for."

They laughed happily and waited for Nikolaus's answer, but as soon as they actually looked at the younger man, it was obvious that something had gone wrong. He could barely look Shawn in the eye, and he was looking at the rest of them pleadingly, as if he wanted them to be able to read his mind and save him from having to say the words.

"*Dios mio*," Thiago breathed quietly.

"He's gone," Nikolaus told them brokenly. "They got him," he said after taking a deep breath.

"Who? What do you mean 'got him'?" Shawn asked urgently, and Brandt placed a steadying hand on the older man's shoulder.

"It was McTiernan."

"Oh, God," Carl murmured.

"Fuck," Brandt said simply, watching the pain seep into Shawn's features and struggling to keep from shouting out in frustration. They had lost one of their own. Carl looked just as heartbroken as Brandt was suddenly feeling, and Thiago stood with a stony expression as his jaw clenched repeatedly.

"When?" Shawn asked with difficulty.

"Four days ago. We were in Missouri. It was McTiernan," Nikolaus repeated miserably.

"Is he– did you see it?"

"They took him alive," Nikolaus said as Brandt pulled him close and hugged him comfortingly. Nikolaus buried his face against Brandt's chest and Shawn stared at him disbelievingly.

"We have twenty-four minutes," Carl pointed out hopefully. "He could have escaped."

Thiago was nodding in agreement, and Brandt looked to Shawn hopefully.

"We'll wait 'til four," Shawn ordered in a hoarse voice. "If he's not here by then, he's not coming."

They returned to their table, and Brandt kept a comforting hand on Shawn's back as they all stared morosely at the tabletop. Nikolaus told them about how McTiernan chased he and Remy and finally cornered them, and how Remy sacrificed himself to send Nikolaus on his way.

"Stupid bastard," Thiago murmured as he rubbed his eyes slowly.

Four o'clock came all too quickly, and with it, Shawn's broken voice speaking with an eerie finality.

"He's not coming."

PART THREE: THE CAJUN HOUDINI

I.

REMY came to consciousness slowly, his world spinning in a most sickening manner as the effects of the tranquillizer wore off. He took in his surroundings with chagrin, not quite believing that he'd managed to get himself captured. Well, he'd been captured before, actually, but never quite so easily.

He was slipping. He briefly wondered how Nikolaus had fared and shook his head to clear it. He instantly regretted the action. Pain lanced through his eyes and the back of his head and he immediately went limp, trying to slow the pounding flow of blood through his aching brain.

He cleared his parched throat and fought through the pounding headache to peer out at the sterile white room around him.

"The headache is the worst part, no?" came the familiar voice from somewhere behind him. Remy acknowledged Sir John McTiernan's presence with a slight cock of his head and a long-suffering sigh. "It feels as if your head is twisting off and trying to float into outer space, does it not?"

"I can't imagine how you would know," Remy responded dryly. He cleared his throat again and squeezed his eyes closed, fighting back the rising nausea.

"Oh, even the best of us get caught here and there," McTiernan said cheerfully as the clicks of his shiny black shoes echoed off the plain white walls. Remy opened his eyes as McTiernan came into his line of vision, and he looked up at him blankly. "The best of us, however, manage to escape once more."

"I see. Should I be taking notes?" Remy asked innocently. McTiernan smiled indulgently and shook his head.

"I've seen your work, my boy. You should be writing the book, it would seem."

"Oh," Remy responded as his brain finally caught up with his situation. He knew what he should be doing. He should be milking McTiernan for information even as McTiernan tried to do the same to him. He should stick around until the very last possible moment and gather as much information as he could, and only then should he be thinking of escape. But Remy was terrified, and all he wanted to do was get the fuck away. He had seen McTiernan's work, too, and he certainly didn't want to end up like that.

"You still have a chance to make the right choice, Remy. That's why you're still tied to that chair, you see, instead of hanging from the ceiling," McTiernan informed him as he gestured grandly to the corner of the otherwise bare room, to a complex system of chains and pulleys that made Remy shiver involuntarily. McTiernan was telling him to choose between the Organization and death, apparently. Remy's mind raced trying to consider how to deal with that.

"*This* is your way of offering an olive branch?" Remy asked acidly as he shrugged his shoulders to indicate the ropes, opting for a delaying tactic. McTiernan shrugged noncommittally.

"I enjoy tying young things like you up and watching them squirm," he drawled. "What can I say?"

Remy looked away, choosing to ignore the comment. If he had to use that as a last resort then he certainly would, but his options were still rather numerous.

"You were marked as dead," he accused bitterly,

"Yes, I was," McTiernan said indulgently as he pulled a metal chair in front of Remy and sat down. "What do you make of that, by the way?"

Remy was a bit thrown off by the question. What did he make of it?

"Well, I would beg to differ, as it were," Remy finally responded in an eerily accurate mimicry of McTiernan. This earned a joyous, resonating laugh from his interrogator. At least one of them was enjoying the ordeal.

"Yes, yes, it would seem that I'm not quite as dead as all that after all, wouldn't it?"

"The Organization marked you to throw us off, didn't they," Remy asserted softly. He was grasping at straws, hoping to throw McTiernan off by either hitting the mark or being so completely off that the man would think he'd finally lost it.

His only reaction was an elegantly arched eyebrow.

"I've extended the one and only offer the Organization is willing to give you," McTiernan told him with a smile. "Go back, make amends for the error of your ways, and continue to help find the Archer."

"Or?"

"Or die. Quickly, of course. No torture involved. A nice, honorable warrior's death," McTiernan answered dramatically, a trace of irony lingering in his last words.

"Screw that," Remy murmured, earning another laugh. "You said this was the Organization's last offer. Who else are you speaking for, John?"

"No wonder Shawn enjoyed your presence so," McTiernan said with a fond smile. "You were always so blunt. Pardon me a moment, won't you?"

With that, McTiernan rose and went to the door, pressing a button on what appeared to be an intercom. Remy tensed as the two rent-a-goons from the airport came through the door and glared at him, waiting for McTiernan to give them orders.

"These are my associates," McTiernan said as he walked up to stand in front of Remy. "No need to know their names. You remember them from Atlanta, I should think?" He paused to give Remy a chance to answer, but Remy merely stared at him and so he went on. "They are fresh from the recruiting ranks of the Organization and are so very eager to please."

Remy watched McTiernan with a slight scowl. He wasn't sure what the older man was getting at, but he was pretty sure it wasn't going to be fun.

"They have been chasing you and your young friend over half of the continent for me," McTiernan continued. With that, McTiernan pulled a silenced gun from beneath his ever-present gray coat and aimed it at Remy. Remy looked down the barrel, knowing that these were his last moments and struggling to go out with some form of dignity. In one swift movement, McTiernan turned and put a bullet into the forehead of each of the other two men.

Remy gaped at him.

"How's that, dear boy? Better?" McTiernan queried in a friendly manner. Remy continued to gape. "Before you ask; no, I'm not the Archer," McTiernan continued with a swipe of his hand as he sat once more. He sat with his legs crossed like a gentleman, the gun sitting atop his knee as he rested his other elbow on the back of the chair. Remy blinked at him. "And no, I don't know who the Archer is. I've never met him and so I assume, since I am essentially his right hand, that he is someone I know," John asserted with a narrowed gaze at Remy.

It took several seconds for Remy's mind to catch up to the logic, but when it did, the alarms began to clang around in his head and his eyes widened theatrically.

"You think *I'm* the Archer?" he asked, his voice a bit higher than he would have liked it to be.

"Possibly," McTiernan answered enigmatically, his voice the epitome of nonchalance. "That's the only reason I can see for him to keep his identity from me, you see. If I know him. And there aren't many agents whom I have contact with these days."

"You can't believe– Shawn is no traitor!" Remy shouted heatedly.

"Ah. He may not be, but you wouldn't defend a dead man so passionately, now would you?"

Fuck.

Remy snapped his mouth closed and clenched his jaw in agitation. McTiernan smiled contentedly.

"That's a relief, at least. I can't tell you how saddened I was when you told me he had been killed."

Remy couldn't be certain, but he was pretty sure McTiernan was being sincere, at least in this respect.

"So you're working for the Archer then," Remy murmured as he tried to think his way out of this mess. Being nabbed by the Organization was one thing; you could plead your case and probably be forgiven and reinstated. But being taken by the Archer's man? By Sir John McTiernan, no less! This was beyond bad.

McTiernan stared back at him, apparently content to let Remy formulate in peace. Remy worked at the bonds on his wrists discreetly, careful not to let his muscles tense and give him away.

"I don't believe Shawn is the Archer," McTiernan offered finally, almost as if he were speaking to himself. "He's much too loyal. Sometimes to the wrong people, yes?" McTiernan added with a pointed stare at Remy. Remy ceased his motions and glared back at him. His heart jumped into his throat, and his stomach roiled uncomfortably. He tried to tell himself that it was just the after-effects of the drugs, but he knew what it was. It was guilt.

"I couldn't possibly know what you mean," Remy croaked finally.

"Don't you?" McTiernan asked in amusement. "The two of you were fairly exclusive, were you not? It doesn't do to hold to secrets, my boy."

"What are you now, an expert on trust?" Remy snapped. "Fucking spook," he muttered in annoyance. "Secrets are our lives, John! You know that!"

"Ah, but do you?"

"What the fuck?" Remy sighed, finally admitting that he couldn't keep up with McTiernan's mind to save his life, which was probably exactly what was required to manage that particular feat.

"Don't lose hope," John encouraged in amusement. "We were doing so well! Don't think I don't know what you and your friend have been up to." Remy stared at John impassively, praying he wouldn't show any signs of the surprise he felt. There were so many things McTiernan could be referring to now. "That's right. It doesn't take a fool to know that you've been less than loyal of late," McTiernan said with a sparkle in his clear blue eyes.

"I wouldn't betray Shawn. Ever."

"I'm not so sure about that, Remy," McTiernan tutted.

Remy lowered his head and thought of Shawn desperately, flooding with guilt. His body flushed with shame, and he looked back up at McTiernan pleadingly. He could take physical torture. He could take any kind of mental games McTiernan wanted to throw at him. But not this. Anything but this.

"What does the Archer want?" Remy demanded weakly, finally losing patience with the mind games and hoping to draw McTiernan out into a monologue. If he could distract him long enough to free himself, he would have a chance.

"You."

"What?" Remy asked in surprise, his discreet motions stopping as he stared at the other man.

"Well, that isn't his ultimate goal, of course, lovely as you may be, but he needs you and your five companions in order to accomplish his goals."

"Uh huh," Remy responded disinterestedly as he recommenced his efforts.

"You don't believe me?" McTiernan asked in a mockingly hurt voice. "I swear it's the truth," he said in the same tone, even going so far as to hold his hand up solemnly and place his gun over his heart. "You seem the type to appreciate honesty, even if you don't always practice it, and so I'm being honest."

"I need water," Remy asserted miserably, his head pounding as he tried to figure out McTiernan's game.

"Poor lad," McTiernan murmured with a sympathetic purse of his lips. "Make your choice, Remy. Then we'll see about water."

"What are my options again?" Remy inquired as his head began to spin.

"Let me fill you in on some facts you may be missing," McTiernan growled as he stood suddenly and bent over Remy's sitting form. "There are two forces in play; one wants you dead, the other couldn't have cared less about you until you stepped in his path. Now whose shoes have you been treading upon?"

"Yours, apparently."

"No no, dear boy. I much enjoyed the chase. You stepped into the Archer's path," McTiernan told him with what seemed like pleasure. "And far from wanting to kill you, it seems that you've rather endeared yourself to him. He doesn't want to see you dead. Will you join us? I can assure you the benefits are an improvement from those you've been enjoying."

Remy stared into McTiernan's icy blue eyes, and for the first time he actually thought about what John was offering. The Archer wanted to help them? Impossible. Why would the man who had been killing off agents left and right want to help the group that had been sent to kill him?

"You don't know who the Archer is?" Remy asked carefully. McTiernan shook his head, a smile playing across his lips. "And if you did?"

"I would tell you. For all I know, you are the Archer, and this is all some elaborate game you're playing."

"Fuck you."

"You may as well, my boy, I seem to be the only one you've left out. Does Shawn know?"

Remy's mouth went dry and his entire body tingled with apprehension once more. He hadn't betrayed Shawn, he told himself desperately. He hadn't betrayed him. It was possible that he'd betrayed the Organization by proposing to join the

Archer, but he hadn't betrayed Shawn. The Archer could go fuck himself for all Remy cared, just as long as Shawn was left out of it.

"You have only one way out of this," McTiernan said sternly. "Find your comrades, Remy, and turn them. Kill any that fight you, and meet me in Auckland in two weeks' time."

"What's in Auckland?" Remy questioned resignedly.

"Is that an agreement then?"

"What's in Auckland?" Remy repeated more forcefully, needing to hear McTiernan say the words before he could even begin to think about agreeing to force the others to join public enemy number one.

"The Archer. Or he will be, if you say yes."

"And if I say no?"

"I'll kill you and be on my way."

"What are we to do in the two week interim?"

"Don't get killed," McTiernan ordered with a smile.

Remy blinked several times and finally lowered his head. He had to think this through very carefully. He had to know what succession of events he would be putting into place, and he had to know if that would be to the eventual benefit of his master plan.

'Master plan. Pffft.'

It made him sound like some evil genius. The Archer was the evil genius, Remy was just trying to save his own skin, and that of the other five men he had grown to care for so deeply. This seemed to be the only way to go about it.

"What does the Archer plan to do? What's his goal?"

"He wants to take out the Organization. And though he doesn't need the six of you to do it, he would most certainly benefit from your cooperation."

"Can the Archer promise that we'll be set free after the mission is over?"

"That I can't say."

"Why?"

"Because I'm not the Archer and I can't read minds."

"Ask him."

"What?"

"You know how to contact him. Ask him." Remy shifted in his tight bonds and smiled cheekily. "I'll wait," he said.

McTiernan grinned and reached into his pocket. For a second, Remy thought he was dead. But then he remembered that the gun was already out, and McTiernan brought out a silver flask.

"Water?" he offered. Remy drank what he was offered readily, allowing McTiernan to hold the flask as the water poured into his throat.

"Better," Remy murmured thankfully after he had soothed the ache in his parched throat.

McTiernan brought out a wicked hunting knife that Remy belatedly recognized as his own. "We have a deal then," McTiernan asserted.

Remy fixed his gaze on the knife. Shawn had given it to him. If he did this, Shawn would probably kill him. McTiernan was right; Shawn's loyalties ran deep. And even though Shawn was loyal to Remy, the Organization had twenty years and a whole lot of training on him.

If he didn't do this, he would most certainly be killed. But did he want to live knowing that Shawn would now despise everything he stood for?

Remy closed his eyes and nodded his agreement.

McTiernan sliced through the ropes and Remy stood shakily and turned to face the old gentleman.

"If I'm followed I will kill the tails," Remy warned. "We'll disappear and your Archer will have to go at it alone."

"Yes, I know. Unfortunately I'm working without a net myself now," McTiernan responded as he gestured toward the two bodies on the floor. "I have neither the resources nor the desire to follow you. Besides, if the Archer sees that you've betrayed him, as is your… tendency, apparently, he will kill all of you. That I can promise." McTiernan held out his hand and watched Remy expectantly. "With that in mind, I suppose I'll just have to trust you, won't I?"

"If Shawn finds out– if he finds out I've turned he'll kill me," Remy informed the man sadly, hoping he could convince him that he'd truly agreed to join them as his mind wrestled with what the old spy had just said. The Archer was watching them? How?

"Yes, he will. So you'd best be sneaky about it," McTiernan suggested with a wink as they gripped each other's hands and sealed the dirty dealings.

"I suppose that makes me a real traitor now… all these years," Remy mumbled as McTiernan clapped him on the back.

"It's not so bad as all that. You've just earned yourself a definite raise in pay."

II.

THIAGO stared blankly up at the ceiling as Shawn sat in bed beside him, rocking slightly the way he had when he held Remy's limp body outside the cabin that day. Thiago's chest compressed painfully and he fought the urge to cry as he recalled that painful scene. And Thiago wasn't a crier.

This was a war, and wars suffered losses, but just because it was expected, didn't make it any less of a tragedy.

Thiago's mind kept taking him around in circles until finally he could no longer stand it. He sat up and propped his back against the headboard. He looked over at Shawn, who was mechanically cleaning his gun in a vaguely disturbing fashion, and Thiago desperately tried to come up with something to say to him.

He could think of nothing. What did one say to someone who'd just lost his soulmate? Shawn continued to rock slowly, the movement almost imperceptible, and finally he placed his gun aside and sat staring at the opposite wall blankly. Thiago watched the other man's jaw clench and unclench repeatedly, and finally he put his hand out tentatively and rested it gently on Shawn's shoulder.

The reaction was immediate and so heartbreaking that Thiago finally did begin to cry silently. Shawn let his head fall and his shoulders slumped beneath the weight of Thiago's compassion. He brought a hand up to cover his eyes and one broken sob tore from his throat before he let Thiago pull him into his arms.

Thiago held him and rocked him back and forth slowly, assuming that the motion comforted the other man in some way since he seemed to do it when he was distressed. Shawn clung to him, sobbing silently against his chest as Thiago let several slow tears run down his own face. He couldn't imagine the pain Shawn must have been feeling. He desperately wished he could make it better somehow, but he knew there was nothing he could say or do to ease the loss.

They fell into a restless sleep at some point, and only when a soft brushing sound echoed in the silence of the night did Thiago wake. He managed not to hit the ceiling as the adrenaline and training kicked in, and the only indication he was no longer asleep was a tensing of his muscles. He peered through the veil of his eyelashes and jerked involuntarily when he saw the shadowy figure standing at the foot of the bed.

Shawn must have been awake as well. Shawn tensed at almost the same moment Thiago spotted their intruder, and in a flash they were both up and reaching for their weapons.

The intruder leapt onto the bed and handily disarmed both of them. Before Thiago could fully register the threat he had a knife to his throat, and Shawn was staring down the barrel of his own gun as the man squatted on the bed between them. Thiago forced himself not to swallow nervously, knowing the movement would force the sharp blade into his skin. He tried to calculate the number of people in the world who could disarm two veteran Class One operatives simultaneously.

There weren't many.

"It's just me. I didn't mean to startle you," Carl whispered through the darkness. "I wanted to make sure you were both doing okay."

Thiago began to relax and the knife was removed from his throat. Shawn was still tense, but the gun was handed back to him and Carl removed himself from the bed.

"*Mierda*," Thiago breathed in irritation, more than a little annoyed that he'd been so easily overpowered.

"I'm sorry," Carl said unapologetically. "I heard a noise; I came to check on you both."

"How did you do that?" Shawn asked suspiciously. Thiago could see the white of Carl's teeth gleaming in the darkness as he grinned.

"I could kill you with a pinecone," Carl intoned as he made his way back out of the room. "G'night, mates."

Thiago was left deeply unsettled as Carl pulled the door closed behind him. It took him a long hour before he was able to get back to sleep.

When next he awoke it was not a sound that was the cause, but a hand over his mouth. His eyes snapped open and he stared at the dark form above him. He could just barely see the shadowy figure put a finger to its lips in a shushing motion, and Thiago blinked several times as a familiar voice whispered to him.

"Thi?"

The hand was removed, but he didn't have time to respond before a rush of movement sent him hurtling off the bed and onto the floor.

"Shawn! No!" Thiago called as the smack of a fist on flesh resounded throughout the silent hotel room. Thiago scrambled to reach the two struggling figures and pull them apart. He wrapped his arms around Shawn's shoulders and tried– unsuccessfully– to restrain the other man from landing his blows. Just as he managed to pull Shawn off their new intruder Carl and Brandt ran in, followed closely by Nikolaus, who had the presence of mind to actually flip the light switch on.

Thiago used all his strength to drag Shawn away, and finally threw his body backward and landed with Shawn struggling in his lap on the floor. As soon as the lights flickered on Shawn froze in his arms.

"Remy?" he whispered as his body went lax. Thiago held him close, not sure what to do with him just yet.

Remy sat up with difficulty and gingerly lifted his fingers to the cut on his cheek.

"At least you didn't shoot me in the ass again, *podna*."

III.

TO say that Carl was a little astounded by Remy's sudden appearance would have been an understatement.

Remy sat on the floor where he had landed, and Shawn and Thiago both appeared to be motionless in one another's arms as they stared at him. Carl was aware of an increase of pressure where Brandt's hand gripped his arm, but other than that, not one of them moved after Remy's decidedly nonchalant statement.

Nikolaus was the first to regain his senses.

"Remy?" he questioned tentatively as he moved around Brandt and took a step forwards. Remy turned to look at him and Carl watched the abused face break into a grin.

"Niko!" Remy exclaimed as he continued to flounder on the floor and swipe absently at the blood running in a trickle down his cheek and nose. "I was worried about you!"

"Me? *You* were worried about *me*? *Hurensohn*! We thought you were dead!" Nikolaus cried. Brandt took hold of him and clapped a large hand over his mouth before Nikolaus could shout anything more. Remy didn't seem to be fazed by the outburst. His attitude was as if he had never left them. Never been in danger. Never made them all believe he was dead or in peril.

And Carl was furious. It was the irrational anger of the relieved, he knew this, but he didn't care. How could Remy just waltz back in here like nothing had happened? Shawn was apparently of the same mind. Carl watched him wrest himself free from Thiago's grasp and crawl across the floor to grab Remy by the front of his shirt and shake him violently.

"You little son of a bitch!" Shawn hissed as he pulled Remy to his knees and knelt facing him. "I told you if you ever did that to me again I would kill you!" he whispered in an angry rush of words. "I'll fucking kill you!" he shouted. "Where's my gun!" he demanded as he pushed Remy away from him and fumbled around on the floor for the weapon he had apparently dropped during the melee.

Carl didn't know Shawn well enough to know whether he was serious, and so he took his reactionary cues from Brandt and Remy. Brandt stood by impassively and watched, seemingly unaware that he still held Nikolaus and covered his mouth. Nikolaus looked terrified to say anything, but he was beginning to turn a tad blue so Carl calmly pulled Brandt's hand from the smaller man's mouth by one of his fingers and turned back to watch the show.

Remy scrambled to his feet and kicked the gun away from Shawn's grasp before crouching in a slightly defensive position and watching Shawn warily. Shawn stood swiftly and growled.

Carl's eyes flickered to Thiago, who was still on the floor looking slightly stunned, and then back to the two combatants. He didn't want to get into a fight tonight.

"I'm sorry, Shawn," Remy said sincerely. "It couldn't be helped," he insisted.

Shawn growled again in response and the back of Remy's foot hit the wall as he backed away. Shawn gripped him by the front of his shirt once more and Carl and Brandt moved forward to separate them, but they weren't nearly fast enough.

Shawn's fist flew at Remy's face as Carl watched in shock, but Remy managed to get his hand up in time and he blocked the blow, catching the clenched fist and stopping it just centimeters away from his already bruised face. He lowered it forcefully and used his other hand to grasp the back of Shawn's head, and Carl thought for sure he was going to head butt the other man and start an all-out brawl.

But instead of a violent meeting of foreheads, it was a violent meeting of lips that shocked the observers. It was an open-mouthed, sensual kiss, and Carl stopped short and simply stared.

Remy released Shawn's fist and wrapped both arms around his body as Shawn tried to devour him right there against the wall. It was certainly a nice change of speed from the hitting. At least Carl knew he wouldn't have to break up any fights.

Thiago got slowly to his feet and stared at the two men in disbelief. Carl could sympathize. For perhaps the fiftieth time since their acquaintance, he found himself marveling at the odd relationship. He turned to gauge Brandt's reaction and found the other man watching blankly.

Carl had been expecting trouble from that area. It was easy to see the attachment Brandt and Shawn formed with one another, and Carl was concerned that Brandt and Remy would be at odds when they all reunited. He was concerned until they'd found Nikolaus, anyway. But now Remy was back, and unfortunately it seemed that Carl was right.

"What happened?" Shawn demanded breathlessly, pulling Carl's attention back to the pair.

"I escaped," Remy said with a shrug. Shawn stared at the other man with a hard look that made Carl want to hide behind Brandt, and finally Shawn began to shake ever so slightly.

"Don't lie to me, lad," Shawn growled dangerously, and even Remy's eyes widened a bit at the tone. Carl had never heard that tone of voice from the older man, and it was obvious Remy had rarely heard it, at least not directed at him. "No one escapes from Mac," Shawn added in the same low, dangerous voice.

Remy's eyes flickered around the room as if he was looking for aid, but no one was going to speak against Shawn when he was actually fucking growling. Carl took a step backwards and glanced around for the closest piece of furniture behind which to take cover.

"You're right," Remy conceded quickly, his tone completely open and conciliatory. "I'm sorry. I… I made a deal with him."

Carl tensed visibly and he heard Brandt and Thiago both suck in deep breaths of air. A deal?

"What kind of fucking deal?" Brandt asked almost angrily. Shawn being angry was one thing. But Shawn and Brandt both angry? Carl looked longingly towards the door and his newly purchased weaponry.

"Nothing like that! I didn't give us away!" Remy said in an insulted voice.

"Then what exactly did you give him?" Shawn asked pointedly, his voice still very lethal.

Remy looked back at him as if Shawn had just slapped him in the face. Carl instantly felt sorry for the younger man. He'd been through God only knew what and had probably been expecting a warm welcome or a happy return. Instead, he'd been attacked, attacked again, accused of betraying them, and then accused of being a whore. Poor kid.

"Shawn," Carl murmured hesitantly, thinking to avert a possible disaster. Green eyes turned on him and Carl felt as if he had just been melded to the floor. His mouth snapped shut and he blinked at the older man innocuously.

"You're hurting me," Remy pointed out calmly, and Carl could visibly see the façade sliding back into place. It had taken a while to figure Remy out, but Carl had finally done it. Whenever he felt threatened or didn't know how to react to something, he slipped back into agent mode and dealt with it that way. Carl was impressed with the ability to morph, but at the same time it made him inexplicably sad. It must have been a lonely existence for the younger man, to be able to pull the curtain with such ease. Carl had never seen anyone better at it.

Shawn instantly released the hold he had on Remy's upper arms and took a step back.

"Do you want the full version or the abridged version?" Remy asked in a businesslike manner as he rubbed his arm gingerly.

"Abridged first," Shawn demanded. Carl couldn't understand Shawn's behavior. He'd been devastated when he'd heard of Remy's capture. Carl had heard the heart wrenching sobbing coming from the next room earlier, and he'd seen Shawn begin to fall apart at the seams. Now here Remy was, fit and in one piece, and Shawn was inexplicably angry with him.

"John is working for the Archer," Remy told them without preamble.

"What?" they all echoed simultaneously.

"He's turned. John's turned," Remy said in the same no-nonsense tone as he massaged his arm where Shawn had held him. "He said the Organization had marked him in order to throw us off, so he could tail us if we escaped the blast. But he was working them, waiting for a chance to break and turn completely."

"How do you know this?" Carl asked curiously.

"John told me."

"And you believed him?" Thiago asked incredulously.

"John and I have the same philosophy on the truth," Remy said matter-of-factly. "Yes, I believed him."

"And he just up and offered this information to you?" Shawn asked sarcastically.

"No, Shawn, he did a lovely little choreographed number and tapped it out in Morse Code," Remy spat back at him.

Carl heard a little snort from behind him, and turned to glance disapprovingly at Brandt. Shawn and Remy glared at one another and Carl sighed heavily. Perhaps he would be breaking up a fight tonight after all.

"I don't believe it," Shawn stated finally, crossing his arms defensively and staring Remy down. "John would never turn."

"Think again, *couyon*," Remy said softly, the anger in his voice suddenly gone. If Carl hadn't known better he would have said that Remy sounded almost sad. "Anyone will turn, if they're given the right incentive."

Carl creased his brow in a confused frown. Had he really just said that? What the hell was he trying to do?

"What do you mean?" Shawn asked dangerously.

"I mean he's turned, Shawn! I don't know why! I'm sorry, I know you admired him, but he's turned. He said something about the incentives being much better and–"

Remy was cut off by Shawn slamming him against the wall with so much force that the picture hanging beside them rattled and fell to the ground with a clank.

"What did you do?" Shawn demanded angrily. Carl tensed and waited to pounce in case it got uglier, but instead of fighting back Remy simply went limp and stared into Shawn's eyes as if he were mesmerized.

"I did what I had to do to get the hell out of there," he answered quietly, as if it were the most obvious thing in the world. "I told him I'd take his deal, that I'd play his game. And the bastard just gave me my gear and said 'on you go then, my boy,'" Remy said in what Carl was sure was an imitation of Sir John McTiernan's voice.

"He just let you go?" Thiago asked as he sat down on the bed and rubbed at a carpet burn on his elbow.

"*Mais oui*. He told me the Archer would know if I went back on the deal. I don't know how, but I believe that, too. I think he's watching us somehow, through someone or something. But I think that…." Remy trailed off with a grimace and lowered his eyes, and Carl saw Shawn's fingers tighten around Remy's arms.

"What was the deal?" Nikolaus asked, and Carl turned to look at him. He had almost forgotten Nikolaus was there, the younger man was so quiet.

"The Archer wants us to join him."

"What?" Thiago and Carl asked simultaneously once more.

"John told me that the Archer plans to take down the Organization," Remy responded slowly, his eyes never leaving Shawn's as he spoke. "He wants the six of us to help."

Shawn practically roared, and he slammed Remy against the wall once more.

"And you promised to what? Turn us?" Shawn demanded angrily, finally losing control of his temper. "With your special skills of persuasion, perhaps? And what if we don't turn with you, traitor? Are you supposed to kill us?"

Carl watched the agent seep out of Remy's face as the blood drained from it, and all that remained was the sweet, slightly oblivious young Cajun they all loved, standing there looking uncertain and betrayed.

Carl couldn't take any more. Apparently neither could Thiago or Nikolaus, and they all moved to break up the confrontation at almost the same time.

"That's enough," Thiago said in his own dangerous growl, and Carl wondered what in the hell he'd been thinking earlier when he'd gone in to check on these two. They were scary as fuck; was he suicidal?

They pried Shawn's hands from Remy's arms and pulled him away, holding him back in case he felt the need to do further damage. Remy slumped back against the wall in defeat, and Carl's heart hurt for him all over again.

"It was my only option, Shawn," Remy insisted softly, his voice barely audible. "It was my only way out. I had to make him believe I would take the deal or he was going to kill me."

"One lie," Shawn murmured angrily through gritted teeth, holding up his finger against the restraining arm Nikolaus had around him to illustrate the point in case Remy happened to miss it. "I told you from the beginning. One lie and it was over."

"Shawn," Remy pleaded, his body still attached to the wall as if Shawn had glued him there.

"Decide right now where your loyalties lie," Shawn ordered angrily.

Remy blinked at him, looking as if he'd just been asked if the sky was blue. "With you," he answered simply. "Always with you."

Carl watched Shawn carefully, and he saw the color drain from his face as he heard the words Remy had just spoken. Carl wondered what Shawn had ever done to deserve such loyalty. He certainly didn't deserve it tonight.

It appeared that Shawn was thinking the same thing as he looked at Remy's bruised countenance.

Finally, he seemed to pull himself together, and he swallowed hard before nodding tersely. Nikolaus and Thiago let him loose, and Shawn stood there staring at Remy.

"You're bleeding," he finally said in a confused, tired voice.

IV.

SHAWN had no idea what he was doing. Why was he so angry? Was it fear? Relief? Exhaustion?

Could it be guilt?

That didn't sit well with Shawn's conscience, but he knew that was the driving force behind his lashing out. Guilt.

The look on Remy's face made Shawn want to shoot himself. The younger man leaned against the wall, looking lost and heartbroken, and the blood running freely down his arm where Shawn had squeezed made Shawn's stomach clench uncomfortably. He'd done that.

Remy looked down at the blood disinterestedly and clucked his tongue.

"*Maudit*! I just stole this shirt," he murmured as he pulled at the sleeve and examined the growing stain. "Stitches must have come out."

"I'm sorry," Shawn whispered sincerely. Remy looked up at him, and the blank look in the younger man's eyes hit Shawn just as if it had been a club in Remy's hand.

"No worries. You had every right."

Shawn looked around the room at the others. They all stared at him as if he'd lost his mind. What had he been thinking? At first Remy's nonchalant, 'look at me, I'm alive' attitude upon returning to them had angered Shawn to the point of distraction, but what had really set him off was when Remy had said the word 'escape.'

One did not escape from Sir John McTiernan. You either gave him what he wanted, or you died refusing. Thoughts of Remy giving John what he wanted had flashed through Shawn's head so quickly that he'd seen red. Remy was lying to him.

Why? What had he done that he thought Shawn couldn't handle? What had transpired between him and John that would cause Remy to resort to that stone wall he'd thrown up? Though Shawn had seen it in use many times, especially during that one captivity they had suffered through together, Shawn had never been the focus of it. Never been the reason for it.

Shawn's mind flashed back to the gentle kisses he'd shared with Brandt and his body flushed with ice. What right had he to be angry with Remy? What right had he to blame Remy at all?

Shawn was the one keeping all the secrets here.

Shawn was so distracted by the various questions running through his mind that he failed to register the most important thing Remy had said until well after Carl and Nikolaus had ushered the younger man out of the room and slammed the door in Shawn's face.

V.

NIKOLAUS and Carl whisked Remy out of the room before Shawn could blow his top again. They sat together on the bed as Remy told them about his ordeal with McTiernan and his subsequent trek to Sydney as Carl stitched up the jagged wound on his arm.

"I never dreamed John would turn," Remy murmured after he had finished his narration. "He's fucking upper level, man. Echelon."

Nikolaus kept his eyes carefully averted from the wound and instead watched Remy's face as he spoke. He didn't seem to be all that upset about Shawn's odd welcome of him, but Nikolaus certainly was. He was dumbstruck by Shawn's reaction to Remy's return. What had the man been thinking? Had he not wanted Remy to be alive still?

Sure, Nikolaus had been angry with Remy, inexplicably so when the man had grinned at him and began talking like nothing had ever happened. Emotions did strange things to people, especially people as high-strung as the six of them were of late. And Shawn had certainly been upset. Perhaps the pendulum had just swung too far and caused him to rage like he had. Nikolaus hoped that was it, anyway.

"And you're certain?" Carl asked as he dabbed at Remy's arm gently. Watching Carl tend to Remy's wound with such care struck Nikolaus as odd for some reason.

"Very," Remy responded with a curt nod. "John had no reason to turn me loose like he did. He had no reason to…" Remy trailed off and his eyes widened slightly. "Unless– oh, fuck. Unless they've used me as a tracer. *Mon Dieu*! Trigger, *à l'aide*!" Remy stuttered as he struggled to get off the bed.

Nikolaus watched in confusion as Remy worked himself into a near panic and pawed at his own clothing and flailed around trying to disengage his feet from the bedcovers. Carl seemed to understand the urgency though, and he helped Remy to stand and immediately began to tug at his boots as Remy attacked the fly of his own jeans.

"What are you doing?" Nikolaus questioned.

"*J'étais inconscient*, unconscious, *oui*?" Remy explained hurriedly, his words becoming hurried and his strange accent growing heavier and almost indecipherable as he spoke. "They would've known their only chance of finding you was to use me. If John's still working for the Organization– fuck! *Maudit*! How could I have missed that?"

"What? What'd you miss?" Nikolaus asked. He was too distracted by Remy standing there in his ridiculous Superman boxers and speaking his Frenglish at warp speed as Carl knelt at his feet to be able to think clearly.

"They would have known he'd give a false location, no matter what they used to extract the information," Carl explained as he produced a wicked looking knife from somewhere and tore into the sole of Remy's boot with it. "And they would also have known that you would get us moving right away," he said to Nikolaus as he examined the ruined boot, "so the only way to find us would be to set Dixie here loose and follow him."

"I wasn't followed," Remy stated with certainty.

Carl nodded as he performed the same operation on the other boot. Remy, too, had a knife in his hand, and Nikolaus wondered where the hell it had come from. Did they carry them in their underwear? Remy slashed through the waistband of his jeans and peered into the cut he had made before ripping the hem apart and looking at the tatters intently.

"So the only way they could have followed was by bugging him," Carl continued as he examined the other boot.

"Oh," Nikolaus responded slowly as he realized what they were saying. "In your clothing? But you said your shirt was new, right? Didn't you switch out everything?"

Remy threw the remains of the jeans down in disgust and looked at Nikolaus abashedly. "No. I'm so fucking stupid! How could I not've taken that precaution?" he asked them in disbelief. "I bought a new shirt because the other one was bloody, but I didn't even… it never even crossed my mind to– fuck!"

"You appear to be clean," Carl announced as he placed the boot gently on the ground and looked up to Remy. "Nice boxers."

"You're just jealous," Remy responded absently as he pointed his finger at Carl. "We have to check me over. Everywhere."

"Shouldn't we move first? I mean, if they're following you," Nikolaus said, letting the consequences linger on his last word.

"No," Remy and Carl answered simultaneously.

"If they're after us they'll wait 'til dawn," Remy explained. "If we move and I *am* bugged–"

"Then they'll be able to, and we'll be forced to move again," Carl finished as he stood up and took Remy's hand. Nikolaus trailed after them and stood in the doorway of the bathroom as Remy discarded his dubious Superman boxers and Carl stood watching and waiting, looking around the toilet idly for something he obviously wasn't finding.

"What are you doing?" Nikolaus asked.

"We've got to search him," Carl responded, gesturing vaguely at Remy's body. "Do we have shampoo or lotion or something?"

"You mean…."

"Yeah."

"Fun," Nikolaus said flatly. "Why don't you just submerge him?"

"What?" Remy and Carl questioned together.

"Fill the bath and get in. Stay there for an hour or so. Even a waterproof tag wouldn't last that long," Nikolaus said confidently, finally feeling useful again as his extensive knowledge of electronics came into play. "If it is... on your person, anyway. Bugs aren't made to swim. You'll still have to retrieve it, but…."

Remy and Carl blinked at him, then shared an abashed look before Carl bent over the tap and started the water running.

"Don't make it freezing," Remy requested as he slapped Carl on the ass and winked at Nikolaus. "And can you put some bubbles in there? Had a hard week, *non*?"

Carl swatted at him as he danced away in the small room. Nikolaus smirked as he watched them. Remy smiled at Nikolaus brilliantly. "What would we do without you, Niko?" he asked affectionately.

"All die horrible deaths, probably," Nikolaus responded flatly. "Bubbles might help actually," he added thoughtfully.

"I'm not fixing him a goddamn bubble bath," Carl grumbled as he let his fingers flit through the stream of water and then put the stopper in the drain.

Nikolaus watched as Remy's hand gripped Carl's shoulder for balance and he stepped into the bathtub.

"Niko, will you rip those fucking things to shreds and search them, please," Carl requested maliciously, indicating Remy's boxers. Remy looked at him with a horrified face and whimpered. Carl shrugged and drawled, "Submerge, bitch."

"What about my head?" Remy asked as he eased himself into the water and hissed plaintively. Apparently, Carl had taken his orders to heart, and it was too hot.

"Breathe through your nose," Nikolaus responded in amusement as he took Carl's knife and delightedly ripped the boxers apart.

He had come to the conclusion during their time together, and in watching the other man's various interactions before and since, that Remy enjoyed making others feel superior to him. Whether it was a way to force others to underestimate him or simply a part of his personality, Nikolaus had not yet discerned. The only thing Nikolaus did know was that out of the other five men, Remy was the least likely to cause an opponent concern, and the most likely to cause them damage.

Remy knew perfectly well what he was doing. He'd probably done this a hundred times, but Nikolaus felt pretty sure that he was acting toward the benefit of Nikolaus's ego, and possibly Carl's as well, and Nikolaus for one couldn't help but be a bit grateful for it.

He'd felt so entirely useless up to this point unless he was at a keyboard. Did Remy even know he had this ability? The ability to make people trust themselves and him with hardly a second thought? Surely, he must know.

Nikolaus's eyes followed the movement of the muscles in Remy's back as his own hands worked at feeling through the thin material, and he watched with some sort of voyeuristic interest as Carl's hand ran gently down Remy's spine. Remy shivered and Carl let out a low whistle.

"Scars tell the story of our lives, don't they?" Carl murmured as his finger traced a faded line at the base of Remy's spine. Nikolaus had noticed Remy's numerous scars as well, but had never had the nerve to mention them.

"Mm hmm," Remy hummed uncomfortably as he settled himself. His shoulders sagged slightly under Carl's touch and he hung his head as if he were ashamed. Nikolaus furrowed his brow, wondering what was wrong with his friend. Carl noticed the sudden change, too, because he immediately removed his hand and stood up; looking at Nikolaus worriedly as if asking what he'd done wrong. Nikolaus shrugged.

Remy looked up as Carl took a step away. "Please stay in here with me," he said in a small, ashamed voice. Carl and Nikolaus exchanged another look, and wordlessly made themselves comfortable.

"Are you all right, Remy?" Nikolaus asked softly as he sat on the closed lid of the toilet and leant his elbows on his knees. Carl sat himself down on the floor beside the tub and leant against the edge, looking as if he wanted to touch Remy to comfort him but was unsure of whether he should.

"Scars are badges of honor, y'know. No need to be ashamed of any of them," Carl said softly.

Remy shook his head. "Yeah. It's not that. I don't mind my battle wounds."

"What's wrong then?" Nikolaus asked as Remy continued to avoid his eyes. It was very out of character for the normally ebullient man.

"It's just, you get so used to being part of *something*. A team, I s'pose. And then you're alone again," Remy explained as he brought his wet hand out of the water and snapped his fingers, spraying droplets of water all over himself. "Just like that. I don't feel like being alone anymore."

He looked at them both with wide, pleading eyes, looking for all the world like a lost puppy, and Nikolaus smiled fondly at him. Carl let his hand rest once more on Remy's back and Remy smiled sheepishly at him.

"Dunno when I became so fucking dependant," he muttered good-naturedly.

"Tell us the truth, Dixie," Carl murmured in a coaxing voice as he rubbed soothing circles over Remy's shoulder blades. "Are you really okay? They didn't hurt you at all?"

"I'm fine. Except for a pounding headache that I had for a couple days, I'm just fine."

"What about what happened in there?" Carl ventured as he nodded his head in the vague direction of the other room.

Remy shrugged and sank his body into the water until only the front portion of his face was still above water. Carl got up and sat on the edge of the bath, and Nikolaus moved to sit beside him in order to see Remy as he spoke.

"Shawn is very passionate," Remy said as he closed his eyes and submerged himself. He stayed under briefly, and then came back up and continued speaking as if he had never gone under. Water streamed down his face in fascinating trails as he spoke. "He's also very proud of his ability to control his emotions. Because of those two traits, anger is his standard fallback when he can't properly express what he's feeling," Remy told them, sounding as if he had rehearsed the speech and gurgling slightly as water filled his mouth. He spit it out and sat up a little.

"Does he do that often then? Beat the fuck out of you when you do something miraculous, like escape certain death?" Carl asked, his tone light but the undercurrent very bitter, in Nikolaus's opinion.

"Not really. Once or twice."

"How many times have you escaped certain death?" Nikolaus asked with a laugh.

Remy shrugged. "Here and there," he said vaguely, rubbing absently at a circular scar on his thigh.

Nikolaus was pretty sure it was an old bullet wound, and it looked to be near the femoral artery, if Nikolaus remembered his anatomy correctly. That had been a close one; it had probably bled fast and in quantities.

"So he'll be okay then?" Carl asked as his eyes zeroed in on the movement of Remy's fingers as well. "The two of you will…."

"He'll be fine," Remy said with a sweep of his hand through the air that splashed both Nikolaus and Carl with water. "Sorry!" Remy exclaimed. He snickered and bit his lip quickly to stop it when Carl glared at him. He cleared his throat apologetically. "Sorry," he repeated in a lower voice. "We'll be just fine. He'll probably sneak over to wherever I'm sleeping as soon as everyone's asleep and apologize 'til I have to clonk him upside the head to get him to stop. I remember one time we were on a mission and we got our orders mixed around. We ended up being separated on different sides of this big compound down in South America, but we could still hear one another through our comms. At one point, he stopped talking. Just completely stopped in mid-sentence. Then I heard guns off in the distance and then nothing. No contact for two days. When he finally came staggering back into the rendezvous with a bottle of Jack Daniels to celebrate his safe return I nearly shot him just for the hell of it. Just to watch him bleed."

"What had he been doing?" Nikolaus asked in amusement.

"He said he'd fallen into an old root cellar as he cased the entry point. That he wasn't watching his step as he talked to me and just fell. A root cellar that apparently had a stash of Jack, because he was flat drunk when he made it back. We never did find out what the bastards were shooting at," Remy added contemplatively.

"So that scene back there, that was normal?" Carl asked dubiously.

Remy nodded and winced as his arm hit the side of the tub.

"Tell us more about your plan," Nikolaus said after several minutes of Remy's fussing with the stitches and Carl's batting his hands away from the wound.

"Plan?" Remy echoed as he glared at Carl and poked him playfully in the chest.

"You do have one, right?" Nikolaus asked in concern.

"Uhh… well, my immediate plan was to find all of you. After that I really didn't think much on it."

"Oh, God," Nikolaus groaned wearily as he rested his head in his hands.

"*Mais excusez-moi* for not reading your mind, *ami*," Remy said sarcastically. "I can't do everything at once, *non*? You are a hard critter to track, by the way!"

"Track? You tracked me?"

"I tried to. Tried to catch up with you and let you know I had made it out. Kept losing the trail. Finally, I had to guess ahead and I just went on to the airport."

"Is that how you found us here?" Carl asked curiously.

"*Ja*! How did you find us?" Nikolaus demanded as it suddenly dawned on him that Remy couldn't have known they would travel on to Brisbane from Sydney. "Were you watching at the airport and you never showed yourself?" he asked angrily. If that had been the case then Shawn's outburst would be nothing compared to what

Nikolaus would do to him!

"No! I tried to get there, I really did, but I got held up in San Francisco. I had to trail Shawn's alias. That's how I found your connecting flight and then the hotel. He always uses the initials S.B. no matter which name he uses. That's how I found you. I was gonna wait 'til morning to show myself, but I was too short on blood and rest. I needed a bed."

"You'll get one, mate. Soon as we get you debugged, that is," Carl promised as he tugged lightly at Remy's hair.

"You'll still have to search me, even if we have shorted it."

"Yeah. We'll make it fun though," Carl said with a wink.

Remy smiled and sank down a bit in the water as Nikolaus and Carl sat quietly pondering their own thoughts. Remy submerged himself once more, and Nikolaus counted absently as he remained under. He stayed down; his face completely calm as little bubbles trailed toward the surface from his nose, and Nikolaus and Carl exchanged several worried looks as the seconds ticked by. When he finally came back up, breaking the surface of the water smoothly and barely making a sound as he wiped at his streaming face, Nikolaus estimated he had been under for almost a full three minutes. He was beginning to see more and more of the agent in Remy as he observed him. He wondered if that particular skill was the training or the swamps.

Remy wiped at his eyes and then he looked back up at Carl.

"You heard me when I came in," he said to Carl with certainty. "I tripped over the fucking doorjamb. It barely made a sound, though; you must have terrific hearing! I thought you were going to disembowel me when you came stalking in with that big fucking knife."

"I never saw you," Carl responded, though he didn't sound very surprised at the revelation. Perhaps he'd already figured that out, though. Nikolaus hadn't even known Carl had gone into the other room.

"Good thing, too. I saw how you handled Shawn and Thiago. It was impressive," Remy said with admiration. Carl smiled softly and stared at the surface of the water. Nikolaus had no idea what they were talking about, but he had the sudden idea that he needed to leave the room and let them discuss the subject.

Remy was due for a nice cavity search anyway.

VI.

BRANDT wasn't certain what to think of Shawn at the moment. The man was a wreck; a completely different person from the calm, controlled man with whom Brandt had worked the last three months.

Shawn's outburst had been similar to the ones Brandt's various fires and explosions had produced, but there had been an intense anger present in this one that had never before surfaced.

Brandt had been instantly turned on, and he had stayed that way.

But he also felt badly for Remy. The kid hadn't deserved the verbal pistol whipping Shawn had given him, and Brandt found himself just a bit fucked off with Shawn at the moment.

"Fuck!" Shawn shouted angrily as he paced up and down the length of the room. Thiago and Brandt sat side by side on the bed and watched him with interest. "Did you hear what he said? He said the Organization marked John to throw us off. Throw us off!" Shawn roared as he tugged at his hair until his knuckles turned white. "That means the bastards really did set us up! I can't believe it!"

"So you believe what he said now?" Thiago asked shrewdly.

"Of course I do," Shawn snapped dismissively. "Remy doesn't lie. Ever. He plays with the truth. Stretches and bends it, but he never breaks it."

"I meant McTiernan. You believe what he told Remy?"

"Like Remy said, he and John have the same philosophy on the truth," Shawn answered dismissively. "I can't believe I missed it when he said it!"

"I think we all missed it," Thiago said nonchalantly, "what with him professing his undying loyalty and your calling him a traitor and a whore and… what else was it?" Thiago asked Brandt as he held out his hand expectantly.

"A liar, I think," Brandt supplied helpfully, his glittering eyes never leaving Shawn.

"That's right," Thiago said with a nod. "A traitor, a whore, and a liar. Yeah. That distracted us all from the real meat of the conversation, I think," Thiago said acidly.

Shawn paused in his pacing long enough to give them both a withering glare. "Enough comments from the peanut gallery please," he growled. "Remy's fine. He's fine," Shawn murmured as he ran his hand though his hair.

"I wouldn't be so sure," Brandt mumbled. "I know I'd hate you after that." Shawn stopped again and stared at Brandt with wide, surprised green eyes.

"Yeah?" Shawn asked combatively. Brandt had never seen him like this. He nodded, regardless of Shawn's threatening glare.

"He came through hell just to get back to you. And you went and…." Brandt finished with a sweeping gesture toward the wall and looked at Shawn in disgust.

"You're pissed at me?" Shawn asked in mild surprise. Thiago and Brandt both nodded and continued to stare at him.

"You don't really understand what you have there, do you?" Thiago asked as Shawn stared back at them.

"'Course I do," Shawn spat. "I'm not blind. I'm not stupid either. The two of you may not understand, but Remy certainly does."

Ouch.

Brandt just barely managed not to physically wince at Shawn's words.

"I'm sorry," Shawn sighed in a tired voice. He looked at Brandt pleadingly. "I'm sorry, I didn't mean that. Both of you," he said, looking at Thiago before practically throwing himself down on the end of the bed and letting his head fall into his hands.

Brandt stared at his well-muscled back and wondered what he was missing that made him unable to understand Shawn's emotions. Was it a sentiment he was incapable of experiencing that was playing hell on Shawn? Was that it? Unless it dealt with destruction, lust, or affection, apparently, Brandt freely admitted that he was pretty well lost.

"I had no right to shout at him. You're right. I had no right to say what I did. I had no right… no right at all," Shawn repeated between his periodic curses and inaudible mumblings. Brandt and Thiago shared a look, then returned their eyes to Shawn as he began to rock slightly.

"You're right, Shawn," Thiago said finally as he looked at Shawn's back sympathetically. Apparently, Thiago was quicker to forgive than Brandt was. "You know Remy better than we do. If you say he's fine, then he is."

Shawn shook his head. "No. I've never seen him look like that. Like– "

"Like you had just called him a traitor?" Brandt supplied in a low, even voice.

"Oh, God," Shawn groaned miserably.

"Why don't you go check on him?" Thiago suggested.

"No. No, he's… he needs to rest. I'll just stir him back up if I go in there now."

"The light's still on," Brandt observed as he looked at the bottom of the dividing door.

"I doubt they'll turn it off after all the excitement," Shawn said morosely.

"How the hell did Remy get in here, anyway?" Thiago asked suddenly. "You think that's what woke Carl?"

"Probably," Shawn replied absently. "I told you Remy had special skills. He's like fucking Houdini. He can get out of just about anything. And it's like he flips a switch and goes into full-out stealth mode. I've seen rusty hinges glide and squeaky floorboards go silent when he touches them. I don't know how he does it. One thing's for sure, if he makes a noise it's either because he means to or he's tripped over something," Shawn said fondly. Brandt snorted and Thiago smiled slightly. "There's no telling how long he was in here before he picked his moment," Shawn murmured.

They sat in silence for some time as Shawn mentally kicked himself for his behavior and Brandt pondered over Remy's other special skills. Finally, Brandt took pity on Shawn and softly called his name to get his attention once more.

He understood where the anger came from. He had felt it, too, when Remy had beamed at them all like a little kid handing his mother a frog. Shawn's anger was just compounded by the deeper attachment, and Brandt could understand that.

Shawn turned to look at Brandt questioningly, almost hopefully, and Brandt scooted away from Thiago and patted the bed between them.

"Come up here. Stop beating yourself up."

Shawn stared at the space between them for long seconds before looking back at Brandt gratefully and crawling towards them. He settled down between them with his back against the headboard and sighed heavily, his mind probably still on the near-brawl and the words he spoke in the heat of the moment.

And boy, did Brandt understand the heat of the moment.

Brandt looked over his head at Thiago, who was looking at him expectantly. Brandt hadn't given Thiago nearly enough attention, he realized. The man was amazingly fit. And intuitive. And intelligent. And his eyes had the power to hypnotize Brandt when they glittered like that. They were such an odd color.

"Do you think a good shagging would help him?" Brandt asked conversationally. Thiago pursed his lips and nodded his head.

"Could be," he said in a scholarly fashion that Brandt found highly entertaining. He saw Shawn glance at him out of the corner of his eye, and he noticed the beginnings of a smile tug at the older man's lips. "Would he be content to just watch, do you suppose?" Thiago asked in the same tone as he fingered the cleft in his chin.

"I don't know," Brandt responded innocently, looking off into the corner of the room as if he were seriously thinking on the matter. "He doesn't really seem the type to just watch."

"Yes, he does strike one as the hands-on type," Thiago mused.

"Will you two bugger off?" Shawn grumped, though he couldn't quite hide the laughter in his voice.

A knock on the door to the other room halted the activities Brandt had been trying to initiate, and Shawn started and leaned forwards expectantly.

"Come on," Thiago called in amusement as he watched Shawn closely.

Seconds later Nikolaus poked his head through the door and blinked at the three of them.

"You look like those evil monkeys," he observed with amusement as he stepped in and shut the door behind him.

"Evil monkeys?" Shawn repeated in confusion. Brandt's own brow furrowed as he watched Nikolaus walk further into the room and nod. Sure they all needed haircuts and maybe a shave, but monkeys?

"You know, hear no evil, see no evil… whatever the last one was," Nikolaus explained distractedly as he looked around the room.

"Speak no evil," Thiago supplied with a grin. Nikolaus nodded again.

"That's the one. Is Remy's bag in here?"

"Might be in the corner there," Shawn said with a gesture toward the corner by the other bed. Nikolaus had managed to salvage most of their things, and he had taken Remy's leather satchel with him to give to Shawn. "Does he need a new shirt?" Shawn questioned guiltily.

"Yeah," Nikolaus said as he walked over to pick up the bag. "New everything, actually. He and Carl cut up what he was wearing looking for bugs."

"Bugs?" Brandt asked in alarm.

"They didn't find any. But Remy and uh… well, they're… what I mean is…." Nikolaus looked at Shawn in concern and perhaps fear, and licked his lips nervously. Brandt understood perfectly though.

"Carl's searching his person, yeah?" Brandt asked in amusement, all sense of mercy or pity forgotten. Nikolaus looked at him as if he were in pain and then nodded reluctantly. "Lucky bastard," Brandt murmured.

VII.

REMY examined his fingers intently, frowning at the wrinkles he was forming.

"I think I need to get out," he announced. Carl raised his head and looked at him impassively. He was entertaining himself by making little ripples in the water with his fingers.

"Niko's getting your clothes. Stay in there 'til he gets back at least. What's taking him so long?" Carl wondered aloud as he looked at the door.

"I'm waterlogged. And your fingers are driving me crazy!" Remy yelled as Carl's fingers continued to rub circles over his hip. Carl looked at him in surprise and then down at his fingers as if he thought he had just grown them.

"Sorry!" he said as he pulled them out of the water. "I didn't realize–"

Remy reached out, gripped Carl's arm, and pulled him down. Carl's eyes widened in surprise, and Remy knew his speed had shocked the other man. Normally, he would have toned it down. It never paid to show your full strength, but right then he didn't care. Carl's gentle touches and unassuming manner threw Remy's control over his neglected sex drive into a complete tailspin, and he needed to be touched. Now.

Carl's arm hit the water with a splash, and Remy rose up to meet him as he crushed their mouths together. Carl fought him slightly, and finally Remy lost patience with it and pulled Carl bodily into the tub with him, pajama bottoms and all. He wrapped himself around Carl's body and kissed him hungrily.

Carl finally regained control and propped himself up on his arms to glare down at Remy, who smiled back at him as he dripped.

"You crazy tosser!" Carl gasped. "I'm wet!"

"So'm I. Search me for bugs, Trigger," Remy said in a low, purring voice. Carl shivered above him, but his eyes remained locked with Remy's. "Your eyes are green, aren't they?" Remy murmured as Carl shifted, trying to get away from the now lukewarm water while remaining plastered to Remy's body. It looked to be difficult. Remy swung one leg over the side of the tub and tried to make room for him. Carl settled down between his legs, and Remy knew that at least Carl wanted it as much as he did. He brought his leg back into the tub and hooked it over Carl's hip before the other man could try to get away again.

"No, my eyes aren't green," Carl answered distractedly.

"Hazel then?" Remy asked with a smirk.

"Yes. Mostly, anyway. What the hell are you doing?"

"I should have thought it would be obvious," Remy purred back at him.

"What about… Shawn won't… I don't want to be getting into the middle of anything."

"The only thing you'll be getting into is me," Remy responded with a mischievous smile as he tugged at Carl's long hair and forced him down for another kiss. Carl was hesitant, and he seemed to waver between pulling away and delving deeper. For some reason the hesitance made Remy want him all the more, and he turned the seduction up a notch. His tongue glided behind Carl's upper teeth and then plunged deep into his mouth, swirling around Carl's tongue and coaxing it into activity.

Carl groaned and gripped Remy's arms as their tongues battled; he slid Remy's wet body up the slick side of the tub and pressed him into a semi-sitting position, remaining on his knees between Remy's legs as he did so. The water splashed wildly around them and Remy pawed at Carl's wet pajama pants with his one free hand. He whimpered into Carl's mouth as the gripping fingers dug into his fresh wound, and for the life of him, he couldn't understand why the pain turned him on so much.

Perhaps he was channeling Brandt or something. Didn't matter.

"Please," he whispered as Carl separated for air. "Please," he said again in a stronger voice. Carl shook his head absently and muttered.

"We should get out of the water," he suggested as he thrust forward against Remy's body unconsciously.

"No," Remy groaned. "Too cold out there. Jesus, Trigger," he murmured as Carl's hand tightened around his arm. The pain lanced through his bicep like a fresh bullet whipping past him, but his cock throbbed with desire and he cried out desperately. "Please! Fuck me!"

"Jesus," Carl breathed as he lowered himself further into the water, and it sloshed over the edge of the bathtub. "We're making a mess," he argued desperately.

"We'll be leaving in the morning anyway," Remy panted. "Do you always argue this much?"

"Uhh..."

Remy cut off any possible argument with another searing kiss, and Carl's hips thrust forwards into him once more, causing them both to slip down the sloping side of the bath and into the water once more. Remy moaned into Carl's mouth and tried to pull him closer, but still Carl held him at bay and shook his head violently when he pulled away.

"I'll hurt you," he protested as he struggled to return them both to a sitting position. The water lapped at Remy's chin and sloshed over the side of the tub.

"No more than you already have," Remy argued plaintively as he grabbed for Carl's arm and pulled him close. Carl did a double take when he saw the water around them. The blood was once more running freely down Remy's arm, slowly turning the water a faint pink. Carl looked down at him in horror.

"Jesus!" he hissed. "I'm sorry!"

Remy lunged upwards and attached himself to Carl like a leech, throwing their precarious position off once more, which was difficult and not a little dangerous in the bath full of water. Carl's knees and hands struggled for purchase; he ended up sliding against the slick bottom of the tub, pressed against Remy's body and into his arms. Remy's head banged against the wall and he slid beneath the water as he lost his hold around Carl's neck, but Carl managed to pull him back up with one arm as the other kept them both above water. The trace amount of anger was gone from Carl's eyes, but he maintained the startled look.

"Sorry!" Carl murmured again as he steadied Remy beneath him and held him close to his body, looking at the flowing blood with a grimace.

"Don't be sorry," Remy growled; they struggled to stay upright together and their bodies pressed into one another with a wet sucking sound. "Just do it again."

Carl shook his head vehemently. "No."

Remy kissed him again, trying to break the other man's restraint. He used his still submerged thigh to push between Carl's legs, and pushed just hard enough to make Carl worry about his ability to reproduce before he let up and then pushed again. Carl wasn't fighting him at all, and Remy was impressed with the man's ability to control himself.

"You don't want me?" Remy inquired in a low, sultry voice. Carl closed his eyes and swallowed heavily.

"Remy," he croaked. "Please don't make me do this to you."

Remy furrowed his brow in confusion, but he sensed something dangerous in Carl's voice that made his entire body pulse with need. How much could you poke the sleeping lion before he awoke and bit your head off?

Well, Remy didn't know, but he sure did plan on finding out.

"Do what, Trigger? What will you do to me?" Remy pushed, tightening his grip around Carl's neck and bringing Carl down to him, pressing his wet, naked body against him and giving him little choice but to feel every inch of what he was being offered.

"Oh, God," Carl murmured as Remy breathed heavily over Carl's wet neck and ear. "Out of the water," he requested softly. He gripped Remy tighter and made to pick him up, but Remy kicked out with his leg and dislodged Carl's knee, sending the bigger man toppling down onto him in another great splash of water.

"I like it here," Remy sputtered as the water rose around his mouth. Carl kissed him hard, pressing Remy down into the water with the weight of his body. Remy squeezed his eyes shut and relished the feel of Carl's tongue in his mouth as the water seeped in and trickled down his throat. He was completely under water, and his pulse raced as the added adrenaline kick from the threat of drowning as he attempted to fuck one of his companions entered his bloodstream. Carl began to push him towards the end of the bath once more, and Remy slid until he was once again above water and panting into Carl's open mouth.

He slid his hands down Carl's dripping body and under the soaked waistband of the thin cotton pants Carl had put on when he woke up, and he pushed them down over Carl's hips and gripped his ass, pulling him towards him and upsetting their precarious balance once more. This time though, Carl managed to keep them from going under again, and he growled warningly as his tongue continued to delve further into Remy's mouth. The growl echoed through Remy's body and he shivered happily.

There was the lion. Remy spread his legs open as far as they could go in the confining space, working Carl in between them finally, and Carl automatically edged closer as he lifted his body up and knelt over Remy, never breaking the wet, heated kiss.

"You want it this way?" Carl panted in between a succession of quick, fevered kisses that Remy thought he'd never get enough of.

"Yes," Remy hissed back.

Carl struggled to disrobe, and somehow managed it without either standing or getting out of the bathtub. Remy was intrigued. He ran his soapy hand over Carl's impressive chest and abdomen as Carl knelt between his legs.

"Jesus," Remy muttered lustily as his hands ran over hard muscle and smooth skin. Carl shivered when Remy's hands reached his groin.

Carl growled again suddenly; he swiped his hand through the soap and suds on his chest before grabbing Remy's hip with his other hand and pulling him forcefully until Remy's ass rested on his thighs. Remy's head remained just barely above the water when he had finished sliding. He let it sink until his nose was almost submerged, and his eyes rolled into the back of his head as Carl's soapy fingers thrust into him roughly.

Remy's slick hands scrambled for purchase, but could find none as Carl twisted his fingers and leant forward to kiss him hard. The water rushed into Remy's throat once more, and he writhed in the shallow water as Carl's finger twisted inside him.

He was drowning slowly, but Remy found that he really didn't give a flying fuck as long as Carl's fingers and tongue continued to do what they were doing. It was only when Carl pulled his fingers out that Remy bit the other man's lip to let him know that he could no longer breathe. Carl had apparently picked up on Remy's fascination with the aggression, and he simply pushed Remy back up the slick incline of the tub and continued to kiss him as he guided the head of his cock into Remy's body and brutally plunged in.

Remy whimpered in a muffled cry of pleasure, but the sound made it no further than Carl's smothering mouth and Remy gripped the other man as he thrust into him. With each plunge, the water moved against their motions, and finally it began to slosh over the edges until there was no longer enough left to drown Remy even if he were lying flat. They slid back until Remy laid flat and Carl hovered over him, thrusting into him as hard and deep as he could manage in the space they inhabited. Finally, Carl broke the kiss with a gasp.

"You wanted a bubble bath," he panted as the suds from the body wash swirled around them in the little water that remained.

"Yes," Remy hissed. "Did you find any bugs?" Remy questioned in the same breathless voice Carl was forced to use. Carl smiled and shook his head, rocking his hips and causing Remy to cry out wordlessly.

Carl's hand came to rest on the top of Remy's head to make certain he didn't bash it against the wall as he repeatedly thrust into him. Remy soon lost control of his breathing; it was coming in short gasps as Carl brought him closer and closer to completion. Carl growled and pushed forward, holding up their bodies with his feet against the other wall of the tub.

"I can't get any leverage," he growled as he gripped Remy's hips and spun them around easily in the slick bathtub, sloshing in the water and ending up on his back with Remy straddling him.

Remy's upper body folded and he jerked repeatedly as the movement sent his control flying out the window. He rocked slightly as he came, a hoarse cry escaping as he covered Carl's stomach and chest, and soon Carl thrust upward with all his strength, shouting as he came into Remy's body.

They stayed that way for some minutes, panting slightly. Finally, Remy dipped his hand in what remained of the soapy water and wiped idly at the mess he'd made on Carl's chest. Carl watched him with amusement and shook his head.

"Now we're both waterlogged," he grumbled with a little grin.

"Yes, but, at least now we know I'm clean," Remy said with a cheeky little wink.

VIII.

"WHAT'S taking them so long?" Shawn growled as he sat between Thiago and Brandt and sulked. It had been almost fifteen minutes since Nikolaus had joined them.

The German had been filling them in on what Remy had been telling he and Carl in the other room, but Thiago knew Shawn wasn't listening. His eyes remained glued to the connecting door and his body was tense next to Thiago's.

"They're doing what we should be doing and blowing off some steam," Brandt huffed.

"What do you want, all of us to climb into bed together and fuck?" Shawn snapped at the man.

"Sounds fun to me," Brandt answered with a shit-eating grin and a wink at Nikolaus. The little German rolled his eyes and looked away as Thiago laughed softly.

"How would that work exactly?" Thiago asked with interest.

"Be fun to figure it out," Brandt answered mischievously.

"Both of you shut the fuck up," Shawn growled. "No one's fucking anyone tonight; we've got too much to do."

"*Au contraire*," Thiago responded gleefully in a parodied French accent. He was enjoying the fact that Shawn was suffering a little. It served the man right. "I think Remy and Carl are taking care of that as we speak."

Shawn reached over and smacked him in retaliation. Thiago fell to the side and toppled off the bed, laughing raucously even as Brandt and Nikolaus moved to restrain Shawn from doing any further damage.

"Somebody kick Che Guevera in the nuts for me please!" Shawn demanded angrily. Brandt laughed harder and Nikolaus covered his mouth so Shawn couldn't see him smirking.

Thiago reached up and pulled himself up to peer over the edge of the bed. "*Hinchapelotas*," he hissed at the man with a smirk.

"I don't know what that means, but I know I want to hit you again," Shawn huffed at him.

"*Debe venir a Buenos Aires. No es la humedad que le matará*," Thiago offered with a mischievous grin.

"Did he just threaten me?" Shawn asked no one in particular.

"Yeah," Brandt answered with a grin and a laugh.

"*Quiero* Taco Bell, asshole?" Shawn shot back.

Thiago stood up and pointed a finger at him. "Don't be rude," he chastised.

Before Shawn could respond, the connecting door was thrown open and Carl and Remy stumbled over one another as they burst into the room.

"What's the yelling?" Remy gasped as Carl bumped into him from behind and grabbed him around the chest to keep him from falling over forward. It was a decidedly unimpressive entrance for two such highly trained and highly skilled agents. Thiago thought that perhaps the fact that they were both clad in only towels and dripping wet had something to do with the bad form.

"What happened to your clothes?" Nikolaus asked as he examined Carl's towel-clad body suspiciously from where he sat, still helping to restrain Shawn on the bed.

"What happened to *my* clothes?" Remy asked pointedly as he eyed the other man.

Thiago glanced at the forgotten bag on the floor and chuckled just before Shawn pulled loose from Brandt's grip and smacked him again.

IX.

CARL stood in the doorway and watched in a sort of detached fascination as Shawn lunged and grabbed Thiago by the neck. Thiago snickered as he tried to pry Shawn's hand loose and Brandt and Nikolaus were little help. They were laughing so hard neither man could really breathe. Carl wondered if the crazy was catching.

"What the hell is going on?" he demanded as Remy moved to help.

The other man held his towel to his hips with one hand and grabbed Shawn's wrist with the other. "Shawn," he murmured as he squeezed Shawn's wrist pointedly.

It was as if they had never been apart. The way Shawn instantly calmed as Remy extricated Thiago from his grasp reminded Carl of their first few weeks together. The reaction provided him with a very brief spurt of elation.

"It don't do to try and kill off the minority," Remy chastised before offering Thiago a hand up. "Looks bad," he said with a hint of a smile as Thiago climbed to his feet and snickered.

"He was baiting him," Brandt argued defensively. He reached out and wrapped an arm around Shawn protectively.

The elation sputtered and died as Carl watched tensely, dreading how Remy would react to the possessiveness. Remy cocked his head at them both and then glanced at Thiago.

"I was," Thiago admitted shamelessly.

Remy asked him something in rapid-fire Spanish, and Thiago responded in much the same unintelligible jumble of foreign words. When Remy glanced back at Shawn, he was frowning slightly. "Need a thicker skin, Beignet," he said to him disapprovingly.

"He didn't take kindly to the thought of Carl searching you for bugs," Brandt told him with what could have been an accusatory glare.

Remy glanced over at Carl and raised an eyebrow questioningly, as if asking how this should be handled. Carl shrugged in answer. It wasn't as if any of them were operating under the delusion of chastity.

"Well. If you're going to perform a cavity search, it may as well be fun, right?" Remy finally asked with a smile. Carl closed his eyes and winced.

Shawn huffed and pulled away from Brandt. He rolled off the bed and stood fluidly, shaking his head as if trying to shake off the irritation. Remy took a step as if to follow him, but Brandt reached out quickly and grabbed him around the waist, then tugged him backward and slammed him onto the mattress.

Carl and Thiago both tensed, and Shawn whirled around to stare at the two men in alarm. Brandt had Remy pinned to the bed and looked down at him intently. Remy didn't seem to be alarmed, though.

"What's shaking, Gatorbait?" Remy asked the larger man calmly, not at all fazed from being upended.

"I thought it an opportune time to grope you," Brandt answered brazenly in the same business-like tone.

Thiago began to edge away from the bed and glanced at Carl inquiringly. Carl's lips twitched in amusement and he shrugged again. Both men were fucking insane. It might be interesting to see how this went without outside interference.

"I lost my towel," Remy pointed out accusingly.

Brandt looked down the Cajun's body and then back up to meet his eyes with a nod. "You did," he affirmed calmly.

Before anyone could move, Brandt held Remy to the bed by his shoulders and kissed him savagely, heedless of the wound on his arm or of the bruises. Remy flailed briefly and uttered a muffled exclamation against Brandt's lips, but then he wrapped his good arm around Brandt's neck and returned the kiss with difficulty.

Carl raised an eyebrow as he watched. This was so completely out of the blue, he wasn't even sure if he was really seeing it. He glanced at Shawn and found the man watching in stunned disbelief.

"*Erotomannin*," Nikolaus muttered with a shake of his head and a slight smirk as he sat down on the edge of the other bed. He took his glasses off and began idly cleaning them.

Brandt pushed up onto his hands and knees and growled down at Remy. "I haven't set anything on fire today," he announced.

Carl saw Remy's eyes widen in sudden understanding, and Carl stepped forward to intervene.

Shawn reached out and stopped him with a shake of his head. "We did have a deal," he reminded.

Carl glanced at him with a frown and then looked back at Thiago worriedly. Thiago shrugged helplessly and Carl turned his attention back to the two men on the bed. Unless Remy asked them for help, Carl supposed he couldn't really step in without making a total ass of himself.

Brandt pushed at Remy's hip and Remy rolled over to his stomach as Brandt hovered over him. He knelt behind Remy and glanced over at Shawn as if asking for permission. Shawn nodded to Brandt and the big man wrapped his arms around Remy's waist and lifted him up until he was on his hands and knees. He ran his tongue slowly over Remy's neck and whispered into his ear. Remy's eyes fluttered and almost closed.

Carl glanced at Shawn. The older man watched Remy intently, his jaw set and his eyes hard, and it looked for all the world like he might simply be using Brandt as his very own weapon of Cajun destruction. Carl was slightly disturbed by the concept, but he was too fascinated to go to the rescue. Remy kept his eyes locked on Shawn's as Brandt manhandled him, and it could have been just Remy and Shawn in the room for all the attention they were paying the others.

Brandt slowly pushed his sleep bottoms down as he whispered into Remy's ear again, and this time Carl heard him say, "Are you still full of Trigger's come?"

Carl shivered, and Remy did as well. Remy nodded and thrust his hips backward slightly.

Brandt lifted him further and then pulled him back, his fingers digging into Remy's hip as he slid into him. Remy's mouth opened as if he were about to yell and his head fell forward, but no sound came out save for a small gasp, and his shadowed eyes remained locked on Shawn's. Shawn's eyes flickered uncertainly, but he didn't look away.

Carl didn't know exactly why or how the little public show had begun, and he couldn't decide who was punishing whom. Remy was fucking another man in front of Shawn, either as revenge for Shawn's being a bastard or to make up for his transgressions. Carl didn't know their relationship well enough to know which. Shawn was allowing it to happen, either to punish Remy or as penance for his own mistakes. And Brandt, well, Brandt could either be punishing them both by fucking Remy into oblivion, or he really had just decided to take his 'I didn't blow shit up' treat from Remy tonight.

Carl's head hurt just trying to figure it all out, and he realized that when two very fit and likely insane men were about to fuck, it didn't do to analyze things overly much. He moved slowly toward the other bed, where Nikolaus and Thiago sat, and he crawled in to sit between the two men and watch with his head cocked in interest.

Brandt's hand reached around to rub across Remy's forehead, and his fingers threaded roughly through Remy's hair, pulling the younger man's head back and forcing his chin up. Brandt moaned as he slowly moved his hips forward and further inserted his cock into Remy's body.

Thiago muttered something in Spanish and shook his head. Shawn began to prowl restlessly around the end of the bed, as if he weren't certain what he should do. Carl wondered what it felt like to watch your old love and your new love fucking in your bed. Remy's eyes never left him as Brandt sped his movements.

Carl'd had Brandt inside him before, and he had no idea how Remy remained silent, much less kept his eyes open and focused on Shawn. But he was managing it very well, and while Shawn struggled with his mental state, Brandt pumped into Remy in smooth, controlled thrusts, trying to get him to cry out.

Remy's eyes finally squeezed shut and he let his head fall completely as Brandt's hold tightened around him. He gasped quietly, but it was the only sound he made.

Brandt growled deep in his throat and increased his speed. Carl knew the signs. The man was getting frustrated. He wasn't used to someone resisting the urge to wail when he fucked him. He reached between Remy and the bed, searching for a sound of pleasure.

"Harder," was all Remy murmured. It was the first word he uttered, and Brandt complied with a growl. Remy whimpered and his body arched as Brandt pounded into him.

Carl's gaze flickered to Shawn, who stood motionless at the end of the bed, breathing hard and looking conflicted.

Brandt straightened up and pressed Remy into the bed, forcing him to lay flat and pounding into him with all his strength.

Carl tensed as he saw the fire in Brandt's eyes, and he saw the others do the same. The last thing they needed was for Remy to be injured by an overzealous fucking.

Brandt pumped into Remy as he held Remy's arms captive at his elbows, and though Shawn looked about ready to pounce on them, he remained where he was and continued to observe with an almost pained look. Carl sat forwards and made ready to stand and do something about the violent attack, but as he was about to stand Remy gasped into the bedcovers and laughed tightly.

"Is that all you have?" he whispered tauntingly.

Carl blinked in surprise and Thiago's jaw dropped. Shawn smiled weakly and Brandt growled in response. He pulled out of Remy roughly and rolled both their bodies until they were standing beside the bed, right in front of Carl.

Brandt pushed the smaller man toward the wall, ramming his chest against the wall and then standing behind him and pinning him there like a ragdoll. He pushed into him violently as Remy's hands scrambled for purchase against the smooth wall.

Brandt roared as he pounded into Remy's body, and then he bent his head and sank his teeth into Remy's shoulder as the rest of them watched, stupefied.

Remy finally cried out when the teeth sank into him; a short, surprised shout that sent Brandt over the edge of his precarious control.

When it was all said and done, they were all breathing hard and looking at one another as if they weren't certain of what to do next. Remy stood at the wall and rested his forehead against it, and Brandt fell back onto the bed and panted from the exertion.

Shawn moved slowly, stepping past Carl wordlessly to come up behind Remy and run a gentle hand down his spine. Remy shivered and finally turned around to look at them with a blank expression on his face.

"You two have some things to discuss, take the other room," Thiago said in a low voice. Carl tore his eyes away from Remy and Shawn and threw back the bedcovers woodenly. He didn't know exactly what he'd just seen, but he thought maybe he'd enjoyed it. He burrowed beneath the blankets as Thiago climbed in with him, and when he poked his head back out from beneath the blanket to turn off the lamp, Shawn and Remy were gone. They hadn't made a sound as they left, and Carl shivered as Thiago pulled him close and sighed heavily.

"Trouble brewing?" Thiago asked him softly.

"If there isn't, I'll eat my boots," Carl murmured in answer.

"Go take a shower!" Nikolaus demanded of Brandt as he tried to run him out of the other bed.

X.

SHAWN hesitated briefly as he watched Remy fall onto the bed. He glanced over at the other bed and swayed on his feet, wondering which one he should climb into. Would Remy want him close after he had behaved so horribly? Brandt had said he would have hated Shawn after such a display. Brandt and Remy were so very much alike, Remy probably hated him too.

"Are you okay?" he asked in a whisper as he stood indecisively between the beds.

"*Un transport*," Remy mumbled in answer. Shawn knew from his experience with the Cajun that it meant he couldn't sit still. Usually when he used the phrase, he was referring to having the jitters or being restless. Tonight Shawn thought it had a different meaning. But if Remy could make a joke, then he was okay.

He didn't know what else to say about the little scene in the other room. He couldn't remember ever watching another man fuck Remy just for the pleasure of it. It had been unsettling and, with Brandt the one doing the fucking, it had hammered home a few of the confusing feelings Shawn was dealing with.

He took a dejected step toward the empty bed.

"Please don't," Remy said in a small, pleading voice. Shawn looked at him inquiringly. He sat in the bed now with his back propped against the headboard, looking at Shawn warily.

"Don't what?" Shawn asked carefully as he took a step toward Remy and reached to turn off one of the lamps.

"Please don't sleep over there," Remy said quietly. "Not tonight. It's been three months." If Shawn hadn't known better, he would have thought Remy was about to break down and cry.

Shawn nodded solemnly and crawled into the bed hesitantly. He sat beside Remy, his entire body tense and his brain working on overdrive. He was unsure of what to do. It was an odd feeling for Shawn, who rarely had difficulty deciding on a course of action. But not knowing how to behave with regards to Remy was unheard of for him. He'd never felt discomfort of any sort around Remy. Not until now.

'So this is what guilt feels like,' he thought grimly. He lowered his head in shame as he thought back on some of the things he'd said when Remy startled them all out of their sleep. He didn't even want to begin to think about the feelings he had for Brandt, or about confessing them.

"Shawn?" Remy ventured softly.

"I'm sorry, Dixie," Shawn murmured. He felt Remy move on the bed, but he suddenly knew he couldn't raise his eyes and look into Remy's face. He couldn't face those earnest brown eyes any more than he could look at himself in the mirror right now. The shame washed over him again and he squeezed his eyes closed to combat it.

Remy's hand came to rest lightly on Shawn's shoulder, and the contact startled the older man to the point that he shook off Remy's hand before he could stop the impulse. He couldn't bear to have Remy touch him; he didn't feel worthy of it. Shawn looked up sharply when he heard a noise from Remy he had never thought to hear.

Remy sniffed again and drew his knees up to his chest. He rested his chin miserably on his folded arms and he looked at Shawn pitifully.

"Oh, God, Remy, no. Don't do that. I can't handle that," Shawn stuttered as he watched a tear run slowly down Remy's cheek and into the stubble on his chin. Shawn shook his head as Remy's shoulders slumped. "No. Remy. Please, don't cry on me. Christ," he pleaded desperately as Remy buried his head in his arms and his shoulders began to shake.

Shawn froze and watched in desperation. What was he to do? He had made Remy cry, for fuck's sake! Remy had never cried in his presence before! Even when he'd shot him in the ass, Remy hadn't cried!

He put his hand out tentatively to try and comfort the younger man, and just as his hand made contact with the quivering shoulder, Remy snorted.

"You wanker!" Shawn shouted angrily as Remy looked up at him and grinned impishly. "I thought you were crying, you little twat!"

Remy covered his mouth and laughed silently and Shawn shoved him. Remy sprawled sideways on the bed and Shawn moved quickly to straddle him, digging his fingers into Remy's ribs mercilessly until Remy was laughing so hard he couldn't breathe and was begging for Shawn to stop.

"Don't ever do that to me again," Shawn warned finally, pointing his finger in Remy's face and letting his body relax against the younger man's.

"I couldn't resist it, you looked so… forlorn," Remy said with another snort. He slapped his hand over his mouth to cover the snorts and widened his eyes innocently as he looked up at Shawn.

Shawn rolled his eyes and flopped onto his back, and Remy remained where he was beside him, staring up at the ceiling and sniggering quietly. Shawn marveled at Remy's ability to completely hijack his thoughts and feelings with so little effort. Remy had known Shawn was beating himself up, and this was his way of accepting the apology Shawn had barely even made.

The knowledge made Shawn feel even worse than before. Now he was certain he didn't deserve Remy's loyalty. He didn't think anyone deserved something so pure.

"You deserved it," Remy muttered after several moments of silence.

"What?" Shawn asked in shock. He'd once suspected that Remy could read minds, but that theory had since been debunked. Primarily because a supernaturally enabled Remy really should have been able to sense that bullet heading toward his ass, but also if Remy could read minds he would have killed Shawn by now.

"You a big big *couyon.* You deserved a good fake cry."

"Shut it, you bugger," Shawn grumbled.

"You called me a liar."

"You are a liar."

"Only when I say 'oh Shawn! You're the best I ever had,'" Remy said, his voice going into a horrible falsetto and his hands clasping beneath his chin as he simpered at Shawn.

"Don't bat your eyelashes at me," Shawn growled.

"How do you know I was?" Remy asked innocently

"I just know," Shawn proclaimed confidently.

"You called me a whore," Remy reminded him, apparently choosing to bypass the eyelash conversation for greener pastures.

"You are a whore, Remy. Biggest man-whore I've ever seen."

"Yeah," Remy said wistfully. Shawn grinned and brought his hand up to twirl Remy's hair absently. It had grown long in their absence from one another, and Shawn played with a curl as he let fatigue and relief wash over him. He'd missed the younger man a great deal. They remained silent for some time, and Shawn was almost asleep when Remy's sad voice reached him.

"You called me a traitor," he said quietly. Shawn's eyes snapped open and he sucked in a painful breath. Here was the conversation he had been dreading. One of them, anyway. He looked over at Remy, but the younger man was still looking up at the ceiling unblinkingly. Shawn rolled and placed his hand gently on Remy's cheek and forced him to turn his head and look at him. Remy's dark eyes glistened in the lamplight, and Shawn frowned at him.

"You'd better not be taking the piss again, Dixie, I swear to God–"

"Shawn," Remy said in wavering voice. Shawn snapped his mouth closed and his eyes widened in surprise. Remy was serious this time. "Did you mean it?" the younger man asked.

"What?"

"Do you think me a traitor?" Remy asked miserably.

"Remy," Shawn said hesitantly. Remy looked at him sternly, obviously expecting a real answer. "I didn't– I wasn't thinking clearly."

"*Arrête-toi*. You always think clearly," Remy said in disgust.

"Do you… do you have any idea what it was like?" Shawn asked angrily. Remy furrowed his brow and stared up at Shawn unfalteringly. "I thought you were dead! I thought I'd lost you, and I was trying to get my mind around how I was supposed to live the rest of my life without you! Do you've any idea what that's like?"

Remy's brow knitted further and he swallowed hard as he looked up at Shawn. His eyes darted back and forth as he tried to take in all of Shawn's features at once, and the mix of despair and anger and guilt and lust that Shawn had been feeling throughout the night came surging forth once more.

"It fucks with your mind!" Shawn yelled in frustration, trying to validate his boorish behavior, to both himself and Remy. "When you came waltzing back in here with that stupid fucking grin on your face I didn't know what to think! And then you started talking about John and turning and finding the Archer and joining him and… I could have bloody well killed you! I almost did kill you! What were you thinking, sneaking in like that?"

"*Te en colaire*?" Remy asked in alarm.

"I'm not angry," Shawn answered defensively.

"You sound angry," Remy insisted incredulously. "You're angry that I escaped? You're angry that I came back? Why?"

"M'not angry," Shawn said in a low voice. "Frustrated, maybe," he added softly as he loosened his grip on Remy's arm and pushed away from him.

"*Co faire?*" Remy asked in confusion.

"Would you speak English, please? Knock off the damn mumbo jumbo for one fucking minute," Shawn demanded angrily as he pushed up and away. He knew it was a low blow. Remy always spoke in a jumble when he was distracted or distraught. It was one of the many idiosyncrasies Shawn loved about him, and he knew he shouldn't bitch about it.

"You're trying to distract me," Remy accused in a slightly hurt voice.

Shawn shifted until his back was against the headboard and he huffed. "Is it working?" he asked softly, not bothering to deny it.

"*Mais non*, it's not working," Remy asserted indignantly as he turned to face Shawn and scowled at him.

They stared at one another for several long moments. Shawn knew he was stalling. He knew that what he really needed to do was apologize, then confess all his sins, and then apologize again. But he couldn't possibly confess all his sins. He didn't think even Remy's loyalty stretched that far.

Instead, he simply looked at the younger man, taking in the cuts and the bruises, some of them older than others. His wrists had fading bruises on them and there was a welt across his chest that looked as if he had run into something hot. The wound on his arm was definitely a gunshot wound, and his cheek was turning red where Shawn had hit him. Finally, Shawn couldn't look at him any longer. He looked away and stared at the dark corner of the hotel room.

"You smell like strawberries," he muttered as Remy sat silently beside him.

"Shower stuff," Remy murmured with a flush as he looked away as well.

Shawn smiled slightly and ducked his head. "I'm sorry," he offered softly.

"You feel guilty about something," Remy responded in a whisper.

Shawn huffed and swung his feet out of the bed. He headed toward the bathroom with his head down, unable to face the conversation. He knew he wasn't a coward, but he also knew this was fight he was afraid to have.

"Where are you going?" Remy called after him.

"Toilet," Shawn grunted as he walked unsteadily toward the bathroom.

"Careful, Beignet," Remy called softly. "The floor's wet in there."

"Do I want to know why?" Shawn asked as he flipped on the light and looked around at the several towels on the floor, hypothetically there to soak up the water. The entire room smelled strongly of strawberry. Shawn stood there looking at the scene and wondering which one of those pansies in the other room used strawberry bath crème.

Remy startled him by slipping his arms around Shawn's waist and resting his chin on Shawn's shoulder. He would never get used to how silently Remy could move. Usually Shawn had to key in on the brush of denim or the creak of leather, the click of a boot heel or even the tapping sound Remy's ring made on his gun when he was nervous or impatient. Shawn was able to use all those things to track Remy's movements, but when Remy was unclothed and unarmed, Shawn couldn't for the life of him keep track.

"You don't wanna know," Remy said to him confidently.

"Was he good then?" Shawn asked curiously, his head tilting to the side as he tried to look sideways at Remy.

Remy answered with a slow, slightly unfocused grin.

"Interesting," Shawn murmured thoughtfully. "That's what Thiago said, too."

Remy laughed softly. "We can fight tomorrow," he whispered hopefully.

"*Fais do do*," he announced as the fatigue caught up with him. He turned back around to trudge to the closest bed.

Shawn had asked several times what that phrase meant, and from what he understood it had something to do with going to bed. Or having a big party, depending on which Cajun he asked. He stood in the doorway of the bathroom, watching as Remy's shadowed form slid under the covers.

Shawn quickly washed up and followed. He crawled into the bed uncertainly and rested his head on the pillow next to Remy's. It had been so long since they'd been like this. Shawn felt the guilt begin to ebb, slowly being replaced by the sheer power of Remy's presence.

"Tell me about your three months with Niko," Shawn prompted as Remy lay looking at him in the darkness.

Remy was silent for a long moment. "Not much to tell," he finally answered thoughtfully. "Niko's a scrapper. He'll do okay. How did you and Brandt get on?" he asked.

Shawn caught his breath and closed his eyes. He took a long moment to clear his mind. "I have to tell you something, Dixie," he said slowly, trying to stall so he could formulate his words. "And it's not going to be easy so– "

"Shawn, wait. I–"

"Please let me do this without interrupting," Shawn said in a low voice. "I'll drive myself mad if I don't get it out. I don't know how to say this, so… I think… I think I may have fallen in love with him," Shawn admitted in a whispered rush of words. He saw Remy stiffen in the moonlight that filtered through the heavy drapes. He waited for several long, heartbreaking moments, but Remy neither moved nor spoke and Shawn began to worry about him. He wasn't even breathing. "Dixie?"

Remy responded by letting out a long, slow exhalation, and his body relaxed again in the bed next to Shawn. "I kinda had a feeling it was something like that," he said quietly.

"Remy, I–"

"My indiscretions don't seem so important now," Remy interrupted in a murmur. Shawn swallowed heavily and reached out to touch him. He expected Remy to pull away from him, but to his surprise and relief Remy turned his head to rub his cheek against Shawn's hand.

"I'm sorry," Shawn whispered. "It doesn't change what I said before," he said hopefully, trying to ease the pain of his confession by any means available to him.

Remy sniffed disbelievingly. "Doesn't matter much, now. I was so worried about loyalty…," he sighed and shook his head. Shawn swallowed heavily and waited for the rest of what Remy had to say. "Some of the things McTiernan told me… he's watching us, Shawn."

"Remy…," Shawn responded uncertainly.

Remy wasn't taking his confession exactly the way he had expected. He was also using a classic Bergeron diversion technique; throw a sliver of important information out in order to keep your opponent off balance and move him away from an unwanted discussion. That was how Remy struck. He would wave his hand in one direction and kick you in the ass from the other. He called it the 'Shiny Thing Approach.' Distraction. Diversion. What the fuck ever he wanted to call it, it was damn effective.

"What's this about John watching us, then?" Shawn asked with difficulty.

"Not John. The Archer," Remy responded with a long sigh. "Look, we'll talk about it in the morning. Had a long day."

Shawn could give him that. The younger man had to be exhausted. When Shawn thought of all that Remy had probably put himself through to get to them so quickly, the guilt twisted through him once more. He watched as Remy rolled over carefully and turned away from him, and he cursed himself for all the confused feelings he harbored. It should have been simple. How could he have compared five years to three months? How could he have betrayed that trust so easily?

"Shawn?" Remy ventured finally.

"Hmm?" Shawn responded in a sleepy tone, trying to make Remy think he had been close to sleep instead of close to a nervous breakdown.

"You never answered my question," Remy said accusingly.

"Didn't I?" Shawn asked in confusion.

"*Mais non.* You thought you would distract me by answering other questions, but that only works once a night."

Shawn sighed and reached out to roll Remy over to face him again in the darkness.

"So we're going to do this now, are we?" Shawn asked in near defeat.

"Do you think me a traitor, Shawn?" Remy asked bluntly.

"What would you do, Remy? What would you do if I were the Archer?" Shawn asked suddenly.

Remy blinked at him and stopped breathing as they stared at one another. Finally, he let his breath out in another long, slow exhalation. "You're not, though, so what does it matter?" he asked uncomfortably.

"How do you know I'm not the Archer?" Shawn asked, feeling the need to play Devil's Advocate and harboring suspicions he just couldn't shake. "We were apart for the first time in five years, you realize, before this mission started. For a full two months, Remy. How do you know I wasn't off killing my fellow agents and–"

"Shawn!"

"What would you do?" Shawn demanded. "After I've just told you that I've betrayed your trust and gone and fallen for another man. What would you do if I had betrayed more than that?"

Remy stared at him for what seemed an eternity, and finally the younger man swallowed and blinked at him. "I told you," he said quietly. "I would follow you. Wherever. Even into the very gates of Hell if you felt the need to go. Nothing you can say or do would change that. *Maintenant*, tell me the truth."

"What if it were one of the others?" Shawn asked persistently, ignoring the question and the pounding of his heart. Remy's words had both wounded him and thrilled him at the same time, but he was determined to get his answers.

"What?"

"What if the Archer were one of the others? What if Thiago is the Archer? Or Brandt? Or Carl, or Niko? What if he's one of them? What would you do then?"

Remy stared at him, blinking rapidly as he tried to figure out how Shawn's mind was working. Shawn watched him closely, waiting for the spark of suspicion in Remy's eyes, but it never came.

"I would follow," Remy stated quietly.

Shawn was taken aback by Remy's answer. He hadn't expected that at all. He had expected a vehement protest as to the innocence of his companions or… something.

"Why?" he asked curiously.

"Because they've earned my loyalty, too. And no matter what happens now, they have it."

Shawn closed his eyes and swallowed painfully. "Your loyalty will get you killed one day, Remy," he mumbled.

"My loyalty is the only thing keeping me alive," Remy responded acidly. Shawn's eyes snapped open and he stared at Remy. "You do, then," Remy said painfully. "You think me a traitor for making the deal."

"I never said that," Shawn argued. He was waffling and he knew it, but the truth was that he didn't know what he thought. If Remy wanted to join the Archer then… yeah. That made him a traitor. And Shawn was under orders to kill traitors. Trained to do it. Programmed to do it. His only defense against the impulse was to fool himself into thinking that Remy was still with him. He had to be with them, still.

"Are you the Archer, Shawn?" Remy asked softly

Shawn stared at him, and Remy waited patiently for his answer.

"You shouldn't have to ask," Shawn responded finally.

"Right," Remy said in disgust. "You know what? I don't care who he is, Shawn. I don't care if he's one of us. I want to find him. I want to join him. I want to do whatever he needs me to do to take the fucking Organization down, and then we'll disappear."

"Remy, for fuck's sake what are you–"

"I–"

"Shut it! I don't want to hear about joining the fucking Archer! I don't want to hear about taking the Organization down! Jesus fucking Christ!" Shawn rolled over and tried to roll out of the bed. He needed to pace. Remy grabbed his arm before he could make it all the way out of the bed.

"Shawn! You wanted to be free," Remy said, his voice low and persuasive and incredibly enticing. "We could be free. We'll disappear together. We'll take the others with us! Brandt, you can bring him," Remy added in a hushed whisper. "We'll pool everything we have and we'll buy a fucking island in the Caribbean or–"

"An island?" Shawn asked, his voice wavering between frustration and amusement.

"I hear they're selling cheap," Remy responded with a shrug.

Shawn snorted, close to despair, and sat on the edge of the bed with his head in his hands.

"No more of this, Remy," he said finally.

"But–"

"Please! I'm fucking begging you!" Shawn said as he turned and grabbed Remy by the arm and shook him violently. "Not another fucking word about joining the Archer!"

"John said he would know if I went back on my word," Remy persisted.

"John was talking out his ass."

"And you were there, were you?" Remy challenged seriously.

"I–"

"He was serious, Shawn," Remy interrupted in a low voice. "The Archer is watching us."

"Bollocks! He may be watching us, Remy, but who are you more afraid of? Him or me!" Shawn yelled before he could think through the implications. As soon as the words left his mouth, he blinked in shock and pulled his hand back. He had just threatened Remy. Threatened him! What in the fuck was this mission doing to them?

They were both silent. The room seemed to grow darker as the silence deepened. Shawn could feel Remy moving on the bed, and he waited to discern exactly what the man was doing. Soon he realized Remy was lying flat once more, and he carefully shifted and flattened out beside the man. They were silent, laying on their backs side by side once more, staring at the ceiling and barely breathing.

"We find another way, then," Remy finally murmured. Shawn turned his head to look at Remy. Even in the dark Shawn could see the determined set of Remy's jaw. "The six of us. We get out together or die trying."

XI.

THE Archer lay awake until the dawn, trying to decide on his next move. He had several roadblocks, the largest of which involved actually making contact with the other five as the Archer instead of the man they knew him to be. The next step would, of course, be getting them to follow him. But the Archer liked to take one nearly impossible step at a time.

He lay there despairing as to what to do, thinking perhaps that the best move would be to simply expose himself and hope they didn't kill him. Remy seemed open to the idea of joining him. Perhaps he could take Remy into his confidence and make an ally of him, not as the man Remy knew, but as the Archer. If anything, Remy was loyal to him. To all of them, really. It could possibly work. It could possibly be forcing Remy into choosing between his loyalties, though. That, or Remy would go into a rage and kill him and solve that problem. That certainly wasn't very appealing.

As he thought through his situation, it hit him suddenly. Gray Kincaid was supposed to be in Brisbane, lying low. He could put in a call to Gray and get him to put on a little performance, something to point them in the right direction. Yes! That was it! He would just have to figure out how to contact him without raising any suspicion. And he would have to do it quickly.

Finally, with his plan in place, the Archer drifted off into a restless sleep.

XII.

NIKOLAUS'S head hurt. In fact, his entire body ached with the very distinct pain of fatigue.

He hated having to move again that morning, but they were better off safe than sorry, as Thiago had put it. They moved one at a time to the new location; an empty flat Brandt kept in Brisbane. It was nice, and Nikolaus found himself wondering why a rambling pyro like Brandt had a nice uptown flat instead of a shack in the outback or a hole he'd blown in the ground somewhere. It was a pleasant surprise, though it left Nikolaus feeling slightly uneasy for some reason he could not define.

Nikolaus, Remy, Brandt, and Carl sat at a café table outside, a few blocks from the flat, their various notes, maps and whatnot spread about them haphazardly as they discussed their next move.

"What does Shawn think of it?" Brandt asked as he lounged in his chair and watched the other patrons of the café nonchalantly.

Remy shifted uncomfortably and looked at them all carefully. Nikolaus knew Remy had to be sore after the treatment he had gotten the night before, but he wondered if that was the reason the other man couldn't sit still or if it was nerves.

"Shawn won't go for it," Remy said finally

"Then why are we discussing it?" Brandt asked coolly.

"We're discussing it because I want you to know what we'll be differing from with the plan I've been trying to formulate," Remy responded testily.

Nikolaus glanced at Carl worriedly. Remy and Brandt had been snapping at one another all morning, and they'd just barely been able to restrain themselves when Shawn had been present. If they started sniping at one another without him there to rein them in, Nikolaus didn't think he and Carl would be able to put a lid on it before they attracted unwanted attention.

Nikolaus leant forwards when Remy started cursing inventively.

"You fucking *motier foux*, you kicked me!" Remy hissed as he leant down and rubbed his shin. "Fuck you, you fucking mad fuck."

"Remy!" Carl admonished, his eyes sliding to a mother with two small children sitting several tables away. "You're gaining some undue attention," he hissed. "Let's try to avoid stepping into a minefield, okay?

"Mines?" Brandt repeated with interest as he zeroed in on Carl. Nikolaus and the other two froze and looked at Brandt warily. His eyes gleamed suddenly with renewed passion and Remy and Carl both edged away as they watched him.

"Down, boy," Remy said as he put a tentative hand on Brandt's forearm and patted him carefully. Brandt and Remy looked at one another, their eyes narrowed and their lips twitching briefly before they were both snickering quietly.

"Sorry I kicked you," Brandt snickered finally.

"Yeah well, sorry I 'fucked' at you," Remy responded with a smirk. This got them all snickering again, and when they calmed down finally all the tension was gone from their little group. Nikolaus sat back and looked around at the other patrons idly as the waitress came to bring their food. He supposed there were advantages to being half-crazy.

The mother and her two kids hadn't noticed them. There were several couples sitting around, lost in their own worlds, and a group of young ladies sat staring at the four of them intently. Nikolaus smirked at them and they giggled and blushed in an amusing manner.

At the next table, a man sat reading a newspaper and rocking his head slightly to the music coming from his little white iPod. Nikolaus's eyes lingered on him, thinking he looked vaguely familiar. His red hair was shaggy, and his beard looked as if it needed a trim, but other than that, the portion of his face that Nikolaus could see was fairly unremarkable. Nikolaus shook his head and returned his attention to the others.

"Should we not wait for the others to talk about this plan of yours?" Carl asked as he unwrapped his silverware. He and Nikolaus seemed to be thinking along the same lines. He wanted Shawn there to crack the whip if the discussion went south again. Remy looked at him appraisingly, and Brandt shrugged and looked off into the distance disinterestedly.

"Sure," Remy said eventually. "They should be back soon, *non*? Shall we have another look at those notes then?" Remy asked them. Nikolaus frowned at him and leaned towards him until he could speak and have just Remy hear him.

"Should you not be practicing a little discretion here?" he asked disapprovingly as he gestured at the tabletop covered with their material.

Remy smiled pensively. "You make me proud, Niko," he said with a wink. "But people rarely pay attention to what other people are doing in places like this," he said as he gestured vaguely at the other patrons. "If there's someone here who knows what we're on about, then we're dead already. No need for discretion."

That didn't exactly make Nikolaus feel much better.

"Where's my crispy paper?" Remy asked absently as he fumbled through the stack of papers and files, completely oblivious to Nikolaus's discomfort.

Carl dug through the papers and brought out the message Remy had carried with him throughout all his ordeals. It was burnt and bloodstained and scribbled upon, but it made Nikolaus smile slightly as Remy took it and began to stare at it.

Carl took out the other note, the one Remy had made of the second message Nikolaus had uncovered, and he and Brandt bent their heads over it.

As Nikolaus puzzled over the now familiar jumble of letters and numbers, the music from the redhead's headphones got louder and louder, and finally Nikolaus looked up to glare at the man. He had taken the things out of his ears and put them on the table, turning the volume up all the way and rocking his head back and forth as the surprisingly loud music blared out of his specialized earphones in the otherwise calm atmosphere.

"D'you mind, mate?" Brandt growled as he looked up at the man.

"Hmm?" the man responded absently as he looked up from his newspaper in surprise and turned in his seat slightly to look at Brandt.

"Could you turn that down a bit?" Nikolaus asked politely, even though the man now had his back to him.

"Oh! Yeah, sorry," the man said in a slow, Southern American accent. "Sorry 'bout that. It just makes me feel at home, y'know, hearing that play. It's *Dixie*," he offered as if that was supposed to make it okay.

Nikolaus did a double take and then glanced at Remy, but the Cajun didn't seem to be bothered by the use of his nickname in song.

"That's fascinating, *mon frère,*" Remy murmured disinterestedly as he chewed on his pen and stared at the paper in front of him without ever turning around to look at the man sitting behind him.

The guy shrugged and put the earphones back in his ears before gathering his things and getting up to walk away. Nikolaus watched him go curiously, thinking that he looked awfully familiar and that he seemed to be in quite a hurry for someone who had been so relaxed just moments before. When he glanced back at the table, Nikolaus saw what looked to have been the man's Sudoku puzzle still lying on the table. He frowned and reached out to snag it.

"He wasn't very good at this," he said dubiously as he examined the answers. It was obvious, even on a passing glance, that some of the answers weren't correct. "Hell, he's even got letters in here," Nikolaus laughed as he examined it. Suddenly his laughter died away and he frowned at the puzzle, then looked at the message Remy held in his hands. "*Gott*," he breathed as realization came tumbling down on him.

"What's wrong?" Remy asked quickly as he looked up into Nikolaus's shocked eyes.

"*Mein Gott*," Nikolaus responded slowly as he looked up into the crowd the man had disappeared into.

Out of the corner of his eye, Nikolaus saw Shawn and Thiago running toward them through the crowded plaza.

XIII.

BRANDT spotted Thiago and Shawn at almost the same time as Nikolaus did, and he stood half out of his chair in alarm. What could possibly make those two men lose their cool enough to literally run through a crowded plaza?

Nikolaus sat frozen as he watched them approach, and Carl was tense in his chair as he sat beside Brandt, looking as if he were about to jump into action. Remy sat calmly sipping his drink as he looked at Nikolaus curiously. He wasn't even paying attention to Shawn and Thiago. Brandt spared him a little sneer before looking back to Shawn and Thiago as they jogged up breathlessly.

"What the fuck are you doing?" Thiago asked in heavily accented English as he panted slightly and stared at all of them in disbelief.

What were *they* doing? They were having lunch, that's what they were doing. Not tear-assing through a crowded plaza drawing all kinds of attention to themselves. Brandt got the feeling from the tone of Thiago's voice that he was out of breath not from the small amount of exertion, but from agitation. Severe agitation.

"What are you talking about? What happened?" Carl asked tensely.

Thiago gaped at them and pointed off in the direction the redheaded man had gone. "That was Gray Kincaid you were conversing with so politely!" Thiago hissed in disbelief.

"The guy from the list?" Remy asked in surprise, finally showing a reaction to Thiago and Shawn's obvious concern. "The one you worked with in Florida?"

"Yes!" Thiago yelled. "What the hell were you thinking?"

"We were… he was… uh…," Remy stuttered as he tried to avoid Shawn's piercing eyes and explain.

Brandt had noticed the discomfort between the two of them earlier, and it disturbed him to no end. Remy seemed distracted, nervous even, when Shawn was around. Shawn just seemed distant. It was as if they weren't certain of how to deal with one another now that someone else was in the picture.

"We'd never seen him before. How were we supposed to recognize him?" Carl asked in vexation.

"I got it," Nikolaus said excitedly as he smacked Remy in the arm and then looked around at them all with wide, excited eyes.

"Ow!" Remy huffed accusingly as he rubbed his bicep and looked at Nikolaus in irritation. "Got what?" he asked distractedly as he looked up at Thiago and Shawn, who were both still panting slightly.

Brandt watched Remy's transformation in fascination. As he looked up at them, it was like he pushed a button and went from a slightly absent-minded young man to a cold-blooded killer in no time flat. His eyes went completely black and his jaw clenched tensely. He looked truly threatening just sitting there and Brandt shivered. Brandt didn't know what Remy had seen in Shawn or Thiago's expressions to cause the change, but it was obviously important. Then just as suddenly as it had come, the killer was gone and Remy was back.

"We have to get inside. Back to the flat. I need my computer," Nikolaus said hurriedly as he started gathering the bits and pieces of paper they had spread across the table.

Remy lunged forward and grabbed Nikolaus's arm with a speed that alarmed even Brandt and Brandt watched them in fascination. This was really the first time Brandt had paid attention to Remy and Nikolaus as a unit, and what he saw made him raise an interested eyebrow. They seemed intimate, which was especially odd after the Jekyll and Hyde performance Brandt just witnessed. As Remy pulled Nikolaus closer to him and spoke in low tones, Brandt watched Shawn for a reaction.

"This is where discretion is called for, Niko," Remy murmured as he put his lips just a breath away from Nikolaus's ear. Brandt saw Shawn tense noticeably and inhale sharply as Remy nodded at Nikolaus and rubbed his arm soothingly to let him know he wasn't admonishing, just advising. "You got the message?" Remy whispered inquiringly.

Nikolaus nodded and brushed his cheek against Remy's lips tenderly before allowing himself to be gently nudged back into his chair. Remy ran an affectionate hand through Nikolaus's hair and smiled at him proudly as the rest of them watched disconcertedly. There was a level of intimacy in their interaction that Brandt recognized as one stemming from physical contact and not just mental understanding, and he could see that Shawn saw it too.

Shawn's jaw clenched as he took a seat around the little table beside Nikolaus, and Brandt watched him until their eyes connected. Brandt tilted his head inquiringly when Shawn's hard green eyes landed on him, but Shawn frowned slightly and shook his head. Brandt wasn't sure what the headshake meant, but he didn't need a written sign to tell him that Shawn was upset.

Brandt turned his attention back to Remy and Nikolaus. Remy was standing now, bending down over Nikolaus and speaking to him in hushed tones. Brandt's attention was torn between Remy and Shawn, and he almost missed it when Remy straightened quickly and tugged at Thiago's arm.

"Come on Thi, let's get after him," Remy said. Without another word to the rest of them the two of them darted off after Gray, and in seconds they simply dematerialized into the scenery. As much as Brandt hated to admit it at that moment, he admired Remy and Thiago's skills. He was even slightly jealous of them. Brandt had never been able to simply disappear like that. His stature and presence were far too conspicuous.

Shawn was leaning forwards and looking after the two men as if he wanted to follow. Nikolaus was already chattering excitedly. Brandt and Carl shared a slightly lost, exasperated look and settled back to observe.

"I've got it," Nikolaus kept saying over and over. For perhaps the first time in his recent memory, Brandt didn't really care about the mission. He didn't care about the messages or the Organization or any of that mess. He focused his considerable attention solely on Shawn. The man looked disturbed. Pissed off, even. Brandt wanted to comfort him somehow, but he knew there was really only one person that could do that. And it wasn't Brandt.

"Nikolaus," Shawn said in a low voice.

"Hmm?"

"You've cracked the Archer's code? Is that what you're saying?" Shawn asked carefully.

"Yes! I–"

"Not now," Shawn said sharply as he stood up and looked around the plaza warily. "Not here."

"But Remy told me to tell all of you what I–"

"Remy's not in charge here," Shawn snapped, startling all three of them as he glared down at them all in turn.

Brandt was shocked. Shawn had never snapped like that. Even when his pants caught fire, he'd maintained a modicum of good humor regarding the situation. Had his discussion with Remy the night before gone that badly? What had they said to one another? Had Shawn told Remy about Brandt? Or was it something to do with Nikolaus and the time he'd spent with Remy? Perhaps both, Brandt decided as he observed the tense, angry set of Shawn's jaw as he glared at Nikolaus. "Now gather this shit up and let's get back to the flat," Shawn ordered as he started gathering the stacks of paper.

None of them questioned the order, though Brandt wondered what would happen if Remy and Thiago ran into trouble. Would they know to return to the flat? Would they think something had gone wrong when they came back to find the table vacated? Well, Shawn was more aware of how Remy would operate than was Brandt, and so Brandt followed along obediently regardless of his questions.

When they returned to the flat, Brandt watched Shawn uneasily, as did Carl and Nikolaus. He stomped around the flat like a caged lion, tossing his things haphazardly onto the table and slamming doors and heading straight for the kitchen after growling something incoherent about needing a drink.

"Shawn?" Carl finally ventured when Shawn stomped back into the main room.

Shawn stared at him, but Carl held his ground and stared right back unerringly. Brandt was proud of his friend just then. He didn't think he would have been able to stare Shawn down, especially knowing he was probably the inadvertent cause of Shawn's evil mood in the first place. Finally, Shawn seemed to deflate and he looked at all of them ashamedly.

"I'm sorry," he murmured in disgust. "I don't like being outsmarted repeatedly by this bastard, it's grating," he huffed as he threw himself down on the sofa and rubbed his eyes. "I'm sorry, Niko. I shouldn't have snapped at you like that. Now tell us about this code."

Brandt turned his full attention on Nikolaus, and, for once, it didn't seem to intimidate the other man. Whether it was that Brandt spent the night before holding Nikolaus like a teddy bear or the excitement caused by the other man's revelation, Brandt didn't know. As long as something worked. Brandt was tired of being the scary one.

"Whatshisname gave us the key," Nikolaus started excitedly.

"Kincaid?" Shawn asked in surprise.

"He did?" Carl asked in the same tone at almost the same time. Nikolaus nodded eagerly and retrieved Remy's crispy piece of paper.

"Look it," he said as he pointed to the message.

"He told us that he was listening to a song called *Dixie*," Nikolaus explained for Shawn's benefit. "And then–"

"Dixie?" Shawn asked in alarm. "He said that? How did Remy react?"

Nikolaus shrugged as if he didn't see the importance. "He just mumbled 'fascinating' in that sarcastic voice of his, you know, the one he uses when he's not really paying attention?"

Brandt watched a wave of melancholy flood Shawn's countenance and he looked away.

"But then when he got up to leave–"

"Remy left?" Shawn asked in confusion.

"No! The guy, the… Kincaid! He left when we bitched at him about his music, but he left this," Nikolaus continued as he waved the Sudoku puzzle in the air. "I'm almost positive it's the key! It's the cipher that we were missing!" he finished excitedly.

"I don't… I don't think I understand," Brandt said slowly when he was sure that Nikolaus was done.

"When we were in… I don't remember, Marietta maybe, Remy talked about the different things you use to decipher codes. This was right before we got drunk and thrown in jail."

"Jail?" Shawn asked in surprise.

"Yeah. Anyway, these Sudoku puzzles are released on a daily basis in places. Newspapers, websites. This is the New York Times Sudoku puzzle from the day before the message was sent, look at the date," Nikolaus told them excitedly. His accent was so thick he may as well have been speaking German.

"Jail?" Shawn repeated disbelievingly.

"Are you paying attention?" Nikolaus asked in exasperation.

"I was until I heard jail," Shawn answered distractedly.

"It was nothing," Nikolaus said with a swipe of his hand. "Indecent something or other. Remy enjoyed it a little too much, in my opinion. But that's beside the point! Look!" Nikolaus waved the puzzle around. "They use the Sudoku puzzles to decipher the messages."

"So this is the key we need to decipher this particular message?" Carl asked as he pointed at the written message Remy had carried with him.

"Well, no. I think this is the puzzle we need. But we'd have to do the answers ourselves," Nikolaus answered.

"Right," Shawn huffed. "It wouldn't do any good to use the puzzles as keys if you were using anything besides the right answers."

"Anybody know how to do these Sudoku things?" Nikolaus asked as he waved the puzzle at them.

They all looked at one another blankly as silence fell upon the room.

"I do," Thiago answered as he closed the door behind him with a tiny click and stepped further into the room. Brandt tensed involuntarily. He would never get used to these bastards sneaking around and being in constant stealth mode like they were.

If they could sneak, then he should be able to blow shit up. It was only fair.

"Where's Remy?" Shawn asked immediately, the alarm apparent in his voice. Thiago smirked and nodded his head towards the sliding glass doors that led out onto the balcony. Remy stood out there with his back to them, his elbows resting on the edge of the railing as he looked out on the city. He looked like a man simply out enjoying a smoke. If it weren't for the fact that they were three stories up and Remy had probably scaled the wall to get out there without going through the flat, Brandt would have thought nothing of the scene.

"We didn't know if the shit had hit the fan or what when we got back and you were all gone, so we took the necessary precautions," Thiago explained as he looked out at Remy. Shawn stood, looking as if he wanted to go outside, but Thiago grabbed his arm and shook his head.

"*Está enojado*," Thiago warned in a low voice. "Pissy as hell. We had Kincaid dead to rights. Had him in a headlock and all ready to extract information. Then our feet got tangled somehow and all three of us went down. By the time Remy and I were up, Kincaid was gone."

Shawn nodded slowly and glanced back at Remy before sitting himself down once more.

"He does tend to beat himself up when something goes wrong," Shawn mumbled miserably. "Thinks he has to be perfect all the bloody time."

"Uh huh. He'll be fine. He's watching for any tails. Now what's this about Sudoku puzzles?" Thiago asked curiously as he wedged himself between Carl and Nikolaus on the couch and looked at the note in Nikolaus's hand.

Brandt moved hesitantly to sit on the arm of Shawn's chair, and to his immense relief, Shawn twined their fingers together and began to absently rub at the tip of Brandt's thumb.

"Here," Nikolaus answered, pointing to the note once more. "Do that puzzle. It's the key to the message."

Thiago looked it over carefully and held out his hand for a pen. Carl handed him one wordlessly and Thiago glanced at it as he pressed the end of it. "This had blood on it," he told Carl in distaste.

"Only a little," Carl responded defensively.

Thiago glanced at Shawn and then shook his head, trying not to smile as he scooted to the edge of the couch and began filling in the proper answers.

"What was the corresponding hit?" Carl asked as he leant over Thiago's shoulder and rested his chin there like a puppy, watching. Thiago glanced to the side and smirked, but he didn't shake Carl off.

Brandt smiled affectionately. He'd missed Carl. Carl touched without realizing it. It was endearing, especially in a trained killer, and Brandt loved that about the man. It seemed like Shawn was always aware of his actions, and he rarely displayed the type of physical affection he was at that moment. Brandt's eyes slid to Remy, who stood on the balcony like a stone sentinel as he made certain Thiago hadn't been followed. If Brandt was feeling as guilty as he was right now, then how must Shawn be feeling? Guilt was an extremely unknown sensation for Brandt. He'd always been of the opinion that you had to have a conscience to feel guilty. Surprise, surprise! Brandt suddenly had a conscience!

No wonder Shawn was in a foul mood. This feeling guilty shit was for the birds.

Nikolaus flipped through the many pages of printouts until he found the hit they all thought had been ordered by this particular message. He handed it to Carl.

Carl held the message in one hand and the printout in the other as Thiago worked at the puzzle. It took him roughly ten minutes, but he finally tapped at it as it sat on the coffee table and then slid it toward Carl.

Brandt watched disinterestedly as the three of them worked at the message. They decided that the squares Kincaid had written something in were the ones that were supposed to be used as the key, and from there it seemed to be a simple cipher. They were done in no time.

"So this is it," Carl murmured in surprise as he held up the pages and looked at the key. "It's so simple, in the end," he said with a slightly disappointed scowl.

"Sounds like," Thiago said as he tapped his finger on his lips and hummed absently. "*Ah, soy bueno*," he sighed in satisfaction.

"Impressive, Thi. Really," Nikolaus deadpanned.

"I can't help that Niko and I are both geniuses," Thiago retorted with a wink at the German.

"You did it then?" Shawn asked, the significance finally hitting him through the haze of his agitation. Nikolaus nodded proudly. Brandt's attention was drawn away from Shawn as the balcony door slid open and shut once more. Remy walked in with his hands stuffed in the pockets of his jeans, looking slightly ashamed of himself.

"You okay?" Nikolaus asked in concern.

"I tripped," Remy responded in disgust. "I wasn't even in motion and I fucking tripped," he added as he sulked off into the kitchen. "I'm like the fucking Three Stooges of espionage. All three of 'em. All rolled into one!" he shouted as he moved around in the kitchen and clanked around. He returned with two beers in his hands and handed one to Thiago before opening the other and looking down at Nikolaus.

"Niko was telling us about jail?" Carl teased inquiringly as he looked up at Remy and smiled a little.

"Mmm. Indecent exposure and public lewdness, I think. Something like that, I wasn't really paying attention," Remy said in an off-handed manner as he tossed his head back and took a long gulp of beer. "We spent the night safe and sound in a jail cell and then we were on our way."

"You didn't try to escape?" Shawn asked, sounding to Brandt as if were afraid of speaking to Remy but wanted to all the same.

"The whole point was to be *in* jail," Remy told him with a sneer. Shawn tensed and Brandt bit his lip. Remy and Nikolaus had gotten arrested intentionally in order to get away from whoever had been after them at the time. It was a slightly scary scenario.

"Were they that close on your tail?" Thiago asked curiously.

Remy nodded his head and swallowed the sip of beer he had just taken. "Got into our room."

"How many?" Shawn inquired.

"Three that we saw."

"Just three?" Shawn asked dubiously. "And you had to resort to jail time to get away?"

"We had some rum flow trouble," Remy said enigmatically. Nikolaus snorted and covered his mouth.

"How'd you get arrested?" Carl asked with a smile.

"In Georgia they don't take kindly to, well, much of anything, I guess."

"They don't take kindly to blowjobs being given in hallways," Nikolaus muttered.

Remy smiled around his beer bottle and tipped it back, and Brandt's eyes slid down to look at Shawn fearfully. There was no visible reaction. So he already knew Nikolaus and Remy had been fucking. Now his mood made perfect sense. Guilt plus the pain of betrayal plus the added guilt felt for the hypocrisy from being hurt by the betrayal. Yeah. That would do you a number over.

"Cops got a call from a concerned father of 2.5 children and that was it," Remy answered. "They didn't find the bodies 'til we were long gone."

The others chuckled as they imagined what the arrest must have entailed, but Brandt was still more concerned with Shawn than anything. Shawn listened with a sad smile, and Brandt wondered what he was thinking of. Five years of such adventures, if Brandt had to guess.

"So, the message?" Remy said finally to Nikolaus, changing the subject and steering the conversation back on track.

"We got it," Nikolaus said as he continued to snicker.

"What about the other message?"

"We haven't gotten to it yet."

"Well, let's get to it then," Remy said bluntly. "The Archer sent Kincaid here on purpose. He wanted us to crack these. There's something in these messages he wants us to know."

"Christ, lad, are you still on about that?" Shawn said testily.

"Go to hell, Shawn," Remy responded in a calm, flat voice. He never even looked up at Shawn as he spoke, and Brandt closed his eyes in frustration. These two had to get back on track, and soon, if they were going to have a chance at successfully executing any plan they might be able to cook up. "Where's the other message?" Remy asked as he leant over the couch between Nikolaus and Thiago.

Brandt and Shawn sat in silence as they watched the other four work through the messages.

"Lemme see," Remy ordered, and Nikolaus passed the little pad and his red pen over. "We've got the blocks at least," Remy murmured as he apparently tried to draw out a Sudoku square. The pad was floppy, though, and he was struggling to do it, even resting it on top of Nikolaus's head to steady it at one point. "Fuck it, I can't do this. Here, Thi," he said finally.

Thiago placed the pad back on the table and began to finish the square.

"What are you doing?" Remy asked in a near panic.

"What?" Thiago asked, lifting his pen and looking back at Remy in alarm.

"The pen's blue!"

"What? So?"

"The pen's a different color! Oh, my God, you're killing me!" Remy said in distress as Thiago rolled his eyes and continued to write with the blue pen. "It's *different*," Remy groaned, and he let his head fall onto Thiago's shoulder as his entire body draped limply over the back of the couch.

Brandt grinned as he watched the drama. Everything Remy did had Brandt liking him more and more, no matter how hard he tried not to. For some reason he felt like they were supposed to be rivals or antagonists or something. But Brandt just couldn't find it within himself to dislike the younger man, and Remy was trying his best to act normally around him. That had to mean something. He glanced over at Shawn to see the older man smiling sadly.

"Obsessive compulsive," Nikolaus mumbled in amusement.

"I would rather eat a grenade than make a line with *two different colors*!" Remy responded in a pained voice as he pointed at the pad of paper. Thiago snickered gleefully and continued to torment the Cajun with his blue pen.

Speaking of grenades, though… Brandt had a timing device around here somewhere. What had he done with it?

They continued discussing the message and deciphered four hits before they grew weary. By that time, Remy had whimpered to the point that Thiago had growled in frustration and yanked the red pen from Remy's hand.

"Not in the middle of a fucking word! You insensitive bastard!" Remy keened pathetically as Thiago switched out the pens and began writing in red.

"*Te voy a romper el orto*!" Thiago shouted.

"No! My ass!" Remy wailed dramatically, and he turned and fled into the kitchen for more beer, leaving the other men in the main room laughing raucously. Brandt wondered if Remy's ass really did hurt or if he was just trying to be funny. If it were the former, then Brandt was considering apologizing.

Did you apologize to someone for fucking him through the wall after he had asked you to do it, though? Brandt wasn't sure. Was there etiquette involved with something like that?

Perhaps it was better just not knowing.

XIV.

AS the afternoon drew on, Remy and Thiago helped Nikolaus ferret out other messages, and they were able to match each of them up with a corresponding suspected hit, save for the one. The second message they had found didn't seem to correspond to anything, and Remy was beginning to suspect that the orders weren't for a hit at all, but for something else entirely.

"Check the original location again, Niko," Remy ordered softly as he puzzled over the message in his hand. "Something's not hitting me right about it."

"I don't want pizza, dammit!" Shawn yelled from the kitchen. Remy raised his head and looked in the direction the others had migrated after they had given up on the messages. He cocked an eyebrow at Thiago, who looked at him and shrugged wordlessly.

"If you don't decide on something, and I mean right fucking now, I'm using the microwave," Brandt threatened. "And you remember what happened to the microwave in St. Louis."

"Jesus Christ!" Shawn growled in alarm and frustration.

"Seems the love birds are having a tiff," Remy muttered around the tip of his pen. Nikolaus and Thiago sniggered quietly, and Remy suddenly felt like a ten-year-old who had had a fight with his best friend and was now talking about him behind his back to make himself feel better. It was embarrassing to be taking pleasure in Shawn's obvious annoyance, but he was doing it all the same.

He needed to shoot something. Get it out if his system.

"Take a look," Nikolaus said as he leaned back and made way for Remy to peer over his shoulder. Thiago came over, too, as did Carl, who was apparently tired of trying to play peacemaker in the kitchen.

"What's the original date again?" Remy asked absently as he looked at their scribbling.

"Uhh… wait a minute… it looks… oh, *fick mich*!" Nikolaus exclaimed suddenly.

"What? What is it?" Remy asked excitedly, recognizing one of Nikolaus's revelations and knowing that it could be significant.

"The entry's backdated," Nikolaus said as he began typing furiously. "We thought it was over four months old, but Christ, it was sent out only a couple days after we all separated!"

"We've been looking for the wrong group of hits then?" Thiago asked vaguely. He didn't sound as if he grasped the significance, and from the look on Carl's face, he didn't either. Remy knew it was significant, he just didn't know why.

"There have been no hits since we formed," Nikolaus said hesitantly. "So this message wasn't a hit. You were right, Remy, it's something else."

"Something else?" Shawn asked as he walked slowly towards them. "Like what? A donation to a charity, perhaps? Notes on holiday bonuses for all the traitors in the ranks?"

Brandt walked up behind the older man and smacked him in the back of the head in passing, dancing away gleefully before Shawn could retaliate. Remy glared at Shawn for a brief moment before the melancholy replaced the anger once more and he looked away quickly. Shawn had hurt him badly, but he couldn't let Shawn or any of the others know that. He wouldn't. They had enough to worry about without him acting like a broken-hearted pain in the ass.

"Well, we know the hints. We just have to… hmm," Carl mumbled as he looked at Remy's notes.

"Hmm?" Remy repeated inquiringly.

"This one doesn't follow the same pattern, right? It's not a hit. None of the words make sense even with a complex cipher filling them in."

"So?" Brandt asked curiously as he hovered on the edge of Remy's vision.

"But if you move these block over one," Carl told them as he drew on the sheet of paper to illustrate what he was doing. He took the numbers from the blocks directly left of the original ones and he substituted them in. "It makes actual words," he said as he held it up and showed them the translated message.

'Anchor point has changed,' it read. 'Archer is bare shaft. Take down bow 3.'

"How did you know to do that?" Thiago asked, his tone a mixture of curiosity and suspicion.

"Accident. I'm seriously dyslexic, I get my numbers mixed all the time," Carl answered with a dismissive swipe of his hand. He turned to Brandt as Remy and Thiago looked at one another blankly.

"So what the hell does that mean?" Nikolaus asked as he pointed at what Carl had written.

"These are archery terms," Carl explained as he pointed at the first line. "An anchor point is the reference point an archer uses when he fires an arrow." He put the pad down and held his hands out, mimicking as if he were holding a bow. "When you pull back, your thumb should hit the same point before you release. It's the same every time, whether it's your mouth or your ear or your eyes or whatever. It's always the same or you can't judge range."

They all stared at him as if he were speaking Greek. Carl looked around and rolled his eyes. "Don't look at me like that. I'm a weapons specialist, okay?" he huffed defensively. "If you're changing an anchor point, it means something has seriously gone wrong with your aim, know what I mean?"

"And the bare shaft thing?" Remy asked in interest. "I assume that's lingo as well and not just the Archer saying he liked to bareback."

Carl snorted at him. "Yeah, it is. A bare shaft is what they call an arrow without any fletching or nocks or paint or… you get the idea."

"What's the point?" Shawn asked dubiously.

"So, what if this isn't orders, but a… an employee bulletin, like you said."

"I was taking the piss, Carl," Shawn responded bemusedly.

"I don't mean literally. I mean, what if he's telling someone that his plans have changed and he's working without any backup? Or working on a new plan. Or something," Carl proposed.

"I think you're onto something there," Thiago said appraisingly. "Yeah. Yeah, I like that. He's saying he's had to change his plans around and he's working without a net?"

"I dunno. Seems logical to me, but then I'm not exactly the brains of this operation," Carl replied candidly.

Remy was impressed. Even if they weren't right on with the meanings, Carl had probably hit the nail on the head with his 'company memo' theory.

"So what about the last line?" Nikolaus asked. "Is it an order to take down someone?"

"I don't think so," Carl answered with a shake of his head as he turned the pad around and looked at the message he had written. "A take down bow is actually a portable bow, it can be separated into two or three pieces."

"The numbers are significant," Remy said with certainty upon hearing this. "Three. But three what? Days? Hours? Weeks?"

"Months?" Thiago suggested quietly. "Pairs?"

"You can't think he... you think he knew our plans?" Remy asked in disbelief.

"You've said yourself that you think he's watching us," Thiago responded regretfully.

"But...."

"I don't think it's a time period," Brandt said suddenly as he walked around the room opening and closing drawers and looking into empty cabinets and cupboards. "The fact that he added a number to something that already contained numbers is probably significant, too. Maybe the three and the two are both significant," he finished as he knelt to look in the bottom drawer of the armoire where the television was.

"What are you looking for?" Carl asked him distractedly.

"It's not ticking is it?" Shawn groaned from the armchair he had flopped himself into. Remy took the opportunity to turn and look at the man. A wave of sadness washed over him and he felt his breath catch. He knew this would be their last mission together even if Shawn didn't retire and they both lived through it. No matter what happened, Remy had been replaced.

"No, it's not ticking. At least it shouldn't be," Brandt mumbled, bringing Remy out of his morose thoughts and making him snap to attention.

"You're not about to blow us all up, are you?" he asked wryly, only somewhat serious. Brandt turned to look at him, and they made eye contact for the first time since Shawn had returned from the errand he and Thiago had gone on.

"Not intentionally," Brandt said in a hurt voice.

"Have you really lost a bomb?" Carl asked in horror. "I thought you were kidding!"

"I haven't lost it!" Brandt said defensively as he prowled across the room and toward the bedrooms. "I just can't remember where I put it!" he shouted as he disappeared down the hall.

Remy turned wide eyes on Shawn, who was sitting with his head in his hands and shaking slightly.

"Shawn?" Remy ventured uncertainly.

"This is how I lost my pants," Shawn said regretfully, his accent heavy with agitation. "And how he blew up the petrol station in the desert. Only one for miles."

"Is he serious?" Thiago asked in alarm, as if he had just tuned in to the conversation.

"Ha!" Brandt called triumphantly from the back rooms. "Found it!"

"Oh, my God," Thiago breathed in disbelief.

"Fuck, Shawn. No wonder you've gone crazy," Remy said as Shawn sat back in the chair and stared up at the ceiling.

"I learned that he only sets things on fire when he thinks there's a problem," Shawn mumbled. "I'll have a talk with him tonight. Until then, watch your pants, all of you."

"What do you mean, when he thinks there's a problem?" Thiago asked cautiously.

Shawn made a vague twirling motion with his hand, and Remy looked at Thiago pointedly. Thiago's eyes widened as he looked at Remy and he mouthed a 'sorry.' At least someone had remained oblivious to the tension between Shawn and Remy.

"Uhh…," Nikolaus said by way of getting everyone's attention.

They all turned to look at Nikolaus as he bent over the table and examined the notes.

"Problem?" Remy asked distractedly.

Nikolaus looked up at Remy, and his gray eyes fairly glowed with the light of discovery.

"I don't think these are hits, Remy," Nikolaus said excitedly.

"What?"

"Look. It's that Washburn kid," Nikolaus said as he pointed at the list. Remy scrambled to get to Nikolaus's side, and he looked down at the list of agents they had made from the messages. "And there's Kincaid, too."

"Jesus," Remy breathed as he leaned closer.

"What is it?" Carl asked as he came over and stood beside Remy. His hand rested on the base of Remy's spine and Remy shivered uncontrollably at the gentle touch. Thiago and Shawn stood on the other side of the table, and Brandt wandered in caressing the little mechanism he'd been searching for and sidled up between the two of them to listen.

"When we were running, we ended up in Prague," Remy said slowly, trying to think through the ramifications of what he was saying even as he was saying it. "We tracked down Evan Washburn, the audio tech kid Brandt told us about working with."

"Prague?" Brandt asked in surprise.

"Yeah. Why?" Remy asked uneasily as he looked up into Brandt's dark eyes.

"He worked in Tokyo, is all. Mostly, anyway. How'd you know he'd be in Prague?"

"Tokyo?" Remy repeated in shock.

"Yeah. Japan. If he had worked in Prague I never would have crossed paths with him," Brandt said flippantly as he twirled the deadly little mechanism in the air to illustrate that they were, in fact, in Australia. Everyone flinched back away from it, but he didn't seem to notice.

"I thought you said Prague!" Remy said distractedly as he tried like hell to remember that day at the cabin. They'd all been at the computer gathering information. Remy would swear Brandt had said that Washburn was in Prague. He looked at Nikolaus curiously.

"I heard Tokyo," Nikolaus said when Remy looked at him.

"Well, why the fuck didn't you tell me that when I was looking for him in fucking Prague?" Remy shouted.

"'Cause you looked like you knew what you were doing," Nikolaus said with a defensive shrug.

"I always *look* like I know I what I'm doing!" Remy shouted as he threw his arms up in the air. "But I only do about half the time! Christ, Niko, you should know that by now!" Remy cried as he turned to face Nikolaus completely. He knew the others thought him just slightly saner than Brandt, and situations like this were probably the reason. "When we were looking for Fletcher Barclay, were we in the right country? Were we on the right fucking continent?" Remy shouted with a stomp of his foot.

"We found the kid, so what does it matter?" Nikolaus asked with a little grin on his face. At one time he would have cowered from Remy when he pitched a hissy fit like this, even though Remy knew his hissy fits were often more humorous than threatening. Now Nikolaus just cocked his head and grinned. Remy couldn't help but be proud of Nikolaus's progress, even as he fumed over the Prague situation.

"It matters because it was sheer dumb luck that we even found him! My God, how long would you have let me wander around Prague before you said 'hold up a minute, Helga, this isn't *Japan*!'" Remy spat in a sarcastic imitation of Nikolaus's German-accented English.

"Can we get back to the point of the story?" Carl asked as he tried desperately not to laugh. Remy glared at him.

"You just picked a random city and actually found the person you were looking for?" Thiago asked in stunned disbelief.

Remy transferred the glare to Thiago, but the mix of admiration and amusement on the man's handsome face forced Remy's lips to twitch with the beginnings of a grin.

"I always said I'd rather be lucky than good," Remy murmured as he carefully avoided eye contact with Shawn. He had actually said that to the older man before every mission they had ever gone on together. It was like a tradition they shared.

"Those were the last words I heard before I shot him in the ass," Shawn mumbled.

Remy tried not to laugh. He really did. He so wanted to remain angry with Shawn. He wanted to hate him. Fucking someone else, while hell on the conscience, was acceptable in the relationship they had. But Shawn had fallen in love. He was leaving him. Throwing away their partnership of five years after just a few months with someone else. Remy knew it was childish and stupid and just plain embarrassing to be resentful. After all, no promises had been made, no undying love declared. It hurt nonetheless. Remy tried not to laugh, but the memory of those cocky words followed by the sharp pain of literally being accidentally shot in the ass was just too much. He snorted in amusement and glanced up quickly. Shawn stared at him unerringly, and his clear green eyes caught Remy. They were full of sadness and pain and guilt and amusement.

"Not two minutes after I'd said it," Remy said wryly. "Pop! Right in the ass!"

"I said I was sorry," Shawn said with a hesitant grin.

Remy didn't know what drove the anger back out, but suddenly it was there. Anger so intense he could almost taste it. Was it the grin? Was it the hesitancy, perhaps? Yes, that was it; the kid gloves Shawn was using when he dealt with him. The fact that Shawn knew he had hurt him and was treating him gently because of it really pissed Remy off.

Remy cleared his throat and looked away before Shawn could see the anger in his eyes. He didn't want Shawn knowing he was as angry as he was. He didn't want Shawn having that power over him. Shawn already had too much power over him as it was. He didn't deserve more.

"What were we talking about?" Remy asked, hating himself for being so easily distracted. He'd never let his emotions rule him like he was doing now. If he wasn't more careful it was going to get him killed.

"Prague," Carl supplied uneasily. Remy looked at him closely. Carl always seemed to sense when there was tension long before the others did, Remy could tell simply by the way the man held himself whenever there was about to be a row. He had a built-in Brawl-O-Meter.

Remy was grateful for the other man's sensitivity to the moods of the others, but right then he really hated the concerned look in Carl's eyes. He didn't want concerned. He didn't need concerned, dammit!

Remy took a deep breath, heading off another hissy fit before he had a chance to lose his head again, and he looked down at the lists.

"Anyway!" he huffed. "Right. Prague. We found Washburn and he told– Christ, Niko! Stop giggling!" Remy yelled as Nikolaus snickered at his side. Remy shook his head and refocused on Carl's face as he spoke. He knew he should have been watching the reactions of the others as he relayed this information, but he just couldn't force himself to look at Shawn. He needed neutral ground to remain calm. Carl was perfect for neutral ground. "When we found him he told us that he didn't know who the Archer was, but that he'd been approached. Recruited, almost. In exchange for doing a job for the Archer, they would fake his death and allow him to get out of the Organization. Fucking hell! Why didn't I remember this before?"

"What sort of job?" Thiago asked suspiciously.

"He… he told them how to bug the operations room."

"The…."

"In the Facility in Paris," Remy added hesitantly.

"*Carajo*," Thiago whispered.

"You didn't think to perhaps mention this *before*?" Shawn asked angrily.

"I was a bit distracted when I showed up!" Remy responded heatedly.

"This is a tad more important than you being distracted!" Shawn growled as his hackles raised and he took a step around the table.

"Perhaps you should have thought of that before you fucking tried to kill me!" Remy shouted as he backed away from the table and put his left shoulder facing Shawn, unconsciously assuming a fighting stance as the anger finally began to boil over.

Shawn immediately relaxed, and he looked at Remy as if Remy had just kicked him in the gut. "You're right," he said softly. "I'm sorry," he muttered as he turned around and ran his hand shakily over his face.

That was a classic Shawn in distress signal. The hand over the face. That was usually when Remy would crack a joke, begin a seduction, or shoot someone.

Remy was really liking door number three at this point.

"What else did Washburn tell you?" Thiago asked as he stepped between Shawn and Remy and looked at Remy pointedly.

"Well, I think the most obvious point we're trying to make here," Nikolaus said as he tossed the list of agents who'd been killed on the table and pointed to the name on the list. "Is that Evan Washburn is not, in fact, dead. Neither is Gray Kincaid, obviously. I think we're missing something here, *meine Freunde*."

XV.

THIAGO stood between Shawn and Remy with his hands held out to his sides as if he could keep them from jumping each other if they lost control of their tempers again. He looked at Nikolaus and blinked rapidly as he absorbed what the younger man was saying.

"Of course we're missing something, *bioque*!" Remy growled as he turned away from the rest of them and walked slowly toward the balcony. He stopped at the door, turned and began to pace back and forth, and Thiago relaxed somewhat as he watched the other man get further and further away from Shawn.

"Don't be a bastard, Remy. I mean, I think there's something inherent about the Archer that we've overlooked," Nikolaus said slowly as he watched Remy pace. "Are you alright?"

"*Oui*," Remy spat as he made a pass by the table where Nikolaus stood. Nikolaus raised a dubious eyebrow and looked at Carl uncertainly.

Thiago always thought it funny that whenever a fight started, everyone seemed to look to Carl to make peace. He just had a calming presence, which was amusing considering he was a world-class assassin. Thiago also noticed that the Kiwi was super-sensitive to everyone's mood. It was a nice trait to have, but probably a bit stressful on the poor guy.

Carl shrugged and looked at Thiago. Apparently, he wasn't sure what to do this time. That meant it was up to Thiago to keep the peace, and that meant they were in for trouble.

"Nikolaus," Thiago said in his best authoritative voice. Nikolaus actually jumped at the angry sound of Thiago's voice, and Thiago scolded himself and toned it down a bit. "What is it, exactly, that you think we're missing?" he asked in a gentler voice.

"Well…," Nikolaus trailed off and looked around at them all uneasily.

"Speak up, lad!" Shawn barked angrily as he turned slightly and glared. His flashing green eyes followed Remy's movements like a lion stalking an antelope.

Thiago locked eyes with Brandt, who looked even more distressed now than when his little explosive thingy was missing. Thiago turned his head in time to see Remy halt right behind Nikolaus and glare threateningly back at Shawn. His hand rested on Nikolaus's shoulder protectively, and Thiago was startled to see that he'd once again pulled the cord that brought out the hardened agent. Thiago had seen it back at the hotel, when Shawn jumped the younger man, and the ability fascinated him. It was called cloaking, and Remy was the best Thiago had ever seen. He could change personalities at the drop of a hat.

Right then, he looked like an entirely different person; cold and menacing, and Thiago's alarm bells started clanging once more. This would not be pretty if Remy felt he needed to defend Nikolaus from Shawn. Not pretty at all.

Thiago took a deep breath and hoped he wouldn't regret what he was about to do. So far, he'd managed to hover on the periphery of everyone's consciousness, sort of like Carl. He simply went along and didn't stir up trouble and hoped he would make it through alive. But now their leader was an emotional and mental wreck, their peacemaker was clueless, their brain was scared shitless to open his mouth, their crazy was suddenly disturbingly sane, and the heart of their little group had just blacked over like a Great White shark going in for the kill.

Thiago had to take control, and now.

"Everyone, sit down, shut up, and don't move a fucking muscle!" he shouted. Everyone froze and stared at him as if he had lost his mind. "On the couch! Now!" he shouted again. He gave Shawn a shove and herded them toward the couch with more shoves and curses and growls. "Sit!" he ordered as Remy and Nikolaus walked warily over, and Carl slid onto the end of the couch. Shawn and Brandt sat on the other end, and Nikolaus practically sat down in Carl's lap to avoid being attacked by Shawn, who still seethed quietly. "I said fucking sit!" Thiago shouted as he got right in Remy's face and shoved him.

The younger man reeled backward and landed in between Shawn and Nikolaus, practically on top of them. Thiago was most pleased to see Shawn reach out to catch the falling man, and hold him there protectively against his chest as they all stared at Thiago in silent shock.

Thiago glared at them all, feeling somewhat like an overworked nanny as they all looked up at him with wide eyes.

"Wow, Thi," Remy muttered as he struggled to right himself. He was practically in Shawn's, and Nikolaus's, and Carl's laps, and, since Shawn still held him around his neck and shoulders, he was having difficulty with sitting up straight. "That was… that was incredibly hot," he said with a mischievous grin. Thiago gaped at him as Nikolaus began to snicker. "You should do that more often, *podna*. Really.

Wow." Brandt snorted and clapped his hand over his mouth and Carl began to laugh quietly. Even Shawn was fighting the laughter that showed in the twitching of his lips. "I think I need a moment alone," Remy continued.

"*Que quilombo*," Thiago murmured as he fell back onto the overstuffed chair and stared at them.

"Did he just call you Columbo?" Brandt asked Remy in amusement.

"Columbo was awesome," Remy answered with a huff as he squirmed and tried to remove himself from the laps of his companions.

"*Quilombo*!" Thiago shouted to clarify.

"Means chaos or a mess," Carl supplied helpfully. "He tends to use it when things go to shit."

"Columbo was still awesome," Remy muttered disconsolately.

Thiago snorted and looked at them all fondly as the three men summarily dumped Remy onto the floor.

"Ow! *Salaud*," Remy muttered as he rubbed his hip gingerly. "What were we talking about?"

"We were talking about the Archer. And Nikolaus had a theory," Thiago said patiently. "Now if we could please not threaten the man while he explains his theory, perhaps we could get something done. This is the most useless bunch of *forros* I've ever seen!"

Shawn and Remy had the good grace to look ashamed of their behavior.

"What, exactly, is a *forro*?" Brandt asked curiously. Thiago pursed his lips and twirled his finger in the air next to his ear to indicate that all of them were, in fact, *forros*. Brandt made an 'ah' sound, and that seemed to satisfy him.

Remy crawled over to Thiago and settled himself cross-legged on the floor in front of the chair to watch Nikolaus as he began to speak. Thiago watched Remy curiously, both ridiculously delighted that Remy picked him as a backrest and at the same time wary of the reason. If Remy planned on running to Thiago for comfort while he and Shawn were having a spat, then Thiago could deal with that, he just wanted to know a little bit ahead of time.

"Well, it's been bothering me ever since *Prague*," Nikolaus said with a little laugh he covered by clearing his throat. Remy growled quietly and Thiago absently patted his head. "What if we're… what if we're on the wrong side of this fight?"

"What do you mean?" Brandt asked as he leaned forward and looked at Nikolaus across Shawn's lap.

"I mean, we all know what the Organization does. What if the Archer isn't trying to set up a rival outfit, but… but rather just trying to take it down? Solely for the purpose of being rid of it, I mean."

"Why would he do that?" Carl asked.

"I don't know," Nikolaus responded with a shrug.

"That's not much help," Carl grumbled.

"Maybe he's clearing the way for something," Nikolaus suggested vaguely. "Maybe he wants to set up shop and he knows the Organization would fight it. It's not necessarily a rival just… something the Organization would object to."

"Like what?" Brandt asked.

"I don't know," Nikolaus said with another shrug.

"Christ, Niko, you've been spending too much time with Remy," Shawn said in disgust as he got to his feet and began to pace once more. "You're going around in circles."

Thiago felt Remy tense, but he gripped the younger man's shoulder hard and forced him to remain seated and quiet.

"Sit down, Shawn," Thiago said in a low, threatening voice. Shawn turned to stare at him in surprise. Thiago looked up at him from under lowered brows. "Don't make me say it again," he added in the same low voice.

Shawn stared at him for several more tense moments, then slowly made his way back to the couch and sat down. Thiago let out an inaudible sigh of relief and looked back at Nikolaus.

"You think he's some sort of… what?" Thiago asked, a little lost as to what Nikolaus was talking about.

"He's sort of like Robin Hood. Except instead of stealing money he's stealing agents."

"He made a deal with Washburn for services rendered, then helped him get out after the job was done," Remy murmured thoughtfully.

"So he's what, some sort of guardian angel? Going around and freeing agents who want out before their time?" Thiago asked.

Nikolaus shrugged. "Could be. For a price, of course. I mean, look at Remy. He's got five more years after this, and…." Nikolaus looked at Shawn warily. "And I know there are others like him who just want out. They'd be willing to do whatever to just be free of it all."

"If you wanted out then why didn't you take their deal?" Shawn asked in a low voice without looking up from his hands, clasped tightly in his lap.

"I never said I wanted out," Remy responded evenly.

Shawn looked up at Remy sadly and Thiago unconsciously rubbed his hand over Remy's shoulder in a soothing manner.

"There are only two things I can't imagine not having in my life, Shawn, and if I lost both in one fell swoop I just don't think I'd live through it," Remy said in the same calm, matter-of-fact voice. "You were already leaving. I had to have something to cling to," he finished evenly as the rest of them watched him uneasily, expecting another outburst or a tantrum or something. But no tantrum came. His features returned to the same blank, killer-shark expression he'd worn earlier, and Thiago found himself thinking they'd be seeing a lot more of it from now on.

Remy looked around at them all and then patted Thiago's hand on his shoulder. Thiago removed the hand and Remy stood gracefully. "I need a smoke," he announced quietly as he dug in the pocket of his shirt and made his way slowly toward the balcony.

Thiago watched him go, noticing the lack of the usual bounce in his step and the broken slump of his shoulders. It was heartbreaking, even if Thiago didn't know the whole story. A tussle on the couch drew his attention as Remy slid the door open, and Thiago turned in time to see Brandt actually thump Shawn on the nose.

"If you don't go after him, I will," Brandt growled as Carl and Nikolaus watched tensely.

"We'll finish this later," Thiago murmured as he stood up. "I'll go after him."

The others watched him go in silence, and, as Thiago stepped silently through the still open door, he heard the beginnings of another brawl commence behind him. He really couldn't be bothered with it, though.

Remy leaned against the railing in the same position he'd been earlier, the smoke from his lit cigarette haloing his head in the pale dark of dusk.

"Come to trip me up again?" Remy inquired quietly into the night as Thiago took a silent step toward him.

XVI.

CARL watched Thiago walk hesitantly toward the door. He knew from their time together that the Argentinean wasn't comfortable dealing with personal situations unless he knew he got to kill you afterward and ease the embarrassment, and he wondered if Thiago was as nervous as he looked about going out to speak with Remy.

"Stop thumping me, you fuck!" Shawn roared as he grabbed Brandt and they both spilled off the sofa and onto the floor.

Carl tore his attention away from Thiago and lunged forward, taking hold of Shawn's arm before a blow could be landed. He was pulled into the brawl, like one of those cartoon dust clouds that sucked in all the cats in the alley, and he called out wordlessly as he tried to break it up. He received a kick to the groin for his trouble.

He doubled over, not truly hurt because the foot had missed anything of anatomical importance, but kneeling there in relief and frustration. If he didn't get peace soon, he would simply kill all of them and be on his way to wherever the fuck. He couldn't stand the bickering any longer.

"You bastard!" Brandt shouted in a panic. "You've broken Trigger!"

Carl looked up to see Shawn go rolling across the floor like a dust bunny and Brandt crawling toward him.

"You hurt?" Brandt asked concernedly as he helped Carl to his feet.

"You kicked me," Carl muttered accusingly as he rubbed the inside of his thigh and glared at anything that moved.

"Come on," Brandt said, and before Carl could protest, he was actually physically picked up off the ground and carried out of the room. "Quit being a bastard!" Brandt shouted over his shoulder at Shawn, who was just getting his bearings, sitting up in the middle of the floor and looking after them in irritation.

"What are you doing?" Carl demanded in confusion as he struggled to get loose. Basically being dragged now, he couldn't get free of Brandt to save his life. Come to think of saving his life, where was that explosive thingy? Did Brandt still have it on him? Carl debated whether to call for help. He no longer had any pride when it came to these men, he could call for help.

"It's been a while, Trigger. Too long," Brandt said as he kicked open the closest door and carried Carl into one of the bedrooms. Carl opened his mouth to call out as the door slammed shut.

XVII.

SHAWN heard the pitiful cry for help through the thick door as he sat on the floor dejectedly.

"Bugger," he muttered disgustedly, having no intention of going to Carl's aid. "Crazy wankers. All of them." He looked up at Nikolaus, who was trying to blend into the sofa, and Shawn's mood deteriorated further as he realized what a bastard he was being. He sighed heavily and flopped gracelessly back onto the floor. He just wanted to stay there and wallow for a while, feel sorry for himself and lament the hornet's nest he'd poked his nose into. "I'm a daft bastard," he said as he stared up at the ceiling.

"*Ja*," Nikolaus agreed readily. Shawn looked at him and raised an eyebrow, but at least Nikolaus looked more angry than scared. "How could you do that?" Nikolaus asked angrily.

"Which 'that' would you be referring to?" Shawn asked dryly.

"You broke his heart, is what you did. And instead of having the decency to own up to that, you're letting your guilt force you into snapping at him every chance you get. It's not his fault," Nikolaus snarled at him.

Shawn sat up and looked at him in alarm. How much did the younger man know? So far as Shawn knew, no one else knew about the discussion he and Remy had the night before. Unless Remy told them all at lunch, then no one should know that he'd broken Remy's heart.

Oh, fuck. Broke his heart.

The thought made Shawn physically ill, and a rush of icy nausea raged through his body as Nikolaus glared at him.

"He's the most loyal person I've ever known," Nikolaus was saying. "And instead of welcoming him back like you should have done, you accused him of betraying us!"

Heat rushed back through Shawn's body as he realized what Nikolaus was talking about. It shamed him that he had to pick from a list of wrongdoings in order to follow the admonishments, and yet here he was. Shawn the Bastard.

"He did what he had to do to survive," Nikolaus continued heatedly. "He was willing to die to save the rest of us. Maybe that's something you don't understand."

"I–"

"And then instead of apologizing or being, I don't know, a decent human being, you go and snap at him every chance you get just because you feel guilty. Yeah, you're a bastard. And no, you don't deserve him."

Shawn opened his mouth to respond, but there was nothing he could say in his defense.

XVIII.

NIKOLAUS glared at Shawn as the man sat stricken on the floor. A pang of sympathy lanced through him, but it was brief and inconsequential when Nikolaus thought of the way Remy's eyes had gone black and heartless at the sound of Shawn's voice. Nikolaus had never seen Remy's eyes do that. They were always warm and brown and laughing. It was frightening, like Shawn had simply killed a piece of Remy with everything he'd said to him. Nikolaus knew it was something more than just the argument they'd witnessed. There had to be something else, and Nikolaus was pretty sure it had something to do with Brandt.

"What did you do to him to make him look like that?" Nikolaus asked after Shawn had failed to respond to his last statement.

"Just like you said," Shawn quietly, the sadness in his voice almost palpable. "I broke his heart."

Nikolaus sat silently, waiting for an explanation, and Shawn looked up at him miserably.

"It's Brandt, isn't it?" Nikolaus asked pointedly.

"Yes. I don't… I didn't expect it," Shawn said ashamedly.

"Doesn't make it right."

"No. No, it doesn't."

Nikolaus glanced out toward the balcony. Remy and Thiago hadn't moved at all since Thiago stepped out there. Thiago still stood behind Remy, and Remy was still hunched over the railing, blowing smoke rings into the night. Nikolaus wondered what they were talking about, or if they were talking at all.

He looked back to see Shawn looking out toward the balcony as well. The sadness and confusion on the older man's face broke through most of Nikolaus's righteous anger, and he decided to take pity on him. Sort of.

"Come on," Nikolaus said suddenly. He stood up and looked down at Shawn, who was still sitting on the floor feeling sorry for himself and looking out onto the balcony longingly. Nikolaus walked up to him and smacked him on the side of the head to get his attention. "Leave Remy alone. Let's go," he said harshly.

"Pushy little bastard," Shawn grumbled as he stood up and growled menacingly. Nikolaus suddenly felt a little less brave as Shawn glowered down at him, but he stood his ground and pointed stubbornly toward the hallway and the door behind which Brandt and Carl had just disappeared.

Nikolaus noticed that while Shawn hadn't been able to tear his eyes away from the balcony, he hadn't given the bedroom a second glance.

XIX.

"YOU'RE joking, right?" Carl asked incredulously as Brandt set him down at the foot of the bed and stood looking at him appraisingly.

"No. Been a while since we talked. I'm tired of Shawn being a prick and I'd like to talk to you alone."

"Oh," Carl responded uncertainly as he looked around the room. Brandt studied him intently. He looked nervous.

"You look nervous."

"I am nervous," Carl responded candidly as he looked back at Brandt. "Where's your blow 'em up thingy?"

"Huh?"

"The…." Carl looked around the room uneasily again and made a clicking motion with his hand.

"Oh... the timing device?" Brandt looked down at his hands as if he expected to find it still there. It wasn't. "Fucking hell!" he muttered as his hands flopped to his side. "Now what the fuck have I done with it?"

Carl began to shake slightly. Brandt found it highly amusing. He lunged at the other man, suddenly needing to hug him for some reason, and as he pulled Carl to him, a peculiar warmth spread through Brandt's body.

It wasn't the heat of passion. It was more sedate and calming than that, and it wasn't the fever of Brandt's need for destruction, either. It was something close to comfort. Familiarity. Friendship.

"I missed you, Trigger!" he exclaimed happily.

"I can't breathe!" Carl responded as he tapped at Brandt's shoulder and sputtered slightly.

"Oh, sorry," Brandt said as he pulled away and held Carl at arm's length.

"I missed you too, mate. It was almost dull without you around to instill the fear of God into me here and there," Carl told him with a wry smile.

Brandt grinned at him and pulled him close once more. "Well, as soon as we find that timer we'll have a spot of fun," Brandt said indulgently. "But I need to talk to you first."

"Fun?"

"Yeah. But no worries, we've got a good hour before the thing goes off."

"Uh...."

"Have you ever been in love, Trigger?"

"What?"

"Love."

"Uh... not... not that I know of," Carl answered uneasily as Brandt moved away and flopped himself down on the bed. "Is that... is that what you think has happened? To you, I mean?"

"I thought so. And I think Shawn thought so too. And I think he thought I thought so."

"Wait–"

"But I don't know what I'm supposed to be looking for and–"

"Hold on–"

"And since we both thought the other thought it then we never talked about it we just thought it and–"

"But–"

"When we finally stopped thinking it and started talking we were on the plane and–"

"Wally–"

"We never actually finished talking about it so we just went back to thinking and now something's changed and I don't know what the hell to think and I don't know what he's thinking and I don't know what he thinks I think and I don't know what to do about thinking that something's changed. What do you think?"

"What?" Carl asked desperately as he stared down at Brandt incredulously.

A knock at the door stopped Brandt's response, and he and Carl looked at one another blankly before Brandt called out, "It's open."

Nikolaus opened the door and stepped into the room, dragging Shawn along by the arm. Brandt was a bit surprised to see how miserable Shawn looked.

"What's wrong?" Carl asked immediately as Nikolaus let Shawn's arm drop and closed the door behind them.

"He's a bastard," Nikolaus said without further explanation as he sat himself down on the bed beside Brandt and glared up at Shawn.

"That's all?" Brandt asked distractedly.

"*Ja*. I smacked him for it," Nikolaus responded.

Brandt watched in amusement as Carl walked up to Shawn, looking very sympathetic and understanding, and smacked him on the side of the head.

"Ow! What the hell?" Shawn snarled as he rubbed his ear and glared at the bigger man.

"I wanted to get one in, too," Carl explained with a shrug as he crossed his arms and looked threatening.

Brandt really liked it when Carl looked threatening. It was such a contrast to his gentle character. It was sexy as hell, too.

Was he allowed to think other people were sexy if he thought he was in love? Brandt really didn't know. That was another of those tricky etiquette questions.

As if lightning had struck him, Brandt's entire body began to sizzle with the spark of revelation. He knew now what was going on in his head. The spark was back. That glorious flame of slight madness. He'd been broken. Driven temporarily sane by Shawn's grounding presence. But now he was back to his good old skewed self, and he could see clearly. In pairs, perhaps, they'd needed the added trust of stronger feelings, and maybe they'd manufactured them a bit. Brandt loved Shawn. But no more than he did Carl. Or Nikolaus. Or Remy or Thiago. As a group, they'd been split apart by their pairings, but now Brandt saw the light and he knew how to fix it.

"Fucking hell!" Shawn growled as he looked from Carl to Brandt. "You want one too, do you?"

Brandt lunged to his feet and gave Shawn a good smack before the other man could take back the offer. Then he took him by the shoulders and steered him toward the bed as Shawn swatted at him irritably.

"We have to talk," Brandt said seriously as he knelt in front of Shawn. Shawn stared at him blankly. "Trigger's convinced me that we're not quite so in love as we thought we were."

Shawn's green eyes clouded over and Brandt heard Carl stammer, "What? I... no... but–"

"When you were sitting out there in the floor letting Gizmo work you over, where were your thoughts?" Brandt asked Shawn as the older man looked from Carl to Brandt and back again.

"What?" Shawn asked in confusion.

"Where were your thoughts?" Brandt repeated calmly.

"I don't... I don't understand."

"Were they in here, wondering why Trigger was calling out for help, or were they out there on the balcony having a smoke?"

XX.

REMY stood at the railing, tense and expectant after hearing the sharp inhalation his words caused behind him.

Thiago moved almost as silently as Remy did. Remy would have to remember that from here on out. He was playing a dangerous game. One that could very well get him killed now that he'd lost his only real ally.

Thiago hadn't moved yet, and Remy suspected the other man could sense how tense he was. He tried to relax his body slightly, but he couldn't quite manage it. He had to get off this balcony. Now. Remy inhaled deeply and produced several more hazy little rings as he tried to get hold of his nerves.

"Do you smoke, Thiago?" he asked unsteadily.

"I try not to," Thiago murmured.

"It's a damn nasty habit for a spook to have," Remy said. "I don't wear cologne or use scented shampoo. I don't make noise when I move and I can blend into a shadow like a wraith. But all it takes is the glow or smell of one little cigarette to give away your position," Remy said pointedly, hoping the message was getting across.

"I didn't trip you up," Thiago said defensively as he finally turned to slide the door closed. "Gray Kincaid tripped us up," Thiago added as he walked over and leant backwards on the railing, facing Remy and crossing his arms casually across his chest. "I told you he was good."

Remy glanced at him and snorted as he calmed slightly, watching the shadows move in the night below him.

"Have you come to cheer me up then?" Remy asked curiously.

"If you think it'll help," Thiago said in a neutral voice. "Sometimes it does some good to complain to someone neutral."

"Yeah," Remy said absently as he flicked the ashes over the side of the balcony and looked up at the clear night sky. "You ever look at the stars, Thi?" he asked curiously.

Thiago glanced up and pursed his lips. "I suppose not. Always figured the moment I looked up was the moment I'd get shot," he said thoughtfully.

"Yeah," Remy said sadly. "I remember that feeling. Not having that feeling was always one of the best things about…." Remy closed his eyes sadly as he nodded his head to indicate Shawn inside.

"You're not alone, Remy," Thiago told him softly. Remy shivered as a wave of cold chills swept through him. "You don't have to be alone ever again."

"We never finished our conversation, y'know," Remy said abruptly as he watched the tip of his cigarette burn slowly.

"What conversation?" Thiago asked gently. He had the tone of a man speaking to a little kid who wouldn't come out from under the bed, and Remy hated himself for causing it. Had he become that fragile? First Shawn, and now Thiago. Both of them handling him like a porcelain doll. It made Remy want to kick himself in the ass. He would have tried it, but he knew he'd hurt himself in the process.

"At the cabin," he explained as he glanced at Thiago once more. "You were going to ask me something."

"Right," Thiago whispered slowly, his eyes still on Remy in the soft light that came from within the flat. "I was going to ask you if you liked to be called something besides your name," he recalled absently.

"I've always liked Dixie," Remy answered thoughtfully. "Do you think they're happy?" he asked suddenly.

Thiago raised one expressive eyebrow and looked back inside. "Shawn and Brandt?" he asked as clarification.

Remy nodded. "He says he thinks he's in love," he told Thiago quietly. Thiago showed no visible reaction, and Remy shifted uneasily. "I never thought someone like Brandt would be a threat," he admitted. "I made the mistake of thinking he'd want someone similar to himself," he said as he finally stood up straight and indicated Thiago with his hand. "I thought it might be you. To replace me, I mean. When he retired. To keep him company. You remind me of him. Doesn't matter now, really. As long as he has someone that'll stick by him."

"You and Brandt are a lot alike," Thiago told him as Remy looked at him. "Three months is a long time to be with just one person day in and day out. You felt it with Niko. I felt it with Carl."

"You're suggesting he loves me and merely found a temporary replacement in Wally," Remy surmised flatly.

"It seems to make sense," Thiago responded confidently.

"Shawn's not stupid," Remy argued.

"He's also not very good with emotion," Thiago pointed out with a huff. "You said this yourself. Give him some time; he will realize there's a difference between passion and proximity."

"We don't have the time," Remy whispered bitterly. "*Gar ici*, you saw me out there, Thio. I'm losing it."

"What I saw was a phenomenal ability to track through crowded streets and nail a target. If we hadn't gotten in each other's way we'd have had him."

"*Mon tcheue*. I'm a fuck up, Thi. I'm going to get one of us killed," Remy claimed disgustedly.

"You saved Nikolaus's life. More than once, from what I hear."

"Niko's a doll. He really is. But, if I had just… if I had been more intent on *who* was after us rather than why, then, I mean, McTiernan and–"

"Remy," Thiago said sternly as he took hold of Remy's shoulders and stood facing him. Remy looked at Thiago in surprise and blinked a couple of times. "We're all in odd circumstances, and nobody's perfect. You're allowed to slip here and there."

"Is that a play on words?" Remy asked suspiciously. "'Cause I'm not really in the mood to talk about slipping anywhere. Or be made fun of."

Thiago smiled at him, and Remy was struck by how different the man looked when he grinned like that. He didn't look quite sane, but he looked happy. Remy was also struck by how good it felt to have the other man's hands on him, and before he really knew what he was doing, he grabbed Thiago by the front of his shirt and lunged forward, pressing their lips together in a passionate, needy kiss.

Remy halfway expected Thiago to stop him. To push him away and gently tell him he needed to think about what he was doing. It was obvious to both men that this was caused just as much by Remy's need for comfort as it was by the attraction both men had been fighting.

But Thiago didn't push him away. He didn't whisper Shawn's name in reproach or tell Remy why it wasn't a good idea for them to touch one another. To kiss one another. Instead, he pulled Remy closer and wrapped his arms around him, moaning into his mouth as Remy slipped his arms around Thiago's neck.

"Let's get off this fucking balcony, *oui*?" Remy whispered when Thiago finally halted the kiss and stood holding Remy close to him. Thiago's unsteady breath gusted across his face and Remy shivered.

"*La cama*," Thiago murmured before placing a succession of soft, stunningly erotic kisses across Remy's mouth. For the first time since Thiago had touched him, Remy remembered that they were in plain sight of the others. His eyes flickered briefly toward the main room, but it was empty.

"Bed," Remy confirmed when he realized the others had already broken camp and headed to bed themselves. His heart hurt briefly to think of Shawn and Brandt wrapped in each other's arms, but then Thiago's hand gently caressed the small of Remy's back and acted like a salve on the open wound.

Remy and Thiago floated through the flat like ghosts, silently turning off lights and straightening papers before they made their way to the last bedroom. Remy noticed the light on in the first room and, as they passed, he could hear Brandt and Shawn murmuring on the other side of the door. Thiago slipped an arm around Remy's waist and pulled him closer, seeming to sense that Remy needed the physical contact most.

"How d'you suppose Brandt affords a flat like this?" Remy asked in a barely audible voice as Thiago ushered him into the dark room and closed the door behind them.

"Same way you accumulated all that money," Thiago murmured as he wrapped his arms around Remy from behind and kissed his neck gently.

"I doubt it was exactly the same way," Remy muttered with a smile.

"Been skimming, have we?" Thiago asked as he dipped his fingers below the waistband of the front of Remy's jeans.

"Possibly. Call it a retirement fund," Remy said as he shivered delightedly and tilted his head to the side to allow Thiago further access. "If you want to know any more you'll have to beat it out of me."

"That can be arranged," Thiago whispered into Remy's ear.

Remy found himself being moved slowly towards the bed as his jeans were unbuttoned and pushed down. He allowed Thiago to manhandle him just a little, and lifted his arms so his shirt could be pulled over his head. But Thiago didn't pull the loose flannel up, gently undoing each button from behind instead as he nibbled on Remy's ear.

"One of those, eh?" Remy asked in amusement as Thiago gently pushed him to lay face down on the mattress. He pulled the shirt off Remy from behind, momentarily trapping his arms behind him, and then pulled the jeans the rest of the way down Remy's body.

"One of those what?" Thiago asked softly. The sounds he was making told Remy that he was undressing himself, and Remy smiled indulgently.

"You're not always a top but you're still in control," Remy said in explanation as he lifted himself up onto his elbows and looked over his shoulder.

"Mmm. And do you always go commando?"

"Not really. They shredded my Superman boxers. Didn't have any more," Remy said absently as he let his eyes travel over Thiago's body in the darkness. He wanted to see more of it. "May I turn over?" he asked politely. This seemed to amuse Thiago to no end.

They tussled slightly as Thiago grabbed Remy's hips and rolled him onto his back, only to keep rolling him until he was on the edge of the bed and grasping Thiago's forearms for dear life so as not to fall off. By the time he rolled onto his back and they edged into the middle of the bed, they were both snickering almost uncontrollably.

"'May I?'" Thiago mimicked in a high-pitched voice as he settled his body on top of Remy's. "Are you always so polite just before you get fucked?"

"I'm always polite, *couyon*," Remy seriously as he hooked one leg over one of Thiago's hips.

"Mmm," Thiago acknowledged with a cheeky little nod of his head and a cocked eyebrow.

"You really should smile more often," Remy told him.

Thiago nodded thoughtfully as he looked down at Remy. "Superman boxers?" he queried finally.

"Oh, yeah," Remy whispered feelingly. "Loved 'em. Carl made Niko shred 'em. Bastard. He's a sadistic fuck, y'know. Carl. Under that teddy bear exterior, there lies an evil–"

Thiago kissed him once more, and Remy completely forgot what he was talking about as Thiago's lips and tongue and teeth sent lances of need throughout his entire body. Fun time was over. Screw the foreplay.

"Okay then," Remy gasped as Thiago pulled away and thrust his hips down slightly and into Remy's body.

"I haven't gotten any of my information yet," Thiago said with a grin.

"Fuck it. Go get the lube. Now," Remy ordered authoritatively. Thiago nodded eagerly and pushed himself off Remy's body.

As soon as the contact was gone, Remy's mind wandered down the hall to

Shawn, and he squeezed his eyes closed to combat the sinking feeling in his stomach.

"Thiago," he whispered desperately. "Fuck the lube. Get your Spanish ass back here."

Thiago was back and kissing him hungrily before Remy could open his eyes again, and Remy wrapped his body around Thiago's and pushed all other thoughts from his mind.

"Are you sure you want this?" Thiago murmured questioningly into Remy's mouth as Remy nibbled on Thiago's lower lip.

"Yes, I want it. I think I need it," Remy admitted. He tilted his hips up and let his head fall back as their bodies made contact.

Thiago moaned something unintelligible in Spanish as Remy tried every trick he knew to get the other man going. "I'm Argentine, by the way," Thiago murmured distractedly as his entire body convulsed with pleasure. "Asshole."

"You can call me French then," Remy muttered as he leaned upwards and pulled Thiago down for one more kiss. "Now," he demanded with difficulty as their tongues slid together and their bodies caressed one another.

Thiago thumped the bottle of lubricant down beside Remy's head wordlessly, but instead of allowing Remy to reach for it he gathered the younger man in his arms and pulled them both into a kneeling position on the bed.

"I'm not this skilled," Remy said with a little smirk as Thiago pulled their bodies together and nibbled at his neck. He didn't really see what position Thiago was aiming for, but he was pretty sure there wasn't one they could manage like this.

"I'm not just going to fuck you," Thiago said by way of explanation as he kissed Remy once more. "You need more than that. You deserve more than that *de un amigo*."

Remy's eyes fluttered shut and relief washed over him. They could do this slowly then. It wasn't like a mission where it had to be over and done with quickly. He didn't have to treat it as something he had to do. It was something Thiago wanted just as badly as Remy needed it and they would do it right.

Thiago sat back on his haunches and brought Remy with him until Remy straddled him.

"Like this then?" Remy murmured as he settled down and kissed Thiago gently. "Your knees won't make it," he whispered after Thiago's affirmative hum.

"You don't think so?" Thiago asked softly, distracted by the intense study of Remy's neck that he was doing with his lips and tongue.

"Mmm. I ride hard, Thi," Remy said, just a hint of humor breaking through his seductive tone.

Thiago leant back slightly and grinned again, and he allowed Remy to push him backward until he was lying flat, his head at the foot of the bed.

"Are you always a bottom?" Thiago asked as Remy kissed a trail down his chest and stomach. Remy nodded slowly, letting his nose travel gently over the light fuzz on Thiago's abdomen before he went further and slowly took the head of the Thiago's cock into his mouth. "Fuck," Thiago whispered as he tried not to thrust upwards into Remy's mouth. Remy grinned and took him in more, letting his tongue circle around before he thrust his head down and took him all the way to the back of his throat.

Thiago whimpered and thrust up into Remy's throat, and Remy swallowed convulsively until Thiago was writhing and trembling beneath him.

"*¿Por qué?*" Thiago gasped finally.

Remy let Thiago's cock slip from his mouth and he kissed the tip with a grin before looking up at Thiago and smiling.

"Why, what?" he asked as he reached for the little bottle Thiago had retrieved and took Thiago's clenched hand in his own.

"Why are you always the bottom?" Thiago murmured.

Remy took Thiago's finger and slid it into his mouth, swirling his tongue in the same fashion he had displayed before and then sliding the finger out once more. He popped open the cap on the lube and covered Thiago's fingers as the older man breathed heavily and waited for his answer.

"Because if the bottom does his job, then *he's* the one in charge," Remy finally murmured in answer, and Thiago opened his eyes to lock his gaze with Remy's.

"You're absolutely right," Thiago gasped hoarsely as he took control of his fingers. Remy gasped and gripped Thiago's wrist. "I want one thing from you, Remy," Thiago said harshly as he slowly inserted two fingers inside Remy and twisted them wickedly.

Remy tensed and arched his back, but immediately relaxed and allowed the unexpected intrusion. "What's that?" he asked distractedly, too concerned with the pleasure Thiago was giving him to respond with any of the cheeky comments his brain tried to force out.

"*Mi nombre*. I want to hear you say it," Thiago said as he pulled his fingers out and gripped Remy's hips.

Remy forced his eyes open and he looked down at Thiago. Before he could respond, Thiago pulled him down roughly and Remy actually cried out as pain and pleasure shot through his body.

"*Maudit, fils de putain*!" Remy gasped as Thiago closed his eyes and fought back the urge to thrust up into him.

Remy gripped Thiago's shoulders and leaned forward until he was eye to eye with the man. He grinned down at him and tightened every muscle in his body, causing Thiago to cry out and buck.

"Please," Thiago said as his hands dug into Remy's hips hard enough to leave bruises, and Remy began to move slowly.

"Why do you need it?" Remy whispered curiously into Thiago's ear as he sped up his movements. He barely kept himself from crying out loud as he found the right angle, and his grip on Thiago tightened as the pleasure began to build in the pit of his stomach.

"I need to be sure you know it's me," Thiago answered with difficulty as his hands moved upward to grip Remy's waist. He rolled them in a flurry of movement, and Remy was left slightly stunned as Thiago settled in between his legs and began to thrust into him slowly. His eyes fluttered closed as the pleasure swept over him. "Open your eyes, Remy," Thiago ordered, "*Abre los ojos*."

Remy writhed slowly and forced his eyes open

"*Mi nombre*," Thiago ordered gruffly.

Remy groaned and closed his eyes again. "Thi," he finally breathed as he let himself relax in the other man's hands. He wrapped himself around Thiago and allowed both his body and his mind to gratefully sink into the pleasure of something that had no strings attached.

Hours later, Remy was just barely awake when he heard a door slam down the hall and a shout echo throughout the flat. He and Thiago were both sitting up and on high alert within seconds.

"It's just Shawn bellowing," Remy whispered after a few tense moments of sitting and listening.

"What did he say?" Thiago asked groggily. "I didn't catch it."

"Sounded like 'fucking wankers.' That's his favorite one, anyway," Remy answered wryly as he flopped onto his back.

"You think they're still fighting?" Thiago asked curiously as he snuggled back under the sheets.

"What do you mean, still?" Remy asked.

"Brandt was pissed at him for what he said to you," Thiago told him through a yawn.

"Good. I'm liking Brandt more and more."

Thiago laughed sleepily and rolled onto his side. To Remy's surprise, the other man snuggled up to him and rested himself in the crook of Remy's arm. Remy nuzzled his nose against Thiago's hair and closed his eyes, trying to decide whether to say what was on his mind. Finally, he exhaled deeply and pressed his lips tightly together. He trusted Thiago, but not enough to take the Argentinean into his confidence. Not yet, anyway.

"The bottom's not always in control, Remy," Thiago murmured, sounding almost as if he was talking in his sleep. Remy waited for Thiago to go on, but the man was soon breathing evenly, and Remy decided Thiago was probably dreaming.

A small crisis had been averted tonight, and Remy scolded himself for being careless. He had been extremely lucky. Thiago hadn't seen Gray Kincaid on the balcony below them when he had stepped out to join Remy, and what Remy had said as a wary greeting to Gray had been taken as words of admonishment aimed at Thiago instead.

What would Thiago do if he knew Remy had really turned?

XXI.

THIAGO groaned and rolled onto his side, expecting to meet a warm, hard body and pull it close. Instead, he encountered a cold, soft pillow that had been pushed against him as a consolation prize and he groaned again.

He pulled the pillow to him and slung his leg over it, thinking that it was a damn poor substitute for Remy. They'd spent the night tangled together in each other's arms and taking turns holding one another, and Thiago had thoroughly enjoyed the experience. He stayed in the warm spot of the bed his body had created for several more moments, thinking about the night before with a little grin on his face.

Remy was something of an enigma to Thiago. He was so capable and yet so… innocent. Thiago felt the need to protect him half the time, and the other half he spent watching the younger man warily and waiting for him to draw his gun and start blasting everyone away. They had all been wary of Brandt at first because the big man was so obviously unstable, but in Thiago's opinion, Remy was just as unstable, if not more so. He was a wild card, a loose cannon, and there really wasn't ever any way to tell what Remy was thinking.

Thiago had thought that after bedding the younger man he might somehow magically be able to understand him, but it didn't seem to be working. The only thing he knew for sure was that Remy was upset. Unstable and upset and probably too emotionally involved with the whole mess to be of much use to the group at all. Thiago wondered just how volatile Remy was. And where he was.

Some of the things Remy had said the night before began to drift back through Thiago's mind, and he opened his eyes to stare at the wall as he remembered the look in Remy's eyes.

"I'm losing it… I'm a fuck up, Thi. I'm going to get one of us killed… there are only two things I can't imagine not having in my life, Shawn, and if I lost both in one fell swoop I just don't think I'd live through it."

"*Mierda*," Thiago hissed. He shot out of bed in a panic and looked around wildly for his jeans. "You little fuck. If you left us...," he muttered in Spanish as he hopped around on one leg and pulled his jeans on. He grabbed his shirt and his shoulder holster and darted for the door, wondering how long Remy had been gone and whether he and Shawn would be able to track the younger man. Shawn knew Remy's habits well, that might give them just enough of an advantage to find Remy before he did something stupid and probably self-destructive.

Thiago threw open the door and tore down the hall, skidding to a halt in the kitchen and staring wild eyed at the four men who stood around conversing quietly and making breakfast. They all froze and stared back at him. It was all very domestic, except for the gun Shawn was cleaning and the several Ramboesque knives lying about.

"Where's Remy?" Thiago demanded apprehensively, already knowing what the answer would be.

"Wasn't he with you? Last night?" Carl asked as he turned the stove off and swatted Brandt's hand away from the hot pan.

"He's not come out. We haven't been up long, though, he may have slipped past," Brandt said distractedly as he glared at Carl and reached for the pan once more.

"Fuck!" Thiago ground out as he locked eyes with Shawn. The other man was staring at him blankly.

"Twenty minutes, at most," Carl offered as he smacked Brandt in the arm. "No fire!" he shouted.

Brandt sulked at him, but then he seemed to sense Thiago's distress and he turned his attention away from the stove to look at Thiago in growing concern.

"He's left?" Nikolaus asked in alarm.

Thiago ran his fingers though his hair and made a helpless sound.

Shawn lunged forward suddenly and gripped Thiago's arm. "What did he say? What happened?" he demanded. He didn't sound nearly concerned enough for Thiago's taste.

"We have to go after him. He's going to do something stupid if we don't find him. He's going to hurt himself," Thiago insisted as he shook himself free and turned to head for the door.

"Why would he leave?" Nikolaus asked in agitation as they all gathered their various means of destruction and prepared to go with Thiago. "After all he went through to find us again, why would he just leave?"

Thiago spared Shawn an accusing stare before he shrugged his shirt on and turned to the door. "You two, stay here with Niko," he ordered as Carl and Brandt came up behind him.

"But–"

"Stay here!" Thiago barked at Carl, who had been trying to object. Carl looked at him in a wounded manner, but nodded obediently. He placed a hand across Brandt's chest to restrain him from following, and Thiago turned his glare on Shawn. "Where would he go first?"

Shawn looked stricken. He appeared to be trying to come to terms with the fact that Remy would just up and leave, and while Thiago felt an inkling of pity for him, he didn't have the time to dole out sympathy.

"Shawn!" he yelled in frustration. "Where would he go?"

"There's no telling," Shawn said in a hoarse voice. "If he's… there's just… no way to know with him. What did he say?"

"He said he was slipping. That he was fucking up too much and that he was going to get one of us killed," Thiago said as he checked his gun.

Shawn looked at Thiago skeptically. "That doesn't sound at all like Remy," he said dubiously. "He doesn't slip. And he doesn't doubt himself."

"He didn't, you mean," Nikolaus mumbled as he glared at Shawn. "He gravitates toward food, Thi," Nikolaus said in a businesslike manner as he tossed Thiago an extra sidearm and nodded at him.

Thiago was too worried to even find the solemn advice as funny as it should have been, and he simply nodded in return and slipped the extra gun into the back of his jeans.

"No," Shawn said, shaking his head. "Remy wouldn't just abandon us without so much as a–"

"Fine. You wait here as well," Thiago spat as he turned to the door and flung it open. The figure hovering outside the door startled him, and before he could stop himself, his gun was drawn and pointed at the surprised man on the other side of the threshold. Thiago was even more startled when he found himself staring at the business end of the other man's weapon. The reaction had been almost as fast as Thiago's, and he found himself slightly disturbed by the realization that Remy was probably faster than he was on the draw. Good Lord, that was a scary thought.

"I'm gone for one whole hour and you're ready to shoot me when I get back?" Remy asked in an amused voice as he uncocked the revolver and slid it easily back into the holster under his arm. Thiago didn't see how Remy had drawn the weapon, seeing as he was balancing a cardboard tray full of breakfast pastries in one hand and had a nondescript little brown box cradled in the crook of his elbow.

"Where the hell have you been?" Thiago demanded, not certain whether to be angry or relieved that the younger man had reappeared. Remy widened his eyes innocently and raised the tray slightly.

"Breakfast," he said cheerfully. "Can I come in or are you just gonna shoot me and get it over with?" he asked after Thiago had gaped at him for several seconds. Thiago stepped aside without further comment and Remy smiled brilliantly at him. "Morning, *mes amis*. Where's the fire?" Remy asked as he sidestepped around Thiago and took several steps into the room, taking in their various stages of agitation and fortification. He looked at Brandt askance and turned to Carl in alarm. "There's not really a fire, is there?" he asked quickly.

Carl smiled slightly and shook his head.

"We thought you'd left," Shawn told him in a low, even voice.

Thiago tensed as he watched the younger man's reaction to Shawn's words. A flash of pain shot through his eyes before they blacked over once more. Thiago was starting to think of Remy as more of the gator than the Cajun lately. It was the eyes. They were lifeless and soulless. Eyes like that were capable of anything, and it scared Thiago witless to see them appear so easily. Just as quickly as the killer eyes had come, they were gone, and Remy seemed to go completely still. So still, in fact, that Thiago could have mistaken him for a photograph.

"I'm sorry," Remy offered evenly. "I should have thought to leave a note." He turned on his heel to walk toward the kitchen without waiting for a response and he continued to talk as if they all weren't standing there tense and armed to the teeth. "I was up for about an hour before I left. I got hungry. And bored. I didn't want to wake anyone by cooking… trying to cook, anyway. So I finally went out to forage when no one else got up."

Thiago followed Remy's voice into the kitchen, and he and Nikolaus stood there in the entryway as Remy laid the tray down and continued talking. His voice lowered to the point that it probably didn't carry to the others. Thiago was pretty certain he wasn't doing it on purpose, considering what he was saying wasn't exactly sensitive material.

"Hell, I can't cook anyway," he muttered as he turned around and leaned against the counter. He met Thiago's eyes and smiled wanly. "I didn't want to burn down Brandt's flat trying," he added wryly. He was smiling, but Thiago could see right through it. He was upset, and rightly so. Only it was Thiago with whom he should be upset. Not Shawn. Apparently Nikolaus could see through the smile as well, and he walked over to Remy and looked at him closely before turning his attention to the food.

Thiago didn't know what sort of connection the two younger men had, but there was obviously some sort of understanding there. Remy's shoulders straightened slightly and the smile became slightly more genuine.

"Carl was making eggs," Nikolaus said absently as he picked up a scone and examined it briefly before biting into it.

"Mmm," Remy acknowledged as he looked at Thiago over Nikolaus's shoulder. "You okay, *podna*? You look a little winded."

"I thought you had left," Thiago murmured as he took a step further into the kitchen. "It wasn't Shawn. I thought…."

Remy stared at him for several long seconds before he nodded slowly as if he understood and plucked the scone from Nikolaus's hand.

"Hey!"

"Mine," Remy growled as he moved to the refrigerator and began rummaging around inside it. "You can have anything but the scones."

Thiago felt a presence directly behind him, but he didn't turn to see which one of his companions it was. His attention was fixed on Remy, waiting for the gator to resurface after his tentative admission.

When Remy peered over the door of the refrigerator Thiago's breath caught in his throat. Remy's eyes were flashing dangerously. It wasn't the gator, but it was dangerous all the same. A throat cleared at Thiago's ear, and he assumed that Shawn was the man standing behind him. At least he hoped so. He didn't want Remy looking at *him* like that.

"Anyone else want juice?" Remy asked in a steely voice.

"Remy," Shawn said softly from just behind Thiago. "Sit down a minute."

"Go to hell, Shawn. I went to get our fucking breakfast," Remy responded angrily as he slammed the door closed. Thiago heard the various glass bottles and containers clang around as the fridge rocked slightly. "I wasn't aware that I had to report my movements to anyone!"

"Remy," Thiago said gently, trying to head off another brawl. "I was the one who thought you'd left. I woke up and you were gone and–"

"And you've known me personally for a grand total of what, ten days?" Remy asked sarcastically. "He should have known better!" Remy yelled as he drew his gun and waved it in Shawn's direction.

Thiago threw his body back against Shawn, trying to get out of firing range.

Remy turned smoothly to point the gun at Nikolaus and yelled, "Nikolaus! I swear to God, if you eat another one of those scones, I'll kill you. And my aim is much better than Shawn's," he growled as Nikolaus dropped the little pastry and sat with a thump into the nearest chair, ostensibly to protect his ass from being shot.

Thiago blinked a couple times when he realized that Shawn was holding him around the chest, using him as a shield, more or less.

"What the hell, Shawn?" Thiago mumbled as he yanked away and turned around to smack the other man in the side of the head.

"He had a gun!" Shawn grumbled defensively as he rubbed his head and glared at Thiago. Remy reholstered his weapon and grabbed the little carton of juice he had set down.

"He always has a gun! Stop pissing him off!" Thiago hissed as he glared at Shawn and smacked him again for good measure.

"I swear, the next person that hits me– oomph!" Shawn growled as Remy walked past and smacked him on the other side of his head with the little brown box in passing.

Thiago glared at Shawn once more and followed Remy into the main room. "What's in the box?" he asked carefully.

"Parts," Remy said succinctly as he set the box and his juice down and made his way back into the kitchen to rescue his scones. Thiago watched him warily.

"Parts for what?"

"In a minute, *podna*, I need food."

"Told you he gravitates toward the food," Nikolaus mumbled as he picked through the pastries.

"Remy," Thiago ventured, wanting to make certain it was clear that he'd been the one to think Remy had gone and not Shawn. That Shawn had actually defended him.

"Look, I understand," Remy said as he walked past them again and sat down at the big dining table. "You caught me at my worst last night, and I can see why you'd think I'd bail."

"I didn't think you'd bailed on us," Thiago said as he walked over and sat at the table beside Remy. "I thought you'd… I thought you were suicidal or something."

Remy stopped chewing and looked at Thiago with wide eyes. "Why would I be suicidal? You weren't that bad, Thi," he said with a grin and a barely concealed snicker.

"Oh, that's great. Why do I even bother?" Thiago muttered as he stood up and went to find something to eat, leaving Remy snickering at the table behind him.

XXII.

CARL watched the interaction tensely, only vaguely aware that he was still holding onto Brandt and absently fingering the trigger of his gun as it rested in its holster beneath his arm. He relaxed slightly when Remy began to snicker and bite into his scone, but the air was still tense and Shawn looked positively miserable.

Brandt nudged him and Carl glanced at the man briefly before looking back at Thiago and Shawn.

"What do we do?" Brandt whispered into his ear. Carl glanced at him again and shrugged.

He had no idea what to do. After the melee he had witnessed between Shawn and Brandt the night before and the continued tension between Remy and Shawn now, Carl was at a loss as to who to try to fix first. He didn't even know if he *could* fix either one of them.

"What's the plan for today then?" Remy asked as he turned around in his chair and straddled it, a scone in one hand and his glass in the other. They all looked at one another uncomfortably. "Jesus! We can't just sit here and twiddle our thumbs. Who's the brains of this outfit, anyway?"

"I think that was Shawn," Carl said wryly as his mind landed on an idea. "Before he went mad, that is. Now I suppose it's you, God help us."

"What the hell is that supposed to mean?" Shawn asked in a hurt voice. "I've not gone mad!"

"Uh huh. What's the plan, Dixie?" Carl asked as he spared Shawn a glance before turning his gaze back on Remy. Remy blinked at him.

"You can't put him in charge," Shawn protested. "We'll be in the shit and he'll stop to get an ice cream, for fuck's sake!"

"What's wrong with ice cream?" Remy asked in an insulted voice.

"I think you missed the point of the comment," Thiago muttered as he sat down in the kitchen beside Nikolaus.

"I didn't miss the point," Remy called from the dining area. "I just don't see what's wrong with ice cream."

"I didn't say there was anything wrong with ice cream!" Shawn yelled in frustration.

"You were the one who made us stop that time for–"

"Remy," Shawn growled.

"Well, you did!"

"That has absolutely no bearing on this discussion. If anything, Thiago should be in charge."

"What?" Thiago said as if he hadn't truly been listening but had simply heard his name.

"I think you're doing a fine job of it, Beignet," Remy said sarcastically. "I mean we're all in one piece, aren't we? You haven't shot any of us yet."

"I told you that was an accident!"

Remy responded with that odd hissing sound he made and then shouted, "I couldn't sit for a fucking month, you bastard!"

"Where do I have to shoot you to get your mouth to stop running?" Shawn asked sarcastically.

"Care for me to demonstrate?" Remy asked casually as his hand moved slightly toward his weapon.

Remy and Shawn glared at one another warily and Carl smirked a little. He leant into Brandt and whispered just loud enough for the others to hear.

"Maybe we'd be better off splitting up again."

Brandt looked at him with narrowed eyes. Miraculously, he seemed to catch on to what Carl was trying to do, and he played along.

"Do you think it would help?" the big man asked casually.

"No!" Remy and Shawn yelled in unison.

Carl raised an eyebrow at them and Thiago and Nikolaus both perked up from where they sat in the kitchen. That was probably the first thing Shawn and Remy had agreed on since they reunited. That was progress, as far as Carl was concerned.

Remy looked down at his half-eaten scone and Shawn shifted uncomfortably against the wall as he glared at Carl.

"Jesus, Shawn," Remy murmured thoughtfully.

"What's wrong?" Shawn asked distractedly as he continued to study Carl and Brandt suspiciously.

"We really are a couple of silly *bioques*," Remy sighed decisively as he looked back up, and Carl was relieved to see a slight smile on the younger man's face. Perhaps this would be easier than Carl had thought. Nothing like a little reverse psychology to screw with the heads of your mates.

"What?" Shawn asked in surprise as he turned back to look at Remy.

"*Mais c'est vrai.* Five years, Shawn. Five years together, and all it takes is one little rogue to send us into a spiral?"

Everyone was silent as Shawn and Remy looked at one another thoughtfully. Carl hadn't quite grasped the amount of turmoil they were in until that point. He wasn't certain any of them had, not even Shawn and Remy.

Five years. In the nomadic life they led, five years was an eternity. No wonder Shawn and Remy were both a mess.

"You're right," Shawn said quietly after several moments.

Remy was up and out of his chair before Carl really registered the movement, and in several long strides, the Cajun had closed the distance between himself and Shawn and pulled him into a tight hug. Remy was getting crumbs from his scone all over Shawn's hair, but neither of them seemed to mind.

Shawn murmured something into Remy's ear as he wrapped his arms gratefully around Remy's body, but Carl couldn't quite make it out.

"Doesn't matter," Remy said determinedly. "We can't forget all we've been through. *Sommes des amis* first, understand?" he added as his voice broke slightly.

Carl felt as if he were intruding as he watched the two of them clutch at one another, and he glanced at Brandt uncertainly before he realized how pointless it was to look to Brandt Everett for his social cues.

Thiago smiled into his coffee mug, and Nikolaus watched with a shy smile. Brandt grinned like a fool, and Carl found himself wondering if Remy and Shawn realized it wasn't just the two of them anymore. They had others to fall back on now. They had all been loners for so long, it was hard to get accustomed to the fact that there was now someone else there, but Carl was coming to realize this, and he hoped the rest of them were as well.

"Well, now that that's settled, on to the real business. I need some supplies," Brandt announced suddenly as Shawn clung to Remy for dear life.

Carl's blood ran cold at the thought of what supplies Brandt needed exactly. "What, uh, what sorts of supplies are we talking about here?" he asked tentatively.

"Explosives, Trigger! Timers, casings, leads, powder…."

"Oh, fuck."

"Ooh! And dynamite! Remotes, grids, wires of all colors… did you know people always cut the blue wire when they're trying to defuse a bomb? Never cut the blue, Trigger. It'll blow you all to Hell. Well… hold on… no, wait, I take that back. Always cut the blue, Trigger. Always cut the blue."

Brandt started down the hall toward the bedrooms, and Carl stood gaping after him. He could hear Thiago and Nikolaus sniggering in the kitchen, and he glanced at them questioningly. They both watched him in amusement. Shawn held Remy's face in his hands and spoke in low tones as Remy looked at him intently, and Carl didn't think either one of them had even heard what Brandt had said. Surely, they would look more concerned if they'd heard that.

Carl stood there debating over what he should do. Should he follow after Brandt and make certain nothing got blown up in Brandt's fervent excitement, or should he sit down and finally eat the breakfast he'd cooked?

Carl's shoulders slumped and he trudged after Brandt dejectedly.

"Hey, Trigger!" he heard from the first bedroom on the right. "I need help!"

Carl broke into a trot and stepped into the doorframe just in time to see a little burst of yellow flame and be assaulted with a smell similar to that of rotten eggs.

"Christ! What are you doing?" Carl yelled as he covered the lower part of his face with his forearm and squinted to combat the smoke and stench.

"That was the last of it," Brandt answered sadly as he stared down at the puff of smoke rising from the cutting board on the floor.

"What was it?" Carl coughed as he waved his hand at the remnants of smoke and the other four men joined him in the doorway.

"A combination of zinc metal powder and sulphur. When used correctly it'll do, well, that," Brandt said as he waved his hand at the ruined cutting board.

"Where'd you get the board?" Remy asked as he poked his head around the corner. He didn't seem at all concerned with the explosion aspect of the event, just the inane details. Carl spared him a worried glance before returning his gaze to Brandt.

"Kitchen," Brandt said tersely as he turned to his bag.

"What was the point of that?" Thiago asked curiously as he slid around Carl and into the room. He looked down at the pile of yellow powder and frowned.

Brandt shrugged and began digging through his bag once more. "There wasn't much of it. And it looked lonely," he said matter-of-factly, and they all froze and stared at him. Just when they thought he was almost normal, he went and did or said something completely odd. Carl wondered if he did it on purpose. "I need supplies!" Brandt wailed finally, and Carl watched in fascination as the man flailed his hands through the air and flopped onto the bed like a little kid throwing a fit. Probably not on purpose, then.

"This is your region, Wally," Carl drawled in amusement. "We all need supplies. So where do we get them?"

Brandt perked up and Carl had to actively concentrate on not hiding behind Shawn as Brandt looked at him with that gleam in his eyes.

"There's a woman in Melbourne," Brandt said excitedly.

"Melbourne?" Remy repeated unnecessarily as he slipped past Carl and walked over to look down at the cutting board on the floor.

Brandt nodded. "She travels between Melbourne and Perth actually, but I'm pretty sure she's in Melbourne now."

"Can we trust her?" Shawn asked skeptically.

"She's a top-class arms dealer. Been in it for years. I get all my equipment from her. If it's in Australia, she'll find it for you, Trigger," Brandt said with a wink.

"Yes, but, that was before," Remy said as he knelt and poked at the ashes. Carl wasn't certain what it was about the action that disturbed him, but he shivered nonetheless. "Word travels, y'know. Can you still trust her?"

Brandt was silent as he watched Remy thoughtfully.

"You think they think we turned and then let it out? You think they've made her think we've turned?" he asked.

Remy looked up and cocked an eyebrow. "What?" he asked in confusion.

Carl knew how he felt.

"I think what Remy's asking," Shawn offered slowly, "is she a company girl, or is she freelance? Will she care whose side we're supposedly on?"

"So far as I know, she's a free agent," Brandt said as he knelt at the foot of the bed in front of Remy and pointed at something in the ashes that Carl couldn't see. Remy nodded and looked up into Brandt's face and grinned. Out of the corner of his eye, Carl could see Thiago and Nikolaus share a worried look, and Carl's blood ran cold once more as the two men on the floor looked at one another gleefully.

Brandt was manageable in his madness because he seemed to know that he was crazy. Remy was a different story, in Carl's opinion. He didn't seem to realize that he was a card or two short of a full deck, and that made him dangerous. If Remy caught the firebug from Brandt, then he would be out of everyone's control, save for maybe Shawn.

'Please God, don't let Brandt and Remy spend too much time together,' Carl pleaded silently.

"Uh...." Shawn said nothing further and he turned to look at Carl warily. Carl shrugged in return and knew that Shawn was thinking the same thing he had been. "Well, come out of this God-awful stink and we'll make ourselves a plan," Shawn urged finally, trying to tactfully usher the two younger men away from the pile of smoldering powder.

As Carl exited the room and made his way down the hall he heard Remy whisper, "You'll have to teach me how to do that."

Carl turned in time to see Brandt nod delightedly. Despite the relatively comfortable temperature of the flat, Carl found himself with the urge to shiver throughout the entire planning session.

"What's this bird's name?" Shawn asked as Brandt sat in the middle of the sofa beside Carl.

Carl was always interested in how they aligned themselves during these little conferences. It was the best way of determining the mood of the group. Right now, Carl was flanked on either side by Brandt and Nikolaus, and Thiago took up residence in the overstuffed chair opposite the sofa. Shawn stood over them with his arms folded across his chest, and Remy simply dematerialized. Carl glanced around casually and wondered to himself how the Cajun did that, exactly.

"Her name's Melinda," Brandt said as he picked at a loose thread on Carl's khaki pants. Carl swatted his hand away. "Melinda Oliver."

Remy walked in holding a pastry and plopped himself gracelessly onto the floor in front of Thiago. Thiago spread his legs wider without seeming to be aware that he was moving at all, and Remy settled in between them happily. Shawn watched them thoughtfully and everyone waited for someone else to say something. It should have been an awkward silence but, for some reason, it wasn't. Carl smiled slightly and narrowed his eyes at Thiago and Remy. So that's what they'd been doing last night. Carl wondered if Shawn knew.

"How do we contact her?" Remy asked in between bites, seemingly oblivious that everyone's attention was still on him.

"Well, that's where we might hit problems," Brandt said thoughtfully.

"You don't know how?" Thiago asked irritably.

"Well, yes and no," Brandt said as he leaned forward and absently plucked at the thread again. Carl watched him briefly before swatting at his hand once more. "Ow. Bastard. We'll have to be careful about it. Even if she's not a company player they may still be watching her. She has a set schedule, you see."

"A set schedule?" Remy repeated incredulously. "She's either very confident or very stupid."

"She's not stupid, mate," Brandt said assuredly. "She sits outside the same café every Saturday from ten in the morning 'til noon. If you want her for business you drop a flower at her table in passing."

"A flower?" Shawn asked dubiously. Carl didn't much like the sound of it, either. It sounded far too staged. Too spy novel to actually be real.

"What kind of flower?" Nikolaus asked curiously.

"Depends on the job," Brandt said as he looked at Shawn steadily. Carl was still worried about them. It seemed that Shawn and Remy had made their peace, at least temporarily. But Shawn and Brandt had really had it out the night before, and though Carl couldn't see a single difference in the way they behaved, something didn't feel right about it. He would have to watch them closely.

"Care to elaborate on that?" Nikolaus asked.

Brandt was very close-mouthed all of a sudden, and getting information out of him was like pulling teeth. Carl took a deep breath and closed his eyes. He was getting a headache.

"We need to be fully equipped," Brandt said evasively. "It's going to take… uh… fuck."

"You can't remember?" Shawn asked flatly.

"It's been a long fucking while since I've been this low on supplies, okay? It'll come to me."

"Doesn't matter what type of fucking flower we lay down," Thiago said quietly, his eyes unfocused and his voice far away. "If she's being watched the deliverer will have to disguise himself somehow."

"How does she know how to get in touch with you after you give her the flower?" Remy asked curiously as he sprawled himself out upside down onto the floor and rested his feet in Thiago's lap. Carl looked at him curiously, wondering how many facets of personality the man had. He seemed so childlike sometimes. It was frighteningly disarming. "How does she know which customer is requesting what?" he asked as he looked up at them from the floor.

"She always has in the past," Brandt said with an unconcerned shrug. "It's not my job to know her business. Just mine."

"And yours would be picking flowers?" Remy asked with a grin as he looked at Brandt upside down. He looked completely ridiculous. And though Carl hated to use the word in reference to the young killer, completely adorable. It was no wonder Shawn couldn't resist him.

"I blow shit up," Brandt replied with a grin.

Remy raised an upside down eyebrow and smiled brilliantly, and Carl barely kept himself from groaning as he saw Shawn stiffen ever so slightly. This just kept getting worse and worse. Carl wondered whether Brandt and Remy were flirting with the express purpose of pissing Shawn off. If they were, it seemed to be working.

"What sort of disguise?" Nikolaus inquired of Thiago. Both of them seemed to be blissfully unaware of anything other than the discussion they *should* have been having, and Carl wondered if he was the only one able to sense these kinds of emotional disasters waiting to happen. Sometimes it seemed that way.

"Well, one of us can't just waltz up there with a rose between his teeth," Shawn said irritably. "If she's being observed, which she almost certainly is–"

"Roses!" Brandt said triumphantly.

They all looked at him blankly as he beamed back at them.

"What color?" Remy asked finally, and for some reason, Carl found the innocent inquiry phenomenally amusing. He bit his bottom lip in hopes of refraining from laughing.

"Different colors mean different things, *ja*?" Nikolaus offered as he leaned forward and looked at Brandt. Carl snorted and clapped his hand over his mouth.

"There's yellow, pink, red, white… aren't there black roses?" Shawn said seriously as he looked across the room at Thiago.

Carl began to laugh silently, his shoulders shaking as he tried to contain it. Remy snickered slightly, and Thiago smiled fondly at Carl as he tried to control himself. Carl shook his head as if to say that he had no idea why he was laughing, and Remy began to laugh.

"There's different colors of red, too," Nikolaus offered helpfully. "They all mean something different, socially, I mean."

"I doubt there's one for 'I wanna blow shit up!'" Carl wheezed as the conversation finally overtook him and he began to laugh raucously.

His laughter set off Remy, who doubled up on his side and clutched at his stomach as he laughed silently, and even Thiago covered his mouth with his hand as he looked up at Shawn apologetically. Shawn narrowed his eyes and huffed, and Carl buried his face in Brandt's shoulder so he couldn't see Shawn glaring at him.

"You blokes are hopeless," Shawn said in disgust as he walked away toward the kitchen.

Two hours later Carl was still laughing raucously, but they were far beyond the flowers. They were discussing costumes, and who should be the one to deliver the flowers to the table.

"They're after two men," Remy said for the fifth time. "That's what the Washburn kid told us."

"Yes, Remy, we heard you," Shawn said testily. "You'll observe from somewhere close, if there's suitable cover. We'll have to keep you out of sight. Nikolaus as well, since you two are the ones they're really after now."

"That's not my point," Remy said irritably, having been interrupted for the fifth time. "They'll be watching every *man* that goes near her."

"No."

"Shawn!"

"No!"

"What's the problem?" Thiago asked carefully.

"He's trying to make one of us dress as a woman," Shawn said accusingly, and Carl laughed merrily at the insulted look on Shawn's face.

"Well, why not make Dixie do it?" Brandt asked. "He's pretty like a girl."

"Hey!"

"No one is dressing as a girl!" Shawn shouted as he stood and began to pace.

Carl briefly wondered why he was so adamantly against what was decidedly their best option. He and Nikolaus were once more afflicted with the giggles as they both imagined any of the others in a dress, and Carl decided not to worry about Shawn's reasons. He thought it was funny simply because he knew it wouldn't be *him* in the dress, and for that reason Carl could afford to laugh.

"Don't be making a *bahbin* about it," Remy said good-naturedly. "You'll make a lovely woman."

Shawn growled at the younger man as Remy snickered quietly.

"Making a what?" Carl asked in amusement.

"He says I'm pouting," Shawn huffed in explanation.

"Well, it's either you or Thiago," Remy reasoned with a laugh. "Brandt and Carl are both too big to pull it off. And you've already made it clear that Niko and I are to stay out of sight. So… what… do you want to draw straws, or… ooh we could dress you both up and see who looks better!"

Carl and Nikolaus both laughed gleefully, and Brandt leaned forwards and smiled expectantly, looking like a lion preparing to pounce.

"I will not wear a dress," Shawn growled dangerously.

"Oh, come on! It's not like you haven't done it before!" Remy shouted at him with a laugh.

"That was different!" Shawn squeaked.

"Oh? Was our life on the line then, too?"

"Well… yes, but… that was different!" Shawn repeated desperately as he paced back and forth.

"How many exits are there, Brandt?" Thiago asked as he ignored Shawn's pacing.

"She's outside," Brandt said with a shrug.

"I think what he means is…." Carl looked at Thiago for permission to continue, and Thiago nodded. "If you were going to trap her, how many things would you blow up to block the path?" Carl asked with a little smile.

"Three," Brandt said without hesitating.

Carl had finally figured out how Brandt's brain worked. That in itself was a frightening concept. Carl made a note to check up on his own sanity with one of the others tonight. Thiago or Nikolaus, maybe. Perhaps Shawn. Definitely not Remy.

"There are three distinct lanes," Brandt said as Carl winked at Thiago and received a grin in return. Shawn still paced and Remy watched him in amusement. Carl leaned back and threw his hand over the back of the couch, and Nikolaus settled into the crook of his arm as naturally as if they had been doing it for all their lives. "One person could cover each one with little to no difficulty. Though, with only the handguns, Trigger'd have to be at the largest one, since I assume he's the best shot. I can wire the smallest with what I have laying around here and blow it all to Hell if need be."

"What exactly do you have 'laying around?'" Remy asked in alarm as he tore his attention away from Shawn.

Carl's mind went back to that timer that was missing yesterday, and he looked at Brandt in concern. Had it ever been found? Carl couldn't remember.

"I'll put something together," Brandt said with a shrug. "If Dixie and Gizmo have to lay low, then you'll have to decide which of the two of you is the best shot, and conversely, which one can slip away the easiest if it goes to shit."

Carl was impressed with the logic, and apparently so were the others. Brandt never ceased to surprise him. In that respect, the big man reminded Carl of Remy, and vice versa. Carl suddenly felt very sorry for Shawn. No wonder he was so fucking confused. Thiago blinked at Brandt blankly, and Shawn stopped pacing and stared at him.

"That's settled then!" Remy declared with a smile as he jumped to his feet and turned to grin at Shawn. "Seeing as how you're the only one in the room to have ever shot someone else in the ass, accidentally or otherwise," he said maliciously as Shawn growled wordlessly at him. "What do you suppose?" Remy asked as he turned to look first at Thiago and then at Brandt, Carl, and Nikolaus. "He's a what, ten? Twelve, maybe?"

"Might need to take him to be fitted," Carl snickered as he hid behind Brandt once more.

XXIII.

SHAWN couldn't quite believe what he was hearing. If these bastards thought they were going to get him in a dress and out in public without a gun held to his head, they were sadly mistaken. Yes, he'd worn that getup several years back, but their lives had been in immediate danger and Shawn had been bleeding quite profusely at the time. It had been necessary. That's right. Necessary.

Their lives were not now in immediate danger, though. And no one was bleeding. Not yet, anyway. If Remy took one more step with that measuring tape, then blood would definitely flow.

"Come now, Beignet, be a sport," Remy said coaxingly as Shawn growled at him like a cornered animal. He *was* cornered. They had him boxed in, Remy and Brandt, and Shawn was simply trying to decide which one to go after first before he attacked. This was their revenge for his being such a bastard, apparently, and though Shawn was more than willing to make amends for his behavior in many ways, this was not the way he planned on doing it.

"I will not 'be a sport'," Shawn spat. "There are other ways of doing this. You're just being a twat for the hell of it."

"So? You fuck around with people's minds for the hell of it," Remy said bluntly. "And this is what you get as punishment."

"Well then, I want to see Brandt in ruffles," Shawn shouted angrily, pointing at Brandt as he glared at Remy. "You're not the only one who got fucked with here!"

"I didn't fuck with you," Brandt said indignantly as he took a step closer. He looked like he was preparing to lunge forward and Shawn turned to face him, chalking Remy up as the lesser threat at the moment.

"Fuck you, Everett," Shawn growled angrily. "You may be crazier than fuck, but it's no excuse for what you said."

Brandt's eyes narrowed dangerously, but Shawn didn't care. He was still stinging from the 'discussion' they'd had the night before, and he wanted to lash out. He wanted to hurt something. Brandt, preferably. Maybe he would take a page from Brandt's book and blow something up. What Brandt had said to him hadn't bothered him quite so much as it probably should have, but knowing he had hurt Remy so needlessly made it hard to look anyone in the eye, especially Brandt or Remy. He felt guilty and hurt and more than a little confused, and he vented those unfamiliar emotions in the only way he knew how. Anger.

"Perhaps later," Brandt responded haughtily as he took another step forward. Shawn growled wordlessly in warning and saw Remy step closer in the periphery of his vision. He knew he was done for when Remy's movement distracted him, but he put up a fight worthy of a Class One agent, regardless of the odds stacked against him.

Brandt lunged forward and wrapped his muscular arms around Shawn, pinning his arms to his sides and pressing their torsos together so hard that Shawn was bereft of the ability to breathe for precious seconds as Remy leapt into the fray.

Shawn struggled and growled and cursed and kicked and even got a bite in on someone's hand as all three of them went crashing to the floor, but it was all in vain. He landed on top of Remy, who immediately thrust the measuring tape forward around Shawn's waist and then wrapped his sinewy arms and legs around Shawn's body from behind. Brandt made certain that Remy had Shawn's arms pinned before he reached down and took the tape in his own hands, winding it around Shawn's midsection.

"Quit squirming!" Brandt yelled irritably as he tried to read the tape, and Shawn got in a good knee to his ribs in retaliation. He didn't want to hurt either of these men or he would have been free some time ago and having a nice relaxing cigarette as they both bled to death on the expensive white carpet, but he didn't mind causing a few bruises here and there. He smiled grimly as Brandt whuffed and cursed colorfully. Brandt spared him a glare before jabbing Shawn in the ribs with his fist. The pain was just sharp enough to make Shawn stop struggling long enough for Brandt to get a read on him. "Eighty centimeters," he gasped as he pressed his weight down on Shawn to keep him from going anywhere.

Remy was probably being squished with the weight of both men on him, but Shawn found he really didn't give a fuck. You reap what you sow.

"Eighty centimeters is roughly thirty-one inches, isn't it?" Thiago asked casually as he walked up to look at the three men struggling on the floor.

"Thiago! Help," Shawn panted pitifully. Thiago looked at him sympathetically, but shook his head and took a casual sip of the God-awful *mate* he always drank.

"Sorry, *amigo*," Thiago said sorrowfully. "If it's not you, it'd be me, and I'd like to keep my dignity, *gracias*."

Shawn narrowed his eyes at the other man and growled in the back of his throat. Brandt attempted to slip the measuring tape under his arms without making Remy let up on the pressure he was exerting, and Shawn began to struggle again.

"That's right, Zed, keep your dignity," Carl said happily as he came to stand beside Thiago and looked down at them as well. "Eighty… thirty-one. So what dress size is that?"

Thiago shrugged and Nikolaus came up to stand beside them and observe as well as Shawn struggled with Brandt and Remy and the Measuring Tape of Doom. Another swift punch to the ribs knocked the breath out of him and before he could recover, Brandt slid the tape mostly under his arms and up his body. He now looked directly into Brandt's amused brown eyes, and he narrowed his own eyes hatefully and growled again.

"Thirty-one inches is a… uh… ow! Fuck! Bastard! Hold still!" Remy ground out as Shawn shifted his body weight and dug his hip into Remy's groin. "It's a size fourteen."

"How do you know that?" Thiago asked suspiciously.

Remy laughed with difficulty, and Shawn thrust his hips upwards and back down hard to accentuate the point that Remy should *not* reveal where he got that information, or why they had needed it. And it wasn't just because it would be slightly embarrassing to explain. Some things went beyond pride.

"I am sorry, *mes amis*," Remy gasped as he tightened his hold on Shawn. "That's Classified. Top Secret, if you will," he said cheekily before biting down hard on Shawn's shoulder.

Shawn cried out in anger and surprise and pain and almost managed to dislodge Brandt as he bucked upward.

Carl turned to Nikolaus and Thiago and murmured, "Ten to one they end up fucking."

"Twenty," Thiago and Nikolaus responded in automatic voices.

Shawn grew angrier than ever. He was not going to drop some stupid fucking flower on some stupid fucking table like some stupid fucking spook in some stupid fucking spy novel, and he was not going to wear some stupid fucking dress while doing it.

"Stupid fucking bastards," he ground out as he tried desperately to free himself.

"So that size, is that U.S. or U.K.?" Nikolaus asked curiously after several more moments of silent struggling.

"U.S.," Remy offered in a strained voice as Shawn pressed his body backward and tried to squeeze the life out of the younger man.

"What's the conversion?" Nikolaus asked.

No one answered and Brandt finally got the tape wrapped around Shawn's chest. As he tried to read it he relaxed slightly, and Shawn took the opportunity to wrap his legs around the bigger man and squeeze right at his lower back. If done correctly, the move would snap the spinal cord, but as much as Shawn felt the urge to murder, he didn't want to paralyze the other man. Then they would have to take care of the fucker. So, he simply exerted enough pressure to hurt like a bitch.

Brandt arched his back and cried out in pain, and Remy's grip on Shawn instantly loosened. Shawn flipped himself and Brandt and landed the other man on his back beside Remy on the floor. He stayed there, straddling Brandt and glaring down at him as Remy sat up and smacked him on the head.

"That's not playing fair!" Remy chastised, and he pushed Shawn sideways off Brandt's body and sent him sprawling across the floor. Shawn rolled and ended in a crouch, ready for another onslaught, but it never came. Remy leaned over Brandt, looking at him in concern, and Brandt was just lying there, nodding and grinning. Thiago made a 'pay up' gesture with his hand in Carl's direction as he gazed at Shawn in satisfaction. Carl and Nikolaus both ignored Thiago and smirked at Remy and Brandt.

Shawn could have killed them all at that point. Stupid fucking bastards. Where was his fucking gun?

XXIV

THE Archer wasn't certain if he was happy with this most recent turn of events. Melinda Oliver *was* a free agent, the Archer and his men had used her numerous times before, but she had no loyalties to speak of and she sold her wares to the highest bidder. She would also gladly sell information if she had it and the price was high enough. She also wasn't stupid. If she was being watched, she would know it, and she would certainly know why.

If they went waltzing up to her like they planned and requested the amount of weaponry they needed to request, it would be a dead giveaway that they were the ones everyone was after. Melinda wouldn't know whose side they were on, only that both the Organization's men and the Archer's own men were looking for them, and she would probably call in both sides to let them fight it out and take the money and run.

The Archer was in this too deep to rely on anyone other than himself and the five men he was with. He couldn't get any messages out now that they were all together again, and he couldn't count on mercy from either side. Even his own men didn't know he was one of the Six. If they were called in, they would kill the six of them much sooner than the Organization was likely to.

The Archer sighed and closed his eyes as he tried to refocus on the activity around him. He really hated that name. The Archer. It was a stupidass name. Next time he decided to go all evil genius on the world, he was going to pick his own fucking name.

XXV.

NIKOLAUS blinked and cleared his vision slightly. He'd slept like shit last night and he seemed to be phasing out a lot today, despite all the excitement. At least he didn't seem to be the only one.

The activity had ceased and they all seemed tired and unfocused. Shawn still crouched warily, but he paid more attention to a spot of carpet next to Remy and Brandt than he did to anything else. Carl and Thiago stared at their companions with smirks on their faces, and Remy petted Brandt and cooed to him like one would to calm a large animal. Brandt's hand had found its way to the small of Remy's back, ostensibly to show him where Shawn had hurt him, but it looked extremely sexual to Nikolaus. The entire picture was most unnerving, and Nikolaus wanted it stopped. He cleared his throat.

Everyone snapped out of it and they all turned to look at him.

"Shawn," Nikolaus said commandingly. "If you don't like the dress idea, come up with a better one."

Shawn blinked at him, and Nikolaus knew he had surprised him by not being timid and afraid to speak. Fuck that. He knew now that none of these men were going to hurt him, and though they were all quite scary in their own ways, Nikolaus wasn't exactly the lightweight he had made out to be. He could fend for himself, and he was sick of the inactivity.

"Well…." Shawn looked at them all shiftily as he stood up and shook himself. "I need a smoke. Let me think," he said finally as he walked past Carl and Thiago and made his way out to the balcony.

Nikolaus watched Shawn step onto the balcony and close the door behind him before he returned his gaze to Brandt and Remy. It appeared that Shawn had truly hurt Brandt, and Carl was now helping Remy get the big man to his feet.

"Come on, I've got some salve we can rub on you," Remy said as he helped Brandt from the room and toward the bedrooms. Thiago and Nikolaus watched them go, and when they both turned back around Carl was grinning at them.

"Ten to one they end up fucking," the man crooned happily.

XXVI.

BRANDT allowed Remy to lead him back to the furthest bedroom, and he sat unmoving on the end of the bed as Remy dug through his bag.

"Take your shirt off, Wally," Remy said without turning around to face him. "This shit gets everywhere. It'll ruin your clothes," the younger man added as he proceeded to slip his own T-shirt over his head and let it flutter to the ground.

Brandt stared at the myriad of scars that covered Remy's torso, and his eyes were drawn to the slender hips where two thumbprints could clearly be seen just above the waistband of Remy's briefs. There was also a faded bruise on Remy's shoulder that looked vaguely like the marks of a bite, and Brandt's body flushed with hot ice.

Brandt remembered making those marks on the night he'd tried to screw Remy into the wall while the others watched. Brandt shifted uncomfortably at the memory. His back protested the movement and he stiffened.

"I'm sorry," Brandt said softly, and Remy ceased his rummaging and looked over his shoulder at Brandt.

"What was that?" he asked as he straightened up.

"I'm sorry for everything. For hurting you," Brandt said as he waved his hand vaguely through the air.

Remy cocked his head and looked down at the little tin of salve he held in his hand. Brandt saw him lick his lips nervously and then look at the door, and he wondered what the other man was thinking.

"You didn't hurt me," Remy finally said with a weak smile. "It was Shawn's bony ass that did all the damage," he added with a stronger smile and he took a step toward the bed and twirled his finger through the air. "Turn over and lie flat," he ordered. "This'll take the sore out."

Brandt looked at him blankly and Remy's smile faltered. They stared at one another for long seconds before Remy looked down once more. He bounced the tin of salve in his hand and made a clicking sound with his tongue, and Brandt watched him unblinkingly.

"You didn't hurt me," Remy repeated slowly. Brandt's gaze drifted down to the fingerprints at Remy's hipbones and he looked back up at Remy pointedly. He was surprised to see deep brown eyes staring at him curiously. "How big is the hole in your marble bag, really?" Remy asked suddenly.

Brandt blinked at him. No one had ever asked him to what degree his insanity ran, not in quite that exact phrase, anyway.

"I'm not sure," he said finally, not certain of how to answer.

Remy smiled wanly and knelt in front of Brandt, placing his hand on one knee and the tin of salve on the other as he looked up at him earnestly.

"Can I trust you?" Remy asked quietly, his eyes never leaving Brandt's.

"Yes," Brandt said without hesitation. Remy nodded and stood once more.

"Then it doesn't matter how many bats you got in your belfry, does it? Roll over," he said with another twirl of his finger.

"But–"

"If we don't get it on quickly, it won't do any good. He probably bruised you pretty good and you'll need it," Remy said as he pulled at Brandt's shirt impatiently. Brandt pulled the shirt off obediently and stood up. He knew Remy was distracting him on purpose, trying to avoid the painful subject of what had happened with Shawn, but his back did hurt something awful.

He would have expected Remy to take a step back and allow Brandt the room to undo the fly of his jeans, but Remy remained planted where he stood, and he tilted his head slightly as his nose and mouth brushed against Brandt's chin. Brandt breathed in deeply and found his hands suddenly lightly gripping Remy's elbows as the other man undid his jeans for him. He watched the movements of Remy's hands as if mesmerized, and when he finally looked up, he found Remy's eyes on him once more. The jeans fell to the floor as they stared at one another, and Remy's eyes sparkled as he ran his hands under the waistband of Brandt's boxers.

"Wouldn't want to ruin them," he said in a low voice.

A thrill ran through Brandt's body at the sensual sound and he nodded silently. He inhaled deeply one last time as his boxers were pushed past his hips and to the floor, and then he turned and stretched out naked on the bed.

Brandt felt the bed dip slightly just before Remy straddled him, and he tensed involuntarily as Remy's salve-covered hands met his body.

"I shouldn't have pushed this meeting," Brandt blurted, desperately needing something to say as Remy's hands worked the mentholated salve into his back.

"What do you mean?" Remy murmured as his fingers dug into Brandt's sore back.

"Melinda. It's too much trouble," Brandt said succinctly.

"Nah. Shawn'll come round. That or he'll think up a way out of it. And it's not like our planner is overloaded with tasks lately."

"Hmm."

"Do you love him?" Remy asked quietly, his hands never ceasing in the slow massage. Brandt tensed again. He knew he'd been the cause of all the strife in the group of late, and the guilt had been slowly driving him back to sanity. He didn't like it at all. Perhaps a nice chat with Remy was just what he needed.

"What type of love do you mean?" Brandt asked, wanting to be entirely clear with his answer.

Remy froze above him, and Brandt wondered what he had done wrong now. He really had to get someone to give him a crash course in etiquette.

"You know, the more I talk to you, the more I like you," Remy said, and Brandt could hear the smile in the other man's voice. Brandt grinned in relief. "Do you think I'm crazy?"

Brandt furrowed his brow and tried to look over his shoulder at Remy. "Yes," he said, as if it were the most obvious thing in the world.

"Really?" Remy asked dubiously. "Shawn's called me crazy for years, but am I really, d'you think?"

Brandt tried to roll over so he could look at Remy as they spoke, and Remy rose up onto his knees to let him do so. Brandt lay there looking up at Remy, and Remy settled back down onto Brandt's hips and chewed on his lower lip as he waited for Brandt to answer him.

"Okay, there are different types of crazy, just like there are different types of love," Brandt said with certainty. "I love Shawn. I do. But no more than any of the rest of you." Remy's eyes widened at that. Brandt reached up and took Remy's face in his hands, pulling him down by his head until Remy bent over completely and flailed slightly. He had his hands out to his sides to keep the salve from ruining the duvet, and the only thing holding him up was Brandt's hold on his face. He blinked several times as he looked down at Brandt, and Brandt couldn't help but think how adorable he was, even if he was a trained killer. "Don't think I don't care about you," Brandt growled.

Remy blinked rapidly but said nothing, and Brandt pulled him the rest of the way down and kissed him gently. Remy's hands came to rest on Brandt's ribs, and the hot/cold of the salve sent shivers through Brandt's body. The shivers ignited a subtle burn in the pit of his stomach, and all memory of what they were discussing was gone as Remy muttered and opened his mouth wider to deepen the kiss.

"You've ruined your bed," Remy murmured as Brandt wrapped his arms around Remy's body and pulled him down, pressing their bodies together. Brandt could feel the duvet sticking to his back, but he didn't care. What was a little grease spot on a duvet when you could burn the damn thing anyway?

"Let's make it worthwhile then, shall we?" he growled as he flipped them over and kissed Remy as gently as the fire rushing through his veins would allow.

Remy wrapped himself around Brandt, and somehow Brandt managed to undo Remy's jeans and slide them far enough down for Remy to kick them off.

"There's lube," Remy gasped as he pointed vaguely toward the pillows. Apparently, Remy had the same philosophy on foreplay that Brandt did. He knew there was a reason he loved these blokes.

"Getting to know Thiago better, were we?" Brandt murmured as he dragged both their bodies up the bed and rooted around beneath the pillows.

"Mmm," Remy responded as he nipped lightly at Brandt's neck and shoulder.

"Bastard's fit, isn't he?" Brandt asked in amusement as his hand finally found the lube and he bent down to take Remy's mouth in another, rougher kiss. Remy nodded against Brandt's mouth and spread his legs wider, hooking them over Brandt's hips as Brandt's hand travelled down the smooth torso.

Remy groaned and Brandt smiled against the other man's mouth. He popped the tube open and poured lube out all over Remy's chest.

"Cold!" Remy hissed.

"You'll be warm soon enough," Brandt said in a low voice as he trailed his fingers though the goo. The head of his cock nudged against Remy, and Remy spread his legs wider, inviting entry. "Not yet," Brandt murmured into Remy's ear as he bent over to kiss him once more. Remy whimpered, but Brandt didn't care. "You think you're mad?" he inquired softly as he trailed his fingers down Remy's stomach. Remy forced his eyes open and looked up at Brandt blankly.

"I think I might be," Remy whispered pleadingly. He sounded lost and desperate and confused. Brandt remembered that feeling. That feeling of being alone even in company and not knowing why. Brandt wanted to help Remy see the light, and he nibbled lightly on Remy's ear as his fingers entered Remy's body slowly. Remy groaned and lifted his hips upward, but Brandt carefully avoided his prostate. "Please," Remy whimpered.

"I want to show you the burn, Dixie," Brandt whispered. "Then you'll see what it truly means to be mad," he growled as the heat raged within his own body, and he made certain the younger man was ready before he slipped his fingers back out and slowly pushed into him.

XXVII.

REMY was still wondering where their conversation would have led if Brandt hadn't kissed him. He didn't really care, just so long as Brandt's hands and lips and tongue continued to do what they were doing. But he was curious all the same. Detached curiosity. Definitely detached.

He'd fucked Brandt before, but in Remy's mind that time didn't really count. There had been far too much else going on, both physically and mentally, for Remy to consider that time a real fuck. This was obviously going to be different.

Brandt entered him slowly, being phenomenally careful as Remy squirmed, trying to get more contact. Trying to get Brandt to push deeper. Harder. To pound into him and chase away the demons.

But Brandt did none of those. He rocked into Remy gently, eliciting moans and pleas and sighs and the most phenomenal need Remy had ever experienced. He could feel the pleasure beginning to build in the pit of his stomach, but it was faint and warm and so enticingly close that Remy thought he might scream in frustration.

Was that what Brandt meant by 'the burn?' Because it was enough to drive anyone mad, not to mention someone who thought they were already half crazy to begin with. Remy scrabbled for something on Brandt's body to grip, and finally Brandt reached back, took both of Remy's wrists into his own hand, and pinned Remy to the bed.

"You feel it, Dixie?" Brandt gasped into Remy's ear as Remy's eyes rolled into the back of his head. His body was completely restrained now, and that had always fuelled Remy's lust. But now, with this torturously slow pace added into the mix, Remy thought he might not live through it. "The burn?" Brandt whispered, and Remy moaned wantonly as the hot breath gusted across his face.

Was this what Brandt felt all the time? A burn like this? No wonder he was obsessed with fire!

"Please," Remy murmured as Brandt buried his face in Remy's neck and his grip tightened around Remy's wrists. Remy found himself unable to move at all. He was completely at Brandt's mercy and, with that thought, the pleasure grew stronger and began to spread.

Brandt whispered to him now, unintelligible words that had Remy groaning and trying to buck upwards, but the slow rhythm never changed and his pleas fell on deaf ears. The warmth had spread to every single bit of his body, and he thought that if Brandt would just speed up or go harder or touch him, then he would come. He just needed that last bit of stimulation to push him over the edge.

"Please," he begged again.

"Burn for me," Brandt whispered harshly as Remy moaned piteously and tried once more to move.

"Yes," Remy responded desperately.

"Burn for me, Dixie," Brandt ordered again.

Remy began whimpering in a jumble of bayou French and English. He couldn't take any more. He needed Brandt to make him come. He had to be rid of that wonderfully tortuous feeling before it pushed him over the edge. "Please!" he cried as he tried desperately to move. "I'm burning. I am," he gasped into Brandt's open mouth just before their lips were crushed together in a needy kiss.

"Come for me, Dixie," Brandt finally commanded in a hoarse voice. He pulled almost completely out of Remy's body and then slammed back into him, hitting Remy's prostate just as surely as if he'd aimed for it with a rifle and scope. Remy cried out and bucked again, and Brandt continued to pound into him as Remy came all over his own stomach.

Brandt didn't come though, and he didn't slow the brutal pace until Remy saw stars and gripped at Brandt's body as he came yet again, shouting wordlessly this time as Brandt's cock hit his prostate repeatedly and Brandt's hand encircled his cock and pumped it. They were both covered in sweat and salve and come, and Brandt still continued to thrust into him.

If being crazy gave you this sort of stamina, then Remy was ready to run and grab his purple crayon and sign the fuck up!

Remy was about to plead for mercy when Brandt rose up onto his knees and took hold of Remy's hips, dragging him upwards and holding him there as he pounded into him. Remy's hand braced against the headboard and he screamed, actually fucking screamed, as he came for a third time. Brandt groaned and leant forwards, rocking his hips slightly as the contractions of Remy's muscles finally brought on his climax.

Remy's world had gone white and his ears were ringing. He couldn't see. He couldn't hear. He couldn't move. Every muscle in his body was on fire.

"Burns," he murmured as Brandt pulled out of him and flopped down beside him.

"Means you're crazy," Brandt said softly as he pulled Remy closer and nuzzled into his hair.

"Really?" Remy asked exhaustedly.

"I dunno. I know I burn. And I'm crazy, right?"

"Oh, fuck," Remy responded flatly.

"Mmm. Do you love him, Dixie?"

Remy stiffened slightly in Brandt's arms before relaxing once more.

"Yes," he said simply.

"There wasn't a day he didn't mention you. Think of you. He even called me 'Remy' without realizing it sometimes. I know it's hard, but you'll be miserable until you forgive him."

Remy nodded despondently against Brandt's chest and burrowed into the muscular protection the bigger man was offering.

"Can I ask you something?" Brandt asked after some time.

"Mm hmm," Remy sleepily, expecting another difficult question.

"Why does Trigger call Thiago 'Zed?'"

"What?" Remy asked as he looked up at Brandt in amusement.

"He called him 'Zed' out there," Brandt said by way of explanation. "Do you know why?"

"No. Why does he call you 'Wally?'" Remy asked in return.

"I dunno," Brandt said with a little shrug.

"Hmm," Remy said thoughtfully as he snuggled back into Brandt's arms.

"Maybe we can recruit Trigger to the Crazy Club too," Brandt rumbled as he spoke against Remy's curls.

Remy snorted and offered Brandt a little jab to the ribs before he sighed contentedly and drifted into a light sleep.

XXVIII.

THIAGO'S head jerked up and he lunged half out of his chair before he realized he'd been dozing. Had he heard a scream? He looked at the others to see their reactions, but they were all looking at him with expressions ranging from concern to amusement.

Shawn glanced at him before standing up and taking a step toward the bedrooms.

"He's fine," Carl said without taking his amused eyes off Thiago.

"But–"

"He's fine," Carl repeated sternly as he turned hard eyes on Shawn. Thiago watched in fascination as Shawn's shoulders slumped and he trudged back to the couch. When had Carl taken charge of their merry little band? Probably when Shawn had lost his mind. That was an interesting turn of events, nevertheless.

Thiago hoped Carl would remain in charge if Shawn didn't take back the lead. The thought of Remy leading them made Thiago shiver involuntarily. The younger man was certainly a capable leader and tactician, but he just wasn't all there. Thiago was beginning to be of the opinion that Brandt wasn't really the resident crazy after all. Remy was the crazy. The dangerous kind of crazy you didn't know was crazy until he got you killed. The bad kind of crazy.

"Shawn," Nikolaus said softly. "What's your plan?"

Thiago wondered if the German was trying to keep Shawn's mind off what Brandt might be doing to Remy, or if he was just antsy and needed something to do. Thiago thought it might be both.

"I'm not wearing a dress," Shawn growled dangerously, and unlike Brandt and Remy, Thiago and Carl were not crazy enough to poke the bear.

Nikolaus, however, seemed to be low on the self-preservation fuel. "Then come up with something better," he said testily.

"Well, the only plan I have requires weaponry. Lots of it," Shawn said somberly. "And that leads us right back to this Oliver woman."

"What's your plan?"

"We need to wait for them," Shawn said firmly, and the command in the voice was all too clear. Perhaps Carl's brief stint of leadership was over. Thiago couldn't help but think that Carl looked relieved at this.

Thiago leaned forward and cocked his head at Carl.

"What are you suddenly so smiley about?" Thiago asked suspiciously.

Carl's eyes slid to Shawn before he grinned at Thiago. "Knowing Brandt's…," Carl cleared his throat through a laugh and schooled his features into a serious scowl that wasn't fooling anyone. "Knowing Brandt's, uh, mating habits, it'll be a while."

Nikolaus snickered and Shawn rolled his eyes.

Thiago smiled affectionately at Carl. "What do you suggest to pass the time?" he asked good-humoredly. Carl grinned evilly at Thiago, and Thiago shook his head and leaned back into his chair.

"Huh uh," Thiago said with a laugh. "I'm not in the same league as Remy, I like to keep my tally down to one person a week."

Carl narrowed his eyes and glanced at Nikolaus with a smirk. Nikolaus widened his eyes and pointed at Thiago. "What he said," Nikolaus said quickly. Shawn was rubbing his eyes distractedly, not following the conversation.

Thiago was certain that if he had been paying attention at all, he would have defended himself.

XXIX.

CARL was on Shawn before the other man had a chance to remove his hand from over his eyes. He gripped the older man by the shoulders and yanked him roughly out of his seat.

"What the–"

Carl slammed him against the nearest hard surface, which happened to be Thiago as the Argentinean stood to intervene, and Carl herded them both towards the sofa like a snow plow mowing down everything in its path.

Thiago's ass hit the arm of the sofa and he went sprawling over it as Carl shoved Shawn into him. Carl gripped Shawn in a bear hug to keep him upright as Thiago went ass over tit and rolled off the other side of the sofa with a thump and a muffled curse.

"Sorry!" Carl called cheerfully, not meaning a syllable of it.

Shawn stared at Carl in surprise and Nikolaus laughed gleefully as he pointed at Thiago and covered his grin with his hand. Thiago glared at Carl and rubbed his hip gingerly but remained on the ground where he had fallen.

"What are you doing, you mad fuck?" Shawn asked in confusion, his voice more amused than angry. If he had seen Thiago's acrobatics, he would have been fucking rolling on the floor with laughter.

Carl snickered. "Passing the time," he growled before he pressed their lips together and pulled Shawn closer. Though Carl was most certainly interested in the activity he was somewhat forcefully suggesting, he had ulterior motives. He was fucking sick and tired of Shawn and Remy and Brandt and whatever the fuck they had going.

Brandt and Remy seemed to be over their little drama and on to greener pastures, so to speak, but Shawn was wallowing. Carl hated to see a man as great as Shawn wallow, and if nothing else, he wanted to shake the older man up a bit. Get his mind off everything and distract him.

Shawn managed a muffled protest and a little frenzy of movement.

Through all the various sexual encounters the group had so far, Carl had never actually kissed Shawn. Shawn was fighting him slightly. Not enough to make Carl stop, but enough that it made the kiss interesting. Very interesting.

Carl had never forced himself on anyone before, unless you counted attacking someone to slit his throat of course, but that didn't really count. He was fairly certain he was reading Shawn correctly in this, that the fight was more instinct than actual desire to get away. The man needed a distraction– a nice knockdown, drag-out fight– and Carl could give it to him.

Shawn broke their kiss with a gasp and shoved at him, and Carl took a step or two backwards, smiling mischievously at Shawn as the other man stared at him in shock. Carl cocked his head to the side in a silent challenge and Shawn blinked. Once. Twice. A third time. He turned to look at Thiago and Nikolaus respectively, as if for verification that he had just been thoroughly groped.

Nikolaus grinned and Thiago still sat on the ground, looking at Carl with the same surprised look Shawn did. Nikolaus raised his eyebrows questioningly and smiled even wider. Thiago shook his head and muttered something unintelligible as he began making his way slowly to his feet.

Carl was still watching Thiago when Shawn's body hit him in a full-on rugby tackle. The two of them toppled to the ground with Carl's body cushioning Shawn's fall nicely, and Shawn pinned him there with an iron grip. Carl continued to grin up at him, and Shawn glared at him for a full two seconds before Carl bucked and flipped Shawn up and over his own head. Shawn landed flat on his back with a grunt and lay stunned just long enough for Carl to spring to his feet and turn around.

"Is that all you have, then?" Carl asked lightly. "I've just molested you, Beignet. Put up a bit of a fight, yeah?"

Shawn growled wordlessly in response, and Carl looked down at him as Shawn rolled into a crouch, then Carl grinned impudently at him. The grin seemed to infuriate the older man, so Carl kept doing it. Shawn rose slowly and they circled one another warily.

"Perhaps that's what you need, lovey," Carl crooned as he sidestepped almost casually toward the kitchen. Shawn's eyes narrowed. "A nice forceful shagging, hmm? Take up your real position as the bottom we all know you are," he goaded with a lascivious wink. He had no intention of fucking Shawn, or being fucked by him. Not today anyway, they had too much to do. But his job was to study the weaknesses of a mark and exploit them, and he'd noticed that Shawn never bottomed, no matter who his partner was. He knew instinctively that it was a big red button, just waiting for someone wearing Kevlar to push it.

He also knew he was seriously pushing his luck. Like, could end up with a knife in his chest kind of pushing his luck, but Carl had little doubt he could physically win this fight. He was ninety percent sure. Yeah, okay, seventy-five.

He'd just called Shawn a bottom, though, and Shawn looked pissed. Call Remy a bottom and he would jump you and let you screw his brains out. Call Thiago a bottom and he would look at you for five minutes, shrug, and then go about his business. Call Nikolaus a bottom and he might cry. Call Brandt a bottom and you might get a blowjob, you might just get blown up. But call Shawn a bottom?

Carl supposed he was about to find out what happened when you called Shawn a bottom. Carl wasn't so sure he liked his plan anymore, and the look in Shawn's eyes told him that Shawn knew it. Nevertheless, they circled until Carl found his back to the kitchen. He moved toward it, never taking his eyes off Shawn and never changing his stance, and as soon as he reached the tile floor of the kitchen, Shawn pounced again.

This, however, was not the same sort of pounce. Shawn wrapped his arms around Carl's neck and pressed their lips together hungrily. Carl whuffed in surprise. He hadn't expected Shawn to actually respond to his advances. Shawn lifted him completely off the ground and slammed him up against the wall beside the entryway to the kitchen as they did their best to devour one another.

"Think they'll make it to the bedroom?" Nikolaus asked in amusement.

"I wouldn't eat on that table in there 'til we get some Lysol or something," Thiago responded drily. "My fucking ass hurts!" he called accusingly.

Shawn's lips formed a smile against Carl's, and Carl pressed closer into Shawn's body. Shawn bit his lip in warning.

"I don't bottom," Shawn growled menacingly even as he pulled Carl closer and hooked his leg over Carl's hip.

"We'll see about that," Carl responded in the same menacing growl, and his hand travelled down the side of Shawn's body, over his hip, and down his thigh to grip the back of Shawn's knee and heft it higher. Shawn bit his lip again and Carl thrust his hips forwards as they battled for dominance with their tongues.

"Lube," Shawn grunted demandingly as Carl reached down and started fussing with the zipper of his jeans.

"No dinner or anything first? You're an easy one," Carl observed in satisfaction. He smiled as Shawn's fingers tightened in his hair and yanked slightly, but he pressed forward more and lifted Shawn completely off the ground. He knew he couldn't hold the other man there for long, nor could he fuck him into the wall like he truly wanted to do. He wasn't really all that much larger than Shawn was. He couldn't do either of those things, but for a few minutes it was nice to stand there and kiss the man senseless, even if his back would pay for it later.

Shawn's hand was tangled in his hair, pulling almost painfully, and Carl had no clue where the man's other hand was. He didn't care, as long as there wasn't a knife in it.

"I thought you assassin types always came prepared," Shawn taunted breathlessly when they parted once more and Carl let him slide down the wall to the floor. He still held Shawn's leg in his hand, and he insinuated his body between Shawn's limbs, trying to get as close as he could as he nibbled on Shawn's neck.

"We always come, anyway," Carl murmured into Shawn's neck with a grin.

"You'll come, all right," Shawn growled. "All over that fucking table I'm about to bend you over. Lube," he demanded again.

"Got a whole kitchen full," Carl muttered against Shawn's mouth as he finally let go of Shawn's leg and used both hands to rid Shawn of his jeans.

"I've seen you cook," Shawn growled as he pushed Carl away and forced him back against the little breakfast table. "Too fucking messy," he added before attacking Carl once more.

Carl's thighs hit the table and he fell backwards in a Thiago-esque fashion as Shawn hovered over him, and for the first time he wondered if he really could have won the fight he instigated. Maybe fucking instead of fighting was a better plan, in the end. Fuck it. A distraction was a distraction, no matter who topped.

Shawn pulled him up by the front of his shirt and crushed their mouths together briefly before pushing him away again and fumbling at his sweats to get them off his body. Carl was sitting on the edge of the table with his legs wrapped around Shawn's waist, and he simply raised his hips off the surface as Shawn yanked the blue material down to his knees.

Carl had fully intended to maintain control over this encounter, but somehow he'd lost it. And he didn't mind, not one bit.

The sweats didn't make it any further than his knees before Shawn grabbed his hips and slipped him off the table. He kissed him hard once more before forcing him to turn around.

Carl could have fought, and probably won, at this point. He was pretty sure he could have, anyway. But he was too fucking turned on now to try. All he wanted was for Shawn to bend him over this table and fuck him into next week.

Shawn pushed him, right between the shoulder blades, and forced him over– Carl's chest hit the table with a thump. He groaned wantonly and pushed his hips against Shawn's hard cock as Shawn pressed against him. He felt Shawn reaching for something on the other side of the table, but he neither knew nor cared what it was.

They were both still fully clothed, though Carl's sweats were now around his ankles and Shawn's jeans were riding low around his thighs, and Carl spread his hands flat on the table as he realized how completely debauched the whole scene was. They ate on this table.

Fucking beautiful.

It wasn't gentle, and it wasn't slow. But goddamn, did it feel good. Carl moaned against the pain and his body jerked when the fingers brushed his prostate. He had started this in a brutal manner; it looked like Shawn was going to end it the same way.

XXX.

SHAWN had needed this more than he'd known. Something with no strings and no deeper meaning attached. Something physical and slightly violent to vent the frustration and anger and sadness. He gripped Carl hard as his entire body suffered through the pleasurable spasms of orgasm.

At some point during their impromptu therapy session, Remy and Brandt joined them. Neither man seemed surprised to find Shawn and Carl fucking on the kitchen table. Brandt, in fact, took a seat to watch the show from the first row.

Shawn could feel Remy behind him. He let his head fall back against Remy's shoulder and his entire body went limp as the anger and frustration and exhaustion of the past several days slipped away. Remy whispered to him softly, and Shawn's eyes drifted closed as he felt himself being pulled backward. Before he knew it, he was on the floor cradled in Remy's arms and watching Brandt tackle Carl to the floor. Brandt took Carl's cock in his mouth and sucked him off until he writhed and begged him not to stop.

"Fuck," Shawn breathed as he watched Carl's fingers thread through Brandt's hair and his hips thrust upwards into Brandt's mouth desperately.

Remy's lips were at Shawn's ear, and he heard the younger man whisper in amusement. "You should have let Carl fuck you," he said. "He's fucking amazing."

"Mmm," was all Shawn managed as he tried to regain his wits. "What the hell?" Shawn groaned, not certain of what exactly he meant. Apparently, Remy took it as a question.

"Brandt didn't want the table getting… messy," Remy explained as Carl bucked again and went into spasms. "We eat there."

Shawn's brow furrowed and he thought he should be smiling, but he didn't feel the urge to do so.

"Jesus," Remy whispered into Shawn's ear as they watched.

Shawn was still breathing heavily from the exertion, harder than he should have been, and he felt a little light-headed, but he wasn't certain why. He hadn't expended that much energy. Not nearly that much.

Remy's arms tightened around him, and Shawn suddenly realized what the feeling must be. He sat on the cold tile of the kitchen with his jeans hanging off his hips and watched the man he'd just fucked being sucked off by another man, a man Shawn had thought he loved. But he was being held by the man that he did love. Truly loved.

Son of a bitch.

Shawn liked that saying. It had no real meaning when said correctly, it was all tone and inflection and *feeling*, and when you said it with just the right amount of disgust, it was perfect.

Was that it? He had loved Remy for a long fucking time, why would 'realizing' it just now make him light-headed?

"Wait, what?" Shawn asked aloud, not realizing that he was no longer speaking just to himself.

"Fucking hot, aren't they?" Remy murmured into his ear.

Shawn nodded distractedly. He had loved Remy for a long time. A long fucking time. He had never been able to admit it, though, not even to himself. Fuck, what had he been thinking?

Son of a bitch!

But he loved him. He really fucking loved the little bastard. Now what was he supposed to do? Tell him? After all this time? And what the fuck was he supposed to say about Brandt? He wasn't even sure himself what that had been.

Shawn blinked stupidly as he sat in Remy's arms. He did know. Brandt reminded him of Remy. A flush of heat flooded Shawn's body as he thought that, and he thought it again just to make sure it was correct. Brandt reminded him of Remy. Yes. They were a lot alike. Hell, they even looked alike, in a way. They had the same eyes. Remy's eyes gleamed like that every now and then, too.

Son of a bitch.

Brandt had told him the night before that they really didn't feel what they thought they felt. Shawn knew if he tried to remember the exact words Brandt had used he'd give himself a headache, but that was the gist of it. They weren't in love. It had been the proximity.

"I missed you, Shawn," Remy said to him quietly, and Shawn could hear the smile in his voice, feel it against the skin of his neck. He so very rarely called him by his name unless he was angry. The tender note in the name struck a chord somewhere very deep, and Shawn closed his eyes as an entirely new feeling washed over him. Yes. This was love. Devotion. Adoration. He was smitten. He had been smite-ed. Whatever you called it.

"Now about this dress."

"Son of a bitch."

Almost an hour later, Shawn was still fighting tooth and nail to stay out of anything resembling a dress.

"What about a nice pantsuit?" Brandt asked in all seriousness as they sat in the main room and argued with him. "You'd look good in purple, I think."

Shawn stared at him, trying to decide if Brandt was serious. Finally, he decided that he wasn't and threw a pillow at Brandt in retaliation. Brandt grinned and giggled ridiculously, and Shawn once again thought he should be smiling. He knew he should be, in fact. But he wasn't.

"He can't wear a pantsuit, it'd look like a suit," Nikolaus protested.

"Yeah, Niko," Remy agreed eagerly. "He needs a dress, right? A skirt, at least."

"And heels," Carl murmured with a cheeky wink.

Shawn growled unhappily at them all and shivered.

"Let's think this over rationally," Thiago suggested finally, and Shawn looked at him gratefully.

Thiago stared at Remy thoughtfully, though, and Shawn couldn't help feeling he was missing something. Missing something inherent, not only in the general mood of the group, but something within himself. Why did he feel so fucking out of it? Everyone was acting oddly, even himself, and Shawn frowned as he tried to decide why. Was it real or was it imagined on his part? He didn't know. He wasn't sure of much of anything right now.

He shook his head and tried desperately to pull himself back into the conversation.

XXXI.

"SHAWN? You okay?" Thiago asked in a voice laced with concern, and Nikolaus turned to look at Shawn curiously.

The older man nodded, albeit uncertainly, and Nikolaus turned back around only to discover that he was no longer 'alone' on the sofa. Brandt sat beside him with his arm draped over the back of the sofa, smiling crookedly.

How in the fuck had the big man moved that quickly? How had Nikolaus not felt the cushion dip? Why was he grinning? Nikolaus's stomach flipped unnervingly and he blurted, "I don't have anything flammable!"

Brandt chuckled wickedly and said, "That's what you think."

Nikolaus swallowed uncomfortably and blinked slowly, not sure of what to say. Technically, he supposed *he* was flammable. Ooh, now he felt sort of nauseous. Not good. But Brandt winked at him and turned his attention back to the group at large, and Nikolaus tried to relax. Remy smiled winningly at him, and Nikolaus wondered if Remy wasn't maybe just a little crazy too. He had seriously considered that possibility when they were on the run together, but it seemed more likely now than it had then. Nikolaus idly wondered why that was, as Thiago continued speaking.

"Now, Shawn, you said earlier that there were other options besides the one we're discussing," the Argentinean prompted.

"I did?" Shawn asked in surprise.

Thiago's brow wrinkled and he cocked his head curiously. "Yeah," he said, sounding half amused. "You said there were other options and that Remy and Brandt were just being twats."

"He's right," Brandt said happily.

"You did say that," Remy affirmed with a worried little frown.

"Oh," Shawn said, sounding lost and a little confused.

"You also said you had a plan of action for after we met with the Oliver woman," Thiago supplied as he leaned forward and rubbed his eyes as if he were tired.

"I did?" Shawn asked again.

Nikolaus did a double take. What the hell was wrong with him?

"You said it required weaponry, though. So, what was it?" Thiago asked slowly as he looked at Shawn carefully.

Shawn edged forward and looked at them all with a frown. Nikolaus examined him closely. He looked pale. Sick, even. Nikolaus glanced at Remy and saw that he too was looking at Shawn in concern. This probably wasn't good.

"You alright there, Beignet?" Brandt asked carefully as he scooted forward and sat on the edge of the sofa, looking at Shawn like a hawk would a mouse. Nikolaus was still looking at Brandt when he saw Remy lunge out of his chair and pounce across the room. He was so quick that Nikolaus only had the time to turn his head around to look before Remy reached Shawn, and Remy was just in time to catch the other man as he went limp and slid forward out of his chair.

Nikolaus and Brandt both jumped up to help but, when Nikolaus got to his feet, it was as if he hit an invisible wall. He gasped and literally fell back into the sofa as the room spun and his stomach lurched.

'What the fuck?' he thought dazedly as the room went slowly black.

XXXII.

Brandt watched in alarm as Shawn and Remy sank to the ground together, and he felt more than saw Nikolaus fall back onto the sofa. He reached back blindly but missed grabbing the smaller man as he fell. Remy looked up at him pleadingly for help but Brandt's attention was drawn by a soft gasp from the other side of the room. He turned in time to see Thiago slowly sink to his knees, as if his legs had simply turned to putty when he had jumped to help Shawn, and Carl was at the older man's side almost instantly trying to give him aid. Thiago fell forward and Carl wrapped strong arms around him and pulled him back until Thiago's unconscious body was cradled in the Kiwi's lap.

"What the fuck's wrong with 'em?" Brandt asked in agitation as he turned to look at Nikolaus. The smaller man was limp and unresponsive, and Brandt quickly bent to take his pulse as his own heart raced in fear. He couldn't find one, and Brandt began to panic slightly. He didn't know exactly where to look, but that wasn't much consolation. "Gizmo?" he said softly as he gave Nikolaus's face a couple of gentle slaps. He got no reaction. Brandt turned back to look at Carl when he realized he hadn't yet gotten an answer from the other man.

"Don't feel so hot myself, Wally," Carl mumbled as he checked Thiago's pulse. "I can't," he said weakly as he took a deep breath and exhaled slowly. He closed his eyes as if trying to steady himself.

"Trigger?" Brandt ventured as he straightened up and took a step closer. Brandt blinked as Carl's body slumped back against the chair, his arms still wrapped protectively around Thiago dragging the older man back with him.

Brandt turned and looked at Remy in confusion and desperation.

Remy was kneeling on the floor beside Shawn's body, laying Shawn's head gently onto a throw pillow, and when he looked up his eyes were dark and sad and dangerous.

Brandt cocked his head, trying to understand what was happening, and Remy stood slowly. He seemed to unfurl, rolling his shoulders and looking up at Brandt through lowered lashes, and Brandt was suddenly reminded of a film he'd once seen.

He couldn't remember the name of it, or even the plot really, but it had been one of those good versus evil things where the evil things were big winged creatures with horns and the good were pure and beautiful and righteously indignant. At this moment, Remy looked like that final evil creature as it rose from its fire pit and unfurled its wings. Brandt was so distraught by the thought that even the image of the fire pit didn't distract him.

"I'm sorry for this," Remy said softly, his voice hard as steel and his eyes black and deadly and soulless. "Even as big as you are, I thought a little exertion would make it hit you sooner, but…." Remy pursed his lips and shrugged apologetically. "I'm truly sorry, but I can't wait for yours to take effect."

Brandt tensed as Remy drew the gun from the waistband of his jeans and aimed it at him. He didn't have time to do anything more than raise his hands in an automatic gesture of self-defense before Remy pulled the trigger.

PART FOUR: BLUE-ON-BLUE

I.

REMY dropped the tranquillizer gun as soon as the dart was shot and lunged forward. He wrapped his arms around Brandt and tried his best to ease the bigger man back onto the sofa instead of just letting him fall to the ground. Brandt's body was nearly a dead weight, though, and despite Remy's best efforts, they sank to the ground slowly.

"Bastard," Brandt whispered disjointedly as they slid down the front of the sofa and to the floor together. Remy hit the ground with a thump and he pulled Brandt gently into his lap and nodded sympathetically.

"I'm sorry," he whispered into Brandt's ear. "If you'd just eaten more of the fucking pastries, man," he continued sadly

Brandt struggled against him, trying to sit back up. Remy was amazed that the other man was still conscious. He could have knocked an elephant flat on its ass with the amount of sedative he'd loaded in those darts. Brandt gripped Remy's bicep painfully and writhed slowly, fighting unconsciousness, and Remy held him close as he plucked the dart out of Brandt's chest. Brandt growled and whimpered a little.

"I'm sorry," Remy whispered again. "It's okay," he added soothingly, his heart breaking as Brandt struggled against him. "You'll just sleep for a while, then you'll be good as new."

Brandt growled wordlessly again, then his eyes drifted shut and he finally went completely limp in Remy's arms. Remy stared down at him sadly. This would complicate matters a bit. Brandt didn't seem the type to take kindly to being shot, even if it was just a tranquillizer dart.

The plan had been for the others not to know who had drugged them. They were supposed to be knocked out, and then wake up in the warehouse dazed, confused, and completely unaware of a traitor in their midst. But Remy was on a time limit. They were all given very small dosages, and if Brandt was as resistant as Remy thought he was then it was entirely possible the big man would still have been struggling against the effects by the time the others were waking up. Remy simply couldn't have that, and he had been forced to dart him.

"If this is the treatment your allies get, I think perhaps I'm on the wrong side," Gray Kincaid's soft voice observed wryly as it wafted into the room from the area of the balcony.

"*Va-t'à la merde, salaud,*" Remy hissed bitterly as he brushed the long curls away from Brandt's eyes and unconsciously rocked him back and forth. "This is your fault."

"Oh, they'll get over it," Gray told him carelessly as he stepped into the room and examined the scene with entirely too much amusement for Remy's taste.

"Get over it?" Remy repeated angrily.

"Well, maybe not, but we couldn't have one of them hearing me, now could we? I don't want my ass shot off before I even make an entrance!" Gray told him defensively as he walked around the end of the couch and looked down at Remy.

Remy looked up and glared at him. "What makes you so sure I won't do the honors myself, hmm? Look what I've fucking done, Gray!"

"You made your bed, Remy. I gave you options," Gray clucked disapprovingly.

"Options? Ha! 'Drug and kidnap them, or shoot them in their sleep, Remy, it's your choice.'" Remy mimicked in an almost perfect imitation of Gray's Deep South accent. "Some fucking options!"

"Yes, well, you can't have everything," Gray responded flippantly as he walked over to Carl and Thiago and checked both of them for a pulse. "Nice and steady," he murmured. "How much did you use?"

"Not enough to keep them down long," Remy answered miserably. "Too much would have changed the taste of the pastries."

Gray sniggered and mumbled, "Death by muffin."

"*Salaud*," Remy muttered irritably as he removed himself from Brandt's limp body and stood up. He put his hands on his hips and looked around at the destruction he had caused.

Nikolaus had fallen back onto the couch and remained where he had landed, slumped over slightly and looking like he had simply had one too many cocktails the night before. Remy had managed to position Brandt beside the base of the sofa on the soft carpet, and now, at least, he looked peaceful. Shawn was laid carefully on the floor, his head on a pillow and one of his hands draped over his stomach as the other lay palm up, out to his side. Carl had managed to pull Thiago against him before passing out, and now the Argentinean was cradled against Carl's chest protectively as Carl leaned back against the chair.

Gray knelt next to the two of them and gently ran his knuckles over each of their faces in turn, checking their temperatures and making certain of their unconscious states. Remy looked at them all sadly and wondered if they'd be able to forgive him.

He doubted that very much.

"I know him," Gray murmured as he pushed Thiago's hair off his brow with gentle fingers. "I worked with him in Florida once."

"Did you?" Remy asked absently as he looked down at Shawn. "He said he knew a guy who'd worked with you, not that he did himself."

"Yeah, well, Thiago never tells the truth unless he has to," Gray replied with a shrug.

"He recognized you in the plaza, even with that awful wig you were wearing," Remy told Gray as he glanced up at him. His hair was still slightly shaggy, but it was back to its natural strawberry blond as opposed to the red it had been the day before, as was the goatee he had always favored. "That's why we had to chase after you," Remy told him. "He's the one we tripped up."

"Uh huh. He's a real hard-ass," Gray said as he stood up and looked at Remy carefully.

"Who, Thi? Nah. He's just a little… slow to warm," Remy responded sadly as he examined Shawn's peaceful features. His chest constricted painfully as he thought of the consequences of his actions. Fucking Brandt! Why couldn't the man have just eaten his drugs like a good little pyro and gone down like the rest of them? Why did he have to be so fucking difficult? "Fuck," Remy murmured softly. It came out as more of a plea than a curse.

He turned back to see Gray looking at him sympathetically. "You had to do it. If you had waited any longer, you would have missed the timeframe. Then it would all have been pointless. We should restrain them all now," the man added regretfully.

Remy's stomach flipped once more. "Yeah," he agreed sadly. "I've got some rope in my bag. Stay with them," he ordered as he walked off toward the bedrooms to retrieve several lengths of rope. He would need a good amount of it. He didn't want to hurt any of them by tying them too tightly. Speaking of being hurt….

"Disarm them all, Boss!" he called to Gray as an afterthought. He didn't want one of them hurting him or Gray, either.

When he came back, Gray had carefully placed the assortment of weapons on the table beside Remy's little brown box of 'parts', and he was standing at attention beside the sofa.

"What the fuck are you doing?" Remy asked as Gray looked at him in amusement.

"Waiting for my orders," Gray told him matter-of-factly.

Remy rolled his eyes and tossed Gray a handful of rope. "I thought you were in charge," Remy retorted caustically.

"I was. But this is your show, now," Gray replied cheerfully. He was too damn cheerful for such dirty work.

"Tie them in front," Remy instructed.

"Won't they be able to get loose easily?" Gray asked with a knowing smile and a raised eyebrow.

"Yes, but they also won't be hurt by it," Remy responded testily.

The two of them made quick work of tying up Remy's five companions. Gray reached Brandt first, and he quickly took the big man's pulse before trying to tug him away from the sofa.

"Goddamn," he breathed irritably. "Big fucker, isn't he?" he said with a little smile as he stood up and stretched his back.

Remy stared at them, but didn't truly see anything. His eyes were unfocused and his mind had gone blank.

"Dixie?" Gray ventured.

"You've got a nice voice, Boss. Has anyone ever told you that?" Remy said distantly. "Very soothing."

"Uhh, why don't you sit down for a bit," Gray suggested uneasily as he looked at Remy closely. "You didn't eat a muffin, did you?" he asked suspiciously.

Remy sniffed and closed his eyes, trying to shake the somber mood that had overtaken him. "No. I feel like something's sucked my brain out through my nose, though," he said finally as he shook himself and looked at Gray ruefully.

Gray's mouth quirked, and Remy looked away before he could see the sympathy he knew would be there soon.

"Those drugs do things to people's minds, Dixie," Gray said thoughtfully. "Isn't this dude a little odd anyway?"

"He's not 'odd.' He's fucking insane," Remy said as he bent and ran his fingers through Shawn's soft hair affectionately and checked his knots.

"Well, maybe I could tie you up too, y'know," Gray suggested as he stood with his hands on his hips and looked down at Brandt thoughtfully. "Maybe they won't believe him. Maybe he's crazy enough he won't even remember."

"Would *you* remember my shooting you?" Remy asked wryly.

"Probably," Gray answered in the same thoughtful tone.

"You can't tie me up," Remy told him. "You'd enjoy it too much."

"True that," Gray agreed happily. "So, who in this room haven't you fucked, huh?"

Remy stood and turned to glare at the other man.

"Wow," Gray said in awe. "You do get around, don't you?"

"You knew what you were getting," Remy told him in clipped tones as he walked over to the table and picked up his box.

"Yeah, I didn't get nearly enough of it, though," Gray said cheekily, and Remy couldn't help but smile.

"I am glad you're okay, Boss," Remy conceded softly. "I was a little worried about you," he added as he glanced at Gray.

"A little? Just a little?" Gray asked teasingly as he walked over and stood at Remy's shoulder.

"I was really fucking worried about you, all right?" Remy said testily. "When I heard that goddamn song in my ear at that café I almost jumped out of my fucking skin, I was so relieved," he asserted as he fumbled absently with the box in his hands.

Gray slipped his hands around Remy's body and slid them slowly down Remy's arms to take hold of the box and set it down on the table. Remy relaxed backward into the contact as Gray pressed against him from behind. He let his head fall back against Gray's shoulder and wished that he could relax completely. Let his guard down just for one fucking moment.

"I was in Mexico when I got word you'd been captured," Gray murmured into the side of Remy's neck. Remy shivered and let his eyes drift shut. "Drinking boat drinks and working on my tan. Then I heard John had you– I almost choked on my little pink umbrella."

Remy snorted. "Did you know John was with us?" he asked as Gray's arms encircled him and pulled him close.

"No. That's the one thing. I understand why it's necessary, but it's a damn nuisance not knowing who's on our side and who's not. What if he'd killed you, huh? Then what?"

"Then the Archer'd have to find another mole, yeah?"

"That's not funny."

Remy smiled sadly. It wasn't funny, but it was true. He and Gray had spent the better part of two months together, digging their way through the Organization and poking holes in the almost airtight defenses. Two months of bickering and slowly coming to terms with the fact that they were essentially the same personality split into two different bodies. Two months of arguing over who was in charge and trying like hell to hate one another. Two months of tense, really fucking amazing sex. The two months just prior to this assignment. The two months away from Shawn.

Remy closed his eyes as pain lanced through his chest and his veins flooded with ice.

The Archer had sent Gray after Remy. Not Remy specifically, but after a Class One agent susceptible to bribery, trickery, coercion, or all of the above. Gray had given Remy the details and convinced him that the only way to get himself and Shawn out, and get out in one piece, was to go this traitorous, godforsaken route.

And Remy had done it. His goal had been to turn Shawn by any means possible as soon as he could, but it just hadn't happened that way. And now, now Shawn was unconscious on the floor, drugged and restrained at Remy's hands, and Remy knew there was no hope. He had known the moment he'd returned to the group several nights ago and been faced with Shawn's rage that the man would never turn. Now it was too late to go back. Now, whichever way Remy went, it was just too fucking late.

Remy turned slightly and looked at the five men who'd trusted him with their lives. They all slept soundly now, but soon they would awake. And they wouldn't be happy. And they wouldn't understand why he had done this. There would be yelling. Lots of it.

"What do we do now?" Remy asked, feeling lost and forlorn. He didn't like this turn of events. Not one bit. He didn't know where to go from here, and the arguments he'd been thinking of using in order to defend his actions suddenly sounded very weak.

"We need to go over what we'll be telling them," Gray told him softly. Remy shivered as the other man's breath ghosted across his neck, and he relaxed further into the embrace. "You smell like sex," Gray observed in amusement. "Up to your old tricks, I see."

"Stop trying to distract me. And if it goes badly? If they won't accept the offer? Or they don't believe what you tell them?"

"Then you'll come with me and be done with this bunch," Gray said confidently, and he kissed Remy's jaw affectionately before releasing him and reaching around to pick up the little box. "And if I wanted to distract you, I'd just wave something shiny in front of you. Or food." Remy snorted in response, and Gray gripped his shoulder comfortingly. "I know you love him, Dixie," he added sympathetically. "But this…."

"I know," Remy said sadly as he finally turned to look at Gray. "This is more important."

Gray nodded and smiled at him, and Remy's lips quirked into a little half smile. Remy was glad to see the cheeky Southerner again, despite the circumstances. He liked Gray, he really did. He enjoyed his company and he thought of him as one of his few friends. Now that he had drugged and hogtied his only other friends in the world, Gray might very well be his *last* friend.

"So how much do we tell them?" Gray asked cheerfully as he shook the box a little and looked at it curiously.

"Hey, careful with the goods there, Boss! They're fragile!"

"Sorry! What's in there, anyway?" Gray asked as he looked at the box more warily and held it out to Remy.

"None of your business, ya bastard," Remy said as he snagged the box and held it to his chest protectively.

"Mm hmm," Gray responded suspiciously. Remy glared at him self-consciously and set the box down gently on the table once more. "How much longer do we have?"

Remy looked at his watch and tried to estimate the doses he had administered. "Hard to tell, really. Niko was going to town on those fucking doughnut hole thingies, and he's a little guy. But Shawn and Thiago barely ate anything that I brought in, I had to slip it into their drinks later as we all sat around. I think I gave Shawn too much, actually. It made him sick. Carl ate later too. He ate a lot since his eggs went cold, but he's a big bloke. Brandt, well, I shot the fuck out of Brandt. He'll be out a good while."

"But they're all okay, right?" Gray asked in concern as he walked back over to look at the assortment of bodies they had collected.

"Yeah," Remy said confidently as he walked up to stand beside Gray.

"So?" Gray said expectantly.

"So what?"

"So what are we telling them?"

"The truth," Remy answered with a shrug.

"How much of the truth?" Gray asked persistently.

"Oh. Not all of it. They can't know that I… that we…."

"That we've been working against them from the start and that you're on the Archer's payroll?" Gray supplied in amusement.

"Now I remember why I didn't like you," Remy mumbled as he cast a sideways glance at Gray and grimaced.

"Seriously. Which ones would have a problem with it?"

"All of them. Niko would be crushed to know it. Brandt and Carl and definitely Thiago would all be severely fucked off that they were left out of the loop. Shawn would kill me."

"Oh, come on," Gray said with a tilt of his head and a smile. Remy looked at him seriously and the smile faded.

"I'm serious, Boss. He'll kill me if he finds out. When he finds out, rather. I have to turn him, but I have to make him think it was his idea… or that I was… I dunno… forced into it. Otherwise he'll hunt me down no matter where I run."

"You *were* forced into it, in case you'd forgotten. I'm a persistent bastard, remember? And from what you told me this morning about your triumphant return, he didn't seem to think that the threat of John torturing you was enough force. What would be acceptable to him? You don't have any family to threaten. You don't give a flying fuck for your own safety."

"I could tell him the truth," Remy said softly.

"You're talking in circles again, Dixie," Gray told him with a soft smile.

"No, you're right. I have to coerce him into it. He can't know why… he.…"

"Why is it so fucking hard for you to say?" Gray asked irritably. "He was on that list, Remy. We both saw it. He's marked, and whether he lives through *this* or not, they will kill him. He can't go back to the Facility. He can't resurface on the Organization's radar."

"I know," Remy said sadly.

After several moments of contemplative silence, Gray clucked his tongue and asked, "Just how exactly did you plan to move them?"

Remy turned to look at him in surprise. "You said you were bringing a crew."

"I did?"

"Gray! We can't move them all by ourselves!"

"Well fuck, Remy, thanks for pointing that out!" Gray shouted as he put his hands on his hips and turned to face Remy square on. Remy turned as well and pointed his finger in Gray's face.

"You said–"

"No! *You* said you'd take care of it. *I* said I was bringing reinforcements," Gray said heatedly. Remy flailed his hands and made a gesture that clearly said 'well?' Gray thumped his chest and shouted, "Reinforcements!"

"One worthless bastard is not 'reinforcements!'" Remy squeaked. "The 's' implies multiples, Gray!" he shouted angrily, spitting out the other man's name like a curse.

"You're the super agent, *Remy*," Gray shot back. "I'm working without a fucking net, where am I supposed to get reinforcements?"

"You're the fucking loner! Jesus! Not only am I without a net but I'm with five other fucking men who can't know what I'm doing!" Remy shouted in frustration as he ran his hands through his hair. "This is the most unorganized clusterfuck of an operation I've ever been involved with!"

"Well, you're the spearhead, Sweetums," Gray responded angrily.

They stared blankly at one another for several seconds.

"Sweetums?" Remy repeated questioningly, unable to keep the smile from his lips. "Really?" he asked dubiously.

Gray shrugged. "I can't call you Dixie in front of them, now can I?"

"*Mais non*, but Sweetums– there's a keeper," Remy deadpanned.

"Shut up."

"You shut up."

"Don't make me hurt you."

"I'd like to see you try, Sugarlips," Remy said with a wicked grin.

Gray lost his scowl and thumped Remy on the nose playfully. "Okay so, we can't move them. On to Plan B."

"You have a Plan B?" Remy asked hopefully.

"No, but, how long do we have?"

"An hour, give or take. Brandt and Niko will both be out longer. Thiago, he'll wake up sooner, probably."

"Well, fuck."

"Yeah."

Gray and Remy stood side by side for several more minutes, staring at the still bodies of the other five and unconsciously mimicking one another as they both tilted their heads to the side and pursed their lips thoughtfully.

"I got it," Gray said finally, sounding more resigned than triumphant. Remy watched him walk over to the table curiously.

"You gonna share, or– what are you doing?" Remy asked as Gray picked up one of the handguns on the table. "You can't do that, Gray!" Remy said forcefully as he took a step toward the other man. "You promised not to kill them!"

"Is this a real gun?" Gray asked as he examined the unearthly looking weapon.

"Yes. Put that down, it's Carl's. It's got a fucking hair trigger. And it fires off ballistic missiles or some shit, you'll shoot your foot off," Remy cautioned as he took the large gun carefully and set it on the table. "Why do you want a real gun?" Remy asked suspiciously, his heart sinking. He thought he had an idea, but he really wasn't looking forward to it.

"So I can finally do what every spook in the world wants to do," Gray said gleefully as he looked at Remy with sparkling blue eyes.

"Shawn beat you to it. My ass still hurts when I think of it."

"Come on, Dixie," Gray said eagerly. "Let me shoot you."

"No!"

"Please?"

"No!" Remy repeated with a disbelieving laugh.

"Remy, look, you're gonna have to choose. You can either show yourself as the traitor you are, or get shot in the ass and stick with these guys to the end."

"Christ, Boss, there has to be some other… please don't shoot me in the ass!" Remy said desperately.

Gray smiled and took another step toward Remy. He took him by the arms and looked at him solemnly. "You're the brightest, most inventive agent I've ever worked with, Remy. Stop thinking with your heart for one fucking minute, and start thinking like the cold-blooded killer you really are."

Remy blinked and swallowed with difficulty. Gray was right. He was trying to get around getting his heart broken. He couldn't avoid that. It was time to buckle down and take care of this fucking thing.

"Okay," he sighed resignedly. He took a moment to think on the situation form a completely neutral standpoint, "Here's what we do," he finally said confidently. "We have an hour, so we're not in a hurry."

"If we're moving them, then we're in a hurry," Gray pointed out, his hands still gripping Remy's upper arms.

"We can't move them, just the two of us. Can't be done. So, you get to shoot me, Boss," Remy said resignedly.

"Yes!" Gray shouted happily and reached for his shoulder holster.

"Not with that, gun though!" Remy said hastily as he grabbed Gray's hand. "With the tranq gun."

"Fuck it, Dixie! If you're gonna do something, do it right!"

"Gray Kincaid, I swear to God if you shoot me, you won't live to regret it," Remy warned sternly as he pulled Gray closer to him, trying to make certain Gray couldn't pull his weapon.

"Mmm, I love it when you go all tough on me," Gray said cheekily.

Remy snorted in amusement and Gray kissed him. Remy felt a pang of guilt as his lips parted automatically. There was definitely something twisted about standing there kissing someone right after drugging and tying up the man he loved. But fuck it all, Gray was a good kisser.

II.

THIAGO was fighting his way back to consciousness with all his might, but it was a long, cold battle. Finally, he managed to crack one eye open, and he moaned miserably before he could stop himself.

Thiago hated being drugged. He despised being drugged! It always left him with the worst fucking headaches! Goddammit. Someone would pay for this misery.

He sat there with one eye cracked open, the other forgotten as the light lanced through his eyeball and straight into his brain. A shadowy figure walked into his narrowed vision and seemed to kneel down in front of him.

"Coming around, are we?" the shadow said cheerfully. Thiago had never wanted to kill something more in his life. Fucker. "I'm sorry?" the shadow asked, and Thiago's vision focused more. Had he said that out loud? "Did you call me a fucker?" Apparently so. Progress. At least his tongue worked. "Well, I suppose, technically, you're right," the shadow said happily.

In Thiago's mind, the shadow was already dead and buried. Moments like this were why people weren't given supernatural powers, Thiago mused dazedly. Every jerk-off in the world would be dead just like that. Death by Thiago.

A warm hand touched his forehead and Thiago finally remembered to open the other eye. It wasn't happy about it, but it finally opened as well and Thiago focused on the man in front of him.

"Gray?"

"Hey there, Thi," Gray said cheerfully. "Bad day, huh?"

"Bastard… son of a… cock-sucking whore," Thiago grumbled as his head throbbed unpleasantly.

"You always were a little grumpy," Gray said thoughtfully.

Thiago reached out, fully intending to throttle the other man, but his hands met with resistance and wouldn't reach.

"Untie me so I can kill you," Thiago demanded groggily.

Gray laughed gleefully and stood up. "I would, darling, but I think you'd regret it later," he said as Thiago glared up at him.

"I'd learn to live with the guilt," Thiago grumbled as the ceiling above Gray's head began to spin in a sickening manner. Thiago was slightly confused to realize that he was still in Brandt's apartment. He looked for the others in a panic and was relieved to find them all in various stages of restraint. If they were tied up, they were still alive. "What have you done?" he asked warily as his mind began to clear.

"That should be fairly obvious," Gray answered.

"How?"

"I had a little help," Gray answered sorrowfully.

"Who?"

"'What, how, who?'' Gray mimicked. "Never have I encountered such a demanding, inquisitive–"

"Who helped you?" Thiago demanded forcefully, and Gray knelt back down to look at him with renewed interest.

"You don't know?" Gray asked with a wicked little smile.

Thiago glared at him.

"Well, then, I'm not telling," Gray drawled gleefully

Thiago mentally killed the man for perhaps the fortieth time as he stood and walked away.

III.

CARL wasn't entirely sure where he was, but he knew he wasn't about to open his eyes until he did know. He was on the ground. He was tied. He was hung over. His head hurt. Fuck… he was definitely not opening his eyes.

He could hear someone or something near him growling, but he remained still. He simply hoped he hadn't been tossed into an animal's cage or something.

What had happened? It was obvious that they'd all been drugged. He didn't waste time worrying about the others. If he was alive and unhurt, then it stood to reason that they were as well. He moved his head imperceptibly and his cheek brushed along the plush carpet.

They were still in Brandt's flat, then. Why would someone drug them, tie them up, and then leave them where they had fallen? Unless… no, Carl's brain couldn't come up with anything else. There was no unless. It just didn't make sense.

The growling grew louder and Carl's eyes snapped open in alarm. If he was about to be eaten, he at least wanted to know what would be doing it.

"Morning, Sunshine," a friendly American accent said, right above Carl's ear, as if the man were kneeling over him. Carl lunged upward and made contact with the voice's owner, and as the white light of the head butt flashed before his eyes, he heard muffled curses and gleeful laughter coming from somewhere above and to the right of his head.

"Oh, that was beautiful," Thiago crooned joyously as Carl twisted and looked up at him.

So Thiago had been growling. Interesting. A blond man sat on the floor holding his nose gingerly and glaring at Carl, and Carl glared right back at him.

"Carl," Thiago said helpfully as he struggled idly with the rope around his wrists, "this is Asshole. Asshole, that was Carl." Thiago looked like he'd been working at the ropes for a while, but the blond man known as Asshole didn't seem to mind his blatant attempt at escape.

"You're Gray Kincaid," Carl said in a hoarse voice. He cleared his throat automatically and closed his eyes against the pounding in his head. Perhaps the head butt hadn't been such a good idea.

"And you are not a morning person," Gray said nasally as he pinched his nose shut to stop the bleeding.

IV.

SHAWN was sick. He didn't like being sick. He didn't handle being sick well. Like all men, Shawn reverted into a little boy when he was sick. He didn't want to be sick, dammit.

What the hell had happened? The last thing he remembered was Thiago talking to him about a plan and then nothing. He couldn't remember having felt so disjointed since....

Wait....

Oh, fucking hell!

He had been drugged!

"Son of a bitch," he murmured, even before he thought of moving or opening his eyes. Perfect tone. Perfect inflection. Perfectly disgusted curse.

"And we have our third contestant!" a cheerful voice said from the darkness of Shawn's half-consciousness. "You really are an unpleasant bunch to wake up," the voice continued as if talking to itself.

"I'll kill you," Shawn murmured, still lying on his back with his eyes closed. His hands were tied around his waist and, apparently, his feet were tied together and attached to his hands somehow, but he was fairly certain he could do it. Mind over matter and all that rot.

"That's sort of what the other two came out with," the voice said, closer now. "I was hoping you would be original about it."

"I'll kill you with Carl," Shawn mumbled as he finally forced one eye open. A handsome blond man stood over him and looked over his shoulder warily. "I see you've already met Carl," Shawn said with satisfaction as he took in the slight bruising on the man's face and the general direction he was looking.

"I could kill you with a pinecone," Carl's irritated voice threatened, and Shawn actually smiled.

He belatedly recognized the man as Gray Kincaid, and if the American was working by himself, he stood no chance. Knowing this group as Shawn did, he could guess what they were all doing. Nikolaus was distracting Kincaid by pretending to be frightened, Remy was already free of his restraints and acquiring a weapon, Brandt was rigging something explosive out of a dust bunny, and Carl and Thiago were joining Shawn in his mental efforts to strike Kincaid down dead. This was fine. This was not a problem.

Shawn closed his eyes again and divided his mental efforts. Half went to wishing Kincaid dead, the other half went to curtailing the nausea. He would let the others handle this one.

V.

NIKOLAUS'S world came crashing back just as quickly as it had abandoned him, and he jumped theatrically when consciousness hit him. It took him a split second to take in his surroundings; Thiago, Carl, Shawn, and a fourth man stared at him with wide eyes from various positions of restraint. Brandt and Remy were unconscious. Nikolaus himself was tied and had most likely been drugged, as had the others. The man who did it was working alone and therefore probably wasn't going to live through it as soon as everyone woke up.

It was odd, the way he was tied. It was probably easy to escape, and therefore the man who Nikolaus suddenly recognized as Gray Kincaid probably didn't intend to hurt them. That or he intended to kill them anyway and would just shoot anyone who got loose. That wasn't good. Nikolaus also recognized that Remy and Brandt had been dosed a lot more or a lot later than the others, and that he'd been hit harder because of his size.

All these observations and realizations came to him in a flood so fast that it made him slightly ill.

"I hate life," he mumbled as he scooted himself into a sitting position on the couch.

"No threats?" Gray asked warily as all four men watched him. Apparently, it wasn't normal for someone to go from unconscious to sitting bolt upright and completely aware in one second flat. Nikolaus knew that much just from the splitting pain in his head when he shook it in answer to Gray's query.

"Do you have any aspirin?" Nikolaus asked pitifully.

VI.

BRANDT'S entire body was on fire with rage, even before he was fully awake. That little bastard had shot him! Fucking shot him! That was the last time Brandt would fuck him, that was for sure. He liked it rough, but fucking hell, there was a limit!

Jesus Blazing Christ, did Brandt not like being shot. Or drugged. Or in this half-conscious state in which he was unable to kill something.

He couldn't open his eyes. He couldn't move his limbs. He couldn't feel the burn! He needed the burn! A low growling noise started deep in his chest, and he let it progress of its own accord until it bubbled up into his throat and emitted as an enraged howl.

He let the energy of the howl and the anger and the need to *kill* fuel his body, and the next thing he was aware of, he was standing in the middle of the room on full seek and destroy mode.

He took in the others, still tied up and looking up at him in shock. He took in his own bindings, somehow magically loose and crumpled on the floor at his feet. He took in the surprised stranger with the gun pointed at him. He took in Remy, unconscious and bound on the floor.

Target acquired.

VII.

REMY'S first thought when he heard the yelling through the heavy cloak of the drugs was that the others weren't taking the situation so well. He expected that, though. Apparently, Brandt was especially upset.

"No! Brandt! Stop!"

That was Carl.

Lord God, did Remy hate being drugged.

"Shoot him!"

His head was already hurting and the sedatives hadn't even begun to wear off. That had sounded like Nikolaus. Remy hoped they weren't shooting Gray. That would suck for him.

"No! Don't shoot him!"

His neck hurt too, for some reason. That had been Carl again.

"He's gonna kill him!"

If Gray had propped him in a position where his neck would cramp, he would kill the bastard himself.

"For fuck's sake, man, do *something*!"

Thiago sounded panicked. Why was Thiago panicking? Thiago didn't panic....

"You just told me not to shoot him!"

Gray?

Air?

"Well, tackle the fucker! He's killing him!"

This didn't sound good.

Remy's mind cleared slightly, but the world was still bleary and heavy. Everything was heavy. Even the air was heavy.

Why couldn't he breathe?

VIII.

"JESUS fucking Christ, Gray, do something!" Thiago yelled in a half-panic as Brandt's large hands closed around Remy's neck and lifted the younger man's limp body clear off the couch. Gray stood at Thiago's shoulder and gaped, and Thiago tried desperately to free himself from the loose restraints. Fuck! If Brandt could break through his ropes half-drugged and half conscious, then Thiago should be able to do it after three hours of working on them.

He was almost free when a flash of movement at his side produced a knife in Gray's hand. Thiago flinched, but Gray sliced through the ropes and freed him just before lunging forward and wrapping himself around Brandt's neck and shoulders. Thiago followed suit, and together they managed to force Brandt into releasing Remy's body. Remy fell back limply against the couch, and Brandt stood there furiously trying to rid himself of the two men. Thiago wasn't certain he and Gray could hold the enraged man, and he was even more uncertain of why in the world Brandt was trying to kill Remy. Had the man finally cracked for good?

"Calm down, Wally!" Thiago heard Carl yelling. He wondered if it would be worth letting go long enough to untie Carl. Carl was a big guy, and he and Brandt had an understanding. Carl could get him under control. If not, Carl could at least kill him creatively.

Brandt roared angrily and flailed, and Thiago was thrown to the floor with a thud and rolled. Gray somehow managed to hang on, but he wasn't able to keep Brandt from wrapping his hands around Remy's throat once more, even though Thiago could see him trying to squeeze the pressure points that should have dropped Brandt like a ton of bricks.

Thiago could see Remy struggling weakly, but he wasn't nearly fighting for his life like he should've been. Thiago prayed that the sedatives would wear off in time for Remy to come fully awake, but he didn't think they would. They needed help. Thiago crawled to Carl and swiftly cut his ropes with Gray's discarded knife.

"Take him down, Carl," Thiago gasped. He watched in fascinated horror as Carl sprang forward and deftly separated the combatants. He quickly brought Brandt to the ground with a well-aimed jab to the kidney and a kick to the back of the knee.

Thiago was up and ready to attack by the time the two men hit the ground, his mind going to thoughts of escape, but Gray was quicker and he stood calmly to the side with his gun in hand, waiting for someone to make a wrong move.

"He shot me!" Brandt roared from the floor. Carl practically laid on top of him, and he wrapped an arm around Brandt's neck, a leg around his waist, and rolled them both until he held Brandt's body in his lap and restrained him with all four limbs. It probably wasn't the most effective way of doing it, but Thiago suspected that

Carl was going more for calming Brandt than stopping him.

"No one shot you, Wally," Carl soothed with difficulty as Brandt struggled against him. "That bastard over there slipped us something. Drugs, Wally. You ever been drugged? It fucks with your mind. Makes you dream and think you're seeing things that aren't there."

"He fucking shot me, Trigger! He shot me with one of those feather things!"

"Feather things?" Nikolaus muttered questioningly, and Thiago crouched low, wondering which problem he needed to deal with first.

"Get him under control!" Gray ordered impatiently as he sidestepped toward Thiago. "Don't make a move, Thi, I have you pegged," he added carefully.

"If I could fucking get him under control, I would have done!" Carl shouted just before Brandt elbowed him in the ribs and shot forward toward Remy once more.

Gray's gun trained on the big man, and Thiago knew he had to move. He lunged as Gray's finger tightened on the trigger, and the soft pop of the silencer sounded as Thiago's body made contact with Gray's and sent them both toppling to the ground.

Thiago heard a pained howl and he knew someone had been shot. He struggled with Gray while trying to figure out who it had been. Shawn was on the ground, languishing where he'd fallen, and Thiago was pretty sure that the man was too low to have been hit. The rest of them were fair game, though.

"You bastard! You shot me!" Brandt yelled, drawing Thiago's attention just long enough to allow Gray to straddle him, pin him, and aim his gun at Carl.

"Goddammit!" Thiago growled in frustration as Gray's other hand closed around his throat.

"Behave yourself," Gray panted. "Don't move," he added to Carl commandingly, and Thiago saw Carl freeze as the weapon trained on him.

"Who's been shot?" Thiago demanded.

Gray shook his head absently.

"Is Brandt shot?" Thiago persisted, hoping someone would answer him. Gray's hand tightened around his neck and Thiago gagged slightly. He could take a hint, and he stopped struggling.

Thiago's air was slowly being cut off, and the spots were flying in front of his eyes, when Gray was suddenly hit from the side and went tumbling off across the floor. Thiago scrambled to get up, his mind already racing to decide which of his companions to save first, but what he saw shocked him into immobility.

It hadn't been Carl who had tackled Gray. It had been Nikolaus. And Nikolaus was now beating the shit out of Gray, much like Brandt was doing to Remy.

"Bad Dixie! No more sex for you!" Brandt yelled as he picked Remy up and shook him.

Thiago fought back the insane urge to laugh.

IX.

CARL did laugh. He laughed at the entirely too ridiculous scene before him.

Brandt was shaking Remy and scolding him, threatening him with abstinence if he ever shot him again.

Nikolaus was shaking Gray in much the same manner, threatening him with far more unpleasant things if he moved. Who knew the kid could move like that?

Thiago was crouched next to them, watching in utter fascination, and Shawn was wallowing on the floor moaning, because, in all likelihood, he had been overdosed. Carl. Well, Carl was bleeding quite profusely from the bullet wound in his side.

That part wasn't all that funny, come to think of it.

X.

SHAWN struggled to sit up, and when he did his world tilted and he fell back against the floor with a groan.

What the fuck was going on? There was fighting. And blood, he could smell blood.

He shook his head, trying to clear the cobwebs, but that merely made his stomach roil violently and he slumped back to the ground.

What the fuck…?

XI.

"DON'T you move, you bastard, or Thiago'll shoot you to shit," Nikolaus growled as he pressed his knee further into Gray's neck.

Thiago looked slightly startled by the assertion that he had a gun, but Gray was duly convinced and he remained motionless.

Nikolaus looked up to see how many pieces Remy had been torn into. Brandt was holding Remy to his chest and rocking him back and forth, and for a brief, horrific moment Nikolaus thought Remy was dead.

But then he saw a weak flail of the Cajun's arms, and Brandt rubbed Remy's head affectionately and set him down. Nikolaus was suddenly reminded of that cartoon with the big white abominable snowman. Or had he been blue? The one where he picked up the bunny dude and hugged him and rubbed him and loved on him and called him George, all the while slowly squeezing the life out of him. Yeah, Brandt was the abominable snowman.

Apparently, whatever had bothered Brandt was no longer a problem. Remy remained motionless on the ground, too drugged to do more than flail a little. Shawn remained motionless on the ground, too sick to move. Gray remained motionless beneath Nikolaus, too smart to even blink.

Brandt crawled to where Carl knelt and pushed him gently onto his back.

Nikolaus watched in horror as Brandt pawed at Carl's torso and brought his bloody hand up to reach out for the pillow Thiago handed him. That was a lot of blood. Fuck. Nikolaus really didn't like blood.

XII.

"GUT shot, Trigger?" Brandt asked shakily.

Carl shook his head. "Glanced off my ribs, I think," he said in a pained voice. "Fuck, but it's bleeding, isn't it?" he asked with a little laugh. "Always was a bleeder."

Brandt nodded distractedly and pressed the pillow down hard.

Carl grimaced, but didn't cry out. "You didn't kill Dixie, did you?" he asked tightly.

"No. I won't kill him 'til he wakes up completely."

"Good. Can't have everyone down at once," Carl responded distantly, and Brandt looked up at Thiago in concern.

An hour later, Gray Kincaid was tied securely to a dining chair, Shawn was resting his aching head on the table, Remy was slumped groggily in the chair beside him, and Carl was stretched out on the couch asleep.

Brandt, Thiago, and Nikolaus surveyed the damage together.

"Bastard," Brandt spat as he prowled past Gray. "You shot my Trigger," he growled menacingly.

Gray looked at him uneasily, but said nothing. His silence angered Brandt even further, and if Thiago hadn't stepped in front of him Brandt would simply have annihilated the man right then and there.

"Shawn," Thiago barked commandingly. "Snap the fuck out of it. We need guidance, goddammit!"

"What's wrong with your brain, *Zed?* Aren't you our guidance system?" Shawn mumbled without raising his head.

Thiago's eyes narrowed, but he looked at Brandt appraisingly.

"Remy shot you?" Thiago asked carefully.

Brandt nodded and looked at Remy fondly. He couldn't really hate the man. It had been a fine piece of subterfuge. He also felt sorry for Remy. Even a blind man could tell he'd been forced into this. Hell, even *Brandt* could tell that! All they had to do was wait for Remy to come around enough to give them an explanation.

"I'm sorry," Remy mumbled as he looked up at them pitifully.

Shawn's hand shot out and gripped Remy's throat. Remy gurgled and held onto Shawn's wrist helplessly as Shawn raised his head and turned it slowly to glare at the younger man. Brandt watched in fascination, and he couldn't help but be a little turned on by the anger in Shawn's eyes.

"You're sorry?" Shawn asked calmly.

Remy's brown eyes widened theatrically. "Beignet, please."

"Please, Remy? *Please?* Do you have any fucking idea how much I fucking hate being drugged?" Shawn roared as he stood up and brought Remy up with him by his throat. "It was you! You sniveling little backstabbing traitor! All this time they've been a step ahead and it was you!"

"No!" Remy protested weakly.

Brandt took a step forward, as did Thiago. This was about to get ugly.

"Why, Remy? Hmm? What could they have possibly used on you to make you turn? What in God's name could have been so fucking important for you to give up everything?"

Brandt took another step forward as Remy's eyes glistened and he looked at Shawn miserably. He wasn't even trying to get free, he was simply dangling from Shawn's hand.

"You," Remy answered weakly. "They used you."

XIII.

REMY watched Shawn's face contort into a mask of pain, but then all emotion drained from the beloved features and Remy stared into the clear green eyes of a stone cold killer.

"I'm sorry, Shawn," was all he could think to say. "Please."

"Quit whingeing," Shawn snarled in disgust, and his fingers tightened around Remy's throat. Remy could easily have gotten loose, but he didn't want to. This was poetic justice. Let Shawn kill him for all he had done. It would serve him right. "I trusted you with my life. For five years, you were the only thing I knew!"

"I'd never let anything happen to you," Remy protested in a hoarse voice. "That's why I did this! I love you, Shawn! I–"

"Shut it!" Shawn snapped, disregarding Remy's declaration as if he had just said the sky was green or that Brandt was sane. "We won't take any more excuses. You turned on us. You lied to us. Was it John? Or was it earlier? Hmm? Was it you let this bastard in here?" he asked, gesturing toward Gray. "Were you the one set the bomb back at the cabin?"

"No! Shawn, please!" Remy repeated desperately. He had to make Shawn understand. He'd done this to get them out. Shawn was marked for death on that fucking list and this had been Remy's only chance to save him. He had to let him know.

"Brandt!" Shawn barked commandingly, all traces of the overdose gone. All traces of Shawn were gone, too. This was a different man than the one Remy had known. This was a vengeful, angry, betrayed man, and Remy didn't think he would be getting out of this. Brandt shuffled over warily and Remy looked at the big man beseechingly. "Gag our young friend," Shawn ordered, and Brandt looked at them both uncertainly.

"Not so sure about that, Beignet," Brandt said softly

"No worries. We'll put the two of them in the back bedroom," Shawn said quietly. "The one with no windows. Then we'll decide what to do with them and go from there. I'm just sick of his fucking voice."

Remy rolled his eyes to look at the other men, but he saw only sadness and uncertainty on their faces. Carl was standing and walking toward them gingerly. Thank God he wasn't hurt badly. Nikolaus looked angry and betrayed. Thiago looked confused and a little lost for words. Brandt's eyes darted back and forth between Shawn and Remy, but he finally turned on his heel and went to retrieve a length of cloth.

So this was it, then. This was the end. Remy's heart broke as Brandt forced the gag into his mouth, and the glint in Shawn's eyes as Brandt and Thiago took hold of him and led him away was something Remy would remember until his dying day.

He hoped he didn't have to carry it with him for long.

XIV.

THE Archer sat at the table staring at the other four men and waiting for his chance to move.

Fucking Gray, he shouldn't be here. The Archer had to get him out. And Remy, too. Son of a bitch! Remy had been working for him all along and he hadn't even known it.

Fucking Gray! No more of this networking shit; from now on, he would do all the recruiting himself!

Fucking Gray! Fucking Remy! Never have underlings with initiative. It was far too much fucking trouble!

The discussion finally began to wane, and the Archer stood, stretched, and announced he was going to check on the 'prisoners' before heading for bed. He got disinterested nods and exhausted yawns in answer, and he walked casually to the back bedroom.

He let himself through the door and closed it softly, locking it behind him. He didn't turn on the light, but simply stood in the darkness until his eyes adjusted enough to see Remy and Gray, both naked, gagged and attached to the furniture with rope.

Remy didn't move. He didn't even twitch as the Archer walked toward the bed he was laid out on.

"Is he still drugged?" the Archer asked softly.

"I think he's heartbroken, actually," Gray said softly through the gag from the chair he was bound to.

"Gag doesn't do much good there, does it?" the Archer asked caustically.

Gray shook his head shamelessly and continued working on the ropes that bound his wrists.

"Hey," Remy said weakly from the bed.

The Archer looked at him closely. He *was* still drugged; he looked completely out of it. That or he was faking. He could very well be faking, trying to escape. Remy didn't know they were still on the same side yet. "Have you come to make me feel like shit, too?"

"Someone else was in here?" the Archer asked quickly, looking at Gray for his answer.

Gray shook his head sadly.

"He was hallucinating before," he said with difficulty through the gag. The Archer took a step and lowered Gray's gag to allow him to speak easier. "Said something about pinecones and purple crayons and talked to someone named Rougarou. He's cracked," Gray explained.

"Fuck me," the Archer breathed in distress as he looked back at Remy.

"You don't strike me as the type to bottom," Remy slurred quietly.

"How'd he get his gag off?" the Archer asked, ignoring the comment for the moment.

Gray shrugged in response. "He has special talents," he answered carelessly.

"They're going to kill me," Remy said softly. The Archer knelt on the bed and ran his knuckles over Remy's cheekbone. Remy nuzzled into the contact.

"I won't let them hurt you," the Archer whispered into Remy's ear.

"I knew you wouldn't," Remy murmured as he tried to wrap his bound arms around the Archer's neck. "Please untie me," he begged as he strained for more contact with the Archer's body.

"Fuck," the Archer breathed as his entire body tingled at Remy's touch. He knew what Remy was trying to do. It wouldn't have worked even if it had been necessary, but it was an admirable attempt nonetheless.

"Fuck," Gray huffed from his chair. "Untie me too."

The Archer chuckled and sat back up.

"We won't run," Remy said earnestly. "Please, please untie him."

"Him?" the Archer repeated in slight amusement. "Just him?"

Remy nodded and arched his back, straining at the bindings and whimpering for contact. The Archer looked at him longingly, and then turned to look at Gray. The man leaned forward, his eyes wide and a slight smile on his face. He was obviously enjoying the Archer's predicament.

"This is your fault," the Archer told him sternly, pointing a finger at Gray and wagging it in his face. "You don't get untied."

"But–"

"You have to watch," the Archer said evilly as he bent back down and kissed Remy slowly.

Remy and Gray had both been tied up wearing no clothing to prohibit their getting free by utilizing anything hidden on their bodies. Remy's naked body writhed beneath the Archer's, and Gray whimpered pitifully from his chair beside them.

The Archer was slightly shocked to see Remy's hands pawing at him, urging him to disrobe.

"How did you do that?" he demanded breathlessly as Remy shoved at his jeans, pushing them down over his hips. The Archer mindlessly allowed Remy to push the jeans down with his feet and then wrap strong legs around his now naked waist.

"Do what?" Remy asked disinterestedly as he latched on to the Archer's neck and sucked at the tender skin.

"You're free," the Archer gasped as his hips thrust forward automatically.

"Not entirely. I usually get dinner first," Remy murmured as he slipped his hand under the pillow. The Archer tensed and grabbed Remy's wrist, pinning it to the bed. "Fuck!" Remy snarled as his legs tightened around the Archer's waist.

"No tricks, now," the Archer warned, and he wondered what exactly he had gotten himself into. Or on top of, rather. He should have untied Gray, for protection if nothing else. Remy thrust his hips upward and the Archer groaned involuntarily.

"It's just lube," Remy said softly. "No tricks. Trust me, *podna*, I just want to be fucked into next week before the execution."

"I could help with that if he won't," Gray offered eagerly.

"Shut up, Gray," Remy and the Archer both ordered as they looked at one another.

"Fuck me," Remy said softly. "Fuck me like you did before. Make him watch, it'll serve him right."

The Archer narrowed his eyes and then smirked slightly. He wasn't exactly long on time, but if he did fuck Remy it would at least give him an excuse for being back here.

"You're both evil," Gray groaned, and he shut his eyes as the Archer positioned himself over Remy's body. Remy grunted and whimpered in pleasure, but there were no cries as the Archer fucked him.

The kid knew clandestine, that was for fucking certain.

Gray cursed at them creatively as he watched, and the Archer knew he couldn't leave the man in the state he was in. Just as soon as he had come, he pulled out of Remy and slid liquidly down the side of the bed to the floor. Remy was limp and hanging his arms and head off the edge of the bed, and Gray squirmed uncomfortably in his chair.

"Bastard," Gray spat angrily as the Archer stood and looked at him.

"You should get Remy to teach you his rope trick," the Archer said cheekily before dropping dramatically to his knees and taking Gray's cock into his mouth.

Gray cried out quietly and bucked as best he could, and the Archer could just imagine Remy's head shooting up to watch. Gray had had quite enough stimulation already, and it didn't take but several moments of the Archer's talented tongue to have him cursing and writhing and coming into the back of the Archer's throat.

"Fuck," Gray muttered again after the Archer had backed way and wiped his mouth with the back of his hand.

They stared at one another in a post-orgasmic sort of vacuum for several seconds before the Archer remembered how fucked off he was at both these men. If they had simply done what they had been ordered and nothing more, none of this would have happened.

"You stupid fuck!" the Archer spat angrily as he loosened Gray's ropes and stood back up, looking around for his bits of discarded clothing. "What the fuck were you thinking? How do you get 'drug everyone and then get captured' from the order 'show them the message'?"

"Well, how was I supposed to know you were one of the fucking Six?" Gray whispered heatedly as he struggled out of the rope.

"That's what they're calling us? The Fucking Six?" the Archer asked distractedly as he gathered the various pieces of clothing and began dressing.

"Six. One of the Six, you fuck. Knowing Remy, though, it fits," Gray said acerbically as he rubbed his sore wrists.

"What the fuck did you think you were doing, coming in here like this?" the Archer asked as Gray stood and faced him.

"What are you doing?" Remy asked weakly as he finally raised his head and looked at them. "Are you untying–"

"Hush!" the Archer warned as he helped Gray to balance and stretch his sore legs.

"Oh, my God, you're one of us!" Remy hissed. "*Maudit*!"

"Shhh!" the Archer and Gray both hissed.

"Jesus Christ, Dixie! Get a grip!" Gray added quietly as he walked over and patted Remy on the head to calm him.

"You knew he was one of us? Why didn't you contact him, too? Why'd you throw me to the fucking wolves?" Remy whispered demandingly of Gray as he got to his knees and growled.

"Calm down," the Archer said as he sat on the bed and looked up at Gray blankly.

How should he do this? Should he tie them back up loosely in case one of the others checked on them before they made their escape? Should he leave the door unlocked or provide them with a key? Should he go with them?

"I didn't know he was here. And then after I did, I didn't know you didn't know," Gray told Remy defensively. "I mean fuck, you've been working for him for almost a year and–"

"What?" Remy asked as he stared up at Gray with wide eyes.

"What?" Gray repeated warily, looking from Remy to the Archer in alarm.

"Working *for* him?" Remy hissed as he transferred his gaze to the Archer. "You're… you're the fucking Ar–"

The Archer leaped forward and clapped his hand over Remy's mouth.

"He's not taking the news very well," Gray mused as he stood with his hands on his hips and watched as Remy tried to bite off the Archer's fingers.

"Would you be taking the news well, you stupid fuck?" the Archer asked as he put all of his weight onto Remy's body.

Suddenly, Remy was free of his restraining hands and had the Archer around the neck, and they rolled off the bed and to the floor. It was like trying to wrestle Jell-O! How in the fuck did he do that?

"You bastard!" Remy hissed, keeping his voice low even while he tried to strangle the Archer and get a hand on Gray as the man danced away all at the same time. "I trusted you! I trusted you!"

"And I trusted you," the Archer croaked as Remy's hands tightened around his throat. "I still do, Remy," he gasped as a last resort. Remy relaxed and his fingers loosened, and the Archer saw Gray's hand rest lightly on Remy's shoulder.

"You bastard," Remy whispered brokenly.

"I know," the Archer said sorrowfully as Remy slumped back and fell against the bed. Gray knelt beside him and looked into his face in concern. "Remy," the Archer said as he got to his knees and crawled to sit in front of the other man.

"Traitor," Remy spat. "And you've made into one, too."

The Archer looked at Gray in amazement. "He doesn't know?"

"You told me to give him absolutely no information that wasn't needed," Gray said defensively. "He didn't need to know."

"He followed you without knowing?" the Archer asked in awe.

"All I needed to see was that list," Remy said in disgust. "What are you talking about? What don't I know?"

"We're not the traitors here, Remy," the Archer said quickly. Remy sniffed disbelievingly.

"It's true," Gray said as he sat down beside Remy and took his hand. "There's a whole lot of history that you don't know, and there's a lot of shit going down at the Organization that'll get a lot of agents killed if we don't get them out. Soon."

"You mean the agents on the list?" Remy asked with a disturbing sort of innocence.

Gray and the Archer shared a look. The Archer had no idea what list Remy was talking about. It would seem that Gray had used a little sleight-of-hand to coerce Remy to their side. That could be very, very bad if Remy found out after all that had happened to him.

"Look, we don't have a lot of time," the Archer said quickly.

"Oh, why, didn't you drug the others before you waltzed in here to instigate the Great Escape?"

"No," the Archer responded angrily. "If I'm not mistaken the drugs were a brilliant concoction of your two great minds."

"Fuck you," Remy growled.

"We don't have time, darling," the Archer responded sweetly. "I have to get back out there, and then the two of you have to get the hell out."

"What? I'm not leaving," Remy said in surprise.

"And I'm certainly not leaving him here alone," Gray said defiantly.

"Oh, for...," the Archer bit his tongue and rubbed his tired eyes in frustration. "Listen, Gray, you're as good as dead if you don't run. I can't hold them off without blowing my cover. And Remy... same goes for you now, too."

"They're still mad, huh?" Remy said sadly.

"Yes. Now–"

"We've got some serious Blue-On-Blue action going on here," Remy muttered musingly. The Archer raised an eyebrow and waited for him to continue. "Inadvertent hostile activity between allies," he explained to them as if anyone in the business wouldn't know what Blue-On-Blue meant. "I never got the irony of how funny that concept was. I mean this is serious blowback."

"Is he okay?" the Archer asked Gray worriedly as Remy continued to ramble to himself.

Gray shrugged in response and petted Remy on the top of the head soothingly. "Drugs make him loopy," he provided.

"Oh, that's just great," the Archer grumbled. "Will you be able to handle him?"

"Come with us," Remy said to him suddenly. The Archer blinked at him in the darkness. "Come with us," Remy repeated persuasively. "You can't hide from them forever, they'll find you out eventually, and then they'll kill you. You won't have anyone to watch your back. Come with us."

"I can't," the Archer told him sadly. "This has got to be goodbye."

Remy blinked rapidly and then nodded in acceptance as he looked away. The Archer stood and looked down at them both. They both sat there, looking up at him like scolded puppies, and his heart broke as he thought that one or both of them would probably be killed because of him.

"Take care of each other," the Archer said softly, running his hands over each of their heads affectionately before turning and walking toward the door.

"Good luck, Thi," Remy whispered sadly in return.

XV.

THIAGO pulled the door closed behind him and stood motionless in the dark hallway. If he had known how fucking hard this was going to be, he never would have gotten involved. How many lives could you save to justify the loss of one? Especially if that one was someone you cared deeply for? It was a tricky question, and Thiago didn't want to think about it. He rubbed his eyes as something Remy said at the cabin came back to him.

"Even trained killers have their moral quirks, I suppose," he had said.

Wasn't that the truth. The memory of Remy's voice and that little smirk of his made Thiago want to turn around, go back into that room, and pull the younger man to him. Just hold him and never let him go. And then there was Gray, who had remained unquestioningly loyal throughout, among other things.

"Fuck," Thiago breathed quietly.

Remy and Gray were both just feet away from him, easily within reach. They were still present and real and tangible, but he was already thinking of them as gone. He felt he'd never see either of them again, and his throat constricted at the thought. He stood at the door indecisively. The desire to go with them, like Remy had begged him to do, was overwhelming. But then he thought of the others. Carl and Nikolaus. Brandt and Shawn. He could still save them. At least, he thought he could. He had to try.

He sighed dejectedly and trudged back out into the living room. Shawn and Nikolaus sat at the table still, but Brandt and Carl were both gone. Thiago looked at the two remaining men warily. He wondered how strongly he smelled of sex and how guilty he looked. Thiago was pretty sure he had perfected the 'not up to anything' look, but the scent of Remy on him was unmistakable. Why hadn't he thought of just going on to bed? Or taking a fucking shower?

"Did he have anything to say?" Shawn asked flatly. Thiago took a seat opposite the other man and looked from him to Nikolaus questioningly. Nikolaus shrugged and looked down at the table. "You were in there for quite a while," Shawn pointed out dangerously.

Thiago could see that Shawn already knew part of what he had been doing. That was what Thiago had planned.

"He said he knew we were going to kill them," he answered softly.

Shawn flinched and looked away, and Thiago fought with the inexplicable urge to hurt the man. He knew he couldn't simply take out his gun and shoot him, he liked Shawn too much to kill him yet. Oh, but he could inflict mental damage, no problem. Make Shawn's heart ache like he knew Remy's was.

"It took him that long to say that?" Nikolaus asked dubiously, giving Thiago the perfect opening. Now he could inflict maximum damage with a few little words and plead that he was simply answering the question. God, did he love subterfuge.

"No," he answered curtly. "I was fucking him for the rest of the time."

Shawn's head whipped back around and Thiago almost regretted the admission when he saw the murderous look in Shawn's eyes. Perhaps that hadn't been the best thing to say. He had probably done Remy more damage than good by doing that, but it was too late to cry over it now. Didn't matter anyway, Remy would be long gone by morning. Out of Shawn's reach.

"Did you set him free?" Shawn asked angrily, rising half out of his chair and clenching his fists.

"No," Thiago said truthfully. "How does he do that, anyway? Get out of restraints like that?"

"It's amazing, isn't it?" Nikolaus asked, leaning forward and looking at Thiago with sparkling gray eyes. "He tried to teach me how to do it but it just takes natural talent, I guess. One minute you've got him tied to the headboard, the next he's loose and flipping you onto your back."

Thiago nodded enthusiastically, forgetting for the moment that Shawn was hovering over them and fuming. "I was trying to get my shirt unbuttoned and suddenly there were two more hands helping me," Thiago told Nikolaus, gesturing to the front of his shirt as he turned slightly in his seat.

Shawn growled angrily and slammed his hands down on the table. Thiago and Nikolaus both jumped and looked up at him with wide eyes.

"Did you tie him back up when you were done *fucking* him?" Shawn asked through gritted teeth.

"No, Shawn," Thiago said in his best sarcastic voice. "I left him untied. I untied Gray too, y'know, just in case they feel the urge to fuck each other into the mattress before you execute them," he added snappishly. Hey, there was nothing like being honest!

Shawn's jaw clenched and he sat back down with a thump.

They sat staring angrily at one another for several minutes. Shawn had a right to be angry, and that made Thiago enjoy it all the more. Let the bastard suffer. Let the bastard realize just how much he'd thrown away by being a stubborn ass. Thiago knew he'd give up everything he knew for the person who loved him like Remy loved Shawn, but Shawn was clinging to his goddamn loyalty like there was no tomorrow. *Pedazo de pelotudo.*

"Wasn't my idea, Shawn," Thiago said maliciously. "He begged me to fuck him. He said, and I'm quoting, 'I wanna be fucked into next week before the execution.' Made me glad I was the one to go check on them."

"I checked on them, too," Nikolaus grumbled. "He was still drugged when I went in there."

"Yeah, he wasn't exactly coherent, come to think of it. Kincaid said he's been talking to his motorcycle," Thiago said distantly as he looked at Nikolaus closely.

Shawn was up and gripping Thiago's shirtfront from across the table before Thiago even registered the movement. Shawn pulled him out of his chair and practically dragged him across the table, cursing and growling and threatening to dismember him.

Thiago grabbed at Shawn's wrists, trying to stop his forward motion, but it was no use. Shawn pulled him completely across the table and dumped him unceremoniously onto the floor before laying into him.

"Brandt!" Nikolaus called in a panic as he ran around the table and threw his arms around Shawn's shoulders, trying to restrain him. "Shawn's trying to kill Thiago!" Nikolaus shouted as Shawn landed a stinging blow across Thiago's chin.

Thiago swung his fist blindly in retaliation for the blow and connected with something, but since Shawn continued trying his damnedest to throttle him, Thiago assumed he had hit Nikolaus.

Great. He had just knocked out the only assistance he was likely to get.

"You fucking bastard! What did you do to him?" Shawn snarled.

Thiago understood. He didn't blame Shawn for trying to kill him. If Remy really had been drugged and not simply faking in order to escape, Thiago would never have touched him. But the evil part of Thiago needed Shawn to suffer for being a bastard, and so he carried on with the charade.

"What's wrong, Shawn?" he said in his best sneer. "You're gonna kill him anyway, right? Besides," Thiago added with a little smirk as he forced his knee between Shawn's legs. "I think he probably enjoyed it." Shawn's eyes went black with rage and Thiago gave the man his best shit-eating grin. "What I did is no worse than breaking his heart," he added, whacking the last nail into the coffin.

'Suffer, punta, suffer!' Thiago thought maliciously as he saw the pain flash through Shawn's eyes. He was about to ram his knee into Shawn's groin when two large hands entered Thiago's vision and grabbed them each around the neck.

Thiago had never been lifted into the air by his neck, and he decided that it was an experience he never wanted to have again. Brandt squeezed Thiago's throat until he thought his head might just pop off, and Thiago cringed submissively on his knees as Brandt bent over them. Shawn didn't seem to be faring much better, and Thiago held onto Brandt's wrist and tried to pry his fingers loose in order to get air.

"Bad!" Brandt yelled at them both, shaking them until Thiago thought his brains would simply leak out of his ears.

"You hit me," Nikolaus stated accusingly as he sat up and rubbed his cheek gingerly.

"You hit Gizmo?" Brandt asked in disbelief. He dropped Shawn and Thiago like lead weights and reached to grab something from the top of the table. "Which one did it?" he roared, and when he turned around Thiago saw that he was holding a magazine in his hand and rolling it into a tight roll. Nikolaus pointed at Thiago, and Thiago turned his head to look at Shawn disbelievingly just before Brandt whacked him in the head with the magazine roll. The blow sent him toppling sideways, and he remained on the ground, staring up at Brandt with wide eyes. "That's for hitting Gizmo! Now who started it?"

Thiago pointed at Shawn, and Shawn glared at him angrily.

"He–"

"Shut up! If you wake Trigger up, you'll both be sorry," Brandt said, adding a whack to Shawn's head for good measure. "And that's for starting it!"

"Jesus," Thiago muttered as he rubbed his stinging ear gingerly. "That thing fucking hurts," he mumbled.

"I know it hurts, that's why I did it! Now, I don't give a fuck what you're fighting over!" Brandt hissed.

"But he–"

"Shut it, Beignet! You've been a dick and I hope you get a nosebleed! Now you, go to your room!" Brandt shouted at Shawn as he pointed to the dark hall.

"Are you fucking pissing me?" Shawn said in disbelief as he finally got to his feet and stared at Brandt. Brandt whacked him in the head again.

"That's for being a dick," he said. He then dropped the magazine and dug around in his pocket until he pulled out an object, yanked at it, and thrust it into Shawn's horrified face.

Shawn backed away a few steps as Thiago finally got to his feet, and Thiago's heart stopped when he realized Brandt had just pulled the pin out of a grenade.

"I'll stick this so far up your ass, the smoke will come out your ears," Brandt growled.

"Holy hell!" Nikolaus exclaimed. "Can you put that thing back in that?" he asked as he scooted backward on the ground.

"We won't find out unless Beignet moves his ass!" Brandt said gleefully. "Zed, you too! Move it! And if I hear any more fighting I'll make you sit on the sofa and hold hands all fucking night!"

Thiago and Shawn scrambled away, leaving Nikolaus alone to discover if a pin could be reinserted into a grenade.

XVI.

CARL groaned and rolled to shield his eyes against the sudden burst of light, but the movement caused a bolt of burning pain to shoot up his ribcage and he groaned again.

Fucking hell. Being shot was a bitch. Carl cracked his eyes open and looked up at Brandt.

"Sorry," Brandt whispered as he pushed the door shut and stepped closer to the bed. "How you feeling, Trigger?"

"Been better," Carl mumbled. "What was all the yelling about?"

"Oh, nothing. Beignet was trying to kill Zed, I think. No big deal," Brandt said as he sat carefully on the side of the bed and leaned over, placing a hand on the mattress next to Carl's other side and looking down at him affectionately.

Carl's eyes widened in alarm. "Why? What happened?"

"I dunno," Brandt answered with a shrug. His free hand came to rest on Carl's forehead and Carl closed his eyes and enjoyed the feeling of the tender touch.

"What did Zed do to Dixie?" Carl asked as he struggled against sleep.

"What makes you think he did anything to Dixie?" Brandt asked curiously.

"Never seen Shawn lose control unless it was over Remy," Carl said seriously as he opened his eyes again.

"Hmm. Guess I should have asked, huh?" Brandt said nonchalantly as he got up and went to the bureau.

"Probably," Carl said with a slight smile. "What are you doing?"

"Time to change the dressing."

"Oh, fuck."

"No no, I know what I'm doing this time," Brandt insisted as he walked back over and turned on the lamp at the side of the bed.

"But… but why don't you call Zed, yeah? We can find out what happened while he's dressing it," Carl suggested desperately as Brandt pulled the covers back off his body. Carl tried to scoot away, but he was too weak and tired and slow.

"Nah!" Brandt said as he ripped the tape away from Carl's skin and yanked the bloody dressing from his body. It not only tore away hair and skin, but also the dried blood that had attached to the open wound. Carl whimpered and bit his lip. Brandt grinned winningly. Sadistic bastard. "We'll find out what happened in the morning," Brandt added absently as he fiddled with a roll of gauze. "Did I get all that tape?"

"If you do that again, I may piss myself," Carl mumbled weakly.

"Well, can you stand up then? Don't want to get the bed wet," Brandt requested distractedly as he put the gauze down and took the little brown bottle he had retrieved and opened it carefully.

"Fucking hell, Wally. Go get Thiago," Carl pleaded miserably.

"It's just disinfectant," Brandt said defensively. "I can't pour it on you when you're laying in bed."

The hurt brown eyes staring down at Carl almost convinced him to go ahead and let Brandt change the dressing. He was so protective and caring and almost gentle, and he so wanted to help. Carl almost decided to let Brandt go ahead and change the dressing again. Almost.

"It's not disinfectant, Wally! It's rubbing alcohol!" he yelled desperately.

"But–"

"Go get Thiago!"

XVII.

Shawn stared up at the dark ceiling and fumed. Remy had betrayed him. He'd trampled all over Shawn's trust and practically laughed in his face afterwards, trying to use *him* as an excuse for the betrayal.

Shawn was so angry that he was disregarding several facts about his and Remy's relationship. The whole goddamn thing was based on a betrayal. Shawn's betrayal. But Shawn was conveniently pushing that to the far reaches of his mind and holding desperately to his anger. The anger was his safe mode. He knew how to be angry.

There was a light scratching at the door, but Shawn barely moved when the door cracked open and then closed again.

"Did you get the pin back in?" he asked his new companion.

"Brandt took care of it," Nikolaus said as he slipped out of his shoes and sat on the edge of the bed to remove his socks. "Does it bother anyone else that Brandt always looks confused when someone else is terrified? I mean, he doesn't seem to understand that normal human beings don't like the prospect of being blown up."

Shawn hummed noncommittally and Nikolaus turned to look at him as he stripped off his T-shirt.

"I thought you might want company," Nikolaus said softly. "If not I can leave you alone. Sleep in there with Thiago."

Shawn looked at Nikolaus then and scowled in the moonlight.

"I'm afraid I wouldn't be very good company tonight," Shawn responded gruffly, and Nikolaus nodded.

"I hate to tell you, Shawn, but you're never very good company," he said with a smile.

Shawn glared at him, but he had to give the young German credit for being brave enough to say it.

"Thiago would never hurt Remy, y'know," Nikolaus said assuredly.

Shawn shot into a sitting position on the bed and took Nikolaus by the throat, pulling him closer and growling when their faces almost touched.

"You heard what he said," Shawn snarled.

"And you know Remy better than that," Nikolaus stated with difficulty. Shawn frowned as his grip loosened. He didn't follow. "You know that one, Remy's never as drugged, oblivious, helpless, tied up, lost, confused, or clumsy as he acts. And two, that if Thiago had wanted to fuck him, Remy wouldn't have refused him, drugged or not."

Shawn growled again and shoved Nikolaus backwards, but the younger man caught himself before toppling over the edge of the bed and he turned around on his knees to face Shawn angrily.

"You're being a stubborn fuck," he spat.

Shawn gaped at him. Wow. Nikolaus was angry. Shawn had never seen him angry before.

"He loves you, Shawn. And you're not only willing to throw that away for some fucked up sense of loyalty, but you're willing to take his life over it. And you love him! That's the worst part of it! If there were any doubts before, seeing you fucking pull Thiago across that table was enough to convince me. Why are you doing this to yourself?"

"This is the way it is, Niko," Shawn said sternly. "Once trust is lost in this game there's nothing left."

"This isn't a fucking game, Shawn! Will you actually be able to point a gun at Remy and pull the trigger? Because none of us will do it for you, that's for fucking certain! Can you squeeze that trigger and know that you'll never see him again?"

"Nikolaus–"

"Know that you'll never hear his voice again? Never hold him close to you and feel his body next to yours? Never–"

"Stop it!"

"No! Because you have to think about those things! You have to think about what the rest of your life will be like without him! And you'll have to think about the look in his eyes when he looks at you that last time. You'll have to see those heartbreaking, pleading eyes every time you close your own. He'll haunt you 'til your dying day, Shawn, and you'll be miserable and empty for it."

Shawn had been angry. He'd been fuming. Seething, even. But as Nikolaus's words sank in, a knot formed in Shawn's throat and he couldn't breathe. He could picture it just as surely as if he had done it already. Remy on his knees, bound hand and foot, looking up at him with those deep brown eyes. Shawn knew what he'd see in those eyes as he pointed the gun. He would see pain and betrayal. He would see hope and supplication. He would see despair and regret. Worst of all, though, he would see love and forgiveness.

Shawn slumped back onto the mattress and covered his face with his hands.

"What do I do, Niko?" he asked miserably

"That's easy," Nikolaus said immediately. "You have to talk to him. Get his side of the story."

"Right," Shawn said after a moment of silence. "Right," he repeated quietly as he let his hands fall to his sides and he looked up at Nikolaus. "Thank you," he said quietly.

Nikolaus nodded and settled down cross-legged on the bed. "You want to be left alone tonight? You wanna go talk to him now?"

"No. We'll give him the night to calm down, get those fucking drugs out of his system. Give me the night to calm down, too."

"Fair enough," Nikolaus said softly, and he swung his legs around to hang off the side of the bed and made to get up.

"Niko?" Shawn ventured as he put out his hand to stop Nikolaus from leaving. "Keep me company?"

XVIII.

NIKOLAUS knew if he didn't stay with Shawn tonight, no one would. He also knew Shawn didn't need to be alone. He needed to have company to keep him from brooding, because in a man like Shawn, brooding was dangerous. Nikolaus suspected he was the only one who actually felt sorry for Shawn right now. But he could understand where Shawn was coming from. Nikolaus felt betrayed, too.

All that time and Remy had been working against them. Or had he? Had it been John who turned him? Nikolaus didn't know, but he knew how Shawn felt. Angry. Betrayed. Lost. He was definitely in need of a commiseration. Why not share in the misery?

XVIV

BRANDT didn't get what the problem was. He could change a dressing. A little burn from the alcohol, a little gauze, a lot of tape. Ta da! You had a dressing!

Carl was being a pansy.

Nevertheless, Brandt had gone and gotten Thiago, as requested. He sat on the end of the bed, watching like a hawk to make sure Thiago didn't hurt Carl. But Thiago's movements were quick and gentle, and Carl didn't cry out once, so Brandt reckoned he was okay.

"There," Thiago said finally, and he rested his hand on Carl's forehead briefly before sitting back into the chair he'd dragged over to the bed.

Thiago looked tense and drawn, and every sound that issued from the outer rooms, whether it was big or small, made him glance at the closed door worriedly.

"Beignet wouldn't hurt Dixie," Brandt told him confidently, and Thiago glanced at him and nodded. "Did you hurt Dixie?" Brandt asked calmly, though his eyes flashed in warning, and Thiago swallowed with difficulty when he looked at him.

"Of course not," Thiago said softly. "But I'm afraid I made Shawn think I did."

"Why?" Carl asked curiously as he settled himself back into his warm little cocoon.

Thiago looked at them both apologetically. "Was sort of a… a rash decision on my part. I was just so fucking angry with him. Wanted him to suffer. I know it probably wasn't the smartest course of action, but…."

"I'm sure you had good reason, Zed. It'll work out."

Brandt and Thiago sat staring at Carl for several moments, and then Thiago glanced quickly at Brandt before sitting forward and asking, "Can I ask you a question?"

"Sure," Carl responded sleepily.

"I understand Beignet and Dixie. There're reasons. I understand Gizmo and Trigger, 'cause those are kind of obvious. But Wally and Zed? Where the fuck did you get those?"

Brandt sat forward and watched Carl curiously. He and Remy had been wondering that earlier. Maybe he would get an answer.

"I dunno," Carl said lazily as his eyes drifted back open. "He kinda looks like a Wally, doesn't he?"

Thiago and Brandt looked at each other.

"What's a Wally?" Thiago asked in confusion.

"Australian who likes to blow shit up," Carl answered.

"True that," Brandt agreed happily.

"And a Zed?" Thiago asked. "Isn't that what the Brits call the last letter of the alphabet?"

Brandt nodded affirmatively. "So do Aussies and Kiwis."

"Zed," Carl answered in a far off, dazed voice, "is Djed. Was an Egyptian symbol."

"Oh," Thiago answered after a moment of confused silence.

"It was a pillar," Carl murmured. "Stood for stability.

Brandt and Thiago were both silent.

"You're a fucking pillar, mate," Carl murmured as he drifted off.

XX.

REMY stood at the door, listening intently. He was pretty sure that everyone was occupied. It was now or never.

"C'mon, Boss. Time for you to go," Remy said quietly.

Gray was by his side in an instant and staring at him angrily. "I'm not leaving without you," he said determinedly. "That bastard will kill you, Remy. Just because you love him, doesn't mean it's mutual."

"I know," Remy said softly. "But I can't leave Thiago here alone."

"Remy! For Christ's sake, listen to reason! They will kill us," Gray said to him slowly. "Thiago's fine. No one suspects a fucking thing and he knows what he's doing. He's made it this far, hasn't he?"

"So did I, Boss," Remy said calmly. "Everyone slips up. And Thiago's the fucking mastermind, you know? He'll need help."

"You really do love him, don't you?" Gray asked resignedly.

"Thiago?" Remy asked in shock.

"Shawn," Gray corrected with an exasperated sigh.

"Yes," Remy answered instantly. "If he's going to kill me, then… then he'll do it. But I love him. I don't want to be without him."

"Remy, there are other people in this world who love you and aren't looking to kill you," Gray said softly.

"Gray…."

"I'm not just talking about me. Thiago'll kill me if anything happens to you. And that big crazy bloke was ready to defend you, too. They all love you. Don't throw your life away like this."

Remy couldn't think of anything to say in response, and he gaped at Gray for several seconds, searching for words.

"I don't… okay," was all he could come up with in the end.

Gray sighed wearily and cupped Remy's face with his hands. "We'll follow them, then, if that will make you feel better," he said finally. "We'll watch from afar and make certain Thi gets through it."

"All of them," Remy corrected.

"What?"

"Make certain all of them get through it."

Gray smiled slightly and nodded. "Your loyalty knows no bounds, does it?" he asked sadly.

"I suppose not," Remy murmured. "Now's our only chance if we're going," he whispered with a heavy heart. "Let's do it."

XXI.

THIAGO awoke in his own bed with Brandt's body wrapped firmly around him. They'd left Carl to sleep alone so as not to further injure him with Brandt's nocturnal flailing, and Thiago had taken the punishment instead. He had to admit, though, waking up holding someone was a very nice feeling. Brandt murmured something that sounded disturbingly like 'bam' and nuzzled closer, and Thiago smiled slightly.

Then it hit him like an anvil falling from the ceiling. Remy and Gray would be gone by now. Suddenly, Thiago was inexplicably lonely, even knowing he still had four companions with him. The loss of one was an incredible blow. Thiago was just disentangling himself from Brandt's grasp when the door was kicked open and Shawn stormed into the room like an angel of death intent upon taking Thiago with him.

"What–"

"They're gone!" Shawn roared as he took hold of Thiago and pulled him the rest of the way out of the bed.

"What? Who? Remy?" Thiago stuttered, so surprised by Shawn's entrance that his shock sounded completely natural.

"No, the fucking tapestries!" Shawn spat sarcastically. "Yes, Remy! They've fucking escaped!"

"But… but, how did… what…."

"Come with me," Shawn growled as he dragged Thiago out of the room. Brandt was up and following, if not entirely aware yet, and Nikolaus danced back and forth in the hallway like he was afraid to stand still lest Shawn catch him. "We have to find them," Shawn said as he pushed Thiago into the room where Remy and Gray had been held. There was no hint of recent inhabitancy. Everything was neat and orderly, and every trace of the two men was gone. Their clothing, their bindings…

even the bed was made.

"Jesus," Thiago breathed. "It's like they were never here," he murmured as he looked around the room. Brandt and Nikolaus followed Shawn in, and when Thiago turned around he was surprised to see Carl standing in the doorway with one hand on his sore ribs and the other holding a very large gun. "You should be in bed," Thiago chastised automatically.

"Heard shouting. Thought maybe I had the chance to shoot something," Carl responded succinctly.

Thiago raised his eyebrows questioningly, but said nothing.

"C'mon, Thi," Shawn said urgently. "I need your help."

"What do you plan to do?" Thiago asked warily as he followed Shawn out of the room and down the hallway toward the living room. He knew they'd never be able to track Remy and Gray, even if Thiago didn't plan on sabotaging the efforts.

"I've got to find him," Shawn said quickly as he went to the dining table and gathered various weapons and began strapping them to his person. Thiago stood slightly behind him and fought back an onslaught of doubt. What if they hadn't had enough time to get far enough away? Shawn might be able to find them. Thiago hadn't counted on Shawn being set on revenge like this. He'd assumed that Shawn would just let them go and vow to catch them later. This was not good.

Shawn was still speaking, talking about Remy's habits of going to ground near the coast as he walked toward the kitchen to retrieve his knife. Thiago's head snapped around when Shawn cut off in mid-sentence. Thiago saw him standing frozen in the entryway of the kitchen and his heart sank. He hurried to stand behind Shawn and see what he was looking at, and the sight made his breath catch.

"Didn't see that coming," Carl murmured into Thiago's ear as he came up behind him. Thiago would have responded, but he couldn't seem to find his tongue.

This was bad. This was very bad.

XXII.

"REMY?" Nikolaus whispered into the stunned silence that followed Shawn's discovery.

Carl swayed on his feet and gripped the closest thing to him to steady himself, which just happened to be Thiago. Thiago held Carl upright, and they both glanced at Shawn warily.

The man stood like a stone statue. His jaw was set, as if he was gritting his teeth, and his eyes were flat and dangerous as they fixed on Remy. Thiago's body was tense beneath Carl's hands, but then Carl supposed he was a bit tense as well.

Remy was either very brave or very suicidal. Carl couldn't decide which.

Maybe he was both.

Remy sat at the kitchen table, idly stirring a cup of coffee. He wasn't exactly on edge, but he certainly wasn't relaxed, either. He casually leaned back in the chair, his hand on the spoon moving it in slow circles, but he was keeping both feet firmly planted on the ground as if prepared for a sudden movement, and his free hand was clenched into a fist in his lap. He stared unblinkingly back at Shawn, his face completely devoid of expression.

Carl shivered uncontrollably, whether from his recent exertion and loss of blood, or from the overwhelming emotion of the scene, he wasn't sure. The younger man had had the chance to run and yet there he sat, calmly awaiting his doom at Shawn's betrayed hands.

"I would have made breakfast, but I didn't figure any of you would eat it, considering…," Remy said softly with a small gesture to the tray of leftover pastries.

A low growling started from some unidentifiable source, and Carl looked around in alarm when he realized it was coming from Shawn. Carl knew Remy needed protection; one of them needed to restrain Shawn before he did something they would all regret, but Carl's body wasn't functioning properly and he felt himself sinking slowly back into the oblivion of blood loss. Thiago held him close and they slowly slid to the floor together, unable to do anything but watch in horror as Shawn pounced forward like a panther attacking a bunny.

'Poor Dixie,' Carl thought disjointedly as the loss of blood finally overwhelmed his brain.

XXIII.

SHAWN was aware of the commotion behind him but he didn't care what it was about. His world consisted solely of Remy sitting in front of him and the overwhelming ache in his own chest. He never wanted to feel like this again. He had to be rid of the ache once and for all.

Remy stood hastily and put his hands out in front of him as Shawn quickly crossed the room. The mug of coffee toppled over and the steaming liquid splashed across the table as Remy backed up and nudged his chair with the back of his leg.

"Shawn, please," Remy said softly. "Let me explain before you–"

Shawn didn't let him finish. He grabbed Remy by his upper arms and pulled him toward him, crushing their mouths together and holding Remy to him as if he might be ripped away at any moment.

Remy was rigid and tense in his arms, but as soon as he realized Shawn wasn't trying to do him any physical damage, he wrapped his arms around Shawn's torso and returned the kiss hungrily. Shawn's world completely imploded as he felt Remy in his arms once more. God, he'd missed this feeling.

"I thought you'd left," Shawn panted in between the short, heated kisses they shared. "I thought you'd gone for good," he whispered as he took Remy's face in his hands and drank in the features he'd dreamed of the whole night before.

Remy dug his fingers into Shawn's back and pressed their bodies even closer, and he shook his head wordlessly as Shawn buried his face in Remy's neck and breathed in his scent. They stood there in the middle of the kitchen for several long minutes, clinging to one another desperately and completely disregarding the small amount of panic Carl's collapse caused the others.

"I couldn't," Remy gasped as he ran his hand up Shawn's back and into Shawn's hair. "I couldn't leave you. Any of you. I couldn't just... I love you, Shawn," Remy whispered desperately, and Shawn's throat constricted painfully. "Please don't be angry anymore. I couldn't bear it if–"

Shawn squeezed Remy tight, cutting off his words. He raised his head and looked into Remy's liquid brown eyes. He was an utter prick. A complete and total bastard and he didn't deserve this. He didn't deserve to be loved like this. Especially not after all he had done, and all that he still had to do.

"God help you, Remy," he breathed finally. "Your loyalty is gonna get you killed," he whispered with a sad smile as he backed out of Remy's arms.

Remy swallowed with difficulty and a single tear trailed down his face as he broke their eye contact and looked down. Shawn reached into the waistband of his jeans and withdrew the knife he'd stuffed there earlier. Remy's eyes followed the movement. He looked back up at Shawn as the blade flashed in the yellow light of the kitchen.

Shawn saw it then; the look that had haunted his dreams. Loving and pleading and resigned. Desperate. Forgiving.

Forgiving of the fact that Shawn was about to run him through with his own knife.

It was the forgiveness that forced the tears to finally flow, tears that Shawn had been holding back for too long. Shawn didn't bother to wipe them away as he flipped the knife in his hand and handed it to Remy, handle first.

"I believe this is yours," Shawn said with difficulty.

Remy stared at the knife for several breathless seconds before his eyes slowly rose to meet Shawn's once more.

"I don't...." He trailed off and shook his head. "I don't understand, Shawn."

"Take it, lad," Shawn urged as several tears made wet trails down the sides of his face. "You're with me 'til the end now. I won't have you face it unarmed," he added with a little smile.

XXIV.

NIKOLAUS found himself unable to fully express how relieved he was.

Remy was there with them, unharmed and sort of forgiven. Shawn was no longer sulking or mean. Carl was awake again and unsuccessfully trying to fend off Brandt's repeated attempts to pour orange juice down his throat. Thiago was quiet and contemplative, but then Thiago was always quiet and contemplative, and as long as he didn't mind Nikolaus cuddling up next to him in the oversized chair, Nikolaus didn't care what he was contemplating.

Shawn and Remy sat together on the sofa, not exactly touching one another, but close enough that a jerk of the leg or a twitch of the arm would create contact. Remy kept sneaking worried looks at Shawn as the six of them discussed this new turn of events, and when Shawn saw him, the man would run his hands through Remy's hair reassuringly. Nikolaus was so focused on watching them that he almost couldn't concentrate on the conversation.

"So tell us, Dixie, how long have you been conspiring with Asshole, exactly?" Carl asked in a weak, irritated voice as he swatted Brandt's hand away from his forehead.

"Well," Remy shifted uncomfortably and his eyes darted back and forth between the four of them. "Conspiring is a bit…."

"Remy," Shawn said softly, and Remy immediately snapped to attention. "No more skipping around."

"Right," Remy said immediately, looking down at his hands as he clasped them together and let them hang between his knees. "Six months, give or take."

Nikolaus gaped, as much at the information that Remy had been a subversive element the whole time as the fact that five little words from Shawn would make him admit it. Apparently, Remy was desperate to make amends, and he was trying hard to come clean with them. Nikolaus appreciated the effort, though he didn't know how any of them would be able to completely trust the man now. In all honesty, Nikolaus was still smarting from the betrayal. He was pretty sure they all were.

"Six months," Brandt repeated flatly. Remy swallowed heavily and looked back at Brandt unerringly. "Did you blow up the cabin?"

"No," Remy said immediately. He sat forward, looking as if he were about to defend himself, but Shawn gripped his arm and Remy turned to look at him.

"Why are you working for him?" Shawn asked sadly.

Remy looked at him guiltily. "That's complicated," he said with difficulty, unable to meet Shawn's piercing green eyes.

"We agreed, Remy," Shawn said sternly. "No more lies. No more half-truths. There had to be a reason, I know you too well to think otherwise. Now what was it?"

"Gray came to me. Told me that if I didn't help him that...," Remy licked his lips and his eyes flicked to the side before he turned to face Shawn completely. "That–"

"Who is Gray working for, Remy?" Thiago asked suddenly, and Nikolaus was glad the older man had taken pity on Remy. Nikolaus was squirming, and he hadn't even done anything wrong yet.

Remy turned to look at Thiago and didn't even blink before speaking.

"I never really knew," Remy said almost defiantly. "When he came to me I had never heard of any of the names he dropped, or of the Archer. I just knew that he was threatening me and that I had no choice but to comply."

"Is Gray working for the Archer?" Shawn asked as he glared at Thiago.

"I honestly never found out before it all went to shit," Remy said flatly. "Though, I think it's probably safe to assume that he is, considering everything that's come to light recently."

"Gray giving us the key to the message, for instance?" Nikolaus asked uncomfortably.

Remy nodded and turned to look at Shawn. "Whether he was telling me the truth or not, I don't know, but I couldn't take the chance," he said quietly. "He told me you were in danger and–"

"Why didn't you come to me?" Shawn asked almost desperately.

"You were on a mission, Shawn. You were out of reach."

Shawn sat quietly, letting that sink in. Nikolaus was surprised to see Shawn break the eye contact guiltily before speaking. "What was the threat?" he asked softly. It looked as if Shawn felt badly for grilling Remy on the whole matter, but they all knew it had to be done.

"I... I don't know," Remy said resignedly.

Even Nikolaus could tell Remy didn't want to answer the question. Whether he was telling the truth was questionable, but Shawn simply nodded and ran his fingertips lightly down the side of Remy's face.

"All right, then," Shawn said softly before turning to address the rest of them. "Starting right now... Brandt! Pay attention, for fuck's sake! He doesn't need any more juice! Christ, Remy, will you do something with him?" Shawn shouted in agitation as he got up to rescue Carl.

Brandt stood up protectively in front of Carl, who was reclining on the sofa and looking in desperate need of rescue, and Nikolaus sensed a fight coming as Shawn squared his shoulders and growled at Brandt.

"Wally!" Remy called as he dug in his pocket. "C'mere, *podna*," he said as he brought out a green Bic lighter and flicked it open.

Brandt's eyes lit up and his entire posture relaxed as the flame flickered in Remy's hand.

"There's a good nutter," Remy said in satisfaction as Brandt glared at Shawn in passing and flopped down beside Remy. He pulled Remy to him and tried unsuccessfully to simultaneously smother him and take the lighter.

"God. What was I saying?" Shawn asked irritably as he slid to the floor in front of Carl's sofa and sighed heavily.

"Uhh…," Nikolaus and Thiago answered simultaneously as they watched Remy struggle away from Brandt's grasp. Brandt was now thoroughly molesting the younger man; Remy looked like a wet kitten trying to climb out of the toilet, and if they expected any more answers out of him, they would need to rescue him as well.

"Hey, Niko," Thiago whispered.

A dreadful feeling began to rise in Nikolaus's chest, and he suddenly knew how the bait in a trap must feel.

"No," he protested desperately as he sank further into the chair cushion. "Remy can handle him."

Thiago snickered, and they watched Brandt wrap his arms around Remy, pull him into a bear hug, and snatch the lighter. After getting his hands on it, he immediately settled down, and Remy looked at Thiago and Nikolaus and rolled his eyes as he was stuffed under Brandt's arm like a teddy bear and held captive there.

"You were saying from now on, something something," Remy supplied in a muffled voice as he continued to unsuccessfully try to free himself.

"Right," Shawn said grimly. "I don't care where our allegiances were before." His eyes held firmly with Remy's as he spoke. "From now on, we are loyal only to one another," he said slowly.

The words hit chords in Nikolaus's body that he hadn't known existed. The hair on his arms raised, and he shivered slightly as Thiago nodded beside him.

"Does everyone understand?" Shawn asked softly.

There were murmured affirmatives and nods, and Remy's eyes reflected the lights in the room liquidly as he looked at Shawn gratefully. Nikolaus felt like crying for him, he looked so relieved.

"So what's the plan?" Carl asked as he struggled to sit up.

Shawn got to his feet and helped the man to sit, and he sat next to him on the sofa and allowed Carl to lean back against him. Nikolaus watched in interest as Shawn's fingers absently twirled around Carl's hair, and he slid his gaze to Remy. The younger man watched Shawn intently, but Nikolaus could see nothing in his demeanor but affection and an eagerness to obey. Hopefully, this would mark the end of all the relationship strife they'd suffered. There were no more pairs or trios. They were six now. Just the Six.

"Remy?" Thiago asked as he shifted slightly against Nikolaus's body. Remy peered out from under Brandt's enveloping arms and raised his eyebrows inquiringly. "What was your and Gray's plan?"

"Well, I was sort of just acting under orders," Remy apologetically. "I only knew the basics, but the only reason I didn't fight it was because he was after the same thing we were."

"What do you mean?" Nikolaus asked.

"He was going to help us get to the Oliver woman."

"What?" Thiago and Shawn both practically shouted. Remy flinched and Brandt cradled him protectively. Nikolaus watched in amusement as Remy flailed uselessly and was literally pulled into Brandt's lap. Finally, he gave up and simply lay there with his chest against Brandt's thighs as Brandt rocked him like a baby and glared at Shawn and Thiago. Nikolaus smirked at Brandt and tried to pay attention to what was being said.

"I told you! That's why I went along with his… his drugging plan," Remy said miserably as he rested his cheek against Brandt's forearm. "I couldn't just come out and tell you that I had a way to get to her, but I knew we had to do it. We're weaponless, after all."

"So the fuss you made about my getting into drag?" Shawn asked wryly.

"I knew it would cause a fight," Remy admitted in the same miserable tone. "The more activity… you know…."

"The faster the drugs would hit us," Shawn said knowingly as he nodded slightly.

"How'd you get them into us?" Brandt asked with interest. "Aside from, you know, shooting me."

"They were in the breakfast pastries I brought in. The muffins, mostly."

"Is that why I couldn't eat your fucking scones?" Nikolaus asked irritably. Remy nodded and hid his face against the crook of Brandt's elbow.

"But I didn't eat any of it," Thiago said in confusion.

"I may have slipped you and Shawn some in your drinks. I figured with that nasty tea you drink, you'd never notice. And Shawn's… sorry, *podna*, I may have overloaded yours a bit."

"You little fuck," Shawn said with a smile.

"Sorry, Beignet. Consider it my shot in the ass back at you," Remy said with a cheeky salute and a smirk he tried unsuccessfully to hide.

"Sneaky little bastard," Brandt grumbled. Remy struggled to turn and looked up over his shoulder at the big man.

"I'm really sorry I shot you, man," he said sincerely.

"S'okay, Dixie," Brandt said affectionately as he ruffled Remy's curls. "You're a good enough shag that it made up for it. We're even."

"Right," Remy muttered in a slightly befuddled voice. "If that's the case, then do you think you can you let me go, now? Since we're even and all?"

"Why would I do that?" Brandt asked with a grin.

"Brandt, watch his back," Shawn cautioned seriously. "He's got problems with it."

"What sort of problems?" Nikolaus asked curiously.

"Doesn't matter," Remy said with a careless sweep of his hand as he was gently placed onto the cushion beside Brandt and cuddled in a manner most unseemly for a man of Brandt's size and temperament. "So, what's the plan?"

"I think it's pretty obvious," Thiago said quietly, drawing everyone's attention to him. "We have to find Gray."

"How?" Carl asked.

"Remy?" Thiago prompted.

Remy looked at them all carefully. "When he thought I was leaving with him, he said that we would follow all of you, to watch over you."

"Watch over us?" Nikolaus repeated disbelievingly.

"Gray's not all that bad a guy," Remy said defensively. Shawn made a 'pfft' noise and Remy glared at him. Remy sighed heavily before disentangling himself from Brandt's grasp and standing up.

"So? Are we going after Gray or… my God, Wally! Is that a grenade?" Remy asked in a near panic as he pointed at the oversized chair on which Nikolaus and Thiago were sitting.

Nikolaus and Thiago moved almost instantly, scampering away from the chair and taking cover discreetly behind the two sofas.

"No worries, Dixie, it's not live," Brandt said as he stretched his hands over his head and relaxed back onto the sofa.

"Holy hell!" Shawn exclaimed, and he was up and dragging Carl off the sofa and toward the hall before the rest of them could register his obvious terror.

"Shawn? What?" Thiago asked in distress.

"That's what he said in Albuquerque!" Shawn shouted before he slammed the bedroom door behind him and Carl.

"Bugger," Brandt breathed. "That one came from a bad batch," he told them all defensively. "The pin had been out of it for nearly a week and then one day–BAM!" he yelled theatrically.

"Fucking hell, Wally!" Remy cried as he scrambled over Brandt's body and over the back of the sofa. He crouched on the floor and shouted, "What batch did *this* grenade come from? Is the pin out of it, too?"

"Hmm? Oh… uhh, well it was one of the ones I had here as a backup so… those were… hold on, I know this one… H17 no 19… no wait…," Brandt murmured as he looked up, accessing his memory and thinking hard.

Thiago grabbed Nikolaus's shirtfront and slowly dragged him down until they, too, were cowering behind the sofa.

"Hmm… H17. Yeah, it was the batch before the duds."

"They're not duds if they go off, you wanker!" Shawn yelled from the hall. "Remy! Thiago! Get your asses over here. Brandt! Clean up that fucking bomb!"

"It's not a bomb, you ignorant fuck! It's a grenade!"

"If it explodes, it's a bomb in my world. Get it the fuck out of here!" Shawn yelled as Nikolaus and Thiago crawled toward him. "You said he took care of it," Shawn hissed at Nikolaus as they reached the relative safety of the hallway.

"I thought he did! Apparently to Brandt, stuffing it under the furniture *is* taking care of it!" Nikolaus snapped quietly.

"C'mon, Wally," Remy coaxed from behind the sofa. "C'mon, mate, it's a fuck of a lot safer over here, yeah?"

"Well, do you want me to hide, or do you want me to get rid of it?" Brandt asked irritably as he leaned over the back of the sofa and looked down at Remy curiously.

"I'd really prefer you get rid of it," Remy answered matter-of-factly as he looked up at Brandt from his spot on the floor. He didn't seem at all ashamed of hiding behind the sofa, but then again, Nikolaus and the others were hiding in the hallway, so Nikolaus couldn't really judge the man.

"Help me, then," Brandt said as he scruffed Remy by the back of his collar and pulled him back over the sofa.

Nikolaus and the others watched from the hallway, and Nikolaus could practically feel Shawn vibrating next to him as Brandt dragged Remy back over the sofa to help retrieve the stray grenade.

"Fucking hell! I just got him back. I can't sit here and watch him be blown to smithereens now," Shawn growled finally and he started crawling forward. Thiago's hand shot out and gripped him by his arm.

"Shawn, we can't afford to lose all three of you," Thiago said regretfully.

Shawn's jaw clenched but he nodded. Nikolaus was slightly surprised to realize that Carl crouched behind him.

"Get back in there, Trigger," Shawn hissed.

"Fuck you, Beignet. It's a fucking scratch. If Wally's gonna get blown up, I at least want to be there to nurse him back to health," Carl said with a certain sadistic pleasure that made Nikolaus do a double take. Carl looked scary now. And slightly mad.

'God, please don't let the madness be catching,' Nikolaus prayed. They'd already lost Remy to it.

They could no longer see Remy and Brandt, and Nikolaus huffed slightly. "Why do you call him 'Wally?'" he asked Carl in a whisper.

"He told us that he looks like a Wally," Thiago answered absently, his gruff whisper ghosting across Nikolaus's ear and sending shivers down his spine.

"I did not," Carl protested in the same whisper the others were using, as if a voice any louder would set off the bomb. Grenade. Whateverthefuck.

"You did so," Thiago said as he turned to look at Carl.

"When?"

"Apparently, when you were delirious," Thiago said with a shrug. "So why do you call him 'Wally' then?"

"Cause he's Australian."

"What?" the three of them echoed, the grenade/bomb forgotten as they all turned to look at Carl. Yep. The madness was definitely catching.

"You know, Australia? Wally? All of 'em really. What the fuck is wrong with you three?" Carl asked irritably.

"So why do you call me 'Zed' again?" Thiago asked curiously.

Carl shrugged and grinned. "You kinda look like one," he said with a cheeky grin and wink.

"You son of a–"

"Wally!" Remy's panicked voice cried out just before the explosion interrupted their trivialities.

XXV.

BRANDT coughed and sputtered and waved his hands through the cloud of smoke, and his eyes landed on Remy as the younger man rolled back and forth on the ground. Brandt pounced on him and beat him until the flames went out.

Brandt straddled him and held him down to keep him from panicking as his jacket smoldered, leaning over to look into Remy's wide, frightened eyes.

"*Fah-yuh*," Remy muttered as he blinked up at him.

"You're awfully sexy when you're flaming, you know that?" Brandt told him with a smile.

Remy's eyes widened further and he began to shake. "I was on fucking fire, you… *bracque*!" Remy cried in an irritated squeak as he tried to squirm out from under Brandt's grasp.

"Mmm," Brandt responded thoughtfully, and he licked his lips as he looked over Remy's body for injuries. "Not hurt then, are you?" he asked finally. Remy's tongue had just barely touched the back of his teeth to form the word 'no' when Brandt bent down and kissed him hungrily. Remy made a surprised noise into Brandt's mouth, and Brandt pressed into him, still able to feel the heat from the flames he had just put out.

"Jesus, somebody get a fucking water hose," Thiago mumbled as the rest of them came up to investigate the small blast. Remy wrapped his arms around Brandt's neck and deepened the kiss before gripping Brandt's shaggy curls and yanking his head back. Remy glared up at him, and Brandt grinned widely.

"You did that on purpose," Remy growled angrily.

"Yeah," Brandt said happily. "Well, you said to get rid of it."

"I didn't mean to set fire to the fucking thing! What if it had gone off? It could have killed us all! Not to mention the fact that I was holding it in my fucking hands, you wank!" Remy shouted as he shook Brandt's head by his hair.

"But you're not on fire anymore," Brandt pointed out reasonably. "And you're not permanently damaged, so–"

"I think I pissed myself," Remy admitted with a slight smile. "That was pretty fucking awesome, though. Will you show me how you did that?" he asked eagerly, and he and Brandt grinned at one another.

"Yeah. Later. I definitely need to fuck something now," Brandt said as Thiago and Nikolaus both rolled their eyes and walked away. Brandt looked at Shawn, who scowled down at both of them. "Perhaps we can discuss this later," Brandt murmured as he hefted his body off Remy's and pulled the other man up with him. Remy staggered and held on to Brandt as Brandt righted him, and they both looked at Shawn sheepishly.

"Are you all right?" Shawn asked them both.

Brandt and Remy both nodded.

"Can we get back to what we were doing now?" Thiago asked irritably, and Brandt frowned at him, trying to remember what they'd been doing before the grenade was found. It wouldn't have blown up on them, Brandt was certain of that.

The bastards, they just didn't understand the intricacies of blowing shit up.

"What were we doing?" Remy asked regretfully.

Thiago and Shawn both sighed heavily, and Brandt met Carl's eyes. Carl was trying hard not to laugh. Brandt figured it must hurt him to laugh.

"Poor Trigger," he said as he released Remy and went over to Carl.

"I'm not hurt!" Carl declared in a panic as Brandt closed in on him, and Brandt shook his head as he picked Carl up and gently carried him over to the sofa.

Carl grunted unhappily as Brandt set him down. "Good Trigger," Brandt said as he patted Carl on the head and sat down next to him. Carl sighed heavily and shifted into Brandt's arms, resting his head in Brandt's lap contentedly.

Shawn pawed over Remy, checking him for burns, and Thiago settled down onto the other sofa as Nikolaus walked back into the room.

"I need food," Nikolaus announced as he walked up and plopped down on Carl's other side. "Only thing we have in there are some tainted donuts. What kind of a psychopath ruins donuts like that?" Nikolaus wondered aloud.

"Sorry," Remy mumbled as Shawn took Remy's face in his hands and looked at him closely.

"You're all right, then," Shawn murmured, as if trying to reassure himself. Remy nodded, but Shawn didn't release him.

Brandt watched them fondly. It was good to have them back to normal. Almost normal anyway. Sort of normal. As normal as Shawn and Remy could be.

"You know what, lads?" Shawn said to all of them. They all looked at him expectantly, but he seemed lost in thought as he looked into Remy's face. Finally, he said, "Get some food. Take care of whatever you need." He was still looking at Remy intently, and Remy looked back at him with wide eyes. "Do whatever you need to do, and be back here in four hours. Then we'll start this."

Brandt watched in amusement as Shawn led Remy out of the room, nodding at all of them in passing, and the four remaining men stared at one another in bemused silence for several long minutes.

"You think four hours is enough time for them to make up for all that lost time?" Nikolaus asked in amusement.

"No. But it gives us enough time to go forage for breakfast," Carl answered as he struggled to his feet. "C'mon kiddies, let's leave them to it."

XXVI.

REMY let Shawn lead him down the hall and pull him into one of the bedrooms. He watched tensely as Shawn closed the door to the bedroom and turned around to face him.

Remy stared at him warily, wondering where the lines were now drawn. Before this mission, he'd known Shawn's moods like he knew his own, and he'd always known what the appropriate response was. A year ago, had Shawn been angry with him, Remy would have teased and joked and seduced until Shawn could no longer remember why he was angry. Shawn could always see right through the ploy, of course, but he enjoyed the process, nonetheless. He always allowed it to cheer him up.

But Remy wasn't certain what he should do now. Was he still allowed to do those things? Was he allowed to touch Shawn whenever he wanted? Was he allowed to tease him and make light like he used to? He felt as if he'd lost the privilege. He couldn't even tell if Shawn was still angry.

Remy looked at his companion miserably as Shawn stood at the door and stared blankly at him.

"Remy," Shawn whispered tentatively as he flicked the light switch off, and they stood in the dim light of the bedside lamp.

That was bad. It was always easier to have difficult discussions in the dark. That meant this was going to be a difficult discussion, and that meant that Remy's heart was about to be broken. Again.

"Shawn," Remy replied in a lost voice as Shawn took a step toward him, unable to think of anything else to say in his distress.

"I owe you an apology, lad," Shawn told him as he stepped up and slid his hands gently around Remy's waist.

Remy's hands automatically rested on Shawn's forearms, and he looked at Shawn questioningly. "I think you have that a little backwards, *non*?" he said uncomfortably.

Shawn shook his head and slid one hand around Remy's body as the other came up to cup Remy's face gently. It was an odd position for Remy, considering he was leaning away as he tried to see into Shawn's eyes, but Shawn held him close all the same.

"No. No, I owe you an apology. So many that I've lost count," Shawn whispered as he looked into Remy's eyes steadily.

"Shawn," Remy whispered again uncertainly. He was dumbfounded by Shawn's behavior, and unsure of what to do or say. He'd seen Shawn loving and sincere before, but never like this. There was an underlying sadness to this, and it scared Remy more than any amount of anger ever could. What could Shawn possibly have to apologize for that would cause that level of sadness? Unless… unless he was ending it for good, and this was a pre-emptive apology for finally turning Remy out.

For sending him away.

Remy slid his hands slowly up Shawn's arms, up under the sleeves of the T-shirt he wore and then back down to his forearms. He desperately wanted to feel every inch of Shawn's body under his fingertips, inhale every scent, take in every line and curve.

"I'm sorry, Remy. For all of this," Shawn whispered as his fingers threaded through Remy's curls and his other hand slid beneath the waistband of Remy's jeans and pulled him closer. "There's more, though," he said with difficultly. "We have to talk."

"No," Remy said automatically, trying desperately to avoid the inevitable. "I'll answer whatever you want, Shawn, please. Please, don't do this," Remy begged as a slow, cold panic took over his entire body. "Please, don't send me away, Shawn. I need to be here with you. Just ask me whatever you–"

"Shh shh shh," Shawn soothed as he stroked Remy's cheek gently. "I'm not letting you go anywhere," Shawn said quickly. "You're stuck with me now, whether you like it or not," he added with a small grin. Remy was so relieved he felt a little light-headed as Shawn grinned at him. "You're bloody adorable when you're panicking," Shawn said fondly.

"Well, what the hell, man, you can't pull that 'we have to talk' shit on me and just–"

"Consider it payback for the fake cry," Shawn growled as he leaned in and took Remy's mouth in a slow, gentle kiss.

"That's not funny," Remy mumbled as Shawn slowly kissed the edge of his mouth and then the tip of his chin and then the line of his jaw. Remy shivered.

"Wasn't meant to be," Shawn whispered as he pressed his nose to Remy's temple and inhaled softly. "We've quite a lot to discuss," he added, his lips moving against the skin of Remy's cheek as he spoke. "I didn't think I'd ever have this again."

"I know how you felt," Remy murmured. He looked back up at Shawn and smiled sadly. He'd come so close to ruining this. And he was still playing a dangerous game, a game of carefully phrased answers and omitted truths. But if Shawn found out about Thiago, all hell would break loose. Someone would end up dead. Remy had no choice. "I'm sorry I lied to you, Shawn," he said softly.

"No worries about that now, love," Shawn said with a smile. Remy blinked in surprise at the endearment, and his entire body tingled from the feeling it gave him to hear Shawn say that.

Remy found he had no more words to say, and Shawn took advantage of the silence. Remy allowed him to slowly run his hands up under the flannel shirt he wore and arched his back into the feeling of Shawn's warm hands on his bare skin as he pressed himself against Shawn's bare chest.

Remy hadn't really registered it before, but he realized suddenly that all the others were still in their nightclothes; a variety of boxers, briefs, sweat pants and T-shirts. Shawn must have discovered he was missing first thing. Suddenly, the memories from the morning flooded Remy's brain, and he snickered. Shawn had been strapping on weaponry, getting ready to head out in his bare feet and his thin pajama bottoms.

"Something funny?" Shawn growled mischievously.

Remy's eyes widened innocently. He tried not to snicker, but it was no use. "What were you gonna do, Beignet?" Remy laughed. "Go out in your bunny slippers looking for me?"

"You know damn well my bunny slippers got toasted back at the cabin," Shawn growled teasingly with a smirk.

"That's right. We'll get you some more," Remy murmured seriously just before Shawn kissed him hungrily. Remy wrapped his arms around him and grinned into the kiss.

"I missed you," Shawn murmured to him.

"*Arrête-toi*," Remy breathed as he hugged Shawn close and buried Shawn's face in the hollow of his own neck as he held him. The proximity brought out Shawn's smell so strongly that Remy was momentarily lost in a sea of scent-induced memory, and he let himself enjoy the moment. "Come to bed," he coaxed.

Shawn followed his gentle tug without resistance, and they crawled into the bed and curled up together, enjoying a stolen moment of peace. Remy faded in and out of sleep for the next two or so hours, finally feeling somewhat secure in his position in Shawn's life once more. He hadn't slept the night before, and his batteries were in desperate need of recharging, now that his mind was relatively at ease.

"Remy?" Shawn ventured after a long silence.

"Hmm?"

"Why did Gray shoot you?"

Remy cuddled closer to Shawn, trying to hide his face. He'd vowed to tell the truth whenever he could, and this truth would only hurt him, not Thiago. "The plan was originally to drug you all and not reveal that I was… that I was a mole," he began with difficulty. To his surprise Shawn squeezed him tighter and nuzzled at his hair tentatively. "But then, Brandt just wouldn't go down. We were on short time, so I had to shoot him with a dart."

"So you really did shoot him," Shawn murmured. "I'm not sure I really believed him."

Remy blushed, but he soldiered on with his explanation. "Then Gray came up with this harebrained idea to make you all think I had been coerced, which in a way I had been, but we thought if I were drugged, too, then it… then it might…."

“Take some of the blame from you?” Shawn supplied quietly.

“Something like that,” Remy mumbled miserably. “It was a stupid idea. If we find Boss again, don’t let him make any decisions. Don’t even let him dress himself.”

Shawn laughed quietly, and Remy held him close.

“You two, you worked together for quite a while, didn’t you?” Shawn asked softly.

Remy raised his head. “How did you know?” he asked resignedly.

“You call him Boss,” Shawn answered readily. “You slipped the other day. Called me that when everything was going to shit.” Remy snorted and burrowed his face into Shawn’s chest.

“Gray’s plans always go to shit. Must have been a Pavlovian response.”

“I assume it was a sarcastic kind of thing, then? You calling him that? Then it turned into affection maybe?” Shawn ventured tentatively.

“Jesus, you never cease to amaze me, you know that?” Remy said fondly. “Gray’s good at almost everything. But he’s shit at giving orders.”

“How long were you together?”

“Roughly two months.”

“This was… this was just before you found me in South Dakota?” Shawn asked as his brow creased worriedly. Remy nodded. “What were you doing?”

“Being subversive,” Remy said miserably, and he rolled onto his back and stared at the ceiling.

“So you were the mole they were having fits over,” Shawn whispered, sounding more like he was talking to himself. “There were two of you.”

“Fits?”

“They were onto you, Remy. Well not *you*, specifically, but they were after a mole.”

Remy stared into the shadows of the room thoughtfully. That wasn’t good. He and Gray had spent a lot of time gathering information, and if they had been pinged then some of that information could be tainted. He had to tell Thiago as soon as he could get the man alone.

“Was he good?” Shawn asked after another long silence.

“Hmm? Gray?”

“Mm hmm. Good shag?”

“Most certainly,” Remy said with a little grin.

That was another of their traditions. They always shared notes on their various sexual encounters. Some of their past conversations had gotten pretty wild. Things weren't back to the way they had been and probably never would be, but with that casual query Remy felt as if they were settling back into their own skins once more.

"Missed you, Beignet," Remy murmured contentedly as he nuzzled into Shawn's arms.

"Missed you too, Dixie," Shawn whispered into Remy's curls.

"Why do you sound so sad?" Remy asked carefully as he played with the fine hair on Shawn's chest.

Shawn didn't answer, and Remy could feel the uneven rise and fall of the other man's chest as he tried to regulate his breathing. The dread Remy had experienced earlier returned in full force, and he propped himself on one elbow as he looked down at Shawn in the dim light.

"I'll do anything you want me to, Shawn," he said in a soft voice as Shawn looked up at him and absently twirled a lock of his hair. "I know I fucked up. I know I–"

"Remy," Shawn interrupted quickly. "That's all in the past. We're starting over," he said firmly. "And it's not… it's not you," he added, any trace of his usual confidence gone.

"Then what's wrong, Shawn?" Remy asked desperately.

"I need to tell you this. And it's going to be difficult, so don't interrupt, okay?"

Remy looked at him carefully, wondering what could be so horrible that Shawn would resort to a pre-emptive no interrupting clause. "Okay," Remy finally agreed slowly.

Shawn took a deep breath as he prepared to speak, but before he could utter a word the door burst open and Thiago stumbled into the room, panting and fluttering his arms as if he'd lost his mind. Remy and Shawn both shot to attention and Thiago pointed into the hall breathlessly.

"Gotta see this," he finally managed before running back out like some bad stage act.

Remy and Shawn looked at one another blankly for several seconds before jumping out of bed and scrambling for the door.

XXVII.

BRANDT hit the floor again. Hard.

Carl laughed raucously and Thiago grinned from ear to ear. Remy and Shawn came hopping up to him, both of them still trying to achieve some semblance of being clothed, and they both stopped dead in their tracks when they saw Brandt and Nikolaus on the floor.

"Why are they fighting?" Remy asked quickly as he rounded the sofa to break up the wrestling match. Thiago reached out and grabbed him by the arm.

"They're wrestling," Thiago corrected. "Nikolaus took him down five times in a row."

"What?" Shawn and Remy echoed.

"Watch."

Thiago turned his eyes back in time to see Nikolaus and Brandt circle one another once again. It was a ridiculous sight considering their difference in size, but when Brandt went to grab Nikolaus, the smaller man moved in a flash and hooked his leg around Brandt's knee, throwing him off balance and twisting him, sending him crashing to the ground.

Carl was laughing so hard that he was actually doubled over in pain, and Thiago was afraid that the other man would start bleeding again if he didn't put a stop to the festivities.

"All right guys, that's enough," Thiago said regretfully. Brandt looked up at him gratefully, and Nikolaus beamed up at him as he got to his feet. Remy and Shawn were both glaring at Thiago, but Thiago didn't care. They'd had their time to make nice. It was time to get back to business.

"Come here, Gizmo," Carl said happily, laughter still in his voice as he beckoned to Nikolaus. Nikolaus practically strutted over to him and plopped down next to him, and Thiago went to help Brandt to his feet.

"You got royally smacked down," Thiago offered observantly.

"Gizmo's a quick little bastard, isn't he?" Brandt huffed as he got to his feet. "Oh hey, the lovebirds are back," he observed happily as his eyes landed on Shawn and Remy. "We brought you food," he added evilly.

"Uhh, thanks," Remy muttered with a wary glance at the table. Thiago watched Remy give Shawn a little shove and whisper, "You try it first."

Shawn simply shook his head and remained firmly planted in his spot.

"Shall we get to it, then?" Carl asked as he put his arm around Nikolaus and petted him affectionately. "It's not drugged, Beignet, no worries."

Shawn's eyes remained fixed on the food as he nodded and rubbed his chin thoughtfully.

"Right. Remy, can you contact Gray?" Thiago asked before any of the others could start in on the questioning. Thiago could tell that Remy was walking that fine line between being honest with his answers and protecting Thiago, and Thiago intended to give him as much help as he could.

"I could try," Remy said with a shrug. "It would have to wait 'til morning, though."

"Why?" Shawn asked as he snuck up to the table, as if the food had to be caught off guard in order to be eaten.

Thiago and Brandt both smothered their snickers, and Remy smiled fondly at the other man.

"Cause he only checks the drop once a day. If– wait," Remy murmured to himself as he began to pace. Thiago noticed that his accent had returned in full force, and when he spoke, he did it so quickly that it was hard to understand him. "If he be worried about me, which he no doubt is, he'll be checking it for sure!" Remy told them excitedly. The last words came out sounding like *fo show*. "We can snag him then!"

"When does he check it?" Carl asked.

"Noon," Remy said flatly as he looked at his watch. "We'd never have time to set it up today. It's almost eleven. And I'll need to find it first."

"*Can* you find it? Where is it?" Shawn asked as he circled the table stealthily.

"I can find it," Remy said assuredly.

Several hours later, Thiago sat alone on the couch. He and Brandt had been left behind while the others went about their various tasks. They decided that it was a good idea to leave a Class One in each pairing whenever they needed to split up from now on, and since Thiago didn't know the area, he'd remained behind. Brandt insisted upon staying behind with Thiago in order to gather the equipment he had spread throughout the flat. Shawn and Carl had gone in search of the nearest sporting goods store for ammunition, and Remy and Nikolaus were trying to find Gray's drop spot from Remy's store of memory.

Thiago was close to nodding off as Brandt did something frightening and probably flammable to a roll of copper wire, and he shook his head sleepily and watched Brandt with vague interest. It worried Thiago that Brandt had neither tried to blow something up, nor tried to fuck him at all during the two hours they'd been alone together, and Thiago's alarm bells were clanging away.

"You all right, Brandt?" Thiago finally asked tentatively. Brandt's hands continued to twist the copper wire into spirals around his index finger even as he looked up and fixed Thiago with a clear, piercing gaze. Thiago went so far as to blink in surprise when Brandt cocked his head thoughtfully. What was wrong with him? He looked normal.

"What do you think of this business?" Brandt asked as he twirled his finger in the air, sending the roll of copper wire flying off the coffee table and onto the floor. They both watched it roll until it came to a stop at the base of the couch on which Thiago sat. Thiago blinked at it, then looked back up at Brandt.

"What do you mean? What business?"

"The whole 'loyal only to each other' business. What do you think of it?"

"I think it's exactly what we need, considering," Thiago said immediately. Thankfully, Thiago didn't have the same issues with the truth that Remy seemed to have. He didn't mind lying to someone's face. Brandt nodded and started pulling the copper roll back to him.

"What about Dixie?" he asked thoughtfully.

"What about him?" Thiago asked uneasily.

"You think he's telling us the truth?"

Thiago stared Brandt down, trying to decipher any hidden meanings from the conversation. Brandt's behavior was way off, but Thiago found it hard to fault someone for acting calm and normal.

"I think he is, *sí*," Thiago finally answered. "I don't think we have to worry about Remy's loyalty."

"Hmm," Brandt said noncommittally.

Thiago leaned forward to look at him more closely. "What?"

"I think… I think you and Shawn don't have to worry about his loyalty. And I have no doubt he'd die for any one of us, but– "

"But?" Thiago coaxed, both intrigued by this sudden wave of coherent thought from Brandt and dreading where it might lead.

"But. I think if someone presents him with a better option, and by better, I mean one he thinks we can take and all six of us live through it, then he'll take it. He'll take it, whether we all agree to it or not. Just like the miffins," Brandt added bitterly as he gestured to his chest.

Thiago assumed that was where the dart had hit him. "Brandt?"

"Hmm?"

"What's a miffin?"

"Trippy muffin," Brandt explained as he finally got his wire rolled back up.

"I see," Thiago said with a slight smile. "So, you don't trust him?"

"No, I do. We're on the same side, you see," Brandt said absently. Thiago perked up and leaned forward even further. Which side did Brandt mean, exactly? Because, technically speaking, Remy was playing for both teams in this. "I mean, if Remy's loyal to the Six, then that's enough for me. I guess. We're our own side now."

"Right," Thiago said slowly as he sank back into the couch in relief.

"Do you know what 'Wally' means?" Brandt asked quietly after a short silence.

"Hmm? You mean it isn't an Australian who likes to blow shit up?" Thiago asked in amusement.

"If someone calls you a Wally it means you're…." Brandt trailed off and flipped his hand through the air again, sending the roll flying off once more. He and Thiago stared after it as it rolled. "I'm not stupid though, Zed," Brandt said seriously as he looked back at Thiago. "Crazy, yes, but not stupid."

"Brandt, I'm not following what you're -"

"What will you do?" Brandt asked intently.

"What?" Thiago asked in confusion. He'd completely lost the conversation, which seemed to happen to him a lot since he'd made Brandt's acquaintance.

"The Six. There are three sides now, Zed. The Organization. The Archer. And the Six. And Carl was right, you're the pillar. So, I'll follow your lead in this. Do you go with the Six, or do you stay with your previous loyalties?"

Thiago's mind raced to come up with a decent answer. That Brandt was looking to him for leadership was both surprising and flattering. Thiago would have thought Brandt's devotion would have gone with Shawn, no matter what.

"I think it's pretty clear that our previous loyalties are now trying to kill us," Thiago finally said with a little smile. Brandt cocked his head at Thiago and looked at him thoughtfully. After a full minute of silent observation, Thiago felt the need to squirm, but he resisted.

"Previous loyalties, yeah," Brandt mumbled as the *loco* returned in full force.

Thiago watched him worriedly, wondering what he'd been on about. There was really no telling what was going on in Brandt's head, especially now that the curtain of madness had apparently dropped again.

"You just remember that, Zed," Brandt said softly as he stood up and turned away to retrieve his roll. "I'll follow your lead."

XXVIII.

CARL was feeling pretty all right for a man who had just recently been shot. Of course, he wasn't actually required to do anything strenuous at the moment, and he also suspected that maybe he'd been slipped some painkillers

He had been careful to stay away from Remy and any offers of food or drink, but it was a bit more difficult to keep away from Brandt. Or Thiago. Or Shawn. Or Nikolaus, for that manner. Fuckers.

They were all preparing to go out on the attack, strapping on weapons and dressing in black combat gear. Well, except for Remy and Brandt, who would be on the ground. In public. With people. Did they really want to set Brandt and Remy loose on the public? With only two snipers– who weren't likely to shoot either of them anyway– present to save the plaza from some sort of exploding muffin attack?

Exploding muffins sounded like a real buzz kill… yep. Definitely drugged.

"You okay there, Trigger?" Remy inquired gently as he came up to kneel in front of the sofa. He put a hand on Carl's knee and patted it comfortingly.

"You little bastard," Carl said distantly.

"Wasn't me, *podna*," Remy said sympathetically.

"He did provide the goods, though," Thiago whispered conspiratorially as he whisked by with an armload of electronics for Nikolaus.

"Bastard," Carl muttered again as his mind floated between happy and pissed off and just plain gone.

"It's just hydrocodone," Remy said reassuringly. "Vicodin. It won't hurt you, just make you forget you got your ass shot."

"Who do I get to kill when I wake up?" Carl asked groggily.

"Thiago," Remy said happily before standing up and running his hand through Carl's hair affectionately. "Niko'll be here with you in case you need anything."

"I should be going," Carl murmured unhappily as his world began to fade.

Bastards. If anything happened to one of them… because he wasn't there to back them up… bastards.

XXIX.

SHAWN tapped at his earpiece and looked at Nikolaus questioningly.

"Coming in loud and clear," Nikolaus assured him.

"Shawn," Remy said in a low voice as he came up to stand beside Shawn.

Shawn hummed inquiringly as he fiddled with his comm unit, but he didn't look up. He knew what Remy wanted and he would just as soon avoid the discussion, thank you very much.

"Shawn," Remy repeated more insistently, and he grabbed Shawn's arm and squeezed it.

Shawn looked up in surprise, and Remy stared back at him with black, flat eyes. Shawn froze. The cold-blooded killer was back, but Shawn didn't know exactly why. Maybe he hadn't guessed right about Remy's subject of choice after all.

"Let me be point on this," Remy said. It was more of an order rather than a request.

"No," Shawn said immediately, even as he watched the dangerous flash of Remy's eyes. He'd rarely seen Remy looking like this over so trivial a manner, but he certainly wasn't frightened easily, and so he held his ground.

"I have to be point on this, Shawn," Remy insisted as he stepped closer and got right in Shawn's face.

"I said no, Remy," Shawn growled dangerously.

"Why? Because you don't trust me?" Remy asked angrily.

"Why do *you* have to do it, hmm?" Shawn asked in the same angry growl. "Thiago and I both are just as capable as you are. What needs to be said between you and Gray that we can't hear, eh?"

"Fuck you, Shawn. He's dangerous."

"If he's so fucking dangerous then why do you have to be down there?"

"It has to be me 'cause he's better than any one of us, and if he sees you coming at him, he'll kill you," Remy said through gritted teeth.

Shawn stared at Remy and tried to think about what the younger man was saying from an unbiased point of view. It wasn't easy, considering how desperate Shawn was to keep Remy out of the line of fire. To keep him safe.

"He left me here, Shawn. He didn't want to. He thought– no. He *knew* you were going to kill me. He was so convinced that he would never see me alive again that he started… if he sees you come waltzing up there at his drop, he'll immediately think I was tortured for the location and then killed. He won't think twice before he retaliates. He'll lose his head and he'll attack you."

"So you're protecting him?" Shawn asked thoughtfully.

What Remy said made sense. Shawn just didn't want Remy out in the open. Vulnerable. Targetable.

"I'm protecting *you*, you *wowarou*!" Remy yelled and he shoved Shawn in anger.

All the activity in the flat seemed to cease immediately. Remy rarely lost control when planning a mission, and Shawn was floored by the outburst. "I'm not even sure I know what that word means," he informed Remy uncertainly.

"Listen to what I'm saying, Shawn! He will kill you," Remy ground out angrily as he poked his finger into Shawn's chest with each word.

"Okay," Shawn conceded softly as he took Remy's face in his hands.

Remy immediately calmed, and his brown eyes were once again soft and gentle.

"You're on point," Shawn assured him. "But if anything happens to you, I swear to God, I'll kill the bastard myself."

"Nothing will happen," Remy said gently, and he gripped Shawn's elbows as Shawn cupped his face.

Shawn wasn't aware of what the others were doing at that point. He didn't care. He stared at Remy worriedly as a sinking feeling started in his stomach. "Promise me," he requested softly.

Remy frowned and nodded slightly. "Promise."

"I hope you've thought this through," Nikolaus murmured from behind Remy, and Shawn looked over Remy's shoulder at him. "Suddenly this plan isn't sounding so brilliant."

"I'd rather be lucky than good, right, Shawn?" Remy replied with a smile and a wink.

Shawn smiled back at him and nodded. As the familiar words wafted over him, he resisted the urge to kiss the other man. Shawn thought somehow that it would end up feeling like a kiss goodbye.

XXX.

NIKOLAUS checked on Carl before grabbing himself some chips and a drink and settling into the little command station he'd set up at the dining table. There was a monitor, several speakers, and a microphone Nikolaus couldn't use. It was shit for a command station, really. It was more of an observation post.

He and Remy placed cameras around the plaza on their earlier outing, and Nikolaus would be able to watch most of the action from where he was. He could also hear the chatter of the other four men through the earpieces as they made their way to the rendezvous, but they hadn't been able to acquire the equipment necessary for Nikolaus to communicate with them. Normally this would have troubled Nikolaus, not being able to give aid if something went awry, but he had complete faith in the ability of these men. Even without Carl there to help protect them, Nikolaus wasn't very worried about anyone's safety. Except for maybe Gray's. Yeah, but Nikolaus wouldn't mind all too much if that bastard got his ass shot.

Carl shifted and moaned from his spot on the sofa. Nikolaus turned to look at him for several long seconds. Carl hadn't developed a fever, which was a good thing all around, and the furrow the bullet had created along his ribcage was healing nicely. Drugging him had been more of a preventative measure than anything else. And, Nikolaus suspected that Remy and Thiago just liked to do that sort of thing. They'd slipped the little pills to the assassin with something like unholy glee.

Carl shifted again and groaned, his face contorted into a frown, and his fists clenched convulsively. Knowing Carl, he was probably just fucked off about being drugged against his will. Again. Hell, knowing Carl, he was probably trying to strangle someone in his sleep. He had a right to be angry, though. Lord knew Brandt was pissed off about it.

"Well, I don't see why you had to drug him," Brandt was even then grumbling through Nikolaus's speakers. Carl moaned again as if in answer, and Nikolaus turned back around to turn the volume down a bit. The last thing he wanted was to wake the man and have to deal with his wrath alone.

"He would have insisted on coming along, Wally," Remy's voice said regretfully. "He's hurt and might have injured himself further."

"Had to be done," Thiago murmured in agreement. Nikolaus imagined that Thiago was sitting in the back of the rental car with Brandt, probably trying to be invisible as he spoke.

"You could have asked him if he needed them," Brandt spat angrily.

"He did need them," Shawn said sternly. "It would have been nice to have his gun around today, but you saw, just like we did, that he was hurting. Did you really want him suffering anymore?" Shawn asked, his voice low and coaxing.

"No," Brandt mumbled like a sulking child.

Nikolaus heard Remy snicker, and then a dull thump and a whoosh of rushing air. Nikolaus was pretty certain that one of them had just hit another, and he tried to contain his amusement as he listened in.

"*Bracque*," Remy muttered.

"You're not helping," Shawn said through obviously gritted teeth.

"What'd I do? *Aiee*! Turn left!"

Nikolaus heard a distinct squealing of tires, accompanied by several muttered curses and what sounded like an unbuckled body thumping against the side of the car.

"Remy!"

"*Mais*, if you wouldn't yell at me, it would not distract me!"

"You haven't seen yelling yet! Pay attention!"

"You deal with your onions, Beignet."

"Remy, I swear to God," Thiago growled angrily. "If you don't get your head out of your ass, I'll remove it for you."

Nikolaus smirked and tried not to snicker.

"Oh, you think that's funny, do you, Niko?" Remy asked in an evil voice.

Nikolaus didn't answer. He actually couldn't answer, considering that the radios weren't two-ways. How did Remy know he was snickering when the radios didn't go both ways? Was he that predictable?

There was silence in the vehicle, and Nikolaus strained to hear anything. He thought he heard a slight snickering, and he leaned forward and turned the volume on the speakers higher, but no sound came. He leaned even closer and turned them up to the max. He could hear what sounded like whispers and a whooshing sound that could possibly have been wind moving over the earpieces as someone moved quickly. Nikolaus cocked his head and strained to listen.

"HEY, GIZMO!" Remy and Brandt finally shouted as loudly as they could. The words echoed through the speakers and practically bounced off the walls of the flat. Carl shot bolt upright on the sofa. Nikolaus yipped in surprise and toppled over the back of his chair. From the floor, he could hear the four men snickering.

"You think the comms are working, then?" Shawn asked through his laughter.

"Bastards," Nikolaus muttered as he got back to his feet.

"Bastards," Carl groaned as he eased back onto the sofa.

XXXI.

BRANDT was positioned in the plaza, the thinking being that in a pinch he could probably scare someone into immobility by simply looking at them. More so than Shawn or Thiago could, anyway.

Shawn and Thiago were both on rooftops overlooking the drop spot, both with short-range sights and itchy trigger fingers, and Remy hovered near the area Gray had set up as a drop. Brandt tried to keep his eyes on Remy, but the man was just too good at being invisible. Brandt kept losing him in the crowd, and the crowd couldn't exactly be described as bustling.

Brandt had lost count of how many times and in how many ways Shawn had told Remy to be careful. It was really quite endearing. Brandt found himself regretting some of the harsh words he had said to Shawn several nights previous. There were feelings there that neither Brandt nor Shawn could deny, and though they'd successfully avoided each other, Brandt still felt the pull of the other man. Like a moth drawn to the flame.

Brandt shook his head free of his thoughts when he realized that he had lost Remy again.

"Hey, Dixie," he said quietly, trying not to move his lips as he spoke. "Stand the fuck still."

"I am standing still," Remy responded in the same close-mouthed voice.

"Where are you, Dixie?" Shawn asked in agitation. "I lost sight of you, too."

"I'm by the trash bin. I haven't moved," Remy said irritably.

"Well don't."

"I haven't."

"Good then."

"Good then."

"Will you two shut up and pay attention!"

Brandt rolled his eyes and looked up at the building he knew Thiago sat atop and nodded approvingly. At least someone was still sane in this group.

XXXII.

REMY stared straight ahead, his eyes unfocused and his vision somewhat blurred. It was easier to see on the periphery that way, and that was how he saw Gray slipping through the small crowd toward him even before Shawn gave the heads up.

"Dixie, at your three," Shawn's gruff voice warned him.

"I've got him," Remy murmured. He stepped away from the bin he hovered next to and into Gray's line of vision.

Gray stutter stepped, but he kept moving forward, directly toward Remy.

"Dixie?" he said urgently as he came up to Remy.

"We need to talk, Boss," Remy said in a low voice. He didn't really have much left to hide from the others, but for some reason he was still nervous about Gray saying something that would set one of the others off. It was incredible how desperate Remy was to walk the straight and narrow now. As long as Shawn kept him by his side, he would do anything.

"Talk?" Gray repeated incredulously.

"Back at the flat," Remy said with a nod.

Gray's face clouded over and Remy slid his hand into his pocket to grip his gun. "Oh, shit," Gray said softly. "What did they do? Did they hurt you? Where are they?"

Remy kept his eyes on Gray, careful not to give away the positions of his companions by looking at them. "It's okay, Boss," he said softly, trying to convey that these were Thiago's orders, but coming off sounding more threatening than reassuring.

"Fuck this, I'm taking you with me," Gray said as he closed the distance between them and gripped Remy's arm.

"Boss, calm down," Remy warned sternly.

"He gets closer and I'm taking him down, Dixie," Shawn growled.

"Gray, step back," Remy said in alarm. He knew Shawn would shoot the other man first and then apologize later. Scratch that. He probably wouldn't even apologize. Remy couldn't have Gray's death on his conscience. Shawn's position was now at Remy's ten, and if Gray took one more step, he would have a clear shot of Gray without the risk of hitting Remy.

"Shawn, stand down," Thiago's voice ordered.

"Gray, step back!" Remy shouted as he took a step back himself, trying to get in Shawn's line of fire. Gray looked at him in shock and his hand traveled to his shoulder holster. Remy heard Shawn's sharp exhalation. The one that always signified he was about to take a shot.

You were always steadier just after letting out your breath.

That was Remy's last thought before he lunged forward and grabbed Gray, spinning the man around and pushing him away. The bullet sliced through Remy just before the report was heard. It echoed throughout the plaza, and people looked around in confusion. Some didn't even stop what they were doing, but others recognized the sound for what it was and took cover. A woman with her daughter screamed as Remy fell into Gray, and Gray cursed imaginatively as he cradled Remy in his arms and tried to keep him on his feet.

"Jesus," Gray breathed as he tried to get his arms around Remy.

Remy knew it was just a flesh wound, figuratively speaking. The bullet had passed through him cleanly, high in his shoulder. No organs, no arteries, no lungs or anything. But holy fuck, did it burn. Thank God Shawn wasn't working with his usual ammo. Remy and Gray both would have been shot to shit. Not to mention the trash bin. And the bench. And the pavement. And the sewer system beneath the pavement.

"Come on, Dixie, come on," Gray repeated under his breath as he tried to pull Remy away and into the cover of the panicking crowd.

"Son of a bitch!" Shawn yelled desperately. "I shot him!"

Remy tried to speak, but he knew he was swiftly going into shock. He couldn't get his tongue to work properly.

"Man down, Brandt," Thiago yelled in Remy's ear. "Man down! Get in there! Help them!"

"Boss," Remy croaked as Gray dragged him toward the parking lot. He lurched forward slightly as his head swam, but Gray held him close and kept him upright. "Wally," Remy gasped disjointedly.

"I'm coming, Dixie!" Brandt responded, his voice low and serious and rushed. He almost didn't sound like Brandt. He sounded normal.

"Dixie!" Shawn shouted desperately. Remy could tell the man was moving, probably running down the several flights of stairs he had to in order to get to the ground floor. "Dixie, where are you hit? Talk to me, lad!"

Remy opened his mouth to speak, to reassure Shawn that yes, he had been shot. Not in the ass this time, but shot, nonetheless. And yes, he did plan on kicking Shawn in the nuts later, because really, there were only so many times your best friend and sometimes lover could shoot you before your world started looking sort of grim.

Gray clapped a hand over Remy's mouth. "They're trying to kill you, Dixie, or don't you get that yet?" Gray hissed into Remy's ear. "Keep your mouth shut and they'll leave you for dead."

"If you touch him, Kincaid, I'll rip you apart!" Shawn shouted through Remy's earpiece.

Remy could hear all sorts of chatter coming through the lines. Shawn was yelling obscenities at Gray and begging Remy to speak. Thiago's continuous undertone of curses and orders were being ignored by all parties. Brandt's attempts to get through the panicking crowd to them. Remy could just imagine Nikolaus back at the flat going mad trying to figure out what was going on.

Gray continued to whisper in Remy's ear, encouraging him to move. "Come on, Dixie," Gray urged. "We have to move. Jesus, I can't believe the bastard shot you."

"Dixie! Gimme your six!" Brandt yelled. He was close enough that Remy could hear him yelling even without the earpiece.

"Remy! Bloody hell, woman, move!" Shawn shouted, and Remy imagined him struggling his way through the crowd. And yet, despite his best efforts, Remy couldn't say a word to either of them.

"Remy! Gray!" Thiago said authoritatively. "Stand down, both of you!"

Remy heard the order, but Gray was too busy trying to force his way through what had become a throng of panicked civilians to hear it. They were all trying to get out of the same archway, and Remy felt himself slowly sinking as the press of the crowd invaded his senses.

"Dixie? Dixie? Just a bit further, brother, come on."

"Remy!" Shawn shouted desperately.

Gray wrapped Remy's arm around his neck and forced his way through the press of people.

Remy caught sight of Brandt, making his way like a bulldozer through the crowd.

"Gray," Remy said weakly. "Gray, *arrête-toi.* I need them," he begged disjointedly.

"Thiago! Take the shot!" Shawn yelled, his accent so deep with agitation that he was barely understandable. Remy felt like weeping for him. "Take it, dammit!"

"We need him alive," Thiago hissed. "I won't risk hitting anyone else."

"Goddammit! Brandt! Take him down! Now!"

"Gray," Remy breathed again, this time in warning.

Brandt was just feet away from them, and he reached his hand out through the crowd trying to grab at them. Remy raised his arm to grasp Brandt's fingers desperately, even though the pain it caused him almost cost him his consciousness. He squeezed the fingers as Brandt tried to take hold of him, and he murmured into his comm, "Take care of them, Wally."

"No!" Shawn and Brandt both shouted as Gray finally ducked through the last clog of people and dragged Remy out and toward his car.

XXXIII.

"Mierda," Thiago breathed as he watched Gray and Remy slip through the entrance to the closed plaza through the scope of his rifle. He lowered it and stood at the edge of the roof, shaking with anger and frustration.

That had certainly not gone as planned.

"Fucking hell!" Shawn cried, his voice cracking as he tried to push through the crowd. Thiago could see him clearly from his viewpoint on the roof, and he could see Brandt, too. The big man was on his knees now, his head hanging and his shoulders sagging pitifully.

Thiago could tell that Shawn wouldn't be getting through in time. Remy's comm was still on, and he could hear the car running and Gray talking to Remy, coaxing him to stay conscious.

They were long gone. Son of a bitch.

Shawn dropped to the ground beside Brandt as he finally made his way to him in the nearly empty plaza.

"Are you hurt?" Thiago heard Shawn ask.

"I had him, Shawn," Brandt said brokenly. Thiago blinked in surprise and raised his rifle to look through the scope at the two men. That was the first time Thiago could remember hearing Brandt say someone's actual name in a long time. "I had him… my hand," Brandt murmured as he held his hand out and cupped it, looking at it then up at Shawn pitifully.

Shawn ran his hand over Brandt's hair slowly and pulled the big man's head to rest against his chest. He looked up to where he knew Thiago was and said, "Can you see them?"

"They're gone," Thiago answered curtly.

Gone. Thiago knew Gray well enough to know that he would disappear and never be heard from again. But if Remy were with him… Remy was more talented than any agent Thiago had ever come across. If Remy didn't want to be found, they had no hope of ever tracking them. But Thiago didn't think that was the case. Remy hadn't gone of his own volition. He'd been wounded. Severely wounded, judging from the amount left of blood on the sidewalk. Thank God Shawn had aimed low, though.

"I shot him," Shawn said distantly. He held Brandt and rocked him.

This was the perfect time for Thiago to drop a big fat 'I told you so,' but Thiago didn't have the heart to do it.

"He stepped into it," Shawn continued in a dazed voice. Thiago couldn't be sure, but he thought he heard Brandt sniffling through his earpiece. "He saved that bastard's life. If one hair on his head is harmed, I swear to God–"

"Shawn, the only one here who's ever hurt him, is you," Thiago spat angrily as he gathered his equipment and hurried to leave the roof. The local authorities would be there soon. They had to be clear.

Shawn didn't respond, and Thiago could no longer see him as he hurried down the stairwell.

"Both of you get your shit together and meet me in the parking lot," Thiago said sternly. "He's not dead yet, and Gray won't hurt him. Listen to your comms!"

"Beignet didn't mean to shoot him," Brandt said miserably as Thiago strained to hear Gray and Remy speaking. Soon they would be out of range.

"If *Beignet* had listened, then no one would have got shot!" Thiago snapped.

The plaza was completely deserted now, and Thiago skirted the edges until he was in the parking lot beside their rental. Shawn and Brandt came staggering up at almost the same time, and they all got into the car in an awkward silence. "Doesn't anybody ever listen to a fucking order anymore?" Thiago mumbled angrily as he started up the car.

Brandt sat beside him, his shoulders slumped miserably. Shawn sat in the back, desperately trying to hear through his earpiece.

Thiago could hear Gray's soft voice speaking, but then a sudden note of panic hit and Thiago's heart raced. Gray rarely panicked.

"Remy! No, brother! Fight it! Come back, Dixie, come on, son, Remy… oh, God no…." Gray's voice faded and finally died out, and Thiago felt his chest constrict painfully.

"Oh, God," Shawn moaned as he began rocking once more.

Thiago didn't know what to say. What did you say to a man who had just shot and possibly killed his lover? Brandt was silent, though several tears graced his bearded cheeks, and Thiago was surprised to find his own eyes damp.

Shawn was beside himself with grief, and Thiago turned just in time to see the man slump down in the seat and reach for the pocket in his pants leg. Thiago always kept a backup gun in that pocket. Whether Shawn did or not didn't need to be discovered at that point. Thiago crawled over the seat and practically tackled Shawn, pinning his arms to his side and reaching into the pocket to retrieve what Shawn had been after.

"M'not gonna kill meself," Shawn murmured weakly as Thiago looked at the cell phone in relief.

"Brandt, get us home," Thiago ordered over his shoulder.

"Was gonna call Niko… I shot him, Thi," Shawn said dazedly as he looked up at Thiago.

Thiago repositioned himself so that he was kneeling in the back seat and he pulled Shawn to him. Shawn clung to him and shook violently.

"I killed him. He stepped into it. I fucking killed him."

Thiago held Shawn tight as his own tears threatened. He had faith in Gray, though. Gray would take care of Remy just as well as they would have had he been with them.

If he was still alive.

XXXIV.

NIKOLAUS'S anguished cry roused Carl from his fitful sleep, and they listened together in horror as the drama unfolded. Carl hovered over Nikolaus's shoulder, listening intently to the muffled sounds of traffic and hushed sobbing coming through the speakers.

"Tell me I'm hearing things," Carl muttered dazedly. Nikolaus shook his head in response and turned the speakers up to the max. Carl could hear Thiago murmuring to Shawn in the car, but he couldn't make out what was being said. "Can you close in on Dixie's comm?" Carl asked quietly.

Nikolaus's hand moved automatically to fiddle with the dials, and soon they could hear snatches of Gray's voice as he begged Remy to stay conscious. The final words they heard uttered were, "… he's dead you… you hear this… bastards…."

Carl blinked and tried to shake away the haze of the drugs, but his world was still fuzzy and confusing.

"Did he say dead?" Nikolaus asked disbelievingly. "Did he say…."

Carl nodded and sat down with a thump in the chair beside Nikolaus. They sat in a daze for what seemed an eternity, and the next thing they knew the door to the flat was thrown open and Thiago and Brandt entered, dragging Shawn between them.

"What the hell happened out there?" Nikolaus screamed almost before the door clicked shut.

"I killed him," Shawn murmured as Thiago shoved him roughly toward the sofa.

Thiago turned on Nikolaus and growled wordlessly. Carl could tell the man was seriously fucked off, and he wondered how much of his mood was from despair. Shawn had obviously lost any composure he had left, and Brandt was in shock as well. Carl watched the big man trudge to the sofa and sit beside Shawn dejectedly. Carl and Nikolaus came over to stare at them in shock.

"Did you hear anything?" Thiago asked quietly as Carl came up to stand beside him. He gestured toward Nikolaus's command station. "Your frequency was stronger than ours, yes?"

"He's dead," Carl answered quietly, hoping Shawn and Brandt wouldn't hear him. They did, however, and a choked little sob drew Carl and Thiago's attention.

Nikolaus sat down hard on the closest piece of furniture, tears flowing freely, and Brandt let his head fall into his hands. Shawn sat in a daze, rocking slightly. Thiago paled visibly when Carl spoke the words.

"How do you know? Are you sure?" Thiago demanded.

"Kincaid so much as told us," Carl said flatly as he watched Shawn and Brandt sympathetically. Thiago clutched the back of the sofa as if for support and lowered his head dejectedly.

Carl was trying not to think of Remy. If he thought of Remy, the easy smile, the gentle brown eyes, the undying devotion… if he thought of those things, he was going to cry. And Carl wasn't supposed to cry.

"I had him," Brandt said softly through the mask of his hands, his voice wavering. "He was right there."

Carl swallowed hard and forced back the tears. He was not going to cry.

"I killed him," Shawn repeated in the same soft, lost voice.

Carl's vision blurred and he blinked away the tears. Finally, he brought his hand up and wiped at his eyes. When he lowered his hand again, he shouted in alarm as Shawn moved with lightning quick speed and reached for the handgun Brandt had in the holster beneath his jacket.

"No!" Thiago and Carl shouted together.

Shawn shoved at Brandt as the bigger man tried to retrieve the weapon, and stood up with the gun clutched in his hand.

"Shawn," Thiago said warily as he and Carl instinctively spread out and tried to surround the grieving man. "Shawn, put down the gun."

"I killed him, Thi," Shawn said sadly as he shook his head slowly. "I killed Remy. What the hell do I have left?"

"Beignet, put down the gun," Brandt said in a low soothing voice as he got slowly to his feet. He put out a hand as if to calm a spooked horse and took a tentative step forward. Carl continued on his circuitous route, trying to get behind Shawn as the other two distracted him.

Shawn shook his head and went about checking that the weapon was loaded while still managing to keep a suspicious eye on Thiago and Brandt.

"Shawn, come on, you've still got us, yeah?" Nikolaus pleaded as he stood nervously to the side. "Please put down the gun."

"Shawn," Brandt whispered, his voice close to pleading.

Carl actually froze and looked at Brandt in surprise. Shawn froze as well, his fingers clutching the gun so tightly that his knuckles were white and his hand was shaking. His whole body was shaking, in fact.

"Please, Shawn," Brandt continued as he crept closer. "Everything I said the other night… I didn't mean it. I need you here, Shawn. *We* need you here."

"I killed him, Brandt," Shawn said as he cocked the gun and looked at it pensively. If one of them tackled him now the fucking thing would probably go off and kill one of them. Carl had already been accidentally shot once. He didn't relish a second helping just yet. "First I crushed him," Shawn murmured. "And then I fucking killed him."

"No!" Brandt cried as Shawn lifted the gun to his temple.

Thiago and Carl moved at the same time and grabbed for the man. His gun hand was forced up and the gun went off, the bullet tearing through the ceiling and spraying plaster all over them as they tackled Shawn to the ground. Thank God they were on the top floor.

Brandt spread his body over Shawn's and held him down as Carl and Thiago struggled to pry the gun from Shawn's hand.

Several minutes later, Shawn was tied to a chair and complaining loudly about it. Brandt was kneeling in front of him, trying to calm him.

"What now?" Nikolaus asked with difficulty.

Thiago opened his mouth to speak, but Brandt stood up suddenly and turned on them all, like a tiger preparing to pounce.

"We have to find him," he growled.

"Wally," Carl said miserably.

"We can't give up on him until we know for sure. Not until he's here with us again. Dead or alive," Brandt said as tears flowed silently down the sides of his face.

Shawn looked up at them all hopefully.

Thiago started to object, but upon seeing the desperate look in Shawn's eyes, he snapped his mouth shut and looked at the rest of them somewhat nervously.

"Right then," Thiago said resignedly. "I think… I think it's about time I told you all–"

The only sounds the shot made were the shattering of the sliding glass doors and the dull thud when it hit its target.

Carl grabbed Nikolaus and forced him to take cover on the ground as another shot found its mark. He shielded Nikolaus with his body and looked over at the others. Brandt dragged Shawn, chair and all, to the ground and covered him in much the same manner, but he had been too late to prevent Shawn being hit by the first shot. Thiago had been wounded by the second, but he was sliding snake-like along the floor toward the doors through the small pool of blood his wound had left.

More shots followed the first two, breaking more glass and imbedding in the furniture, walls, and floor. Carl started Nikolaus forward with a little nudge, and they both slithered toward Brandt and Shawn. Shawn was hit, but not as badly as Carl had thought. The only real threat to him at that moment was the possibility of Brandt smothering him. Carl reached out and yanked at one of the knots as another shot hit the chair Shawn was tied to, and finally they got him untied. Brandt rubbed his hand protectively over Shawn's head and then Carl's and Nikolaus's, as if petting prized dogs, before he went crawling over to the cupboards near the door.

Thiago reached the gaping hole that had once been the sliding glass doors and he yanked the string to the blinds, closing them and providing the rest of them with enough cover to crouch and scramble for safety.

Carl pulled Nikolaus to his feet and shoved him toward the bedrooms. "Gather whatever you can! The essentials!" he ordered as he hit the interior lights and turned them all off. He then went straight for the high-powered rifle Thiago had been using at the plaza and set himself up at the doors. He stayed behind the wavering blinds, careful not to poke them with the muzzle and careful not to let his scope reflect the bright sun. He searched the rooftops and balconies through the scope, but found nothing. Finally, he found a black hole in a building down the street where a window had once been. The angle wasn't right for him to be able to see inside.

"We have to move," he shouted finally. "Everyone. Grab what you can and go. Now!"

XXXV.

SHAWN didn't move. He'd been shot, but it was more of a graze than an actual hit, and Shawn was pissed off about it. The least the bastard could do was have the decency to hit him. A nice kill shot and Shawn's misery would have been over.

"That the best the bastard can do?" Shawn growled angrily from the floor where he remained sprawled. "A fucking professional marksman with a target that's tied to a fucking chair, his whole fucking chest exposed for the taking, and all he can hit is the fucking arm?!" he yelled at no one in particular. "Open those blinds! Give him a second chance, the worthless fuck! We'll paint a fucking bull's eye for him this time!"

"C'mon, Beignet," Brandt urged insistently as he practically dragged Shawn across the floor and to the door.

Shawn allowed himself to be dragged. He didn't care whether he made it through now. He'd lost the only thing he truly cared for. He'd known Remy was important to him, he just hadn't realized how little life would be worth living if Remy were no longer in it. He had always told himself that something would be there for him to care about. He had taken for granted the knowledge that there were certain things, certain obligations and certain loyalties he thought would always take priority over Remy. Now he knew he'd been wrong. Remy had always been the priority, even when Shawn had been working against the younger man.

Shawn's head swirled as guilt overcame him. He'd always been Remy's priority. Why had it taken five years for Shawn to give him the same respect? Why had it taken Shawn five years to begin to want to earn what he got from Remy?

Why hadn't Shawn told Remy about that mission? He'd tried to, but only once. Only once in five years had he tried to tell Remy the truth about how they'd come to know one another. Only once in five years had he tried to be honest.

But now Remy was dead. Dead by his hands. At least he could go back to the Organization and finally say 'mission accomplished, mates, now I'm going home.'

But home was Remy. And Remy was gone.

The Organization could go fuck itself for all he cared. Mission fucking accomplished, indeed.

Remy was gone, and that was all that mattered.

"C'mon, Beignet, stay with me," Brandt murmured pleadingly into Shawn's ear as he dragged him to his feet.

Brandt was using emotional manipulation to keep Shawn from killing himself. Brandt had said that he hadn't meant all the things he had said the night they had fought, but Shawn had seen the look in his eyes. And unless Brandt was seriously more talented than Shawn gave him credit for– which was possible– Shawn didn't believe him. You didn't tell someone to their face that you didn't love them unless you truly didn't, Shawn didn't care how fucking angry or crazy or both you were.

Why had it taken so little to convince Shawn he was in love with Brandt anyway? It had taken five years of loving Remy before he had realized it, but Brandt had been almost instantaneous. Why was that? Shawn supposed it had to do with his guilty conscience. He wasn't supposed to fall in love with Remy, and so he had denied the fact. Was that it? Shawn didn't know. He loved Brandt, sure. But nowhere near like he did Remy.

Brandt wasn't enough to keep him from putting that muzzle to his temple and pulling the trigger now. Brandt wasn't Remy.

Brandt could go fuck himself, too. If Shawn wanted to kill himself then, by fuck, he was going to do it. Brandt, the Organization, Thiago, Carl, Niko. Gray. John. Thierry. Whoever the fuck else was out there gunning for them. They could all go fuck themselves. And Shawn would get the job done, one way or another. He had nothing left. He would go out on his own terms, preferably suitably liquored up, and he would take whoever stood in his way down with him when he went.

XXXVI.

"WHO'S shooting at us?" Nikolaus yelled as the five of them ducked through the door and out into the hallway.

Thiago was bleeding profusely from what looked like a wound on his neck or shoulder. It dripped down his arm and left a trail behind him as he walked. Shawn was bleeding from the graze on his arm and complaining about the shooter's bad aim.

Nikolaus wondered how long they would have to keep Shawn restrained before the suicidal urge went away. If Nikolaus had been the one to shoot Remy– yeah, well, maybe they could keep Shawn in handcuffs or something. They were easier to haul around than ropes.

"Whoever it is, we have to get the fuck out of Australia," Thiago said in a weak voice as they moved cautiously down the stairwell and to their rental vehicle.

"Where do we go?" Nikolaus asked as he watched Carl and Brandt clear their path through the parking garage. They moved forward quickly. Thiago and Shawn were helping one another along as Brandt and Carl stayed on either side of the group with their weapons. The few items Nikolaus rescued and tossed into a duffel bag, Remy's duffel bag, were thrown into the trunk, and Nikolaus took the keys from Carl and got into the driver's seat.

"Just drive," Thiago muttered as Brandt shoved him and Shawn into the back seat. Thiago looked a little worse for the wear, but he was conscious, and that was always a good thing. He held a bandana to his collarbone and Shawn sat fuming and muttering as Brandt fussed with his arm.

"Fucker missed," Shawn kept mumbling angrily.

Nikolaus tore out of the garage and headed south.

XXXVII.

BRANDT looked back at the receding building and pulled the switch out of his pocket. He'd managed to recover it from its hiding place in the cupboard and now he grinned as he fixated on the building.

"Cover your ears," he ordered just before flipping the device and placing his own hands over Shawn's ears. The man was listless and without hope at the moment. Brandt would need to do something. Something drastic. Something like… tell him the truth. Fucking hell, Brandt hated telling the truth.

The top floor of the building didn't exactly explode. Not in the traditional sense of the word. It crumpled first, then the centre blew up and out like an erupting volcano. Brandt watched it with intense glee. He'd wanted to blow that fucking place up for years now.

He turned back to the others. Nikolaus watched the blast in his mirrors as he drove, and Carl turned in his seat to look at Brandt pointedly.

"Was that strictly necessary?" Carl asked finally in exasperation.

"No," Brandt replied joyously as he petted Shawn and rubbed the man's head like a dog. "But it was fun."

Carl rolled his eyes and turned back around, trying to hide his smirk, but Brandt saw it anyway. Thiago hissed in pain and Brandt leaned over Shawn, who slumped dejectedly in the middle of the back seat, and began helping Thiago get his shirt off.

"Shawn, did you and Remy have a predetermined place to meet?" Thiago asked as Brandt looked over his wound. It wasn't deep, but it was bleeding quite a lot. They would have to get Thiago and Shawn looking somewhat presentable if they were to be going anywhere public. They were both covered in blood.

"Doesn't matter," Shawn said quietly as he laid his head against the seat and closed his eyes. "He's dead. Doesn't matter."

"Shawn! Get your head out of your ass, please, and think!" Thiago growled angrily. "Gray was trying to protect Remy, just like we were."

Shawn growled and snorted at this, but Thiago continued regardless.

"Do you really think Gray would have told us Remy was dead? The only thing he would tell us was what he wanted us to know, and he knows that if we thought Remy was dead we wouldn't come after him."

"You think he's alive then?" Carl asked from the front seat.

"I don't know. But we have to operate under the assumption that he is, and that he'll try to get back to us," Thiago said gruffly as Brandt poked at the wound. "Stop it, dammit! That hurts!"

"It's stopped bleeding, hasn't it?" Brandt responded defensively as he stuffed the bandana into the gaping wound.

"Then stop messing with it!" Thiago shouted.

Brandt huffed and sat back in his seat, after one more poke for good measure. Shawn slid against him and buried his head in Brandt's chest. Brandt wrapped a protective arm around the man.

"Shawn," Thiago persisted.

"What?" Shawn said miserably.

"Did you have a location? A fallback?"

"There's a bar in the French Quarter," Shawn said in a hoarse, muffled voice. Brandt held him closer and he could feel Shawn shaking uncontrollably.

"The French Quarter? You're talking New Orleans? Like… Louisiana?" Nikolaus asked as he negotiated the traffic distractedly.

"Yeah," Shawn affirmed and he cleared his throat and sat back up. "It's called The Morgue," Shawn said wryly.

"The Morgue?" Thiago asked incredulously.

"Remy's idea of humor. If we're separated for any reason, we… we wait a month," Shawn told them with difficulty. "Then, after the month, we spend two hours every night for a week, ten to midnight, at The Morgue. Waiting," he said sadly. "But that was before Katrina hit."

"Do you think it's still there?" Carl asked doubtfully.

"No," Shawn answered. "No, it closed down before the storm. We never thought to make new arrangements. I don't know what's in its place, now."

"If you don't have new ones, then we follow the old ones. We don't have any other choice," Thiago said as he twisted and tried to get a look at his wound.

"We go to ground for a month? Where?" Nikolaus asked.

"*No sé*," Thiago admitted candidly. "Just keep driving. We'll think of something."

Part Five: Pepper In The Gumbo

I.

"REMY?" the soft voice inquired through the haze

"Go 'way."

"Remy, open your eyes," the voice ordered insistently.

"*Fiank.*"

"Well, if you feel well enough to cuss at me, then you're doing better than I thought," Gray said quietly.

Remy scrunched his eyes tight before trying to open them. Only one of them actually managed the feat, but that was enough to allow him to survey his surroundings. He was in yet another hotel room. Gray sat in a chair beside the bed, looking down at him worriedly.

"Where are *mes pattes*?" Remy asked finally, referring to his 'paws.'

"You've still got them," Gray said with a slight smile, knowing Remy and his language well enough to know that he was asking where his toes were. "I gave you some morphine. You've been shot."

"*Mes pattes*," Remy muttered as he drifted back into oblivion. "I want my toes back."

Several hours later, Remy awoke to a dark room. His toes were back, the little vagrants, and so was the pain in his upper body. Fucking toes. They always caused problems.

Remy turned his head slightly and saw Gray sitting in the same chair. The man was slumped slightly, and Remy was fairly certain he was asleep. Remy cleared his throat and whispered Gray's name. Gray jumped to his feet, his hand on his gun, and Remy watched him with wide eyes.

"Remy?" Gray said quietly as he took a step closer to the bed and looked down at Remy.

"What happened?" Remy asked in a hoarse voice.

"You were shot," Gray explained.

"I remember that part. Why did you drag me away, Boss?" Remy asked in a weak voice. He wanted to be angry but he didn't have the energy.

"He tried to kill you," Gray answered in surprise.

"No," Remy protested as he shook his head back and forth. "No, he tried to kill *you*."

"But–"

"Thiago wanted you with us. We needed your help."

"But–"

"We couldn't tell the others you were working for Thi," Remy said as his voice got stronger.

"But–"

"Contact Thiago, Boss. Tell him we're both okay."

"I've been trying. I've been rethinking my original plan a bit, but I can't get him."

"What? Why not?"

"I don't know," Gray said sadly. He passed his hand over Remy's forehead and whispered, "Go back to sleep, Dixie."

"What plan?" Remy asked as the gentle hand threatened to lull him back to sleep.

"They think you're dead. I told them as much before I turned off your comm. You're free of them, if you want to be."

Remy opened his mouth to protest, but sleep overtook him before he managed it.

A week later, Remy and Gray stood side by side across the street from the building in which Brandt's flat had been located. Remy's shoulders slumped dejectedly as he took in the remains of the flat.

"What the hell?" Gray said under his breath.

"Brandt," Remy responded with certainty.

"He blew up the flat?"

"Looks like."

"Why?"

Remy shrugged as best he could in the makeshift sling and looked up at the sky idly. "Get rid of evidence, I suppose," he murmured as he looked around at the surrounding building. A work crew on one of the larger buildings was working busily on a platform, replacing a missing window. "Look there," Remy murmured with a nod of his chin.

Gray turned and peered up at the building. "Sniper," he observed softly.

"Someone found them. C'mon."

"Where are we going now? You shouldn't be traipsing around the city in your condition," Gray scolded as they made their way down the pavement.

"That's not what you were saying last night," Remy said with a slight smile.

Gray had the good grace to blush. "You started it," he mumbled.

"After a week of lying on your back with no lovin', yeah. Anyone would start it," Remy muttered.

"Remy...."

"I have to find them, Boss." Remy stopped and turned to look at Gray. "I have to find him."

Gray sighed heavily and looked away. "And what do you plan to do once you find them?" he asked finally.

Remy blinked slowly and looked down at his feet. What did he plan on doing? He knew his loyalties were with the Six now. But could the rest of them say the same thing? He had a bad habit of misplacing his loyalty and getting being shot for it.

"That's a good question," he finally said. "Tell me about the List, Boss. How much of it was real, and how much of it was you being full of shit?"

Gray's head whipped back around and he looked at Remy in surprise. "I don't–"

"Don't fuck with me," Remy warned in a low, dangerous voice. "I'm not in the mood for it. And I'm not as stupid as I look, thank God. I saw the way Thiago looked at you. He didn't know what you were talking about."

Gray clenched his jaw and looked away again. "Come on, Dixie, I'll buy you lunch. You were always easier to deal with when you were being fed."

"No. Tell me now," Remy demanded stubbornly. Gray licked his lips nervously and Remy's heart sank. "There is no list, is there? Shawn was never in danger. You used me. You used him against me."

"We needed you, Remy," Gray hissed in disgust. "You were the only one–hey! Don't walk away from me. Listen," Gray murmured as he grabbed Remy's elbow gently, ever mindful of Remy's admittedly fragile state. "I was given one job; find someone who could move right under the Organization's nose without being caught. I went through hundreds of files, Remy. *Hundreds*. You were the *only* one that could have done what we did."

"That's supposed to justify what you've done? What Thiago's done?"

"No," Gray said grimly. "But the ends justify the means, in this case. Besides–"

"Fuck you, Boss."

"No. What's it matter anyway, huh? He forgave you, right?" Gray said flippantly. "Or did he? He did shoot you, after all."

Remy growled low in his throat and swung at Gray with what little strength he had left. It ended up being more like a left-handed bitch-slap than a punch, but Remy was happy with it all the same. The contact and sound were satisfying, anyway. Gray shook his head and looked back at Remy ruefully.

"I deserved that," Gray admitted candidly. "I apologize. Can we go sit before you pass out?"

"Yeah," Remy said flatly as he realized suddenly that he was a bit light-headed. One bitch-slap a day, then. That's all he could handle. Fucking hell, he hated being shot. The recovery was a bitch. He allowed Gray to lead him back to the car, but he didn't allow Gray to stop explaining as they searched for a place to eat.

"So what are these all-important ends?" he asked pointedly.

Gray sighed and glanced sideways at Remy. "Thiago didn't explain any of this?"

"Nope. That's your job, *Boss*," Remy said caustically.

"Where to start…."

"How 'bout you start at the point that you decided to drag my fuzzy ass into this?"

"I told you, we needed you."

"Why?"

"Because we needed someone who had never been under suspicion. Of course, if I had known then about you and Shawn and how you met I never would have–"

"What does that have to do with it?"

"What?" Gray asked in a shocked voice.

"What does how we met have to do with my never having been under suspicion?"

"Shawn never told you?" Gray asked incredulously.

"Told me what?" Remy asked warily. He didn't know how many more betrayals and secrets he could handle.

"Jesus, Remy," Gray said in exasperation. "You're not in many loops, are you?"

"Apparently not," Remy shot back in agitation. "What hasn't Shawn told me?"

"This is gonna take more than lunch," Gray said grimly. "We might need like… a buffet, or something."

II.

THEY stayed under the radar for the month, traveling from Australia to New Zealand to Japan to Europe, and finally to the States. Nikolaus begged them to go to Los Angeles and retrieve his motorcycle, but Thiago refused the request. They were short on time and they needed to get to Louisiana.

When they arrived in New Orleans, Shawn led them through the airport terminal, down to the long term parking garage. Thiago and the rest of them watched Shawn warily as he walked slowly up to a classic Ford Mustang and ran his hand over the car lovingly. It was a bright, flashy yellow, with a black hood and black hockey stripes down the side. The rear window was louvered and the trunk sported a chin spoiler. Inside the black lines along the side were the words 'Boss 302.'

Thiago couldn't help but whistle at it. It was a beautiful, rare car. He knew he had to have cost upward of $500,000 US.

"That's Remy's car, isn't it?" Nikolaus asked softly.

"How do you know?" Carl asked curiously.

"It's a '69 model," Nikolaus said with a small smile.

"Yeah," Shawn said sadly. "It's his."

Shawn dangled a set of house keys in front of Thiago and started walking toward an older model white Toyota 4Runner without another word.

"You have a place here?" Thiago asked in surprise as he jogged to catch up. Shawn simply shook his head and gestured for the rest of them to get in as he handed the keys to Thiago.

Shawn said very little lately. In fact, Thiago had only heard perhaps twenty words from the other man in the past thirty days. He knew that Shawn spoke to Brandt; mostly late at night and in hushed tones, but Brandt was the only person to whom Shawn spoke.

If Remy didn't show, Thiago wasn't sure what they would do with Shawn. They'd watched him closely to keep him from killing himself, but he seemed to be just withering away regardless of their attempts. He no longer made decisions. He no longer offered advice or opinions. He no longer touched any of them, even Brandt. He allowed himself to be touched, but he never reached out. Never tried to make contact. He was still with them, physically, but mentally, he was lost.

Thiago had never been to New Orleans, and he tried to keep his thoughts from roaming further as he followed Shawn's gestures and one-word directions through the city, toward what he assumed was the famed French Quarter. At first, the buildings looked no different than any other city Thiago had ever visited, and he was sorely disappointed. He had been expecting a bit more from all the hype over the place. But then it was as if they crossed over a line, and were transported back to the eighteenth century. The scenery went from gray, grubby office buildings to festively decorated and lively two- and three-story homes and storefronts in the blink of an eye, and Thiago slowed the vehicle to avoid hitting a horse-drawn carriage in front of them. It was a beautiful area, and Thiago found it hard to keep his eyes off the iron-trellised balconies and the cobblestone streets as he drove.

Shawn gestured to one of the buildings Thiago was admiring, and Thiago pulled the 4Runner into an almost hidden garage behind the building. The brick structure was lovely; a classic example of what Thiago pictured when he thought of New Orleans. It sat on a corner of a block of Royal Street, with a covered balcony wrapping all the way around the second level.

"Wow," Nikolaus murmured as he unbuckled.

Shawn looked out at the house sadly for several seconds, and then got out of the car without a word.

"Is that one house or is it apartments?" Thiago heard Carl murmur curiously as he put the car in park and turned off the ignition.

"Has to be several homes. This must have cost him a fortune," Nikolaus answered under his breath.

Thiago nodded in agreement and they retrieved their bags from the back of the 4Runner and walked out of the garage and up to the front entrance to join Shawn there.

"Is this yours, Beignet?" Carl asked gently as they walked up to stand behind the man.

Shawn shook his head and went about unlocking the door for them. They all gaped at their surroundings like tourists as the key jiggled in the lock.

"It's his," Shawn said softly as he pushed the door open and let them in.

III.

CARL and Nikolaus explored the massive house together, like two little kids in a candy shop. Carl had been floored when Shawn had informed them that the entire building belonged to Remy and that it was indeed a single home. How many people did Remy work for, anyway? And what the fuck was he using to supplement his income, exactly? This place must have cost a fortune, and it was full of an odd mixture of expensive antique and modern furniture that made it one of the most pleasant homes Carl had ever been in.

Carl made good money with what he did, but this was phenomenal wealth. Ill-earned wealth, in Carl's mind.

"Hey, Carl?" Nikolaus finally ventured softly as they found the kitchen once more.

"Hmm?" Carl responded as he looked out the back windows into the private courtyard.

"You think Shawn'll be okay? I mean… if Remy… I mean… I don't think Remy's… I don't think he's coming. Do you?"

Carl looked at Nikolaus sadly for several long seconds. Did Carl think Remy would be meeting them here? It was hard to decipher between hope and belief. He certainly *hoped* Remy would show up. But did he really believe that he would?

"I dunno, Gizmo. All we can do is wait and hope."

"Hope for what?" Thiago's gruff voice asked as the man walked silently into the kitchen from the opposite direction they had.

Carl tried not to jump, but he just could not get used to the way Shawn and Thiago moved. They were so silent. It was unnerving. Carl could be quiet, but he couldn't be completely devoid of noise the way the others were.

"Remy," Nikolaus answered quietly.

Thiago nodded and glided over to the refrigerator. Carl watched him curiously.

"How's Shawn?" he asked as Thiago stood in front of the open appliance.

"Did you two go grocery shopping?" Thiago asked in place of an answer.

"No. We were exploring. Why?" Carl asked as his alarms began to sound.

"This fucking thing is full," Thiago said in a shocked voice.

"What do you mean, full?" Nikolaus asked as he and Carl crowded behind Thiago and looked over his shoulders. The refrigerator was indeed fully stocked, and it all looked to be fresh foods. Fruits and vegetables, deli meats, sodas and beers, and even several different kinds of ice creams graced the freezer.

"The hell?" Carl murmured as hope reared its ugly head once more. Had Remy been here? That would certainly be an appropriate way for Remy to let his presence be known. With food.

"Do you think it was him?" Nikolaus asked in a hopeful whisper.

"No," Shawn said softly from behind them. All three of them jumped and turned around to look at him, like guilty schoolchildren being caught by the headmaster. Brandt stood off to the side looking at Shawn worriedly, but Shawn simply shrugged and gestured toward the cabinets. "I made a call, had it taken care of before we got here."

Carl's heart sank with the man's words. Hope looked to be dwindling the closer they got to nightfall.

Shawn disappeared just as quietly as he had come, and after a tense silence, Thiago followed after the man him.

"How is he?" Carl asked Brandt as soon as he was sure the others were out of earshot.

"If Dixie doesn't show…." Brandt sighed and let his shoulders slump as he sat down at the island in the middle of the kitchen. "If Dixie doesn't show, we'll have to… I dunno… he won't make it, Trigger. He'll get careless. And he'll get himself killed."

IV.

"SHAWN? Wait," Thiago called softly as Shawn mounted the stairs.

Shawn kept moving though. He didn't want another of Thiago's talks. Thiago had been pissed at him, and rightly so. If he'd simply stood down when Thiago told him to, Remy would still be with them. But fucking hell, didn't the man think he was suffering enough without the weekly lectures?

"Shawn!"

"I'm just going to lay down," Shawn mumbled morosely as he reached the top of the staircase and took a left toward the master bedroom. He stopped short and stared at the hallway in horror. Thiago caught up to him, and almost ran into him, as Shawn stood frozen in the middle of the narrow hall.

"What's wrong? Shawn?" Thiago asked as he gripped Shawn's shoulder and shook him slightly, trying to lean around him and get a look at his face.

"Autopilot," Shawn mumbled as he tried to back away from the master bedroom.

Thiago stood behind him like a brick wall and wouldn't let him go anywhere. "What? Shawn… what are you…."

That was the bedroom he and Remy shared when they were between missions. That was the direction his body always went when he climbed these stairs. That was where his feet always took him. To Remy.

"I was on autopilot," Shawn murmured as he tried to get away from the familiar territory.

Shawn could smell him. Remy's scent lingered in the rooms he'd inhabited. He could hear the easy laughter and feel the smile against his face. Remy was everywhere, and yet Shawn couldn't touch him. Couldn't speak to him and hear his voice, save for in his memories. Shawn tried to back away again, and Thiago wrapped his arms around Shawn's shoulders and held him close.

"I can't go in there," Shawn finally croaked. "Please, don't make me."

Thiago pressed into him and growled wordlessly. "Goddammit, Shawn, get hold of yourself and be a fucking man!" Thiago ordered angrily as he shoved Shawn toward the bedroom.

Shawn saw red as memories and pain invaded his senses, and when he calmed once more he was holding Thiago backward over the railing of the stairs. Thiago's feet didn't touch the ground and he balanced on the one-hundred-year-old railing, gripping Shawn's clutching hands and staring at him with wide blue eyes.

"Fuck you, mate!" Shawn yelled as his hands tightened around Thiago's neck. If he hadn't been trying to strangle him, Thiago would already have dropped. The chandelier hanging in the stairwell swayed from the force of their movements and Shawn growled wordlessly as he tried to decide how best to kill the man. Drop or strangle; oh, the choices this business forced him to make.

"You're not the only one who lost him, Shawn," Thiago managed to say as Shawn tried to choke the life out of him.

Shawn's hands loosened their grip as he realized just what it was he was doing, and Thiago scrambled for something to grab onto as he started to fall backward. Shawn cried out in alarm and grabbed the falling man by the shoulders, pulling him back over the railing and falling back against the wall with Thiago clasped tightly in his arms.

"*Boludo*," Thiago panted as he rested his head against Shawn's shoulder.

"Sorry," Shawn mumbled as he looked at the railing warily, as if it had had something to do with Thiago's near-demise. "I can't go in there, Thi," Shawn whispered with a sideways glance at the bedroom. "He's in there. I can't face him yet."

"Okay," Thiago agreed hoarsely. Neither of them moved for long seconds, they simply breathed heavily and stared at the railing accusingly together.

"What did you want to talk to me about?" Shawn finally asked with dread. The least he could do was listen to a lecture after almost killing the man.

"I wanted to see if you were okay," Thiago said as he rolled to his knees and stood up shakily. He looked down at Shawn and offered him a hand. Shawn took it and let Thiago help him up, unable to meet the Argentinean's piercing blue eyes.

"M'okay," Shawn mumbled with another glance at the master bedroom. He edged sideways away from it, and Thiago seemed to take pity on him and stepped into his line of vision.

"We've got about five hours before we even need to do a dry run," he told Shawn gently. "Why don't you show me around? What about the other bedrooms? You can nap in there."

Shawn nodded and shuffled his way down the hall toward the other three bedrooms. He realized with some chagrin that he'd never been in any of these rooms.

At least that meant no memories would assault him here.

"I don't wanna talk, Thi," Shawn said before Thiago closed the door behind them and turned to look at Shawn pointedly.

"You need to, though," Thiago said.

"No. No, I think *you* need to. I think it makes you feel better to give me these little talks, but you know what, Thi? Every time you come to me and tell me 'I told you so,' Brandt comes in after you and ties me to the fucking bed to make sure I don't kill myself!" Shawn yelled angrily. Thiago looked fairly shocked by his outburst, but Shawn continued anyway. "I'm tired of being tied to the bed, Thi!" Shawn shouted as he got close to hysterical thinking about another night tied to the bedposts with his guns and knives out of reach. "Why can't you people just let me kill myself in peace, eh? What the fuck does it matter to you?"

Shawn swatted at Thiago as the man tried to take hold of him, and he continued to rant as he stalked around the room.

"I killed him! He's not showing up this week because I don't bloody well miss when I aim! I killed him, and you know what, Thiago?"

"Shawn, calm down."

"No! I killed him, and I mean to follow him! I never did right by him when I had the chance, the least I can do is rid the world of myself before I go and kill anyone else I love! Christ! I almost pushed you down the fucking stairs!" Shawn yelled as he gestured toward Thiago and turned around to face him.

"Shawn, just– what?" Thiago asked as he froze in mid-step.

"What?" Shawn asked in wary confusion, unsure of what he had said that would make Thiago look so shocked.

"*¿Qué dijo?*" Thiago asked with a slight smile.

"I don't know. Why?" Shawn asked warily as he backed away further.

Thiago advanced on him and pointed a finger at him. "You just said you loved me," he said with a sly smile.

"I did no such thing," Shawn protested as the backs of his thighs hit the mattress. He glanced backwards, looking for something to use as a weapon in case Thiago had lost his mind.

"Yes, you did. You said you loved me," Thiago said as he closed the distance between them. "That means you can't kill yourself," Thiago said softly as he took Shawn's face in his hands.

"Can so," Shawn replied weakly.

"No. Brandt loves you; he wouldn't tie you to the bed if he didn't. Carl and Niko love you. They worry about you, more than you know. I love you," Thiago admitted hesitantly. "And you love us back, you just admitted it. So you can't kill yourself."

Shawn glared at him. He didn't want this. He didn't want logic or professions of love. He wanted to wallow in misery and self-pity like he had been for the past month. That had been nice and masochistic and he wanted to go back to that. Thiago was saying that he loved him. That the others loved him and cared for him. That Shawn wasn't alone like he thought he was and that it wasn't as bad as it seemed. Shawn didn't want that, damn it! Why couldn't they just let him be miserable and die like a good little spy?

"I'm sorry for all the… what was it you called them? Lectures?" Thiago said softly.

His voice wafted over Shawn like a soothing balm over a wound, but Shawn fought the feelings it gave him. He didn't deserve to feel that. He didn't deserve to feel comforted and happy.

"I was trying to get you to… to *feel* something. Anger. Rage. Something besides self-loathing. I was baiting you, hoping you'd fight back. It finally worked. You stood up for yourself."

"You're a bastard," Shawn whispered as his eyes welled with tears.

Thiago nodded in agreement and kissed him gently. Shawn's entire body went limp when Thiago's lips touched his, and Thiago held him close as Shawn groaned pitifully and let his eyes drift shut.

"It'll be okay," Thiago whispered against his temple.

"How?" Shawn asked desperately.

"He'll come, Shawn. I can feel it," Thiago assured him gently as he pressed their foreheads together. Shawn squeezed his eyes closed and breathed in Thiago's scent.

"Oh, God," he moaned, sounding as if he were pain as he clung to Thiago.

"What?"

"You smell like him, Thi," Shawn whispered sorrowfully.

Thiago made to back away from him but Shawn gripped him hard and kissed him once more as the music from the darkening streets wafted to them. He closed his eyes and breathed in Thiago's scent deeply. It did smell like Remy, but it was different as well. It was earthier, like Thiago smoked Remy's cigarettes and then played in a sandbox.

He clung to Thiago tighter and whimpered slightly as he forced himself not to cry. He was a fucking pussy, is what he was. Remy would hate him if he saw him behaving like this.

V.

NIKOLAUS stared worriedly at the doorway through which Shawn and Thiago had disappeared as Carl and Brandt conversed.

"Did you hear that?" he asked them.

"What?" Carl asked as he and Brandt stopped talking and both cocked their heads to listen.

"Sounded like a shout. A cry, maybe," Nikolaus whispered as he strained to hear.

"Better go get the ropes," Brandt mumbled unhappily as he turned to head back out to the car.

"Wally, wait," Carl said sympathetically. He reached out and grabbed Brandt by the arm, and Nikolaus ducked instinctively. It had become a habit of Nikolaus's lately, to flinch when someone else was touched.

If you touched Thiago, someone got yelled at. If you touched Shawn, someone got hit. If you touched Brandt, something caught fire. Carl and Nikolaus had resorted to sleeping in the same room every night just so they could touch each other without fear of one of the three happening.

Waking up on fire was not high on Nikolaus's to do list.

"If Zed's yelling at him again, we'll need to Beignet-proof this entire fucking house," Brandt said testily as he turned around to look at Carl. "No razors, no glass, no scissors… anything club-like; candlesticks, screwdrivers, even the fucking chandeliers. Christ, the fucking balconies. We'll have to take his belts, his shoelaces, anything electric in that fucking toilet. Find all the rat poison, Drano, window cleaner… cling wrap, tin foil, those little plastic things drinks come in. Not to mention the knives, guns, and all my fucking C4! Can't you keep that bastard under control and tell him to stop yelling at him?"

"Yeah. About as well as you can keep Shawn from trying to slit his wrists with a safety razor," Carl spat back.

Nikolaus rolled his eyes and groaned inwardly. Another night, another fight.

"He's a sneaky fuck, all right?" Brandt yelled. "You try to keep a trained killer from killing himself, for fuck's sake!"

"Did you think of maybe *not* physically restraining him every night? Give him some space, some time to grieve."

"What would you know about grieving, Trigger?" Brandt shouted angrily. "How many mother's sons have you killed without a second thought?"

"*Bitte*," Nikolaus cursed under his breath.

He watched Carl's handsome, pleasant features morph into a hard, cold mask and he wondered whether he should hide under the table, hide in a cupboard, or run for help. He sure as fuck wasn't going to interfere.

VI.

EVEN as the words left his mouth, Brandt knew he had made a mistake. A big mistake. A life-threatening mistake. Carl was no longer Carl. He was flat and lifeless and brimming over with anger; Brandt knew he was in danger.

"Trigger, I'm sorry, I didn't–"

Carl moved so quickly that Brandt didn't even have enough time to throw up his hands to defend himself. He hit the ground hard and sucked in a great breath of air. He tried to, anyway. The side of Carl's hand had connected with his windpipe and it felt as if it had been crushed. He couldn't breathe. He couldn't speak to apologize. He couldn't cry for help.

Carl wrapped his arms around Brandt and picked him up off the ground by his neck. Brandt gasped and flailed, but Carl didn't seem bothered by the resistance, and he slammed Brandt face first into the closest wall.

"How many?" Carl hissed. It wasn't Carl's voice. This was something different and evil.

Brandt tried to speak, but it still only came out as a strangled gurgle. Carl took Brandt's arm and twisted it, pinning it behind his back, and Brandt sank to his knees as pain flared through him. This was not the good kind of pain.

A blade came to rest against the pulsing vein in Brandt's neck and Carl whispered, "You can count them when you get to Hell."

"Carl!" Nikolaus's panicked voice cried as the blade cut into Brandt's neck. "Kick his ass, Carl, but don't kill him! Please!"

The blade remained where it was, but the tension in the body holding Brandt slowly ebbed, and finally Carl released him and Brandt fell to the ground with a thump. He sucked in air with difficulty and let his cheek rest against the cool tile of the kitchen floor. Never had cold felt so good.

"I never have second thoughts," Carl said in a calm, icy voice.

When Brandt finally got the strength to look up, Carl was seated calmly at the bar eating a carrot and watching Brandt as if he were a Saturday morning cartoon.

Brandt got to his hands and knees and dabbed at the cut on his neck gingerly.

"Are you okay?" Nikolaus asked concernedly as he helped Brandt to his feet.

Brandt nodded and looked at Carl warily. "Bad Trigger," he muttered accusingly.

Carl shrugged. "You had it coming," he said nonchalantly before biting off another piece of carrot. "Wanker," he added as he chewed.

VII.

REMY sat in the dark hotel room, slumped in one of the two chairs, a glass in one hand and two plane tickets and a joint in the other. He stared at the tickets as if he could make them burst into flame, and like clockwork every twenty seconds, he would lift the glass to his lips and take a sip. It never crossed his mind to set joint to ticket and actually set the things aflame. Where was Brandt when you needed him?

The electronic lock on the door sounded, and the door swung open and closed quietly. "That's not a cigarette I smell," Gray observed in a flat voice as he walked over to the bed and switched on the bedside lamp. "I don't see how getting drunk and high and whatever else you're planning to do helps us at this point," he informed Remy caustically from where he stood by the bed.

"It may not be helping you, but it's certainly making me feel better," Remy said quietly as he glared up at Gray from beneath lowered brows.

"Dixie, look–"

"Don't call me that," Remy said in a low, dangerous voice.

Gray stopped in mid-sentence and snapped his mouth shut.

Remy took another sip of the drink he held and looked back down at the tickets. "I'll be damned if I'm going down there, Boss. You may as well get your money back," Remy said as he tossed the two tickets onto the floor and stared at Gray defiantly.

Gray looked at the tickets for several long seconds, then back up at Remy. "What about Thiago? What about the others? You can just walk away from them?"

"You bet your ass I can," Remy growled before throwing back the rest of the drink and standing up quickly. His world spun and he flopped back down onto the chair inelegantly. Gray snickered and came to kneel in front of Remy.

"Loss of blood plus four cocktails on an empty stomach make Remy a dizzy boy, hmm?"

"Fuck you, Boss," Remy muttered as he took a long drag and then held his breath as Gray glared at him.

"As tempting as the offer is, I must decline this time. We have a plane to catch."

"No," Remy said in a strained voice before deliberately blowing the smoke back out into Gray's face.

"Remy–"

"I'm not going, Gray! Every word he ever said to me was a fucking lie. A *mission*," Remy spat. "He… he fucking tried to kill me!"

"I thought he was protecting you from me?" Gray asked gently.

"I thought so too, but I loved him, Boss… I… every day was a lie."

"I know you love him, doll," Gray said sadly as he patted Remy's knee.

"Oh my God, do you think he was trying to kill me when he shot me in the ass?" Remy asked in horror.

"He shot you in the ass?"

"That bastard! I'll kill him!" Remy growled, not taking into account the fact that Shawn could have flipped him on the nose and taken him down at that point, if he had been present.

"I thought you refused to believe it until I showed you proof," Gray observed slyly. Remy glared at him.

"We've been through that, *non*? I demand proof; you say you can't give me proof without a team of at least five. I say we can do it the two of us, you say we'd need more weapons. We can't get weapons without Melinda Oliver, and we can't get Melinda without Brandt, and we can't get Brandt without Shawn, and I want nothing to do with Shawn 'til I have proof! Goddammit! I want proof, Gray! I don't fucking believe you!" Remy yelled as his brain did a merry dance around his common sense.

"And here we go again," Gray muttered as he got up and rubbed his eyes.

"You've lied to me before, why should I believe you now?" Remy asked as he tried to stand.

"Because you do," Gray said simply as Remy fell back against the chair once more.

"How do you know?" Remy asked obstinately.

"Because you said you did," Gray said with another sly smile.

"The fuck I did… when?" Remy asked suspiciously.

"Before you started drinking. About two weeks ago, in case you'd like a reference point."

Remy blinked up at Gray and mulled that over. "Two weeks?"

"I'm sorry; do I need to use smaller words?" Gray asked mockingly.

"That means…."

"That's right, Sherlock. You're supposed to be in New Orleans. Tonight."

"But–"

"Remy, you're a bright kid. The best out there, in fact. Now please tell me it was the booze and weed and not your undying love for this man that's killed that many brain cells," Gray requested sarcastically. "You don't have to let on that you know everything you know. We'll go to New Orleans. We'll find the others, propose our plan, and let them choose their own paths from there."

"And Shawn?"

"Keep your friends close, Remy, but your enemies closer, right?" Gray advised sagely.

"Shawn's not my enemy," Remy muttered.

"Oh? Then why don't you explain to me why–"

"He was under orders!" Remy shouted angrily.

He and Gray stared one another down, but considering that Remy was seeing two Grays, and they both looked pretty pissed off, he didn't stand much of a chance in that contest.

"You know, it would probably make a lot more sense if you weren't stoned out of your mind," Gray said after a long silence.

"What were we talking about?" Remy asked as he squinted up at Gray.

Gray sighed in exasperation and sat down on the bed in front of Remy. "You have a couple choices here, Remy. I'll lay them out for you. First choice; either you believe me, or you don't. My advice would be to believe me, 'cause really," Gray huffed with a gesture, the meaning of which Remy couldn't quite identify. "Second choice; if you do believe me, which you should, you then have to decide whether or not you're going to forgive and forget and live happily ever after with the man you obviously love, or whether you're going to kill him. Me, I'd opt for Door Number Two there, 'cause Shawn's a bit of a bastard, after all. Third–"

"Wait, you lost me at Door Number Two," Remy muttered in confusion. He really didn't need to be this altered at this stage in life. He silently handed the joint over to Gray and watched sadly as Gray snuffed it out and tossed it away.

"Third choice! If you decide to kill Shawn, I'll be happy to help. If not, then you've got more choices."

"Hey, Boss?"

"Hmm?"

"You really are telling me the truth, aren't you?" Remy asked sadly.

"Yeah," Gray answered regretfully. "No matter which way you cut it, Remy, Shawn's not who he says he is."

VII.

THIAGO listened to the rhythmic beat of the music as it drifted to them through the windows. The sun had barely gone down, but the nightlife was already lively. The music was soothing and exhilarating and somehow strangely familiar, even though Thiago knew he'd never heard it before. He felt at ease and, strangely enough, at home. Thiago decided right then and there, as he lay in the bed with Shawn stretched out next to him, that if ever he were to get out of this business, New Orleans would be a good place to disappear.

"Did you hear that?" Shawn murmured as he rolled onto his side and looked at the closed door warily.

"Music?" Thiago suggested hopefully. He didn't want to move. He didn't want to deal with anything sharp or hot or trigger-happy.

"Sounded like a thump?" Shawn said uncertainly. "A fight, maybe?"

"Get dressed?" Thiago asked quietly, hoping that Shawn would say 'no' and they could just remain where they were. Shawn looked at him thoughtfully for several seconds, his fingers playing over the hairs on Thiago's chest. Finally, he sighed regretfully and nodded.

"Which one snapped, d'you think?" Shawn asked as he slid out of bed and reached for his khakis. "My money's on Carl."

"Nah. Not unless Brandt poked him with a stick of dynamite. I'm betting Niko," Thiago said with a little grin. "Poor guy, he's due, don't you think?"

Shawn smiled wanly and nodded.

The two men padded down the hallway warily, both shirtless and barefoot but still gripping their guns. They paused at the top of the stairs and listened intently, and the sound of soft conversation coming from somewhere on the lower floor allowed them both to relax slightly and exchange wry glances.

Thiago's eyes drifted to Shawn's bare torso, and Shawn cocked an eyebrow at him. Shawn's hand slid up Thiago's chest to his shoulder and wrapped around the back of his neck. Thiago watched Shawn's eyes wordlessly, noting the spark of desire that mingled with the now-constant sadness, and Shawn met his eyes as he pulled him close and kissed him gently. When he pulled back, Thiago could plainly see the war going on in Shawn's head. He felt guilty, and probably lost. Thiago patted him on the head for lack of a better action to express his sympathy, and they both smiled and snickered in a most inappropriate manner. Without a word, they both turned around and went to retrieve the rest of their clothing.

"Hey," Thiago said softly as he pulled a white T-shirt from his bag and twisted it nervously in his hands. Shawn straightened from where he was bent over his own bag and turned to look at Thiago. "If you need to talk, we're all here, y'know." Shawn looked at him silently and then nodded. "I mean…." Thiago stepped forward and took hold of Shawn's shoulder.

"Thiago, calm down," Shawn said with a small smile as he ran a hand through Thiago's hair. "We fucked. It was good and we'll be doing it again, I'm sure.

I don't need therapy," he said with a small smile.

Thiago smiled in return, though he wasn't so sure about the truth of the statement. Shawn had secrets, that much was obvious. Thiago would hear them eventually, one way or another.

When Thiago and Shawn entered the kitchen, Carl sat at the island, reading a newspaper and eating what looked to be a stick of celery from a plate that was full of other such healthy stuff. Brandt and Nikolaus huddled at the other end of the island, intermittently casting furtive glances at Carl and whispering. If Thiago didn't know better, he would have thought they were scared. That couldn't be right. The only things that scared Brandt were water and fire extinguishers.

"You two all right?" Carl asked nonchalantly as Thiago stopped in the doorway to examine the scene.

"Yeah," Thiago answered slowly in a tone that he was sure sounded suspicious.

Shawn stood at Thiago's shoulder, and Thiago could almost feel the man's eyes burning into Brandt, so intense was his concentration. Shawn appeared to be back in the land of the living, momentarily at least, and he obviously thought the scene somewhat odd as well.

"You're bleeding," Shawn observed as he walked past Thiago and circled the island slowly. His eyes never left Brandt, and Brandt sat up straighter, looking like a dog whose master had just walked into the room. "What happened?" Shawn asked sternly as he eyed each of the three men.

Thiago felt a thrill go through his body. Was it possible that Shawn was really back? He'd been completely unresponsive for almost an entire month. Even when Brandt had accidentally set Thiago on fire, Shawn had just sat and watched as Carl and Nikolaus rolled him on the floor. He wasn't crazy in the sense that he had taken pleasure in watching Thiago be set on fire, like Brandt had. He just hadn't cared. But now he appeared to actually give a shit about them again.

"We had a…." Nikolaus trailed off and looked at Brandt. Brandt's eyes widened and he looked at Carl as if for guidance.

"An episode," Carl supplied easily as he turned the page he was reading.

Shawn cocked an eyebrow disbelievingly and Thiago looked at Carl a little closer.

"Did you finally try to kill him?" Shawn asked as he took one of Carl's celery sticks and bit the end off it.

Brandt slumped dejectedly and Thiago frowned as Carl looked up at Shawn blankly. "I didn't *try*," Carl informed icily. "If I had *tried* to kill him, we'd be cleaning up the puddle."

Brandt's hand went to his neck and Thiago's frown deepened. "Is this something we need to fix?" Thiago asked uneasily. "Or has it been settled already?"

"All's well that ends well, yeah?" Carl said flippantly as he rolled up the newspaper and tossed it at Brandt. "Set that on fire, Wally, you'll feel better."

Brandt glared at him for several seconds, but then a slow smile spread on his handsome face and he and Carl grinned at one another.

"I think I need dinner," Nikolaus muttered suddenly, and they all looked at him as if he had lost his mind. "I mean, I could eat, y'know? Food?"

"Niko?" Thiago said as he pointed his finger and beckoned Nikolaus to come to him. Something was definitely amiss, and Nikolaus was the only one in the group Thiago knew he could intimidate into telling him what had happened. "We need to talk."

"Talk later," Shawn said authoritatively as he threw the celery stick at Brandt. Nikolaus looked at him gratefully. "Food now."

"Are you back, then?" Carl asked curiously as he stood and looked at Shawn.

"Back?" Shawn asked warily.

Carl took a step closer and looked at Shawn intently. There was something slightly different about Carl at that moment, but Thiago couldn't quite put his finger on it. Whatever it was, Thiago didn't like it. It gave him goose bumps and made him shiver, as if Carl were the ice to Brandt's flame.

Carl hummed noncommittally, and he turned around to look at Thiago questioningly. Thiago shrugged, and Carl shrugged back at him. "What are you in the mood for, Gizmo?" he asked as he started walking casually toward the door. "*Étouffée*? *Fricassee*?" he asked with a smile as he walked out of the kitchen into the private courtyard. "Gator?" he asked with a smirk as he walked out of view and finally out of earshot.

"Is he okay?" Thiago asked no one in particular.

"He's just stressed," Brandt mumbled as he grabbed Nikolaus and dragged the smaller man out into the courtyard.

Nikolaus mumbled something that sounded suspiciously like 'crazy fuckers' as he was swept past, but Thiago didn't quite hear it. He and Shawn looked at one another blankly before shrugging simultaneously and following.

Shawn led them to a tiny restaurant called The Gumbo Shop. Dinner there was an interesting affair, simply because it went smoothly, to Thiago's complete and utter shock. There were no fights, no napkins spontaneously combusting, no groping under the table, and no undue attention being paid to the five of them. It was really quite pleasant. They rarely ate out for these obvious reasons, but it seemed they all felt safe here, and Shawn even knew several of the passers-by by name.

He returned their greetings softly as the five of them walked casually through the streets after dinner. The people were calling him Sumner, and Thiago couldn't figure out whether the alias was supposed to be Shawn's first name or his last. Either way, Thiago was enjoying himself. Shawn told the stories and histories of the various buildings and sites as they walked, and Thiago felt ridiculously normal and safe.

Carl and Brandt seemed to be on good terms once more, and Nikolaus bounced excitedly between them like a pinball as they took in the sights and sounds and smells. They walked one block from the restaurant, and Shawn stopped as they came upon an entire city block of grass, trees, paths, and noble-looking statues.

"That's Jackson Square," Shawn said in his soft fake accent. It was a decent imitation of Remy's Cajun. Thiago had been a little surprised to hear it at first. He had to keep reminding himself that Shawn apparently spent a lot of time down here, and he had to keep up appearances. "You wouldn't believe the amount of shit he could get into down here," Shawn said softly as he looked around.

They were all aware of whom he spoke, and the French Quarter had been the locale of several of Remy's adventures, judging from the wistful way in which Shawn looked out on it.

"It's, uh, it's about eight o'clock," Nikolaus said softly. "Shouldn't we be getting on?"

"Yeah," Shawn said in a soft voice.

Thiago put a tentative hand on Shawn's elbow, and Shawn seemed to shake himself and started walking once more, in the opposite direction from which they had come. They passed by the Café du Monde, where Shawn looked over all the patrons in the outdoor sitting area carefully before heading on.

Horses clopped by drawing carriages and drunken couples and groups swayed around them, laughing and giggling. Music wafted from the many bars and restaurants, and the smells of food and coffee and river mud mingled in the air. Thiago could definitely see why Remy and Shawn picked this place for their occasional down time. There was so much activity, they could have walked around in black trench coats with machine guns and no one would have thought it odd.

Even as he thought it, a man walked swiftly past them wearing a long black cape, a top hat, and carrying a cane with a silver skull on the handle. Yeah. Even Brandt wouldn't stand out down here.

Shawn didn't give the man a second glance, merely nodded at him idly in passing and continued on his way. He turned them left on Rue St. Phillip, and they walked several blocks in silence. Shawn stopped dead in his tracks just as they were coming up on Royal Street once more and stared at the establishment on his left in abject horror.

"Something wrong?" Carl asked softly as he edged up to Shawn.

"It's gone," Shawn whispered, forgetting his affected accent momentarily.

"What?"

"The bar. It's not here," Shawn hissed.

"We knew that," Carl reminded in a low voice as he came closer to Shawn. "You told us it closed down."

"But… the *bar*," Shawn breathed. "It's been fronted over. There's nothing here."

"What do you mean? Not here?" Brandt said as he lit a woman's cigarette for her and nodded as she thanked him and then moved on.

"Must be a private residence now," Shawn murmured as he ran his hands through his hair in agitation.

"What now?" Thiago asked in a patient voice as the man in the cape walked by them again and entered the pub across the street. Thiago looked after the man suspiciously. What was he doing, laps?

"Are you sure you didn't have a Plan B, Shawn?" Nikolaus asked in a quiet voice as the five of them unconsciously huddled together in the street.

"This is Beignet and Dixie you're talking about, mate," Carl said caustically. "We're lucky they had a Plan A."

Thiago jabbed him in the ribs and glared at him even as he tried not to snicker. Carl put his arm around Thiago and leaned closer to the others as Shawn frowned in concentration.

"I don't know. I don't know where he'd go if he… if…."

"Yeah you do, Beignet," Brandt said gently. "Just think for a minute. What would he do?"

Shawn stared at Brandt for several seconds, then turned his head to look at the bar across the street. Flanagan's Pub. A sign sat out front advertising nightly Ghost Tours, and Shawn walked over to it slowly as the others followed in his wake.

"These used to start from The Morgue," Shawn murmured as he pointed at the sign. "Wonder if they're the same ones?" he said as he turned to look at Thiago questioningly.

"Let's just see about tickets then, shall we?" Thiago said pleasantly as he dragged Carl with him into the pub.

VIII.

CARL looked around the pub warily. It was small. And it was dark. And it was crowded. And it was loud. Carl did not like small, dark, crowded, and loud, not unless his target was there. It was so easy to kill someone in a place like this.

The others seemed to know this, too, and even Nikolaus was hanging back in the entryway warily. The more Carl saw of Nikolaus's instincts, the more impressed he was with the man.

"See the cape?" Thiago murmured into Carl's ear. Carl nodded. He had noticed the man earlier, it was hard not to. "Does that look like a getup Remy would wear?"

"Certainly does," Carl muttered.

He and Thiago separated without another word and spread out, and Shawn walked up to the bar, heedless of the danger, to inquire of the bartender what had become of the spot where the Morgue had once stood. He was still taking unnecessary risks, seemingly not giving a shit whether he was putting himself in danger. Carl worried about him, and he worried about the rest of the group. Remy's absence and Shawn's indifference were destroying them, one day at a time.

Carl watched the man with the cape, trying to decide whether his mannerisms and stature matched those of Remy. He didn't think they did, but then, he had seen Remy morph from frightened little boy into hardcore assassin right in front of his eyes, so he couldn't really be sure.

Just as Thiago re-entered Carl's line of sight, the man in the cape jumped onto a table and began banging his cane on the scarred tabletop. Carl blinked at him, his hand already at the gun in his shoulder holster, even if it was out of reach beneath the sweatshirt he wore, but the pub went silent and everyone turned to the caped man and listened raptly.

"Good evening, ladies and gentlemen! Will everyone here for the Ghost Tour please migrate over here to me? Thanks folks, if you can just… scoot… there… nice…." Carl lost what he was saying as the chatter started up once more. Ghost Tour leader. How appropriate.

Carl shot Thiago a wry look across the room and started making his way back toward Brandt and Nikolaus at the door.

"Sir? Sir? Please," a small voice said from behind Carl, and it took him a moment to realize that the woman was speaking to him. She tugged on the hood of his sweatshirt and he turned around to look at her. She was young and petite and sort of plain, not pretty but certainly not hard to look at. She blinked up at Carl as if he had surprised her, and he waited patiently for her to find her tongue, all the while keeping most of his attention on the patrons around him. Thiago was warily sidling closer to them, and Brandt and Nikolaus had begun to move toward him as well. "I was– that is– we were wondering if you– my friends and I– if you would maybe… do us a, uh… a favor," the girl stuttered as she gestured toward two other women, both similar in height and build to her. Carl looked at them silently and then back at her, waiting for her to spit it out. "There are these guys… they've been following us around all night…," she drifted off and her brown eyes widened theatrically.

Carl felt a presence behind him and turned slightly to see a man loitering at his left shoulder. The girl's eyes widened further and she actually took a step backwards.

Carl looked at the man and then back at the three girls, who were now fairly cowering, and he turned to let his shoulder face the man in a subtly combative stance. Carl's eyes found Brandt, and Brandt's eyes flicked to where Carl knew Nikolaus to be. Thiago and Shawn were probably hovering around somewhere as well, and this man and his two buddies didn't stand a chance if they decided to pick a fight.

"Can I help you, mate?" Carl asked coolly as he stepped in front of the little brunette and into the path of the man's drunken glare.

"Mate?" the man mimicked, and he turned to his two friends to have a nice little chuckle.

Carl looked over his shoulder at the woman and raised his eyebrows inquiringly. She nodded and stepped closer to him for protection.

"Please make them go away," she pleaded in a whisper.

Carl turned back around to look at the three giggling morons and sighed inwardly. This would take finesse. Carl wasn't in the mood for finesse, goddammit! He wanted to kill something!

He restrained the natural instinct to reach out and snap the man's neck with his pinkie finger, and he turned his back on the three men to face the girls once more.

"Were we going on this Ghost Tour, then?" he asked cheerfully, and they all looked up at him gratefully. Carl put his hands out to the sides in a friendly manner, and they drifted toward him as if the circle of his arms would protect them from the three now angry men. With his outstretched hand, he gestured subtly for Brandt to join him.

"*Oi! Mate!*," the Head Moron said sarcastically in a horrible imitation of Carl's accent. "I think you need to mind your own business."

Brandt made his way through the tight crowd like a heated knife cutting through butter, and Carl turned deliberately around to look at the men again. When he was facing the Three Morons once more, Brandt was standing beside him, his arms crossed and his silver lighter in his hand, flicking, lighting, snapping closed. Nikolaus materialized from out of the crowd and stood on Carl's other side, introducing himself to the three frightened women and calming them with easy smiles and humor.

Carl took a step toward the first man and smiled pleasantly. "Are you trying to enlighten us as to what our business may be?" Carl asked icily, and he heard Brandt's lighter flare and snap closed behind him.

The man's eyes widened and he backed away slightly, shaking his head. The Three Morons made their retreat, and Carl turned to grin at Brandt. He hadn't gotten to kill anything, but it had been rather fun, regardless.

Carl caught Thiago's eye as he turned, and Thiago slid through the crowd to speak to him.

"Looks like we're going ghostbusting," Carl murmured as he watched Nikolaus chat up the three women.

Brandt hovered as only Brandt could, and though the three women gave him several wary glances, they looked to be more relaxed now that the immediate threat was gone.

"Keep an eye out. Shawn told me that Remy loves these things," Thiago whispered as he gestured toward the man in the cape. "The tours and ghost stories and shit. Watch for anything that might appeal to him. Tell Niko as well, he seems to know Remy's… whatever it is. Preferences."

Carl nodded and stepped toward the others, but Thiago grabbed him and looked at him carefully.

"Stay out of trouble, if you can. And watch for Remy. He may be here."

"Got it. What about you?"

"We'll be around. Meet you back at the house in three."

Carl nodded again and Thiago was gone, disappearing into the crowd. Carl sighed heavily and turned around to look at the others.

Nikolaus smiled at him and said, "And that's Barney," Nikolaus said to the three women. They all smiled shyly at him and Carl nodded.

"Thanks so much for that. They were really starting to creep us out," the alpha girl said sincerely.

Carl smiled. "No problem," he said softly. It looked as if they would be stuck with these women for several hours. The three of them turned to listen to the rest of what the Caped Crusader was saying, and Carl glared at Nikolaus. "Barney?" he hissed.

"Hey, I could've used one of Remy's names," Nikolaus whispered back. "You could've been Beauregard or Cletus or something, so no bitching."

IX.

SHAWN and Thiago stepped back out into the cool night air together, and Shawn sighed heavily.

"I've got shit for luck," Shawn murmured as he looked at what used to be the Morgue.

"Quit your sulking," Thiago chastised with a slight smile to soften the blow of his words. Shawn nodded and pursed his lips. "What did the bartender say?"

"The Morgue closed back in March of 2003," Shawn said as he dug in his pocket for his cigarettes. He laughed humorlessly and shook his head. "It's a private residence now. Fucking place," he said as he lit his cigarette and offered the pack to Thiago.

"What's the plan, then?" Thiago asked as he took a cigarette out of the proffered pack and leaned in to light it with Shawn's. Through the smoke, Shawn could smell Thiago's scent, and even as his body responded to the erotic memories it produced, his heart felt heavy with sadness and guilt.

It wasn't a rational guilt. He and Remy had never been anything close to exclusive. They'd shared notes on partners in the past, and by Shawn's count, Remy had been with each of the other four men at least once. And that was the way both men liked it. But now, Shawn felt guilty at the drop of a hat.

"I'll give you a tour," Shawn told Thiago gruffly.

They headed toward Royal Street, walking slowly and without purpose, simply enjoying the atmosphere and the semi-solitude. Shawn pointed up the street to indicate where the house was located, just to allow Thiago to regain his bearings.

"How did Remy afford that?" Thiago asked carefully as they walked.

"I never asked," Shawn responded sadly. "I never asked him a lot of things I should have."

"He'll be here, Shawn," Thiago said sympathetically. "I can feel it."

"Wish I could say the same," Shawn said just before he grabbed Thiago and pulled him out of the road as a vehicle flew by. Thiago looked at him with wide blue eyes and snorted. "Louisiana is one of the only places in the world where pedestrians aren't given the right of way," Shawn said as he patted Thiago on the head and grinned. "They're allowed to run you over. Which, when combined with the fact that pedestrians are allowed to carry open alcoholic beverages as they stumble through the streets, is probably not all that good a combination," he added thoughtfully as a group of tourists walked by. Many of them held plastic cups with various kinds of almost lethal concoctions. Thiago smiled in amusement.

"Lovely, that," Thiago murmured as they continued on.

It reminded Shawn of so many nights in the past when he and Remy had walked like this. Just walked and enjoyed the companionship. They didn't get much down time, but when they did, they always came here. Shawn closed his eyes and breathed in the familiar scents. He could see Remy, walking beside him and smiling, gesticulating wildly as he told a story and waving to strangers and acquaintances alike. He could feel Remy's body pressed to him, gripping him and pulling him into a side street for a stolen kiss, and he could hear him laughing merrily when they were caught by drunken tourists. He could smell him, that sweet familiar smell that was so like Thiago's and yet unique. He could taste him.

God, he missed him.

Shawn's breath caught in his throat and he choked back the threat of tears. If Remy didn't show, he would end it. He would end it and put himself out of this misery. Take the easy way out. The pain and guilt were almost unbearable now, and what little good his earlier cleansing had done was suddenly wiped away as the ghosts of New Orleans assaulted him.

Suddenly the hairs on the back of Shawn's neck pricked up, and he knew instinctively he was being watched. He felt Thiago stiffen almost imperceptibly beside him, and he turned his head casually to look at the other man.

Thiago was on the alert, a trained eye could tell that much, and they shared a concerned look before Thiago slowly bent down to tie his shoe. Shawn watched him, looking for movement out of the corners of his eyes, and Thiago took the opportunity to look behind them as he knelt.

"Anyone there?" Shawn asked without moving his slightly parted lips.

"I thought… someone's out there, but I can't see anything," Thiago murmured as he stood back up and they continued walking.

Shawn said nothing and kept his head down as he walked. Did he dare to hope that it could be Remy? If it was, then they wouldn't catch a glimpse of him. They wouldn't know it until Remy wanted him to know. Them. They wouldn't know it until Remy wanted *them* to know.

X.

THE Painter stood in the shadows of the sunken doorway he'd stepped into as refuge from the Argentinean's seeking eyes. He watched as the two men walked slowly away. They hadn't seen him, but he'd gotten careless and they'd marked him somehow.

His job was to watch and wait. He was, essentially, the laser that painted the target, and he'd followed them all the way from Sydney without them sensing his presence. But the amount of unbridled activity in this town made him edgy, and he'd been afraid of losing them. He had moved in closer and overstepped, and now they'd marked him.

"Fuck," the Painter muttered as he looked at his watch and sighed. Two more days of this and the Hunter would be here to clean up this mess.

He would have to back off and follow the other three. Trying to get close to two Class One agents had been an idiotic thing to do, and the Painter mentally kicked himself for trying it. He waited until the two men had walked far enough away, then he started back down Royal Street toward Flanagan's.

A little Ghost Tour never hurt anyone.

XI.

"WHERE'D you disappear off to?" Brandt asked as Nikolaus came scurrying up to the back of the tour group.

"Had to take care of business," Nikolaus said defensively.

"So where are y'all from?" the brunette asked them as Nikolaus and Brandt looked at one another warily. "Australia? Germany?"

"Yeah," Brandt answered without taking his eyes off Nikolaus. Carl shook his head in irritation and poked at Nikolaus to make him move forward faster. They were losing the tour.

"And he's from New Zealand," Brandt provided with a jerk of his thumb at Carl. "He likes sheep."

Carl smothered a snort and whapped Brandt in the arm, and Nikolaus's voice wavered as he said, "In town for a company conference."

That explanation seemed to satisfy the three women, and they carried on with the tour in relative silence, listening to the stories the guide told them. Nikolaus had expected more simpering and batting of eyelashes from them, but the three women were surprisingly uninterested in the three of them. Perhaps it was obvious the men had spent the last four or so months shagging one another senseless, Nikolaus reasoned. Good to know.

Carl seemed to be a little too alert for Nikolaus's liking, and Nikolaus was worried about the other man. He had lifted off into Assassin Mode, but he'd somehow burned out before re-entry. He was now orbiting somewhere out there between their old, sweet teddy bear Carl and this new 'kill it if it moves' evil-teddy version. It was frightening and beyond disturbing. Nikolaus was having serious second thoughts about their sleeping arrangements. He didn't want to be in bed with the evil-teddy version of Carl.

XII.

AS they walked, they heard several different ghost stories, saw several people fall down because they were all drinking copiously, and got into one minor fight when Brandt poked Carl in the eye for calling him a wanker earlier.

Delayed reactions were worth the effort sometimes, just to see people's reactions to them.

The three women set off Brandt's rusty alarm bells, but so far they'd had no problems from them, aside from a little bit of ass-grabbing Brandt was fairly certain hadn't been one of the girls after all.

"Okay, which of you grabbed my ass?" Brandt asked jokingly as they came up on what looked to be a church. The three girls looked at him in horror, blushed, and all proceeded to shrug and babble and point at each other accusingly. Brandt looked at Carl and Nikolaus suspiciously. Nikolaus just rolled his eyes, but Carl grinned maliciously at him.

"If I wanted to grab your ass, I'd just do it, mate," Carl said as he took a step closer and grabbed Brandt's ass and squeezed. He hummed appraisingly and looked Brandt up and down like one would a used car. "Good stock. Could use a good shearing, though."

"Baaa," Brandt responded with a cheeky grin.

The girls giggled and tried their best not to look, and Nikolaus snickered to himself as they came to a halt and waited for the tour guide to go into his next story.

Brandt observed the area closely, thinking that this looked like a place Remy would like. It was old and beautiful, with a decidedly sinister Church-nunnery air about it. Old, dry wood. It would go up in flames in seconds.

He zoned back in just as the guide said the words 'vampiric attacks.'

"Whathuh?" Brandt whispered in Carl's ear. Carl leant over and pointed at the top floor of the part-church part-nunnery part-tinderbox.

"He says they keep coffins up there. Windows and doors to the top floor are nailed shut and sealed. People get eaten."

"Ah," Brandt said as if that had caught him up.

"The students were found on the steps of this very church the next morning," the guide was saying as he gestured grandly with his cane. "Their throats ripped open and their bodies completely drained of blood," he added with a certain malicious glee. At least he enjoyed his job. "Now, are there any doctors or nurses in the crowd? Does anyone know what it takes to completely drain a body of blood?"

"Filet knife," Carl muttered under his breath as he stood with his arms crossed and his head lowered. Brandt snorted and Nikolaus looked at them both askance.

"Even if you hang someone upside down and slit their throat," the tour guide continued. "All the blood wouldn't drain from the body. The blood pools inside your limbs, you see. And there was no blood around the bodies of the two students. Not a drop was ever found. Where did that blood go, I ask you?" the man finished with another grand sweep of his hand toward the mysterious top floor.

There were murmurs and excited chattering from the crowd and Brandt would have sworn Carl was grinning.

"Now those windows up there are nailed closed. Every year more nails are added, blessed by Holy Water. Now that's over one-hundred and fifty years worth of nails. Would any of you like to try to explain why, once or twice a year, those windows are found open in the morning?"

The crowd murmured nervously.

"Now my advice to you, my friends, is to not walk by this building at night without the safety of numbers. And if ever you do happen upon it and see those windows open… run for your lives," the man finished gravely.

Brandt felt chills go up and down his spine, and Nikolaus shivered beside him. The three girls they protected scooted closer to them, and even Carl seemed affected by the tale. Brandt was glad when they moved on.

An hour later, the tour was over, and Carl, Brandt, and Nikolaus walked the three girls to their hotel to ensure their safety. They were thanked with fluttering eyelashes and kisses on their cheeks, and with that, their job was done. They set off for the house on Royal Street.

Walking back through the nearly deserted streets, Brandt shivered uncontrollably. It was like they were being watched, but every time Brandt turned around, he could see nothing suspicious. Carl seemed on edge as well, and Nikolaus was practically pissing himself as he walked.

"Starting to wish we'd brought Thiago with us," Nikolaus mumbled.

"You think Thiago's scarier than we are?" Carl asked good-humouredly.

"No. You're certainly the scariest with your…." Nikolaus flailed for a moment and then waved his hand through the air dismissively. "But Thi's definitely smarter than we are," he grumbled as they walked through the middle of the street. Carl snorted and Brandt grinned.

There was something exhilarating about what they were doing, walking down the middle of the street in the middle of the night as a party raged on several streets away. Brandt didn't know what it was exactly. It gave him the same little burst of pleasure that flicking his lighter did. He reached into his pocket to finger the precious piece of silver, but he stopped dead in his tracks when he saw where they were.

His lighter all but forgotten, he stared up at the tinderbox church thing in horror.

"Hey, Wally? You all right, mate?" Carl asked in concern when he realized Brandt was no longer beside him.

"Look at the windows, Trigger," Brandt whispered.

Carl and Nikolaus turned to look up at the building, and when they saw the gaping black holes of the open windows, they both unconsciously began to back away from the structure.

"Uhh," Carl said uncertainly as he looked around. The street was deserted, though they could see activity further down. It was as if this block was being purposefully avoided.

"I'll run if you run," Brandt whispered to the other two. They all exchanged wary glances. "No one tells a soul," Brandt proposed.

Nikolaus nodded furiously and backed away. Carl blinked at Brandt, licked his lips nervously, and then he turned and pushed Nikolaus along and skittered away from the building. Brandt ran after them, and not one of them looked back until they stood in front of the house on Royal Street, panting ever so slightly and shivering.

"I get to sleep with Carl tonight," Nikolaus proclaimed as they let themselves into the house.

"No. Mine," Brandt growled.

"Safety in numbers," Carl suggested nervously as they headed up the stairs to the bedroom, where they could plainly hear Shawn and Thiago fucking.

Safety in numbers sounded just fine to Brandt.

XIII.

REMY and Gray stood on the street, looking up into the unlit windows of the structure Remy referred to as Les Bon Temps Royale. It was well into the early morning hours, and all activity within the house ceased some time ago.

"How do we get in?" Gray asked in a low voice. There were still people on the street, not many, but enough to make Gray a little twitchy. Remy looked at him in surprise.

"I'm not going in there," he said with a little gesture of the hand that was still in his coat pocket. "Did you see how keyed up they all were? Something spooked them tonight. No way I'm trying to sneak up on any of them."

Gray nodded and stared at Remy for several long seconds. Remy stared back at him.

"Still a little high?" Gray asked finally.

"Little bit, yeah," Remy answered immediately, and they both turned to stare at the house some more.

"So how do we get in?" Gray asked after several more moments of staring. He seemed to know that, despite Remy's declaration he wouldn't be going into the house, they would be going anyway. Remy smiled grimly.

"Gallery would be the best bet," he answered thoughtfully. "Though, the Romeo Catchers are a problem. Not so much going up, but coming down, *podna*, they'll tear you a new one. Several new ones."

"The what? And what's a gallery?" Gray asked in confusion.

Remy blinked at him, then turned and pointed up at the gallery under which they were standing.

"This is a gallery. Balcony with two levels. And see those little spiky-barb things on the poles? Those are Romeo Catchers. Back when all of these houses belonged to wealthy landowners and society types, they had to protect the virtue of their daughters, see. So they put those barbs on the supports of the galleries to keep suitors from scaling them."

"You sound like a tour guide," Gray said dryly.

Remy shrugged. "I be *cadien*," he said nonchalantly. "Anyway, you can get up them okay, 'cause they don't really keep them sharp no more, but making a swift retreat down might be painful, I think."

"Lovely," Gray murmured as he looked up at the night sky. "Dawn'll be here soon," he added, and he looked up both ways of Royal Street. "Are we going in, then?"

"Yeah," Remy said grimly.

"How? You're in no shape to be shimmying up polls and scaling walls there, Romeo," Gray said wryly.

Remy shivered uncontrollably and tried to clear his mind of the lingering buzz. Five hours on a plane, with a perpetually bleeding knife wound on your arm and a lot of alcohol and weed in your system, did not make for a clear head. His right arm was really not having a good year. He dug around in his pocket and produced a set of house keys, and he smiled as he dangled them in front of Gray.

"It my house, Boss," he informed the man with a grin.

Gray rolled his eyes and looked back at the house. "On we go, then," he murmured.

They crossed the street silently and made their way to the private courtyard through a back alley. Remy let them in and Gray looked around in silent awe as Remy eased the door shut once more. He went to the little alarm pad and punched in a code, then turned around to look at Gray blankly. Gray mouthed the word 'nice.'

Remy nodded, then pointed up and gave Gray four fingers to let him know how many bedrooms there were. They moved silently through the lower level, clearing it of anything dangerous, awake, or both, and then they made their way to the staircase in the great room. The lower level was clear and Remy leaned against the banister and looked up into the open stairwell. All was dark and silent, but his heart was thumping in his chest so hard that he was beginning to get dizzy.

It could have been the loss of blood or the booze, but Remy thought maybe it was adrenaline. Or all three. It wasn't Shawn, though. Nope. Not Shawn at all.

Reasons for the dizzy be damned, he had to do this while he was still high enough to go through with it. They moved slowly up the stairs, pausing at each creak of the old floorboards, and Gray kept one hand on the small of Remy's back as they went. Remy wondered if he looked that unsteady, or if Gray was offering support for what he knew would be a difficult task. Either way, Remy appreciated the gesture.

When they got to the top of the stairs, Remy looked first left, then right. The three smaller bedrooms were on the right, and Remy suspected that was where they would find most of them. Shawn would probably be in the master bedroom. With whomever he had chosen to lie to next, of course.

Remy held up his hand and pointed Gray to the right, and Remy crept silently toward the master bedroom as Gray went in the opposite direction. It felt odd to be sneaking in such a manner and not have his gun drawn, but Remy was edgy enough that he didn't have it out. The last thing he wanted to do was shoot one of the others or Shawn. Not before he could get his answers, anyway.

Fucking lying bastard son of a bitch. Remy would show him shot in the ass.

He crept to the closed door of the master bedroom and steeled himself for what he might see. Would Shawn be with one of the others? Had he been fucking any of them? Did Remy even care? He hadn't exactly been celibate for the past month. But yes, he did care. No matter which way he cut it, he still loved Shawn. Still felt drawn to him. He still needed him. And that was why he had to be rid of him. He couldn't live the rest of his life being emotionally dependant on a person he couldn't trust.

Remy pushed the door open and peered around the corner of the doorway cautiously. This was the last time Remy would see Shawn, but Remy didn't want Shawn to see him first. He couldn't handle any more blood loss at this stage. He needed to catch the older man off guard and subdue him properly.

Remy blinked at the empty room and turned around to peer down the hall. Gray walked silently toward him with a quizzical look on his face and he held up five fingers to indicate that he'd found all five marks. Remy motioned with his head for Gray to follow him into the room.

"Something spooked them," Gray told him in a soft voice as they both looked around the room warily. It looked untouched. No one had been here, and that worried Remy a little. Why wouldn't Shawn have come in here? Why wouldn't he sleep in here?

"How do you mean?" Remy asked distractedly as he walked to the window and looked out, careful to stay out of the light.

"I mean, the big crazy one and the little tech guy are both in there, curled around that mean bastard that almost broke my nose like he's gonna save them from the Apocalypse or something."

"They have names, Boss," Remy said in the same distracted tone as he watched a shadow move on the street below.

"Yeah. We're like the fucking Seven Dwarfs, the lot of us," Gray responded wryly as he looked out the other window.

Remy backed away from the window and looked at Gray curiously. Gray returned the look with a blank expression. "What do you think spooked them?" Remy asked as he went to the other window to look from a different angle.

"I don't know, Snow White?" Gray answered sarcastically as he returned his gun to its holster.

"Heigh ho," Remy murmured as the shadow settled into a sunken doorway and remained there.

Remy moved back and looked at Gray. "Who's who?"

"I dunno," Gray shrugged. Remy nodded and looked at Gray blankly for several seconds. "We going after him or what?" Gray finally asked in a tired voice.

Remy glanced at the window and pursed his lips thoughtfully. "*Mais non*," he decided after a while. "We tail him. See what we can get from him. Find out who he is and what he's doing. Hell, he may even be working for us," he added bitterly.

Gray nodded and went to sit on the king-sized four-poster bed. He huffed and looked at Remy in irritation.

Remy cocked an eyebrow at him and removed the leather jacket he was wearing. "Damn, I'd love to speak to Thiago," Remy sighed as he walked slowly over to the bed and ran his hand over the duvet.

Shawn was a bastard. Every night they'd ever spent together down here was a lie. Remy looked up to check once more that the door was closed and they weren't likely to be caught. They weren't making much noise, but someone should have been on watch. Someone should know they were here by now. The others were getting lax. Remy idly wondered if they even knew they were being watched by that bastard down on the street.

"Seven Dwarfs, huh?" he murmured as he looked at the door.

"Gropey, Sappy, Humpy, Sleazy, Creepy," Gray murmured as he counted on his fingers. "Can't think of two more."

Remy snorted softly and bit his lip to keep from laughing. "That about sums it up," he agreed as he turned from the door and looked back down at the bed. "You know, I was going to have you fuck me, but now I'll be thinking about the goddamned Seven Dwarfs and trying to remember the names of the last two," Remy told him testily.

"Tease," Gray whispered affectionately.

"Mmm," Remy responded noncommittally as he lowered his head again and stared at the pattern of the duvet.

"I think you get off on the rush," Gray observed.

"What rush?" Remy asked distractedly.

"Of having sex with the seriously uptight trained killers in the next room," Gray whispered in amusement. "Romeo."

"Spoilsport," Remy accused with a huff as he moved away from the bed and back toward the window.

Gray smirked and watched Remy in the darkness for a long moment. "How's your arm?" he asked after a while.

Remy looked down at his right arm and shrugged lopsidedly. The wound from Shawn's shot was healing nicely, but the newest one, the one from the knife fight he and Gray had inexplicably found themselves in just the night before, was still worrisome. The gauze around his bicep was stained red with blood, and the arm hurt like fuck to move.

"Hurts," he admitted as he looked out the window once more to see if their guest was still out there. "I think he's a Paint, Boss," he murmured as he looked down at the man. "A Painter." It was hard to see his features, but the dawn was approaching and soon they'd be able to make out more. The downside, of course, was that they too would be visible.

"Hmm, c'mon then. We'll find out," Gray muttered. Remy followed him out of the room, giving it one last sweep to make sure it was left as they had found it.

They made their way back to the staircase, but where Gray should have turned he continued on. Remy couldn't call to him, so he simply followed him curiously. Gray had a shit sense of direction, but surely he couldn't get lost in a hallway with one stairway down.

Gray stopped outside the first two doors and pointed to his right. Remy looked at him curiously, then stepped forward and looked left, taking in Carl and Brandt and Nikolaus as they slept curled around one another. Remy's stomach flipped. Lord, he had missed them.

He turned his head slowly to the right to peer into the other bedroom and felt his breath catch. Shawn and Thiago were there, both sleeping peacefully. The only anomaly was the handcuffs. Why was Shawn handcuffed? Had Thiago found him out and exposed him to the others? Was he a prisoner now?

Remy was about to gesture to Gray to check out the third bedroom when a crash sounded downstairs.

XIV.

"THIAGO!" the voice yelled in something close to a panic. Thiago was instantly awake and when he rolled over, he met two wide green eyes staring at him. "Unlock me, Thi!" Shawn urged as he strained against the cuffs they'd forced him into the night before. "Someone's in the fucking house! Let me loose!"

"Vampires!" someone shouted from the other room as Thiago deftly unlocked the chains and then sprinted out the door. He and Carl ran into one another in the hallway and went tumbling to the ground.

"Move, y'wankers!" Shawn grunted as he jumped over the tangle of limbs Thiago and Carl created and made his way down the stairs.

Thiago finally managed to disengage himself, and when he and the other three got to the bottom of the stairs, Thiago stopped dead in his tracks.

Gray Kincaid and Remy Bergeron stood in the middle of the great room, panting and bloodied and looking a little worse for the wear. Shawn was vapor-locked at the bottom of the stairs, his gun held limply at his side, and no one seemed to be moving at all. Thiago was afraid to blink. He and Carl and Brandt and Nikolaus stood tiered on the stairs like kids on Christmas morning, peeking in to see if Santa had come, and Thiago felt rather ridiculous for being so stunned by the scene.

An older man lay on the floor, looking even more bloodied than Gray and Remy did. Everyone tensed when he moaned and rolled and looked up at Remy and Gray accusingly.

"I knew it was you," the man said in an English accent. "Bloody… traitors," he spat.

Shawn moved with the speed of a striking snake, raising his gun and aiming at Gray before Thiago could even open his mouth to speak. The popping sound of the silenced gunshot resounded throughout the old house.

Thiago blinked in disbelief as he watched Shawn fall back against the wall of the stairwell and slide slowly to the ground, leaving a red trail of blood smeared against the wall as he fell.

Remy stood like an Angel of Death in the middle of the room, his long leather coat hanging off his shoulders like a cape and his eyes black and lifeless, his gun smoking as he kept it trained on Shawn.

XV.

CARL watched the scene in horror. It was like the whole thing was happening in slow motion, and all of them were powerless to stop it.

Shawn slid slowly down the wall, as if his body knew that it would never be upright again and was trying to remain so for as long as possible, and he looked out at

Remy in shock. He dropped his gun, sending it clattering to the ground, and he reached down and covered the wound with his hand.

Remy watched him impassively, only lowering his own weapon after Shawn dropped his.

The rest of them all stared raptly at Shawn, as if watching him fall and mentally willing him to get back up again would do any good. He looked down at the blood on his hands like he couldn't understand where it was coming from, then back up at Remy as he finally sank to the ground with a soft thump.

"You shot me," he stated in a hoarse, surprised voice.

"That's right. Asshole," Remy responded heatedly as he finally moved. He stalked closer to Shawn and pointed the gun in the stricken man's face. "And *that* is what getting shot in the ass feels like!"

Everyone stared at Remy in shock. Carl was pretty sure that no one even blinked.

"You sort of missed his ass there, Romeo," Gray murmured out of the side of his mouth as he looked at all of them warily and held the stranger down with his foot.

"Well, I couldn't very well ask him to turn around and wait while I took aim, now could I?" Remy snapped as he waved his gun through the air in an expressive gesture. Everyone on the staircase ducked and covered and Remy glared at them all. "You," he said to Gray. "Are an ungrateful prick. I just saved your life. Again! And you," he said accusingly as he whirled around and pointed his gun at Shawn. "Are a bastard. And stop bleeding on my floor!"

"That's uh… kind of difficult to… you fucking shot me!" Shawn murmured in disbelief as he tried to stop the bleeding from the wound in his shoulder.

"Well fuck, Beignet, you've been trying to do it for weeks now," Brandt said as he carefully descended the steps. "What's the difference in who does the job, right? As long as it gets done."

"Stop moving, Wally," Remy said, his tone of voice suddenly all business once more. Carl still covered Nikolaus protectively on the stairs, and he didn't intend to move until someone explained to him just what the fuck was going on. But if Remy kept waving that gun around, someone was getting his ass kicked.

"You gonna shoot me too, Dixie?" Brandt asked nonchalantly as he took another step toward Shawn and looked at Remy challengingly.

"Don't call me that," Remy said in a flat, lifeless voice just before he pulled the trigger. The bullet thumped into the wall right in front of Brandt, and Brandt stumbled backward and fell back onto the uneven steps. Carl growled wordlessly and stood up. Remy had either lost his mind or turned on them, and either way, Carl figured he needed a refresher course in loyalty. Nobody tried to kill Brandt but him, goddammit!

Remy swung his eyes in Carl's direction as Carl drew the throwing dagger he had strapped to his thigh before going to bed, and for an instant Carl thought Remy was going to shoot him as well. Remy's eyes flickered hesitantly, and he lowered the gun deliberately. Carl lowered his arm warily in turn, and they stared at one another for several tense seconds.

"Please don't fucking throw that thing at me, mate. I think right now a paper cut would do me in," Remy said in a tired voice.

The stranger whom Gray was keeping pressed to the floor with his foot laughed wickedly. Remy stalked over to him and kicked him. Hard.

"Remy!" Gray shouted in reprimand.

"Gray," Remy responded mockingly as he glared at the other man.

"Jesus, Carl, do you sleep with a full arsenal?" Thiago whispered in a slightly horrified voice as Remy and Gray bickered over the proper treatment of a prisoner.

Carl looked down at Thiago and then at the knife ashamedly and shrugged as he slid it back into its sheath. "Kinda antsy tonight, is all," Carl murmured.

"Antsy?" Thiago hissed.

"Yeah, with the…." Carl blushed slightly as he realized that everyone else was listening.

"Vampires?" Gray provided with a smirk and they all turned to glare at him. He cleared his throat and then looked at Remy and shrugged nervously. "Sorry."

Remy rolled his eyes and looked down at the man on the ground, who was wheezing and carrying on about his ribs, then he looked up at the rest of them.

"The next person who attempts to shoot, stab, strangle, maim, maul, or manipulate me in any way, shape, or form is going to have one *fuck* of a hissy fit to deal with!" he shouted angrily and actually stomped his foot in the process. "That goes for you too!" he shouted at Gray as an afterthought.

Gray shrugged innocently, and Carl watched Remy warily. His behavior was odd: erratic and almost sluggish. He'd implied that he was low on blood, and it was obvious he was injured, but he appeared to be drunk as well. Or high. Or all of the above, perhaps?

"Christ," Shawn said in a weak voice. "You're fucking stoned."

Brandt took another step toward him and Remy whirled around to glare at them both.

"I've had a bad fucking month, Shawn!" he shouted. "Would you rather I had been completely sober when I shot you? Would that make you feel a bit better? A little more fucking secure with your position in life?" he spat angrily.

"Remy, calm down, man," Gray requested quietly, and Carl tried his best to keep an eye on everyone at the same time.

Thiago and Nikolaus were in vapor lock; neither had moved since they had ducked away from Remy's erratic movements, and both still knelt on the stairs. Brandt had eyes only for Shawn, and Shawn was holding his shoulder and looking at Remy like a dog following its master's movements and hoping to be noticed.

Gray divided his attention between the mystery man on the ground and trying to get Remy calmed. Said mystery man had ceased his whining, and Remy was practically vibrating, he was so keyed up. All in all, it looked to be a disaster waiting to happen.

"Calm down?" Remy repeated disbelievingly. "This fucker just whacked me over the head with a piece of priceless fucking artwork!" he yelled, gesturing to the splinters of wood and ripped canvass on the floor that Carl had failed to notice before.

"Is that an art attack?" Gray asked, seemingly unfazed by Remy's ranting.

"Priceless!" Remy shouted with emphasis, ignoring the other man as they all stared at them both. "And he just… we just… everyone's fucking sound asleep when we… we just *waltzed* right in here," he continued heatedly. He was gesticulating wildly as he ranted and he was definitely a little altered. His accent was heavy and his words were coming almost twice as fast as normal.

"Hey, Ragin' Cajun," Gray huffed. "No one can understand what the hell you're saying," he pointed out.

"What sort of fucking shoddy operation are you running here, Thi?" Remy continued, undeterred, as he paced back and forth. "If we hadn't been breaking into the goddamned place ourselves, then none of you would have even heard him! No guard, no alarms, no tripwires no fucking anything to stop anyone from… quit laughing, you fucking *galette*!" he yelled suddenly at the chuckling man on the floor. "My God, can I kill him yet?"

"No!" Gray and Thiago both yelled angrily.

Remy looked at them all once more, his eyes still black and hard and lifeless, then his gaze returned to Shawn and his features finally relaxed. He looked at Brandt, who was still edging toward Shawn, and he gestured at Shawn with a flick of his gun.

"See to him, would you?" he asked softly.

"You shot me," Shawn said in the same surprised voice he'd used earlier as Brandt knelt beside him.

"It was only a twenty-two," Remy responded testily. "It barely even counts."

"But you bloody well shot me! What the hell?"

Remy glared at Shawn and then turned back around to look at Gray.

"Who is this?" he asked with a flip of his gun toward the man on the floor.

"I don't know," Gray answered with a shrug. "Same dude as before, though."

"Well fuck," Remy said in disgust just before he disappeared through the door to the kitchen. The man on the floor began to laugh once more, and Carl tensed inadvertently as Remy stomped back into the room and kicked him again. "Jackass!" he yelled for good measure as he once again exited the room in a huff.

XVI.

"HE'S gone mad," Shawn murmured as he watched Remy disappear into the darkness of the kitchen, the long coat he wore trailing after him and flaring out as he turned the corner. "I've never seen him like…." Shawn turned his eyes to Gray, who was keeping his gun trained on the stranger and looking at them all warily. "What in God's name have you done to him?" Shawn asked in a whisper as Brandt pressed a handkerchief to his shoulder and made white lights of pain flash in his vision. It may have only been a twenty-two, but it still hurt like a son of a bitch.

"What've *I* done to him?" Gray asked incredulously. "Oh, you have some nerve, buddy."

"Can you stand?" Brandt asked as he glared over his shoulder at Gray.

"I– he shot me," Shawn answered disbelievingly as Brandt nodded and pulled him gently to his feet. Shawn clung to him and allowed the bigger man to press him against the wall in order to keep him standing, but his eyes never left Gray.

Shawn had expected anything from Sir John McTiernan to Nikolaus and Brandt's dreaded vampires when he had descended the steps, but he hadn't been prepared for what he had seen.

Remy. Remy, alive and well. Alive and well, if not covered in blood and kicking the shit out of some stranger in the middle of the floor. Shawn's heart had almost stopped. He'd been so sure Remy was dead. So sure, in fact, that he'd spent almost every day for the past month attempting to end his life in various creative and not so effective ways.

Then he had seen Gray. Gray, standing behind Remy with his gun drawn and pointed at the man on the floor. Gray. The source of all Shawn's mental anguish. Well, most of it, anyway. Possibly just a third of it.

He'd aimed his gun without thinking, and then he'd been in pain and bleeding, staring at the killer shell of Remy and wondering what the fuck just happened.

"All right, then?" Brandt murmured as Shawn tore his eyes away from Gray and looked up into Brandt's worried brown eyes. Shawn nodded and looked over Brandt's shoulder at the others.

Thiago was staring at Gray fixedly, but Shawn couldn't see the expression on his face. Carl was watching Brandt, but his eyes kept sliding warily to the side to make certain that Gray was still doing what he was supposed to be doing, and Nikolaus was sitting on the stairs, looking at Shawn with wide gray eyes.

As Shawn looked at him, Nikolaus stood up in a huff and stomped down the steps, past Shawn and Brandt, past Gray and their mystery guest, and down the dark hallway toward the kitchen.

"What're you talking about?" Shawn asked in a low, angry voice. The room was tilted unpleasantly, but he could see Gray clearly enough to hate him.

"Eye for an eye, man. That's all I'm saying," Gray said with a shrug as he placed his foot on the stranger's neck and growled at him to stay down. "Seriously," he said in a low voice as he looked back up at Shawn. "If I were you, I'd watch my ass for the next couple hours. Remy's on a revenge kick."

Shawn blinked at him as he finally understood.

Remy was angry.

Shawn had spent so much time worrying over whether the younger man had been killed, he hadn't thought to worry about him being angry.

"Fuck me," Shawn murmured.

XVII.

"WHAT the fuck, Remy?" Nikolaus demanded angrily as he entered the dark kitchen. The sun was just barely up, and it hadn't yet found its way into the courtyard outside. Light spilled into the room from the refrigerator, however, and Nikolaus focused on Remy's leather-clad back as the other man foraged for food in the freezer. "Remy! Turn the fuck around and look at me!"

Remy backed his head out of the freezer and straightened slowly. Nikolaus grew angrier when he became aware of the fact that Remy was trying to intimidate him with the slow, deliberate movements.

Fuck that. He'd put up with a horny Brandt and an evil teddy Carl and real-life fucking vampires all night, a pissed off Remy in a leather coat with a gun was not going to scare him. Much. Not much. He wasn't scared.

But then Remy turned around completely to look at him, and Nikolaus realized that something was definitely wrong with him. He wasn't trying to be intimidating, he just couldn't move well.

"I need peas, Niko," Remy told him in a weak voice. "Bag of 'em, preferably."

"What?" Nikolaus asked in confusion.

"They work better than ice," Remy mumbled as he turned back around and began digging in the freezer once more. "Frozen peas."

"Shit," Nikolaus breathed as he walked around the island and came to stand by Remy. "Where are you hurt?"

"My head needs ice. Peas. My arm's bleeding again, too. I swear, Niko, not much left in me," Remy slurred slightly.

Nikolaus led him to the nearest stool and sat him down.

"Take off that coat," he ordered, and Remy did as he was told. He was wearing nothing but a white sleeveless shirt beneath the coat, and his bare arm was soaked with blood. Nikolaus could only just make out a bandage beneath the blood. "Is that from Shawn?" Nikolaus asked tentatively as he wet a dishtowel under the faucet and looked over his shoulder at Remy.

He watched Remy's shoulders slump dejectedly. Remy shook his head in answer and opened his mouth to speak, but then he straightened suddenly and whipped his head around to stare at the dark hallway.

A moment later, Carl padded into the room silently and Remy relaxed once more. Nikolaus loved having these guys around. They were better than Dobermans.

"You don't look so hot," Carl observed casually as he pulled out the stool next to Remy's and sat down. He never took his piercing hazel eyes off Remy, and Remy shrugged lopsidedly, not meeting them.

"Been better. Need peas," he mumbled.

"Yeah," Carl agreed. He stood up and went to the freezer as Nikolaus rung out the towel, and he fished out a bag of frozen peas and plopped it down on the counter. "Want me to do that, Gizmo?"

"Please," Nikolaus said with difficulty as he handed the towel over. Nikolaus really didn't like the blood. He could handle it, but if someone else was willing to do it, then by all means, Nikolaus was willing to let them.

Carl sat next to Remy and removed the bandage carefully, then he squeezed the towel over the wound before wiping gently at Remy's arm. Nikolaus's stomach turned as the diluted blood ran down Remy's arm in rivulets. Remy shivered, and Carl slid the peas across the counter with his free hand until they sat in front of Remy.

"Thank you," Remy murmured. He picked up the peas and placed them gingerly on the left side of his face before sitting up straighter and turning to look at Nikolaus. "Both of you," he added with a little smile. "God, it's good to see you again. *Ai*!"

"Sorry," Carl said softly, though he didn't sound very sincere.

"Is Shawn okay?" Remy asked timidly.

"He's a little shocked, I think," Carl said in a clipped tone. "Been waiting four weeks to see if you were still alive, and the only greeting he gets is a bullet."

"I couldn't let him shoot Gray," Remy said defensively. "And I couldn't exactly take the bullet for the bastard again," Remy muttered. He sighed and his shoulders slumped again when he realized Carl and Nikolaus weren't all too pleased with him.

Carl continued to clean what was apparently a knife wound in silence. As Nikolaus pondered where in the hell Remy had found himself a knife wound, Thiago and Gray walked into the kitchen together. Carl stiffened noticeably and glared at Gray, and Nikolaus was surprised to find himself snarling at the blond man.

"Where's the asshole?" Remy asked in a weak voice without looking up from his peas.

"He's tied up– wait, which one did you mean?" Gray asked distractedly as he edged away from Carl.

"The fucker that busted my face, Boss," Remy said wearily. "Where did you tie him?"

"To the banister," Thiago said as he placed a calming hand on Carl's shoulder. Carl growled like a bristling dog and Remy flinched away from his hands.

"How's Shawn?" Remy asked Thiago without looking up to meet his eyes.

"He's fine. A little wobbly. Brandt's trying to take him upstairs," Thiago told him, his hand tightening on Carl's shoulder as Gray moved to sit on Remy's other side.

"Goddammit!" Shawn bellowed from the other room. "Let me go, you bastard!"

"Maybe not," Thiago murmured.

Shawn shuffled into the room sideways, holding his arm to his torso protectively and swatting behind him with the other as Brandt pawed at him. When he turned around, he stopped short and fell back against the wall as if he had lost his balance, and they all tensed as he looked at Remy.

Remy sat with his shoulders slumped and his head resting in his hand, the bag of peas pressed to the side of his face. He hadn't yet turned to look at Shawn, and Nikolaus wondered if he was afraid to face him.

"I thought you were dead," Shawn said, his tone close to accusing as he slid slowly to the ground.

Brandt grabbed him and propped him up once more, and they all waited breathlessly for Remy's response.

Finally, Remy turned slowly and looked at Shawn sadly. "I am," he said softly.

XVIII.

BRANDT wasn't sure if Shawn heard Remy's response, and at that point he didn't care. Shawn's strength had finally given out and was almost a dead weight in Brandt's arms, but Brandt picked him up easily and hugged his body close. Shawn clung to him, and Brandt turned to glare at the others.

Remy and Carl got to their feet when Shawn fell, though Remy swayed and plopped back down almost immediately, and Thiago was by Brandt's side trying to give him aid. Brandt growled at them all.

"Bastards and wankers stay here. Gizmo, Trigger, come with me," he ordered as he dragged Shawn out of the kitchen toward the great room and the stairs.

"Hey!" Thiago called in a hurt voice. "What did I do wrong?"

Brandt didn't bother to answer him.

XIX.

"WHAT was that all about?" Gray asked as the others stalked out of the kitchen.

Thiago looked askance at Remy and Gray and shrugged. "I think he's finally gone *el loco final*," he said irritably. "And he's taken the other two with him."

Remy slowly sank his head to the counter and rested his forehead on the cool marble. His arm hurt. His face hurt. His heart hurt. "Maybe he knows you've been fucking his Beignet," he said a little more caustically than he intended. He cracked one eye open to see Thiago looking at him in shock.

"How long have you been tailing us?" Thiago demanded angrily.

"We haven't been tailing you," Remy said with a grim smile as he closed his eye once more. "But it is a good guess, *non*?"

"Son of a bitch," Thiago muttered irritably.

"Do they know?" Gray asked as he rested his hand on Remy's head and patted him absent-mindedly.

"Know?" Thiago asked in a distracted voice.

Remy opened his eyes to look up at the other man. He looked strained and drawn and just a bit neurotic. He'd always been wound a little tight, but this seemed to be a new level of stress. Interesting. Remy was too far gone to be able to draw any conclusions from that, but he knew it was interesting, all the same.

"Thi?" he ventured curiously. Thiago tore his eyes away from the dark hallway and looked at Remy. Remy sat up straight and examined him closely "Do they know that you're the Archer?" Remy asked in a low voice.

Thiago shook his head and turned to face them both. He pulled on his ear nervously and then rested his elbows against the counter and eyed Gray and Remy.

"So what's wrong with you, then?" Remy asked hesitantly.

Thiago squeezed his eyes closed and rubbed at his temples as if to ward off an impending headache. "Shawn's just… and Carl has… and Brandt is fucking… for Christ's sake," he muttered brokenly. He looked up and eyed them both angrily. "Where the fuck have you been? And why do you look like death warmed over?" he demanded of Remy.

"*Mais*," Remy said with difficulty. How to explain? "We had… you see… we, uh…."

"Remy got caught," Gray informed Thiago gleefully, with the air of a child tattling on a sibling to a parent.

"Caught?" Thiago repeated in alarm. "Where? When?"

"For once, this wasn't my fault. And 'caught' is a little harsh, don't you think, Boss?" Remy added angrily. Gray grinned at him.

"Not harsh if it's true, Romeo. Besides– "

"Being attacked by your tail in the men's room of an airport is not being 'caught'," Remy spat angrily.

"You had a tail?" Thiago asked with interest.

"As did you," Gray said confidently.

"And stop calling me 'Romeo'!" Remy demanded petulantly.

"A Paint, to be more precise," Gray told Thiago with a grin, disregarding Remy as if he hadn't said anything. "I'm ninety-nine percent sure that the jackoff out there is the same one that was following your boys earlier."

"They were so fucking worried about ghosts and vampires they probably didn't even notice," Thiago said in frustration. "I assume you questioned yours in this little episode that you had? What did you get out of him?"

"Well…."

"You see…."

"We sort of…."

"We kinda had to kill him," Remy admitted.

"Before he could tell us anything," Gray added.

"Well, goddammit!" Thiago hissed angrily.

"He had a knife to my throat!" Remy said defensively. "And one in my arm, thank you very much. It wasn't the proper time for pleasantries!" he yelled as he stood up angrily. His world immediately tilted and swirled in a most disturbing manner and he fell back against the refrigerator with a crash. Thiago and Gray both leapt forward and grabbed for him, and he blinked away the blurriness at the edges of his vision as they righted him. "Sorry," he murmured as they eased him back onto the stool.

"Jesus, you're worse off than you look, aren't you?" Thiago said as he brushed his hand over Remy's forehead and frowned.

"If I looked like I felt, you would have put me out of my misery already," Remy admitted candidly. He felt horrible. He needed sleep.

"He's running a fever," Thiago murmured to Gray. Gray frowned.

"He wasn't earlier. He was doing fine when we… we, uh… broke in," Gray stuttered as he placed his hand against Remy's cheek.

"I don't have a fever," Remy insisted as he batted their hands away. "I just got bashed on the head with a picture frame. What I want is answers. I say we go in there and pound on that *bioque* until he tells us what he's up to."

"Later. The longer he sits there, the more he'll fidget. I want answers too," Thiago demanded in a commanding voice. "What are you two up to? And don't even get me started on how pissed I am at you, Kincaid," he added with a pointed finger in Gray's face.

"Gray has a plan," Remy murmured around the bag of peas he had reapplied to his face. "Can you believe that fucker hit me with a goddamned painting? A goddamn priceless oil painting! The frame alone was worth thirteen hundred dollars!"

"Well, now it's scrap," Gray responded joyously. "As is your face. I'm with Remy, Thi. I want to know what he was doing. We saw him earlier, out on the street. He was planted out there. What made him decide to try and break in? It could be *pertinent*, y'know?" he said with emphasis. "And what did he mean by 'he knew it was us'? I've never seen the guy before."

Remy nodded in agreement and looked at Thiago. Thiago sighed heavily and gnawed on his lower lip.

"Besides, the others will want to know our plan, too," Remy said coaxingly.

"All right. Remy, you're taking a shower and getting into bed. You look like hell. Gray, you help him. I'll get Brandt and Carl and Niko and we'll see what we can get out of this *chacon*."

"You want me to keep watch on Remy and Shawn?" Gray asked in surprise.

"No, I want you to help Remy to bed and then come back down here. They'll be fine."

Remy swallowed heavily and nodded to Thiago as Gray helped him to stand. He didn't know what to do now that he'd actually seen Shawn once more. He knew in his heart that Gray was telling him the truth about him. But it was Shawn! He needed him.

"Hey," Thiago said softly, his voice no longer authoritative. Gray and Remy both turned and looked at him expectantly. He put an affectionate hand on both of them, his fingers curling around the back of Remy's neck and causing him to shiver. "I'm glad you're both safe," he said as he looked at them both in turn. Remy closed his eyes and enjoyed the feeling of Thiago's gentle hand. "Now," Thiago growled as his fingers tightened. "If either of you go getting shot or disappearing on me again, I'll kill you both myself." Thiago then leant forward and kissed Remy gently on his temple. The side that wasn't covered with dripping peas. He looked at Gray and murmured, "Have you been injured at all?"

"No," Gray said quietly. "Unfortunately, Remy's taken the brunt of the beatings."

Thiago nodded and looked at Remy almost apologetically before he pulled Gray to him and kissed him passionately. Remy blinked in shock as he watched Thiago and Gray attempt to devour one another with the kiss.

XX.

"When the hell did this happen?" Remy asked in shock.

Thiago stole one last kiss and then pulled away from Gray to look at him. He smirked and shrugged.

Gray huffed at Remy and took his good arm to lead him away. "You're a bloody tease, Thi," he murmured with a soft smile.

Thiago grinned crookedly and ran his hand over Remy's short hair as Gray dragged him out, and he wondered why Remy had cut off the curls. Thiago had been fond of the curls, though Remy did look more threatening now, for some reason. Perhaps it was more the knowledge of severe mental instability than his actual physical appearance. He watched as they retreated, smiling dazedly over the kiss he had managed to steal. Time with Remy had suited Gray well. Thiago had missed him.

"*Va te faire enculer*!" Remy's voice shouted, just about the time they would have walked past the Paint tied to the banister.

Thiago smiled and chuckled. It was such a relief to have Remy back that Thiago was almost disregarding the fact that Remy had actually shot Shawn. Shot him! What had he been thinking? Yes, the action had saved Gray's life. And yes, after a month of Shawn's dealing with the guilt and hatred and misery, the only thing that would have kept him from killing Gray would have been to shoot him. Or shoot at him. But did Remy have to shoot him in the arm? Couldn't he have missed him, like he had Brandt? Or hit him somewhere a bit less painful? Well, Thiago supposed it didn't matter where you got shot, it was still painful, regardless.

Thiago shrugged it off and made his way back into the other room. He came to stand over the man tied to the banister and snarled menacingly at him.

"Thiago," the Watcher said in mock courtesy.

"Bernard," Thiago responded in the same tone. "You've got some explaining to do."

XXI.

CARL heard Gray and Remy come up the stairs, bickering and cursing at one another as they went.

"If you call me Romeo one more time, Boss, I swear to God–"

"You couldn't thump me in the nose, the shape you're in. Ow! Damn you! I didn't say it!"

"You were thinking it!"

"How do you know? I could've been thinking about… uh… ow!! Fucking hell, that hurts! My fucking nose!"

Carl forced himself not to smile as Remy's snickering echoed through the otherwise silent upper level of the house.

Brandt sat on the bed next to Shawn, who had grudgingly surrendered to a dose of the dreaded rubbing alcohol and a duct taping and was now propped up in the middle of the bed. Nikolaus sat in the corner, his head in his hands as he rocked slightly, and Carl leaned against the wall by the door.

Shawn's shoulders slumped further as the bickering faded away, and Carl looked at the man sympathetically. It must have been hell on him to hear Remy being chummy like that with someone else. Especially after a month of despairing and then being shot upon the happy reunion.

"Can anyone tell me what just happened?" Nikolaus asked after a long, uncomfortable silence.

"Remy's pissed off," Shawn observed in a childish, surprised voice.

"Just a bit, mate," Carl murmured in amusement.

"He shot me," Shawn said in the same tone of voice.

Carl snorted before he could stop himself.

"Oh, that's just great, Trigger. Just fucking great," Brandt said angrily as he got off the bed and stalked toward Carl.

Carl pushed away from the wall and flexed himself, preparing for a nice brawl, and Brandt growled at him. Before any fur could fly, Thiago stepped into the room and looked at them all warily.

"Everything okay in here?" he asked gruffly.

They all nodded, looking like naughty children who'd just been caught in the act, and Thiago glared at them all before beckoning them to come with him.

Carl watched Brandt tuck Shawn in, despite the older man's protests, and waited for him in the hallway.

"Don't be mad, Wally," Carl whispered coaxingly, running his fingers through Brandt's thick hair and pulling his head down so he could kiss him on the forehead.

"Hmph," Brandt offered as he tried to hide a grin, and they walked down the stairs together, trailing after Thiago and Nikolaus.

Their visitor sat tied to the banister, looking at all of them with a self-satisfied grin that Carl really felt needed to be kicked off his face.

"Gentlemen, this is Bernard," Thiago said as he gestured to the man and took a seat in one of the wingback chairs nearby. "He's a Class One from the early days, as well as a state-of-the-art jackass. He also knows something that we don't, and our job here today is to get it out of him."

Bernard smiled unpleasantly at Thiago, and Thiago looked back at him blankly.

"And how exactly do you go about getting a Class One agent to spill his guts?" Nikolaus asked curiously.

Carl grinned wickedly and looked at the man, and Bernard's eyes flickered over him hesitantly.

"Filet knife," Carl answered with a joyous growl.

XXII.

SHAWN waited until he heard the door to the master bedroom close. He waited still further until he was certain that no one was lurking outside, ready to pounce on him and force him back into bed. The duct tape was bad enough. It pulled at Shawn's chest hair every time he so much as blinked, he didn't need Brandt sitting on him as well. Fucking duct tape. They couldn't have found some real medical tape? Or a nice roll of linen, maybe?

He got out of bed carefully, wincing as the tape pulled, and he sat on the edge of the bed, straining to hear what was going on. Finally, he sighed and hefted himself out of bed. He would have to get closer if he wanted to hear what was being said downstairs.

He shuffled out the door and looked both ways down the hall before making his way to the railing, and he stood at the balcony listening to the conversation below. They didn't seem to be making much progress with the man whom Thiago was calling Bernard, but that would probably change as soon as Carl went all batshit again. Shawn knew *he* would spill what he knew if Carl Travers stood over him with a knife in his hand.

Shawn leaned over the railing and looked down, then turned his head slightly and looked down the hall toward the master bedroom as he listened.

Remy. He was so close, but Shawn couldn't make himself get any closer. The guilt and the pain were overwhelming, and knowing Remy was angry with him made it all that much worse.

He looked at the door longingly for several seconds, and then returned his gaze to the stairwell. He couldn't see any of the action, but he could hear it. As he listened to Thiago explaining to the others how he knew Bernard, Shawn heard the door at the end of the hall creak open slowly. His heartbeat quickened. He flicked his eyes to the side, but didn't turn his head. He couldn't bear to look the younger man in the eye.

Remy was dressed in nothing but a pair of white linen pajama bottoms and Shawn's eyes surreptitiously raked over the scars on Remy's otherwise perfect, tanned skin as the younger man walked silently toward him. The newest one; a nasty, jagged, glaring red oval, adorned his left shoulder. Shawn swallowed hard and ducked his head again, trying to fight back the nausea. He had done that to Remy.

"I'm sorry I shot you," Remy said to him in a soft voice as he stopped in the middle of the hallway and cocked his head to the side to listen.

"I deserved it," Shawn responded quietly as Remy resumed his movement and glided toward him.

"Maybe so," Remy agreed. "But I'm still sorry."

Remy approached him slowly, as he would a wild animal or a spooked horse, and finally Shawn found him close enough that he could smell the other man. He closed his eyes and savored the scent. When he opened them again, Remy stood beside him, leaning over the railing with him. Shawn could sense that sort of movement. Most people could, in fact, and it was a talent that could be honed. But Remy's talent to move soundlessly, and what was more, to move *indiscernibly*, was without question a natural thing. It was also highly frustrating at times.

"You must not be too hurt, if you can still move like that," Shawn observed with a small smile.

Remy cocked his head and looked at Shawn expressionlessly. Shawn swallowed nervously and finally turned his head to look at Remy. He let his eyes roam over Remy's features.

"You cut your hair," he observed sadly. He'd enjoyed Remy's curls, though he hadn't had much time with them. Remy's hair had been short when they'd met up in South Dakota and had grown long during their separation.

"Actually, Gray cut it," Remy informed him without moving a muscle other than those required for speech.

"Why?" Shawn asked as anger and jealousy flared briefly through his body. It all went back to Gray Kincaid, didn't it?

"It became a liability," Remy answered flatly. "Why were you handcuffed to the bed, Shawn?"

"What?"

"Why were you handcuffed to the bed?" Remy repeated slowly.

Shawn hadn't known that Remy had seen him in bed. He really had gotten slack. Of course, better men than Shawn'd had Remy sneak up on them. Shawn was just lucky he had lived through it.

"Did they think *you* were a liability?" Remy asked in the same flat voice after Shawn didn't answer his question.

Shawn blinked at him in surprise. "What?"

"Hmm," Remy responded as he looked at Shawn appraisingly. "Why then?"

"I… I was giving them a spot of trouble," Shawn muttered, blushing at the thought. He couldn't let Remy know how many times he'd tried to end his life. It was too shameful for him to think of.

Remy's eyes narrowed and he turned to look at Shawn. Shawn looked up to see the flat black of Remy's Kill Mode, and he swallowed nervously. If Remy wanted to do the job for him, then so be it. Shawn had already established that you could toss someone over the balcony.

"I was so angry with you," Remy said through gritted teeth, "I could taste your blood at night."

Shawn looked at him in shock and despair as a shout sounded from below.

"Is that all you have, you bastards?" Bernard's strained voice shouted.

"What, that? That was just the stretching exercise, son," Gray drawled from below. "Wait 'til we get started before you start your evil monologue, 'kay?"

Shawn frowned and Remy's eyes flickered. "He's very good at what he does," Remy murmured.

"And has he been doing it to you?" Shawn asked in a low voice, knowing that it was the wrong thing to say, but unable to stop himself.

Remy's jaw tightened and he rested his elbows on the balcony once more. "We've got a lot to talk about," he stated grimly. They stood in silence, listening to the occasional thump of fist hitting flesh from below. "What's a Hunter, Shawn?" Remy asked in a quiet, dangerous voice.

Shawn's blood seemed to run cold as he stood there, and his body went completely still as his mind raced, trying to come up with an appropriate response. There was no point in avoiding this conversation, though every instinct Shawn had told him to dance around the issue or just flat out lie.

But Remy knew. No wonder he'd shot him.

"When did you find out?" he asked in a defeated voice.

"You mean, at what point in our five years together did I discover that every word you said was a lie? A simple means to an end?" Remy hissed angrily as he finally lost control and turned around to face Shawn. He pushed at Shawn's shoulder and pain flared though Shawn's body as he stumbled backward. "Well, you didn't complete that fucking mission, Shawn. Whoops! Remy didn't die!" the younger man said with another shove.

"Remy, please," Shawn begged desperately as Remy backed him up against the wall. "I tried to tell you, I tried to–"

"Five years!" Remy hissed.

Shawn swallowed with difficulty and looked into Remy's enraged black eyes.

"I've spent the last month thinking of how I'd have you suffer. Thinking of how every time you looked me in the eye and opened your mouth, it was a line. When did they put you on me, Shawn? Were you supposed to kill me? Did they threaten you when we came limping back into the Facility together? Hmm? Why did you stick with me all this time after they cleared me, Shawn?"

"Remy, please let me explain."

"Fuck you, Shawn!" Remy growled angrily, his voice still so low that the others wouldn't be able to hear him. "Your explanations always involve orders and loyalty, and I don't want to fucking hear them! I spent every night plotting painful ways for you to die and then every fucking morning I would wake up with memories, Shawn. I couldn't get you out of my fucking head! I could smell you. Feel you there with me, and so help me God, if I knew I wouldn't blow my fucking brains out right after I slit your throat, I would do it," he said as he turned around and ran his hands through his short hair in agitation.

Shawn blinked at him in surprise. It had been roundabout and scattered, but had Remy just forgiven him? "Remy?"

"I would!" Remy protested. He turned and looked at Shawn wearily. "If I thought I'd be able to exist without you, I'd kill you."

Shawn nodded. He certainly knew how that felt. He had lived through five years of that feeling.

Remy went completely still, and for a brief moment Shawn thought he was going to attack him anyway. Then, Remy launched himself at Shawn, disregarding both their injuries, and wrapped his arms around Shawn's neck as he kissed him thoroughly.

XXIII.

NIKOLAUS winced as Gray's fist made contact with Bernard's exposed torso once more, and he forced himself not to look away. There was a certain moral question that Nikolaus was dealing with that the others didn't seem to have trouble with; if he couldn't stand to look at what was being done, was it right to be a party to it? Nikolaus decided that the question was something he would have to deal with later; he wanted answers just as badly as the others did.

"What are you up to, Bernie?" Gray asked as he paced back and forth in front of the man. They'd retied him, with his hands over his head, and he slumped slightly against the banister of the staircase. He was still grinning, though.

"Brandt?" Gray requested as he turned around to look at the other man. "I assume you have a lighter with you somewhere?"

"In my pants," Brandt said grudgingly as he nodded his head toward the stairs. There had been a silent agreement to treat Gray as one of their own in front of Bernard, to show a united front, if nothing else.

"Are you sure?" Gray asked as he held up a silver lighter and showed it to Brandt. Brandt's eyes flashed angrily and he growled deep in his chest. Gray tossed it to him and pointed at Bernard, who was still grinning.

"Guess that explains who grabbed your ass," Carl murmured. "Did you fuck with the windows, too?"

Bernard looked at him blankly.

"Why would he take Brandt's lighter?" Nikolaus whispered in Thiago's ear.

"I can only assume he feared losing us," Thiago murmured. "He knew Brandt wouldn't leave that behind, so he took it and probably bugged it with the intention of replacing it. Is that why you're in here getting yourself caught?" Thiago asked in a louder voice. "Were you trying to return it?"

"If your whirlwind up there hadn't jumped on me, I wouldn't have been caught," Bernard said testily, the first words he had spoken other than taunting. "You're not the only ones who were on that tour, yeah? I saw those windows, too. You stand in an old house like this and have someone jump on you from above. Fucking leather coat."

Nikolaus actually snickered. The thought of what Remy must have looked like in the dark as he jumped over the banister, his leather coat flaring out behind him, was enough to make anyone piss their pants.

"You didn't open the windows?" Brandt asked in a small voice.

Thiago cleared his throat and glared at them all. "I think that's not exactly the point," he admonished. "Bernard, be a good man and tell us who sent you and why."

"Fuck you, Thiago. You know better than to think I'll be telling you anything, you may as well go ahead and kill me."

Carl took a step closer and put his face right up to Bernard's. "Did you know that even if you hang someone by his toes and slit his throat, you won't get all the blood out?" he asked pleasantly.

Bernard stared at him and blinked several times. "I heard the tour guide, too, there, Sport. Interesting trivia, all the same."

"Hmm. Trivia, yes," Carl murmured thoughtfully. "I ask, you see, because I don't think it's true. I think I *could* get all the blood out," Carl said in a low voice as he ran the serrated edge of a knife along Bernard's cheek. "I'd sure like to try, anyway."

Nikolaus didn't know where Carl had pulled the knife from, or how it had made its way into Carl's hand so quickly, but he swallowed with just as much difficulty as Bernard did, and thanked God that Carl was on their side. The knife sliced into the skin and Bernard hissed and flinched away.

"That would take a while, Trigger," Brandt observed seriously. "And we already know how Dixie feels about blood on his floor. I say we just set fire to him."

"That wouldn't help the state of the floor, either," Gray observed with a small grin.

Brandt looked at him for several long seconds and finally he pursed his lips and nodded. "True. Would be fun, though."

Gray smiled and walked up to stand beside Carl. "Really, Bernie, you're gonna die either way," he said as he looked down at the man. "Now, either I can do it and be nice and quick about it, or I can set one of these mad hatters on you. I hear they eat their wounded."

"Doesn't have to be wounded," Carl growled. "As long as it screams."

Bernard's eyes widened and he swallowed again, but he clamped his jaw shut and looked at them stubbornly.

"Come now, *Freund*, don't make me watch them torture you," Nikolaus pleaded.

XXIV.

BRANDT did feel a little sorry for Nikolaus. The man wasn't accustomed to this sort of thing. Neither was Brandt, really, but he was enjoying it immensely. The prospect of setting the stranger on fire had Brandt supremely excited, especially after the bastard had pilfered and desecrated his lighter.

They were getting nowhere with threats and the small amount of physical damage Carl and Gray had inflicted, a process Brandt had found surprisingly entertaining. Maybe Gray wasn't such a bad guy, after all. He seemed to enjoy inflicting pain, at any rate. That made him okay in Brandt's book.

They needed a more effective way of extracting information, though.

Even as Brandt thought it, his eye was drawn to Remy as he made his way slowly down the stairs. Shawn trailed after him, and Brandt tensed as he saw the looks on both their faces. Shawn looked like a whipped puppy, and Remy looked, well, evil. Tired, beat up, and evil. Everyone in the room froze, as if they all sensed that Remy wasn't in the mood to be jerked around. If someone could make Shawn look like that, then they meant business.

Remy looked at them all for a second or two, then he turned to look at Bernard.

"Who sent you?" Remy asked in a calm, soft voice.

"Go to Hell," the man responded calmly.

Remy walked over to Gray with deliberate steps and held out his hand for the man's gun. Gray looked at him warily for a brief, tense moment, then he handed the weapon over wordlessly. Remy didn't say another word before he aimed at Bernard's kneecap and pulled the trigger.

The scream was deafening, and Brandt finally saw Nikolaus close his eyes and look away. No one else moved, and even Brandt was a little stunned.

"You've only got two of them, would you care to lose the other?" Remy asked cordially.

"The Organization sent me!" the man panted as the tears ran down his cheeks and he squirmed in pain. His kneecap was shattered.

"And what is your purpose here?" Remy asked calmly as he knelt and looked at the Paint with interest.

"Follow. Just to follow," Bernard insisted readily. "I was painting them."

Brandt knew painting. You followed and made reports of the mark's location. Then an agent would follow your directions and take out the mark. Painting was for agents who were either overloaded or incompetent. The overloaded ones were scary. It meant they were in high demand. And that meant they were good at what they did.

"I see," Remy said as he nodded understandingly. "Have you made your reports?"

"No," the man claimed with a vigorous shake of his head. "No, I report in at noon. I had to be sure they were stationary first."

"Hmm. Wrong answer, man," Remy said before he jerked his arm flippantly and fired again. The Paint cried out in anguish and screamed for mercy as he looked down at his other newly shattered knee.

"You mad fuck!" he screamed. "Jesus fucking Christ!"

"I don't appreciate being lied to," Remy informed him icily. Brandt saw Shawn squeeze his eyes closed, and Brandt frowned worriedly. Something was amiss. Brandt was so tired of the secrets he could have screamed.

"I reported," Bernard panted. "He'll be here… at sixteen hundred… tomorrow," he said as his body shivered with the beginnings of shock.

"Who? Do you know his name?"

"Just the Hunter."

"The Hunter?" Thiago echoed worriedly.

Brandt glanced at him curiously, and out of the corner of his eye, he saw Shawn shift slightly.

"Hunter," the Paint said as he looked up at Remy. "Please," he said pitifully. "Please, end it." Remy stood up and looked around at the others inquiringly, his gaze lingering on Shawn.

"What do you know about the Hunter?" Thiago asked as he stood for the first time and looked down at Bernard.

But Brandt wasn't watching the prisoner. He was watching Remy and Shawn. Remy stared the older man down, and Shawn shifted again and failed to meet Remy's eyes.

"They… please," Bernard grunted weakly, and Remy lifted his hand and pulled the trigger one last time, his eyes never leaving Shawn's as the bullet hit dead center between the Paint's eyebrows.

"Jesus!" Thiago yelled as Nikolaus recoiled completely and Carl and Gray gaped at Remy.

"What the hell?" Gray growled angrily as he snatched the gun from Remy and glared at the younger man.

"He was in pain," Remy said with a shrug. "I need to speak with you, Kincaid," he added menacingly, and he grabbed Gray's arm and dragged him away into the kitchen.

Brandt stood stunned, just like the rest of them, looking down at the body of the prisoner.

Remy had cracked. And for Brandt to make that observation meant that the younger man was pretty far gone.

"No more drugs for him," Thiago said softly.

Carl and Brandt looked at him blankly and both nodded their heads, and Nikolaus clapped his hand over his mouth and mumbled, "I think I may be sick."

Shawn stood staring at the floor and looking fairly pale, and finally Thiago moved as if in slow motion and untied the body from the banister. "We're going to have to get this cleaned up," he said softly.

Several moments later, Remy came back through the room. Gray was conspicuously absent, and Brandt found himself inexplicably worried about the man's safety. Remy gave them all one last look and proceeded back up the steps. "We have a little over twenty-four hours, gentlemen," he informed them all. "I suggest you all make the most of it. I'm going to bed."

"What if he was lying about the time?" Carl asked incredulously.

"Then we'll deal with the Hunter when he gets here," Remy answered bitterly without stopping.

XXV.

REMY walked slowly back up the stairs, knowing that all eyes were on him and not caring. It wasn't the first time he had killed someone in cold blood, and it wouldn't be the last. He'd given Shawn's secret a bit more time, and that was all that really mattered. Now he just wanted to curl up in bed and sleep for ten years.

He barely had the energy to get to bed, though. He stood in the doorway and stared at the room for several seconds, guilt and anger and shame washing over him. He could feel the presence of someone else in the hallway and he knew instinctively that it was Shawn. He didn't have the energy left to be angry with Shawn.

He continued on into the room and stood by the bed, looking down at it as if it were about to open up and swallow him whole. Technically, he and Gray hadn't fucked on the bed. But they'd been close enough to play hell with Remy's conscience, all the same. The door closed softly behind him and Remy turned his head slightly as he fussed with the bedcovers.

"That was risky, don't you think?" Shawn asked softly.

"So is being a traitor in this group, if you'll remember," Remy responded flatly.

Shawn didn't respond, and Remy wondered if the same memories he had were assaulting Shawn as well. Expecting a welcome only to be attacked and accused of being a traitor. Remy was beginning to grow angry once more as he thought of that night. How dare Shawn berate and threaten him for doing what Shawn had been doing all along! He shivered and looked down at the bed.

"It's funny, Shawn," he said malevolently, the need to wound the other man so great that it was overwhelming. "I just shot a man and yet, the only thing I feel guilty for is fucking someone besides you in this room."

He couldn't see Shawn's reaction, but he could hear it. The soft footsteps that neared him ceased and the sudden intake of breath made Remy feel slightly gratified. Gratified, but guiltier than ever.

"We all have our cross to bear, I suppose," Shawn responded with difficulty.

"Am I your cross?" Remy asked as his throat constricted.

"Never," Shawn whispered. He was suddenly behind Remy, his hand snaking under Remy's arm to wrap around his waist. Remy's eyes closed against his will, and his head tilted to the side as Shawn kissed his neck gently.

So many questions whirred through Remy's head that he could hardly keep them straight, but the exhaustion and the pain were overwhelming. He let his head fall back to rest on Shawn's shoulder, and Shawn tightened his grip.

"I missed you," Shawn whispered into his ear. "So fucking much it hurt to breathe, sometimes."

Remy knew how he felt.

"I spent half my time cursing you," he said as Shawn buried his face in Remy's neck and breathed in deeply. "The other half I spent wishing you were there."

"I'm here now," Shawn responded thickly. "When they find me out, they'll kill me, Remy. You can't protect me for long. But I'm here now," he said just before Remy turned in his embrace and kissed him.

Shawn moaned like a man dying of thirst who'd just been given water, and Remy wrapped his arms around Shawn's neck despite the pain in his arm.

"What's with the duct tape?" Remy asked as an edge of the duct tape on Shawn's shoulder caught his skin and pulled at it.

"Brandt," Shawn growled as he brought Remy to him for another kiss. "Pull it off," he murmured into Remy's mouth.

"Hmm. Huh uh," Remy said as he pushed away from Shawn and really examined the monstrosity for the first time.

Shawn looked like he was in full body armor. The duct tape went over his shoulder and under his arm and across his chest to circle his torso, and then around again to hold his arm to his body. Remy recognized that it was well done– if it had been an Ace bandage or something. He winced at the mere thought of what it would take to get it off.

"Why did you let him do this to you?" he asked with a little laugh.

"I had just been shot, if you'll recall," Shawn responded wryly.

"You shot me in the ass, but I didn't let you roll me up in sparkly ribbon," Remy pointed out.

They both stared at the silver wrap, as best Shawn could stare at it, anyway, and they looked at one another at almost the same moment and smiled.

"Shower?" Remy suggested hopefully, and Shawn grinned and kissed him hungrily one last time before taking his hand and pulling him toward the bathroom.

XXVI.

THIAGO watched wearily as Carl and Brandt loaded Bernard's body into the back of Shawn's 4Runner.

Bernard had been a first-class asshole and a second-rate agent, which probably explained why he'd been relegated to Paint duty in the first place, and Thiago wasn't lamenting his death. He was, however, worried about Remy's mental state. He was also concerned about Brandt's exceedingly odd behavior toward him, and Gray's sudden lack of smartass remarks.

In fact, where was Gray? Thiago pushed away from the wall he had been leaning against and looked around in concern. If that little bastard had slipped away, Thiago was going to kill him. Find him, fuck him, then kill him.

As he scanned the dark garage, he heard Gray's voice and relaxed slightly.

"Just, you know, breathe," the American was saying in a soothing voice.

"He just shot him," Nikolaus's horrified voice said as the footsteps got closer to Thiago. "Just like that."

"That's his job, kiddo. It's what he does. It's what we all do," Gray justified as they walked through the doorway.

Gray turned to look at Thiago and shrugged, and Thiago raised an inquiring eyebrow. Nikolaus walked on to the car and Carl put a comforting arm around him in greeting.

Gray stood beside Thiago and whispered, "Been sheltering him, have you?"

"Maybe," Thiago said in a low voice. It was true. Every time in the last five or so months that someone had needed killing, Nikolaus had never been present. To Thiago's knowledge, even Remy had managed to shield Nikolaus from the brunt of the carnage he'd been forced to inflict during those three months the two of them were alone. Nikolaus was a scrapper, but there were some things a glorified computer tech just didn't need to know. "What did Remy say to you earlier?"

Gray shrugged and began fishing around in his pockets for something. "Just… you know… Remybabble… where the hell did my… ?" He trailed off as Brandt came to stand in front of them. The big Australian was obviously off kilter, and he seemed to have doubled in size for some reason. Even Thiago swallowed nervously. Brandt held out his hand and offered Gray a pack of cigarettes.

"Left 'em on the counter," Brandt said in a friendly voice. What passed for Brandt-friendly, anyway.

"Err… thanks," Gray replied uncertainly as he took the pack from Brandt and continued to slowly pat himself down as he pulled one of the cigarettes out of the pack with his teeth. Brandt held out his other hand and flicked his silver lighter open. Gray blinked and looked at him warily, but allowed him to light the cigarette anyway and then nodded in thanks.

Thiago watched suspiciously. Seeing Brandt be nice to anyone outside of their little group was an extreme novelty, and Thiago could smell something fishy burning somewhere.

"Did you get the transmitter out of that thing?" Thiago asked Brandt carefully.

"No. I was going to stay behind and do it now," Brandt said cheerfully. "That is, of course, if Asshole here is willing to take my place," Brandt added with a friendly clap on Gray's shoulder.

"Uhh… sure," Gray said with a sideways glance at Thiago. Thiago shrugged and the three of them walked to the car together. Thiago strolled up to the driver's side window and tapped Carl on the shoulder.

"Gray is under my protection, got it?" he informed the man, feeling a bit stupid saying the words. Like he was some mob boss or something. It didn't matter, though, it got the point across. "We need him," he added as Carl looked at him strangely.

"I won't hurt him," Carl insisted with a little smile.

"No 'he slipped into the river' or any of that shit," Thiago warned with a grin.

"No worries, mate."

Thiago and Brandt walked back and stood by the door as Carl pulled out of the garage, and as soon as they were out of sight and the door had closed, Thiago turned to Brandt to ask if he wanted help with his lighter.

Brandt grabbed him and threw him up against the wall, knocking the wind out of him and shaking him angrily.

"Tired of your bullshit, bossman! I want answers and I want them now!"

"What the… what are you talking about?"

"Jesus, Zed! You really *have* been networking!" Brandt said in surprise as he let Thiago slide down the wall and touch his feet to the ground once more. "No wonder you haven't been letting me in on the big secrets. You didn't know I was working for you, did you?"

"You… wait, what?" Thiago asked as Brandt's words sank in.

"Code name Pyre, at your service," Brandt said with a cheeky little salute and a grin.

"Pyre?" Thiago gasped as he looked at Brandt closer. Brandt nodded happily. "Jesus fucking Christ, Everett! Why didn't you say something sooner?" Thiago yelled as he smacked Brandt on the arm. "Do you know how fucking insane I've been going?"

"Yeah, I can see that," Brandt said with a nod as he turned to head back to the kitchen. "Hey, what the hell kind of name is the Archer, anyway? It's bloody stupid."

Thiago watched him go with a grim smile.

"So," Thiago said as he jogged to catch up with the other man. "So, the whole act was just to throw the others off?"

"What act?" Brandt asked as he flicked the lighter open and looked at Thiago with that same old gleam in his eyes.

"Never mind," Thiago mumbled.

XXVII.

REMY had given Gray directions to the best place to dump a body, and Carl negotiated the early morning traffic as Gray quietly gave him driving instructions. Because of this, Nikolaus was forced to sit in the back, and the poor man was white as a sheet because of his proximity to the body.

He kept sneaking looks to the side where the rolled-up floor rug containing the body sat leaning against the back of the seat, and Carl couldn't help but feel sorry for him. They had tried so hard to shield him from the violence all these weeks, and then Remy had just swooped in and shot all their hard work all to hell. Literally.

"So, tell me," Carl said suddenly as he eased the car to a stop at an intersection and turned to look at Gray. "When exactly did Remy crack?"

Gray looked at him steadily for several seconds, his arm hanging casually out the open window as he let his lit cigarette dangle from the tips of his fingers. Carl frowned at him when he realized that the man had yet to take a drag of it.

"Afraid he rigged it, are you?" Carl asked with a small grin.

"Yes," Gray answered readily. "I'm just waiting for it to take my hand off when it explodes."

"Well, you may want to toss that one out and try a new one then, mate. 'Cause he most definitely did something to it."

Gray hurriedly flicked the cigarette out the window and watched it suspiciously as it tumbled toward the curb and rolled to a stop, still glowing red at its tip. He accepted the new one from Carl with a wary look.

"It was probably in the filter," Carl informed him with gleeful malice. He didn't think Brandt had actually put anything explosive in Gray's cigarette, of course, but a little psychological warfare never hurt anyone. Much.

"Fucker's mad as a hatter, that's what Remy kept warning me about," Gray said as he lit the cigarette with the car's lighter and looked in the side-view mirror.

"Maybe so, but we're used to it," Carl said with a fond smile. "Remy, on the other hand, he's usually more... contained," he observed worriedly.

"Remy had a difficult month, wouldn't you say?" Gray replied dryly as he inhaled deeply and relaxed back into his seat. "But you're right, he's not himself. And I doubt he will be again," he added softly before blowing out a stream of smoke and closing his eyes with a grateful sigh.

"Is it something I'll have to kill you for?" Carl asked as he pressed the gas and took them out of the French Quarter. "Are you the cause?"

"Not me, sonny," Gray answered as he flicked the ashes out the window.

"Who then? What happened to him to make him go all batshit?" Carl demanded as he took a turn and Nikolaus squeaked as the rug slid toward him.

"From what I understand he was nearly blown up, shot, taken prisoner, tortured, attacked repeatedly and then shot by his lover of five years, kidnapped, abandoned, and then stabbed... several times over, actually. But worst of all, he was betrayed," Gray said matter-of-factly. "I mean, I've never had a friend or lover close to me like Shawn and Remy were, or are, I suppose, but I know that would hurt. Hell, it would hurt if *Remy* tried to kill me, and we've only known one another for, fuck, half a year? Christ, it feels like longer," Gray mused with a weary groan as he rubbed his eyes with his thumb and forefinger.

"Close quarters with Remy always does," Nikolaus murmured from the back seat as he poked at the rug with his finger, trying to slide it back to its rightful spot. "Does he have names for you?"

Gray turned around, his eyes sparkling and a genuine smile on his lips. Carl had to look at him twice as he drove. He was quite a handsome guy, once you got around the all-encompassing and overwhelming urge to kill him.

"He had all kinds of fucking names for me at first!" Gray said with a little laugh. "I thought it was 'cause he couldn't remember my name, and that brought on all sorts of... y'know... concerns over his effectiveness as an agent, y'know?"

"Oh, believe me, I know," Nikolaus said with a long-suffering look that made Carl smile as he watched the younger man in his rear-view mirror. They had heard most of the stories from Remy and Nikolaus's three months together. Carl thanked the heavens that he'd gotten Thiago on that venture. Thiago was nice and safe and calm and *sane*.

"But when we were planning or whatever, he always called me 'Boss' with this, I don't know, snide little...." Gray waved his hand through the air as he tried to come up with the right word.

"Sneer?" Carl supplied with a small smile. He knew that look well.

"Yes," Gray said with a smile and a nod at Carl as he turned back around to watch the scenery pass. "Sarcasm in its purest form. I was giving the orders, but technically, he outranked me, you see, and it really chafed him at first, I think. But then we got closer, y'know? And it became more of an endearment, I suppose. He still uses the sarcasm occasionally, but now at least it's tempered with friendship."

"I don't think any of us really took note of the fact that the two of you had history," Carl realized softly, suddenly understanding Gray and Remy's actions better. "He saved your life, yeah? And in turn you tried to save his."

Gray nodded slowly. "I thought Shawn was trying to kill him. If I'd known the whole story, I, well, I'm not sure what I would have done. Would've still gotten him out of that square, for sure, but…."

"Why would Shawn try to kill him?" Nikolaus asked distractedly as he poked at the rug again.

Carl looked over in time to see Gray's jaw clench. "I don't know the guy," he answered in a tight voice. "But when Remy forced me to leave him with all of you, Shawn had just tied us both up and we were awaiting our executions, remember? That seems a pretty good reason not to trust him to me."

"Right," Nikolaus said softly, sounding slightly chastised. "Forgot about that."

"Must be a nice habit," Gray responded wryly.

XXVIII.

REMY'S back hit the wall of the tiny shower stall with a wet thud, and Shawn pressed into him as the shower's spray beat down on his own back.

"Fuck me, Shawn," Remy breathed pleadingly, just before their mouths crushed together.

The hot water beating down on Shawn's brand new gunshot wound had been agonizing at first, as had the removal of the copious amounts of duct tape, but Remy had tempered the pain with heated kisses and periodic grinding of their bodies together. Now, Shawn didn't notice that he was in pain or bleeding.

"Now," Remy ordered in a low growl that sent shivers all over Shawn's body.

Shawn knew that they weren't anywhere close to being okay again, but he also knew that they both needed a release; the type of release they could only give one another. They would deal with all the other problems later.

Shawn slid his hand down Remy's slick body, feeling the hard muscles of Remy's torso bunch as he tensed with anticipation, and then he leaned in to kiss him hungrily as he slid his hand between Remy's slightly parted legs. Remy groaned and let his head fall back against the tile wall. They'd fucked in this shower before, but they had both been healthy at the time. Shawn didn't know how well he could hold Remy up in the slick stall and still pound into him like he wanted. And God did he need to pound into him. Now.

He slipped his soapy finger into Remy's body and Remy groaned wantonly, wriggling his hips slightly and sliding down the wall a little more as his legs parted further, trying to get Shawn's finger deeper inside him.

Remy's hands grasped for purchase on Shawn's wet body. He seemed to be disregarding his own injuries as well as Shawn's, and Shawn's primal instincts began to take over. Remy began to mutter in an indecipherable mash of French, Cajun, and English.

Shawn kissed him brutally once more, and Remy pushed his head forwards, meeting the momentum of Shawn's kiss and opening his mouth wide to welcome Shawn's tongue with his own. Shawn allowed the other man to suck on his tongue and paw at him for several long, agonizingly pleasurable moments before he pulled away and curled his fingers once more, watching in fascination as Remy's mouth fell open and his eyes drifted shut in pleasure.

His other hand gripped the back of Remy's neck and pulled his head forward. "Do you want to be fucked, Dixie?" he growled hungrily.

"Fuck," Remy murmured as his eyes glazed over.

Shawn recognized that look, he had seen it often enough to know what it meant. The lust had overtaken Remy's brain, and Shawn knew that the man was simply listening to the growling cadence of Shawn's voice now, not really hearing what was being said.

Shawn picked him up by the backs of his thighs and pushed his hard cock into Remy's body in one swift movement. Remy cried out again and scrambled to get into a position that allowed Shawn to do what he wanted.

"Fuck, yes!" he cried once more, and one of his hands pressed against the stall door as Shawn held him by the backs of his thighs and pressed his shoulders hard against the wall. Shawn bit into his collarbone as he rocked into Remy's body, waiting for the other man to right himself. The last thing they needed was to bust one or both of their heads open by falling in the shower.

"Brace yourself, lad," Shawn rasped into Remy's ear, his accent thick and hoarse as need coursed through his body.

"Fuck," Remy breathed as he wrapped one arm around Shawn's neck and pressed his foot against the opposite wall to steady himself. It wasn't a large shower stall, just barely big enough for the both of them to shower together and not bump the walls, and its size was perfect for this particular activity.

As soon as Shawn felt some of the weight of Remy's body lift off his aching arms he slammed into the younger man with every bit of force he could muster, and Remy cried out and threw his head back, banging it on the tile wall. He didn't seem to care though, and so neither did Shawn.

Shawn continued to thrust into him, forcing Remy's lower back to hit the wall with each powerful thrust. The give of Remy's body as he suspended himself between the walls made it difficult for Shawn to get as deep or go as hard as he wanted, and he kept increasing the power of his thrusts, trying to go deeper and harder and faster. Some primal urge buried in his brain was screaming at him to maim, and his body was responding. Finally, Remy pushed away from the wall using his shoulders and his abdominal muscles, and he held his hips away from the wall with a strength that would have shocked Shawn if he hadn't been so busy fucking the other man through the wall.

With that move, Shawn's thrusts finally met the resistance he had needed, and he growled into the wet skin of Remy's neck as he slammed into him. Remy's hand squeaked against the stall door as he lost the strength that had been holding it there and the water beat down on Shawn's back in a dull, thumping rhythm that only added to Shawn's need to devour the other man.

"Fuck! Shawn! Fuck, yes!" Remy called as his blunt fingernails made red, ragged trails across Shawn's shoulder blade. He finally gave up on the wall and he brought his other hand to tangle in Shawn's hair as his body shuddered uncontrollably.

Shawn was holding more of his weight now, but he didn't care. All he cared about was the hot, wet body pressed against his, and the feeling of his cock once again surrounded by Remy's more than willing warmth. Remy hissed as his muscles convulsed around Shawn's cock, and his come spurted onto both their bodies. When Shawn finally fought through the fog of lust, he realized that Remy was repeatedly whispering his name as he rode out his orgasm.

Shawn came with a plaintive roar, his movements never ceasing as he tried desperately to keep Remy pressed against the wall and within fucking distance. Remy clung to him, moaning almost continually until Shawn's movements finally stopped and he slid slowly out of Remy's body. Remy hugged Shawn close and let his feet fall to the ground. Shawn held him almost tenderly as he regained his footing in the slick shower.

Remy slouched against the wall and panted as he looked up at Shawn. Shawn leaned over him, his hands on either side of the other man's head.

Remy looked up at him unblinkingly for several seconds, and Shawn tried several times to meet his eyes, but couldn't.

"I'm sorry, Shawn," Remy offered finally.

Shawn had known him long enough, and seen him in action enough times, to be able to recognize a real emotion from a fake one. The pain and regret in Remy's voice were real enough to make Shawn's heart ache. Shawn closed his eyes and leaned over to rest his forehead against the tile beside Remy's head as the water continued to beat down on his now tender back. It was running lukewarm, and Remy reached to switch it off. As he did so his chest and arm made contact with Shawn's torso, and Remy hissed in pain and pulled away.

"You're bleeding," Shawn observed belatedly as he took Remy's elbow in an iron grip and examined the wound on Remy's bicep. It was deep and clean, an obvious knife wound, and Shawn frowned at it. "How did you get this, exactly?" he asked, hoping to not only find out what had happened, but also to turn the conversation away from the painful subjects of who had fucked whom and for what reason.

"Knife," Remy replied curtly as he tried to wrench his arm away and climb out of the shower.

Shawn growled menacingly and pressed Remy back into the wall. Remy didn't fight him. Shawn didn't even see the spark that usually lit Remy's eyes when they sparred like this, and Shawn knew then that Remy was in far worse condition than he made out to be. Shawn had never seen Remy's eyes so lacking in life.

He released the younger man and let him make his escape, but he followed closely behind. He grabbed a terry cloth robe from the back of the door and shrugged into it with a pained wince as Remy stalked out into the bedroom and began to pace with a towel slung low around his waist.

Shawn watched him prowl back and forth at the foot of the bed, examining the lithe body for other wounds that his passion may have caused him to miss. There was the knife wound on his arm, the healing bullet wound on his shoulder, and the purpling bruise on the side of his face, as well as several other nasty bruises along his ribcage and his arms and legs. There was also a long, thin red line just under his chin that Shawn had failed to notice earlier, partially because it could only be seen when Remy was in mid-pace and tilting his head to the side.

Brandt had a similar mark; the slice Carl had made when he had apparently almost slit the big man's throat.

The thought of Brandt suddenly slammed into Shawn as he stood there, and all of his anger was knocked from him like the air whooshing out of a balloon. How could he be angry with Remy? He himself had done far worse than simply fuck someone else out of spite. He'd been ready to discard the younger man. Shawn's stomach flipped uncomfortably and he squeezed his eyes closed before going to sit on the bed in defeat.

"You look guilty," Remy observed as he stopped pacing long enough to look at Shawn through narrowed eyes.

"It's a horrible feeling, that," Shawn mumbled. "I've never done right by you, Remy. Not in five years of…." Shawn trailed off and swallowed heavily. What did he even call it? It seemed condescending to call what they had shared merely a 'relationship' or a 'partnership' or, God forbid, an 'acquaintance.'

"Tell me," Remy begged in a soft, pleading voice as he crawled onto the bed and toward where Shawn sat. He sounded almost desperate. Was he desperate to find out the truth? Or desperate to have it told to him so he didn't have to dig for it? Was that it? Did he want Shawn to tell him so badly because he knew he would find out sooner or later? Or did he already know? Was this a test? Was he testing Shawn's supposed newfound loyalty by trying to get him to talk first? Was he trying to save Shawn after all that Shawn had done?

"I don't deserve you," Shawn said sadly. "I never will."

Remy's good hand snaked around to grip Shawn's chin, and he pulled Shawn's head to the side until Shawn was looking into his sad brown eyes.

"Lies and the truth both have one thing in common, Shawn," Remy said in a low, steady voice. "They both have their consequences."

XXVIV.

NIKOLAUS stood lookout while Carl and Gray took care of the body, and he couldn't have been happier to do it. He knew killing and torture were part of the job, and he wasn't so oblivious that he didn't realize the others had been shielding him from a lot of this sort of thing over the past four or so months, but that didn't make it any easier for him to deal with.

He heard a distant splash and Nikolaus shivered as he thought about what was happening. Remy had directed them to a little town called Lafitte, full of signs that offered Swamp Tours and bayous that stretched on forever. He had instructed them to dump the body in the water and make certain that it was under something heavy, so it would rot and attract the alligators.

Finally, Nikolaus turned his head slightly to see Carl and Gray walking casually back toward him, and he jogged over to the car to jump in with them.

"Everything all right, then?" he asked cautiously as he shut the door and scooted forward in the seat just to see Carl's face.

"Yep," Carl responded as he put the 4Runner in drive and sped away. "If what Remy said is true, it'll never be found."

"Not in one piece, anyway," Gray mumbled.

The car fell silent as they were all left with their own thoughts.

Nikolaus's thoughts flittered quite a bit, bouncing from the body they had just dropped into the bayou, to worrying over Remy's mental well-being, to wondering if they could really trust Gray, to thinking how fucking hot Carl looked in the flannel shirt he was wearing with his hair all shaggy and long like it had become.

They had all become shaggy, really. Even Gray was a little on the shaggy side, and he seemed the type to be sort of prim and proper.

Why had Remy cut off his hair?

Nikolaus shook his head in agitation, trying to will his brain to pick one thing to think about and stick with it. Christ, if this sort of mental rambling was what Remy dealt with all the time it was no wonder the other man was so flighty. When he looked around, he saw the familiar buildings of the French Quarter gliding past.

"Hey, look!" Carl shouted excitedly as he slammed on the brakes and sent Nikolaus splatting into the back of the passenger seat.

"What the hell?" Nikolaus muttered angrily as he tried to untangle his limbs and right himself.

"I think my seat belt just slit open an artery," Gray murmured as he rubbed his neck and glared at the other man.

Carl fumbled with his own belt and hurriedly exited the vehicle, leaving the door hanging open and the 4Runner both running and still in drive.

Gray cursed and lunged forward as the vehicle rolled slowly, and he yelped again as the belt restrained him once more. The more he struggled to be free of it the tighter it got, and Nikolaus found himself snickering helplessly as he tried to wedge himself between the two front seats and reach the brake pedal with his hand.

Carl came traipsing back and looked at them both impatiently. "Come on!" he said as Nikolaus finally managed to press the brake and Gray threw the car into park.

They both glared out the open door at the larger man as he huffed impatiently. Nikolaus squeaked when Carl grabbed him under the arms and yanked him head first out of the vehicle.

"What… Carl! *Affenschwanz*," Nikolaus grumbled as Carl carried him under his arm like a piece of baggage for several steps and then set him down with a jarring thump on the pavement.

Gray barked a laugh, obviously having understood that Carl had just been called a monkey's dick in German.

"Look!" Carl said excitedly, ignoring them both as he walked over to a storefront and peered into the window.

Nikolaus looked at Gray and they shrugged at one another.

"Uh, we're not exactly loaded with extra time for browsing here, man," Gray said uncomfortably as he stepped up behind Carl and bent down to look at the objects Carl was frowning over. "Oh, for Christ's sake, are you serious?" Gray asked incredulously when he got close.

His curiosity piqued, Nikolaus shuffled up to the window and looked in. An array of silver, gold, mother-of-pearl, and cheaper multi-colored cigarette lighters were arranged in a case, along with various forms of paraphernalia that Nikolaus was pretty certain weren't legal, and other assorted shiny treasures.

"Jesus, Carl, you've got one fuck of a sharp eye," Nikolaus murmured.

Carl looked at him blankly and pointed at his own chest. "Sniper," he said sarcastically. Gray snickered and Nikolaus rolled his eyes and nodded. "I have to get him one. Is this place open yet, d'you think?" Carl said as a strange light shone in his eyes and he headed for the door to the establishment.

Nikolaus and Gray shared another blank look before hurrying to follow.

After an inordinate amount of time spent in the little specialty shop while Carl looked at every lighter present, looking for the perfect one, they were once again in the car and on their way back to the others.

"What exactly compelled you to do that?" Gray asked curiously.

"He needs a new one," Carl answered with a shrug.

Nikolaus was having difficulty understanding why exactly Carl would think Brandt would be apt to toss out anything even remotely flammable, but Carl was convinced Brandt wanted a new lighter.

"The other one's been, I don't know, tainted."

"Tainted?" Gray repeated in disbelief.

Nikolaus groaned. Carl had returned to his normal, sweet self after his little orbiting 'episode,' but Nikolaus was convinced that he'd burned up a whole shitload of brain cells upon re-entry.

Carl nodded vigorously and looked at Gray seriously. "What's important to you, Boss? Do you mind if I call you that?"

Gray opened and closed his mouth several times. "Uhh… no, but… no. It won't piss Shawn off, will it? Will he get the irony of that, d'you think?" Gray asked as he turned around and looked at Nikolaus.

Nikolaus shrugged. Who the hell cared? Whatever they called Gray, Shawn would still kill him in his sleep tonight. Call him Cupcake, for all Nikolaus cared.

"We call the bloke 'Beignet,' for fuck's sake," Carl responded with a little sneer. "I think he understands the concept of irony. You didn't answer my question."

"What was the question?" Gray asked distantly.

"What's important to you?" Carl asked seriously. "Honestly."

Gray shifted uncomfortably and cleared his throat. "If I told you, you wouldn't believe me."

"Try us," Nikolaus urged from his spot in the back seat.

Gray was silent for several seconds, and he finally glanced at them quickly before answering in a quiet voice. "Friendship, I suppose."

Nikolaus found himself with his mouth hanging open and quickly snapped it shut. The double agent traitor bastard who'd blackmailed Remy into service valued friendship above all else?

"Well, think of that being taken from you and warped into something that can be used against you," Carl said in a quiet, solemn voice.

Nikolaus heard all kinds of double meanings, considering what he knew of Gray, and he wondered if that hadn't been Carl's objective all along.

Gray was silent for long minutes, and by the time he looked ready to say something, they were pulling into the garage of the house on Royal Street.

XXX.

"HOW did you know who I was?" Thiago demanded for perhaps the fifth time in as many minutes.

Brandt rolled his eyes and let his head thump onto the dining room table. For a smart man, Thiago really was quite dense at times.

"Listen, Zed, and listen carefully," Brandt mumbled into the tabletop. He looked up and crossed his arms across the table and fixed the other man with a glare. "Concentrate. I know you deal with a lot of people while acting as an evil mastermind, and that you don't recognize every face you see. But when one of your subordinates sees you, we remember. You know me by my code name, yeah? Therefore, you know that I've been with you since the beginning."

"But how did I not… how did you… how did…."

"Concentrate!" Brandt hissed, not really believing that he was the one having to say that to Thiago. Usually it was the other way around. "I was a member of your group on that raid five years ago. The one where we found the files that started this whole fucking thing. You remember *that*, yeah?" Brandt asked sarcastically, wondering if he was going to have to give Thiago a brief 'History of Being the Bad Guy' for good measure.

Thiago cocked his head and squinted at Brandt. "Yeah. Shit. You were the one who blew the door for us. You had short hair then. And you were clean-shaven," Thiago said as realization dawned. "It changes your look a lot."

"Yeah, that's sort of the point. Jesus, you need a nap or something," Brandt said as he rubbed his eyes and yawned.

"And you were a hell of lot more wiry," Thiago muttered as he cocked his head at Brandt.

"I bulked up some," Brandt huffed defensively.

A thump sounded from somewhere in the house and Brandt cocked his head to the side to listen. It could have simply been a door shutting. But then, it could also have been a body hitting the floor upstairs. "Should we check on Beignet and Dixie?"

"No," Thiago said absently as he stared at Brandt. "I can't believe I didn't recognize you."

"It happens," Brandt said flippantly. "And it's not really like we had much interaction on that mission. Group leaders rarely look their subordinates in the eye. Makes it hard to order them to their deaths, I suppose. Look–"

"Why didn't you say something earlier?"

"Well, you're the boss, right? I assumed you had a reason for completely ignoring one of your most trusted lieutenants. Now–"

"But when we were alone, you could have said something."

"When we were alone I was fucking you. Seems to me, a conversation of this sort would be a bit of a mood killer, don't you think? Besides, I tried to. In Sydney, remember? I told you I was with you no matter what you decided. I love these blokes, every one of them, but you say 'strike' and I'll get the matches, yeah? I won't kill Trigger, though, or Beignet or Dixie, or Gizmo for that matter. Actually, I won't kill any of them, but… is Asshole by any chance in need of killing?"

"Gray's code name is Friday. You've dealt with him before," Thiago answered in low voice.

"You're shitting me! Gray is Friday?" Brandt hissed in a disbelieving whisper. Thiago nodded. "But– goddammit, I liked Friday! Now I can't kill him, either! Wait, so if Friday and Chimera were the ones doing the inside work, then…."

"Remy is Chimera, yes. Jesus, I can't believe this. First Remy, now you. Who the fuck else is working for me that I don't know about? Fuck me, I really need to make an employee roster or something," Thiago murmured disgustedly as he ran his hands through his hair. "I can't fucking keep track of you all."

"You've got a lot of employees," Remy's soft voice said from the doorway.

Brandt flinched and looked over at the other man in surprise. He was leaning casually against the doorframe, but Brandt could see the flames licking just beneath the calm surface. It took crazy to see crazy, and man, could Brandt see it now.

"Maybe you should recruit personally instead of sending your flunkies to do it," Remy suggested icily as he prowled into the room. "Beignet, they're in here!" he called in a voice that was louder than strictly necessary.

What the hell had happened to the man? Brandt had known that he was a borderline case from the beginning, and from time to time, he could see the wildfire spark in Remy's actions, but this was a constant, controlled crazy now. Something had to have triggered it. Brandt tensed in expectation of the inevitable 'bam' that always came when someone who was teetering on the edge finally took the final plunge.

He watched the Cajun prowl around the room with interest. He was still shirtless and the white linen pants were still riding low on his tanned hips. But his hair was wet, and his wound was bleeding as if from overexertion. At least he and Shawn hadn't been fighting.

Brandt felt a slight stab of jealousy at the thought of Shawn and Remy fucking, but at least now he recognized it as lust, and not love. Shawn was a good fuck, especially when he was in a temper. Over the last month Brandt had been the only one Shawn had really spoken to or touched at all, and they'd had plenty of sleepless nights to work out their feelings for one another.

Shawn loved Remy and always would, that much was clear. Brandt found that he was glad for it. He wanted to see Remy and Shawn together. He wanted them both happy, so long as he still got to fuck both of them occasionally.

Brandt enjoyed being dominated by Shawn, and he enjoyed the interaction he had with the other man. But it wasn't love, and Brandt was fine with that.

Shawn tolerated him, and was, perhaps, amused by him. But he didn't understand him. Not really.

"Hey, Dix– uh… what am I calling you now?" Brandt asked uncomfortably, belatedly realizing that his attempt to calm the younger man may simply have wound him up further. Brandt didn't want to be shot at again.

"I don't fucking know," Remy spat. He stopped and stared at Brandt for several seconds and his countenance softened. "I'm sorry I shot at you, Wally. Again. I missed on purpose, y'know," he added with a little shake of his finger.

Brandt nodded in recognition and looked at Thiago briefly. The Argentinean was watching Remy keenly, but he looked more amused than wary, and Brandt relaxed a bit further. If Thiago trusted the man still, then so did Brandt. "What's your code name, Wally? Which one are you?" Remy asked suddenly.

"What?" Brandt asked in alarm. He frowned worriedly. This was bad. How much had Remy heard? How much did he know already and how much could Brandt tell him without jeopardizing everything? Thiago had been unclear about that during their brief little talk.

Remy walked over and bent over him, leaning his hand against the table and getting right into Brandt's face. He stayed there, looking at Brandt closely. "You're the one who got Evan Washburn out, aren't you?"

Brandt blinked at him. "How did you… how did you know that?"

"He said the agent sent for him pulled out all his teeth and then set his van on fire. Blew it up. That was you, wasn't it, you crazy bastard? You knew him. But it wasn't on some mission in fucking Asia or wherever. It was in Prague. I did hear you say Prague that day at the cabin."

"Wait, wait… you're right about all that, mate, but I didn't say Prague," Brandt insisted." How you skewed that one, I don't know, but–"

"Are you sure?" Remy asked almost desperately. He was so cute when he was desperate, Brandt just wanted to grab him and fuck him into oblivion. Well, he always wanted to do that, but even more so now.

"Positive, mate," Brandt responded after licking his lips and drinking in Remy's scent. "You must have linked him to Prague through something else."

"Fuck me," Remy cursed as he stood back up.

"Whenever you're ready, Dixie," Brandt said with a cheeky little wink.

Remy growled at him and started pacing once more.

"As soon as the others get back, we're having the come to Jesus meeting," Remy said in a low, tired growl.

"We're what?" Thiago asked in alarm.

"Everyone is spilling. Including you, *canaille*. Sneaky bastard."

"Remy?" Shawn's voice called from the stairs.

"In here!" Remy yelled without taking his eyes off Thiago.

"Are you two okay?" Thiago asked in a low voice, nodding his head at the other room to indicate that he was talking about Shawn and Remy. "Did you talk at all?'

"No, we didn't! And I'm tired of the fucking secrets, Thi!" Remy bellowed at almost the exact moment that Gray, Nikolaus, and Carl walked through the door from the kitchen.

"Uh oh," Gray murmured as Shawn came in through another entryway, and they all stood staring at one another blankly.

"Everybody, sit the fuck down, don't move a fucking muscle, and only speak when I fucking tell you to! Now!" Remy shouted from the corner of the room where he prowled around in a restless circle.

Brandt caught sight of the gun stuck in the waistband of Remy's linen pants as he turned around, and he shifted uncomfortably in his chair.

This didn't bode well for group unity and all that. Or for Remy's sanity, for that matter.

Brandt looked at Carl as the man shuffled toward him and sat in the chair beside him with a questioning glance. A stab of guilt shot through Brandt, and his entire body flushed unpleasantly. Now there was a man who understood the way

Brandt worked. He hadn't been bothered with his position in the group until he'd found himself connecting with Carl more and more. Then the charade had played hell on what little conscience Brandt had retained over the years.

Brandt had never had a real friend. Someone who had understood him and was able to meet both his mental and physical moves blow for blow. He'd never felt safe before. Not like this. And Carl was the reason for it. And even though Brandt hadn't necessarily been lying to the other man, he'd certainly been withholding the truth.

Hell, Remy was right. Brandt was tired of the lies, too.

He sighed and watched Remy warily as Carl unconsciously rested his hand on Brandt's shoulder. Brandt shivered at the gentle touch and resigned himself to losing the only true companion he had ever known.

XXXI.

REMY clenched his fists as he looked at the six pairs of wide, wary eyes looking up at him from around the large dining table. He resisted the urge to throw a proper hissy fit as they all gaped at him. He was so fucking frustrated. Every one of them had a secret. Every one of them was hiding something, and though Remy had sniffed out bits and pieces of each one, he didn't know any of the full stories.

"This is the end," he growled as he started to pace once more. Everything he'd ever learned about proper interrogation techniques and intimidation and subtlety and anything else that would probably be good to use right now was all being thrown out the window and gleefully pissed on from above. Remy was too far past his tolerance of bullshit for utilizing subtlety.

"We're going to have it out right here, right now. Anyone I suspect of lying, fibbing, stretching the truth, qualifying, prevaricating, looking at me the wrong way, or breathing my fucking air, will be shot!" he shouted, drawing his gun and waving it through the air.

Everyone flinched and Gray actually ducked. Remy growled at him.

"Did we, uh, miss something?" Gray asked uneasily as his eyes slid to look at Thiago carefully.

"Yes!!" Remy shouted emphatically. "You missed your chance to escape the fucking heart to heart we're all about to have, *couyon*!" he snarled as he picked up one of the dining chairs by the back and slammed it back down forcefully. It creaked and he backed away until he was standing in the open, away from anything small and heavy and *breakable*. This was his stuff, damn it, and it was all valuable to him for one reason or another. If he needed to start throwing things, he was going to start tearing body parts off the others and tossing them around before he destroyed his own fucking furniture.

"Who wants to fucking start?" he growled.

XXXII.

THEY sat and stared at Remy like ill-prepared schoolchildren hoping not to be the one the teacher picked to answer a difficult question.

Thiago watched Remy warily, his brain running at full speed, trying to judge the ups and downs of having his identity released in this manner. He knew Brandt and Gray would have his back, and he knew Shawn would turn on him, but the others were all toss-ups. Carl had developed an unwavering loyalty to both Brandt and Nikolaus, and Nikolaus, in turn, seemed to admire Thiago a great deal. Remy had cracked. He was just as likely to go *loco* and kill them all as he was to pick sides.

"All right, fine, I'll go first!" Remy yelled angrily as his pacing kicked up a notch.

"Remy, calm down," Shawn said in a low voice. He sounded tired and frustrated and… scared? Nervous?

Why would Shawn be frightened of what Remy had to say? If Remy was right and they were each and every one of them keeping secrets, Thiago wanted to know them. Shawn's hesitancy just piqued his curiosity further.

"Fuck calm! Tell them, Shawn!" Remy shouted as he waved his good arm at the rest of them. "Tell them what a Hunter is!"

Shawn paled visibly and his jaw clenched, but he didn't move a muscle and he didn't take his eyes off Remy.

Thiago felt his heart stutter to a stop. "The Hunter?" he repeated in a hoarse voice. He looked at Shawn in horror. "Are you the Hunter?" Shawn glanced at him briefly but didn't answer.

Remy stopped and stared at Shawn for several seconds before stepping up to the table and slamming both of his hands down on it. He leaned over and glared at the other man menacingly, and when he spoke it was in a low, ominous purr. "Tell them, Shawn. Or I'll have Gray do it."

Shawn's jaw clenched again and his eyelashes fluttered as he tried his best not to blink in the face of Remy's quiet rage. "It's not… it's not *the* Hunter," he whispered. He shifted and glanced around at the startled and confused faces around him. "They're a group," he said with difficulty, his eyes fixed on the shiny top of the table.

"How many? What are they?" Thiago asked eagerly.

"There are thirteen, give or take a few, depending on each one's status. They act as a… a sort of Internal Affairs for the Organization," Shawn said slowly. "They single out agents who have turned or are suspected of being disloyal."

"And do what with them?" Nikolaus asked. "Watch them? Kill them?"

Shawn shrugged noncommittally.

"Whatever's called for," he said as his eyes flickered up to Remy's face.

"How do you know this?" Carl asked with a hint of dread in his voice.

"Because I'm one of them," Shawn whispered.

A heavy silence descended upon the room, and Thiago found himself stunned into immobility. The repercussions were so far-reaching that he couldn't even begin to understand them.

"What was your objective?" Remy asked in a harsh, unforgiving voice. Shawn flinched and ducked his head. "Start from the beginning."

"I can't," Shawn said sadly. "I was assigned to you, Remy, that much you know. I swore to them up and down that you were loyal, that you would never turn. But now… they'll kill us, now. Doesn't matter what I tell them."

Thiago stared at the other man as Remy backed away and circled the table. He knelt beside Shawn, placing one hand on Shawn's knee and the other on the man's shoulder.

"Shawn," he whispered pleadingly.

Shawn closed his eyes and turned his head slowly to face the younger man. He forced his eyes open and looked as though he were looking into the sun when he tried to meet Remy's gaze.

"Please," Remy begged in a barely audible whisper. "If we know everything, we can live through this. Together, Shawn. Be the man I thought you were… be the man I love, and help us."

Shawn swallowed with difficulty and he looked into Remy's eyes as if mesmerized. Thiago couldn't see Remy's face, but he knew that any man in his right mind would do anything those pleading brown eyes asked him to do.

"There's too much, too much to explain," Shawn said breathlessly. "I wouldn't know where to begin."

"How about us? What do you know about why we were put together?" Carl asked as he leaned forward and looked at Shawn with bright eyes. "You were sent to kill us, weren't you?"

"Yes," Shawn whispered, his green eyes never leaving Remy's. "You were all considered risks of some sort. All but the two of us," he added.

Remy winced.

"Did you blow up the cabin?" Nikolaus asked in a horrified voice.

"No," Shawn said in an insistent, hoarse voice. "I swear to you all, that wasn't me."

"Why didn't you just shoot us, if you were sent to kill us? Why did you let us live?" Carl demanded. He seemed to be the only one capable of complex thought at that moment. Thiago certainly wasn't.

"But then who blew up the cabin?" Nikolaus squeaked in agitation.

"I don't know," Shawn said desperately as Remy stood up and backed away from him. Shawn turned slightly and looked at them all. "I don't know who blew it up, and that's why I didn't kill you then. I realized that they had sent a backup and I wondered why. I also… I care for all of you. Well," he turned to look at Gray almost apologetically. "Not you, mate. Sorry, but I quite hate you still."

"Feeling's mutual," Gray said graciously.

"It was because of me, wasn't it?" Remy asked as he walked slowly around the room. It was unnerving to have him pacing like that, and Thiago suspected he was doing it on purpose. "You failed your mission before, when I was the target, and so you thought they didn't trust you. That's why you thought they sent a backup plan."

"I didn't fail that mission. I was called off," Shawn said in an odd, flat voice. "They had targeted you as a liability, but then… then they decided to put me on you as a sleeper instead of eliminating you."

"And that's why you stuck with me," Remy asked in a slightly hurt voice. "You were waiting for me to turn traitor. You were supposed to worm your way into my trust and then turn me over when I flipped."

"Remy," Shawn begged as the rest of them watched tensely. Remy stared at him blankly for several long seconds. "I may have been on a mission those first several days, but not after. Not after you… please," he said miserably.

Remy's eyes softened slightly, but his jaw remained set. "We'll come back to that," he finally whispered.

"What are you talking about when you say you were assigned? The Purges?" Carl asked carefully.

Shawn and Remy stared at one another and didn't answer. Finally, Shawn took a shaky breath and said, "The Purging wasn't a computer virus. It was an aid to the Hunters."

"An aid?" Carl echoed.

Shawn nodded.

"A raid the month before had gone bad, and a group of agents came across some information they weren't supposed to see. Files and the like, detailing the Organization's activities."

"What activities?" Carl demanded.

"I don't know. Whatever it was, it was bad enough to warrant the mass extermination of the entire group. We were ordered to clear out the roster from that mission, and any individuals they had come into contact with. There's only thirteen of us. We were overworked. We needed help."

"So, they had someone create this virus?" Thiago asked as his brain finally kicked back into gear. "The targets weren't random. Those nine agents who lost their lives were all successful hits. They were all part of that raid."

"Aye. All but one. One of those nine deaths was a Hunter."

Thiago looked at Brandt and Gray sharply to ensure that they said nothing about the raid. "He was killed by his mark?" he asked.

"Yes," Shawn murmured.

"And that's where our Nikolaus comes in. Isn't it, Niko?" Remy murmured in a low, dangerous voice as he looked at Nikolaus from under lowered lashes.

Thiago and the rest all looked at Remy and then at Nikolaus in surprise.

"I… you see… but… well…," Nikolaus stammered as he squirmed in his seat and looked at them all with dread. "I don't… how did you know that?" he asked desperately.

"It's the only reason you would have been included in the group that needed exterminating, Niko. I wasn't sure until just now."

"Son of a bitch!" Nikolaus muttered as he looked at Remy fearfully.

"No one'll hurt you, mate," Carl said soothingly as he glared at Remy to make his point. "Tell us."

"They came to me during my first week," Nikolaus blurted out. "They told me the scenario they wanted to set up and asked if it was possible. I said it was and they gave me the numbers to make the protocol. I didn't know they were going to use it! I thought it was just how they tested newbies!"

"You created the Purge virus?" Thiago asked in shock.

"Yes!" Nikolaus cried in anguish. "And I remember the results of the data I entered. Shawn was supposed to kill you. Both of you!" he murmured as he gestured at Thiago and Remy.

Shawn's eyes widened and he turned to look at Thiago.

"You were the covert I never caught sight of?" he asked in a whisper. Thiago blinked at him and Shawn stared back in shock. "Why would they have put you… and then here… unless… my God," Shawn stuttered as he pushed away from the table and stood up quickly, sending his chair toppling backward.

Thiago jumped out of his seat as well and pulled his gun, pointing it at Shawn even as Shawn mimicked the gesture and drew his own weapon.

Thiago froze when the cold barrel of a pistol nudged his temple in warning, and he rolled his eyes slightly to see Remy's flat black eyes on him. Shawn was in much the same position, looking out of the sides of his eyes at Brandt, who'd drawn Carl's gun and had it trained on the other man. How the two of them had moved so quickly Thiago didn't want to know, but it was definitely not a good idea for Brandt and Remy to both be armed, angry, and in charge of things. Not good at all.

Gray and Carl grabbed Nikolaus and pulled him away from the table by the collar of his shirt. They crouched by the wall and Gray stood in front of Nikolaus protectively.

"That's, uh, that's called a Mexican standoff, Gizmo," Carl whispered carefully, sounding like a tour guide in a museum. "Don't see those every day."

"I think technically for it to be a Mexican standoff, Brandt and Remy would both need another gun," Gray whispered.

'Smartass until the end, that one,' Thiago thought with a slight smile.

"Let's all just sit back down, shall we?" Remy suggested calmly as he stepped in front of Thiago, shielding Thiago from Shawn's line of fire, while at the same time blocking Thiago's vision. He was protecting them both, and Thiago relaxed slightly as he looked at Remy's calm face. "We're going to get through this without maiming one another," the Cajun pronounced as everyone filtered back to their seats. "Guns on the table. All of you," he ordered as he threw his own weapon down. "Brandt, anything flammable, if you please. Your lighter too."

Brandt sniffed as if he were insulted. "Threw it away," he snarled. "Bastard did unholy things to it," he said sadly.

They stared at him uneasily for several long seconds, then everyone seemed to shake out of the Brandt-induced stupor and look around warily.

"Where were we?" Remy asked pleasantly. "In case we all didn't follow; Shawn is a special Organization assassin sent to kill us all, Thiago is the Archer and therefore the reason we're all here to begin with, Brandt and Gray both work for Thiago, perhaps since the beginning, yeah?" Remy said slowly as he eyed the Australian carefully. "And Nikolaus knew a whole lot more than he ever let on, because it turns out that he orchestrated the whole fucking thing. Did I miss anything?"

"You missed yourself," Thiago growled angrily. "Whose fucking side are you on, anyway?"

"Ours," Remy said succinctly. "I made a promise. I am loyal to you," he said, enunciating each word with care as he waved his hand at all of them. "And only you," he said softly. "I feel compelled to add Gray to our agreement. I quite like the bastard," he added with a faint smile as he looked at Gray. As his words sank in. everyone seemed to relax further.

"So wait, what?" Nikolaus asked in confusion. "Who's working for who?

Thiago's the Archer?"

"I hate that fucking name!" Thiago shouted angrily as he banged his fist against the table. "Whoever the hell came up with that name should be shot!" They all stared at him, and suddenly he knew how Brandt must have felt most of the time. "Sorry," he mumbled as he let his head fall onto his crossed arms.

"I'm sorry about the whole trying to kill you thing," Shawn mumbled. "Just sort of instinct," he added with a shrug.

"No problem," Thiago murmured as he looked over at Shawn and smiled slightly.

"If you hate the name 'Archer,' then what do your subordinates call you?" Carl asked curiously.

Brandt shifted beside him and studied his hands as if he had never seen them before.

"I don't know," Thiago said with a shrug. "Shitface over here is the only one I ever deal with directly," he added as he nodded at Gray.

"You know, there is just too much Kincaid love in this room right now," Gray said in exasperation as he threw his hands up and let them flop back onto the table. "Jesus fucking Christ. No, no! Don't everyone rush to adore me at once, now!"

Thiago grinned at him and watched Carl put his arm around Gray and squeeze him consolingly. That was new. Maybe the others would be accepting of Gray after all, especially considering that they now knew he was technically on the same side as Thiago and Brandt.

"We just call him the Archer," Brandt answered softly. Carl turned to look at him, but Brandt didn't look up.

"And what do they call you?" Carl asked in a soft voice.

Brandt shifted under the man's intense scrutiny. "Pyre," he said hoarsely. "My code name is Pyre."

Carl simply nodded and looked at Gray and Remy in turn. "And what are your code names, may I ask?" he asked in the same strangely calm voice.

Remy and Gray looked at one another blankly for several seconds, and Thiago wondered what they were thinking. Were they sensing the same strange vibe that he was? This was getting too confusing too quickly, and Thiago wanted it stopped. Now.

"*Escuche*, we don't have the time for this right now," Thiago said as he stood slowly. "We can go over all this later, but right now we need to clean up and clear out. Shawn? Who's coming after us tomorrow?"

"I don't know," Shawn said as he looked up at Thiago warily.

"Shawn," Thiago growled warningly.

"I can make an educated guess, Thiago, but I don't know," Shawn growled in return. "I've not been in contact since the cabin was blown."

"I still want to know who blew up the fucking cabin!" Nikolaus demanded with a huff.

"I did," Remy murmured in answer.

Everyone stared at him in shocked horror.

"What?" Shawn finally breathed.

"I blew up the cabin," Remy answered calmly. "I had to convince you that the Organization was–"

"I fucking asked you," Shawn hissed. "Right to your face!"

"I lied," Remy responded flatly as he crossed his arms over his chest and looked down at Shawn blankly.

He was barraged by a flurry of questions, and he ignored every single one of them as he stared at Shawn unerringly.

"Wait, wait," Brandt muttered as he stood up and leaned over the table to look at Remy keenly. "Just answer me one thing," he requested. Remy nodded and looked down at the tabletop. "Did you mistime it?"

Remy looked up at him slowly, his eyes black and hard. "No," he answered.

"So you set that charge, and then put yourself right smack in the blast radius?" Brandt asked with what might have been open admiration. Remy nodded curtly. "Marry me," Brandt requested with unholy glee.

Remy cracked a smile and Carl laughed softly at Brandt's side. Shawn and Nikolaus both sat motionless, staring at Remy disbelievingly. Thiago rolled his eyes and cleared his throat. Nothing Remy did surprised him, now.

"Shawn," he sighed. "Make your educated guess."

"What?" Shawn asked dazedly as he tore his eyes away from Remy.

"Who is coming for us?" Thiago asked slowly.

"My guess would be that it's Mikhail," Shawn answered in a distant voice as his eyes were drawn back to Remy.

"Is that the dude with the last name I could never pronounce?" Remy asked idly. Shawn nodded. "Well, fuck me," Remy breathed.

"Chamov. He's one of the best," Shawn said with another nod.

"Gray?" Thiago ventured after a tense silence. "You and Remy go on upstairs, get some sleep. Shawn, you too. We leave at first light."

"But–"

"Wait a minute–"

"I still have questions."

"I don't care," Thiago answered. "Later."

"What do you plan to do?" Remy asked curiously.

"We have to move, we'll plan the rest as we go. Go on, all of you. Carl, Brandt?"

"Hmm?" they both answered distractedly.

Thiago stared at them curiously for several seconds. After a moment of thought, he said, "You two go rest up as well. We'll need you keeping watch tonight. Niko? We have some things to take care of."

Thiago watched the others shuffle out, and he took special notice of the long, tense look Gray and Remy shared before Gray nodded to Thiago and ducked out of the room. What the hell was that about?

Thiago followed them to the staircase to make certain that his orders were followed.

Carl waited until the others passed by him, and he fell into step with Brandt as the man trudged up next to him. Thiago couldn't help but feel sorry for Brandt.

"Does anyone else feel like they've just been sent to bed for being naughty?" Thiago heard Gray ask as he reached the top of the stairs and looked back at them all.

"Keep moving, Boss, I'm tired," Remy growled as he pushed Gray on the ass and caused him to stumble away from the stairs.

"Yeah, hissy fits of massive proportions such as the one you just threw tend to take a lot out of you," Gray responded wryly. Remy kicked him in the shin. "Ow!"

"It was not a hissy fit!" Remy yelled and Gray thumped him on the nose. "Ow! Dickface!"

"Fuckhead!"

A sharp growl from Shawn stopped the argument. Carl snickered as he got to the top of the stairs and watched Gray limp away to the smallest bedroom.

"You rarely see a good kick to the shin from a trained agent anymore," Carl teased. Remy looked at him and blushed. "That's old school smack down," he said with a wink.

"That's playground smack down, you twisted fuck!" Gray called as he slammed the door behind him. Even Thiago could hear the smile in the other man's voice, though, and he snickered uncontrollably as he walked back into the dining room to speak to Nikolaus.

XXXIII.

SHAWN and Remy stood in the hallway with Carl and Brandt, both of them avoiding looking at one another. They may as well have been shuffling their feet and blushing. Carl rolled his eyes and gave Brandt a discreet shove toward the bedroom they'd shared with Nikolaus last night. If Shawn and Remy needed time alone in separate beds, then they'd have that option. Besides, Carl wasn't tired and he wanted Brandt's company.

Brandt opened the door and stepped through, going directly to stand in front of the window and look out on the courtyard below. He looked sad, and Carl's heart ached for the normally ebullient man.

"Hey, Wally," Carl said softly as he closed the door to the bedroom behind him and stepped into the room.

"Yeah?" Brandt said in a slow, sad voice.

"I have something for you," Carl murmured as he walked closer to Brandt and stood beside him, putting a gentle hand on the small of the other man's back.

"Please don't kill me yet," Brandt requested miserably as he pressed his forehead to the glass of the window and closed his eyes.

Carl frowned and started rubbing slow circles on Brandt's back with the tips of his fingers.

"I couldn't tell you any of it," Brandt insisted miserably.

"I'm not going to kill you, Wally," Carl whispered with an indulgent smile and a little laugh. "I understand why you didn't say anything. If it had been me, I wouldn't have said anything, either. That's your job, to protect your loyalties," he whispered in a soothing voice as he closed in and spoke into Brandt's ear. "I'm not angry. Come here," he coaxed as he tugged at the back of Brandt's shirt.

Brandt shivered and turned to look at him, his brown eyes huge and strangely innocent. How Carl could think that someone like Brandt was innocent in any sense of the word was beyond his comprehension, but there it was all the same. Carl looked into the other man's eyes and smiled reassuringly. A flash showed in Brandt's eyes as he smiled tentatively back.

There was his Brandt.

"You have something for me?" Brandt asked in something close to his usual carefree tone.

"Yeah," Carl said excitedly. He'd been so concerned about the other man's mental state he'd almost forgotten what he was supposed to be doing! He dug around in his pocket and retrieved the little gift box. "I saw it this morning while we were out," Carl told him as he held it out in the palm of his hand, his casual tone completely disregarding the fact that 'out' had been a body dump. "I knew you would want a replacement."

Brandt looked at the box for several seconds and then back up at Carl with a smile that lit up his entire countenance. Carl grinned back at him.

There was his Brandt.

Carl knew Brandt had guessed what he was being given. He knew because he and Brandt had melded somehow. They were one now, even if neither of them had really realized it before. They walked the same path, even if one side of the path was engulfed in flames and the other was covered in ice. They were the same, and the knowledge made Carl happier than he had been in some time. He was no longer alone, and Brandt was the reason for it.

"Are you asking me to marry you then?" Brandt said with a cheeky, almost shy smile as he took the box from Carl and sat on the bed to unwrap it.

"I'm not really the marrying sort," Carl murmured, and he stuffed his hands in his pockets and watched Brandt open the box with a small smile on his face.

"What's wrong, Trigger, I'm not your type? I can baaaa with the best of them. I'd even wear wool for you," Brandt teased as he let the paper fall to the floor and held the box in the palm of his hand.

He looked up at Carl with a smile, and Carl felt the overwhelming urge to kiss him. Not the fierce, primal kisses they had always shared before, but a slow, tender kiss. One that would convey the emotions Carl was feeling.

Brandt's smile slipped slightly as he saw the slightly stricken look Carl had acquired as he thought. "What–"

"Do that again," Carl ordered quietly as he took several steps and took Brandt's face in his hands.

"What, baa like a sheep?" Brandt asked in confusion.

"Smile for me, Brandt," Carl whispered as he leaned over slightly and looked Brandt in the eyes. Brandt blinked and opened his mouth to say something, then snapped it shut again as a slow smile spread across his face.

"You called me Brandt," he said with another shy smile, and Carl kissed him gently.

Brandt's hands moved slowly up Carl's forearms, rubbing up and down several times before he wrapped his fingers around Carl's wrists and tilted his head slightly to allow Carl better access to his mouth.

Carl's pulse raced as he slowly slid his tongue over Brandt's. "Is that not your name?" he asked breathlessly.

"I can't remember," Brandt responded in the same tone.

Carl smiled again and kissed him once more. He pressed into him this time, and Brandt wrapped his arms around Carl's neck as Carl pushed him slowly back to lie on the bed. Brandt groaned and gripped him tighter.

"You didn't open your present," Carl murmured in between slow, sensual kisses. He slid his hands up Brandt's forearms, which were still wrapped around his neck, and he pulled at them to bring Brandt's hands down to the bed. He laced their fingers together and allowed his thumbs to rub lightly back and forth along Brandt's wrists as he pinned Brandt's hands down.

Brandt looked up at him longingly. "I'd rather do this," he said in a low, growling voice.

Carl had always wondered which activity held the highest rank on Brandt's Big List of Fun Shit. Apparently, sex was higher than fire. Today, anyway.

Carl let go of Brandt's wrists and slid his way slowly down Brandt's body until he was standing at the edge of the bed with Brandt looking up at him curiously.

"Pyre, huh?" Carl asked he unbuckled his own belt and let his jeans fall to the floor. He stepped out of them as Brandt watched him hungrily and then pulled his flannel shirt over his head without bothering to unbutton it. "Do you like to burn, Wally?" he asked in a low, seductive voice as he stood naked at Brandt's feet.

"Are you going to make me?" Brandt breathed as he disrobed slowly, staring at Carl's eyes and moving as if in a daze. Carl reached down and pulled Brandt's jeans off for him. He gestured for the other man to scoot to the head of the bed and crawled onto the bed after him, settling between Brandt's legs comfortably. "Are you sure you're not very mad, Trigger? I wanted to tell you, I just…," Brandt murmured as he licked his lower lip nervously and looked up at Carl with worried eyes.

"You know better. Don't make me take your treat away," Carl threatened cheekily.

"Mmm, I thought *you* were my treat," Brandt responded with the same cheeky tone as he rotated his hips and groaned slightly. Neither of them was much on foreplay. They both preferred to have a nice, satisfying fuck and then revel in one another's presence after. Carl smiled and said nothing, and as they looked at one another, Brandt's eyes suddenly cleared and he whispered, "Fuck me, Trigger."

"No," Carl said as he leaned over Brandt and stroked him in a lazy rhythm. Brandt groaned and thrust his hips upward into Carl's hand.

"Please," Brandt breathed as his hand came to tangle in Carl's long hair.

"I won't fuck you. But I will make love to you, if that's what you want," Carl whispered to him, his lips ghosting over the tender skin of Brandt's collarbone as he spoke.

"Oh, God, yes. Please," Brandt groaned with more passion than Carl had expected.

Their encounters had never been anything but fast and hard. In fact, as far as Carl was aware, all of Brandt's encounters had been brutal to some degree. To this day, the thought of Brandt trying his best to fuck Remy through the wall could make Carl instantly hard.

"Where's the–"

"No, no lube. Nothing. I want to *feel* you," Brandt said in a hoarse voice as he wrapped strong arms around Carl and pulled him closer for an open-mouthed, wet kiss.

Carl gave Brandt's cock several more strokes before tearing away from the kiss regretfully and sliding down Brandt's body.

"Never on a warm up, remember," Brandt said plaintively as he rose up onto his elbows to watch what Carl was doing. "You'll hurt your jaw," he warned cheekily.

"Have I ever sucked you off, Wally?" Carl asked as he bit at the soft skin covering Brandt's hipbone.

"I, uhh, holy hell, that feels good," Brandt moaned as his eyelids fluttered.

"You'll come on the warm up, all right," Carl growled evilly.

Brandt's eyes fluttered closed and both hands reached to press against the headboard as Carl did his best to make him scream. Finally, he was writhing and thrusting into Carl's mouth almost uncontrollably.

"Please," he gasped as he opened his eyes and looked down at Carl pleadingly. "I want you inside me. I want you to feel me come, Trigger. Please!" Carl closed his eyes and moaned as he raised his head. That did sound like a good idea. But if Brandt didn't come for him, he needed something else to use as lube.

Brandt's breathing was still erratic as he tried to calm his overheated body, and Carl crawled up to kneel beside his head. Brandt needed no prompting, and he immediately rolled to the side and took Carl's throbbing cock into his mouth. His hand slid around to rest on the back of Carl's hip and he pulled at him, urging Carl to thrust forward, to fuck his mouth as he moaned and sucked.

Carl cradled Brandt's head with his hand, desperately trying to hold back, and after only seconds, he knew that he couldn't take any more and he pulled at Brandt's curls to make him stop.

Brandt looked up at him, licking his lips slowly, and said, "Fuck me. Make me burn, Trigger. I'll make you feel it, too."

Carl repositioned himself between Brandt's legs and locked eyes with the other man as he slowly pushed into him. Brandt moaned and tried to push down with his hips, but Carl's fingers dug into his hipbones and stopped him. Words flew in one ear and out the other with Brandt, and this was the only way Carl knew to let Brandt know how he felt. He intended to do it right.

Brandt shuddered as Carl finally sheathed himself completely; they both gasped and stared at one another raptly. Carl kept his movements slow and deliberate, just the way he liked it, and soon Brandt was begging and whimpering, pleading with him to go faster.

"Please! Fuck me, Trigger! Please go harder, please make me burn!" the man begged.

But Carl had no intention of making Brandt burn. For once, he wanted Brandt to feel what *he* felt: a slow, cold swelling of emotion.

"Come for me, Brandt," Carl whispered, savoring the name as it came out of his mouth. "Come all over yourself. Let me feel you. Let me see you."

Brandt groaned and his cock jumped against Carl's body. Carl gripped Brandt's hips and thrust into him, pulling at him and sitting back on his knees as he did so. Brandt allowed himself to be manhandled until his hips were resting on top of Carl's thighs and Carl was just barely moving inside him.

"Come all over yourself," Carl repeated enticingly as he took Brandt's cock in his hand and began a fast, steady rhythm. "I want to see it." Brandt's hand went to the headboard and scrambled for something to grip as his entire body began to shake. He was so close; Carl could feel the rhythmic tensing of his muscles as he fucked him. "I want you to come. I want to lick you clean," he coaxed as he started moving faster inside the other man.

"Fuck yes! Carl!" Brandt cried out, the first time either of them had ever heard Carl's name spoken by the other man. He groaned and shuddered, and thrust into Carl's hand with a muted roar as Carl jerked him off. His come spurted across his muscular stomach, and Carl immediately rubbed his free hand slowly through the milky fluid even as more covered the backs of his fingers.

Brandt was breathing hard and moaning constantly, and his head thrashed back and forth with each of Carl's powerful thrusts into him. Carl spread his hands over Brandt's stomach and massaged his torso as he pushed into him, and when Brandt finally looked down to investigate Carl's activities, he groaned wantonly at what he saw. Carl was leaning over him, holding Brandt by his sticky waist, his fingers digging into Brandt's ribs as his hips moved faster. Brandt's orgasm had destroyed Carl's self-control, and he thrust into Brandt's body with as much force as he could manage as he licked over Brandt's chest and sucked on his nipples one by one.

Carl continued to lick and rub Brandt's come into the man's skin, and by the time he lost complete control and was forced to shift and really begin pounding into the other man, Brandt was shivering as the cold air hit his moistened body.

"That's what I feel," Carl gasped as he thrust into Brandt and they both moaned in pleasure. "You feel the cold?"

Brandt groaned in response and dug his fingers into the bedcovers.

Carl pounded into him and marveled at how stunning the man was laid out like this. The heat engulfed him and Brandt's clenching body surrounded him as he moved. He pulled almost completely out and then rammed back in with all his might. Brandt called out his name again and sent Carl plummeting over the edge.

"Fuck, yes," he murmured over and over as he rocked his hips and clung to Brandt. He cried out wordlessly as he came hard into Brandt's shivering body.

He collapsed against Brandt as soon as the aftershocks had ceased, and Brandt held him close as their sweating bodies stuck together pleasantly.

"You feel that?" Brandt panted as he wrapped his arms around Carl and pulled him up to stretch out by his side. "You feel cold like that? All the time?" he asked with a hint of sorrow in his soft voice.

They both lay on their sides, facing one another and breathing heavily. Carl slid his arm beneath Brandt's head and kissed his forehead tenderly. Brandt slung his leg over Carl's hip as they stared into one another's glazed eyes.

"My whole world is cold, Wally," Carl whispered matter-of-factly. "It's all cold steel and cold nights… turning off emotions in order to do a job. Well, it was, until you blew it all to Hell."

Brandt smiled and rolled slightly until he was half on top of Carl, and he reached to the edge of the bed where the forgotten box remained. He picked it up and rolled back to his previous position, cuddled into Carl's embrace. He opened the box slowly and looked inside.

"You got me another lighter," he said in a soft, pleased voice. "The other one was tainted. But you knew that, didn't you? You got me another one," he murmured as he tore his eyes away from the new lighter and looked up into Carl's eyes.

"Yeah," Carl whispered as he ran his knuckles over Brandt's cheekbone and licked his lips nervously. There was no other time to do this. Soon, they would be running again, and Carl was good enough at his job to know that anything could happen to any of these men at any time, no matter how much he loved them. "Promise me something," he requested in a tentative whisper as he rubbed his hands up and down Brandt's hard, muscular chest.

"Anything," Brandt whispered as his eyes closed slowly and he arched sideways into Carl's touch.

Carl scooted forward and kissed Brandt chastely before moving to whisper in his ear. "Promise you'll stay with me," he pleaded, his voice tinged with desperation.

"Stay with you?" Brandt asked in a breathless voice as he unconsciously slid his body closer and rubbed against Carl like a puppy trying to get comfortable. "What do you… where? When?"

"Anywhere," Carl said as he kissed Brandt's temple. "For as long as you can stand me. I want you with me," Carl admitted in a barely audible voice.

Brandt froze and his breath caught as Carl's heart beat wildly in his throat.

"So you *were* asking me to marry you," Brandt finally teased with an amused grin as he nuzzled his face against Carl's chest and inhaled deeply.

Carl smiled despite the evasive manner of the response.

"You're stuck with me now, Trigger," Brandt whispered, so softly that Carl almost missed it.

"You'll stay with me?" Carl asked hopefully, his tone almost disbelieving as he hugged Brandt close.

Brandt shimmied even further into the embrace and wrapped his arms around Carl's body before looking up and kissing him on the tip of his chin. "I'll stay with you. I'll keep you warm," he whispered.

XXXIV.

SHAWN watched Remy closely, trying to decipher the other man's mood before he said or did anything that would exacerbate Remy's irritation. He desperately needed Remy to give him some sign that he could follow him to the master bedroom; if that sign didn't come, then Shawn knew all was lost for the two of them. All he wanted was to talk to the other man and hold him. Just hold him.

Remy stood and watched Carl and Brandt withdraw into the bedroom, and then he turned and shuffled down the hall away from Shawn without another word. Shawn's heart sank, and he stood with his head bowed, watching Remy's feet as they moved away from him. Remy stopped as he reached the doorway and turned around. Shawn looked up quickly and met Remy's soft brown eyes.

"Coming?" Remy asked softly.

Shawn swallowed the lump in his throat and ducked his head gratefully as he started forward. Once inside the room, Shawn leaned against the closed door, feeling as if there was nowhere left to hide. He wanted to hide. He needed to hide almost as much as he needed to tell Remy everything.

"So you're a Hunter?" Remy asked in a low voice as he padded over to the bed and stood beside it, looking down at it idly.

Shawn had a strange sense of déjà vu as he watched the other man. "Yes," he answered gruffly.

"Will you tell me about it?" Remy asked as he turned to look at Shawn appraisingly.

"Yes," Shawn said eagerly, and he took a step forward.

Remy smiled and turned back to the bed. "What should I call you, then?" he asked as he looked at Shawn over his shoulder. "Elmer?"

Shawn snorted and grinned before he could stop himself. He took several tentative steps toward the other man. Remy had always made it easy. Easy to love him. Easy to forgive him. Easy to be forgiven. He closed the distance between them slowly.

"Which is it, Mr. Fudd?" Remy asked. His eyes were twinkling even as his voice grew low and mockingly serious. "Duck season or rabbit season?"

"Silly wabbit," Shawn murmured as he circled his arms around Remy in a gentle embrace and kissed him slowly.

Remy muttered something unintelligible and wrapped both of his arms around Shawn's neck, but almost immediately he hissed and jerked away. Shawn let him loose as if he'd suddenly been burned.

Remy looked at him apologetically. "Shit," he breathed as he let his right arm hang limply by his side and rubbed it gingerly. "Sometimes I forget that it hurts," he said ashamedly. He closed his eyes and hummed quietly as Shawn ran gentle fingers over his cheekbone and down the side of his face.

"How did it happen?" Shawn asked curiously as he let his fingers travel up and through Remy's short hair. "And why did you cut your hair?" he asked sadly

"Those two events are shockingly related, actually," Remy said absently as he looked at Shawn. "God, I missed you," he said dazedly as he stepped closer and hugged Shawn to him. His arms slipped around Shawn's waist carefully and he buried his face in Shawn's neck as he pulled him close. Shawn stood there stiffly for several seconds, his brain not fully realizing that he should be performing some sort of action in return. Remy was hugging him. Not seducing him or kissing him or embracing him passionately, but simply hugging him.

Shawn thought he might cry. He hugged Remy back, wrapping him in a soft, tender embrace.

"Will you hold me, Shawn?" Remy asked in a voice muffled by Shawn's skin and the gauze in which Remy had wrapped him after their shower.

"Forever," Shawn murmured into Remy's short hair. Even now the damp hair was trying to curl, and Shawn smiled into the shower fresh scent of the other man.

They both laughed softly at the words. They had never been very romantic with one another, and even now, even when it felt good to commit and say the words, it still struck them both as funny.

"C'mon," Shawn laughed gently as he pried Remy loose and pushed him gently toward the bed. "Do you want me to wrap your arm first?"

"Yeah," Remy said as he ran his hand idly over Shawn's chest. He sat on the edge of the bed and Shawn gathered the gauze and peroxide Remy had used earlier. "He caught up to us in Los Angeles, at the airport," Remy said as his eyes followed

Shawn's movements. "We knew he had been following us, but we didn't expect him to attack us. He was just a Paint, y'know? I've never heard of one attacking like that."

Shawn nodded and sat beside Remy. "It is unusual. He did this, then?" Shawn asked as he indicated the knife wound on Remy's arm. Remy nodded and Shawn's eyes were drawn to the red line beneath his chin. "And this?" he inquired as he let his knuckles brush over Remy's jaw.

"That too," Remy said. "I went to the bathroom while Gray was checking the message drop Thiago always used."

"You were in contact with Thiago?" Shawn asked as cold rage threatened to boil up. If Thiago had known all along that Remy was alive and he hadn't told Shawn, there would be hell to pay!

"No, no," Remy said quickly as he patted Shawn's knee soothingly. "But we checked by phone every day, just in case. Anyway, he attacked me in the toilet. Didn't even have the decency to let me zip back up first!" Remy continued in outrage.

Shawn grinned and dabbed at the wound. That was so like Remy, to be insulted by the fact that he'd been attacked with his willy out instead of by the fact that he'd actually been attacked.

"Ow."

"Sorry," Shawn murmured as he looked at the wound. His eyes were carefully avoiding the urge to dart up and look at the pink scar his own bullet had created, and instead he examined the knife wound. It was deep, probably a defensive wound. Shawn could imagine Remy standing at the urinal and hearing the scuff of a shoe behind him, then turning just in time to block the killing blow. Shawn shivered as the mental image played itself over and over.

"That's okay," Remy muttered. "We scuffled for a bit, but he overpowered me. I couldn't use my right arm, you see," he went on almost defensively. "When Gray finally came in, the guy had me on my stomach, holding my head back by my hair and getting ready to slice my throat open. That's where this came from," he said with a wave of his hand at his throat. "Gray killed him just as the knife cut into me. He threw a dagger at him. Really cool move," he finished with a small appreciative smile.

"Had you by your hair, huh," Shawn said as he wrapped the wound with gauze. "That's why you cut it?"

"Yeah. We figured we needed to eliminate as many useful handles as we could," Remy muttered almost shyly.

Shawn ran his fingers through Remy's hair affectionately. "All done," he said quietly.

"Good. Now it's your turn. I want to know everything. From the beginning."

XXXV.

"THREE hundred dollars for a train ticket?" Thiago yelled into the phone.

Nikolaus looked at the words Thiago had written on his little white pad as he spoke to the person from Amtrak, and he furrowed his brow in confusion.

"Is that for all seven or… Jesus Christ, I don't want to buy the damn thing, I just want to ride on it! Fine, fine. It'll take how long? Are they still laying the fucking track? All right, all right. Yes, that'll do. Seven, yes. Thank you."

Thiago slammed the phone down and looked at Nikolaus disbelievingly.

"Why are we going through D.C. and Chicago to get to Spokane?" Nikolaus asked as he pointed to the scribbles Thiago had made. "Would it not be quicker to, you know, walk or crawl maybe?"

"I don't know," Thiago huffed is disgust. "Probably. Why are we paying more than we would for a plane ticket to do it?" he countered in agitation.

"Remy seems to be fully loaded, I don't think he'll mind the expense," Nikolaus pointed out as he sat back and looked at Thiago carefully. "Does all this money come from you and your activities?" he asked suspiciously.

"No. I don't know where he gets it from," Thiago answered uneasily.

"Are you really the Archer?" Nikolaus asked suddenly, unable to control his sudden urge to inquire further into the matter.

Thiago stared at him steadily for several long seconds, his icy blue eyes making Nikolaus squirm. "I am," Thiago finally answered, his tone apologetic.

"Then why the hell don't you ever know what's going on?" Nikolaus demanded angrily. "I mean, you have agents running wild every which way and people trying to kill us and–"

"I think, perhaps, the situation is no longer within my grasp," Thiago murmured grimly. "The only option we have left open to us now is to turn tail and run."

XXXVI.

BRANDT was drifting somewhere between awareness and sleep, but when he heard the dull thump his eyes snapped open and he was immediately awake and tense. He remained still, his head resting on Carl's shoulder and his leg still slung over the other man's hip possessively.

Carl was awake; Brandt could feel him breathing shallowly. You never held your breath when you were trying to listen. Shawn had taught Brandt that. You ended up hearing the blood rushing through your body and your own heartbeat, instead of external sounds. On remembering this, Brandt released the breath he was holding and listened intently. He started to move but Carl tightened his grip and Brandt froze.

"It's okay," Carl whispered into Brandt's hair. "It's just Zed."

"How do you know?" Brandt whispered back as his body relaxed against Carl's. It struck him then, just how much he trusted the other man. For the first time he could remember, Brandt was entrusting someone else with his life. The realization made him smile.

"He mumbles to himself when he's fucked off," Carl answered with a smile against Brandt's temple. "Listen."

Brandt grinned and strained his hearing. Sure enough, he could hear Thiago's gruff voice as the man passed by their door. A sudden thump on the door almost made Brandt jump out of skin. He gripped Carl so tightly that the other man squeaked in surprise.

"You two better be resting in there, goddammit!" Thiago yelled through the door.

Brandt bit back a snicker, and Carl shook against him as he laughed silently.

"We're leaving in two hours!"

"Two hours?" Brandt whispered questioningly.

"Three more quality fucks," Carl answered. They both sniggered and shushed one another as Thiago growled wordlessly at them.

"Where do you think we're going?" Brandt whispered conspiratorially after Thiago stomped away. He tilted his head upwards and nuzzled against Carl's scruffy jaw.

"Mmm… don't know. Hopefully they'll have beds there, though," Carl murmured as he rolled into Brandt's body and forced him to his back. He wrapped himself around Brandt and they both hummed contentedly.

Brandt fingered his new lighter thoughtfully as he held the other man, wondering how Remy and Shawn were doing and what Nikolaus was up to if Thiago was up here and prowling around in the hall. He also wondered how he'd actually gotten the lighter in his hand, and he realized with a grin that Carl had handed it to him.

"Don't even think about lighting that thing," Carl murmured sleepily. "I'm not flame retardant."

Brandt smiled contentedly and breathed in the smell of soap and sex and sweat that marked their previous activities.

"You know, I think we're going to ground," Brandt said quietly.

"Probably," Carl murmured sleepily, his lips moving against the skin of Brandt's neck as he nuzzled closer.

"We can't run forever," Brandt said matter-of-factly.

"No. We can't," Carl agreed.

"We're going to have to turn and fight, eventually."

"Yeah."

"It's going to be fun when we do, Trigger," Brandt growled with relish.

"Yeah," Carl responded quietly.

XXXVII

SHAWN sat with his shoulders resting against the headboard of the antique four-poster bed. He'd tried to lay flat, but when did he complained that he was able to feel his heartbeat throbbing in his fresh wound, and was forced to sit back up.

Remy was sprawled out next to him, with his feet resting in Shawn's lap and his head hanging off the corner of the bed.

Remy didn't know why the pretence of hanging upside down always relaxed him, but it did. Shawn had always found it slightly odd, but Remy didn't care. Hanging upside down was a nice affinity to have if you were being tortured, at any rate.

He lifted his head warily when the thump sounded out in the hall, and they both cocked their heads to listen as Thiago banged on Carl and Brandt's door and growled at them.

"Thiago's pissy," Remy murmured as he let his head flop back down onto the corner of the mattress and stared at the upside down room. His sore back popped, and he groaned in relief.

"You'll give yourself a headache doing that," Shawn warned as Remy brought his arms up gingerly and stretched them out over his head, making him look like an upside down Superman, trying to fly.

"Too late," Remy groaned as he flopped his arms back onto the mattress and lifted his head to look at Shawn. "So, I get that you were assigned to take me down way back when," he said, changing the subject abruptly as he struggled to sit back up, like a turtle stuck on its shell. Shawn reached down and grabbed him by the forearm and pulled him upright with a grunt. "Thanks. But why was I a target in the first place? And why didn't you just kill me when you had the chance? What made them change your objective? And–"

"Remy, stop," Shawn murmured with a grimace. They sat staring at one another for several seconds, blinking and waiting for the other to speak first. The silence stretched into uncomfortable territory, and they both jumped when Thiago banged on the door.

"Two hours, *chicos*," his gruff voice called from the hallway.

"Thi?" Remy called.

The door creaked open, and Thiago stuck his head in. "*Mierda.* I thought I'd see something naked," he said in mock disappointment.

"My ass hurts," Remy responded matter-of-factly in explanation for his apparently inexplicably half-clothed state. "What did you work out?"

"Train to Spokane, up in Washington."

"What are you doing?" Remy asked with a small smirk after he nodded in recognition of the answer.

"Well, I sent Nikolaus out to pick up some last-minute necessities and–"

"You sent him out alone?" Shawn asked incredulously.

Thiago shrugged. "He volunteered," he said defensively. "I'm going to make Brandt and Carl keep watch for a bit so I can go irritate Gray. How much time will you need to get ready?"

"Thirty minutes to get our things," Remy said with a quick look at Shawn for confirmation. Shawn nodded distractedly. "Irritate him, *non*?" Remy said mischievously.

"Mind your own business," Thiago huffed with a grin as he withdrew his head and closed the door behind him.

"You deal with your onions, Thi!" Remy called after him with a smirk. "Where were we?" he asked Shawn with a furrowed brow.

Shawn looked at him fondly and shrugged. "Thiago and Gray?" he asked dubiously.

"Gray's got it bad, too," Remy answered absently as he examined his hands thoroughly. Remy didn't want to talk about Gray, not with Shawn. He cursed himself for making the joke in the first place.

"We're running, you know," Shawn said softly. "That's what Thiago plans."

Remy crossed his legs and sat with his forearms resting on his knees, his fingers dangling just above the duvet. He looked at Shawn blankly and cocked his head. He said nothing and Shawn shifted uncomfortably.

"I want to run," the older man stated. "I don't want to go back. Even if I could convince them that I was still loyal to them and not be killed for my trouble, they would take you from me."

"Hmm," Remy responded noncommittally as he looked at Shawn thoughtfully. A plan was beginning to form.

XXXVIII.

GRAY awoke with a start when the weight of Thiago's body settled over his and a callused hand clapped over his mouth and nose. Thiago was aware that Gray knew better than to struggle. They had played this game before. Thiago's blue eyes blazed with anger and he mumbled and grumbled to himself still as he straddled Gray and moved to pin Gray's hands to the mattress.

"What the fuck are you playing at?" Thiago demanded of him.

"Thi," Gray whispered as he shifted slightly. "I… uh… well," he licked his lips and his eyes darted back and forth, taking in Thiago's features quickly. Thiago knew what he was thinking; wait to see what he was being accused of before he confessed to anything. "What?" he finally asked innocently after several seconds of stuttering.

Thiago sighed heavily and closed his eyes. "That may work for Remy, but it doesn't suit you," he said angrily in regards to Gray's stalling tactics. "You knew about Shawn."

"Yes," Gray admitted immediately.

"For how long?" Thiago asked through gritted teeth.

"I found out a month into our mission. By then, we were so deep I couldn't get the information out to you without Remy knowing. I didn't know if we could trust him then."

"But you told him, obviously," Thiago growled.

"Only when I had to. It was either that, or have him go crazy and kill me," Gray said defensively.

"Why didn't you tell me when you got here?" Thiago demanded, switching gears and tightening his grip on Gray's wrists.

"Remy threatened me," Gray huffed. "That's what he pulled me away for this morning. He said he would get the truth out of Shawn, and until he did, I wasn't to say anything. Sorry, *amigo*, but between the two of you, I think he's more likely to follow through with the threat. He's fucking scary, Thi."

"I know he is," Thiago said with a small smile.

Gray watched him carefully, probably wondering if Thiago was over his little fit yet. He let out a little gasp when Thiago lunged forward and kissed him hungrily.

Gray moaned and flexed his fingers, trying to get Thiago to loosen his grip so he could touch him. Thiago sat back up and released him. Gray ran his hands under Thiago's shirt and looked at him curiously.

"What about Niko?" Thiago asked as he pulled the shirt over his head and idly unbuckled his belt as he looked down at Gray.

"What?" Gray asked in surprise.

"Something funny with you two. What is it?"

"I don't–"

Thiago growled in warning and grabbed Gray's throat with one powerful hand, pulling him up into a sitting position by his neck and glaring at him as he straddled him. Gray clutched at Thiago's wrist and looked up at him with wide, slightly frightened eyes.

"I won't be fucked around, Gray," Thiago spat. "You and I both know I've lost control of this thing, but I will get it back. Starting with you," he said in a low, dangerous voice.

Gray swallowed with difficulty and nodded slightly. They both knew that Thiago didn't make idle threats.

"I have… I don't think Faust is who he says he is," Gray said uncertainly.

Thiago understood the hesitance. It was one thing to have suspicions. It was entirely another to voice them to your boss who had the power and the inclination to kill the person you suspected. Thiago's eyes narrowed suspiciously, and he turned his head slightly as he looked at Gray. He suspected Nikolaus of something? Gray's instincts were rarely wrong.

"I… Thio… I can't really breathe, here," Gray stuttered as his fingers tightened around Thiago's wrist.

Thiago's fingers loosened around his throat. He cocked his head the other way and let go of Gray completely. He sat back and looked at Gray in unnerving silence for a full minute. Gray shifted slightly beneath the weight of Thiago's body and licked his lips nervously.

"To be honest, Gray, we'll have to deal with that later. My brain can't get any further than wanting to fuck you through the mattress," Thiago finally said matter-of-factly before he lunged forward once more and crushed their mouths together, forcing Gray back down to the mattress in a flurry of flailing limbs, muffled laughs and curses.

Gray's hands fumbled to slide Thiago's unbuckled pants off his hips as Thiago struggled to remove the layer of bedding that separated their bodies. He nipped at Gray's lower lip and Gray groaned as they struggled with the sheets. Thiago tried to raise his knees one at a time to remove himself of his clothing and Gray snickered into his mouth as they fumbled.

Thiago grinned and rolled to the side, pulling Gray with him and finally getting out of his pants and under the covers.

"You're not worried about making a quick escape?" Thiago asked as he slipped his arm under Gray's head and pressed their naked bodies together. "Tsk tsk. Always sleep in clothing, Gray, you know better."

"Thought you might come see me," Gray muttered huskily in between hungry kisses.

"I couldn't get up here fast enough," Thiago growled as he rolled them again and found himself atop Gray's body once more.

They both jumped when the banging on the door sounded; soft snickers followed and Carl's mockingly serious voice called, "You two better be resting in there!"

"They aren't sane, are they?" Gray asked with a grin as Thiago let his forehead fall against Gray's shoulder.

"You'll learn to love them," Thiago sighed against Gray's skin.

"God help us all," Gray muttered.

Thiago laughed softly and shook his head. "Now I understand the meaning of scaring the fuck out of someone," he huffed disconsolately. "Give me a minute."

Gray laughed softly and wrapped his arms around Thiago's neck slowly. "I missed you," he admitted in a whisper after several moments of heavy silence.

Thiago pulled him closer and let his chin rest on the other man's head. Gray nuzzled into the hollow of his neck, and Thiago smiled contentedly.

"I missed you too… *Boss*," Thiago said with a grin.

Gray snorted and pinched his nipple, and Thiago yipped plaintively. He shook Gray a little bit in retaliation and growled.

"Now," he huffed, "tell me about this theory of yours."

XXXIX.

CARL sat staring out the door to the courtyard, his mind elsewhere as he played absently with Remy's knife.

"Earth to Trigger."

"Hmm?" Carl answered, his eyes still focused on the empty doorway and his hand rubbing absently over a catch on the handle of the knife that should not have been there.

"Hey!" Brandt shouted as he pushed at Carl's shoulder and almost sent him sprawling to the floor. The sharp blade of the knife sliced through Carl's palm, and he touched a toe to the ground to steady himself.

"What?" he asked as he turned to look at Brandt and thrust his bloody hand at the other man accusingly.

Brandt smiled softly at him and flicked his new lighter. Carl watched the flame flicker and die as Brandt spoke.

"He's all right. Gizmo can take care of himself," Brandt said as he flicked the lighter and let it flame, then shut the lid with a snap.

"Hmm," Carl responded absently as he rubbed the pads of his fingers through the blood on his hand and watched the motion of Brandt's fingers like a moth being drawn to the proverbial flame. Flick. Flare. Snap. No wonder the man was so easily distracted by fire. It was quite fascinating.

"Hey," Brandt said as he flicked the cover to the lighter closed and leaned forward to catch Carl's wavering attention. "You're not worrying about Gizmo, are you?" he asked with certainty.

Carl lowered his gaze guiltily. To be fair, he *had* given Nikolaus's welfare a passing thought. Admittedly, it hadn't been a very long one. "Not really," he admitted ashamedly.

Brandt didn't respond. He simply sat there like a huge Labrador Retriever, staring at Carl with those inquiring brown eyes and a hint of a smile.

Carl started to fidget beneath his unerring gaze. "Stop that," he growled finally.

"Stop what?" Brandt asked as he flicked the lighter again.

"Thinking about whatever it is you were thinking about setting aflame," Carl said irritably as he turned on his stool and rolled his neck, trying to get it to crack.

"I wouldn't set Dixie's house on fire," Brandt protested in an insulted voice.

"You want to, though," Carl countered with a knowing grin.

"Yeah," Brandt admitted with a self-satisfied smile, and his eyes returned to the flame emitting from the lighter.

With Brandt suitably distracted, Carl returned his thoughts to where they'd been drifting and stifled a disturbed sigh.

It didn't matter what they did, whether they ran or whether they turned and fought. The Organization wouldn't let up until they were all dead, and Carl knew it. It might be a good fight, and Carl knew with a cold certainly that he would enjoy it.

But it was a fight they couldn't win.

XL.

"I don't know why they marked you as a liability," Shawn said quietly, keeping eye contact with Remy even though it was difficult. "And I don't know why they changed their minds. It was never my job to ask."

"At what point did I go from a mark to a…." Remy swallowed with difficulty. "A resource?" he asked bitterly as he looked down at his hands and fiddled with one of his thumb rings absently.

"After we got back to the Facility," Shawn answered regretfully. "When we got the messages, my orders had been to cease and desist all operations and simply to come back in. I think they realized you were still innocent and panicked."

"You weren't ordered to bring me in?"

"No," Shawn answered quietly. "That was a field decision."

Remy snorted. "Field decision," he muttered. "So how did we end up together?"

"That's why we were asked so many questions when we were debriefed."

"And that first week?" Remy asked tentatively.

"I didn't know what they had planned," Shawn said urgently. He needed Remy to know that. That first week they had spent together, fighting their way back home, had been the spark that started their relationship. It hadn't been a lie. Shawn desperately needed Remy to believe that.

Remy stared at him for several long seconds and then nodded. "When did… do you… fuck," Remy muttered as he shook his head and rubbed the back of his neck in frustration.

Shawn frowned and waited, unsure of what Remy was trying to ask.

Remy shook his head again and seemed to mentally switch gears. "What was your objective, exactly?"

"The powers that be suspected a coup," Shawn started with difficulty.

"Stemming from the raid that I've never heard of before today?"

"Yes. I don't know a lot about it. There were twelve agents involved. Eight were killed in the Purge. I don't know what they found or why it caused such a fuss. But something in your files flagged you as a danger. They put me on you so that when– *if* you turned…."

"I would trust you enough to take you with me," Remy finished as he looked away and sighed heavily.

"After four years of vouching for you, I… that's why I was so fucking angry when I found you'd actually done it, Remy," Shawn said with difficulty as he leaned forward and took Remy's face in his hands.

"I'm sorry I let you down, Shawn," Remy said flatly. His eyes were black and emotionless and Shawn could almost feel the other man's spirit simply seeping away. "I'm sorry I turned like I did."

"You didn't let anyone down," Shawn said sternly. He pulled on Remy slightly and Remy crawled forward obediently and allowed Shawn to guide him until he was straddling Shawn's hips. "I never needed to… I always wanted you," he said softly as Remy looked at him blankly. "I…."

"Okay. No more apologies, *non*?" Remy said as he braced himself with his hands on Shawn's shoulders. "I'm tired of saying I'm sorry. And I'm tired of hearing it, too. We both fucked up beyond belief, and we both blew our tops with our reactions. I just need… I need to know one thing, okay?"

"What's that?" Shawn whispered as he looked up into Remy's eyes and a little seed of dread formed in the pit of his stomach.

"Did you ever mean it?" Remy asked after a long silence. "Any of it? Did you ever mean any of the things you said?"

"I meant some of them," Shawn said hoarsely as guilt forced his entire body to flush. He could remember the only time he'd told the other man he loved him. He hadn't meant it then, not completely.

"When you told me you loved me?" Remy asked as he sat back and looked at Shawn patiently, seemingly able to read his mind.

Shawn opened his mouth to lie. He would lie and tell Remy that he had meant it then, because even though he hadn't meant it then, he knew that he meant it now. What difference did a couple of years and a belated realization make?

Remy saw the look in his eyes, though, and he nodded tightly and clenched his jaw as he looked down at Shawn's chest.

"That's okay," he said quietly.

Shawn's words caught in his throat, and he tried desperately to say something, anything to take that look off Remy's face. That hard, vacant mask he pulled on when he didn't want to feel. Shawn had seen it so many times before, just before a kill.

"Are you still in love with Brandt?" Remy asked in a casual voice as he slid off Shawn's body and sprawled back onto the lower half of the bed.

Shawn grabbed for him and missed. "No," he croaked as he leaned forward to take hold of the other man once more. Remy batted his hands away and waited for an answer. "I never was. I was wrong. *We* were wrong," Shawn added, wondering if he should tell Remy about the various talks he and Brandt had gone through while Brandt had tried to convince him not to kill himself. "Remy, please–"

"I don't mind that you lied, Shawn," Remy said in an even voice. "I know you care about me, that's enough for me."

"But–"

Remy sat up quickly and looked at Shawn with a gleam in his eye that Shawn had rarely seen aimed at him. "Can I trust you?" the man asked breathlessly.

"Yes," Shawn breathed immediately.

"You're no longer a Hunter? You're no longer an O.R.G. agent?"

"No," Shawn answered urgently as he shook his head.

"You're one of us?"

"Yes."

"Then that's all I need to know," Remy said flippantly. He sounded casual, but there was a hard glint in his eye that made Shawn shiver.

"What… what happened to you, Dixie?" Shawn asked in something close to dread. It was the same man he'd known sitting before him, but he was somehow different. Harder. Definitely more unstable.

Remy blinked several times and then nodded. "I think I blew a fuse. I think… I think you finally drove me crazy."

"Insane people don't think they're insane," Shawn said before completely thinking through the wisdom of saying the words.

"That's not true. Brandt's crazy as hell and he knows it. I think… I think I may be, too," Remy said with a tinge of desperation.

"Why?" Shawn asked in fascination.

"Because I don't want to run. Thiago will have us run, but I want to fight them, Shawn," he hissed, his eyes flashing and his accent thick and rich. "I want to take them on and take them down," Remy growled as his eyes unfocused and he clenched his fist in the bedcovers.

Shawn's heart fluttered slightly and he sucked in a breath of air. Take on the Organization? Just the seven of them, and whoever else Thiago had up his sleeve? It was suicidal. It couldn't be done.

"You're right," he breathed as he leaned unconsciously away from the younger man and propped against the headboard once more. "I think you've fucking cracked."

XLI.

NIKOLAUS was more nervous now than he ever had been before. If Remy had discovered he'd been the one to create the Purge virus just by process of elimination, what else did Remy know? Did he know what Nikolaus had been doing this whole time? Surely not. Surely, he would have called Nikolaus out the moment he found out.

Nikolaus took care of what Thiago sent him out to do as quickly as possible; buying the basic travel supplies they'd need for what was essentially a six-day train ride. After taking care of that with his usual efficiency, he practically ran to the Café du Monde to give him enough time to fill his contact from the BND in on what was happening.

There were advantages to being seen as the weak link in a crew. You weren't subject to the normal suspicions, and you were given leeway where others weren't. Nikolaus had used this to his full advantage so far. He felt certain that Thiago would not have let any of the others do this on their own, no matter how much he trusted them. Nikolaus skidded to a halt in front of Jackson Square and shook his head sadly. He stared across the street into the outdoor eating area of the café until he caught sight of the man he was looking for.

The BND, or *Bundesnachrichtendienst*, was a German foreign intelligence agency. Much like the CIA or MI6, its job was to protect German interests from threats overseas. Before Nikolaus had been recruited by the Organization, he'd worked in the *Technische Unterstützung*, the technical support section of the BND. He still did.

Nikolaus stood and watched the other man from the cover of the crowded pavement. He spotted four others in and around the café, and he smiled ruefully to himself. Yes, he was a computer nerd. Yes, he was smaller in stature than the others. But that was the essence of his cover; seemingly weak and unsuspecting, inexperienced and naïve. That was how he appeared. Highly trained and with a specific mission from the BND; that was what he was. He knew that Gray suspected him, but the others had never done. Now, even if they believed what Gray had to say, it was too late for them to counter his actions. Wasn't it?

Nikolaus sighed heavily. He hadn't expected to grow so fond of his companions. He didn't want them to be hurt. Was there another way around this? His contact wasn't an O.R.G. man, and therefore Nikolaus had a little leeway. He shifted uneasily and took a deep breath to steady himself.

The Organization wasn't helmed by idiots, and they were well aware of far more than even Nikolaus knew. Sometimes, Nikolaus wondered if they had known all along that Thiago was the Archer. If they had known, then they were playing a stupid, dangerous game. Thiago struck Nikolaus as being slightly flustered right now, and maybe even a little lacking in organizational skills, but he was a dangerous man, nonetheless. Regardless of whether or not they knew Thiago's specific identity, the Organization certainly knew there was a threat, and they knew this group of six– or seven– posed the greatest threat of them all.

They knew because they'd engineered it that way.

From what Nikolaus had been told before the start of the mission, Thiago and Brandt were both known to have turned, and though there had never been enough evidence gathered to say for certain, Remy was suspected as well. Shawn was under suspicion simply because of his relationship with Remy and his constant insistence that Remy was clean, though it was now clear to Nikolaus that Shawn should never have been here. The man was loyal, and Nikolaus thought that if they got into trouble, Shawn's loyalty would sway back to the Organization.

Love versus twenty years of service was a tough call, but Shawn liked order. Loving Remy was anything but ordered.

Nikolaus had been placed with the group by a joint O.R.G./MI6/BND decision, and his sole purpose was to observe the others and report back. His reports would be the deciding factor on when punishments started raining down. So far, he'd been able to report that the Six were simply attempting to figure out who or what was trying to kill them, and they'd been left to their own devices. What he was hearing now was rebellion and subversion and taking down the Organization. That couldn't happen, and though Nikolaus was painfully aware of the hopelessness of their situation, he couldn't allow six desperate men to destroy the entire Organization.

It never crossed Nikolaus's mind that they couldn't do it.

Nikolaus frowned as he realized that his thoughts were rambling, and he crossed the street with a heavy heart. This was it. This was when he gave himself over to the agents from MI6 and allowed them to take the other six down. This was when his mission ended.

He walked up to the contact and looked down at the man disdainfully as the agent jumped and sputtered coffee in response to Nikolaus's sudden appearance. Nikolaus knew this *Fotze*. The man was a complete and utter bastard, and just sitting across from him at the small table made Nikolaus want to shower. Nikolaus hadn't questioned his own loyalties up until this point, but as the British agent droned on and on about duty to Queen and country– disregarding the fact that Nikolaus didn't give a damn about Great Britain– and how his companions would be put away until they were old and gray or killed as an example to future traitors, Nikolaus questioned his decisions.

If this *Wichser* was one of the good guys, then Nikolaus wasn't sure he wanted to be one.

"Traitors, the lot of them," the man sniffed quietly as he sipped at his coffee.

Nikolaus bristled slightly, but held his tongue. The man wasn't even trying to keep his voice down, and Nikolaus looked around warily. No one was paying them any attention, but that didn't mean that no one was listening. Nikolaus sniffed scornfully and shifted. Even he could see that this man wasn't a field agent. Why would they send a paper-pusher to do this job?

"O.R.G. has done too much good for the world in the past five decades to be brought down by this group of rabble. They cannot simply be let off with a slap on the wrist. I personally can't wait to see them all hang."

"Hang?" Nikolaus repeated in a quiet, calm voice.

"Figuratively speaking, of course. This has been the most serious internal threat since the Third Reich; they'll be made examples of, the lot of them. Ugh, this sludge cannot be called suitable for human consumption. Don't these blasted Yanks believe in tea?"

Nikolaus bit his tongue and tried to shrink into the metal chair as several patrons turned to look at his vocal companion.

"So, where shall I have the men set up, hmm? Where are your lot going?"

Nikolaus stared at the greasy man with a new hatred and made a decision that would probably end up costing him his life. He didn't care. Loyalty deserved loyalty, after all. It was the least he owed the others, and it was never too late to make amends for all the damage he had probably done. Good guys be damned, he would hang with the rest of them.

"We're leaving in five hours, heading for the port," he said calmly, surprised at how easily the lying came to him. "I suggest you have your men set up there as soon as possible."

"Five hours? Why not just tell us where they are now and have us go in, guns blazing?" the man asked with relish.

"Because if you attack them on their turf, you'll all die," Nikolaus said with certainty. "Taking them at the port will take them unawares. Believe me, you want them unawares."

"Wonderful," the man said happily, no trace of suspicion evident. Nikolaus stood and nodded to him. "And where are you going?" the man asked officiously.

"If I don't go back to them, they'll suspect something and simply disappear," Nikolaus sighed, rolling his eyes behind his sunglasses. This man was beyond dense. At least they had made it easy for Nikolaus to finally turn.

"Ah. Yes, of course," the man said as he stood and stuck out his hand. "Good luck to you."

Nikolaus stared at the man's hand for several seconds, then let his eyes travel up the man's pale, chubby body to land on his greasy face. He looked at him from over the top of his sunglasses with barely concealed contempt.

"No, mate. Good luck to *you*," he said with a little smirk. "You're going to need it."

XLII.

BRANDT was practically vibrating with anger.

They were all gathered in the kitchen, their bags stacked by the door, listening to Gray's theory about Nikolaus.

Remy and Thiago were both frowning slightly as Gray spoke, and Shawn looked ready to throttle Gray just for breathing his air. Gray kept throwing the man wary glances and edging further away, but he was edging closer and closer to Brandt, and Brandt was just waiting to grab him and choke the life out of him. Carl was looking particularly blank, as though he either had previous knowledge of Nikolaus's activities or he simply didn't give a flying fuck.

Well, Brandt gave a fuck. He was pissed off beyond belief, whether at Gray for making the accusation or at Nikolaus if it was true, he didn't care. He needed to kill something. Nikolaus wasn't here. Gray was.

"Gizmo wouldn't do that," he growled, pushing away from the counter finally and taking a threatening step toward Gray.

Gray straightened slightly and looked at Thiago and Remy briefly as if for permission to get into a fight. Brandt growled and took another step, but Carl's hand wrapped around his bicep and pulled him back before he could do any damage. Brandt turned to look at the man in shock.

"Someone's running," Carl announced in a flat voice.

They all looked at him as if he had lost his mind, but he simply stared back at Brandt with an inexplicably sad expression. Brandt frowned and looked at him questioningly, but got no response. Remy cocked his head and took a couple of silent steps toward the door to the courtyard, and finally Brandt heard the hurried footfalls on the pavement outside.

Brandt turned again just in time to see Nikolaus skid through the door and barrel into Remy, taking them both to the ground in a flurry of curses and grunts and flailing limbs.

"We have to move," Nikolaus huffed. He struggled to his knees and looked down at Remy as the other man lay spread-eagled below him and blinking up at him in shock. "We have to go now," he said urgently as he looked up at the others.

No one asked questions as their training kicked in, and in less than two minutes the house was deserted and the seven men were in the garage area loading up. Remy tugged at Brandt and Carl and nodded toward the street.

"With me," he said quietly as he started toward the street. Brandt and Carl both fell into step beside him, but a soft call from Shawn halted them.

"Listen, lad," he said as he came up to them.

Remy turned to look at him curiously, and Brandt let Carl pull him to the side as they watched. Shawn took Remy's face in his hands, wincing at the pain in his fresh wound, and he looked at him for several long, precious seconds. Brandt could feel Carl twitching beside him. He knew they had to be moving, but it seemed no one had the heart to say anything and cut the encounter short. Remy's eyes darted back and forth across Shawn's face almost uncertainly, and he finally looked down and nodded and started to pull away. Shawn gripped him harder and pulled him back, kissing him gently.

Brandt saw Remy tense, and as the two men pulled apart, it was obvious that Remy was holding his breath as Shawn struggled to speak. Brandt was holding his breath as well, for that matter. *'Just say it, you daft bugger,'* Brandt thought desperately.

"Be careful," Shawn finally said with difficulty as he let Remy go and stepped away.

Brandt deflated slightly, and he heard Carl growl behind him. Shawn and Remy were both fucking idiots.

"And you," Remy said quietly as he nodded once more and turned to go.

Brandt gave Shawn one last scathing glance and then jogged to catch up to the other two.

XLIII.

"WHAT the hell?" Carl muttered under his breath as he and Remy walked swiftly away from Les Bon Temps Royale. Remy didn't look back as he heard Shawn's 4Runner start, or allow his pace to slow when Brandt called him softly.

"Dixie," Brandt hissed again as he jogged to catch up to them. Remy didn't know how much more drama he could handle. He was convinced that it was, in fact, Brandt's fault that he'd cracked so easily. Ambient insanity, that was it. "Why can't you just–"

"Don't start, Wally," Remy growled angrily.

"But–"

Remy stopped and whirled around, letting the larger man bump into him and stumble backward as he pointed his finger in Brandt's face. "I'm trying my damnedest to blame you for all that fucking mess, but it's fucking hard when you keep trying to help!" he yelled as he waved his hands through the air and stomped his foot. "Why do you have to be so fucking likable, huh?"

Brandt looked mildly surprised at his outburst, and Carl's hand slipped around Remy's waist, pulling him gently onwards as they started moving again.

"I didn't–"

"You don't just say you're falling in love with someone and then turn around and take it back! Especially not Shawn!" Remy shouted, and Carl tightened his grip to the point of pain, ending Remy's rant with a little squeak.

"He said that?" Brandt asked in disbelief.

Remy clenched his jaw and forced his brain to switch gears. Now was not the time or the place to start acting like a jilted teenager.

"Gray and I left the car just down… shit, can either of you monsters fit in the back of a Mustang?" Remy said as it struck him suddenly that he shouldn't have picked the two largest men in the group to accompany him. He'd simply grabbed the two closest bodies.

"I, for one, have never tried," Carl muttered testily.

"What was that back there?" Brandt demanded persistently. "Why can't you just tell him you love him? And what the hell is going on? Was what Gray said true?"

"How the hell should I know?" Remy retorted defensively. They came upon the yellow Mustang and Remy reached for the door handle, but Brandt's hand on the car door stopped him. "And I have told him," Remy added quietly as he looked down at Brandt's hand over his. "I got tired of not hearing it in return."

Remy glanced up at Brandt and saw pity briefly flit across his handsome features before the anger returned.

"You know a lot that we don't," the bigger man growled suddenly.

Remy's eyes flickered over his face and quickly to Carl as the other man sidestepped to position himself behind Remy. Remy turned slightly to open up his door before turning his head once more to look Brandt in the eyes. Carl didn't exactly look like his usual and relaxed self, and when Remy's eyes once more found Brandt the man was inexplicably holding his lighter and what appeared to be a tampon.

"What the hell are you doing with that?" Remy asked, his voice wavering between irritation and amusement.

"Wick," Brandt said simply as he flipped open the cover to the Mustang's gas tank.

"Oh, holy hell!" Remy cried in a near-panic. He lunged forward but was stopped literally in mid-air when Carl wrapped his arms around his torso and pulled him back with a warning hiss.

Brandt twisted the top off the gas tank and looked at Remy questioningly. "It's not hard to tell that you're keeping something from us, Dixie," he said as he stuffed the tampon into the gas tank. Remy's jaw dropped as he watched the string of the thing saturate with gas and droop as it grew heavier. On a newer model car this might not have been possible, but on his classic… his baby… it was entirely too possible.

"You sick fuck!" Remy cried in anguish as he went limp against Carl's body. "What did she ever do to you?"

"Tell us what you know, and she'll make it to the train station," Brandt bargained with barely repressed glee as he flicked his shiny new lighter open.

"We really don't have time for this, gentlemen," Carl hissed as Remy stared in horror at the flickering flame. "Remy, just swear to us you'll spill it so we can drive to the fucking place instead of hitching."

"I swear," Remy cried desperately. "I'll tell you anything you want to know. I'll read you a fucking encyclopedia. Just please don't toast her!"

XLIV.

THIAGO sat in the back of Shawn's 4Runner as the man whipped through the streets of New Orleans, driving toward the train station. He was unbuckled, being thrown around slightly, and he was bearing down on Nikolaus as if he were about to devour the smaller man.

Nikolaus cowered, his eyes darting around in search of assistance that wasn't anywhere near coming.

"You're in some serious shit unless you start talking, *hijo*, and I mean yesterday," Thiago growled as he glared at the younger man.

Nikolaus swallowed hard and nodded. "Anything, I'll tell you anything," he stuttered obediently.

"Oh, for Christ's sake. Cut the fucking act, you little bastard," Gray snarled from the front passenger seat.

Thiago saw Nikolaus stiffen and then slump against the door with a roll of his eyes.

"Unless you want to be thrown through the fucking windscreen, keep your fucking mouth shut," Shawn shot back at Gray angrily.

"Oh, now you want me to shut it?" Gray shouted sarcastically. "What happened to tying me up and torturing me for information, huh? What happened to shoot first, apologize to my mother at the funeral? Make up your fucking mind, you fuck!"

Thiago growled wordlessly and pulled out his pistol, leveling it at the rear view mirror and firing without a second thought. Gray turned his head slightly just before Thiago pulled the trigger and managed to shy away from the blast, while Nikolaus balled up in the back seat and covered his head with a warning shout. The unsilenced blast reverberated throughout the enclosed space, and Shawn yelled in surprise and swerved the car briefly before regaining control. His hand went immediately to his ear and he turned to shout at Thiago.

"Next person who speaks without my say will be re-upholstering the inside of this fucking car," Thiago said in a low, menacing growl that he was sure none of the other three men had ever heard before.

Shawn's mouth snapped shut when he saw the look in Thiago's eyes, and Gray and Nikolaus both watched him warily, looking like kicked puppies. Thiago had somehow vastly lost control of this operation, and like he had told Gray before, it was time to get it back.

"You," he snarled, pointing the gun at Nikolaus and growling. "Speak."

"I don't… I… I'm sorry!" Nikolaus blurted out, his panic now obviously genuine. "If I had known before… about how… what you all were… I never would've… I… I'm sorry!"

"Sorry for what? What have you done?" Thiago pressed on, still utilizing the adrenaline and the anger to push the now terrified man, even though he wasn't enjoying the experience all that much himself.

"I've been in contact with… with various agents from the Organization, BND, and MI6," Nikolaus admitted hesitantly.

"MI6?" Shawn yelled questioningly as he turned to look back briefly. Thiago cocked the gun and glared at him, but Shawn shrugged and turned around again to watch the road. "My fucking eardrums!" he shouted angrily with a gesture toward his ear.

Thiago noticed with a slight pang of guilt that Shawn's ear was bleeding. It could have been from the puff of hot powder emitted by the gun, or from the shattering debris of the rearview mirror, but the shot could very well have busted the man's eardrum.

"Cocksucker," Shawn added, though since he apparently couldn't hear it came out fairly loud.

Gray snorted and clapped his hand over his mouth, and Thiago rolled his eyes. Nikolaus was the only one left he could intimidate, apparently, and it was no fun since he felt so goddamned guilty about doing it. He clapped Gray upside the head for no other reason than to make himself feel better, and he turned back to Nikolaus.

"When you say in contact, what do you mean?" he asked wearily.

"I've been sending reports of our movements and the group's decisions," Nikolaus said calmly, realizing now that Thiago wasn't going to really shoot him. "I was supposed to give warning if we decided to attack the Organization. Today was the day they were going to move in and take you all down."

"Did you fucking tattle on us again?" Gray shouted angrily as he turned in his seat to look back at Nikolaus. "Did you tell them where we're headed?"

"I told them we were leaving from the port," Nikolaus said as he met Gray's glare. "I thought they were the good guys, but I'm not so sure anymore."

"Well, by all means, take your fucking time deciding!" Thiago shouted angrily.

"Well, excuse me, Mister Big Bad Archer Man!" Nikolaus shot back, his gray eyes blazing angrily. "I wasn't the only one keeping secrets, was I? Who else is working for you that you don't know about?"

Thiago was momentarily stunned by the anger, and he blinked at Nikolaus several times before mentally conceding that point. When the fuck had he so completely lost control of this thing?

"Jesus," Gray muttered as he turned back around. "Remy's a double, Niko's a plant, Brandt and Thiago were working together but didn't fucking know it, and Shawn's been trying to kill the lot of you for four fucking months without doing much more damage than to get himself shot! What about Carl? Is he the Grand

Poobah of the fucking Underground, just here for shits and giggles? You six are the most unorganized, half-assed group of slipshod piece of shit agents I've ever had the displeasure of being captured by!" he spat as he gestured and squirmed in a fashion disturbingly reminiscent of their Cajun friend.

Shawn turned to look at him with narrowed eyes, and Thiago saw Gray shrink away from the man slightly. Thiago braced himself for one of Shawn's tirades.

Shawn tugged at his bleeding ear and shouted, "What?"

XLV.

THEY somehow stuffed Brandt into the back seat of the Mustang, and he was hanging in between the front seats, breathing in Carl's ear and accompanying Remy's monologue with soft growls.

For his part, Carl was listening quietly, only prompting Remy every now and then with pointed questions.

"Gray and I uncovered a lot of shit, though now that I know the Organization knew about us, it's hard to tell what was planted and what was real," Remy told them as he negotiated the narrow streets. "I don't know where to start. I didn't know anything about that raid or why the Archer– Thiago– started what he did. I just knew that something bad was going down. We found out that the Organization has a... I don't even know what to call it. A subversive element. At least we think so."

"Why do you think that?" Carl asked curiously.

"Well, we all do our own thing, no one ever knows what anyone else is working on. And have you ever heard of a retired agent?" Remy asked as he glanced over at Carl.

"No. But then we wouldn't, would we?"

"I think they kill them off. The Organization. I don't think they let us out when our contracts are up. I think that's what Thiago and his men found on that raid, and I think that's why he went under, freeing agents by saying he had killed them and then recruiting some to help him."

"That was your job, yeah?" Carl asked as he turned to look at Brandt.

Brandt flushed slightly under Carl's steady gaze and nodded. "Dixie's right," he murmured. "There are two sides to the Organization; a legitimate one and an Underground."

"How do you know that?" Carl asked sadly, though he already knew the answer.

"I was on that raid," Brandt answered quietly.

"What?" Remy cried angrily as he almost ran off the road. "Then you know more than I do, you crazy fuck! Why'd you need to blow up my fucking–"

"I needed to blow something up, goddammit!"

"Not a classic fucking '69 Boss 302!" Remy cried, his voice cracking with distress.

"Hush!" Carl shouted, his voice booming in the small vehicle and immediately silencing the other two. "I have questions. If I don't get answers, there will be hell to pay, you both understand?" he said authoritatively.

"Yes," they both responded obediently.

"Why did you blow up the cabin in North Dakota?" Carl asked bluntly.

Remy looked into the rearview mirror apprehensively and then shrugged. "My goal was to try and turn all of you, make you think the Organization was trying to kill us."

"Are you saying they *aren't* trying to kill is?" Carl asked angrily.

"No, they are trying to kill us," Remy insisted.

"Then why did you have to fake an explosion to convince us if they're really trying to kill us?"

"I didn't know they were trying to kill us at the time," Remy responded defensively.

"Jesus, Remy," Carl groaned as he looked away and rubbed his face in agitation. "Where does all your money come from?" he asked.

"What?" Remy asked in what appeared to be genuine shock.

"Your money. No agent makes this sort of coin without something on the side. That goes for Wally, too. Does it come from the Archer's dealings?"

"No," Remy said defensively.

"What do you mean, that goes for me, too? I don't have that kind of money," Brandt said angrily with a flick of his thumb over his shoulder to indicate the house from which they had just come.

"That was a nice building you blew up in Sydney, mate. Not another body in sight. Did you own the whole thing?" Carl asked shrewdly.

"I… well… I resent the implication that I'm dirty," Brandt said testily as he tried to fold his arms and sulk in the cramped back seat.

Carl found it highly amusing that both men were so insulted by the implication that they'd been somehow earning ill-gained money when they'd both been playing both sides of this fight from the start.

"Nosy bastard. Fuck," Remy muttered to himself as he pulled into the parking lot of the train station. The 4Runner sat several spaces down, empty. They'd gone different routes, and the one Remy took had been the long way around. The others were probably already on the train. "I'm not dirty, either."

"And?" Carl pressed.

"Well, there are legitimate ways of dealing with money, you know," Remy said as he turned to look at Carl with wide eyes.

"What, like the stock market and shit?" Carl asked incredulously.

"Well, when you're the one assassinating politicians and CEOs, it's easy to judge the ups and downs of the stock exchange, *non*?" Remy asked sarcastically.

Carl stared at Remy in shock. Assassinating politicians and CEOs? What the hell?

"That's what you do for the Organization?" Brandt asked after a short stunned silence.

Remy blinked several times as he belatedly realized that perhaps this was a bad thing to have made public.

"Jesus," Remy breathed irritably. He unbuckled slowly and placed one hand carefully on the handle of the door. The other he rested on the steering wheel, both in plain sight of Carl. "We've never been on the same fucking side, have we?" he asked slowly as his body tensed. Carl could only stare at the other man in shock. "You're the fucking good guys," Remy whispered in anguish as he stared sadly out the window of the Mustang.

XLVI.

SHAWN sat in the corner of the lower bunk of one of their three sleeping compartments, stuffed behind a ladder he was pretty sure they could have removed if they weren't so busy fighting. He tried to force his tense muscles to relax. His ears were still ringing and he could barely hear Thiago and Gray speaking, even though Gray sat on the bed with him and Thiago stood just steps away in the tiny compartment.

They were speaking in low tones to avoid being overheard, and their voices were simply a murmur of white noise beneath the overwhelming ringing in Shawn's head. Nikolaus was crouched in the corner of the small compartment, his eyes darting back and forth between Thiago and Gray as he followed their heated conversation. He reminded Shawn of a small child watching his parents have it out.

Considering that Nikolaus had revealed his treachery to them in the car, Shawn assumed that at least half of the argument had to do with the German tech. Some of it, however, seemed to deal with him as well. Every now and then, Gray would gesture toward Shawn emphatically and snarl and Thiago would respond with an angry wave of his hands or a shake of his head. Shawn had never felt so lost in his life. He needed to be able to hear.

He didn't know if it was something he did that was causing the heated discussion, or if it was the fact that Thiago had maimed him. He doubted that Gray was worried over any harm done to him, though. The man was probably upset that Shawn couldn't now be used for guard duty and they wouldn't get as much sleep. Bastard.

Shawn watched Thiago, who stood facing him, trying to read his lips as he spoke. He could catch pieces of what was said, but it was a skill he'd never tried to improve, and he wasn't able to follow very well. His hearing seemed to be getting worse rather than better. Maybe Thiago really had busted his eardrum. Bastard.

As Shawn sat watching, Thiago tensed and turned slightly to look over his shoulder at the door. Gray lunged forward quickly to stand with him. It was close quarters, and Gray was forced to stand slightly behind Thiago as they waited for whatever they had heard. Shawn saw the man place a hand on the small of Thiago's back, and Thiago visibly relaxed.

Whatever they shared didn't matter to Shawn, though. Shawn still didn't like the bastard.

The door burst open and Shawn sat forward, unable to do more than watch in the cramped compartment as Remy barreled into Thiago and Gray, followed by a very pissed off Brandt. Carl stood out in the aisle looking first to his right and then to his left nervously. He actually looked quite distraught.

Shawn hoped the assassin wasn't claustrophobic. Thiago caught Remy by wrapping his arms around the man, and Shawn immediately tensed once more as he saw the look on Remy's face. He was as close to panicking as Shawn had ever seen him.

Remy's eyes landed on Shawn, and he immediately began to struggle in Thiago's grasp. Brandt pointed at Remy and then Shawn and started speaking harshly to Thiago. Thiago and Gray tried to get out of Remy's way as he struggled past them. Remy spoke to Shawn in what appeared to be a hurried whisper, but Shawn could only frown back at him helplessly.

He had no idea what was going on, and he couldn't hear a fucking thing.

Remy clambered onto the bed and knelt right in front of him, pawing at him as if he hadn't expected him to be there. He caught Shawn's face in his hands and looked Shawn in the eye. His mouth was moving, but no sound was reaching Shawn's ears. Shawn could read his lips, though.

"Are you okay?" he was asking.

"I'm fine," Shawn answered in a harsh whisper as he jerked his head away. Remy's hand on his ear was a bit more painful than Shawn would have expected.

Remy pulled away from him as if he'd been struck, and Shawn supposed that his tone of voice had sounded rather severe. He knew it was basic instinct to speak loudly when one couldn't hear in an effort to hear your own words, so he'd been keeping his voice low and flat intentionally. But to Remy, who had apparently rushed in to find him, worried over his well-being for some reason, the tone had probably sounded harsh and reprimanding.

Shawn berated himself mentally as Remy shrank back into the other corner of the bunk. Could he not do a damn thing right anymore? Remy nodded sedately in response and looked back at Brandt, who glared at them both. Shawn blinked back at him, wondering what happened to get the normally calm pyromaniac so riled up.

Brandt turned slightly and threw his hands up in exasperation as he looked at Carl. He reached out and grabbed the man by his shirtfront and dragged him inside, sliding the door shut violently as he pushed at Thiago and Gray to back them up and make more room.

Gray lost his balance and Shawn instinctively reached out to grab him before he fell and cracked his head open on the ladder, or some other equally desirable fate. He pulled him toward him and Gray fell onto the bottom bunk to sprawl on top of Remy and Shawn. The three of them remained there, barely breathing and hoping to remain inconspicuous as Brandt got in Carl's face and snarled, then turned on Thiago and started motioning angrily toward them once more.

Remy was struggling with Gray and looking slightly dejected as he helped the man out of Shawn's lap. Nikolaus was edging further and further into the corner and looking at Shawn and Remy with a look of ever-increasing horror, and Thiago and Brandt were bristling as they argued. Carl simply looked trapped in the corner beside the closed door, and Gray was now smacking Remy upside the head and yelling at him.

All this Shawn was observing with a sinking feeling, but the only thing he could completely focus on was the ringing in his ears.

XLVII.

REMY and Shawn were killers? Well sure, they all were. Killers for hire? On the wrong side? Bad guys, essentially? Not possible. The Organization didn't do that sort of thing.

Did they?

Nikolaus couldn't quite understand what Brandt was ranting about, though he was shamefully glad that it was taking the focus off him, for the moment.

"I'm telling you, mate, I don't like being in the dark," Brandt growled as he took a threatening step toward Thiago.

The compartment was tiny, and Nikolaus scrambled out of Thiago's way as the man stumbled backwards. Nikolaus climbed the ladder to the top bunk and watched the scene unfold below him. Brandt grabbed Thiago to keep him from falling and pulled him close.

"If you don't spill every goddamn thing you know, and I mean right fucking now, I will kill you. Slowly."

To the surprise of everyone in the small space, Carl stepped forward, grabbed Brandt around the neck, and pulled on him, throwing him up against the side of the wall and pinning him there. Thiago fell back against the window as he was let loose and stared at the two men in confusion, and Nikolaus saw Gray and Remy shift uneasily below him. Shawn watched the drama unfold warily, but it was pretty obvious that the man wasn't following it.

"Calm the fuck down," Carl growled in a low, even voice.

Brandt blinked at him with wide brown eyes, and Nikolaus wondered if the big man was having flashbacks to his near-death experience in Remy's kitchen. Nikolaus certainly was.

"What the hell is going on?" Thiago asked in frustration as he pushed away from the window and turned around to close the curtain.

"Seems we've had a little miscommunication," Carl answered calmly without taking his eyes off Brandt.

"Ha!" Remy cried from beneath Nikolaus's bunk. "Yeah, apparently not all the guns for hire got the fucking memo this time around!" he spat disgustedly. "Fucking misunderstanding," he grumbled. "You're a fucking master of the obvious, you know that, Trigger?"

Nikolaus leaned over the bunk to look at the three men beneath him. Shawn and Gray were looking at Remy warily, and Remy sat in the far corner with his arms crossed over his chest, looking very much like a scolded child. Shawn leaned forward and tugged on Gray's shirtsleeve, and Gray leaned toward him.

"What's going on?" Shawn asked in a low voice.

Gray did a double take and then tilted his head up to glare at Thiago pointedly. "See?" he said angrily as he jabbed his finger at Shawn. "He can't hear a fucking thing!"

"What do you mean, he can't hear?" Remy asked concernedly, and Carl and Brandt stopped glaring at one another long enough to look at Gray in alarm. "And who shot at you on the way here? Were you followed?"

"No one shot at us," Gray spat. "Thiago fired his gun through the freaking windshield, right by Shawn's ear."

"Why?" Remy asked curiously, his concern ebbing. Nikolaus wondered how Remy knew a gun had been fired, and it suddenly struck him that the three men must have seen the bullet hole in the front of the 4Runner as they came in. No wonder Remy had been panicked when he found Shawn with blood running down the side of his face.

"Seemed like a good idea at the time," Thiago said with an angry glare at

Gray. "Certainly made me feel better."

"Move, Boss," Remy ordered as he crawled behind Gray and they struggled around one another until Remy was sitting next to Shawn and examining the side of his face. He put his mouth right next to Shawn's ear, his lips moving almost imperceptibly as he spoke. Shawn nodded slowly in response and shivered slightly. "You'll be okay then," Remy said reassuringly as he patted Shawn's head and ran his hand through Shawn's hair.

"Someone explain before I lose my mind," Thiago said, his eyes still absently on Remy and Shawn.

"It would seem that someone in the upper echelons of the Organization has been having a good laugh with us," Carl said calmly.

"What?" Gray asked in a frustrated voice.

"They're fucking villains, is what!" Brandt shouted as he pointed his finger at Shawn and Remy.

Nikolaus cringed, expecting an outburst of protest from the two men, but Shawn simply looked at Brandt with a confused frown and Remy wrapped an arm protectively around Shawn and stared back at Brandt defiantly.

"Yes, we've established that, Wally," Carl said sharply. "Sit down."

To Nikolaus's utter astonishment Brandt obeyed with very little fuss and actually sat down on the lower bunk beside Gray. Nikolaus was rather glad for his bird's eye advantage just then. They looked crowded down there.

"What do you know?" Thiago asked Carl shrewdly as Carl leaned against the wall and smiled.

"Probably more than you do," Carl responded assuredly. "First things first, though, yeah?" Carl said as he pushed away from the wall and removed his gun from his shoulder holster. He checked the number of rounds idly and looked up at Brandt and gave the man a small smile as he replaced the gun. "We should secure the train before it leaves. It'll give us some peace of mind on the way to D.C., at least."

"Right," Gray said a brief silence. "Pairs?"

"I don't think we have the time for pairs," Thiago said quietly. "Especially since there'll just be three of us working the entire thing."

"Why three?" Nikolaus asked with a sort of dread, speaking for the first time since they had boarded the train.

Thiago looked up at Nikolaus briefly and then moved his eyes down to stare at Remy and Shawn sadly for several seconds. "Because someone will have to make sure you three don't get loose. Brandt, Gray… tie them up."

XLVIII.

BRANDT tried to avoid looking Shawn in the eye as he tied a twisted sheet around the man's hands and feet, but he failed and nearly froze in place when he met the cold green eyes.

Shawn had fought them at first, but Remy had whispered in his ear for a good minute, probably explaining to him that they'd been found out for the killers they were and that they were not, in fact, all on the same side, if Brandt had to guess.

After that, Shawn and Remy both remained alarmingly sedate as they allowed themselves to be tied up. Brandt and Gray went easy on them, since they were both not only injured, but also friends. Brandt didn't want to think of either of them as the enemy. It broke his heart.

Brandt didn't understand why Nikolaus needed to be tied up, but the smaller man had simply held out his hands and nodded, and Gray wrapped him up with a little bit more enjoyment than Brandt supposed was necessary.

"Why is he being restrained? What has he done?" Remy asked as his eyes followed Gray's hands.

"He's been informing on us. We'll tell you all about it when we get back," Thiago said in a hard, flat voice.

Brandt sat counting the seconds that Carl, Thiago, and Gray were gone, casting guilty glances at Shawn as he sat next to the prostrate man on the lower bunk. Remy and Nikolaus above them were unusually quiet, and Shawn simply laid there, staring at Brandt balefully like some affronted, green-eyed cow. Or a sheep, maybe. Could you insult a sheep? Or a cow, for that matter?

Brandt shook his head and sat forward. He couldn't take it any longer. It had been twenty minutes. They should have been back by now.

"Hey, Wally?" Remy ventured softly just as Brandt was about to jump up and begin to pace.

"Hmm?"

"Can Beignet hear me?"

Brandt glanced over at Shawn to try and discern whether the man had recovered any of his ability to hear, but it didn't appear that he had. "I don't think so," he responded doubtfully.

"We're not bad people," Remy asserted in the same soft, sad voice.

"You kill innocent people for money," Brandt spat in disgust. "What do you consider yourself, if not bad?"

Remy was silent for some time, and Brandt clenched his jaw angrily.

"I suppose you're right," Remy finally said softly. "Doesn't change who we both are, though. You love him; I can see it in the way you look at him."

"Maybe so. He's still a killer."

"As are we all," Remy said in a tone that signified the end of the short conversation.

Brandt flopped back against the wall and looked at Shawn sideways, wanting to vent his anger but knowing the older man didn't deserve to be the target. Especially when he wasn't even really aware of what was going on.

"What'd he say?" Shawn asked softly.

Brandt supposed he spoke in such a low tone to avoid yelling. Brandt had seen it plenty of times after an explosion; people couldn't hear themselves when they spoke, and so they yelled, thinking that others couldn't hear them either. At least Shawn had realized that was not the case and kept his voice down.

Brandt felt a pang of pity for the man, thinking he must be reeling from losing one of the senses he depended on most. But then, he remembered what Shawn was and he tried his best to harden himself against the myriad of sympathetic feelings running through him.

"Tell him something, Wally," Remy said softly as the bunk above Brandt's head creaked and rustled with one or both of the shifting bodies of the two men above.

"He was trying to get me to untie him," Brandt answered finally, lying through his teeth and wondering why, even now, he was protecting Remy from Shawn's judgment. Remy obviously hadn't wanted Shawn to hear his words.

"Liar," Shawn said simply as he lowered his head back onto his pillow.

Brandt blinked and sighed heavily. He ran his hand through his hair and looked around the room for something to hold his attention.

"Should we go look for them?" Remy asked quietly after several more uneventful minutes.

"You're not going anywhere," Brandt said flatly.

"Think about it, *podna*, we're all in this shit, here," Remy said heatedly. "We're all on the same side, dammit!"

"The hell we are!" Brandt yelled angrily. "We've spent the last five years fighting and dying against your lot, and don't you dare to think you can tell me we're the same!"

Shawn had raised his head again to look at Brandt, tilting his good ear toward Brandt as he shouted.

"You may have been fighting us, but we weren't fighting you," Remy said calmly.

Brandt lunged forward and stood, turning around to face Remy angrily. He was quite shocked to find the younger man sitting cross-legged on the bunk, his back to the wall and his hands on his knees in an unthreatening manner. Nikolaus sat in the corner, holding his knees to his chest and looking as if he simply wanted to sleep.

"Bugger!" Brandt shouted in frustration.

"Sorry, *podna*, it was killing my shoulder. Can we untie Shawn, too? Or were you a little gentler with him than Boss was with me and Niko?"

"Get back in your sheets!" Brandt shouted as he pointed at the bundle beside Remy's knee.

Remy shook his head regretfully. "Can't. That was one fuck of a knot he had me in."

"Son of a bitch," Brandt sighed as he rubbed his eyes tiredly. "I can't let you run, Dixie. I just can't."

"I'm not asking you to let me run. If I were going to run, I would have simply jumped down, snapped your neck, untied Shawn, and been gone an hour ago."

"I call bullshit," Brandt said with a little smile. "You couldn't jump off that bunk; you'd catch your foot in the sheets, splat against the wall, and knock yourself unconscious."

Nikolaus snorted and covered his mouth, and a slow smile spread over Remy's lips.

"Shut up," Remy finally responded with a grin.

XLIX

"ARE you two done arguing?" Nikolaus asked testily as Remy and Brandt smiled at one another. They looked at him blankly, as if they had both forgotten he was there. "Can someone please explain what the hell is going on?" he asked in frustration.

"Untie Beignet first," Remy requested as he looked back at Brandt. "Please? His arm must be killing him," Remy added as Brandt looked at him doubtfully. "Come on, Wally, don't make me knock myself unconscious," he added with a sly grin. Brandt snorted and looked at him warily for several long seconds. "Wally, it's still me. It's still all of us," Remy coaxed as he gestured toward Nikolaus. "We swore our loyalty."

Remy heard Nikolaus sniff and risked a glance at him. The man had buried his face in his arms and was shaking his head miserably from side to side. Brandt and Remy shared a puzzled look, but Brandt finally held out his hand to aid Remy in getting down. Remy smiled at him gratefully before slithering down to the floor and crawling onto the bottom bunk with Shawn

Shawn looked at him in mild amusement as Remy worked at the sheets, and when he got the last knot undone, Remy ran his fingers through Shawn's hair and sat back on the man's thighs, hunching over as his head hit the bottom of the top bunk.

"You can talk your way out of anything, can't you?" Shawn said in a low, even voice. Remy didn't know if it was meant as a compliment or an insult, but he smiled weakly and nodded, anyway.

"Can you hear me?" Remy asked in a deliberately low voice.

"No," Shawn responded in the same tone.

"You can read my lips?" Remy asked hopefully.

Shawn frowned and shook his head, tilting it to the side in an attempt to better hear Remy's words.

Remy leaned forward and put his mouth to Shawn's ear. "Can you read my lips?" he asked.

"Yes, but just when I think I know what you're going to say," Shawn answered, his breath ghosting over Remy's ear and making him shiver. "Just the predictable things, I mean."

"Is it getting better or worse?" Remy asked.

"The same, I think," Shawn said in the same flat voice he had been using. "It pops a bit when I open my mouth wide, like at high altitudes, but that's it. The ringing's still there. It hasn't gotten any worse, but it's not improving, either."

"What about your other ear?" Remy asked as he turned his head slightly and let his lips brush across Shawn's earlobe.

Shawn closed his eyes and let out a shuddering breath, and Remy's world began to shrink until he and Shawn were the only people left in it.

"I think it's having sympathy ringing," Shawn finally whispered as he turned his head to brush his cheek against Remy's.

Remy lingered there, enjoying the feel of Shawn's body beneath him until Brandt cleared his throat impatiently and brought him crashing back down to the present. He sat back and rubbed his eyes, wondering how in the hell they would get through the mess he knew was coming, especially with Shawn not being able to really follow what was going to be said.

"Nothing for it but to wait it out," he said slowly in a loud voice.

Shawn nodded in acknowledgement.

The door swung open as Remy opened his mouth to speak to Brandt, and Thiago stopped dead in his tracks as he looked at them all.

"Jesus fucking Christ, Brandt!" he finally yelled, and Carl shoved at him from behind to crowd them all into the tiny compartment once more and close the door behind him.

"Where's Gray?" Remy asked immediately.

"I told you to watch him!" Thiago shouted as he pointed at Remy. "He's like Gumby, for Christ's sake! You have to fucking staple him to the wall!"

"Who the fuck is Gumby?" Carl asked absently as he locked the door and looked at Remy and Shawn with interest.

"Where's Gray?" Remy demanded again as Shawn took hold of his shoulder and shook him to get him to move off his body.

"I *was* watching him!" Brandt yelled. "Sort of," he added in a smaller voice. "And how do you not know who Gumby is?" he added as he looked over Thiago's shoulder at Carl.

"Shut up!" Shawn yelled angrily as he pushed Remy off him and stood.

Remy fell back and banged his head on the wall, and he simply flopped into the corner, watching Shawn fume at the others in the tiny space. They all stared at Shawn in slight shock, and he reached out and grabbed Thiago by the shirt collar and pulled him close. "If I can hear you then the whole bloody train can," he snarled. "Now, where is Gray?" he demanded slowly.

"He– wait, he's not back?" Thiago asked as panic began to seep into his angry blue eyes.

"Shit," Remy breathed as he sat back up and rubbed his head gingerly. Gray was missing. That wasn't good by any stretch of the imagination.

"Did he run, do you think?" Carl asked calmly.

"He wouldn't do that," Thiago said heatedly as he pushed Shawn away and stepped toward the door.

Remy leaned forward to stand but Shawn placed a hand on his shoulder and forced him to stay seated.

"Are you okay?" he asked as he looked at the back of Remy's head.

Brandt and Carl were trying to get out of Thiago's way, jostling Shawn and causing his hands to clench around the back of Remy's neck as he almost lost his balance. Remy winced, but nodded anyway and looked up into Shawn's eyes as Thiago unlocked the door and yanked it open.

Gray stood in the aisle, his hand reaching for the knob that was no longer there and his blue eyes registering only mild surprise. Thiago reached out and grabbed him, pulling him close and hugging him as if he'd just been reunited with his favorite teddy bear. Carl rolled his eyes and pulled them both back into the compartment, then closed the door again.

"I got held up with this old couple," Gray huffed in explanation for his tardiness as Thiago squeezed the life out of him. "They needed help with their– ow– luggage," Gray wheezed. "Why are they up?" he asked as Thiago released him and petted him in a manner quite unbecoming a trained killer.

"Brandt let them go," Thiago growled as he checked Gray over for injuries, ignoring the swatting Gray did in protest of the treatment.

"I did no such thing," Brandt said indignantly.

"When we left, they were tied. When we got back, they weren't. That means you let them go."

"They let themselves go!"

"Then you let them escape. Same fucking difference!"

"Stop!" Carl yelled finally. His eyes flashed dangerously and Brandt discreetly shoved at Shawn and sent him headlong onto the lower bunk and into Remy's lap. Brandt followed the movement by slinking sideways and squeezing into the bunk with them, and he settled in beside Shawn to look up at Carl obediently.

Remy couldn't help but stare at the man, dumbfounded. When had Carl taken control of the group? From his pointed, concise questions in the Mustang, to being the only one willing to wade into the chaos and try to stop it by being the voice of reason, Carl was making a pretty effective point to revolve around.

Remy and Shawn shared a look and looked up at Carl in mimicry of Brandt's obedient attitude. At least someone was trying to remain in control. Carl rubbed his eyes as if they hurt, and Thiago and Gray watched him warily as they tried to stand together in the small space in front of the door.

"We have a lot of shit to go over, and very little time in which to do it," Carl said quietly. "First; what did you two find, no one tailing us?"

"No," Thiago responded succinctly.

"It's all clear," Gray affirmed.

"Good," Carl said with a little nod. "What issue shall we address first, then?" he asked with a little grin.

"Issue?" Remy repeated disbelievingly. "How about, we address why all of a sudden you seem to know a lot more than the rest of us? How about–"

"Why don't we address just what exactly you two do, huh?" Brandt interrupted angrily.

"Stop! If this is going to happen it has to be done in something resembling an orderly fashion," Carl growled as the train lurched and they all tensed to keep upright.

"Isn't there supposed to be an announcement or something when they do that?" Thiago grumbled as he and Gray stumbled to the side.

"There was," Gray said as he wrapped his arms around Thiago and held him until the rocking motion stopped. Remy watched them with interest, wondering why he'd never guessed at the extent of the connection they shared. He'd suspected Gray was smitten with the Archer, who happened to be Thiago, but he hadn't known the feeling was mutual.

"First thing, I want to know why we tied Niko up," Carl said, pointing at Nikolaus in the top bunk. Remy was struck by the fact that he had momentarily forgotten about Nikolaus being up there.

"He's a plant," Gray spat angrily. "Been informing on you all along."

"What?" Remy cried.

Shawn gripped his arm and tugged at him. Remy turned to see the frustration and concern in Shawn's eyes, and he immediately calmed. He realized Shawn was taking his cues from Remy's reactions, and he vowed to remain calm through this.

"Sorry," he said softly as he scooted back and placed his arm around Shawn's shoulders. He positioned himself so Shawn's ear was at his mouth. He would have to act almost as a translator, whispering in Shawn's ear what was being said as the others spoke.

This was no way for Shawn to be when their lives depended on their survival skills.

L.

"NIKOLAUS'S been working for someone else all along," Gray continued as Thiago tried to calm him with a hand on his back. "I think now's a good time to tell us about your little meeting this morning, Niko," he growled, looking up at the man who'd remained essentially silent since he'd confessed in the car.

"I told you," Nikolaus said quietly.

Thiago watched as Remy whispered in Shawn's ear, and Shawn nodded in response. He supposed that since Carl and Brandt accused the two of them of something, something as yet unknown to Thiago, they shouldn't be allowed to whisper. Thiago just didn't see them as a threat.

"Why did you change your mind so suddenly?" Thiago asked Nikolaus. "All this time, even after swearing loyalty, you've been in contact with them. Why turn today?"

"He said… my contact was talking about seeing you all executed. He said they'd hang you as an example and–"

"Hang?" Carl broke in questioningly.

"Did he say hang?" Shawn asked in confusion.

"They don't hang people anymore, Gizmo," Carl said doubtfully.

"I'm just telling you what the man said, all right?" Nikolaus said in a tired voice.

"Who was this?" Remy asked worriedly.

"Nikolaus's MI6 contact," Thiago answered.

"MI6 certainly doesn't hang people anymore," Remy said slowly. He looked at Shawn and they shared a concerned look. "But we know who does," he added slowly.

Silence fell in the cramped cabin, and finally Thiago breathed deeply and said, "Maybe we should start with you two then."

"We're going to need like, uh… a diagram or something," Remy said with a resigned nod.

LI.

ALL Carl had been able to find for Remy to write on was a napkin, but Remy was making do. He was using Shawn's back as a hard surface to write on, since the man couldn't really follow the conversation anyway, and they all hovered over the two of them as Shawn sat on the edge of the bunk with his head hanging between his knees.

Carl recognized that it took a lot of trust on Shawn's part to allow Remy to defend the two of them by himself, and he wondered if Remy knew how much Shawn was counting on him.

"Okay," Remy sighed finally. "We have the standard intelligence agencies from all over the world over here," Remy said as he pointed his pen to the left side of the napkin. "CIA, KGB, MI6, GSS, ASIO, BND, Mossad, SAVAK, Al Amn Al-Khas, AVB," Remy said, rattling off the names of intelligence agencies.

"We know the agencies, just get on with it!" Brandt said testily.

Remy gave him a glare but continued.

"They all feed into O.R.G. This, too, we all know, and the Organization acts as a sort of an Interpol of spies, handling and coordinating anything that's too big for one or two groups to go at alone. What is not common knowledge, however, is that the Organization has two sides to it," Remy said as he drew two lines from the symbol he had made to represent the Organization, making his diagram look sort of spider-like.

"What do you mean, two sides?" Nikolaus asked as he hung over the edge of the top bunk and looked down at them all.

"The legit side, and the black side," Remy answered as he wrote the words and circled them. "We call it the Underground, for lack of a better term."

"So you two really are the bad guys," Thiago said in disbelief.

"I resent the term bad guy," Remy responded angrily.

"My neck is starting to hurt, people," Shawn said in a muffled voice. "I know you're arguing. I can smell it. Stop it and get on with it."

There was a brief silence before Gray snorted in amusement and actually reached down and patted the back of Shawn's head, earning a sloppy upside down smack for his trouble.

"Too bad he's such a bastard," Gray whispered to Thiago. "I quite like him."

Thiago rolled his eyes and motioned for Remy to continue.

"Think of it like this," Remy said as he drew a circle. "You have your legit agency, let's say MI6 or the CIA. They handle everything that's out there in the open, so to speak. But then you have your higher branches; say, the NSA, black ops that handle both the legit and the not so legitimate jobs. Follow?" he asked of everyone. Everyone nodded. "That's what we are. We know about you, but you don't know about us. And if ever your kind were to find out about our kind, well, we're supposed to handle it. But basically, we're you," Remy said as he pointed at all of them. "Simply without a conscience or committee oversight."

Carl stared at him incredulously. Talk about drawing it out in purple crayon.

"Is that what you and your boys found out on that raid, Thiago?" Nikolaus asked curiously after several more moments of silent contemplation over Remy's words.

"Not exactly," Thiago said hesitantly. He looked at Gray and then at Brandt, then sighed heavily. "Gray and Brandt were there as well. There were twelve of us. As we've recently discovered, eight were killed in the purges."

"That didn't strike you as, I don't know, alarming?" Remy asked sarcastically.

"I didn't know they were all the same men," Thiago said defensively. "I didn't keep track of them, not then."

"You're not exactly aces at keeping track of us now," Brandt mumbled.

"We've had some difficulties," Thiago spat angrily.

"Uh huh. Go on," Remy prodded as he reclined and patted Shawn on the back to let him know they were done with using him as a table. Shawn sat up and turned to look at Remy, his face flushed from being upside down for so long.

"Whoa, head rush," he murmured as he reached out to steady himself on the wooden ladder. The others snickered and he looked up at them quickly. "Hey! I can hear!" he said happily, his face lighting up like Carl hadn't seen it do since before the cabin blew up.

Remy grinned and patted Shawn on the shoulder. "Good then, just in time to hear Thi spill it."

"Hmm… I can kind of hear, anyway," Shawn said as he rubbed his ear gingerly and turned his head from side to side. "Better than nothing, though," he said as he turned to look at Remy happily.

Remy smiled at him and nodded, then turned and frowned and asked, "So who was the twelfth man?"

"We don't know," Thiago admitted with a shrug. "He was our outrider."

"Outrider?" Remy repeated in confusion. "Why would you need someone on surveillance outside? Wasn't this your basic, straightforward raid?"

"Not at first. It was a bait and tackle. What it turned into was a fuck up. We were given bad intel, whether on purpose or not, I don't know. What we thought was a drug runner's outpost turned out to be one of the Organization's backup document storage buildings. We were never supposed to go inside. We were never even supposed to know it was there."

"So let me get this straight," Shawn said, holding out his hand and closing his eyes. "Eleven of you accidentally raided what was, essentially, an Organization satellite storage, found backups of compromising documents– that eventually got most of you killed– and this twelfth man heard every word of it, but never surfaced after it was all over?"

Thiago pursed his lips and nodded. "Basically," he said tightly.

"And then when they tried to off him for what he knew, he turned around and killed his own marker and faded away, yet again?" Shawn clarified.

"Apparently," Thiago said uncomfortably.

"Wow. Smart son of a bitch, yeah?" Shawn claimed in a soft voice.

"Yeah," Thiago said uncomfortably.

"Too bad he's not on our side," Shawn huffed.

Thiago rolled his eyes and sighed.

"So what did you find?" Nikolaus asked hesitantly. "I mean, what made you turn and start… what exactly do you do, anyway?"

"We found documents that detailed the extermination of agents," Thiago answered in a slow, tired voice. By now this wasn't so much of a shock to anyone, and so Thiago continued without much fanfare. "In a nutshell, they don't let you retire, *chicos*. Too much of a liability to have us running around in society."

"What, so they do it to protect themselves? Or to protect society?" Remy asked in a strange voice. "They think we'll all go psycho one day and start randomly killing innocent people for the fun of it?"

Thiago bit his lip and tried not to look Remy in the eye, and Carl saw Shawn turn his head to look at Brandt, who sat glowering at them all in the corner of the bunk. Carl couldn't help but smile at the other man. Brandt and Remy were the most likely candidates to go crazy one day and start randomly killing people. That's why Carl loved them so much.

"So that's it?" Nikolaus asked incredulously. "All you were doing was pretending to kill off agents in order to save them?"

"Yes," Thiago said with another shrug as he crossed his arms over his chest. "My guess is the Organization thought we were amassing some kind of army out of the agents we set loose. But most of them just went to ground. Went home. Disappeared. I don't know. We just wanted out," Thiago said in a soft, sad voice.

"None of this is adding up," Shawn said in a gruff voice that indicated that he probably still couldn't hear much. "We're missing something."

"Yes, Beignet, let's make a chart, shall we?" Remy said in a fake, posh British accent that sounded disturbingly like Sherlock Holmes. "Off with your shirt then," he said as he popped the cap off his pen and leered at Shawn.

Shawn glared back at him. "I was drunk," he growled.

"Which made it all the funnier," Remy said with a raised eyebrow.

"What the fuck are you two on about?" Carl asked as they glared at one another.

"Last time Shawn got confused about a mission, he made a chart of it to help him keep track of our information. Of course, we were in a foxhole, so all he had was me to write on. I say it's payback time."

"Give me that," Shawn growled as he snatched the pen away from the younger man and tossed it at Gray.

"Hey!" Gray cried as the pen bounced off his chest and hit the ground. "If you're going to throw pointy objects, at least do it with feeling. Use that big mother of a knife Remy carries," Gray said as he bent to pick up the pen and stick it behind his ear.

"Don't tempt me," Shawn growled.

Carl perked up at this, and he leaned over and looked at Remy. "I meant to ask you about that thing," he said as he remembered the odd catch on the handle of Remy's knife that he'd played with earlier.

"Uh huh," Remy said flatly. "I'll give you the damn thing if you tell us all what you know."

Carl glared at him, but stood back up and looked at everyone briefly before sighing and scratching his head resignedly.

"All right. I knew about the raid and the executions. I knew about the Underground and its job within the Organization, though I wasn't a part of it. By the way, Gizmo, the Underground makes a public to do of hanging their rogues to instill loyalty. Your contact from MI6 was probably an Organization man and let it slip."

"What?" Nikolaus cried in disbelief.

"Yeah," Carl said regretfully. "I doubt the Organization would allow MI6 or the BND to stick its nose into an internal cleanup like this. You were the reason we were almost killed so many times, even if it wasn't intentional."

"Internal cleanup?" Thiago asked as Nikolaus paled visibly. "What the hell are you talking about? And how did you know about the raid? And how did–"

"Okay, listen. I'm going to go over this, and I'm going to do it slowly so everyone will follow. When you have an outrider on a multi-asset assignment, what Class do they usually assign there?" Carl asked, hoping to have them all clue into it themselves.

"A Four," Thiago whispered as realization dawned.

"You were our twelfth man?" Gray asked in disbelief. The others weren't quite as quick on the mark, but Carl didn't care. He nodded and Gray gritted his teeth. "Then why didn't you join us? You had to have heard–"

"Quite honestly, I didn't care," Carl said quietly. "The work was all I had, and as far as I was concerned, when I got too old or too slow to do it, they could kill me off if they wanted to."

"Jesus," Nikolaus breathed.

Carl looked up at him, then at the others. It was slightly alarming to see Remy looking back at him with a sympathetic little frown, and Carl instantly knew that Remy was familiar with that feeling. His eyes went to Brandt, who sat smiling sadly at him, and he smiled back at the other man. No words needed to be exchanged at this point.

"So how did you know all this, is the question," Remy said finally.

"We all know Thierry St. John, right?" Carl asked as he flushed a little under their combined gaze.

"Yeah, he's the one who placed me," Remy said suspiciously.

"Me too," Shawn said quietly.

"But wait, do you mean St. John's a Hunter, too?" Remy asked in horror.

"Yep," was all Shawn said in response.

"That son of a bitch," Remy growled.

"Carl," Thiago said sternly in order to silence the two men. "What about Thierry? How did you get all this information from him?"

"I was fucking him, and he likes to talk," Carl said simply as he put his hands behind his back and waited for the onslaught of questions.

LII.

THE compartment fell into a stunned silence after Carl's admission. Shawn sat wedged in between Remy and Brandt, barely breathing as he looked up at Carl in shock.

"Thierry told you all this?" Shawn finally asked in a hoarse voice. "He's been leaking information? For how long? When did it start? Why did–"

Remy squeezed Shawn's shoulder and hissed slightly, and Shawn fell silent.

Carl looked back at him blankly and then looked at the others questioningly.

"Any other questions before I start? No? Okay then," he said in a pleasant voice as he crossed his arms over his chest. "First of all, no, I wasn't fucking him to get information. I didn't give a flying pigmy fuck about information then, and I still don't."

"Then why... never mind," Brandt said softly as he looked away from Carl and watched intently as he flipped his lighter over and over in his hands.

Shawn absently reached out and let his hand rest on the bigger man's thigh in a comforting gesture.

Carl's calm façade faltered briefly as he looked at Brandt, but he took a deep breath and continued. "It started about seven years ago, I guess. Don't ask me how because, quite frankly, I don't remember. It just sort of happened. It went on for a couple years, no big love affair or anything, just fucking whenever we saw one another."

"Years?" Brandt asked in a hard voice.

"It's over now," Carl said almost instantly. "Has been for a while. It ended just after the raid."

Shawn examined Brandt closely, noting the flash in Brandt's brown eyes and his rigid posture as he glared at Carl. He understood that all of this was difficult for Brandt to hear. Hell, Shawn hated the thought that *Brandt* was involved with anyone else, and he instantly hated himself for the pang of jealousy he experienced. Remy's hand on his shoulder made his throat tighten painfully and he bit back a curse. He was such a bastard. Maybe he should have Remy shoot him again, just for good measure.

"I still don't understand how you go from a nice casual fuck to leaking special compartmentalized information," Remy muttered in a lost voice. "Especially not... this particular... I mean... he compromised the entire fucking Underground! He just... told you? Just like that? Were you fucking him at the time? 'Cause, I mean... I would have told you anything you asked me in that bathtub that one time."

Carl snorted and tried not to smile, and Thiago rolled his eyes and rubbed at his temples like an overworked nanny.

"It wouldn't be the first time Thierry used his position for some kind of gain," Shawn murmured. "He told you about my taking the retirement deal, remember?" he asked Remy. "He obviously wanted you on this mission badly enough to do it. The question is, what did he want Carl to do for him?"

"He wasn't leaking anything he didn't mean to," Carl said with certainty. "He was very subtle about what he told me, and no, it wasn't when we were fucking. I think he was recruiting me. Trying to, anyway. When I finally just told him I wasn't interested in playing the games a double-switch would entail, that I was just there to do my job, that was the last we saw of each other."

"He was trying to pull you over?" Thiago asked curiously.

"And then he just dropped you?" Gray asked as he peeked at Carl from behind Thiago.

"Yeah," Carl answered simply as a frown graced his handsome features.

"Why? Did he have a specific purpose for you?" Thiago asked as he turned and glared at Gray pointedly.

"I don't know," Carl answered with a shrug.

"Fair enough. Most of the time *Thierry* doesn't even know what he's up to," Remy grumbled. "All right then, new question. Did Thierry put you on this team? Directly or indirectly, was he responsible for your presence here?"

Carl was silent for several long moments, and then he nodded almost imperceptibly and licked his lips nervously. "He contacted me and said he needed a favor; someone who would be able to clean up a mess if the shit hit the fan and then keep quiet about it. 'Disappear' was the word he used."

"You were his insurance, then," Remy muttered.

Shawn turned even more to glare at the younger man, who was smiling grimly and beginning to chuckle.

"Stop giggling like a halfwit," Shawn growled. "What have your last two brain cells stumbled over now?"

"Thierry heads up the Underground, but is also a major player on the legitimate side of the Organization. He's got to be the one behind all of this," Remy said, his voice still breaking with laughter.

Shawn narrowed his eyes suspiciously. Thierry was a straight player, if not a little… okay yeah, he was an underhanded bastard, but he wasn't this unorganized.

"Just because he's in the position to do so, doesn't mean he did," Shawn said dubiously.

Remy rolled his eyes and pointed at Thiago. "We have not one, not two, but all four of the remaining members of the raid that, by all accounts, started the whole thing rolling," the Cajun said, pointing at each of them in turn as he spoke. "We have the tech who created the Purge virus that would cause a shitload of problems if word ever got out, and who also happens to remember the data he put into said virus. And we have Carl, who was perhaps the only clean agent who knew about the black ops side of the Organization and wasn't personally or professionally invested in keeping it a secret."

Shawn frowned and nodded, and the others looked at one another grimly. "All right, so what about us?" Shawn said slowly.

"Well, they already suspected me, right? I say you were under suspicion too, no matter how undeserved the sentiment. They put all their rats in a trap, Shawn," Remy said with an expressive gesture of his hands that betrayed his frustration. "With the exception of Gray, they had every agent they knew to be a threat in one unit, with you thinking that you were placed to take care of them. This had nothing to do with hunting down the Archer."

"Are you trying to tell me that Thierry put me here to die?" Carl demanded in a low, dangerous voice.

"I think he put us all here to die," Remy said sadly.

"I think you're wrong," Shawn said with a stubborn shake of his head.

"What makes you say that?" Thiago asked curiously.

"That just doesn't feel like Thierry to me. And I gather Carl disagrees, as well," Shawn said with a wave of his hand toward Carl. "I was told that I was put here to eliminate the rest of you, but then Thierry went to what can be considered extraordinary lengths to make certain that Remy was placed here, too. Consider this; the higher-ups knew there was a mole. They knew Gray was snooping around with someone in the know, but they just didn't know who it was. Or so they said, anyway."

"How do you know that?" Gray demanded.

"Because I was the one tracking the mole," Shawn admitted candidly.

Remy's body stiffened next to him.

"Ha! I told you we were being tracked!" Gray yelled angrily as he pointed his finger at Remy triumphantly.

"Tracked and captured are two entirely different things," Remy pointed out flatly.

"What if they already knew it was you two and simply hoped I wouldn't be able to find you?" Shawn suggested, trying to ignore the looks Gray and Remy shot one another. The pang of jealousy hit him again and he closed his eyes as he continued to speak. "And I couldn't find you. God help me, I tried, but you two were good. I should have known Remy was behind most of those covers," Shawn said almost to himself.

"Shawn," Remy whispered as he placed his hand tentatively on Shawn's shoulder. Shawn looked at the younger man and shook his head, smiling slightly.

"So… you think… knew… turned?" Gray asked in a low voice. Shawn turned to look at Gray and leaned forward, cocking his head to the side.

"What?"

"So you think Thierry knew that Remy had turned?" Gray asked in a loud, deliberate voice.

"I don't know," Shawn sighed in frustration. "Fuck, I'm confused. I'd love to get my hands on St. John and squeeze some information out of him. What did you two uncover while you were digging?"

"We were looking more for agent locations and specialties, to be honest," Remy said as Gray opened and closed his mouth quickly.

"Gray?" Shawn growled, ignoring Remy's tense posture.

"That's all we were doing. That's when I found your designator," Gray said with a nod at Shawn.

Shawn narrowed his eyes at the other man, feeling like he was missing something but not certain how to go about extracting it.

"Wait, wait," Nikolaus said from the top bunk where he had remained silent the entire time. "So, since I was… working for the wrong side, apparently, do you think all my information was tainted?"

"Probably," they all answered in a chorus.

"Goddammit. Okay… we agree that we're all here for a reason, the group wasn't put together randomly. What else do the seven of us have in common?" he asked as he hung upside down and looked at Shawn, Remy, and Brandt before disappearing again. "Or the six of us, rather. We all had some type of insider information, just like Remy said. We were all a threat to the security of the Underground. But what else?" There was a silence in which Nikolaus gave them a chance to answer, and when they all simply sat and stared at one another he sighed and said, "We had all worked with that list of agents we pulled up, remember?"

"Shit, man, I'd forgotten about that," Remy murmured.

"Wait, what list?" Gray asked.

"We had a list of eleven agents," Thiago explained. "All of whom had worked with agents we had freed in the past year. All six of us were on it, as were you."

"Who else, anyone remember?" Shawn asked, not in the least ashamed to admit that he didn't.

"John," Remy said almost immediately as he held up his thumb to count. "Evan Washburn. Fletcher Barclay. Lydia Ashton. John and Evan, I can report, are not, in fact, dead as was reported. John's… what side is he on anyway?"

"John's on his own side," Shawn muttered. "What was the point?"

"Uhh," Thiago and Remy responded, and the others shrugged or sighed.

"We'd all worked with them at one point or another, yeah?" Nikolaus asked as he hung over the edge again.

"Yeah?" Remy and Shawn echoed.

"Well, is that normal? For you black ops types to work with… what did you call it? Clean agents?"

"Yes, it is," Remy answered.

"We're all under the same umbrella," Shawn explained as his hearing faded in and out. "The only agents who are part of the Underground are Ones and to a lesser extent, Fours. The rest service both sides without ever really knowing it."

"Oh," Nikolaus said in a disappointed voice.

"And I have to say, Carl," Remy said after another brief silence, "while the hangings aren't exactly 'public,' they do get a lot of publicity."

"Wait. Jesus Christ, that's really true?" Thiago asked in horror.

Shawn smiled grimly at him.

"They don't tolerate fuck-ups, Thi," Remy said in a cold, hard voice. "Have you ever seen a hanging?"

"No," Thiago said in a small voice.

"Pray that you don't. If they catch you, it'll be your own."

Shawn gritted his teeth and watched Thiago shift uncomfortably. "You never really knew what you were getting into, did you?" he asked softly.

"I never wanted to get into it to begin with," Thiago asserted almost angrily. "I was elected," he added, spitting out the last word in disgust.

"That would explain your complete ineptitude," Remy said bitterly.

"Bite me, Remy," Thiago spat.

"I throw you to the gators, let them do it for me!" Remy shot back.

Thiago growled and Gray snickered as he turned to try to hide his smile. Shawn smacked Remy on the thigh and glared at him.

"So where does all this leave us?" Carl finally asked after a moment of uncomfortable silence.

"Hungry," Brandt grunted.

LIII.

NIKOLAUS wasn't feeling very hungry. He felt quite sick, actually. It was bad enough he'd been informing on them all along, but now Carl asserted he'd been informing to the wrong side. Maybe they were taking the hanging comment too literally? But Remy and Shawn confirmed the practice. Nikolaus felt sick, indeed.

"C'mon Niko, we'll get you some food," Remy said softly as he stood up and peered over the top bunk at Nikolaus.

Brandt and Carl had already exited, and Shawn was standing in the open doorway waiting for Remy to join him. Gray and Thiago sat on the lower bunk speaking softly, claiming that they weren't hungry.

"No, thanks," Nikolaus responded despondently.

Remy raised his eyebrows and opened his mouth to protest, but Shawn called softly to him. "Let him be, lad," he ordered gently. "Come on."

Remy looked over his shoulder, then back at Nikolaus and nodded. "Want me to bring you something?" he asked hopefully.

"No, thanks," Nikolaus repeated as he forced a smile.

Remy nodded again and turned to go, closing the door behind him as he went. Nikolaus knew it was coming, and so he simply closed his eyes and waited until Thiago finally cleared his throat and stood.

Nikolaus looked at him steadily as Thiago rested his forearms on the top bunk and leaned his chin on them, his blue eyes boring into Nikolaus in silent contemplation. Gray stood as well and began to pace the short length of the compartment restlessly. This, more than anything, made Nikolaus nervous. If Gray was uncomfortable even though he and Thiago obviously shared something, then Nikolaus probably should be as well.

"You fucked up," Thiago said conversationally.

Nikolaus frowned and nodded.

Thiago's eyes softened and he grinned a little. "Next time you're supposed to be snitching on someone, make sure you don't start fucking them, too," he said with a wink.

Nikolaus's jaw dropped and he stared at Thiago in disbelief. Was that all the reprimand he was going to get? Remy almost was killed for what he did, and Nikolaus's actions were far worse. He'd almost gotten them all killed.

"Oh that's fucking great, Thi," Gray hissed. "Let him off with a wink and grin so he'll be more confident about the backstabbing next time around."

"Gray, *cierre su trucho*," Thiago muttered in a tired voice.

"Fuck you, Thiago," Gray snarled as Thiago turned around to face him. "Fuck. You. You can include yourself in that invite too there, sport," he told Nikolaus angrily before turning to reach for the door handle.

The action was so sudden that Nikolaus blinked and almost missed it. Thiago reached out and grabbed Gray by the elbow, pulling him backward and throwing him onto the lower bunk with an angry growl. Nikolaus lunged forward and swung down onto the floor in time to see

Thiago straddle the stunned man. He took Gray's collar into his hand and lifted his head and shoulders off the mattress as he reared back for a swing.

Gray did nothing to defend himself, he didn't even bring up his hands to try and block the blow. Nikolaus cried out wordlessly and reached out to grab Thiago's hand as he pulled back for the punch.

"What the fuck is wrong with you?" Nikolaus hissed as he fought with Thiago for possession of Thiago's arm. Thiago yanked and pulled Nikolaus onto the mattress with them, eliciting a series of gasps and muffled curses from all three men.

"Let me the fuck go," Thiago growled as he shook Nikolaus off and turned to glare at Gray dangerously. Nikolaus wrapped his arms around Thiago's shoulders and pulled back until he landed at the end of the bunk with Thiago struggling in his lap.

Gray scooted away from them until he leaned against the other wall of the bunk and glared daggers at them both. "Jesus. You never used to be this fucking violent," he muttered as he kicked Thiago in the thigh for good measure.

"*Forrito*," Thiago growled as he continued to struggle with Nikolaus. "Let me go, Niko!"

"You've completely lost it!" Gray practically shouted.

"*Boludo*!"

"Psychopath!"

"*Puto*!"

"What?" Gray asked in a shocked voice. He appeared to have understood the curse and was almost amused, but there was a wary flicker of his eyes toward Nikolaus that told Nikolaus the other man was still hiding things.

"I called you a slut," Thiago hissed pointedly. "You don't think I know what went on?" he asked heatedly as he suddenly stopped struggling and went frighteningly still. "I don't care that you fuck whatever moves, *hijo*, but I wish you'd at least have the decency to admit to it. I know Remy well enough to know what happened!"

"Thi–"

"Do you love him?" Thiago demanded.

Gray paled visibly and Nikolaus suddenly forgot how to breathe as he held onto Thiago. "We… I… no," Gray stuttered in shock.

Thiago snarled as he finally wrenched away from Nikolaus and struggled to his feet. Nikolaus and Gray remained on the bunk, carefully avoiding looking at one another or directly at Thiago.

"Thi, we never… I don't deny fucking him, man, but we aren't… in love," Gray insisted quietly.

"For a Class One agent you're a shit liar, you know that?" Thiago said quietly. He bent over and put his face right in front of Gray's. "Be honest with me, Gray. This is your last chance," he whispered.

Gray sighed and glanced at Nikolaus, but he neither flinched nor stuttered when he looked Thiago in the eye and said, "I don't love him."

Nikolaus snorted in a derogatory manner, and Thiago's jaw clenched angrily.

"Why do I not believe you?" Thiago posed in a flat whisper.

"I think he's telling the truth, Thi," Nikolaus ventured. As much as he disliked Gray at the moment, he couldn't help but want to defend him. "Remy wouldn't–"

"That's fine," Thiago said quietly as he stood up and backed toward the door. Gray struggled to his feet and reached out to grab the other man, but Thiago wrenched away and nodded. "I'm sorry. It's not like I've been faithful. I thought there was something… I was mistaken," he said in the same soft whisper. "*Lo siento.*"

"Thi," Gray sighed as he reached out again and tugged at Thiago's hand.

"What were you two discussing in Sydney?" Thiago asked hoarsely as he allowed himself to be carefully hugged.

"How did you know about that?" Nikolaus asked, so shocked by the fact that he didn't even register the sudden change of subject. "Did Remy tell you?" he demanded as he sat forward.

"No, Niko, I actually do this sort of thing for a living," Thiago mumbled as Gray backed away from him. Thiago looked at Gray and narrowed his eyes. "You didn't have your stories straight. Niko said he checked on Remy, but you told me no one had been there."

"Yeah," Gray said somberly. "Faust came in to check on Remy, and I told him I knew what he was doing. I didn't," he said quickly before Thiago could yell again. "I wanted to see if I could smoke him out before I was executed, give myself a bargaining chip," he explained wryly.

Nikolaus shrugged. "I thought I was on the right side," he said defensively.

"You got good men killed because you were naïve," Gray growled as he stepped away from Thiago and toward Nikolaus.

Nikolaus paled and lowered his eyes. "I know," he said in a small voice.

LIV.

"So…."

Brandt shifted in his corner of the little booth in the dining car of the train and looked at Remy curiously. "So?" he repeated questioningly.

"So what do we do now?" Remy asked in a soft voice. He sat beside Brandt, his hands twisting the paper napkin from around his silverware and his eyes darting back and forth between Shawn, Carl, and the server. Every now and then, he would glance at the door to the dining car as if he expected a dozen ninjas to jump through it at any second.

Brandt wouldn't have been surprised to see ninjas at this point, complete with black pajamas and plastic nunchucks.

"Well, which catastrophe, monstrous lie, or betrayal do you want to address first?" Brandt asked wryly when he saw that neither of the other two was going to answer.

"I don't think we should address any of it," Remy snapped. "I don't give a fuck what happened before or who was–" Remy abruptly cut off his words when the server walked by and gave him an appraising look. He smiled gamely at her and watched her swaying hips from over his shoulder as she strode away. He then turned back around, leaning in closer and whispering harshly, "I don't care who was into what, or who was fucking who before this whole fiasco started. I don't care that Carl was sticking it to St. John every chance he got, or that Niko was the one almost got us killed, or that Shawn has been lying to me at every turn from day fucking one. I just care about getting the fuck out of this shit and living through it."

"What?" Shawn hissed as he leaned forward and cocked his head a little to the side.

Remy glared at him briefly, but then his face softened and he sighed. "Still can't hear anything, can you?" he asked regretfully.

"I can hear until you start whispering," Shawn said defensively. "Then you just hiss like a snake and it all blends into one long Remybabble."

Carl reached over and patted Shawn's hand sympathetically and Shawn swatted him away with a growl. Carl snarled at the man and threw his napkin at him. Brandt watched the interaction sadly. The group was falling apart. They'd never been extremely cohesive for any long period of time, now that Brandt thought back on it, but now they were really fucked.

"Remybabble?" Remy repeated questioningly.

"What?" Shawn asked as he leaned forward further.

The server came back carrying their food, and Remy and Shawn both leaned back to allow her to place it on the table between them. Her gaze lingered on Remy and she gave him a shy smile.

He returned it half-heartedly and nodded. "Thank you," he said softly.

They watched the woman walk slowly away, then leaned in once more to continue their whispered conversation. "I just want to know what we plan to do now," Remy hissed. "Do we turn around and try to fight, or do we keep running, forever looking over our shoulders?" he asked bitterly.

"What?" Shawn demanded in frustration.

"*Va-t'à la merde*, Shawn, I taught you how to read lips. Were you not paying attention?" Remy asked with a flop of his hands onto the table that sent his fork flying through the air and onto the floor beside them. "*Merde*."

"No, I wasn't paying attention," Shawn growled as he watched Remy lean out to retrieve the utensil. "I never pay attention to you, because you babble and ramble and throw shit, and you give me a fucking headache!" he whispered heatedly as the server hurried over to help Remy with his fork.

"Thank you, *mon cher*," Remy said in his soft, sexy Cajun accent, and she smiled winningly at him and murmured something Brandt couldn't hear. Remy shook his head in response and she smiled and walked away once more, even slower this time. Remy winced as he sat back up. "Good then, bastard!" he spat at Shawn angrily, his accent deepening further as his emotions took hold. "So stop saying 'what' and just sit there and not listen to me like you always do. Fucking… fuck!"

Brandt looked at Carl, and they raised their eyebrows in alarm. It was difficult to tell whether one of Shawn and Remy's fights would end up requiring weaponry or lubricant. Or both. It was usually both.

Shawn sat back and stared at Remy blankly, and Remy shifted and glanced at Brandt and Carl before thumping his fork down on the table and reaching for his hamburger. The server came back by with an empty tray and glanced over her shoulder at them as she passed. She set the tray down on the table and filled it with the empty plates and glasses left there, and as she walked back by, her foot got tangled as she made eyes at Remy, and she lost her balance.

Remy reached out in a lightning fast movement and grabbed the woman around her waist as she fell forward. Brandt reached out as well, snagging Remy's hamburger out of his hand so he could use both hands to catch the smitten woman. Remy ended up standing, holding the woman with both arms from behind as the tray of glasses went clattering to the ground. He held her tight, their position close to obscene as he steadied her.

"All right?" Remy asked as he released the woman and held her elbow gently until she regained her balance. From the look of her when she gazed up at Remy, though, Brandt didn't think she would ever regain her balance.

"Yes. I'm so sorry. Oh, my God, I'm not usually that clumsy. How embarrassing," the woman stuttered as she flushed and tried to bow her head to hide her face.

Brandt smiled at her reassuringly, and from the corner of his eye he saw Carl watching her sympathetically. Remy cooed to her gently and patted her on the back and shoulder, trying to console her, and Brandt looked to Shawn curiously. The older man hadn't even flinched throughout it all; he would probably have let the woman fall flat on her face, and now he sat watching Remy like a hawk.

It hit Brandt then that Shawn was jealous. Brandt had never considered that Remy might be bi. The younger man had made no secret of the fact that he was a bottom, so Brandt had simply assumed he was strictly gay. He couldn't exactly bottom in a heterosexual relationship.... Brandt shook his head and told himself not to let his mind wander into that territory. Regardless of his sexual orientation, Remy was being quite charming now, and soon the server giggled and flushed with something other than embarrassment as Remy murmured to her and helped her pick up the scattered plates and glasses.

She practically floated away as Remy slid back into the booth, and he smiled grimly at Brandt when his slightly battered hamburger was returned to him.

"You're bleeding," Carl observed quietly, and he nodded at Remy's arm as he took an unconcerned sip of his drink.

"Hurt like a son of a bitch, too," Remy muttered as he twisted to peer at his own bicep. "Should have let her fall," he whispered to himself.

"Eat quickly," Shawn said in clipped tones. "You can plan all you want back in the room while we rewrap that."

"I think we'll need another room for planning, actually," Brandt said smugly. They all looked at him curiously.

"You think there was bloodshed?" Remy asked flatly as he chewed quickly. "Poor Niko."

"There may have been bloodshed, yeah. But I can almost guarantee you, they're shagging," Brandt said with a wink.

They all stared at him for several seconds, then the quiet activity of eating continued with simple shrugs and nods.

Brandt grinned across the table at Carl, who raised an eyebrow in question and winked. Angry, repressed fucks were always the best.

LV

SHAWN led them to one of the other compartments Thiago reserved. He stood beside the door in the aisle like an irate schoolteacher as they filed past him. Remy gave him a passing glance, but he knew Shawn was angry and embarrassed over not being able to hear, so he kept moving and refrained from saying anything.

"All right, lad, you obviously have a plan," Shawn grumbled as he closed the door and looked at Remy blankly.

"Well, I do," Remy acknowledged slowly as he sat on the lower bunk beside Carl. He licked his lips and looked up at Shawn apologetically. "Sort of. But you're not going to like it."

"We'll just add it the queue of shit I don't like right now," Shawn responded in an angry growl. "Out with it."

"We all know they're going to keep coming and coming until either they kill us all, or the Organization crumbles," Remy started as he looked around at them all for confirmation of his assertions. They all stared back at him impassively and he cocked his head to the side, wondering if they were even paying attention. "Right… uh… so, we all know that the seven of us can't take them on. Even if Thiago did manage to get his shit together, he's made it fairly clear that he doesn't have many men at his disposal. Brandt? Do you know how many others are permanent fixtures, like you and Gray?"

"Well," Brandt responded thoughtfully as he crossed his arms and frowned. "Friday and I were– Gray that is, were the only ones doing the really dirty work."

"Wait, you mean all this chaos has been caused by three of you?" Shawn asked disbelievingly.

"Well, obviously there were others here and there," Brandt said in the same pensive voice.

The tone alarmed Remy, and he wrinkled his brow and looked from Brandt to Shawn in concern. Had they finally lost Brandt's mind for good? Remy knew he himself was no longer firing on all cylinders; it was entirely probable Carl's confessions had kicked Brandt over the edge, too.

"And?" Carl prodded gently.

"I don't know about them," Brandt answered as if it were the most obvious thing in the world. "We were compartmentalized in case we were captured. The only people I had contact with were those two, and the agents I helped set free."

"So wait, you knew Gray from that raid, right?" Remy asked as the plan he'd been forming was pushed to the backburner in favor of questioning Brandt and satisfying his curiosity.

"Yeah."

"Did it never occur to you that he was part of Thiago's… whatever it is? Archer Ring? I mean, you were pretty shocked to see him, before. And then when Thiago told you his codename you–"

"How do you know that?" Brandt asked accusingly.

"You don't think I stood at the door and listened before I walked in?" Remy asked with a smirk as he thought back on the looks on Brandt and Thiago's faces when he surprised them during their argument. "Even if I hadn't known Thiago was the Archer, I would have stopped and listened first to a conversation that heated."

"I knew Gray, yeah, but it just struck me as odd, is all."

"Why?" Carl asked curiously.

"'Cause he was very loyal," Brandt said thoughtfully.

"Wait a goddamn minute," Shawn growled. "First of all, speak the fuck up, all of you. I can't hear a bloody thing. Secondly, I'm not following what the fuck you're talking about, and even if I were, I can't see how any of it pertains to your mysterious plan that will probably get us all killed," he said to Remy.

"Well, yeah, okay. Sorry, we got a little off track," Remy admitted as he scooted further back into the bottom bunk. Brandt came over and sat on Remy's other side and pulled Shawn down with him. Shawn fought him half-heartedly, but eventually allowed himself to be wrangled in and coddled. The four of them sat stuffed into the lower bunk together, none of them able to actually look at any of the others or even really move, and Remy snickered at the picture they painted.

Shawn sighed heavily and mumbled, and Remy tried to control his laughter.

"Okay, here goes," Remy said determinedly. "My point before was that they'll keep looking for us until they kill us, or we disable them somehow."

"Disable them?" Shawn repeated doubtfully.

"Yes. More to the point, one of us will have to, well, sacrifice himself to do it," Remy told them quietly.

"Oh, and I suppose you're going to be the one sacrificing, is that it?" Shawn said angrily as he struggled away from Brandt's grasp and tried to stand back up. "Ow! Fuck me!" he growled as he banged his head on the upper bunk. He stood and glared at Remy as he rubbed the back of his head with his good arm. "I won't stand for it, Remy," he said sternly.

"You don't seem to stand too well, regardless," Carl observed dryly. Remy elbowed the bigger man and bit his own lip to keep from smiling. Shawn narrowed his eyes and Remy sobered immediately.

"Shawn, I–"

"No!" Shawn yelled with a determination that even Remy wasn't willing to argue with. He ran his hands through his hair and over his face in agitation, and when he finally looked back at them, Remy wanted to shrink away from the look in his eyes. "I know what you're thinking, Remy, and I can't have you doing it."

"But Shawn–"

"No. That's final," Shawn declared quietly. He looked at them all grimly and nodded almost imperceptibly. "I'll do it."

LVI.

"I'M tired," Thiago snarled at them both, "of being betrayed."

Nikolaus stared back at him with something like fear in his eyes, and Gray turned back to face him with a hurt look.

"I never betrayed you," Gray hissed. "I did exactly what you asked of me."

"And you fucked it up at every turn! You and that fucking Cajun!" Thiago shouted in frustration. He couldn't quite pinpoint where his anger came from, nor could he explain to himself the very real need to blame Gray for all that had gone wrong.

He saw the way Gray and Remy treated each other. There was a familiarity that spoke of something more than simply fucking. It spoke of emotional involvement, and the thought of Gray emotionally involved with anyone other than him had Thiago so angry he could barely think.

"I refuse to let you do this again, Thiago," Gray snarled as he pointed a finger in Thiago's face. "You're fucking with my mind, and it's not fair to use Remy to do it!" He waved his hands through the air in a gesture that signified the end of the conversation and took a step toward the door.

Thiago reached for him in a burst of movement and slammed the other man up against the wall with more force than Gray was probably accustomed to. He barely registered the look of rage in Gray's eyes or the sinking feeling in the pit of his own stomach before his fist connected with the side of Gray's face.

Gray slid slowly to the ground. Thiago's world went slightly fuzzy as he stared down at his lover in something akin to horror. It was one thing to hit another agent during the course of a mission, or even to deck an acquaintance during a friendly round of drinks. But it was entirely another to hit the man you called your lover during what was decidedly a lover's spat.

"*Hölle*, Thiago!" Nikolaus yelled as he scrambled to come to Gray's aid.

The anger flared again, an uncontrollable force that Thiago could no longer contain, and he grabbed Nikolaus by the arm before he could reach Gray and shoved him back at the bunks.

"Leave him the fuck alone, Thi," Gray said as he pushed against the wall and slid up and to his feet. Thiago rounded on him Gray inclined his head defiantly.

"Don't become this guy," Gray told him as he raised his hand to gingerly swipe the blood from the cut under his eyes. "You're not this guy."

LVII.

CARL knocked on the compartment door gently and waited impatiently for a response. He didn't like loitering outside the door, regardless of how thorough their checks were. He knocked again, a little louder this time. They'd worked out the sleeping and watch arrangements quite easily, after Remy and Shawn finally stopped shouting at one another, and he was there to fill Thiago and the others in on the plan.

They were to stay two to a room, with two men on guard for three-hour shifts, rotating sleeping shifts. Carl needed to let these three know about it before he started off on his rounds. He knocked once more and looked casually up and down the aisle. At least there was no one in sight. If they were in that compartment fucking instead of answering his knocks, then Carl was going to be removing some limbs from their owners.

"Hey, Zed?" he called softly and knocked again. There was a brief shuffling, and Nikolaus finally cracked the door open and peeked out at him. "Whoa, you don't look so good," Carl observed with a hint of alarm. "Are you okay? What happened? Where's–"

"I'm fine," Nikolaus said grimly. "Can't say the same for Gray or Thiago though," he added as he opened up the door and let Carl into the compartment.

Gray sat on the edge of the bottom bunk with his elbows resting on his knees and his head held in his hands. He neither looked up nor moved when Carl entered.

"What happened? Are you all right? Where's Thiago?" Carl asked in alarm as he took a step and knelt in front of Gray.

"Gone," Gray said in a hoarse whisper.

"What do you mean gone?" Carl asked in a harsher voice than he had intended.

Gray finally looked up at him, and Carl frowned as he took note of the burgeoning bruise on Gray's cheekbone.

"Did he do that?" Carl asked as his hand came up to gently run his fingers over the discolored skin. Gray grabbed his wrist and glared at him before he could make contact. "I'm not going to hurt you, mate," Carl said gently.

Gray released him and allowed Carl to look over the bruise. It was going to be a nice one, but Carl had certainly seen worse. The cut on his cheek had probably been made by a ring, but it wouldn't require stitches.

"Doesn't look like anything's cracked or broken. Can you see all right?" Carl murmured as he looked at Gray's eye carefully.

Gray nodded.

"Who fought?" Carl asked as he stood back up and looked at Nikolaus, checking him visually for bruises or cuts.

Gray and Nikolaus made no secret that there was no love lost between them, but Nikolaus looked to be unharmed. The German shrugged and looked at Gray with a frown.

"Thiago did this? Why?" Carl asked before they could answer him.

"We may have pissed him off," Nikolaus mumbled.

"How?" Carl asked, his concern and growing anger taking a brief back seat to curiosity.

He'd seen Thiago angry once, maybe twice. Even with all his plans falling apart around him and one unwelcome surprise after another, Thiago had yet to lose his temper. Well… Gray's face was telling a different story, but before today, he had yet to lose his temper.

"Doesn't matter," Gray said with certainty. "He'll walk it off and be back apologizing in about an hour."

"He does that often, then?" Carl asked angrily as he gestured toward Gray's face. The man didn't flinch away from his waving hand, and that was a good sign as far as Carl was concerned. Thiago never seemed the abusive type to Carl, and he didn't want to think of him that way now.

"Not as such, no," Gray said brusquely. "What did you need?"

Carl frowned at him, but if Gray didn't want to get into it, then Carl couldn't force him. Nikolaus bit his lip and scowled impressively, but Carl nodded all the same and sighed inwardly.

"We're taking shifts on watch," he told them resignedly, hoping that whatever it was between them would work itself out before they were forced to turn and fight. "Rest in pairs, round robin the beds. Try to stay put as best you can, we don't want our faces getting too much light." Carl paused and looked down at Gray, who sat dejectedly on the side of the bed looking at Carl's feet intently. "You sure you're okay?" he asked finally.

"Yeah. What's the watch order?" Gray asked without looking up.

"You and I are on now. Niko, Shawn will come get you when it's your turn. You should rest up 'til then."

"Great," Gray said flatly.

"Anything I should tell Thiago if I see him?" Carl asked carefully before he turned to go. Gray shook his head and looked up at Carl with determined blue eyes.

"Be careful," he said quietly.

"Always," Carl said in a surprised voice. Gray was the last person he would have expected to worry about him. "Is there any particular reason I should be?" he asked suspiciously.

"Thiago's in a rage," Gray said seriously as he looked up and into Carl's eyes unwaveringly. "There's never any telling what he'll do when he's like this."

LVIII.

"I won't let you do it," Remy declared heatedly as soon as Brandt and Carl had left Shawn alone with him.

"You don't really have much say in it," Shawn said pointedly as he unhooked his shoulder holster and laid it carefully on the little built-in seat in the corner of the room.

"You son of a–"

"Remy," Shawn said sternly as he turned quickly, gripping Remy's arms and shaking him slightly. "I'm the only one who can do this, and you know it," he said as he held Remy at arm's length.

"Bullshit! You're looking for an easy fucking way out, and *you* know it. What are you running from, Shawn? Is it me?" Remy asked with a worried expression that broke Shawn's heart. "If it is, then I swear you don't have to. After this is done, I'll disappear and you won't have to deal with me ever again, just don't… don't go back to them, Shawn. Please," Remy begged as Shawn gaped at him.

"I would never run from you," Shawn insisted as his fingers dug into Remy's arms possessively. "I've done you wrong at every possible fucking turn, lad. You have to know that I hate meself for it. But you have to let me do this."

Remy frowned and looked at him intently. "You've never done me wrong, Shawn. Not in my mind you haven't," he said with certainty. Shawn stared at him in disbelief.

"Remy, how can you say that?" he asked in a breathless whisper as he dropped his hands to his sides and took a slightly stunned step backwards. "I've been nothing but horrible to you. I've lied and–"

"You don't need to list your offences, *bebette*, I remember most of them. My ass says to say hello," Remy said in a flat, almost amused voice.

The corners of Shawn's mouth twitched in amusement at the pet name Remy had used. Obviously Remy had forgotten the thrashing he got for calling Sean a 'little monster' the last time.

"*Bebette*?" Shawn repeated in amusement.

Remy shrugged and smirked. "We're both too tired to kick the shit out of each other again. I figure I can use it if I want." His smile disappeared as he looked at Shawn solemnly. "You're the only friend I've ever had, *podna*," he asserted in a soft, serious voice. "That's all I know right now, and that's what I'll take with me when I go."

"Remy," Shawn protested in a stunned voice that he wasn't sure belonged to him.

Go? Remy couldn't go anywhere.

"I won't let you do it," Remy said as he stepped closer to Shawn and held out his hand with his palm up as if asking for Shawn to take something from him. "You're burnt out and you're half-deaf and you've proven to them that you're no longer loyal. I know it hurts you, Shawn, but they can no longer trust you, and you know it. They would never let you back in. I have a much better chance of getting back than any of the rest of you do, and I have the only chance of staying alive once I'm in."

"Fuck," Shawn groaned as he ran his hands through his hair in agitation.

Remy was right. Their only hope was to reinsert a member of their group back into the Organization; someone who could then muck up the investigations enough to allow the other six to go to ground without exposing himself as a mole. Nikolaus, with his computer skills and the access they afforded him, was the most likely of the seven of them to be able to divert the attention they would receive, but he was far too vulnerable. He didn't have the devious quality that would be necessary, regardless of how easily he'd fooled all of them. He'd proven he was far too gullible and trusting, despite his experience as an agent.

Shawn didn't want to risk any of the others on this, anyway. That was why he had volunteered himself, though he probably didn't have the ability to evade detection that Remy did. He could at least take care of himself if he was found out.

Even so, Shawn hated to admit it to himself, but Remy was right.

The younger man was the only one with both the know-how and the charisma to pull it off. Shawn just didn't want to see the other man heading back into the lion's den alone. Never alone.

LIX.

"I don't get it," Nikolaus whispered as he slid down the wall of the compartment to sit on his haunches and look up at Gray, who had yet to move since Carl left them almost an hour before.

"What part of what just happened didn't you follow?" Gray asked flatly. Nikolaus found himself actually missing the smart-ass smirk that was seemingly forever evident in Gray's voice.

"I've never seen Thiago crack like that," Nikolaus said in a soft voice. "He's always the one breaking up fights and sitting on Brandt when he tries to blow something up. He just didn't strike me as the type to… to just… "

"The type to what?" Gray asked in a tired, almost challenging voice as he finally raised his head and looked at Nikolaus. "Be angry when he's betrayed and lied to? Lose it when he finds out his lover and partner of five years has been running around with another man and liking it? He didn't just crack, Faust, he figured me out. He knew I was lying to him and he fucking lost it. Any one of us would've done the same."

"I don't think I would have. Not like that. That was vicious."

"He kills people for a living, he was nowhere near vicious," Gray spat heatedly.

Nikolaus frowned and shook his head.

"Open your fucking eyes!" Gray shouted. Nikolaus looked at the door nervously and made a gesture with his hands for Gray to quiet down. Gray huffed in annoyance. "You're a secret agent," he whispered intently. "A fucking commando. Shit goes down every day that would break a normal person; we live with it and we move on because we aren't fucking normal, Nikolaus. We don't play by life's rules, and–"

"It may go down, but it's never your lover that does it, is it?" Nikolaus asked angrily. "Thiago fucked Remy, too, Gray. And Shawn and Carl," he informed Gray as the man stood up and began to pace restlessly in the confined space. "Why would he take exception to you doing the same? I mean, it's obvious that you and Remy–"

Nikolaus gasped and his words cut off short as Gray darted toward him and grabbed him by the collar of his shirt, pulling him roughly to his feet. He was slammed against the wall with Gray's forearms at his throat. Gray held him on his toes just like Remy had pinned Evan Washburn back in Prague.

"There's a difference between fucking and fucking and then lying about it," Gray snarled. "Especially when it meant more than just getting information," he whispered feelingly as his breath ghosted across Nikolaus's face. "At least it did on my side of it," Gray amended as he let go of Nikolaus's collar and rested his hands instead on Nikolaus's shoulders as he straightened out Nikolaus's shirt in a disturbingly tender gesture.

"You're saying you're in love with Remy?" Nikolaus asked in confusion.

Gray's grip tightened on Nikolaus's shoulders briefly before he pushed away from the other man to resume his pacing.

"Kincaid?" Nikolaus prodded as he looked out at Gray incredulously. Gray closed his eyes and sighed. "But I thought you and Thi were… I mean… what?"

"This is getting too fucking complicated," Gray murmured. Nikolaus watched him sympathetically as he flopped back down onto the lower bunk with a frustrated sigh.

"Do you think him about him every waking minute, Gray?" Nikolaus asked in a businesslike tone.

Gray's head shot up and they locked eyes for several long seconds. "What?"

he asked incredulously.

"You heard me. Do you think about him all the time and worry about his safety when he's gone? Are you barely restraining yourself from jumping up right now and stalking out there to find him?"

"Not really," Gray answered in a hesitant, confused voice.

"I'd wager that, right now, Shawn has him in the other compartment on his knees, fucking him senseless. Are you thinking about that? Picturing it in your mind and letting the jealousy take over your other emotions?"

"I… no. I hadn't really thought of it," Gray said softly as he looked around uncomfortably and finally forced his eyes back to Nikolaus.

"Your mind's on Thiago right now," Nikolaus stated assuredly. "Even after what he did to you, you're still worrying about him, aren't you? Wondering where he is? What he's doing? Whether he's okay? Whether he's gone mad and leapt from the train or called in the Feds to take us all away."

Gray blinked and swallowed with difficulty. "Yes," he whispered in a voice so soft that Nikolaus barely heard it.

"Well then, that's not complicated at all," Nikolaus said with a smile.

"Yes it is," Gray argued in a hoarse voice. "Thiago doesn't… he's not the type to understand this sort of… fuck," he murmured as he rubbed his eyes and let his head fall back into his hands. "I do better with guns than feelings."

Nikolaus frowned sympathetically and tried to remember if Gray had slept at all since he and Remy had reappeared. Nikolaus didn't think he had. He was pretty sure the two of them had endured a long road to get to them, especially considering that Remy had been injured– and decidedly altered– when they arrived. Gray had probably been playing nursemaid for quite a while.

"When was the last time you slept?" Nikolaus asked the other man gently.

"The plane from Sydney," Gray answered without raising his head.

"You should sleep, then."

Gray nodded and rubbed his face, scratching his fingers through the course beard he had managed to grow.

"How long were you under before you showed up in Sydney?" Nikolaus asked as he forced his body to relax.

"Not fucking long enough," Gray mumbled. "Not deep enough, either. I was still hearing all kinds of talk coming through the underground. About you six and–"

"Through the underground?" Nikolaus asked as his interest was piqued and a memory was rekindled.

"Yeah?" Gray said as he looked up at Nikolaus curiously, sensing the change in Nikolaus's interest. "It's a sort of… I don't know, gossip that goes through the Archer's people. It–"

"The underground?" Nikolaus repeated incredulously

"Not the Big Bad Underground of the Organization," Gray said quickly. "That's a coincidence."

"Evan Washburn said something about that in Prague; about hearing something through the underground," Nikolaus said thoughtfully.

"Prague?" Gray asked in alarm. "Evan Washburn was in Prague?"

"Yeah. He–"

"When?"

"About two months ago when Remy and–"

"Fucking hell," Gray cursed as he stood abruptly, barely missing whacking his head on the upper bunk. "I have to find Thiago."

LX.

BRANDT watched the scenery fly by as the train hurried them toward Washington, D.C. He narrowed his eyes at the opaque reflection of himself in the window and cocked his head to the side.

Something was wrong. The hair on the back of his neck stood on end and his every sense told him to move, to get to the others and protect them.

But he simply stood there and shivered, trying to convince himself that the others were safe. They'd checked the train. They'd covered their trail. Carl was on watch and everything was fine.

Carl came in about an hour ago and told him about what happened between Thiago and Gray. That worried Brandt more than he cared to admit. Thiago was a ruthless bastard, to the point that Brandt found his mild, caring behavior around the six of them the past six months quite odd. So odd, in fact, that he'd at first questioned his identification of the other man.

He saw Thiago exhibit some cruel and unusual behavior during their brief mission together five years ago, and the rumors of punishments handed out to the Archer's men who didn't do what they were supposed to do were truly horrific. What he had done to Gray, that was more like the Thiago Brandt knew. But what caused the sudden shift from cruel to unassuming and back to cruel again?

Brandt was so engrossed in his thoughts that when the door to the sleeping compartment opened, he spun around and pulled his gun on Thiago as the other man entered. Thiago stopped short and raised his hands slowly, and he stood staring at Brandt until the gun was lowered.

"You a little tense?" Thiago asked in his calm, gruff voice.

"Could be," Brandt said defensively as he re-holstered his weapon. "Have you seen Trigger?"

"I passed him on the way here," Thiago said softly with a flick of his thumb over his shoulder. "He was in the dining car, doing his rounds. What's wrong?"

"We have to talk, mate," Brandt said as he took off his shoulder holster and flung it onto the upper bunk. Thiago watched Brandt unerringly, the motion of the slinging gun not even causing his eyes to flicker. He was on high alert, and Brandt licked his lips nervously. Why would Thiago be on high alert?

"Okay," Thiago finally said with a little nod. "What about?"

"You have to let me know what's going on. Something's changed, I can feel it."

"Brandt–"

"Don't make me threaten you, mate, I'm too bloody tired to come up with something clever so I may just stick a grenade up your ass and watch you go boom."

"Nothing's changed," Thiago insisted as he walked over to the bunk and sat down heavily. "Just… you know, enjoy the ride. We're safe, for now."

"Uh huh. That why you're so bloody alert? I heard what you did to Kincaid," Brandt hissed accusingly. Thiago didn't look up at him, but he flinched almost imperceptibly and Brandt frowned at him. "Why'd you do it? What happened?"

"I snapped," Thiago admitted in a businesslike tone that Brandt found quite disturbing. "He's hiding something from me. I can feel it."

"Doesn't give you the right to do what you did," Brandt maintained with a frown. "Beat the shit out of a prisoner, sure. Hell, set them on fire, even. But never that to a friend."

"The right?" Thiago asked in a soft, dangerous voice as he looked up at Brandt from under lowered brows. He stood suddenly and looked at Brandt as if he was about to devour him, and Brandt took an involuntary step back. "You forget who's in charge of this thing, my friend," he said in a deliberate, threatening growl.

Brandt thought briefly about reminding Thiago of the extensive fuck up the whole operation had become while under his control, but the look in Thiago's eyes made him think twice about it. This didn't look like someone who would have lost control of any operation, no matter how large or complicated. Was this even the same fucking person?

"You've gone round the bend, mate," Brandt whispered as he took another step back and hit the wall with the heel of his foot. Thiago narrowed his eyes and cocked his head, and then to Brandt's immense surprise, the other man threw his head back and laughed.

Actually fucking laughed.

"Oh, that's fucking rich, coming from you!" Thiago howled as he laughed joyously and flopped back onto the bunk.

Brandt huffed defensively and relaxed a little. "Hey, I know fucking insane when I see it."

LXI.

REMY had briefly fallen into a restless sleep, but now he lay awake and plotting.

How would they go about reinserting him into the Organization? It would have to be a pretty extensive masquerade; a betrayal of some sort. They would have to make it seem that he had turned on the other men, that he had been working for the Organization all along, trying to be subversive, and that he was now getting out and skittering back home like a good little puppy.

The real kicker was that it would have to be done in front of trusted O.R.G. agents, to ensure that the charade was accepted, and it would have to be believable. Bloody, in other words.

Bloodshed was inevitable, it seemed.

Remy jumped when Shawn's feet thumped the ground. He turned his head on the thin pillow and looked at him in surprise as the other man knelt beside him in the position in which he had landed.

"What are you doing?" Remy asked in his normal voice, ever mindful of Shawn's lack of hearing.

"Even I can hear you down here sighing," Shawn responded with a little smile. "Scoot your skinny ass over."

"No. I just got my spot warm. Bastard," Remy protested as Shawn lifted the blanket off him and sat on the edge of the bunk expectantly.

"I'll keep you warm," Shawn assured him with a wink. "Now scoot."

Remy smiled at him briefly and scooted over to the wall. It was a thin bunk, regardless of how much he scooted over, and Shawn slid in behind him and held onto him tightly to keep himself from falling over the edge.

"Want to make a pallet on the floor?" Remy asked in a muffled voice even as he sank into Shawn's familiar embrace. The exhaustion was overwhelming. He just wanted to be held for the rest if his days and die happy.

"If I were planning on shagging you, I would," Shawn said with a little laugh. "But this suits my purposes just fine for now," he added as he buried his nose in Remy's short hair. "Reminds me a bit of Toronto," he said softly after several long minutes of silence.

"Yeah," Remy agreed as his chest tightened painfully.

"Remy–"

"Shawn, don't. Even if you have finally driven me crazy, I can only be broken so many times," Remy said softly. "Doesn't matter if you love me or not. All that matters is that I can't imagine life without you, and I won't let you go back to them."

"Let me say this before you go all Babbling Cajun on me," Shawn said sternly, his breath gusting against the back of Remy's neck.

Something in his voice made Remy's breath catch in his throat, and he was aware of every involuntary twitch of his own body as he rested tensely in Shawn's arms and waited for him to continue. Shawn held him close and seemed to be gathering his thoughts, but finally Remy's patience wore out and he snuggled closer to the other man.

"Just get some rest, *non*?" he said quietly.

"Fuck it," Shawn growled in disgust. Remy tried to turn to face him but Shawn held him tight. "I love you, Remy," Shawn admitted softly. "I should have told you a long while ago, and meant it. I'm a complete shit for not doing it before this, but I will make it up to you."

"Shawn–"

"You can't go back in."

"But–"

"I'll do anything, including resorting to dirty tricks, to make sure you stay with me."

"Pulling out the dirty tricks threat, huh?" Remy said thoughtfully as a smile spread over his lips.

"You've seen what I can do," Shawn said with a grin apparent in his voice as he hugged Remy closer.

Remy nodded, but his smile faded as he thought about what Shawn had just told him. The more he thought about it, the more disturbed he became. Finally, he squirmed and rolled until he was lying on his sore arm and facing Shawn.

Shawn watched him worriedly, looking self-conscious for perhaps the first time in Remy's knowledge.

Remy leaned forward and kissed him chastely. "I love you, Shawn. I do. But it's too late for us," Remy said sadly. "You know I have to do this.

LXII.

THIAGO waited until Brandt's easy, steady breathing indicated that the bigger man was asleep, and he moved silently to the door of the sleeping compartment. He'd expected to have to wait quite a long time, but Brandt's head hit the pillow and he had been out in minutes.

He hesitated at the door and took several deep breaths to calm himself.

He'd done his best to break away, but the pressure had obviously gotten to him. He'd hurt Gray. That wasn't what he was supposed to be. That wasn't who he was. He had to go to him and apologize, even if words couldn't make it right.

He would never be able to make that right.

First, though, he had to take care of this.

He opened the door slowly and listened for footfalls for several long moments. Hearing nothing over the roar of the train, he stepped out quickly and slid the door closed with a muffled thump.

He had to find a phone. A landline, preferably, but a cell phone would do. Thiago knew that they had no hope of escaping the Organization, especially now that both sides were after them. It was time to pick the lesser of two evils and beg for mercy. He had to call Thierry St. John and give himself up. Or give himself back, at any rate.

As Thiago prowled through the cars of the train in search of a phone, he thought back on how this entire fucking mess started. It seemed surreal, even to a man who led the life Thiago led.

The Organization was headed by what was affectionately called the Committee. Up until about five years ago, Thiago had been blissfully unaware of the Organization's dual personalities, but now he knew the Committee was split right down the middle.

Thierry St. John and Sir John McTiernan, who had both proven themselves to be devious, lying bastards, were the Underground's representatives on the Committee. They roped Thiago into this by methods that Thiago still couldn't quite straighten out, and they kept him in it with threats, promises, and just outright bribery.

Hugh Wallace and Claude Bryce-Johnson represented what Thiago had come to think of as the clean side of the Organization. The good side. The side he'd signed up to serve when he had been young and idealistic. They were both good men. Intelligent men. And unfortunately, they were also clueless men, at least as far as the actions of their dark counterparts were concerned.

Eduard Rollins was one mean, scary, war-hardened son of a bitch, and he oversaw the entire thing. Thiago had wondered at times if Rollins was aware of Thierry's machinations, but he'd always been too much of a coward to inquire into it. It wasn't exactly like Thiago had access to Rollins, anyway. He couldn't just stroll into the man's office and start pointing fingers at his underlings. And besides, if Rollins were aware of it all, then it was probably he who instigated the whole thing in the first place, and then Thiago would really be in the shit.

The original plan was simple, but it had taken Thiago a while to finally figure it all out.

Thierry was planning a coup. He'd been planning it all along, and Thiago had simply been his pawn all this time. Thiago knew this. It wasn't a surprise; he'd known it from the beginning. But it still irked him.

His initial instructions were to do just what Thiago was thought to have been doing all along; round up agents and turn them or kill them. It was very simple, and Thiago had at first taken them to be traitors, hence the need to off them. Thierry gave him a specific list of agents to take out, but Thiago later discovered they were all clean agents.

That had started his inquiries. He found out about the Underground and the Black Agents. He found out about the Hunters, and in so doing had begun to wonder what he was doing if the Hunters were charged with the job of taking out traitors and moles.

Then it hit him. Thierry was trying to turn the entire Organization. He was trying to take control of what was likely the most powerful security agency on earth. He was instigating an Organizational Civil War, and he was weakening the other side agent by agent in preparation. Not only that, but he was using Thiago and his recruits to do it.

To subvert Thierry's plan, Thiago ordered his men to simply fake the deaths of the agents they marked. He was no cold-blooded killer, and these were his brothers-in-arms, most of them not even lead agents, but simply technical support.

Thierry knew who the real strength behind the Organization was, and he'd aimed for the jugular. But Thiago threw quite the wrench in Thierry's plans, and when Thiago was ordered to join this crew in order to stop his own detection, only to have the cabin blown up by an unknown who, at the time, he'd been sure was one of his own men, Thiago knew he'd had enough.

He stopped communicating with the Archer ranks. He stopped reporting in to Thierry. He simply existed as one of the Six, and until the secrets were spilled, he was content for the first time in half a decade. Now, though, he had no choice but to go crawling back. It was the only way to save all their lives.

Thiago clenched his fists in anger and frustration as he finally spotted a courtesy phone in the now empty lounge car. It was mid-afternoon, and apparently it was a downtime for the food service people. The server washing down seats paid him no mind, and so he stepped up to the phone and dialed the number from memory.

Thierry answered on the first ring, but Thiago had to attempt speech three times before he was able to speak.

"St. John," he said in a hoarse, angry voice.

"Archer? Bloody hell!" Several obscenities and a flurry of shouted instructions to someone in the background followed, and Thierry's voice came back on the line in an excited rush of words. "Location and status!" he demanded. "Oh, fuck that shit! Where the fuck are–"

"Thierry, shut up and listen," Thiago said through gritted teeth. "There are seven primaries. Location is in transit, heading toward D.C. from New Orleans via train. We have Hunters on our tail, Thierry, you have to call them off."

"General opinion around here is that you've all turned on us, Thiago," Thierry said in a hushed, agitated voice as papers shuffled and what sounded like a cup full of pens scattered across a hard surface.

"I haven't," Thiago answered testily, lying through his teeth and clenching his fist in anger once more. "Things got a bit tight around here, I had to go under."

"That last message you left us indicated that you had indeed turned," Thierry argued in a calmer voice. "Though it was a bit out of character. Care to translate it?"

"I didn't send that message, Thierry," Thiago said worriedly. Quite frankly he'd forgotten about the damn thing. "Someone in the ranks has found us both out. I think it could possibly be Fletcher Barclay."

"Why do you say that?" Thierry asked with interest as something clicked and whirred in the background.

"Because he knew I was one of the Six," Thiago said with a frustrated sigh.

"How in the hell–"

"I told him as a backup," Thiago growled. "In case something happened to me, he was to take the lead. He must have figured it was an opportunity for career advancement and tried to take me out," Thiago reasoned, knowing damn well it wasn't the truth. Fletcher was certainly after him, but it wasn't for career advancement. Fletcher had figured Thierry out, too, and in all likelihood he thought Thiago was in on it. It tore Thiago apart to be the adversary of the good guy. "Someone took a shot at us in Sydney and missed," Thiago continued resignedly. "Remy and Nikolaus tried to find him in Scotland with no luck, and by all other accounts, he's completely off the reservation. It has to be him."

"He's not next in line, though, why didn't you tell Kincaid?"

"*Te voy a romper el orto*, Thierry, I'm a little short on time here!" Thiago hissed as he looked around warily in search of Carl or Gray doing their rounds. "Gray wants no part of heading this shit up. Just find Barclay. Call off the Hunters. Have a whole shitload of agents waiting in D.C. with orders not to fucking kill us, and end this goddamned clusterfuck of a mission before anyone else dies!"

"Will do," Thierry said with urgency, and Thiago could tell that the man was giving orders even as he slammed the phone down angrily. Thierry was an evil bastard, but at least he was efficient. And he took care of his men.

Thiago was practically shaking with frustration. The seven of them wouldn't escape the clutches of the Organization this time. They would be lucky to escape with their lives.

He closed his eyes and shook his head sadly, and as he opened them to turn and go find Gray to beg for forgiveness, the only things he saw were the courtesy phonebook being swung toward his head, and the angry snarl on the face of the man wielding it.

LXIII.

CARL swung through the first blow and winced at the heavy thwack of the phonebook hitting the side of Thiago's face, but he used the momentum of the first blow to swing the thing again in a backhanded uppercut phonebook smackdown, and he caught Thiago under the chin with the second blow. The man went down like a load of bricks, and Carl briefly mused that he would have to patent that move. Death by phonebook.

He immediately dropped the phonebook to land with a heavy thud beside Thiago's unmoving body, and he crossed the dining car with the frightening swiftness and agility of a large cat to grab the server before she could even turn to run. He wrapped one arm around her torso, trapping her arms against her as he picked her up off the ground, and he covered her mouth with his other hand as he held her tight against his own body.

"Quit struggling, dear, I don't want to have to hurt you," he whispered threateningly into her ear.

She continued to utter muffled cries for help and kick her legs uselessly, and Carl used his middle finger to dig into her cheek, right at the tender joint of her jaw, in order to let her know that he was serious. She let loose a muffled cry of pain and went limp obediently.

"There's a good girl," Carl whispered soothingly, hoping to hush the girl without getting any more trouble from her. He had no intention of hurting her, but if she was going to give them away, he'd kill her without a second thought.

Even with the girl motionless and quiet in his arms, Carl still had a problem. He couldn't exactly drag Thiago or the girl through the train to their sleeping compartments, much less both of them. He couldn't let the girl go now, not by any stretch of the imagination, and he couldn't simply leave her and Thiago tied up there in the middle of the dining car while he went to the others to tell them about what he had just overheard.

That didn't include the problem of Thiago himself. He'd betrayed them. Lied to them. Turned them in and forfeited all of their lives for his own safety.

Fucking bastard.

"Listen, darling, and listen carefully," Carl said quietly into the girl's ear. She shivered and trembled, but nodded her obedience enthusiastically, even though she must have been extremely frightened. Carl was impressed. "We're going to walk calmly through this train, together, all the way to my room, and you're going to be very quiet while we do it, understand?" She nodded again. "One misstep and I'll snap your neck," he assured her in a growl.

She nodded vigorously once more, and Carl lowered her carefully until her feet were touching the ground. As soon as her feet had gained purchase, she stomped on the instep of Carl's right foot with a muffled shout and jabbed back at his torso with her elbow. He released her instinctively and doubled over as the wind was temporarily knocked from his lungs, and she ran for the door of the dining car.

It opened as she reached it and she flew into the arms of the man entering, wrapping her arms around his neck in relief and babbling about Carl's attack on the 'poor guy on the phone' and his subsequent attempt to 'kidnap and rape her.' She finished by begging the man to 'kick the shit out of him, please.'

Gray held the girl in his arms comfortingly and looked down at Carl with a confused frown. Carl shook his head and straightened back up, rubbing his stomach gingerly. He quite liked this girl; she had spirit, if not really horrible luck.

"Poor girl," he said to Gray sympathetically. "Shit for luck, really, to run into you as she's trying to get away from me."

Gray nodded absently and held the girl tight as her eyes widened in horror and she tried to wrench away.

"Who have you killed, now?" Gray asked flatly. "Stop struggling, woman, we won't hurt you unless you ask for it," he said testily as he covered her mouth in expectation of a scream.

Carl nodded toward Thiago, who was unmoving on the ground and bleeding from his mouth where his teeth had probably cut into his tongue.

"I caught him on the phone," Carl explained as Gray looked at his boss and lover impassively. "He was speaking to St. John," Carl muttered as he walked over to the other two and looked down at the girl with a frown. "We had a deal, love," he growled at her.

"Don't scare her," Gray scolded as he held her tightly to him, whether to comfort or restrain her, Carl didn't know. "Jesus, you're as bad as Brandt sometimes," he chastised. "Thierry, huh? Then those fucking rumors were true," Gray muttered as if he was talking to himself. "Goddamn you, Thiago," he hissed bitterly.

Carl frowned at him and waited for further explanation, but none came. The girl was beginning to tremble and whimper against Gray's hand. Carl chewed on the inside of his cheek thoughtfully.

"Let's take them both with us, then, get them the fuck out of the open," Carl said after a few moments of pondering their situation. "You can explain what the fuck you're on about to all of us at the same time."

"Yeah, everyone will certainly need to know now," Gray agreed absently. "There's some serious fucking trouble coming our way."

LXIV.

SHAWN didn't wake until he was halfway to the floor. He landed on his back with a whuff and lay there, stunned, until he got his bearings and regained his breath.

Remy had rolled and shoved at him, which was why he was now on the floor with a swiftly developing headache instead of being spooned up behind Remy's warm body. But that didn't explain why Remy stood at the door with a gun held up by his shoulder and his head cocked, listening to something Shawn couldn't even begin to hear.

Shawn rose to his elbows and raised an eyebrow inquiringly at the other man. Remy brought his finger to his lips and shook his head. He then held up three fingers, frowned, and held up four.

Shawn got quickly to his feet and retrieved his gun from its holster, and he stood against the wall opposite the bunks, waiting for Remy's cue.

A soft knock sounded, which threw Shawn briefly, since attackers didn't normally knock first to get your okay. Remy looked at him quizzically before curtain to peer out.

"Jesus!" the younger man hissed just before he threw the door open and pulled their visitors into the compartment.

Shawn watched in confusion as Gray carried the little server girl from earlier into the room. Nikolaus followed them, looking worried and carrying an armload of bed sheets, and Brandt and Carl struggled through the door, carrying Thiago's limp body between them.

"What happened?" Shawn asked hastily as they laid Thiago on the ground and Gray set the unfortunate girl on the lower bunk with a hissed warning to keep quiet. Remy closed the door and looked at all of them in confusion.

"We have a serious problem," Gray told them grimly as he straightened up and turned around.

"That's rather obvious, numbnuts, what the bloody hell have you done?" Shawn demanded angrily.

"I don't happen to be the cause of this particular disaster, asshole!" Gray shot back angrily.

"Both of you, shut it!" Carl said authoritatively as he knelt beside Thiago. "Listen. Thiago's turned us in. I caught him on–"

He was interrupted by the rest of them all spewing questions at once and protesting that Thiago would never turn them in, but Shawn noticed that Gray was silent. Just that fact was enough to tell him that Thiago was entirely capable of turning on them. If his own lover and right-hand man wasn't defending him, then there had to be a good reason.

"Shut up!" Carl shouted in a frustrated, dangerous growl. They all fell obediently silent. "I caught him on the phone with Thierry St. John. I heard him say Thierry's name and tell him that he was short on time. I heard him tell Thierry to call off the Hunters, something about Gray not wanting any part in something, and to find Barclay. He then told Thierry where we were heading and to have men waiting in D.C. He gave specific instructions not to have us killed and to end the mission. Even if he was trying to protect us, he fucking turned us in, all the same."

"Why would Thiago turn us in? To Thierry, of all people?" Nikolaus asked desperately. "Isn't he the… the bad one? I mean, wouldn't Thiago have called Wallace or Bryce-Johnson if he were giving himself up?"

"There was…." Gray trailed off and looked suddenly at the girl, curled up and cowering in the corner trying to escape everyone's attention. At least she wasn't screaming her head off. "Fuck me, what are we going to do with her?"

"Kill her," Shawn ordered immediately. "We don't need to deal with her."

"Hold on," Remy urged as he stepped over Thiago's body and shoved Gray to the side. "Come here, darling," he said softly.

The girl was trembling now and her eyes were darting back and forth between Remy and Shawn like a cornered animal. Shawn narrowed his eyes at her and she shrank further into the corner.

"Shawn! Stop it!" Remy scolded as he turned to glare at Shawn, and he held his hand out to the girl. "It's all right, lovely, no one will hurt you. You remember me, *non*? From before?"

She was practically hyperventilating now, but she looked at Remy carefully and held out a shaking hand to him. He took it firmly in his own and pulled her out from under the bunk.

"P-please, don't hurt me," she begged in a small voice. "I haven't heard anything. I haven't seen anything. I won't tell a soul, I swear, just, please, let me go."

Remy frowned and looked over at Shawn. They all knew she couldn't be let go. Regardless of what she promised, she would eventually tell. And if the people after them knew where they were, she could be in danger as well. But what to do with her?

"All right, sweetheart," Remy said in a deep, soothing voice. "Come with me, then, we'll put you somewhere nice and safe 'til we get this straightened out."

"No! Please!" she cried in a near-panic as she dug her heels into the floor and pulled at his arm as he tried to lead her to the door. "I'll be good! I promise! Please, God, don't kill me!"

Remy clucked at her disapprovingly and pulled her to him forcefully, picking her up easily and turning to look at the others.

"Don't start without me," he requested as Shawn opened the door for him and looked both ways down the deserted aisle to make certain it was clear. As Remy passed with the now softly crying girl in his arms, he looked at Shawn and said, "I won't be long."

Shawn nodded and watched him walk down to the next compartment and open it, setting the girl down and ushering her inside with a gentle hand on her back. Remy paused before he followed her in and looked back at Shawn. Shawn nodded at him and Remy offered him a sad smile before disappearing into the room.

LXV.

NIKOLAUS wanted to pace, but the small, crowded space didn't allow for it.

"What's Remy doing with her?" he asked worriedly. If it had been one of the others, Nikolaus wouldn't have worried about her safety, but knowing that Shawn and Remy were both ruthless killers who had been assassinating innocent people for years didn't make him very comfortable in regards to the girl's fate.

"She'll be fine," Shawn said in hoarse voice.

Shawn, for one, did not look fine. Nor did Gray or Carl. In fact, even Brandt looked overly disturbed. Everyone was tense and tired enough that no one had the heart to tell the big Australian to stop flicking his new silver lighter compulsively. It was a nervous habit, just like Nikolaus's urge to pace, and Shawn's constantly running his fingers through his hair, and Gray's cracking his knuckles.

Carl didn't seem to have a nervous habit. That was disturbing in and of itself.

Remy slipped quietly back into the compartment just as Thiago began to stir. They'd tied the older man with the bed sheets Nikolaus carried in, and they left him on the hard floor where Carl and Brandt dropped him.

"Let's get to it," Remy said in a soft voice as he eased the door shut.

"Did you hurt her?" Nikolaus demanded.

"If I did, it wasn't intentional," Remy answered calmly as he eyed Thiago warily. "Now. What's going on?"

"There are some details you all need to be made aware of," Gray started as he stared down at Thiago, who was groaning and throwing his head from side to side as he fought his way back to consciousness.

"Is this something I'll need to sit down to listen to?" Remy asked in exasperation.

"If you mean will it take a long time, then no," Gray answered snappishly. "But if you're that delicate, then maybe Shawn needs to hold your hand while I talk!"

"Fuck you, Boss," Remy snapped. "I've defended you at every fucking turn, but you're starting to get up my craw! I'd just as soon shoot you as put up with this shit anymore!"

"Can we fight later, please?" Shawn asked in a tired voice.

Remy looked at Shawn with a frown, and Gray cleared his throat apologetically.

"When I was under, I kept hearing rumors," Gray explained without preamble. "Rumors about the six of you, about vigilantes tearing through the ranks, and about the Archer."

"What kinds of rumors?" Brandt asked curiously as he sat down against the wall beside Thiago's head and put his hand on the man's forehead to still his fitful movements.

"That he had been working with St. John all along," Gray answered regretfully as he sat on the edge of the lower bunk beside Nikolaus. "That his goal was not to free agents, but to get rid of them in any way possible in order to weaken the legitimate side of the Organization."

"Why the fuck didn't you tell us this earlier?" Carl demanded angrily.

"Why would I?" Gray shot back. "I don't know any of you. None of you trust me, anyway!"

"I did," Remy pointed out quietly.

Gray's mouth snapped shut and he looked up at Remy apologetically.

"I know," Gray said softly. "But I knew about you, too, that you worked for the Underground. I couldn't let on about all I knew. I didn't know how much you were really involved until it was too late."

Remy pressed his lips together into a thin line and nodded in understanding.

An inexplicable sadness washed over Nikolaus. Gray had well and truly been working without a net this entire mission, all the while thinking he had an ally in Thiago. To learn that Thiago wasn't what he said he was, after all that time, must have crushed the other man. Nikolaus put a tentative hand on Gray's shoulder, and when Gray didn't shake it off, he squeezed slightly and left it there.

"Go on," Shawn said softly.

"Well, there's not much more to tell," Gray said with a shrug. "It's hard to gauge the accuracy of rumors that come through that pipeline, since it's so fucking secretive."

Nikolaus noticed that Gray refrained from calling the rumor pipeline 'the underground,' and he thought that was probably for the best in this environment.

"But there was a lot of static over it," Gray continued with a sigh. "The Archer's people thought they'd been duped. They were angry. They wanted revenge, on Thiago and Thierry and anyone else they thought had been part of the deception."

"What does all this have to with Evan Washburn being in Prague?" Nikolaus asked curiously.

Remy perked up and Gray sighed heavily.

"Why'd you get all excited over that?" Nikolaus prodded.

"One of the messages floating around was for a meeting in Prague," Gray explained. "It was to discuss Thiago's– well, the Archer's position. When you said Washburn had been there, I knew I had to tell Thiago what I'd been hearing. If I'd known it was all true, I wouldn't have bothered looking for him."

"Is that where you got Prague, Remy?" Nikolaus asked.

"How the fuck should I know?" Remy shouted with a frustrated flop of his hands. "I heard him say Prague!" he said with a jab of his finger at Brandt.

"You may have *heard* Prague, mate, but I said fucking Tokyo," Brandt maintained with an amused smile.

"Son of a bitch," Remy murmured in frustration.

Nikolaus caught a sad smile on Shawn's face. "Wouldn't be the first time you lucked out in something like that," the man said fondly.

"Son of a bitch!" Remy huffed again as he stomped his foot.

"Anyway," Gray muttered in a confused voice. "I didn't put much stock in it at first, I mean, there was really nothing to the rumors. But when I heard that Washburn was in Prague instead of the States, I knew we were in trouble. It means all those rumors were true, and it means people are coming for us from every side."

"The States? What about Tokyo?" Nikolaus asked in confusion.

"I knew he was one of ours, of course," Brandt said as he brushed Thiago's long hair from his forehead tenderly and looked at the older man in concern. "I wasn't going to give you his real location, now was I?"

"Has anyone in this fucking room said a single word that was true in the last five fucking months?" Remy asked in exasperation.

"I have," Shawn said softly as he looked up at Remy with a soft smile.

Remy stopped in mid-hissy fit and looked at the other man sadly.

Nikolaus didn't know what the hell was going on there, but the two men looked to be fighting once again. That was just fucking great.

"I don't understand, Boss," Carl sighed with a frown. "What does it matter to us if half the fucking world met in Prague?"

"Well, if Washburn was there, then others were, too," Gray said assuredly. "And I would bet my life that it's not been the Organization after you all this time. It's been Thiago's boys."

LXVI.

"BARCLAY," Thiago croaked in the silence that followed Gray's last assertion. He cracked one eye open painfully and cleared his throat. "It's been Barclay," he said in a hoarse voice.

Brandt patted him on the head gently and motioned to Carl to wet a washcloth for him. Thiago was motionless as he lay on the floor, and he looked up at Carl accusingly.

"You hit me," he muttered in disbelief.

"You gave us up," Carl countered as he handed Brandt the wet cloth.

"You didn't have to hit me," Thiago said as he squirmed a little. "With a fucking phonebook. Twice. That was... *afano*."

"I have to say, I'm not all too sorry about it," Carl admitted. "At least it won't leave a bruise," he added in a mockingly upbeat tone that Thiago didn't seem to find comforting.

"And I didn't give us up," Thiago insisted as Brandt wiped gingerly at the blood on his lip. "I was trying to save all our lives," he asserted as he looked from Carl to Gray. "Gray," he whispered pleadingly. "I'm sorry," he croaked when Gray locked eyes with him. "I have no excuse for what I did. I know I hurt you."

Gray clenched his jaw angrily and looked away, and Brandt saw Shawn and Remy exchange a confused glance. They didn't have time to explain that ordeal to the others, though.

"Doesn't really matter now, does it?" Gray responded casually, though Brandt could clearly hear the hard edge to his voice. "We're as good as dead, thanks to you and your little phone call."

"Not true," Thiago protested in a hoarse voice. "I may have sold our souls temporarily to Thierry, but we won't be killed."

"What do you mean?" Brandt asked.

Thiago turned his head and winced as he looked up at Brandt. "I was working for Thierry," Thiago admitted in a soft voice.

"And you had the fucking nerve to have us tied up before?" Remy yelled angrily as he pointed at Shawn and then himself.

"What did he say?" Shawn asked in frustration. The man was doing much better with reading lips, apparently, to the point that Brandt kept forgetting he couldn't hear much.

"He says he's been working for St. John all this fucking time!" Remy said as he jabbed a finger in Thiago's direction. "The whole Archer operation has been backed by the Underground from the fucking beginning! What was the purpose, Thi? Weaken the other side and then take it over?"

"Basically," Thiago admitted with a groan as his head lolled to the side.

Brandt watched him sympathetically. If Carl had hit him with a phonebook, not once, but twice, the man was going to have one mother of a headache.

"So, are you a clean agent or an Underground agent?" Carl asked in a frustrated voice Brandt had rarely heard the man use.

"I was clean," Thiago said slowly, his eyes never leaving Gray's rigid form. "Until about five years ago. Just before the raid."

"All this fucking time," Gray said with a disgusted shake of his head.

"I'm sorry, *querido*, I–"

"Don't," Gray ground out angrily. "Don't ever call me that again."

The entire compartment was silent, and Brandt felt that this was vaguely familiar territory for them all. The similarities between Thiago and Gray's relationship and Shawn and Remy's relationship were beginning to lean just this side of annoying.

Especially when happy endings seemed so hard to come by.

LXVII.

"SO, what, the raid was a setup?" Remy asked as he began to place the puzzle pieces together.

"Yes. It was a way of kick-starting the men Thierry had chosen," Thiago answered in a defeated voice.

"I don't get it, why didn't he just use us?" Remy asked as he looked at Shawn. "I mean, not us specifically, but why not use Underground agents to do the work?"

"He didn't want to lose any of his own men," Thiago answered bitterly as he squirmed to make his arms comfortable beneath his body. Remy sympathized with the discomfort. He wondered if they could trust Thiago enough to untie him.

"He probably also liked the idea of making Hugh and Claude think one of their own had gone AWOL," Carl added thoughtfully.

"Let's get him untied," Remy said after a few more moments of silence.

"Are you serious?" Gray and Nikolaus asked simultaneously.

Remy frowned at them. "What the hell happened with you three?" he demanded.

Nikolaus immediately clamped his mouth closed, and Gray scowled impressively. Thiago closed his eyes and swallowed with difficulty, and Remy thought maybe he understood at least the basics of what transpired. It was obvious Thiago and Gray had a history. It was just as obvious that Thiago and Gray had gone through some sort of argument. Apparently, Thiago had lashed out at him violently.

"I see," he said softly. "Brandt, untie him."

Gray stood and walked toward the tiny toilet with a disgusted look on his face, and Brandt and Carl swiftly untied Thiago and helped him to his feet.

Nikolaus sniffed disapprovingly, but Remy stared Thiago down and crossed his arms, letting the gun rest against his bicep in a subtle reminder of what would happen if Thiago made a wrong move. Thiago rubbed his shoulders and cracked his neck, looking at Remy gratefully.

"So, what should we be expecting," Shawn asked resignedly.

LXVIII.

THIAGO looked from Remy to Shawn and glanced at Gray's back briefly before sighing heavily. Gray was refusing to look at him, Remy was watching him like a hawk, and Shawn looked even more tired than Thiago felt.

"There will be men in Washington waiting for us," Thiago told them as a sudden scuffle broke out behind him. He turned to see Carl restraining Brandt easily as the bigger man struggled to reach something that had apparently skittered beneath the lower bunk.

"Sit still, you big baby," Carl hissed as he thumped Brandt on the head from behind. "Leave it!"

Thiago closed his eyes and turned back around to look at Remy, who had merely raised an eyebrow at the altercation. Thiago blinked at him and Remy shook his head.

"I have no idea what I was just saying," Thiago admitted solemnly.

"I think you were telling all of us about what a fucking bastard you are," Gray provided caustically from within the little toilet compartment. He walked back out and glared at Thiago briefly before looking around at all the others. "The problem is not who's waiting for us in Washington. The problem is who may be on to us that we hadn't thought to fear before."

"Like Fletcher Barclay," Thiago agreed grimly.

"Why would Fletch even know you're here?" Gray asked with an exasperated sigh. "Unless, of course, that's something else you've been hiding."

"No," Thiago said sadly. "I told him because he was next in line to take over. I didn't think he'd react to the news of who was backing us quite like he has. And I knew that when you found out what was really going down, you would want no part in it. That's why I told you to go home and stay there."

Gray's tense body relaxed slightly as the implications of what Thiago just told him sank in. "You didn't expect to live through this, did you?" he asked sadly. "You weren't even going to say goodbye, were you?"

"I didn't know how," Thiago answered with a helpless shrug.

Carl cleared his throat, and they all turned to look at him. He had managed to sit on top of Brandt to restrain him, and he sat there calmly, holding out his hand with the palm open as if he were about to say something that should have been quite obvious.

"If we're all stuck in one compartment like sardines, we're not exactly hard targets if someone's after us," he said in an irritated voice. "I suggest we all split up now, and then get off at the next stop."

"No. No, Thiago and I have to go to D.C.," Remy countered.

"Remy–"

"I'm tired of arguing, Shawn," Remy said with a finality that Thiago found almost physically painful. "The five of you will get off at the next two stops. Carl, Brandt, and Nikolaus at the first, you and Gray at the second. Thiago and I will carry on to D.C., and we'll cover any trail you happen to leave from there. Shawn?"

Shawn looked up with a frown. "Hmm?"

"I want you to take the girl with you and keep her safe."

"What?"

"We can't in good conscience see her killed," Remy said apologetically. "And you'll need someone to take care of you since you're not likely to let Gray do it," he added softly with a sad smile.

Thiago stared at the other man in disbelief. "It's not going to be that easy, you know," he said in a shocked voice.

"Sure it will," Remy stated with a smile. He stepped closer to Thiago, put his hand on his shoulder, and brought his mouth to Thiago's ear. "I suggest you say your goodbyes, *podna*," he whispered with a discreet nod in Gray's direction. "We've run out of time."

LXIX.

CARL watched impassively as Nikolaus tried to calm the girl they'd essentially kidnapped. Brandt had tried it first, but his attempts nearly sent the poor thing into hysterics, to the point that Carl had been forced to shake her to get the point across that she had to be silent.

Carl didn't like being violent unless his target deserved it or could fight back, and with as many knots as Remy had tied the girl in, she really had no chance at defending herself. No wonder it had taken the younger man a whole fifteen minutes to see to the girl.

Carl had been somewhat relieved to walk into the compartment and find her wrapped up like a mummy in as many sheets as Remy could find. At least they were merely kidnappers, and not rapists as well. Not that the girl would have minded a roll around with Remy, in Carl's opinion. Shawn, though, that was an entirely different matter. One that Carl really didn't want to think about.

"Are we really going to let Remy and Thiago just give themselves over like that?" Brandt asked in a distraught voice as the girl cried quietly in the background of Carl's awareness.

"I really don't see what else we can do," Carl responded with a shrug. He felt more helpless than ever, but he was still trying desperately to keep up the appearance of calm for the other two men. Lord only knew what sort of explosive whatsit Brandt would produce if he felt cornered.

"You've got to think of something, Carl," Nikolaus urged desperately as he gave up on comforting the inconsolable woman. He looked up at Carl pleadingly as he sat on the edge of the bunk. "We can't let them just march to their doom while we saunter on our merry way to safety."

The girl began to hum and sob quietly, and she closed her eyes and started rocking. Carl realized with something akin to admiration that she was humming so she couldn't hear what they were saying. She still hoped they would let her go.

"What do you want me to do, Gizmo?" Carl asked as the desperation began to poke through his façade. "I don't know what to do any more than the rest of you! And it's not like the rest of us will exactly be *sauntering*, either. If any of us live through the year, I'll be quite impressed."

"I know that! But you knew Thierry! You were lovers, for fuck's sake! Call him! Talk to him, get him to let us all go," Nikolaus begged as he grasped for their last straws of hope.

Carl furrowed his brow and sighed sadly, and Brandt put his hand on Carl's shoulder in a familiar, comforting gesture.

"Thierry cares first and foremost for power," Carl explained bitterly. "He won't give a damn about seven men who can't offer him anything in return. All we have to give him is our skills, and to use those he has to own us. No, Thierry won't help us here."

"What about the other side? Hugh or Claude?" Brandt suggested doubtfully.

"We're too much a liability for them to trust our word against Thierry's. They would want us dead faster than St. John would," Carl reasoned mournfully.

The girl sniffed pitifully, and they all looked at her as if she'd just materialized from thin air.

"Could we take her gag out, do you think?" Nikolaus asked hopefully as he looked back at her and then up at Carl and Brandt.

Carl tilted his head and looked down at the girl. She was a pretty little thing, not beautiful by any means, but certainly not plain, either. She was of average height and average build. She had mousy brown hair with blonde streaks throughout, and a clear, healthy complexion. The most striking thing about her, though, was the color of her eyes. They were the same mesmerizing green that Shawn's were, and right now they were filled with terrified tears and looking up at Carl pleadingly.

Perhaps they could risk taking the gag out of her mouth, but they definitely needed to explain a few things to her first.

LXX.

"PLEASE don't make this any harder than it already is!" Remy practically yelled as Shawn gripped both of his arms and held him in place, preventing the younger man from turning away from him and pacing again.

"You've got to be fucking kidding me," Shawn said in disbelief as he searched Remy's brown eyes for any emotion, other than determination. What he found was so much worse. There was sadness so profound that seeing it made Shawn physically ill. His throat constricted painfully before he could get any more words out.

"If you've got any better ideas, I'd love to hear them," Remy said in a hoarse, desperate voice as Shawn's grip loosened.

"No," Shawn admitted softly. "The only thing I can think of is getting you as far away as fucking possible and keeping you safe."

"Beignet," Remy whispered as his hand came up to brush Shawn's cheek affectionately.

"I wouldn't live if I thought you were in danger every day," Shawn whispered urgently as he took a step closer to Remy and took the younger man's face in his hands. "I wouldn't live. I have to know you're out there somewhere, alive and safe. I have to know–"

"Come on, Shawn," Remy interrupted uncomfortably. "You're a rock. You're a fucking hero, man. You don't need me and you never have." The statement wasn't bitter; it was simply a fact put forth in Remy's blunt manner of speaking, and that made it all the more hard to take. Remy actually believed it and accepted it as the way of life.

Shawn laughed miserably. He let go of Remy as he stepped away and retreated to the window of the little compartment. He had always known that Remy's half of their relationship had been a little heavy on the hero worship. Remy had never really known that *he* was the real rock. Well, it was past time to change that.

"Do you have any idea how I spent the last month without you?" Shawn asked softly as he watched the countryside fly by. He could see Remy's form reflected in the window, and he watched the younger man cross his arms across his chest and shrug uncomfortably. "Do you?" he asked again as he turned around to look at Remy.

"No," Remy answered as he looked down at his feet and shuffled a little. "I know Brandt stayed with you," he said in a soft voice.

"Do you know why?" Shawn pressed.

"I think I could guess, if you really wanted to torture me in our last hours together," Remy snapped as he looked up and his eyes blazed briefly before he clamped his mouth shut and looked apologetic once more. "Sorry," he mumbled.

"He stayed with me because…." Shawn met Remy's eyes and wondered once more if he had the courage to tell the younger man the truth. He'd spent five years trying to be the hero Remy thought him to be. It wasn't easy admitting how weak he really was after all that time. He forced the words out before he could second guess himself again. "Because they were trying to keep me from killing myself, Remy. That's why I was handcuffed to the bloody bed when you found us. Every fucking chance I got, I tried to end it. I even let them put me on a bloody helicopter!" he said plaintively.

Remy straightened up and dropped his arms to his sides as he listened, and when Shawn ended abruptly with a shiver in remembrance of the helicopter ride from Hell, Remy blinked twice at him and opened his mouth to speak, then shut it once more with a disbelieving shake of his head.

"Why? Why would you do that?" he finally asked after several tense moments of silence.

"Because you," Shawn said emphatically as he stepped up to Remy once more and took his hand in a surprisingly tender gesture, "you are my world, lad. I didn't want to face the world without you in it. Whether you're with me or not is neither here nor there. I just need to know you're out there. I just need you in it."

Remy swallowed heavily and stared at Shawn for several more long moments before he launched himself at the older man and wrapped his arms around Shawn's neck. Shawn grunted from the sudden onslaught. He closed his eyes and returned the hug until his supply of air was almost cut off.

"I'll still be out there," Remy said with difficulty as he buried his face in Shawn's neck.

"You're not careful," Shawn responded as the lump in his throat threatened to develop into full-fledged tears. "I need to be there to protect you from yourself."

Remy let out a laugh that sounded more like a sob. He didn't let go of Shawn, though, and they stood there clinging tightly to one another, the steady swaying of the train their only movement as they said a final, silent goodbye.

LXXI.

NIKOLAUS frowned worriedly as Carl knelt in front of the unfortunate woman and scowled at her.

Brandt kept his distance out of necessity. For some reason she started hyperventilating every time he came near her, and Nikolaus wondered what he'd said to her earlier to make her so terrified of him.

Carl wasn't much better. He was deliberately trying to be intimidating, and he was doing such a good job that even Nikolaus felt the need to scoot away from him. But he remained by the girl's side and patted her foot comfortingly, for lack of a better body part being reachable through all the sheets in which Remy had wrapped her.

"There are a couple of rules I need to go over with you, love," Carl said in a pleasant enough voice.

The girl nodded her head and widened her eyes as if to signify that she would do anything they wanted.

"Here's the situation. We can't let you go," Carl said without preamble.

Several tears streamed down the girl's face as she looked desperately from Carl to Nikolaus, but she didn't utter a sound and Nikolaus found himself admiring her courage.

"Now, you've probably gathered that there are some very bad people after us. If we leave you here, they will kill you."

She closed her eyes and more silent tears trailed down the side of her face.

"We won't let them hurt you," Nikolaus murmured in a comforting voice as he rubbed her hair and patted her on the head. Her hair had been up in a neat ponytail, but had long since come undone during the excitement.

Carl nodded in agreement. "Now, if we take this gag out, you're going to have to be very quiet," Carl continued in a soothing voice, his gentle manner returning as he started to feel sorry for the girl. "Can you do that?"

She nodded slowly, even though she had yet to open her eyes. Carl gave

Nikolaus a nod and Nikolaus went to untie the complicated knot at the base of the girl's skull.

"Dixie can be a little overzealous when he ties these things," Nikolaus murmured to her as he tried to get it loose. "He seems to think that everyone can get out of them like he can," he added with a little smile.

She sniffed and opened her eyes as Nikolaus messed with the torn sheet.

"Do you need to cut it?" Carl asked in exasperation.

"Have you ever tried to untie one of these things? It's like a five year old's shoelace," Nikolaus griped.

Carl raised an eyebrow and smirked at him.

"Yeah, hand me your knife," Nikolaus sighed as he finally gave up on the thing. "So much for the dramatic unveiling, right *Hasi*?" he whispered to the girl as Carl reached through the hole in his pocket and retrieved the huge dagger he kept strapped to his thigh.

It sliced through the material easily and Nikolaus pulled the gag away as she opened her mouth wide and worked her jaw a little before offering a weak smile.

"Thank you," she whispered as her eyes darted between the three of them. She licked her lips and looked at Carl warily. "I'm sorry I stomped on your foot," she offered tentatively.

Nikolaus looked at Carl with a laugh and Brandt started sniggering.

"And I'm sorry I elbowed you, too," she said even more tentatively.

Carl glared at Brandt, who was giggling behind his hand and snorting in a most unbecoming manner.

"She beat you up?" Brandt finally squeaked as Carl turned to face him. "Well, no wonder you wanted to keep her gagged!" Brandt managed to say before he doubled over laughing.

"Don't mind them," Nikolaus told the girl. "If they don't have their crayons, they get a bit unruly." She smiled shyly and looked from Nikolaus to the other two men, who were now bickering loudly and poking at one another. "What's your name?" Nikolaus asked her.

"Marissa," she answered in a hoarse voice.

"Marissa, I'm Nikolaus," Nikolaus replied in a soft voice.

Behind him, Carl snatched the lighter out of Brandt's hand and held it up in front of him tauntingly before pulling it away and forcing the other man to grab wildly for it.

"Those two will probably kill each other before long, so you don't really need to know their names," he said as Carl took Brandt in a headlock and sent him once more to the ground with a thud, sitting on him and flicking the lighter in his face tauntingly as Brandt struggled to get to it. Nikolaus just sighed and looked at her with a smile. "Don't worry, you'll be going with Shawn when we leave."

"Which one was he?" Marissa asked in a small, worried voice.

"He's the one who wanted to kill you."

"Oh, good," she said in a distant voice as she watched Brandt finally get hold of the lighter and use it to set Carl's sleeve on fire.

LXXII.

"HA!" Brandt cried as Carl rolled off him and beat his burning sleeve out on the ground.

"Goddammit, Wally! I liked this fucking shirt!"

"Well it was awfully flammable for being quality material," Brandt reasoned as he sat up and leaned against the door. He winked at the girl and she shrank behind Nikolaus as best she could, tied up like she was. "Besides, burns give clothing character."

"I'll give you some fucking character," Carl grumbled as he examined his wrist for any permanent damage.

"You big baby," Brandt said with a grin. "Hey, Gizmo, why don't you untie her, yeah? She can't be comfortable in all that."

"You think?" Carl asked distractedly as he looked at his singed cuff.

"She won't run," Nikolaus said confidently as he used Carl's knife to slice carefully though the many layers of material. "Will you?"

"I'll be good, I promise," she said in a stronger voice than she had used before.

"There's a good girl," Brandt said happily. "You'll like Beignet once he gets used to you. Just do what he says; and he'll take care of you," Brandt said with a tinge of sadness. He wished he could say a final goodbye to the other man, but Remy needed this time more than he did.

"Beignet?" the girl said doubtfully.

"I wouldn't suggest you call him that," Carl advised as he rested his back against the wall and settled down.

"Is there nothing else you can do with me?" she asked desperately. "Lock me in a closet or… or throw me off the train?" she suggested hastily.

Carl and Brandt both laughed joyously.

"Shawn's not so bad," Nikolaus told her in amusement as he finished freeing her. "He'll most likely take you somewhere, threaten you not to say anything about all you've heard until you piss yourself, then leave you safe and sound in a Holiday Inn with a couple thousand dollars to get you home. He's a good man; he won't hurt you unless you do something to threaten him."

"Couldn't I go with all of you?" she asked meekly. "I mean…."

Nikolaus looked at the others and they both frowned and shrugged. "Remy surely had a reason for sending you with Shawn. He probably thought Shawn could keep you safe better than we could. Did he say anything to you when he tied you up?"

"Is that his name? Remy?" she asked curiously. Nikolaus nodded and set Carl's knife down on his knee. "He just kept telling me that he wasn't going to hurt me. I thought he was going to… I thought he brought me in here to kill me. But he kept telling me jokes and, no, he didn't really say anything about… I thought you were going to kill me," she finished with a little sniff.

Nikolaus put a tentative hand on her knee and patted her comfortingly.

"When we leave, we'll take you back in there," Carl said quietly. "If Remy says you can go with us, then we'll take you."

"You're not… you're not staying together? I thought you all were friends?" she asked in surprise.

Brandt looked at Carl and then Nikolaus, who both looked as miserable as he felt about the whole thing.

"We're supposed to leave at the next stop," Nikolaus told her quietly.

"But that's about two minutes away if that watch you're wearing is right," she said as she nodded at Nikolaus's wrist.

"Observant little thing, aren't you?" Brandt said with a fond smile. He had never had much use for the female of the species. In his limited experience, they were either afraid of him for no reason, or smarter than him. He didn't like to deal with unwarranted crying, and he didn't like being outsmarted. Granted, this one had cried a little bit, but he supposed that was warranted since he had offered to let her play with one of his grenades to cheer her up. In hindsight, that probably hadn't been the best way to go about it.

Even as Brandt mused, the train began to jerk and slow. Brandt and Carl were both pitched around on the floor as the train pulled to a stop. They sat staring at one another uncertainly as the sounds of passengers disembarking and train whistles greeted them.

"*Herren*?" Nikolaus ventured finally.

Carl looked at Nikolaus and the girl, then turned his head to stare at Brandt for several long seconds. Brandt returned the look unblinkingly. Either way, he and Carl were going to stay together. He'd promised that much. But the thought of leaving the others to the will of Fate didn't settle well with Brandt at all.

"For the first time in my life I have people I call my friends," Carl said finally as his jaw took on a determined set. "I wouldn't like myself very much if I abandoned them now."

Brandt smiled grimly and nodded. "We take it to the end, then," he said gravely.

They sat in silence as the train vibrated beneath them. This was their stop, but they weren't about to get off now. Brandt thought that he'd never felt so relieved in his life. At least they would all go down together.

Suddenly, the door at Brandt's back was forced open, sending him rolling backward as he was caught off balance. Carl jumped to his feet and knocked the first man back with a powerful punch to the face, and Nikolaus stood protectively in front of the girl, wielding the knife Carl had given him as three men invaded their little compartment. Even the girl got in a good kick or two as the intruders grabbed at her, but the compartment was simply too small to allow the four of them to defend themselves, and they were quickly overpowered.

LXXIII.

"OH, shit," Remy breathed as his eye caught movement outside the window of their compartment. Remy pulled away from Shawn's arms and slid around the other man's body.

"What's wrong?" Shawn asked in a voice hoarse from restrained tears as he stood where Remy had left him in the middle of the compartment, facing the door and rubbing his face in an exhausted manner. Remy wiped at his own damp eyes as he stepped to the side of the window and looked out.

"We have guests," Remy announced as he watched the men outside crabwalk along the side of the train and then board it. "Time for Plan B."

"There's a Plan B?" Shawn asked doubtfully as he walked to stand beside Remy and look out. They weren't worried about being seen, it was already too late for that. "If there's a Plan B, then why in the hell were we going through with Plan A?"

"Because in Plan B I have to kill you," Remy said as he bent over and rifled through his bag.

"I think I rather liked Plan A better, in that case," Shawn murmured gloomily as he peered out the window.

Finally, Remy found what he was looking for and he grinned. It was really a miracle that his equipment had survived the entire mission. Remy hadn't been able to spend much time with it, but they had still ended up in the same place, in the end.

Remy stood up and looked at Shawn, preparing to explain his hastily thought out plan further. He stopped and stared before he could a get word out. Shawn looked at him intently and frowned.

"You're going to stab me with that big mother of a knife again, aren't you?" the older man asked in a defeated voice.

Remy smiled affectionately and let his hand come up to brush a stray lock of hair from Shawn's face. "Yeah," he said apologetically. There was an underlying sense of urgency surrounding them, but for several long moments they simply stood there looking at one another longingly. "But don't worry, *podna*," Remy finally said as he shook himself out of a near trance and gave Shawn a cheeky wink. "I've got the hang of the switch this time. Here," he said as he handed Shawn the blood capsule he had fished from his bag. "Makes it more fun," he said in response to Shawn's dubious look.

"Is it real blood?" Shawn asked as he examined the little plastic capsule.

"I don't think so. It's a Halloween thing. You know, you put it in your mouth and bite it… vampire costume," Remy said with a careless wave of his hand just before he unbuttoned his jeans and dropped them to the floor. He then bent and strapped his knife to the inside of his thigh before pulling on the loose pair of track pants he had retrieved from his bag. Shawn handed him a dagger and he cut a hole in the inseam and tore at it until a hand could fit through. "Can you reach it through there?"

"Yeah," Shawn answered readily as he watched Remy's hands move. "We start a fight, then? Close combat?"

"Yep," Remy said as he straightened up and looked at Shawn with a grin. Shawn nodded grimly and looked at Remy sadly. The adrenaline that had started to pump through Remy's body waned as a profound sadness hit him. "There's so much we never said," he murmured as he took a step closer and lifted his hand to smooth out the wrinkled material of Shawn's shirt.

"I love you, lad," Shawn said with difficulty as Remy's hand came up to caress his face once more. "You just remember that every time you think you want to take a stupid chance."

"I will," Remy said as his eyes began to water.

They could hear thumps coming from the next room and they both knew the attacking forces had found some of their companions. It was almost over.

"I'll find you, Shawn," Remy promised just before he moved in and kissed Shawn gently. "I don't know how long I'll be, but I'll find you," he whispered against the other man's mouth.

Shawn kissed him once more and then shoved him away before they could get lost in one another. He nodded and Remy returned the nod with one of his own.

"Let's go get ourselves captured then," Shawn said in a gruff voice.

LXXIV.

THIAGO knew he'd run out of time. He didn't have time to tell Gray how much he cared for him. He didn't have time to tell Gray that he couldn't go an hour in the day without thinking of him. He didn't have time to tell Gray that he'd never been good with words, and that he wasn't likely to develop the ability any time soon.

He didn't have time to tell Gray how sorry he was, and that he loved him and always would, no matter what happened. He only had time to get Gray away. Away and out of danger.

"It's our boys," Gray murmured as he leaned next to Thiago and looked out the window at the men moving discreetly through the crowd. "They're going to kill you, Thi."

"They're going to try," Thiago corrected through gritted teeth as he made a decision he knew would haunt him for the rest of his days. "Get the hell out of here, Gray."

"No. No, I'm staying with you," Gray said determinedly as he straightened and turned to look at Thiago with a weak smile.

Thiago could have killed himself as he looked at the other man. Even after the lies, the deception, and the abuse, Gray was still loyal to him. Probably even still in love with him.

"Did you hear what I said?" Thiago shouted, even though he wanted nothing more than to take the other man in his arms and hold him until the last possible second. This was his only option, though, if he wanted to save the other man. He shoved at Gray's shoulder for good measure. "Get the hell out of here! I don't need you, Gray," Thiago said in the most malicious voice he could muster. "I don't need you, and I don't want you with me."

Gray paled visibly and took a step back as he searched Thiago's eyes for any hint of a lie. But that was one thing that Thiago knew how to do, and he knew that Gray could search from now until the end of time, and he wouldn't find the emotions Thiago was hiding.

Thiago shoved at him again, hard enough that he stumbled backward and caught himself on the handle of the door to the compartment. He looked at Thiago incredulously.

"Thiago," Gray said almost pleadingly. "What the hell are you–"

"Shut your mouth and run like you usually do, you fucking disgrace!" Thiago shouted as desperation began to take him over. Gray had to go. Now. They were coming any minute, and Gray had to be out of sight or they'd take him, too.

Gray's mouth parted in shock and he was breathing heavily as he furrowed his brow and searched for words. "Everything you just said was another lie then," he finally said in a hoarse, barely audible voice.

Thiago's heart broke as he remembered all the words he'd just spoke, not ten minutes ago. He'd tried to convince Gray that he loved him, tried to tell him all the things he no longer had the time to prove through his actions.

And now he was taking it all back.

"Oh, for Christ's sake, Gray, I was trying to get one last fuck before you and Shawn rode off into the sunset!" Thiago said in a condescending voice as he waved his gun through the air dramatically. "You might be shit at everything else you do, but at least you're *una Buena cogida*." Thiago took a step closer and lowered his voice until it was just a menacing, disgusted growl. "If I'm going to make a last stand it won't be beside a whore like you," Thiago spat with as much disgust as he could muster as he looked Gray up and down with a sneer.

Gray's jaw clenched, and after several tense seconds of disbelief, he nodded curtly as his hand pushed at the handle on the door. He turned as he pulled the door open, and Thiago's heart dropped into his toes when he saw the man standing in the aisle with a gun pointed at Gray's face.

Gray moved on reflex only, and he knocked the gun to the side, pinning the man's arm against the doorjamb as his other hand swung toward the man's elbow joint. The arm made a sickly crunching sound when it broke, and Gray's elbow came up to hit the man's chin, knocking him back and to the ground.

Thiago's gun was up and ready as two more men came through the small doorway one at a time, but Gray's body blocked any shot he had, and the two of them were overtaken.

LXXV.

MARISSA closed her eyes and offered up a little prayer to any deity that may have been listening as she and the three men with her were all marched down the center of the train at gunpoint.

She thought she'd been scared when the big man grabbed her in the dining car as she wiped down the tables, but that was nothing compared to the complete and utter terror she was experiencing now. The German who introduced himself as Nikolaus was in front of her, his fingers laced behind his head obediently and, every few seconds risking worried glances over his shoulder to make certain she was okay.

The two bigger men walked ahead of them, each with a gun pointed at his head. The crazy one with the lighter and the grenades bled quite profusely from a cut on the back of his head. It dripped down his neck and onto his shirt, but he paid it no mind.

Marissa spared a brief thought to worry about the other passengers and her fellow employees as the four of them were led through the eerily silent train. These men weren't worrying about being discreet, and that probably meant there were no witnesses around. Wouldn't they have heard gunshots if people had been killed? What did silencers sound like, anyway? Did men like this even need guns to kill?

She kept thinking that this was all a very bad dream and she was going to wake up any second. She squeezed her eyes closed as the man behind her shoved at her to quicken her pace, and she bit her lip to try to keep from crying. Crying would probably just piss them off. She would wake up any second, anyway. Any second, now.

They were taken back to the club car, which was inexplicably empty, even though it was almost dinnertime, and Marissa and the three men were forced to their knees in front of the wall next to the little serving bar.

"Keep your fucking hands there unless you want them shot off," one of the men growled at her. She swallowed convulsively to keep from bursting into tears as he walked away. She tightened her fingers around the back of her neck and closed her eyes.

"Whose boys are these?" the one the others called Carl whispered out of the side of his mouth.

"I think it's safe to say these are not the ones we wanted to run into," the crazy one answered.

"Fuck."

Marissa sniffed and watched as the four other men were brought in. She'd hoped they'd been able to fight off their attackers and would come rescue them, which was silly, really, hoping that your kidnappers would rescue you from a second set of kidnappers. The two Marissa knew as Remy and Shawn didn't even appear to have put up a fight. The other two were in pretty bad shape, though. At least they'd fought back.

She had been afraid when these seven men had taken her hostage, but now she knew that the new players were far more dangerous than the original ones. She tried to count them, but they kept moving around as they forced the others to their knees. She thought there were ten of them. Well, nine and a half, really, if she counted the guy with the broken arm. Of course, if she was subtracting for injured body parts, then it was more like three against five instead of seven against ten. Or was it eight against ten? Did she count as a player on either side? She knew damn well that if a fight broke out, she would be hiding behind something solid, so she didn't think she counted.

There was a shorter man who was dressed all in black. He stood in front of them as soon as they had all been assembled, and in another world Marissa would have thought him to be quite cute. When he spoke, it was with a heavy Scottish accent, and Marissa could barely understand what he was saying.

"We trusted you, Thiago," he said to the man Carl had hit with the phonebook.

Thiago, who was on his knees in the middle of the car and bleeding from his lower lip, squinted up at the smaller man out of a rapidly bruising eye and grinned crookedly. "Likewise, *boludo*," he said angrily.

Shawn, who was furthest away from Marissa, turned to Remy and hissed at him, and Remy turned his head slightly and shrugged in a manner that was sure to infuriate the older man. Sure enough, Shawn began growling angrily, and the Scottish man looked up from his study of Thiago to glare at them.

"Is there a problem, gentlemen?" he asked.

"Not at all," Remy said with a huge smile. "Everything's just right with my world, how about you?"

"Oh no, Dixie," the crazy one groaned under his breath. "Now is definitely not the time to be a smartass."

"Well, what do you want me to do, Shawn?" Remy yelled in response to something Marissa hadn't heard. "They're the wrong fucking people, how was I supposed to know?"

"I don't know, but you should have!" Shawn yelled back, earning them both a whack to the head with the butt of a gun and a shouted order for silence.

Marissa's eyes burned as she struggled not to cry or make a sound. Perhaps if she simply faded into the background, they would forget about her and leave her alone.

"Fletcher," Thiago said in a low voice. The man with the accent looked down at him. "Let them go, Fletch. None of them have anything to do with this."

"You always were a complete shit," Fletcher said with an amused smile. "And even now, you're lying to me. I found out about your little deal with Thierry. And Gray had to have known what you were up to, so he's just as guilty as you are."

Marissa saw Thiago blanch. The other man, who she assumed was Gray, looked at Thiago as if he could simply melt him on the spot.

"The rest of them," Fletcher continued, "I couldn't care less about, but they're not leaving. The boys missed you twice already, but I'm not letting this go any farther. I hope you're all ready to die, gentlemen."

"This is all just one huge fuck up, Barclay," Thiago continued in a hoarse voice. "Let me explain before you–"

"No more talk," one of the other men interrupted angrily. "You've led us through Hell and back, telling us we were going home without any more bloodshed, and all so that evil bastard could take over!"

"No! No, I was trying to save lives!" Thiago insisted. "Sometimes you have to dance with the Devil in order to rectify your sins."

Fletcher rolled his eyes and pulled his weapon, pressing the barrel to Gray's temple and looking at Thiago expectantly. Gray closed his eyes and inhaled deeply. Thiago's mouth hung open as he looked up at Fletcher for several long seconds.

Finally, he clamped his teeth shut with an audible click and shook his head.

"Go ahead, Fletcher," he said casually, almost challengingly. "I don't have any information for you. Not like I give a damn what happens to him now, anyway."

Fletcher raised an eyebrow and Marissa heard two of the men next to her inhale sharply. Remy and Shawn even stopped their muttered bickering and looked on tensely.

"Is that so?" Fletcher asked with interest. "Perhaps it will just be an execution for his treachery, then." He cocked the gun and Marissa squeezed her eyes shut, not wanting to see what would come next.

"We've got company," one of the men said in a low voice, and Marissa's eyes popped back open as she watched Fletcher lower his gun and walk away from Gray and toward the window.

"Son of a bitch," Fletcher hissed angrily. "How did they find us so quickly?"

"Hey, Wally," Carl hissed, and Marissa looked at him in time to see him nod his head toward Remy and Shawn. The man he had called Wally grinned suddenly, and chills ran up and down Marissa's spine.

"If there's going to be trouble, at least let the girl go," Remy called as several guns trained on him.

"I fucking knew it!" Shawn yelled angrily as he let his hands drop away from the back of his head and he turned to glare at Remy.

"Get your hands back up, you bastard!" one of the men yelled as he pointed his gun at Shawn.

"You little shit!" Shawn snarled angrily.

"Fletch!" another one of the men shouted as Shawn growled at Remy, who was looking at him in shock.

"You fucked her, didn't you?" Shawn continued, and Remy's hands dropped, too. Shawn stood angrily, seemingly uncaring of the four weapons now trained on him. "You just can't keep your fucking hands to yourself, can you? Not for one fucking hour!"

Remy stood as well and actually gave Shawn a little shove. "You're such a jealous old biddy, you know that?" he shouted. "Christ, you complain more than the fucking girl does, and God forbid you let anyone else top for once! At least she opened her legs for me! Of course I fucked her!"

Marissa shook her head in denial of ever having been touched by any of them, but no one was paying her any attention. Their captors didn't seem to know what to make of this new development, and they simply stood with their guns at the ready as Shawn and Remy faced off.

"You fucking whore," Shawn growled, and before anyone could move, his fist had connected with Remy's chin and sent the younger man staggering backward. Shawn followed the attack by pouncing on him, and far from trying to throttle the younger man like he appeared to want to do, Shawn reached in between Remy's legs as they all looked on in shock.

Even more startling was when he pulled back with a huge knife in his hand and threw it, underhanded, at the closest man with a gun. That started it, and Marissa edged closer to the wall and curled into a protective ball as a complete melee broke out around her.

Carl reached up onto the bar and grabbed the coffee maker that sat there as Nikolaus and Wally both jumped to their feet and attacked two of the gun-wielding goons. Shawn followed through with his toss and retrieved the knife, and Remy jumped the man closest to him.

Carl threw the coffee pot at the man coming at him, sending scalding hot water and broken glass everywhere. Marissa couldn't keep her eyes off Remy, though, as he sent the man he was fighting with to his knees and then straddled his back. He wrapped one arm under the man's neck and pressed the other hand to the side of his face as an odd glaze filled his black eyes, and there was a sensual sort of pleasure in his expression when he exerted a slow, steady pressure and snapped the struggling man's neck.

Marissa's mouth fell open as she watched, and she wondered what the hell was wrong with her that the act had seemed to her so sexual in its nature.

A fire blazed merrily on the other side of the train car, and Marissa realized that it was a man on fire. The crazy guy with the lighter, who they called Wally, was apparently a pyromaniac. He hadn't been kidding about the grenades. She'd thought it was a metaphor he'd used to indicate that he was going to rape her, but there he stood, grenade in hand as he watched Carl choke the life out of a man with the power cord he'd ripped from the cash register.

Thiago and Gray both fought steadily with two men who just wouldn't give up, and Marissa nearly screamed when Nikolaus came up to her and placed a hand on her shoulder.

"Get the hell down, girl, get behind that counter," he hissed.

She nodded and turned to crawl to safety, but as she did so her eye caught movement behind Nikolaus's head and she screamed and pointed. He ducked as the chair came crashing down, and instead of hitting him in the head it glanced off his shoulder and sent him to his knees.

"Niko!" Gray yelled as he saw the man go down, but he was soon swamped by two men and couldn't get free to come to the German's rescue.

Marissa cowered. The man who had hit Nikolaus pulled a gun and pointed it at his head as Nikolaus struggled to his hands and knees.

Marissa's stomach lurched and she reached for the closest thing she could find, which happened to be the phonebook Carl dropped on the floor when he hit Thiago earlier. She stood suddenly, surprising the man standing there as he pulled back the hammer on the gun, and she threw the phonebook with all her might at the man's hands.

It hit him and knocked the weapon from his hands, and Nikolaus was able to stand and hit the man once, twice, a third time and send him to the floor, bloody and unmoving. He then turned and grabbed her, pushing her down and behind the counter as shots rang out. Nikolaus covered her body protectively with his own and she tried her best to burrow into him and disappear.

"Everybody freeze," a new voice said authoritatively.

"Oh, thank God," Marissa breathed. "It's the police," she said as relief washed over her.

Nikolaus moved to stand, and he pulled her up with him to survey the damage done. But it wasn't the police. It was simply three more black-clad, menacing goons with evil-looking weapons. The man at the head of the goon brigade grinned at them all.

"I've always wanted to say that," he said in a completely different accent from the one he had just used. "Thiago, my boy, you look to be having a bit of trouble."

"Don't 'my boy' me, you rat bastard," Thiago growled as he stepped over a lifeless body and walked up to the new man. "You're fucking late, Mikhail," he said as he snatched the gun from the Mikhail's hand and turned calmly and shot the man he'd battled with. Marissa jumped and grabbed onto Nikolaus, and he held her and shushed her automatically.

The only man left standing of the original ten attackers was the man they called Fletcher Barclay. He didn't look quite as smug as he did before, but he certainly didn't look as terrified as Marissa thought he should.

Thiago looked at the rest of them blankly for several long seconds. Carl and Wally stood side by side, looking like they'd enjoyed themselves entirely too much. Gray calmly put out the fire, and Remy helped Shawn to his feet. The three new men all looked infinitely more professional than anyone else there.

"You got Thierry's message, I assume?" Thiago finally asked.

"Yes. I'm to escort all of you home," Mikhail replied with disgust. Apparently, escorting anyone anywhere was quite beneath him.

"Fuck that," Wally growled as he fingered his lighter dangerously. Carl placed a calming hand in his arm.

"What about Fletcher?" Thiago asked as he glanced at the smaller man.

"Do whatever you want to with him. I'm not a fucking babysitter."

Thiago looked at Fletcher and nodded his head at the door to the dining car. Fletcher narrowed his eyes suspiciously, and then sidestepped out of the room without another word.

"You're just letting him go?" Mikhail asked in disbelief.

"You said I could do whatever I wanted," Thiago said with a shrug. "We've got to have a patsy for this mess, anyway."

"Fine. Whatever," Mikhail said as he waved his gun around carelessly. "Let's get this show on the road."

"You and what fucking army, mate?" Carl asked with a little sneer.

"Oh. This one," Mikhail said as he gestured to Thiago and Shawn. "Bennett, you look a little worse for the wear, though," Mikhail observed with a small smirk.

Shawn stepped forward, wiping the huge, bloody knife on the leg of his pants, and he nodded a little. "Aye. But I'm afraid you won't be taking all of us with you, comrade," he said assuredly.

Several bodies tensed, including Marissa's, but Shawn turned his back to Mikhail and looked at Remy apologetically. Remy frowned at him questioningly, and Shawn took a step closer to him as if to embrace him. He put a hand behind the younger man's neck and pulled him to him, kissing him passionately and seeming to forget the room full of guns and blood and death.

When he pulled away, Remy opened his eyes slowly and Shawn whispered, "I have to do this, lad. I just don't fucking trust you."

"What–"

Marissa screamed when the knife plunged into Remy's stomach, but she couldn't tear her eyes away from the scene. Remy's brown eyes widened in shock, and his hand gripped Shawn's arm for support as his other hand fisted the back of Shawn's shirt. Nikolaus and Wally shouted wordlessly, and Carl and Thiago watched on in silent, unmoving horror.

"I'm sorry, lad," Shawn said brokenly as Remy opened his mouth trying to speak. Shawn kissed him again chastely as he pulled the knife out of his body. A single tear ran down the side of Remy's face as Shawn broke the kiss, and he gripped Shawn's arm harder as Shawn plunged the knife in again.

Remy started coughing up blood, and his knees were no longer holding him upright.

Shawn held him almost tenderly as he gently lowered the mortally wounded man to the ground. He held him down as Remy struggled for breath, murmuring to him soothingly and crying silently. He ran his hand over Remy's damp forehead almost lovingly as Remy's head fell limply to the side, and he let his hand drift over the young Cajun's eyes, closing them for the last time.

Gray moved then, as did Wally, who grabbed Shawn by the collar of his shirt and lifted him off the ground. He practically threw him across the car with a roar and then dropped down beside the unmoving body of their companion with a desperate whimper.

Shawn got to his feet slowly with much more dignity than a man who had just been tossed across the room should have possessed, and he turned to glare at Mikhail. "Happy?" he asked in a choked voice, and he threw the bloody knife to the ground in disgust.

"That was very touching," Mikhail said sarcastically as he pointed his gun warningly at the others, who were growling at Shawn mutinously and practically vibrating. "Now, let's get going before Thierry has another panic and calls in the real cavalry."

"You bastard," Gray growled as he looked up at Shawn. His hands were covered in blood and he was crying silently. Marissa was a little shocked to see that they all were.

"Look, the only ones I care about bringing home at this point are these two, so if the rest of you want to make a bloody mess of this, then be my guest!" Mikhail shouted as he gestured to Shawn and Thiago and trained his gun on the others.

"Mess?" Carl asked in a voice laced with ice and death. He stepped forward and picked up the knife Shawn had thrown down. He squared off against the five men now facing him, two of them men he had called his only friends. That seemed like a lifetime ago. "You've never seen a mess, mate. Not yet."

A hand on his calf stopped whatever he was about to do, and he turned to look down at Wally, who was holding something up and showing it to him, grinning like a kid who'd just dug up a pile of dog shit in a sandbox.

Carl calmly reached down and took the grenade from him. He looked at it, then at the knife in his hand. He frowned as he rubbed his hand over the handle of the weapon. After long seconds, he looked up at the others with an evil grin.

"Carl," Thiago said warningly.

"You're a fucking turncoat, Zed," Carl said angrily. "You'll play for whichever team's winning, and when the chips are down, you simply change sides." Shawn put out a calming hand, but the blood all over it didn't seem to have the right effect on the enraged man. "And you," Carl said through gritted teeth, "have killed a much better man than you could ever hope to be. You'd better never fucking show your face topside again."

Without another word, Carl pulled the pin from the grenade and dropped it at his feet.

There was a moment of utter stillness as realization of what he had just done hit everyone. Then there was a scramble of movement.

The three men with weapons ducked out the way they had come with shouts of anger and frustration. Wally gathered Remy's body in his arms and easily followed Carl toward the opposite door of the car as Shawn's eyes followed their forms sadly. As soon as they had disappeared, he walked slowly backward and then calmly turned to follow Mikhail and the other two men. Nikolaus pulled Marissa with him hastily, but she couldn't seem to tear her eyes off Thiago and Gray, who stood watching each other over the live grenade Carl had dropped on the ground.

"Come on, Thi," Gray whispered desperately as he held out his hand. Thiago stared at it sadly. "Thiago, please," Gray begged as his voice broke. "If you ever loved me, Thi, please come with us," he pleaded.

"Get out of here, Gray, before it blows us both to Hell," Thiago responded in a flat voice as he turned and walked calmly out of the dining car after Shawn.

Gray's hand dropped lifelessly to his side and Nikolaus pushed Marissa to the doorway.

"Come on!" he growled as he ran to Gray and grabbed him by the arm, pulling him with him as they fled.

LXXVI.

SIR JOHN MCTIERNAN sat in a comfortable leather office chair, looking across the large glass table at two of the Organization's top Class One agents. He wrinkled his nose primly and cocked his head.

"You two certainly don't look like the highly trained assets we sent out six months ago," he observed after nearly five full minutes of complete and utter silence. Shawn stared at him balefully and Thiago blinked disinterestedly. "Would you care for a shower or something to eat before we begin? Or perhaps a shower?" John offered pleasantly as he looked them over and sniffed.

"Been a while since you smelled blood and smoke, has it, Mac?" Shawn asked in a low voice.

"As a matter of fact, it has," John responded with another sniff. "There was a shower aboard the jet, you could have availed yourself the luxury of soap. You were on it for more than twenty-four hours, after all."

"We found that sleep was more important," Shawn answered coolly. "You could have waited to do this until tomorrow if you're so offended," he added in a growl.

John examined him closely. Shawn's hands were still stained with the blood of his latest victim, and both he and Thiago were smudged and tattered from the explosion that rocked the train after the grenade dropped.

John had been filled in on all the details of the massive fuck up that occurred back in the States. He looked back into Shawn's flashing green eyes and smiled winningly at him. At least the ordeal hadn't completely exterminated the will to fight from his former protégé. That would have made the whole thing quite tragic.

"How are you, Shawn?" John asked pleasantly. The question was sincere, though the tone was not. John had always thought of Shawn as a son, in his own twisted way. "Not hurt, I hope?"

"No," Shawn answered coldly. "Not hurt."

"And you, Thiago? I trust you're uninjured as well?"

"Yes," Thiago responded in barely a whisper.

"Good, good. We bad pennies always turn up, don't we?" John drawled with a wink.

Thiago stared at him for several seconds and then offered a weak smile in agreement.

"Cut the shit, Mac, what are we waiting for?" Shawn asked impatiently. "Ask your questions and let us get out of here and get cleaned up, for fuck's sake."

John smiled at the two men again and nodded toward the flat screen panel on one side of the room. They both turned in their chairs and looked at it curiously. John flicked on the conference phone in the center of the table with a remote, and a man came up on the screen. He sat behind a large, swanky desk and grinned.

Shawn growled wordlessly and Thiago sighed heavily and let his head fall back to rest on the back of his chair.

"How are you, gentlemen?" Thierry St. John asked pleasantly.

Shawn merely growled at the screen again.

Thiago cleared his throat uncomfortably.

"That glad to see me, eh? Well, no worries, I'm happy enough for the lot of us. Never thought we'd see either of you again. Do you have any idea how much money it takes to train one of you buggers?"

"Why do I have the feeling we're about to get royally fucked?" Shawn mumbled as he leaned forward and spoke into Thiago's ear. Thiago brought his hand up to cover what was probably a grin, and he nodded solemnly as Shawn rested back in his chair once more.

John narrowed his eyes at the two men. They seemed to be friends. Interesting.

"Who wants to start?" Thierry asked as he leaned his elbows against the desk.

"Start?" Thiago asked tentatively.

"Yes. Start. Telling us what the hell happened," Thierry clarified.

"It's pretty clear, is it not?" Shawn asked with a furrowed brow. "The shit hit the fan and everyone fucking died. That's what happened."

"I think we're going to need a bit more detail than that," Thierry said with a scowl.

"Detail?" Shawn echoed angrily.

"Shawn, calm down," John ordered sternly. "The only person who died in all this was the one you were sent to kill."

"Fuck you, John. And you, too, you rat bastard," Shawn said as he turned to the screen once again. "You sent us out there to die!"

"That's not true," Thierry said as he pointed a finger at the screen, "I sent you out there because you were all liabilities. There's a difference."

"Thierry!" Shawn yelled as he slammed his fist down on the table and stood and drew his gun. "Get your ass down here so I can kill you!"

"Uh, no. That would be why I'm staying here," Thierry said with a cheeky grin as he eased back in his chair and laced his fingers behind his head. He gave them a huge smile and tilted back in the posh leather chair. John closed his eyes and shook his head wearily as Thierry leaned back too far and went toppling over backward.

Thiago pinched the bridge of his nose and sighed and Shawn rolled his eyes as Thierry's head popped back up behind the desk and he clawed his way to his feet.

"Sorry… sorry," Thierry mumbled as pens and classified documents went skittering across his desk.

"Oh, for fuck's sake," Shawn grumbled as he rubbed his eyes.

John knew how the man felt. Thierry was difficult to deal with even when you weren't exhausted.

"Sorry, what was I saying?" Thierry asked as he righted his chair and settled himself carefully into it.

"You were explaining to us your thinking behind this brilliant scheme of yours," John supplied.

Shawn looked at him sharply and narrowed his eyes, but John kept his eyes on the screen. He knew Shawn thought he'd been behind the entire thing, but Thierry had constructed this farce all on his own. John never would have put Shawn in that situation.

"Uh… oh! Right, right. We had two backups," Thierry continued. "You two, actually. Thiago, we weren't at all certain of your loyalty any longer, considering that you haven't been doing a damn thing we've told you to–"

"If you wanted someone to do your bidding you should have taken someone from your own fucking ranks," Thiago growled angrily.

"Yes, yes, I believe we've had that conversation before," Thierry said flippantly. "Uhh…"

"For God's sake, Thi, don't distract him," Shawn hissed quietly. "We'll be here all bloody night."

John smiled in amusement and cleared his throat to center Thierry's attention. The man was a brilliant tactician, but sometimes he took the idiot bit a mite too far. Sure, the others in power at the Organization underestimated him because of it, but it was just embarrassing for John to be associated with him at times. Like now.

"And Shawn, for a while there, we thought you'd turned on us as well," Thierry continued reproachfully.

"Well, that was rather the idea, was it not?" Shawn replied icily. "My orders were to take Remy down by any means necessary. It was a field decision to tell him everything and make him think I'd turned on you."

Thiago flinched slightly at this admission, but John wasn't certain what the reaction meant, if it meant anything at all.

"Well, you almost played it too well," Thierry said angrily. "If Mikhail hadn't seen it with his own eyes, I never would have believed you'd killed the little mongrel."

Shawn's jaw clinched angrily and he opened his mouth, then closed it again and sighed.

"What about the others?" John asked as Thiago examined his hands intently and Shawn glared up at the screen.

"What about them?" Shawn finally asked as he turned his chair back to face John.

"You let them get away," John said pointedly.

"I didn't *let* them do anything," Shawn responded tightly. "They dropped a fucking grenade on us."

"And?" Thierry prodded.

"And I'm only speaking for myself here, but I didn't feel like getting blown up at that particular point in time!" Shawn yelled.

"Shawn," Thiago said in a soft voice. Shawn immediately calmed and sat back in his chair once more. "*Escuche*, Thierry, we're both exhausted," Thiago continued in a mild voice. "We've been playing mind games for six fucking months and we both smell like death. Why don't we do this later?"

Before Thierry could respond, John stood gracefully and nodded.

"That's a wonderful idea, my boy," he said kindly. Shawn glared up at him suspiciously, but Thiago looked at him gratefully and stood as well. "We've arranged for quarters for both of you on the top floor until we can move you out to the Estate for a spell, I'm sure you'll find them satisfactory," John said smoothly.

Thiago acknowledged this with another weak smile. He looked up at the screen and nodded to Thierry, then down at Shawn briefly before turning and exiting the room quietly.

Shawn remained where he was for several long moments, studying John and watching suspiciously as John turned the screen off before Thierry could say another word.

"Don't try to play me, John," Shawn finally said quietly as he stood and faced John across the glass expanse. "Whatever you think you have with me changed years ago. I don't trust you one fucking bit, and no amount of handling us with kid gloves is going to change that."

"You're home, Shawn," John responded softly. "Get some rest. You've earned it."

LXXVII.

THE slowest week in the history of the world followed their meeting with John and Thierry. Shawn and Thiago were kept apart and each forced to have four more meetings to relate what happened during their time with the Six, as the group was now officially called.

After John and Thierry were both satisfied with what they told them, they transferred Shawn and Thiago from the Facility, which was nothing more than a military bunker in the wilds of New Zealand, to what was simply called the Estate. They had only been there for three days, and Thiago already found himself going slowly crazy.

The Estate was a huge, ostentatious place the French locals thought belonged to a wealthy oil baron. It was luxury at its finest, and Thiago was beginning to hate every inch of it. The Organization used it for all kinds of different things; meetings, missions, training, and spying on its own spies. Thiago wasn't stupid, he knew John sent them here under the guise of giving them a well-earned rest, only to be able to keep them under a watchful eye for that much longer.

Thiago sighed miserably and opened his eyes. He sat on the great stone veranda, looking out over the vast expanse of green that led to the well-tended forest beyond, and drank every ounce of alcohol he'd been able to scavenge.

After six months of having at least one companion, he was growing heartbreakingly lonely. He kept the hell away from Shawn for obvious reasons, and Shawn was the only other human there. They sent all the servants away by asking, sweet-talking, and threatening them all in turn, and they were left to their own devices. The entire house was bugged and wired and probably had cameras every two feet, anyway, so what did it matter if they were there all by themselves?

Thiago was angry with himself for entirely too many reasons. Shawn had fooled him. Completely and utterly fooled him, and Thiago mourned Remy's death just as he mourned the loss of his lover and his five only friends. If he had had any inkling of Shawn's deception, he might have been able to save Remy. And if he had any brains or self-control, he wouldn't have said the things he had said to Gray in their last minutes together. He would have told him he loved him. He would have gone with him when Gray asked him to.

His was going to be a lonely existence from here on out, if he lived much longer. Not that he didn't deserve what he was getting; not by any means did Thiago think his fate unfair. It still sucked, though.

A shadow fell across his lap as he sat feeling sorry for himself, and he looked down at it in confusion for several long seconds before squinting up at the source.

"Christ, Thiago, how long have you been out here?" Shawn asked in exasperation.

"Long enough that I think I may have pissed myself," Thiago answered as Shawn knelt beside him. "Twice."

"You've drunk all our liquor," Shawn said disapprovingly.

"That I have," Thiago agreed readily as he shifted away from Shawn. He searched his inebriated brain for something to say to the other man. "Have you been down to the wine cellar?" he finally asked desperately. "This place has its own fucking vineyard," he said in an impressed voice. Being drunk helped to alleviate the sense of unease Shawn caused, now that Thiago knew of his treachery.

Shawn sighed heavily and leaned his elbows on Thiago's thigh. "Are you too drunk to ride a horse?" he asked sadly.

"A what?" Thiago asked in surprise.

"A horse, Thi. Surely you've been to the stables on your drunken forays?"

"*No, no todavía*," Thiago admitted with a frown. "What sort of drink do they keep out there?"

"Come on," Shawn sighed as he hefted himself back into a standing position. He reached down and took Thiago's hand and pulled him to his feet. Thiago wavered but Shawn held him tight until the world stopped spinning. "Let's take a walk, shall we?"

Thiago allowed himself to be pulled along, partly because he was curious about what Shawn had to say to him, but mostly because he knew as drunk as he was he had no hope of resisting the other man's efforts.

They walked the grounds in what felt like circles, but finally they came upon the stables. Thiago watched Shawn warily as he saddled one of the horses and then started on a second.

"Do you know what you're doing?" Thiago asked finally.

"Aye. You end up acquiring skills you never thought to acquire when you spend too much time with Remy," Shawn answered wistfully, sounding as if he was mentally reliving a past experience. Thiago shifted uncomfortably at the mention of Remy's name. "Do you?" Shawn asked with a little smile.

"Do I what?" Thiago asked he shook off the memory of Remy's blood on Shawn's hands.

"Do you know how to ride a horse?" Shawn asked in a slow, deliberate voice.

"Of course I do. I grew up riding horses," Thiago said with a touch of pride in his voice. He realized his mistake seconds later when Shawn grinned widely and led the horse from the stall, all saddled up and ready to go.

"Gettyup then, mate," Shawn said with a grin.

Thiago offered him a weak smile, but he couldn't see how the other man could be so cheerful after all that had happened. Thiago had genuinely believed that Shawn loved Remy. If Thiago felt like eating a bullet to rid himself of the memory of the hurt he had caused in Gray's eyes, how could Shawn be Mister Beignet Sunshine after stabbing Remy to death?

"I'm drunk, Shawn," Thiago supplied dubiously as he took the reins and eyed the horse warily. "I can't ride."

"But you grew up riding, Thiago," Shawn cooed indulgently, and with a cheeky grin he led his horse out of the stables and into the blinding sunlight.

When Thiago finally got himself on the horse, Shawn watched him intently from atop his own mount. At least, Thiago thought he was watching him intently. The sunglasses made it difficult to tell.

They set off on one of the trails that led through the grounds without another word, and Thiago frowned as he tried to decide whether to broach the subject of the other men. Several times during their ride, he opened his mouth to ask the question, but each time he changed his mind and remained silent. After over thirty minutes of riding, Shawn pulled ahead and stood his mount in front of Thiago's, stopping him in the middle of the path.

"Why don't you just go ahead and say what's on your mind, Thi? They can't hear us out here," Shawn said as he gestured to the trees around them.

Thiago stared at him unsteadily, wondering if he would regret this when he sobered up completely.

"You killed him," he finally said in a hoarse voice.

Shawn actually had the nerve to look stunned. He pushed his sunglasses onto the top of his head and his green eyes pinned Thiago with an amused stare.

"Thiago," he sighed in exasperation. "Is that why you've been ducking into shadows every time you see me coming?"

"You said you loved him," Thiago said as the anger inside him grew. "You spent an entire month trying to kill yourself because you thought you'd killed him, for Christ's sake!"

"Aye, I did," Shawn said with a little nod as he tugged at the reins and brought the horses side by side. His thigh came to rest against Thiago's knee and Thiago leaned to the side in order to better see him.

His world tilted and he would have completely fallen off his horse had Shawn's arm not shot out and grabbed him by his shirtfront to steady him. Thiago swallowed with difficulty and met Shawn's piercing green stare.

"I want to show you something, Thi," Shawn said pleasantly, and he reached beneath the jacket he was wearing.

Thiago's hand immediately went to the spot where his gun would normally have been, but there was nothing there to grab. "Easy, Shawn," he said as his horse stepped to the side nervously and jostled him.

"It's just my knife, mate," Shawn responded in a soothing voice, as if that were supposed to make Thiago feel better. He pulled the knife out slowly, letting off that unique metallic gliding sound that only a knife coming out of its sheath can make, and Thiago noticed that Shawn had the sheath attached to his belt. Thiago didn't remember him ever having carried a knife during the previous months. Why would he start when they were safer than they had ever been?

"What are you doing?" Thiago asked suspiciously.

"Do you recognize this?" Shawn asked instead of answering. Thiago glanced down at the knife and back up at Shawn, but then he looked closer and realized that he did recognize it.

"It's Remy's," Thiago said in surprise. "I thought Carl walked out with it," he added as an inadvertent shiver ran through him.

"He did. This is mine. Actually, it's one of my backups, mine got lost in the explosion at the cabin. But it's the same as the others. I had them made several years back. They're special, you see," Shawn said with a small smile. "Care to have a look?" he asked as he flipped it into the air and expertly caught it by the blade.

Thiago gave him another suspicious look as he took the proffered knife by its handle and examined it. He bounced it a little in his hand and turned it over to look at the other side. He quirked his eyebrow at Shawn as he handed it back.

"I don't understand," he said in frustration. He really shouldn't have been drinking as much as he had.

"Look," Shawn said patiently as he pointed to a little catch in the side of the handle. He pressed it down with his thumb and then pushed the tip of the knife into

Thiago's saddle horn. He exerted a slight pressure and the knife dug into the soft leather cover, but he kept pushing and the blade began to slowly retract into the handle. Thiago watched in fascination as Shawn pushed the knife all the way to the hilt, and then slowly pulled it back, letting the blade reappear.

"Jesus," Thiago breathed as he met Shawn's sparkling eyes once more. "It was all an act," he said as a vague idea of what had happened began to form.

"You didn't really think I could kill the lad, did you?" Shawn asked with a small smile.

"I... yeah, actually. So wait, all that blood? It was fake?"

"No, unfortunately," Shawn said sadly as he looked off into the distance and put the knife back into its sheath. "The blade retracts, but it needs a little pressure first."

"So you did stab him?"

"Only a little," Shawn answered indignantly. "It probably went in a ways, but not enough to kill him. Believe me, I've had it done to me," he added with a wink.

"I saw him spit blood," Thiago insisted disbelievingly.

"He had one of those blood capsules in his mouth. You bite it and it bursts, sort of thing," Shawn explained with a vague gesture toward his mouth.

"I can't believe Remy went along with that," Thiago said doubtfully.

Shawn clucked his tongue and urged his horse to circle around Thiago's and start forward the way they had been heading.

"He didn't exactly have a choice by the time he figured it out," Shawn said regretfully as they cantered along easily. "I told him I wouldn't allow him to come back. I told him I didn't trust him to keep himself alive. I told him I'd resort to dirty tricks, but he insisted on playing the martyr and giving himself over. I couldn't have that. He was supposed to kill me, you see. That's what we had worked out. But I switched it up on him. He couldn't exactly call me on it, it would have gotten us all killed."

"So when you kissed him, you were transferring the blood capsule," Thiago reasoned. "And you had Carl and Brandt blow the train to cover the deception."

"You're right about the capsule; I pushed it into his mouth when I kissed him. Almost bit the fucking thing myself when that wanker hit me," Shawn muttered thoughtfully. "But the others didn't know what we planned," he continued as they rounded a bend in the path that indicated the trail was almost at its end. "We didn't have time to tell them. Carl dropped that grenade because he's spent too damn much time with Brandt. It wasn't planned, but it allowed them to escape and caused enough chaos that no one had time to ask why either of us did what we did."

"Why did you do it? What purpose did it serve?" Thiago asked as he tried to wrap his brain around what Shawn was telling him.

"You heard Thierry in that first meeting. He never would have believed I'd done it had someone he trusted not witnessed it. Remy's safe now, for the rest of his life, if he keeps his head down," Shawn said with a touch of melancholy.

They stopped at the tree line and Thiago examined Shawn closely. "You sacrificed yourself for him," he finally said sadly.

"Not so much," Shawn said with a grin as he looked at Thiago finally. "I get you out of the deal, right?" he asked with a cheeky wink.

Thiago smiled gamely and looked up at the stables they were heading for. "You brought me out here to tell me something aside from this," Thiago said as he looked at the security cameras that lined the roof of the main house. "You thought I knew about Remy."

"Aye, I did, I would have said something earlier if I'd known you thought me a cold-blooded killer."

"You are a cold-blooded killer, Shawn," Thiago said flatly.

Shawn turned and looked at him again and grinned widely. "Can't argue with that," he said happily. "But there was nothing in particular I wanted to say, really. I was lonely. And restless as hell," Shawn admitted candidly. "Needed to get out of that house for a spell."

"When do we start looking for the others?" Thiago asked as he allowed himself a small smile.

"I don't even know that we should," Shawn answered with a frown. "We'll be watched closely for the next year and a half, Thi. After that, they'll set us free, supposedly, and we'll be on our way. But if we did track the others before that, we could be undoing any good we may be able to do for them here."

"Right," Thiago said quietly.

Shawn turned in his saddle and looked at Thiago. "I say all of this assuming that you'll stick with me, mate," he said seriously.

Thiago smiled and nodded. "Don't know what I'd do without a grumpy old bastard around to make me look good," he responded lightly.

Shawn eyed him and growled playfully. "I may be grumpy, but we'll need a fuck of a lot more than me to make you look good." He sat smiling for several moments before saying innocently, "Speaking of grumpy bastards, did you make things right with Gray before it all went down? Is he out there somewhere waiting for you?"

"No," Thiago answered in a hoarse whisper as a wave of nausea suddenly swept over him. Shawn looked at him in concern and Thiago shook his head. "But he is out there somewhere safe. That's all that matters."

LXXVIII.

Shawn stared up at the dark ceiling through the canopy of the four-poster bed. His talk with Thiago had disturbed him more than he cared to admit, and he couldn't find sleep.

He missed Remy. He missed all his former companions. Even Gray. He wondered if he would ever see any of them again. He had done what he had to in order to get Remy out of the Organization's crosshairs. He and Thiago together would be able to put up a smoke screen for the others until they all went under permanently. They were safe, and Shawn could rest easy knowing that.

So why was he so fucking unsettled?

A tap on the door jolted him out of his thoughts, and he sat up in bed and cocked his head at the door. It cracked open and Thiago peeked inside quietly.

"Hey," he whispered when he saw Shawn sitting up. "I didn't wake you, did I?"

"No," Shawn answered curiously as he looked at the other man.

Thiago stepped into the room and closed the door with a muffled thump. They stared at one another quietly through the darkness, and Shawn grinned slightly.

"My bed's cold," Thiago finally said miserably.

"So's mine," Shawn whispered, and he pushed the bedcovers off his legs and patted the mattress beside him.

Thiago's shoulders sagged slightly, and he padded over to the bed and crawled in beside Shawn with a grateful little sigh.

Shawn settled back under the covers and was slightly surprised when Thiago snuggled up next to him and rested his head on Shawn's shoulder. Shawn held him close and waited for Thiago to say whatever was on his mind.

"These are the old model cameras, right?" Thiago whispered, indicating the camera mounted into the ceiling in the corner of the room.

"Yeah," Shawn whispered back. The old cameras had no microphones on them. Shawn had already swept the room for other bugs, and found none. The camera he had taped over, simply for peace of mind, if nothing else. "We're free to talk in here, if we whisper," he added as he turned his head and nuzzled against Thiago's hair.

"I miss them," Thiago said in a barely audible voice.

Shawn closed his eyes and smiled sadly. "Me too," he admitted.

"You're going to find them, right?" Thiago asked desperately. "They're letting us out in eighteen months, and then we'll find them?"

"Yes," Shawn hissed forcefully as he pulled Thiago closer.

"You know where they are, don't you?" Thiago said accusingly as he lifted his head up and looked down at Shawn.

"I know they split up," Shawn admitted. "Carl and Brandt went one way together, Gray and Nikolaus another. I can't be certain, but I think they separated after a couple days together. Remy, I couldn't find. We'll find them, though. All of them."

"But they're alive. Gray's still…."

Shawn looked up at Thiago sympathetically and lifted his hand to trail slowly down the side of the other man's face. He knew how Thiago felt. They had both lost lovers, if only temporarily. They had both lost companions and friends.

Shawn uttered a surprised little squeak when Thiago lunged forward and pressed their lips together desperately, but soon he warmed to the idea and wrapped his arms around Thiago's body.

As the two men took comfort in one another, their soft moans mingled with the gentle rustling of the curtains that covered the doorway to the balcony, and later that morning, when Shawn finally remembered he'd left the doors open, he was much too tired to care.

LXXVIV.

WHEN Thiago awoke, he was wrapped tightly around the pillow Shawn had shoved against him when the other man got out of bed earlier. Thiago raised his head groggily and found Shawn sitting on the floor of the room in the doorway that opened out onto the balcony. The long white curtains fluttered around him in gauzy swirls, but he paid them no mind as he sat and stared out into nothing.

"Shawn?" Thiago called out in a hoarse voice. "*¿Está bien?*" he asked roughly as he sat up and rubbed his eyes.

"Look at this, Thi," Shawn said with difficulty.

Thiago immediately tensed at the tone of the other man's voice. "What? What's wrong?" he asked as he struggled to disentangle himself from the sheets and limped over to where Shawn was sitting cross-legged near the doorway. In front of him was a nondescript little brown box. "*¿Cuál es?*" Thiago asked uneasily. He eased himself into a sitting position beside the other man. "Jesus, this floor is cold," he muttered.

"It's his box," Shawn whispered as he smiled at Thiago's complaining.

"What?"

"From Sydney. Remember? The one he had when he drugged us all?"

"Where... how did you... have you kept it all this time?" Thiago asked in disbelief.

"No," Shawn said with a little shake of his head. "It was here when I woke up. I haven't touched it."

Thiago stared at the box, realizing that someone had managed to get past every foot of security in the Estate and sneak into the bedroom of two Class One operatives, without leaving a trace of his presence, save for a little brown box. Someone they both knew very well.

"Jesus," Thiago muttered.

"He was here, Thi," Shawn hissed, just barely containing his excitement.

Remy had been there. Last night. "So much for keeping his fucking head down," Thiago observed with a little snicker.

"Little bastard," Shawn muttered happily.

"Well, open it," Thiago urged in amusement.

Shawn looked at him briefly and then at the box. Thiago reached out and nudged it slightly, moving it from the spot where Remy had left it and seemingly breaking the spell it held over Shawn.

Shawn reached for it and picked it up carefully. He turned it over and over in his hands and shook it carefully. Thiago half expected him to smell or lick it. He opened it slowly, as if by touching it he was somehow closer to the man he loved for a brief moment in time, and finally when he peered inside his green eyes sparkled and he actually laughed out loud.

He threw his head back and laughed joyously as he pulled the thing out and showed it to Thiago, and Thiago took it carefully in his hand and laughed along with the other man. It was a Christmas ornament; an alligator with antlers taped on its head, being ridden by a smiling Santa.

His hand found a note attached to the bottom, and he pulled at it and opened it up. It had only five words on it, written in Remy's loopy hand.

"It's written in purple crayon," Shawn whispered gleefully as he held his side and giggled in a most unbecoming manner for a man of his temperament.

Thiago grinned and looked at Shawn as he read aloud the title Remy had given the little alligator figurine.

"Beignet and Dixie Ride Again."

Abigail Roux is a whimsical girl who likes her beer cold and her sex hot. A past volleyball star and current rabid Braves fan, Abigail has a husband, one dog, six cats, a crazyass family, and a cast of thousands in her head. Her stories often feature love, lust and manly men.

Visit Abigail's Blog at http://abigail-roux.insanejournal.com/

Other Novels from Dreamspinner Press

A Summer Place by Ariel Tachna 248 pages
Paperback $11.99 **eBook** $5.99
ISBN: 978-0-9795048-4-6 **ISBN**: 978-0-9795048-5-3

Overseer Nicolas Wells had been coming to Mount Desert Island for ten summers to help build cottages for the rich and powerful. Despite his secrets, he had grown comfortable in the peaceful little island town, getting to know its inhabitants and even to consider some of them friends. The eleventh year, however, he arrived to startling news: the island's peace had been shattered by a murder. At the request of the sheriff, Shawn Parnell, Nicolas agreed to hire Philip Hall, the local blacksmith and the probable next victim, in the hope that the secure construction site would be safer than his house in the village. He never expected the decision to lead to danger. Or to love.

Caught Running by Urban & Roux 236 pages
Paperback $11.99 **eBook** $5.99
ISBN: 978-0-9801018-8-1 **ISBN**: 978-0-9801018-9-8

Ten years after graduation, Jake "the jock" Campbell and Brandon "the nerd" Bartlett are teaching at their old high school and still living in separate worlds. When Brandon is thrown into a coaching job on Jake's baseball team, they find themselves learning more about each other than they'd ever expected. High school is all about image – even for the teachers. Brandon and Jake have to get past their preconceived notions to find the friendship needed to work together. And somewhere along the way, they discover that perceptions can always change for the better.

Cursed by Rhianne Aile 232 pages
Paperback $11.99 **eBook** $5.99
ISBN: 978-0-9795048-2-2 **ISBN**: 978-0-9795048-3-9

Upon their grandmother's death, Tristan Northland and his twin, Will, come into possession of her Book of Shadows and the knowledge that their family is responsible for a centuries old curse. Determined to right the ancient wrong, Tristan sets off across the ocean to reverse the dark magic that affects the Sterling family to this day.

Benjamin Sterling might not be happy with his life, but it is predictable – at least until Tristan Northland shows up in his office, unannounced and with nowhere to stay. He has plenty of reason to distrust witches and Northlands, but instead of caution, he experiences two unexpected emotions: hope and love

Diplomacy by Zahra Owens — 228 pages

Paperback $11.99 — **eBook** $5.99

ISBN: 978-0-9801018-6-7 — **ISBN**: 978-0-9801018-9-8

Jack Christensen has everything he ever wanted. He's a rising star in US Diplomacy, the youngest man to have been appointed as an Ambassador of the United States. A career diplomat who's just been sent to a politically interesting Embassy in Europe, he has the perfect wife, speaks five languages and has all the right credentials, yet there's something missing and he doesn't quite know what.

Then Lucas Carlton walks into an Embassy reception and introduces himself and his American fiancée. From the first handshake, the young Englishman makes an impression on Jack that leaves him confused and uncharacteristically insecure. Lucas' position as the British liaison to the American Embassy means they are forced to work together closely and they have a hard time denying the attraction between them, despite their current relationships.

When their women decide to go on a weekend trip together, Jack and Lucas start a passionate relationship, which continues long after their partners return. Diplomatic circles are notoriously conservative though, and they each know that the right woman by their side makes a very significant contribution to their success. Will they be able to make the right choices in their professional and personal lives? Or will they need to sacrifice one for the other?

Slight Details & Random Events by Eric Arvin — 224 pages

Paperback $11.99 — **eBook** $5.99

ISBN: 978-0-9801018-0-5 — **ISBN**: 978-0-9801018-1-2

A collection of short stories from one of today's most talented and challenging new writers. Eric Arvin covers everything from college love to mystical river sprites, from deep tragedy to bawdy sex comedy, in this collection that takes the everyday and finds the adventure within. It's a read sure to keep you guessing.

Cover art and illustrations by HvH (http://hvhexpo.blogspot.com)

To Love a Cowboy by Rhianne Aile — 228 pages

Paperback $11.99 — **eBook** $5.99

ISBN: 978-0-9795048-8-4 — **ISBN**: 978-0-9795048-9-1

Seven years ago, Roan Bucklin left the family ranch for college, leaving foreman Patrick Lassiter with a mix of sweltering emotions: relief, regret, and nearly overwhelming desire. Afraid that Roan would regret giving himself to an older man, Patrick let him go without a word about his true feelings. But Roan took Patrick's heart with him.

Roan had harbored a crush on Patrick from the time he'd turned fourteen. He thought he'd gotten over it, grown up, moved on, but now he's back and home to stay. After one look, he knows he has something to prove to Patrick – that he wants to be claimed by the cowboy who has always possessed his heart.

Size Still Matters: Short Stories Still Long Enough to Satisfy
A Dreamspinner Anthology of Gay Erotic Novellas

Paperback $20.00
ISBN: 978-0-9801018-2-9

eBook $12.00
ISBN: 978-0-9801018-3-6

Sight Unseen by Shay Kincaid

Famous actor Jackson Prescott wonders if anyone will ever look past the glitz and glamour of his Hollywood persona and love the person behind the name. So after accidentally dialing a wrong number and feeling an instant attraction to Devon Forrester, the stranger on the other end of the line, he decides to test the waters ... using a different name. After getting to know Devon through their daily phone calls, Jackson starts to worry: Will the relationship they've built crumble when they meet face to face? Or will Devon be able to forgive Jackson's deceit?

Take My Picture by Giselle Ellis

Aaron has no idea what he's walking into when he shows up to pose for a famous photographer. Instead of being the focus of the camera, he ends up working as Jake's assistant. Five frustrating, thrilling and crazy years later, Jake discovers Aaron has become the focus of his life, a life that's threatened when Aaron finds someone else, and Jake has to set his beloved muse free.

Start From the Beginning by Chrissy Munder

A heart attack leaves Miles wrangling with a slow recovery and a quiet retreat ... just one cabin down from wounded warrior Drew. Although he's unhappy to have his solitude invaded, Drew finds himself fascinated with Miles, but he can't bring himself to push aside his skittish nerves. Both men fear rejection for different reasons, but what if they've instead found the acceptance they crave?

Evan's Heaven by Nicki Bennett

Actor MacAlester Kerr wanders into a whole new world of pampering and pleasure when his director sends him to *Evan's Heaven* for a pedicure. Right off, he meets *the* Evan and finds himself head over heels. Mac's on Cloud Nine when he finds out Evan feels the same.

Desire Beyond Death: Tales of Eternal Love

A Dreamspinner Anthology of Gay Erotic Novellas

Paperback $20.00
ISBN: 978-0-9801018-4-3

eBook $12.00
ISBN: 978-0-9801018-5-0

Ink: The Tale of a Vampire in Melbourne *by Isabella Rowan*

After too long alone, Dominic enters a tattoo parlor, desperate to find a way to reconnect to life. He meets Michael, an artist who evokes feelings and needs Dominic knows are dangerous. But those emotions and the allure of the handsome human intoxicate Dominic as much as the blood that keeps him alive, and he finds that he – usually the hunter - just can't resist giving in to his prey.

After the Storm by Chrissy Munder

Angry and frustrated with his chronic illness, Vincent Poulsen moves into an old lighthouse to live out the few days he has left. After a dangerous collapse, he meets the ghostly Captain Cason, who shares stories of his distant past. In the process, Vincent stumbles over the tragedy that binds the captain to the lighthouse and his haunted memories. Then fate offers them both a chance to change the future… for better or for worse.

Revenant by Connie Bailey

When Bo Andressen and his salvage crew contract a job in a crumbling castle, they walk into a mystery of murder, intrigue, hidden treasure and greed that has its roots in the far past. Ghosts are only the first suspected danger – the crew, local constable Gavin Gilroy, castle owner Sir Rhys Turcotte and psychic Tristan Andrews have to find out who of a more earthly nature is involved, before more people fall victim to an ancient spectre who seeks to rejoin and conquer the mortal world.

Seeing is Believing by Abigail Roux

Scott Cunningham has a ghost problem, a problem that requires a specialized touch. Enter Zacharias, Leo, and Andy – professionals, if you will – in solving said problems. But solutions don't always come easy, and if Zacharias and his crew can't get the job done, someone innocent might get hurt.

Bittersweet by Madeleine Urban

His business failing and his marriage floundering, Harrison Holden is falling apart. To make things worse, he wakes one morning to see Piers Claybrook, a man he rescued after a car crash the night before, standing in front of him – the same Piers he'd seen dead in the hospital. Now a ghost, Piers believes he's with Harrison to make a difference in the other man's life, and it's up to the two of them to find the key to living – and dying – and how to walk the line in between without being separated by it.

Printed in the United States
125509LV00004B/1-3/P